Praise for Walter Jon Wi

'Walter Jon Williams ha
as Patrick O'Brian and Jane Austen; both comparisons,
bizarrely, make sense. This is classic space opera, elegantly
written and beautifully plotted' *Guardian*

'This is a hugely fun ride. It has empires crashing, civil wars,
aliens, humans, scheming clans, plucky young heroes and
villains fighting space battles in huge starships – what more
can you ask for?' *Alien Online*

'Fearsomely inventive space opera' *SFX*

'Walter Jon Williams has succeeded in creating the perfect
contemporary space opera, revved up and ready to take
the SF genre by force with all the artistry and panache one
could ask for' *Enigma*

'Crammed full with worm-holes, space ships, anti-matter
bombs and all the paraphernalia of high opera, this is
a great read' *The Times*

'Fascinating… this is the new space opera – done with grace
and imagination' *Time Out*

'A writer who can make a formal reception, a dinner party
or a staff meeting as gripping as a fleet action is a rarity and
a treasure and that is just what we have in Williams' *Locus*

'Interstellar adventure has a new king and his name is
Walter John Williams' GEORGE RR MARTIN

Walter Jon Williams has written SF novels since the mid-80s. He has won or been nominated for most of the major SF honours, including the Hugo and Nebula Awards. He lives in New Mexico, USA.

Books by
Walter Jon Williams

CONVENTIONS
OF WAR

ONE

The woman called Caroline Sula watched her commander die. She had liked Lieutenant Captain the Lord Octavius Hong, though she had distrusted his orders, and she was thankful that he didn't stand the torture for long. He had been wounded during capture, apparently, and tortured once already to make him give up his communications protocols; and he was now too weak to last long under the knives. When he passed out, the loop of executioner's wire was passed around his neck and he died.

Hong's execution, as well as all the others, were broadcast live on the channel reserved for punishments, one long summer afternoon of blood and torment, entertainment suitable only for sadists and clinicians. *Which am I?* Sula wondered. Because she needed to hear the announcer read the names of the condemned, she couldn't even turn off the sound to insulate herself against the moans, screams, and the eerie discordant chimes of dying Daimong. Though there were moments when she had to turn away, Sula steeled herself to watch as much as she could, and noted the names of every one who died.

So far as she could tell, the entire secret government died that afternoon, from Military Governor Pahn-ko all the way down to his servants. When Sula had first heard of the secret government's existence, she'd pictured an underground bunker packed with communications gear or a lonely cave in the mountains reached only by a hidden

path; but it appeared that Pahn-ko had been captured in a
country house not far from Zanshaa City.

That was the secret hideaway? Sula thought with disbelieving scorn. Pahn-ko might as well have painted SE-
CRET GOVERNMENT on the roof in large white letters.

The government's military force died with its leadership. Junior Fleet Commander Lord Eshruq, the head of
the action groups that had volunteered to stay behind under
occupation, took a long time to die. Perhaps the knobby-
limbed gray Daimong body was unnaturally hardy, or perhaps the torturers took special care, since one of Eshruq's
action groups had killed some Naxids on the day they rode
in triumph into the captured city.

But most of the condemned went quickly. There were
nearly two hundred loyalists to execute, and a limited number of torturers. Most of the torments were perfunctory,
followed by the garotte, a death merciful compared to what
the state could inflict when it had more time and leisure.

From the bedroom came the amped sounds of saccha-
rine music, mixed with murmurs and moans. One of
Sula's two teammates, Engineer First Class Shawna
Spence, lay wounded on the bed watching a romantic
melodrama, with the sound turned up so she wouldn't hear
her comrades dying.

Sula didn't blame her.

The apartment was close and hot and smelled of dust
and gun oil, disinfectant and sadness. Sula felt the walls
pressing in, the dead weight of dead air. She couldn't stand
it any longer and opened a window. Fresh air flooded in,
and the scent of onions frying on a stone griddle just below
her window, and the sounds of the street, the music and
laughter and shouts of the close-packed neighborhood
called Riverside.

Sula took a few welcome breaths as she scanned the
slow-moving crowds below. Her nerves hummed as she
saw a pair of uniforms, the gray jackets and white peaked
caps of the Urban Patrol. Her lip curled, an old instinct.

Her upbringing, on faraway Spannan, had not been such as to instill in her the greatest respect for law enforcement.

The police traveled in pairs in a place like Riverside. These two were Terran, but Sula didn't know if she could trust that fact to help her. They might not care who their orders came from, so long as their own position remained intact. They'd subjected people to the arbitrary justice that was a feature of the old regime, and the Naxids' orders might not seem any different.

Nor were these two the sort to build confidence. As Sula watched from the window, one ear cocked for the sound of the announcer on the video, she saw one of the cops collect some graft from the lottery seller on the corner, and the other help himself to some spiced fry bread from a vendor.

Choke on it, she thought at him, and withdrew into the apartment before they could see her.

The executions went on. Sula's stylus jotted names and numbers as she busied herself with calculation. Lieutenant Captain Hong had led Action Group Blanche, which was composed of eleven action teams, each of three Terrans, plus his own headquarters group of six, with his extra servants, runners, and a communications tech. Action Group Blanche therefore had thirty-nine personnel. There were four other action groups, one each for the Cree, Daimong, Torminel, and Lai-own species, and though Sula hadn't met any of their members, she assumed they were organized the same way as Action Group Blanche, so that Eshruq's whole command would have constituted 195 members, plus his own headquarters group.

Those identified as members of the action groups— "rebel anarchists and saboteurs," as the Naxids called them, as opposed to the mere "rebels" of Pahn-ko's administration—amounted to only 175. Ten, the announcers said, had been killed while resisting arrest, or in Hong's luckless engagement on the Axtattle Parkway.

Three more—Sula's own Action Team 491—were supposed to have died in an explosion in their apartment at

Grandview, a booby trap that Sula had set off to catch the security forces she knew were closing in. The story of their deaths was pure propaganda—unless by some miraculous coincidence the Naxids actually *had* found three burned Terran bodies in the wreckage—but Sula supposed she might wring some advantage in being officially dead.

But even counting Action Team 491, that added up to only 180. This left at least some of the loyalists unaccounted for, and as she added her columns of figures, Sula saw they were all Torminel.

Relief eased her taut-strung nerves. She and her team weren't entirely alone: there were at least some other Fleet personnel out there, armed and presumably ready to make the Naxids pay for the capital. Torminel might *look* like fat-bottomed plush toys come to life, but that was only until you saw their fangs. They were a species that Sula would rather have on her side than not.

The problem was, she had no means of contacting them. There were backup communications protocols, but these were the very procedures the Naxids had used to capture most of her comrades. Sula didn't dare use them, and she presumed the Torminel wouldn't dare either.

Nor could she communicate with any of her superiors. They were all off-planet, and none of the action teams were provided with appropriate transmitters. Hong had such a transmitter, but it had probably been captured along with him.

The executions continued, messy and bloody now that the executioners were tired. Sula told the video wall to turn off. She had learned all she could.

Despair fell on her like soft rain. Her mouth was dry. She dragged herself to the kitchen and poured a glass of water, and saw the bottles of iarogüt piled casually on a shelf. Iarogüt was the cheapest drunk available, a palate-searing rotgut with a sickening herbal scent, the least attractive form of alcohol Sula knew, but still the sudden urge to drink struck her with the force of a hammer. One or two bottles, she thought, and the whole nightmare afternoon would spin away into chemical oblivion . . .

Her heart throbbed in her chest. Her knees felt watery. She turned and walked back to the front room, clutching her glass of water as if it were her savior. She took a sip, and then another.

Jangly music floated into the room through the open window. "It's *you*," cried a voice from the bedroom. "It's never been anyone but *you!*"

Sula opened the bedroom door and looked at Spence, who was sprawled on her bed, her wounded leg on one pillow, her straw-colored hair strewn over another. "It's over," Sula said. "You can turn down the volume now."

Her voice probably had more bite than she'd intended. Over the last few days she'd had her fill of Spence's romantic videos.

"Yes, my lady!" Spence said in proper military style, and from a position on the bed that approximated attention commanded the wall to silence.

Sula was embarrassed by Spence's overreaction. "Lucy," Sula said. "Call me Lucy." It was her cover name. Then, "Do you need anything?"

"I'm all right, Lucy, thanks." Spence shifted her sturdy hips on the bed.

"Right," Sula said. "Call if you want something."

Sula closed the door and returned to the figures she'd scribbled on her pad. There was a tap on the door, and then it opened to reveal Constable Second Class Gavin Macnamara, the third member of her action team. Tall and curly-haired and ingenuous, he had been Team 491's runner, traveling through the city on his two-wheeler to collect and distribute messages. But that had been in the days when there were people to send messages *to*. Now he wandered Zanshaa's Lower Town at random, collecting what information he could.

He glanced at the video wall as he entered, his expression tentative. "Is it over?" he asked.

"Yes."

"How was it?"

She gave him a look. "A hundred and seventy-five reasons not to surrender."

Macnamara nodded and sat on a chair.

"How are people taking it?" she asked.

Macnamara's open, friendly face clouded over. "They're trying to ignore it, I think. I think they're telling themselves that the condemned were all military, and that it doesn't apply to them."

"And the hostages?"

On arrival in the city the Naxids had grabbed over four hundred hostages from the streets, and announced they would be killed if any more acts of resistance were mounted.

"People are still angry over the hostages," Macnamara said. "But they're starting to be scared too."

"There are thirteen Torminel unaccounted for," Sula said. "At least three action teams, plus their group commander."

Macnamara absorbed this news thoughtfully. "How do we find them?"

Sula could only shrug. "Hang around in Torminel neighborhoods till we hear something?"

It had been a facetious suggestion, but Macnamara took it seriously. "A good way to get arrested. Torminel cops are going to wonder what we're doing there."

Especially as the Torminel were a nocturnal species. Terrans would very much stand out in their neighborhoods, both at night when the Torminel were active or in the day when they weren't.

Sula gave it some thought. "Maybe it's better if we *don't* contact them," she said. "They've got all the supplies they need to conduct a war right where they are. So do we. If we're not in touch, we can't give each other away."

Macnamara nodded. "So we're going to keep on fighting then," he said.

The option to quit had always been there. To stay where

they were and do nothing, to wait for the war to end one way or another. No one would blame them, not once their superiors had died.

"Oh yes." Sula could feel the tension twitching in her jaw muscles. "We're still at war. And I know just where we're going to start."

"Yes?"

"With Lord Makish of the High Court," Sula said. "The Naxid judge who sentenced our friends to death."

An expression of satisfaction settled onto Macnamara's face. "Very well, my lady," he said.

High Judge Makish lived in the Makish Palace in the High City, and for anyone who wasn't a mountaineer, there were only two ways onto Zanshaa's granite acropolis: a funicular railway for pedestrians, and a switchback road for vehicles. Since the seat of the entire government was in the High City, in the midst of a hostile population, Sula supposed the Naxids would be very careful about who got onto the acropolis and who didn't.

After buying Spence supper from Riverside vendors, Macnamara and Sula went to the lower terminus of the funicular railway at suppertime, when many of the High City's servants and workers would be returning to the Lower Town. The usual vendors and street performers had been cleared from the broad apron in front of the terminus, and Sula saw Naxid guards on the roof of the Central Station across the street, but otherwise civilian traffic seemed normal, and the line of buses and cabs on the street was reassuring, though fewer than usual.

"See if you can talk to someone at the bus stop," Sula told Macnamara. "I'll go inside the terminal."

"Are you sure?"

Macnamara's attempts to protect her from danger were endearing in their way, but in the end annoying. Sula said she was sure and walked across the highway.

In the funicular terminus she stood on the far side of the

polished onyx rail and tried to act as if she were waiting for someone. Access to the funicular was controlled, she saw, by a squad of Naxids, all carrying rifles and wearing armor over their centauroid, black-beaded bodies. A petty officer with a hand terminal checked some manner of list as his subordinates checked the identification of anyone trying to board.

Only a squad, she thought, but she knew more Naxids were on hand: they had requisitioned a number of hotels and apartments in this vicinity, and these were probably packed with troops.

Nearly half the departing passengers were Naxids, scuttling over the polished floors and dodging between the other commuters. Many wore the brown uniform of the civil service. Apparently, employment prospects had improved for their species.

Sula pretended she'd seen the person she'd come to meet, then joined a complete stranger for the walk to the outside. She found Macnamara waiting for her.

"Right now the Naxids are working off a list of everyone who lives in the High City," he said. "Workers have to provide documentation from their employers that they're needed. But the rumor is that special identification will be required soon."

Sula gave the matter some thought. "That's good," she said. "A letter would have to come from a *real* employer, one already on the list—and they might check. It'll be easier to get the special badges."

She had ways of getting false documents out of the Records Office.

Her mind was already abuzz with plans.

That night she checked into the Records Office and found that Lieutenant Rashtag's word for the day was *"Observance!"* The newly appointed head of Records Office security was fond of bombastic bulletins, and they always included the single-word exclamation intended to inspire the security staff.

Sula saw that the next day's bulletin was already on file, and that its inspirational word was *"Compliance!"* For a moment she was tempted to alter it to *"Subversion!"* but decided to save that for another day, the day when the loyalist ships appeared above Zanshaa and the Naxid domination was at an end.

She wondered what single-word exclamation Rashtag would utter if he knew that she had free run of the Records Office computers, and with Rashtag's own passwords. With a combination of luck, carelessness on the part of the previous administration, and one long night of caffeine-fueled programming, Sula had gained mastery of the Records Office system before the Naxids had even arrived. Any password created by the head of security was sent to her automatically, so even if she were detected and the passwords changed, she'd still have complete command of the place.

She was now able to access, alter, or create any personnel record. Birth and death certificates, marriage and divorce decrees, records of education, residence, and employment, primary and special identification . . .

Identification. Proper credentials were the key to survival in a world occupied by the enemy, and the key was in her hand. For a person's identification card provided more than just a picture and a serial number. The identification card in Sula's pocket held medical, employment, clan, and credit history, and tax records. It was used as a driver's license for anyone with the proper qualifications. It could be used in bank transfers, could carry cash in electronic form, was used for travel on trains and buses.

Incidentally, it was also used as a library card. Even before the Naxid rebellion, the Shaa Empire had always been interested in the sorts of books and videos that people checked out of or downloaded from the library.

The official IDs weren't foolproof, and there were always forgeries. But it was always possible for the forger to make a mistake, and by far the best and most foolproof of false identity cards were those issued by the government.

Those issued by the Records Office.

Sula had used her command of the Records Office computer to issue her team multiple IDs. At present she carried the identity card of Lucy Daubrac, an unemployed math teacher evacuated from Zanshaa's ring before its demolition. Macnamara and Spence were Matthew Guerin and Stacy Hakim, a married couple, also from the ring. Being from the ring explained why they were new in the neighborhood.

Sula checked to see if a High City identity badge had been designed, but found that if it had, it wasn't as yet in the computer.

As long as she was in the computer, she downloaded every file they had on High Judge Makish and his family. He'd had a lackluster career at the bar, apparently, but his status as a Peer of the highest class had eventually got him a judgeship in one of the lower courts. The arrival of the Naxid rebels had resulted in his promotion to the High Court, where his sentencing of the two-hundred-odd loyalists to torture and death had been his first official act.

She pictured Makish lying in his blood on the Boulevard of the Praxis in the High City. She could feel the weight of the gun in her hand.

But who would ever know? she wondered. The Naxids were censoring the news. If she were to shoot Lord Makish, no one would know but a few witnesses. And even if word leaked out, the Naxids could claim that it was an accident, or an unlikely street crime, or hadn't happened at all . . . there was no way to tell the population that this was a military act, an action by an officer of the Fleet against a traitor and killer.

Sula could feel the energy draining from her at this thought. The reason for the creation of the secret government and its military arm was to let the civilian population know that the war hadn't ended with the fall of the capital, that the legitimate government, the Convocation, and its Fleet were still active, would return, and would punish the rebels and those who aided them.

The secret government had distributed its own clandestine newspaper, *The Loyalist,* sheaves of which Sula and her group had humped up and down the streets of the Lower Town, leaving copies in restaurants, bars, and doorways. Even that primitive form of communication was gone now.

Sula turned as Spence came out of their bedroom, limping only slightly on her wounded leg. She had been shot through the calf during Hong's ill-advised fight on the Axtattle Parkway, and was lucky—no arteries hit, no infection. The swelling had finally receded, and most of what was left was stiffness. Sula had prescribed Spence a regular routine of stretching exercises, and of walking back and forth in the apartment to keep the wound from stiffening.

She hadn't let Spence leave the apartment, even though she could have walked through the neighborhood with only a minimum of discomfort. Sula didn't want Spence seen outside until she could walk normally. A limp attracted attention, struck the eye as a *wrongness.* In fact, she didn't want anyone on her team to attract attention, not when the situation was so unsettled, not when the attention might come from the Urban Patrol or from an informer.

Why is the stranger limping? That was a question Sula *never* wanted her neighbors to ask each other, not when the news broadcasts were full of the Naxid triumph in a pitched battle on the Axtattle Parkway, and even an ordinary person might think of flying bullets and wounds.

She knew that it was perhaps irrational to take these precautions, but she had survived the Naxid occupation so far by taking precautions that others had thought irrational.

"How's the leg?" Sula asked Spence.

"Better, my la— Lucy." She made a turn about the room

and gave a wistful look at the street beyond the window. "Pity I can't leave, on a lovely day like this."

"Work on your walking and your stretching, and you will," Sula said.

Human warmth is not my specialty, she thought.

"Didn't you like your squid?"

Sula looked in surprise at her supper, bits of squid grilled on a skewer, which had sat untouched by her elbow for the last hour.

"I forgot to eat," she said.

"Let me warm it," Spence said, and took the skewer—and the other skewer with mushrooms and vegetables—to the kitchen.

Sula heard the hum of the convection oven as Spence returned to take another turn around the floor.

"You must be working hard on something," Spence said.

"I'd be a lot happier if I *could* work on it," Sula said. She looked down at the displays on the glossy surface of her desk and touched the pad to disconnect her desk from the Records Office computer. "I was trying to think of a way to communicate with people in the city, let them know it's not all over. Replace *The Loyalist* somehow."

Spence considered this, her pug nose wrinkled in thought, then shook her straw-colored hair. "I don't see how. It took all of us several days to distribute those papers last time." An idea struck her. "But Lucy, you've got access to the Records Office computer. Can't you use that to send electronic copies?"

"Only if I want the security forces to go through every line of programming on that computer until they find me," Sula said. "There are invisible tags on every piece of mail that tells you where it came from—and of course a duplicate of every mail goes to the Office of the Censor, and you can imagine what would happen if ten thousand copies of *The Loyalist* turned up in their buffer."

Spence paused in her pacing, a thoughtful frown twitching at her lips. "Lucy," she said, "you've got high access. Couldn't you just tell the computer to lie about all that?"

Sula opened her lips to make a scornful reply, then hesitated. A subtle chime came from the kitchen, and Spence limped there to take Sula's supper from the oven. When she returned, Sula had turned to her desk and was connecting once more to the Records Office computer.

"Eat your supper," Spence said as she dropped the plate on Sula's desk, over the flashing symbols that were appearing in its glowing depths. Juices sizzled faintly in Sula's ear. She picked up the nearest skewer and ate a piece of squid. Reheating had turned the cuttlefish rubbery, but its texture, or for that matter its taste, were by now of little interest. She pushed the plate to one side as the Records Office directory appeared onscreen.

"Make good use of the help files," Spence advised.

As Sula ate her supper, and later drank the sweetened coffee that Spence provided, she discovered that all the Records Office mail—minus the interoffice communications, which remained within the department—went through the same broadcast node, a heavy duty model fully capable of handling the thousands of requests for information delivered to the office every day. The node tagged every mail with its own code before sending the original to its destination, and automatically copied every mail to the Office of the Censor, where it would be subjected to a series of highly secret algorithms to determine any subversive content.

But how easy was it to program the broadcast node? She followed Spence's advice and checked the help files.

Very easy indeed. She was surprised. For someone with the proper user status, the programming features of the node could be turned on or off nearly as easily as flipping a switch.

Her eyes burned from hours of staring at the display. Sula went to the bathroom and removed the brown contact lenses she wore to disguise her green eyes. She looked at herself in the darkened old mirror above the rust-stained sink, checked her hair roots, then touched her skin. Her efforts at disguise extended to dying her blond hair black and giving herself carotene supplements to darken her pale complexion. She was going to have to use the hair dye again soon, she saw.

Her nerves gave a leap as the outer door opened and she realized she was far from the nearest weapon. She tried to calm herself with the thought that it was probably Macnamara returning, and so it proved to be.

Got to keep a gun in the bathroom, she thought as she returned to the front room.

"Shall I sleep here tonight?" Macnamara asked. "Or shall I use my own place?"

Originally, the Riverside apartment had been acquired only for meetings of the team, with the members actually sleeping in their own individual apartments, but the necessity of caring for a wounded team member had changed that.

"You can go home," Sula said. "I'll look after Spence tonight."

Macnamara glanced at the symbols glowing in the depths of the desk. "Working on something?" he asked.

"Yes. A way to communicate with the population."

Macnamara considered this. "I hope it's less work than the last one."

After checking her work several times, Sula produced a program that would do a number of jobs in sequence.

Turn off the broadcast node's logging, so there would be no record of what followed.

Turn off the function that appended an identification tag to the message.

Turn off the function that copied the message to the censor.

Broadcast a message.

Turn on the function that copied messages to the censor.

Turn on the identification function.

And turn on the logging again.

After which the program would remove itself from the node.

She tested her program by sending herself a message—"The information you requested is not available at this department"—and found that it worked. No record of her message, or any of the other tasks she had triggered, appeared in any of the Department logs.

She could send a message now, if she could only work out who to send it to and what the message was.

Before Sula cut the connection and turned off the computer, she checked Rashtag's message for the next day and found that his word was *"Expedite!"*

Exactly, she thought.

Spence had long ago gone to bed, but Sula had drunk too much coffee to sleep. She leaned out the window and took a deep breath of warm midsummer air.

The traffic was gone, the stalls and pushcarts carried away. Energy restrictions had turned off all signs and illuminated only every third streetlight. Under the nearest, a street away, she could see a few figures engaged in intense conversation, their arms gesturing broadly.

She grinned. It was so late that the hustlers could hustle only each other.

Sula left the apartment through the rear door off the kitchen, onto the building's back stair, and climbed to the roof. The roof access had been wedged open for the benefit of some tenant's cat, and she stepped soundlessly onto the flat roof, her shoes silent on the epoxide roofing material. Normally the city's glare permitted only a few stars to be seen, but now the city's subdued glow revealed a blazing spray of brilliants strewn across the night's velvet canopy.

Across the sky gleamed a series of silver arcs, each separated from the next by the starry darkness. These were the silent, empty remains of the accelerator ring that had once circled the planet, that had created the antimatter that fueled its economy, that had berthed its ships, warehoused its goods, and supported the lives of eighty million people. When it had been clear that the Naxids were going to capture Zanshaa, the ring was evacuated and then destroyed, its fragments separating as they rose to a higher orbit.

The ring had circled the planet for over ten thousand years, the greatest and most glorious technical achievement of the Shaa Empire, and it had survived the death of the last Shaa by less than a year. The fragments hanging in the sky, visible from all quarters of the planet, were a silent, reproachful reminder of the fragility of civilization, and of the uncertainty and violence of war.

And it was all my idea. It had been Sula who first suggested destroying the ring, as a way of making it hard for the Naxids to rule the planet they had conquered. Somehow the credit for the idea had lodged with someone else, and somehow Sula herself had gotten lodged on the planet with Hong's action group, instead of flying away with the rest of the Fleet.

I should be up there, she thought as she looked at the stars. In a warship driving deep into enemy territory, bringing the war to the Naxids, instead of living a hunted existence on the surface of the planet, scurrying from one bolt-hole to the next.

She thought of one person she knew was flying among the stars with the Fleet, and a lump formed in her throat.

Martinez, she thought, *you bastard.*

TWO

He could touch the silk of Sula's pale, perfect skin, feel the warmth and soft weight of her hair on his flesh. Her brilliant emerald eyes gazed at him fondly. He scented the rich fragrance of Sandama Twilight, her perfume. He tasted her lips. He felt the warmth of her breath as she whispered in his ear, and strained to catch the words.

The words remained forever beyond his grasp. Lord Gareth Martinez woke with a cry in the darkness of his cabin, and reached with a hand to catch at the phantom that had already fled.

He heard the steady roar of the cruiser's engines, the engines that were propelling *Illustrious* from the Bai-do system. He heard the whisper of air through the ducts. He heard the tread of a pair of shoes outside the cabin door, and felt sweat drying on the back of his neck.

Martinez undid the elastic web that kept him from floating out of his bed during occasional periods of weightlessness, and put his bare feet on the cool parquet floor. He rose from the bed and passed out of his sleeping cabin and into his office. He sat heavily in his chair and gazed down at his desk, at the images he'd set in its display, images of Lady Terza Chen, his wife.

Terza was beautiful, intelligent, accomplished, cultured, and heir to the Chen clan, a clan of the highest possible social standing. In normal circumstances she would be far beyond the reach of someone like Martinez, who came from an affluent but provincial clan, and who spoke with a barbarous accent he'd been unable to polish away. Terza's father served on the Fleet Control Board that determined Martinez's professional future. Her aunt was Martinez's commander. Their families had arranged their marriage just hours after the argument that had destroyed his relationship with Caroline Sula, and they had spent a bare seven days together before his duty called him away.

During those seven days she had conceived his child.

He gazed down at the images of Terza and knew that he didn't deserve her. He didn't desire her either.

He touched a hand to his lips. He could still taste Caroline Sula.

"Lights," he said. He blinked in the sudden brightness, then blinked again at the sight of the wall murals, which for some inconceivable reason were of naked, winged children. He called up the navigation plots for the wormhole jump from the Bai-do system to Termaine.

Chenforce, seven ships of war commanded by Terza's aunt Michi Chen, had bypassed the Naxid fleet securing their conquest at Zanshaa, and had now driven deep into enemy-controlled space. They had wiped out a detachment of ten enemy warships at Protipanu, then raced through a series of systems, destroying merchant shipping, wormhole relay stations, and uncompleted warships.

And several billion people. The raid had worked brilliantly until Chenforce had come to Bai-do, where the Naxids in command had refused Michi Chen's orders and launched missiles from the planet's accelerator ring. In response, Squadron Commander Chen had ordered Bai-do's ring destroyed.

Tens of millions of people lived on the ring, and nearly five billion on the planet below. The great mass of the ring dropping onto the planet must have killed millions outright and imperiled the rest. Clouds of dust and debris rising high into the atmosphere from the impact would shroud the sun and smother the food crops. Without the elevators from the ring to the surface, there would be no way to deliver significant amounts of foodstuffs to the planet.

Most of those who had survived the ring's fall would die a slow, cold death from starvation.

One nightmare like Bai-do was bad enough. What was worse was that there could be more.

In a few days Chenforce would jump through one of Bai-do's wormholes into the Termaine system. Termaine was a wealthy world packed with industry and rich farmland that produced an overabundance of exports. Under normal circumstances Termaine's ring would host a hundred merchant vessels at a time. Naxid warships would probably be found under construction in its shipyards.

And if those warships fired at Chenforce from the ring, as had happened at Bai-do? The ring would be destroyed, along with the billions below it.

Martinez looked down into the depths of the three-dimensional navigation plot, at the little blue sphere, ringed with silver, that represented Termaine. He recalled the sight of the blue sphere of Bai-do as its doomed ring oscillated and then fell with slow, tragic majesty into the atmosphere. He remembered the sight of the impacts, the antimatter sparkling amid the great plumes of steam and dust and ruin.

Let them not call our bluff again, he thought. Perhaps the Naxid high command thought it worthwhile to find out whether the raiders had the stomach for mass murder. But having found out, surely they would not sacrifice more than one world.

He wanted to reach down into the depths of the desk display, scoop up the little world, and carry it to safety.

A zero-gee warning gonged through the ship. Martinez looked at the chronometer, saw that it was a scheduled course change and there was no need for him to strap himself in. Another warning sounded, the distant roar of the engines ceased, and Martinez floated weightless. He kept one hand clamped on his chair bottom to keep himself from drifting away—the chair itself was intelligent enough to know to adhere to the floor. An eddy in his stomach told him that *Illustrious* was rotating onto its new heading, and then there was another warning for the resumption of gravity followed a few seconds later by the punch of the engines. Martinez dropped into his seat again.

The ship was going through the orderly progress of its day. The heading was changed on schedule, watches came on and off, decks were cleaned, parts were replaced on schedule, drills performed.

The only person not going about his routine was Martinez, who was awake and staring into his desk display when he should be in bed.

He told the navigation plot to go away, and the display darkened for an instant, then filled with images of Terza.

Terza smiling, Terza arranging flowers, Terza playing her harp.

Terza, whose soft voice he could barely remember.

He doused the lights and returned to his bed and his uneasy dreams.

The High City was half deserted, with overgrown gardens of summer flowers that rioted beneath the blank, boarded-up windows of the great palaces. Even on the grand Boulevard of the Praxis, motor traffic was scarce. Half those pedestrians on the street were Naxids, and most of these were in uniform. Most prominent was the viridian green of the Fleet, along with the gray jackets of the Urban Patrol and the black and yellow of the Motor Patrol.

Businesses were adapting to the conquerors. Restaurants that had served cuisine tailored to Terran or Torminel tastes now advertised Naxid specialties, and the chairs that served their old customers were being replaced by the short, low couches on which centauroid bodies could take their ease. Tailors' window displays featured Naxid dummies in sumptuous military splendor, chameleon-weave jackets automatically flashing Naxid scale patterns. Pulse-stirring Naxid music, created by beating on the tuned, hollow sticks called *aejai,* clattered from the doors of music stores.

Sula saw no military or police who were not Naxids. Their presence wasn't particularly heavy except in the area of the government buildings clustered under the domed Great Refuge, on the east side of the acropolis, where there were checkpoints and armed Naxids on the roofs of at least some of the buildings. Otherwise, small units were posted at important intersections, and there were wandering patrols.

"It's going to be hard getting away," Sula said. "Harder than doing the thing in the first place."

She and Macnamara had stationed themselves in the Garden of Scents off the Boulevard of the Praxis, where they could look down the boulevard toward the famous statue of The Great Master Delivering the Praxis to Other Peoples, and in the other direction to the Makish Palace, an ancient structure with five bulbous, ornamented towers, each shaped vaguely like an artichoke.

Two days after their reconnaissance to the funicular terminal, the government had announced the special identification card that would be required for all residents and workers of the High City. Sula looked up the requirements in the Records Office computer, then filled out applications for everyone on her team, approved them in the names of high-ranking administrators, and mailed them to the Riverside address. She made them employees of a fictional firm, at a fictional address, that was owned by Naxids—Naxids who were themselves far from fictional, all close relatives of Lady Kushdai, the governor and highest-ranking Naxid in the capital. Police would be unlikely to inquire too closely into Sula's business once they saw those names.

When the cards arrived in the mail, Sula retroactively altered all records of the mailing address to a fictional street number.

The identity cards worked perfectly when, dressed in laborers' coveralls, boots, and caps, Sula and Macnamara had come up the funicular carrying boxes of tools.

"We should just shoot Makish from here," Macnamara said. He had been one of the best marksmen in their firearms training course. He tilted his cap onto the back of his head and gazed up at the fragrant lankish trees overhead, all adrip with trailing pink blossoms. "I could do it from one of the trees."

"That would mean smuggling a rifle into the High City," Sula said. They didn't have weapons with them at present, not knowing whether they could get them past the detectors at the funicular.

"Maybe a bomb then." Macnamara was undeterred. "Plant it just inside his gate, detonate it from a distance when he steps in."

To Sula this seemed a more attractive proposition. "The bomb would make a lot of noise," she said. "Break a lot of windows. The Naxids could never pretend it didn't happen."

"Here comes someone, our target maybe."

Sula tilted her cap brim over her face and busied herself with the contents of her toolbox as she cast covert glances at the three Naxids moving down the broad walk. Two wore the uniforms of the Fleet, the exact color of Zanshaa's viridian sky, with the red cross-belts and armbands of the Military Constabulary. The third was in the brown jacket of the civil service, with badges of high rank and what seemed to be the orange and gold sash of a High Court judge over one shoulder.

"Good of him to walk home," Sula said.

"It's a nice day, why not?"

"Shall we follow?"

They picked up their tools and strolled out of the Garden of Scents. The Naxids moved rapidly on their four feet—Sula had never seen one move slowly unless he was injured—and they had already sped past by the time she and Macnamara left the park. One of the Constabulary guards looked over her shoulder at them as they came out of the park gate but saw little of interest; she turned back to follow the judge, and her jacket flashed a bead-pattern to her partner.

"I wish I knew what she just said," Macnamara muttered.

The black beaded scales on a Naxid's torso and long back were capable of a flashing red, and bead-patterns were used as a form of auxiliary communication. The chameleon-weave fabric of the Naxids' uniforms duplicated the patterns on the scales beneath, so even Naxids in uniform were capable of communicating silently in a private language that few non-Naxids could read.

"I doubt she said anything interesting," Sula said.

"Are you sure that's our judge?" Macnamara asked. "I can't tell them apart, usually."

"I'm reasonably certain," Sula said. "I got a glimpse of his face as he went past and it looked right to me." She offered the world a chill smile. "But even if he's not the judge we're after, he's important enough to rate a couple guards. As far as I'm concerned, that makes him a target."

The Naxids crossed to the opposite side of the boulevard, where the Makish Palace waited. Sula and Macnamara remained on their own side of the street and watched with what she hoped was an appropriate level of disinterest. The judge passed through an elaborate fence of gleaming silver alloy, then entered the house through the formal garden out front. One guard went into the palace with him, and the other stationed herself in the garden.

Sula's eye had already moved on to the building next to the Makish Palace, another ornate structure, a palace of mellow gold sandstone with an intricate, carved facade of radiating, interlinking lines. The place was obviously shut down, and the garden out front had run riot.

"No obvious security besides the two guards," Macnamara said.

"Beg pardon?"

Macnamara repeated his statement. Sula looked at the abandoned palace again.

"I've got an idea," she said.

A gold-accented door opened in front of Sula, the door to a private club. In a whiff of tobacco smoke a well-dressed Terran, braided lapels and fashionably pleated trouser front, stepped out of the club and glanced left and right as he made a minor adjustment to his cuffs.

The door closed behind him. His mouth gaped under its narrow little mustache. *"Lady Sula!"* he gasped.

She stepped forward, took his arm, and steered him down the street. Macnamara, suddenly alert, kept a wary eye behind.

"You're dead!" the man cried.

"For all's sake, PJ," said Sula, "you don't have to make such a fuss about it."

THREE

"Laredo is too far," said Fleet Commander Tork. His melodious voice sounded like wind chimes, and it took a modest effort to separate content from melody. "A message would take eight days each way to Chijimo, and ten to Zanshaa. We are Fleet Control Board; we must remain near the Fleet."

Lord Chen had no desire to join the fleeing Convocation on Laredo, the home of his bumptious in-laws. He had no desire to accept the hospitality of Lord Martinez, and face the daily reminders of his dependent status. He had no wish to see his daughter Terza surrounded by the members of the parvenu family to whom he had sold her.

On the other hand, he was less than enchanted with what Lord Tork seemed to be proposing, if for no other reason than it offered fewer opportunities to escape Tork's company.

The eight members of the Fleet Control Board were traveling together on the *Galactic,* a sumptuous passenger yacht the Fleet maintained in order to ferry dignitaries from one system to another. Though *Galactic* was a large vessel, it was stuffed full of evacuees from Zanshaa—a large staff of secretaries and communications staff, members of the Intelligence Section and the Investigative Service, bureaucrats from the Ministry of Right and Dominion, servants of the board members . . . all people who existed to serve the lords of the Fleet, and who Lord Chen was finding it difficult to escape.

Lord Chen was trapped on a small ship with his job, and he wasn't enjoying himself. At Tork's insistence, the board had followed the rules it had laid down for everyone else, and so Lord Chen was permitted only a single servant, and family members were forbidden to accompany—and in any case Lady Chen, who had strongly disapproved of the arrangement by which her only child and heir was married to a Martinez, would never have consented to visit Laredo. Since boarding *Galactic,* Lord Chen's sole diversion had been frequent communication with his daughter Terza, who was on the Martinez yacht *Ensenada,* traveling a few days ahead.

"What do you have in mind, my lord?" he asked Tork.

A waft of air brought Lord Chen the scent of Tork's decaying flesh, and he took a discreet sniff of the cologne he'd applied to the inside of his wrist. The Control Board met in a room that had been intended as guest quarters for important Fleet dignitaries. It was bright with mosaics that showed ships dashing through wormholes; but now a long table crowded the room and the air was rather close.

The Daimong turned his round black-on-black eyes on Chen and chimed again. "We will divert to Chijimo and remain with the Home Fleet until the time comes for the recapture of Zanshaa."

Lord Chen could not imagine Lord Eino Kangas, who commanded the Home Fleet, being very pleased at the idea of his superiors hovering over him that way.

"My lord," said Lady Seekin, "shouldn't we remain with the Convocation? We may need to contribute our expertise on important matters, and of course our votes."

Lady Seekin, a Torminel, was one of the civilian members of the board, and a convocate. Her comprehension of Fleet matters was imperfect, but she understood the political dimension of her career very well.

"The important votes have already been taken," Tork

said. "Policy has been set and allocations have been made. It is our duty to make certain that the proper policy is implemented, and that no mistakes are made with regard to Fleet deployments and tactical doctrine."

Kangas was going to *love* this, Chen thought.

"I confess to reservations," he said. "Aren't we better employed being Lord Eino's advocate with the Convocation? Few of the Lords Convocate have our experience in—"

"We are best employed by ensuring the destruction of the rebels and the restoration of the Praxis to the capital!" Tork declaimed. His voice took on the harsh, clanging, dogmatic overtones that others on the board had learned to dread. Lord Chen tried not to wince as the discord clashed in his skull.

Junior Fleet Commander Pezzini, the other Terran member of the board, gave a convulsive sneeze. Perhaps he'd gotten too strong a whiff of the chairman.

"My lord," he said, "if we sit on top of Fleet Commander Kangas that way, it's going to look as if we don't trust him."

"We will be ensuring the correct employment of the Home Fleet!" Tork said. His voice was like a razor blade shredding Chen's nerves. Chen took another whiff of cologne.

"We have entrusted Lord Eino to make those deployments," Pezzini said. His voice was firm. "It's not our task to second-guess him."

"We must not take chances!" In the small room the voice sounded like a blaring fire alarm. *"The Fleet has been undermined by subversive activity and unsound doctrines!"*

"The Fleet," Pezzini said patiently, "will be undermined by a crisis of confidence if we spend months looking over Lord Eino's shoulders."

Lord Chen cast Pezzini a grateful look. He and Pezzini were often on opposite sides of board disputes, but at least Pezzini had been a serving officer, and understood how such a preemption of authority would look.

Tork, who had also been a serving officer, had either forgotten or never knew in the first place.

"Kangas must not be permitted any latitude!" Tork cried. *"He must adhere without question to the ways of our ancestors!"*

Lord Chen took a long breath. As Fleet recruits gradually built up a resistance to high gees, he and the others of the board had gradually steeled themselves against the chairman's outbursts.

"Fleet Commander Kangas is not a child," Chen said. "He does not require a nursemaid standing over him, particularly a nursemaid in the form of a committee." As Tork turned his pale, frozen face to reply, Lord Chen slapped the table with his hand, making a sound like a gun crack. The others jumped.

Tork, Chen thought, wasn't the only one in the room who could make a sonic attack.

"We must obey the dictates of the Praxis!" he said. "The Praxis states that there must be a completely clear chain of command, from the Fleet Commander to the lowliest recruit. For the Control Board to interfere in that relationship is a violation of the *empire's . . . fundamental . . . law!*"

He slapped the table again on each of the last three words. Glasses of water and tea jumped. Tork gazed at Chen with his expressionless face, his gaping mouth and round eyes giving the impression of perpetual surprise.

"So can we please go to Laredo?" asked Lady Seekin, her voice a bit plaintive.

Of course they compromised. In the end the decision was taken to go to Antopone, where the board could hover between Laredo and Chijimo, and also supervise the three cruisers that were being constructed on Antopone's ring.

At least *Galactic* would berth on the ring, and Lord Chen knew he would have some time away from his colleagues. He had friends who had fled to Antopone from Zanshaa, and he could count on a gratifying reception from them.

He therefore wouldn't have to put up with Laredo or the Martinez clan, with their rude accents and barbaric manners. And he would have at least a few hours of liberty from Tork and the others. He could look forward to Antopone with satisfaction.

But unfortunately Terza would not be staying with him. Her calm presence was the last reminder of his old life on Zanshaa, the days before Naxids and the Martinez clan became such oppressive presences in his life.

During the weeks it took to reach Antopone, the press of business never slackened. Tork, whatever his other faults, was a peerless organizer: somehow he managed to keep in his gray, bald head the details of recruitment and training, ship building and repair, logistics, and support for the entire Fleet. He read reports and dictated memoranda. He ordered supplies to be shipped from one location or another. He supervised the deployment of recruits from the training camps, and deployed officers to the ships building in the yards.

Lord Eino Kangas, reasonably free of interference, remained orbiting the Chijimo system with Home Fleet, which had lost not only its home but most of its ships. The Home Fleet proper had been reduced to the five survivors of Magaria, all heavy cruisers, to which had been added an additional seven heavy cruisers of Faqforce, the Lai-own divisions commanded by Squadron Commander Do-faq. These twelve vessels were hardly a match for the nearest enemy, the forty-three Naxid ships known to be at Zanshaa.

If the enemy advanced, Kangas would have no choice but to fly before them, surrendering any systems the Naxids chose to threaten. But the Naxids didn't seem to be interested in advancing. They remained at Zanshaa, guarding the capital while their government sank its roots into the soil below. They seemed confident that the remaining loyalists would surrender.

But the loyalists had no intention of surrendering. More than half the loyalist fleet, Chenforce under Michi Chen and Light Squadron 14 under the Torminel Squadron Commander Altasz, plunged on separate raids into rebel-held systems, there to demonstrate that while the rebels might have the capital, the rest of their domain wasn't safe.

The strategy of abandoning the capital and defending nowhere while building forces and raiding into enemy territory was referred to as the Chen Plan. In fact the plan had been developed by Captain Martinez and Lady Sula, but neither of them were sufficiently important or free enough from controversy to deserve having the Fleet's strategic aims named after them. So Lord Chen, who had first presented the plan to the board, had his name appended to it, and his career would rise or fall with its success.

While Tork managed the business of the Fleet, while Kangas orbited Chijimo with his outnumbered force, while warships were building on many worlds, while the representatives of the Investigative Service bickered over fine points of interpretation with their rivals in the Intelligence Service, while the Naxids occupied the capital and Lord Chen's sister and son-in-law advanced with their squadron into the unknown, Lord Chen occupied himself sending messages to his friends on Antopone.

It would be such a relief to see them again.

So much for my clever disguise, Sula thought. Blond hair dyed black, green eyes turned brown, pale skin darkened, and she couldn't even fool someone of PJ Ngeni's . . . extremely localized intelligence.

PJ had recovered his equilibrium somewhat, and the reflexes of a man of fashion came to the fore. "You must let me give you dinner at my club," he said.

Sula dropped PJ's arm and indicated her gray coveralls. "We're not exactly dressed for it, PJ," she said.

He touched his little mustache. "We'll order in, then."

Sula felt a nervous giggle flutter like a butterfly in her abdomen. The jolt of adrenaline that had followed PJ's blurting of her name was followed by an equally powerful impulse to break the tension with laughter.

"I don't think you should be seen with us," Sula said through her breaking smile. "We're wanted by the Naxids. If you're caught with us, you'll be tortured and killed."

PJ waved a hand. "Oh," he said, *"that."*

Lord Pierre J. Ngeni was a tall, slim, elegant man, not quite middle-aged, with a long balding head and clothes of a modish cut. It was generally believed he'd wasted his inheritance on the usual dissipations available to members of his class, and now—for a Peer—he was poor, and living largely on the charity of his clan.

Sula knew PJ because he'd once been engaged to Gareth Martinez's sister Sempronia. This, Martinez had clearly explained to her, had been a sham engagement, yet another of Martinez's attempts to clamber from his obscure provincial origins into the cream of Zanshaa society. An engagement to a member of his patron clan, the Ngenis, would guarantee access for Martinez and his siblings to the highest levels of the city. After Martinez and his family had won access, Sempronia would be at liberty to discover, to her horror, that PJ had led a scandalous life, and then break the engagement.

The chief fault of the plan was that PJ Ngeni, himself, had never realized his engagement was a travesty. He'd fallen in love with Sempronia, who in her turn had rebelled at the very idea of a burlesque engagement and run off with one of Martinez's lieutenants. The resulting scandal had threatened to unhinge the relationship between the Ngenis and Clan Martinez, and another sister entirely had been offered as a family sacrifice. PJ traded a farce of an engagement for a mockery of a marriage.

Since the Martinez family had sensibly cleared out before the Naxids arrived, as had the Ngenis, the fact that the new bridegroom had been left behind did not speak well for PJ's conjugal condition.

"We'll bring in a nice dinner," PJ continued amiably, "and open a bottle of wine. Oh—sorry—I forgot you don't drink."

"PJ," Sula said, "what are you *doing* here?"

PJ shrugged. "I volunteered to stay behind and guard the family's interests on Zanshaa," he said. "Not that there are very many interests left, barring some property. But we still have clients here, and some old servants that we've pensioned off, and I'm doing my best to look after them." He looked at Sula, then glanced over his shoulder at Macnamara. "Do I know your friend?" he asked.

"I don't believe so. Call him Starling." Which was Macnamara's code name.

PJ was amiability itself. "Pleased to meet you, Mr. Starling."

Macnamara gave a terse nod. "My lord."

PJ hesitated as he peered along the street. "If I'm going to give you dinner," he said, "we should be walking in the, ah, the *other* direction." He pointed the way they had come.

"You're staying in the Ngeni Palace?"

"The palace is closed. The servants have been dismissed, and the pensioners sent to our place in the country. I'm in a guest cottage."

"No cooks? No servants?"

"Someone from an agency comes in to clean. And I either eat at one of my clubs or call for delivery from a caterer."

Sula looked at Macnamara, who gave her an equivocal look. *Up to you,* Sula read.

"It sounds safe enough," she ventured. She turned to PJ. "Go ahead of us, please. If we walked together it would look odd."

PJ was bemused but led the way. He passed his smoking club again and then crossed the boulevard, where he led them past the Makish Palace. Sula tried to amble casually along, and as she passed the palace she paused to shift her toolbox from one hand to the next. She paid as much attention to the abandoned palace next door as she did to her target. From the name inscribed in a sunburst over the doorway, *Orghoder,* Sula assumed the empty building had been built by a Torminel clan.

The Ngeni Palace wasn't on the Boulevard of the Praxis, but several streets behind, backed against the gray cliffside for a stunning view of the Lower Town. The palace itself was tall, faced with veined pink marble, and nearly a cube, with a huge glass-fronted, barrel-vaulted hall visible from the street. PJ didn't enter the palace, but took them around by a side entrance, then past a huge old banyan tree that looked as if it might have been standing on the High City since the dawn of time.

His "cottage" was three stories tall and probably had twenty rooms, but PJ seemed only to be living in a small part of it. He ushered his guests into a parlor, one with a view of the flagstone terrace that overlooked the Lower Town. PJ went to the comm unit concealed in a dramatic commode of arculé wood, ordered dinner for three from a caterer who seemed to know him, then closed the commode and turned to his guests.

"Well!" he said brightly. "So you're alive after all, Lady Sula!"

"Yes." The laugh that had been struggling to escape from her finally broke free, and she indulged it. "I hardly expected to see anyone I knew."

"That's lucky, isn't it?" PJ seemed pleased. "I'm glad I'm able to be of service." He reached for the drink trolley. "What may I give you to drink? Whisky, Mr. Starling?"

Sula looked at him. "Whatever you've got that doesn't have alcohol. And what did you mean 'service'?"

PJ looked at her. "You're obviously in, ah, straitened circumstances. You can stay here with me, of course, and I'm good for any tailor's bills you may run up." He patted his pockets. "Do you need any ready money?"

Sula's laugh rose again, unstoppable, and went on for some time. PJ hesitated, a half-hurt expression coming over his face. Sula controlled the laughter.

"PJ, you're wonderful!" she cried, and his expression turned from hurt to pleased. "We don't need money," she told him. "We're just dressed this way because, well, we're just taking a look around, and we don't want people to look at *us*."

PJ nodded, then hesitated again. A massive, startling thought worked its slow way across his face. "Oh!" he said. "Oh! I understand!" He pointed a finger at his two guests. "You're here on a *mission!* You're doing something for the secret government!"

Sula wondered if she should tell PJ that, so far as she knew, she *was* the secret government.

"Actually," she temporized, "we're just taking a look around. We're not on an assignment or anything."

"Well, if there's anything I can do," PJ said, "anything at all, you'll be certain to let me know." He looked at Macnamara. "That was whisky you wanted, was it, Mr. Starling?"

Macnamara looked at Sula. "Feel free," she said.

PJ poured whisky for himself and Macnamara, and gave Sula a Citrine Fling. He pulled his armchair closer to Sula and leaned toward her.

"Lady Sula," he said, "I want you to know that I'm completely at your disposal. Ever since the war began I've wanted to volunteer, I've wanted to prove myself worthy of . . . well," he hesitated, "a certain person."

So he was still in love with Sempronia, Sula thought, even after she'd run off with another man.

Don't feel so superior, she told herself. PJ wasn't the only person in the room to make the mistake of falling for a Martinez.

"I've tried to think of something I could do," PJ said. "I've racked my brains. But I have no military skills, and it's too late to establish a career in the civil service. I even thought about becoming an informer or a spy."

Sula tried not to show her astonishment at this last revelation. So *that's* what he was talking about, she thought as she remembered a drunken monologue from PJ at a reception.

PJ settled back in his chair, a sunny smile breaking onto his face. "And now it's come true. I can be *your* informer. *Your* spy. I can seek enemy secrets right here in the heart of the capital."

Alarm rose in Sula. "No," she said quickly. "Don't try to spy out anything. You'll get caught and killed and put the rest of us in danger." At PJ's downcast expression, she added, "Just live your normal life. You *already* possess considerable knowledge that's of value. Tell me what you know."

PJ seemed uncertain. "What do you mean?"

"What's the news? What do you hear at your clubs? What are the Naxids doing?"

"Well," PJ shrugged, "they're all over the place, aren't they? Taking over the High City. They claim that they're bringing everything back to normal, the way it was under the Shaa, but that's not true." He took a sip of his whisky. "They've got their own people in charge of all the ministries, all the departments."

"So how do people feel about that?"

"They're angry, of course. But . . . baffled." He shrugged again. "Nobody knows what to do. Like Van, who I was talking to in my smoking club. Lord Vandermere Takahashi, I mean."

The Citrine Fling stung Sula's tongue. "Go on," she said.

"He's in the Meteorology Department," PJ said. "He's got a new Naxid supervisor, and he doesn't know how to act. He's loyal, of course, but could he be charged with treason if he followed her orders?"

"He might be shot if he didn't," Sula said.

"Probably not in the Meteorology Department," PJ allowed, "but if he were in anyplace critical, like my friend Sun is at the Ministry of Police, that would be different. He's got Naxids asking him for information all the time, and he doesn't know what they're going to use it for, whether it's an ordinary request or something they could use to prosecute loyalists. And of course he's had to take the oath of allegiance to the new government—does that make him a traitor or not? Will he be prosecuted or killed after we win the war?" He blinked. "The former government—the *real* government, I mean—was quite vehement about cooperation with the Naxids. And Van's worried too, because even the Meteorology Department will have to take the oath sooner or later."

"I see," Sula said. Ideas sizzled through her mind.

She thought she knew the message that she wanted to send to the population.

Martinez spent the transit to Termaine in the Flag Officer Station, strapped to an acceleration couch and wearing a vac suit. *Illustrious* was at general quarters, standard procedure for a warship that might encounter an enemy on the other side of a wormhole. Martinez, as the squadron's tactical officer, sat facing the squadron commander, Lady Michi Chen.

The ship's captain, Lord Gomberg Fletcher, directed *Illustrious* from Command, on another deck. The Flag Officer Station concerned itself only with squadron maneuvers and grand strategy, not with the details of running the cruiser.

The squadron entered "hot," radars and ranging lasers hammering in search of a foe. The Naxids knew Chenforce was coming, and they just might have prepared some kind of surprise.

No surprise was in the offing, though since the Naxids had turned off their own radars, it took some hours for this to become apparent. Termaine Wormhole 1 was a considerable distance from Termaine's primary, outside the heliopause, and it would take days for Chenforce to near the planet. If there were any surprises, they would be farther into the system.

In the meantime, Michi Chen's own demands were being pulsed to Termaine via high-powered communications lasers, and repeated on radio frequencies for the benefit of shipping. All ships in the system were to be destroyed; all crews in transit to abandon ship if they wished to live. All ships on the ring were to be cast off without crews, all docking and construction bays to be opened for inspection, any uncompleted ships thrown into the vacuum with everything else. And Squadron Leader Chen's own message to be broadcast regularly on all planetary media, assuring the inhabitants of the planet that the Fleet still had teeth and were still able to punish rebels . . .

The demands were not negotiable. The destruction of Bai-do had made that clear.

It would be nearly half a day before the commander of the Termaine ring received the orders, and another half day before *Illustrious* could expect a reply. No incoming missiles appeared on the squadron's sensors. The only ships visible were fleeing Chenforce under as many gees as their crews could stand. It seemed that the squadron was safe for the present.

"Inform the squadron they may secure from general quarters," said Squadron Commander Chen. Her fingers rapped in rhythm against the armrest of her couch. "Ships to remain on alert, and point-defense systems to be placed on automatic."

It was not beyond possibility that missiles were incoming at relativistic speed, and the ships' automatic laser defenses would be the most efficient defense against such a threat.

"Yes, my lady," said Lady Ida Li, one of Michi's two aides.

Martinez looked at his commander. "Will you be requiring anything else, my lady?" he asked.

"No. You're at liberty, Lord Captain."

Martinez closed the tactical display, then pushed the display over his head until it locked. He unstrapped from his

acceleration couch, grabbed one of the struts of his acceleration cage, and tilted the couch until his feet touched the
deck. He stood, stretched to bring the blood tingling to his
limbs, and then removed his helmet and took a grateful
breath of fresh—or at any rate fresher—air.

Michi Chen, still on her couch, removed her helmet and
stowed it in the mesh bag intended for that purpose. She
tilted the couch forward to get to her feet, and Martinez, like
a good staff officer, stood by to offer a hand if necessary.

She didn't need his help. The squadron commander was
a handsome, stocky woman, with graying dark hair cut in
straight bangs across her forehead. She looked up at Martinez. "So far, so good," she said. "I keep wondering if
we're going to find an enemy fleet waiting for us."

Martinez, who had been wondering if he was going to
be obliged to kill another four billion people, nodded in
tactful agreement. "I think they're fully committed to Zanshaa. I think they're flying over the capital waiting for us to
surrender."

Her lips gave a twitch of amusement. "I think you're
right. But my job obliges me to worry."

She adjusted the collar of her vac suit to a more comfortable angle, then led the way out of the Flag Officer Station. Martinez followed, wishing that someone had invited
him to dinner.

Martinez ate alone in his office, staring sourly at the
plump buttocks and chubby faces of the naked winged
children that so oddly ornamented his office walls. He was
served by his cook, Perry, and he dined alone.

It was normal for him to eat by himself. A tactical officer
was typically a lieutenant, and would mess in the wardroom, a kind of club for the lieutenants. Martinez, a full
captain, couldn't take a meal in the wardroom without an
invitation. Squadron Leader Chen had her own dining
room, as did the *Illustrious* captain, Gomberg. Unless

someone invited him, or unless he invited others, his unique status on the ship ensured his solitude.

He had left the relatively carefree life of a lieutenant behind, but he missed the companionship that life had once brought him. He would have happily traded that companionship for the loneliness of command, but the fact remained that he *wasn't* in command, and he had to dine alone anyway.

Perry cleared Martinez's plate and offered to pour more wine. Martinez placed his hand over the glass.

"Thank you, Perry," he said. Perry took the glass and left in silence.

Martinez called the tactical display onto the wall, just to make certain nothing new had appeared. Even though the naked children on the walls gazed at the displays as if in fascination, Martinez found there had been no change.

He closed the display and gazed at his desk, at images of Terza floating in the midnight surface. He thought of the child they had made together and he was suddenly possessed by a desperate exaltation, a hunger he could taste far more keenly than he had his meal. The idea of a child was a wonder to him, and he felt a blade-sharp longing for the child that he had never quite felt for Terza.

Suddenly, desperately, he wanted to be with his family aboard the *Ensenada,* the Martinez family yacht that was taking them from abandoned Zanshaa to safety on Laredo. He wanted to be with Terza, to bask in her placid smile and watch the minute progress of the child growing within her. For a brief, intense moment he would have thrown away all ambition in exchange for a quiet life of familial bliss.

There was a knock on the frame of his cabin door, and he looked up to see Lieutenant Chandra Prasad, the one person on *Illustrious* with whom he didn't want to be alone.

"Yes?" he said.

Chandra entered, closed the door behind her, and walked

to his desk. She braced properly at the salute, shoulders flared back, chin high, throat bared—the posture imposed by the empire's Shaa conquerors on all vanquished species, the better to allow their superiors to cut their throats if they felt so inclined.

"Yes, Lieutenant?" Martinez said.

She relaxed and held out a thick envelope. "From Lord Captain Fletcher."

The envelope was of thick smooth paper in a faintly cranberry shade, no doubt custom-made for Captain Fletcher by the foremost papermaker of Harzapid. The seal on the envelope had many quarterings and reflected the captain's illustrious heritage.

Martinez broke the seal and withdrew a card, which invited him to dine with the captain on the next day, to honor the birthday of Squadron Commander Chen. Exigencies of the service permitting, of course.

He looked up at Chandra. She had auburn hair, a pointed chin, and a mischievous glint in her long eyes.

"I'll come, of course," he said.

"Shall I wait for your reply?" Chandra asked.

Even though the captain's quarters were only a few paces away and the invitation nothing a sane officer could possibly decline, custom of the service nevertheless required that Martinez reply to a written invitation with a written reply.

"If you're not required elsewhere," he said.

The mischievous eyes sparkled. "I am entirely at the captain's service," Chandra said.

Which was all too true. Lieutenant Lady Chandra Prasad was Captain Fletcher's lover, a situation dangerous with potential for intrigue and service politics. That potential was all the greater for the fact that she and Martinez, at the time both obscure lieutenants of provincial origin, had once been involved with each other, a tempestuous relationship that featured mutual betrayals and a parting that had left Martinez feeling relieved rather than rueful.

Martinez didn't know if Captain Fletcher knew of his involvement with Chandra, and the lack of certainty made him uneasy. His unease was increased by his knowledge of Chandra's character, which was ambitious, restless, and explosive.

Which was why he didn't want to be alone with her for any length of time.

He got a card and envelope from his desk and in his best hand wrote a brief acceptance. As he sealed the card in its envelope he had a mental picture of Fletcher touching the card stock with his sensitive fingers and shaking his head at its inferior quality.

Martinez offered the envelope to Chandra, who was looking down at his desktop with her head tilted, casting a critical glance at Terza's pictures.

"It's unfair that your wife is beautiful as well as rich and well-connected," she said.

"She's also talented, brave, and highly intelligent," Martinez said, and held the envelope clearly in Chandra's line of sight.

Her full lips gave an amused twist. She took the envelope, then glanced with her long eyes at the naked, winged boy-children fluttering on the office walls. "Do you like the view from your desk?" she asked. "The captain tells me they're called *putti,* and they're an ancient artistic motif from Terra."

"I wish they'd stayed there."

"I imagine you'd prefer naked girls," Chandra said. "I seem to remember that you liked naked girls very well."

Martinez looked up at her and saw the invitation in her eyes. Suddenly he was aware of the nearness of her, the scent of her perfume. He looked away.

"Not in such quantity," he said.

"Don't underestimate yourself. You juggled quite a number of us, back on Zarafan."

He looked at her again. "It's not Zarafan anymore."

Now it was Chandra's turn to look away. Her eyes

passed over the chubby children. "Still," she added, "it's a good deal more cheerful than what the captain has in *his* private quarters."

Martinez told himself that he wasn't interested in what Chandra had seen in her visits to the captain's chambers. "Is that so?" he found himself saying.

"Oh yes." She raised an eyebrow. "It's nothing like what he's got in the public areas."

Pornography, then, Martinez concluded. The thought depressed him. "Thank you, Lieutenant," he said. "I won't take up any more of your time."

"Oh," Chandra said, "I don't have anything to do. I'm not on watch for hours yet."

"*I* have work," Martinez said. Chandra gave a shrug, then braced to the salute.

Martinez again called up the tactical display. Chandra left the room.

Martinez glanced at the display and saw nothing new. In fact he had no work, not until the squadcom found a task for him or something unexpected turned up on the tactical display.

He wished there were more to do. He very much wanted a task in which he could lose himself.

The alternative was to think about what might happen to Termaine if the system's governor refused Michi's demands. Or to think about his marriage. Or think of Chandra, near, available, and dangerous. Or, worst of all, to think about Caroline Sula.

In an attempt to fill the hours till supper, Martinez called up hypertourney on the desktop computer and tried to lose himself within a game of strategy and abstract spacial relationships.

He played both sides, and lost.

FOUR

This is the official newsletter of the loyalist government-in-exile. A loyal friend has suggested that we send this to you. We hope that you duplicate this document and share it with other loyal citizens. *Do not send this through electronic mail!* We distribute this notice through safe means, but you cannot. If you send this electronically, the rebels will trace this message to its place of origin and you will be caught.

If you can, reproduce this newsletter using scanners and duplicators that cannot be traced to you. Remove the image and/or text from the duplicator's buffer afterward, if you can. Share it with friends, or display it in a public place.

If you can't reproduce this material physically, share this information with friends you can trust.

What We Owe Our Government

The fact that we are under occupation by an invader has caused even loyal citizens to question their actions and to wonder what is required of them. They do not know how to respond to the rebels who have seized the capital and whose demands on the population are backed by threats of arrest, torture, and violence. They are uncertain how to respond to the invaders' demands for loyalty. We of the secret government offer the following as a guide.

As loyal citizens, we owe the government-in-exile our trust. We trust that they are fighting on no matter what the Naxids tell us through their controlled media. We trust that our government will return, defeat the rebel forces, and restore legitimate rule. We trust that the rebels will be punished along with those who helped them. Likewise, we trust that those who resist the Naxids will be rewarded by a grateful government after the restoration.

What else do we owe our government?

We owe it to our government to stay alive! We can't resist the usurpers if we're dead. Therefore we should avoid any unnecessary acts of confrontation that will result in our being captured or killed. This doesn't mean that we shouldn't resist the Naxids, just that we should resist wisely, and on our own terms.

In order to resist, we must first organize and share information. Sharing this newsletter with your family and with trustworthy friends is a beginning. If you possess information that may be of value to the secret government, try to pass it to someone who may be able to make use of it. If you discover anything that the Naxids wish kept secret, spread the secret as widely as you can.

We owe the government the use of our minds! Keep track of rebel activities. Note which Naxid gives which orders. Note which of your neighbors and colleagues follows those orders, and with what degree of enthusiasm. Keep your memories clear and fresh. After the war you may be required to testify.

We owe the government our service against the rebels! The enemy can be attacked. Not simply through force of arms, but through other means. Rebel placards can be defaced. Loyalist slogans can be painted on walls. The latest anti-Naxid jokes can and should be circulated.

If you can, you are allowed to attack Naxid officials. They are mortal, and they can die. But remember that you are not required to risk your life needlessly—make sure of your escape route, then strike!

What Do We Owe the Naxids?
We owe the Naxids only what they take at the point of a gun! The Naxids' rule is based on threat of naked force.

Therefore we will cooperate only when that threat is clear and unambiguous.

If a Naxid demands an oath of loyalty, give it. An oath extorted under threat of arrest or dismissal is meaningless. You will not be penalized after the war for taking such an oath, so long as you cooperate with the enemy only when you must.

If a Naxid asks you for directions, you are not required to know the answer.

If a Naxid asks you to identify a friend or a neighbor, you are permitted to feign ignorance.

If a Naxid asks you for information you are known to possess, give the information if you must. Act only according to the letter of your instructions: provide neither more nor less than what is asked for. You are not required to volunteer any additional information that may be in your possession, and if the information contains errors that cannot be traced to you, you cannot be blamed.

If you are asked to inform on a colleague, you are allowed to tell the Naxids that your colleague is their friend. Unless of course he *is* a Naxid sympathizer, in which case you are allowed to cast suspicion upon his activities.

If you are asked to participate in a roundup or arrest of those believed to work against the Naxids, you can hardly be blamed if your information is incorrect, so that the arrest goes wrong and the victim escapes.

If you are asked to work for the Naxids, you are permitted to make mistakes, particularly if the mistakes can't be traced to you. Improper maintenance can result in the destruction of machinery or vehicles. Deliveries can be sent to the wrong address, or to the wrong continent. Food can suffer spoilage or contamination. Videos can accidentally be erased. Labels can be confused. Weapons and explosives can vanish from inventory and appear in the hands of loyalist volunteers.

If you are asked to believe the Naxids propaganda, don't. They say the legitimate government is on the brink of surrender, but it isn't. They say that the Fleet has suffered one defeat after another, but it hasn't. They say that the secret government of Zanshaa has been destroyed, but they lie, and you are looking at the proof right now.

Remember that the rebel government will not last. We owe them only our enmity.

Remember that the legitimate government will return. We owe them our trust.

Remember that you can help the enemy fail. Do what you can to undermine the rebel authority.

Remember to circulate this message as widely as you can.

Remember that the secret government is in more places than you know. Know that we are always working against the enemy, and on your behalf.

Remember that our victory is assured.

Sula glanced once more over the text. She bit her lip as she read through some of her more preposterous declarations—"the secret government is in more places than you know"—and she wondered how many lives her words would claim.

Her own misrepresentations aside, she had far less confidence in the legitimate government than her message alleged. So far they had bungled everything, and any success the government could claim was the result of a few individuals lucky enough to be in the right place, and talented enough to be able to act effectively against the enemy. And—come to think of it—those individuals were so few that she knew most of them personally.

Her newsletter was intended to encourage citizens to act against the Naxids, though she suspected that few would. And of these, many would fail, and be arrested or killed. Most of the rest would probably be totally ineffective.

Even so, she thought she had little choice. The secret government and almost all its military had been tortured to death. Her task, assigned by the government in which she had little faith, was to mobilize opposition to the Naxids. She couldn't mobilize soldiers, and so civilians would have to do.

If they died, they died. *Human warmth not my specialty.*

Sula turned to Spence, who was looking at the text from over her shoulder. "Can you think of anything we've missed?"

Spence shook her head. "I think it's marvelous. It's everything we could think of."

"The newsletter still needs a name."

Macnamara, who was in the kitchen pouring out bottles of iarogüt into the sink, called out, "Our last bulletin was *The Loyalist.*"

"That title's bad luck," Sula said.

" 'The Staunch,' " Spence offered. " 'The Anti-Naxid.' 'The Faithful.' "

Macnamara, carrying three reeking bottles in a sack, passed through the room on his way to the front door. "You could just call it 'What We Owe,' " he said. He tossed a sheet over the bomb to hide it from anyone in the corridor, then opened the front door and placed the empties in the hall for pickup.

Sula's plan for discouraging the neighbors' questions was to give them the answer to a question they hadn't asked: the bottles placed outside the apartment every day marked them as alcoholics unworthy of further curiosity.

" 'The Fighter,' " she said. " 'The Clarion.' "

" 'The Tocsin,' " said Spence.

"That's good," Sula said. The last time the population of Zanshaa had heard the sound of the tocsin was when the accelerator ring had been destroyed.

Macnamara closed the door and sat with crossed legs in front of the disassembled bomb that sat on the small table in front of the sofa.

" 'The Bomb,' " he said.

The Saboteur, Sula thought. " 'The Anarchist,' " she said, and laughed. "Why not? That's what they call *us.*"

She looked at the text again, her eyes skimming words in search of inspiration. "Ah," she said. "Hah."

At the top of the text she called for a larger font, and added the single word *"Resistance."*

The first copy of *Resistance* went to Spence, just to see if Sula's program still worked, and the copy arrived on Spence's hand comm a half second after Sula touched the icon marked "Send."

The next ten thousand copies were sent to citizens chosen randomly, by a sorting program Sula had written, from among those who had done business with the Records Office within the last three years. The program rejected the recipient if he lived outside of the Zanshaa metropolitan area or if his species was indicated as Naxid.

Sula sent *Resistance* in mid-afternoon, at the peak of Records Office activity, on the assumption that a slight delay on the broadcast node would less likely be noticed than if she sent in the dead of night. The entire broadcast took less than twenty-five seconds.

It had occurred to her, as she prepared her message, that if her program removed the code that identified the Records Office broadcast node as the point of origin, she could as easily substitute another code. She'd looked through Rashtag's correspondence and found a note from a colleague at the Hotel Spartex, a building in the Lower Town, near the funicular, that had been requisitioned by the Naxids to house their constabulary. The code for the hotel's node was easy to pinch and insert into all ten thousand copies of *Resistance* as the newsletter's point of origin.

She smiled as she thought of the Naxid authorities turning the Hotel Spartex upside down in search of the minion of the secret government. Especially as every possible suspect was a Naxid.

Sula rewarded herself with a cup of tea while she monitored Rashtag's incoming messages. Nothing alerted him to misuse of the broadcast node, and she began to feel a certain impatience. After all her hard work, the actual experience of sending *Resistance* had been anticlimactic. She wanted the enemy to panic *now*.

Ten thousand copies, she mused, wouldn't go far among Zanshaa's three and a half million population, not to mention the further three million in the metropolitan area. Perhaps another ten thousand were in order.

She sent fifty thousand copies before her nerve finally gave out. There were no alarms flashing in the Records Office, but she had begun to feel exposed, and she decided that the experiment had run enough risks for the day.

She shut down her desk computer and rose. Spence was working on assembling the bomb with Macnamara's help.

Sula walked across the room and leaned out the window with her hands braced on the sill. The street swarmed below her, and the air was scented with the aroma of cilantro, garlic, and hot pavement. Her muscles tingled with the release of tension. She searched the crowd carefully, but nobody seemed to be reading their displays. She wanted to demand of the crowds below, *Did I just change the world or not?*

She turned to the rest of her team. "I declare a holiday," she said.

Spence and Macnamara stared at her. "Are you sure?" Spence asked, in a tone that meant *Are you sure you're feeling all right?*

Sula had never showed an interest in holidays before.

"Yes. Absolutely." Sula shut the window and moved the spider plant to the right-hand side of the windowsill, the position that meant *No one's here, approach with caution.* "Clean up your homework, get on the streets, have some fun." She reached in an inner pocket and handed them each a few zeniths. "Call it a reconnaissance. I want you to take the pulse of the city."

Spence seemed dubious. "Can I leave as well? Because—"

"You walk well enough until you get tired. So see that you don't get tired—take cabs everywhere."

Spence gave a yelp of joy and leaped to her feet. Bomb components vanished into hidden compartments that Macnamara had built into the furniture, and everyone changed into clothing more suitable to a night on the town. At the door to the apartment, they separated like the flying fragments of one of their own explosive devices.

They had been in the same small room far too long.

Sula went toward the entertainment district along the old canals below the High City. She visited a series of clubs and cafés, sitting at the bar where she could encounter people, or at a table where she could overhear others. A number of men wanted to buy her drinks. She sipped mineral water, let them talk, and tried to steer the conversation toward the Naxids.

All showed prudent caution about the topic—one never knew who might be listening—but alcohol eventually loosened their tongues. Several had new Naxid supervisors, but said it was too early to know how that would change things. One man had been demoted, his place in the Transportation Ministry taken by a Naxid: he was on his sixth or seventh drink and in the midst of a deep melancholy. Most were eventually willing to admit they were furious that the Naxids had taken hostages.

"But what can we do?" one said. "We've got to cooperate. The whole planet is hostage now."

None seemed to have encountered the first issue of *Resistance,* let alone absorbed the wisdom Sula had so hopefully packed into it. By now she herself was depressed, and her steps brought her to a derivoo club, where she could be comforted by the existence of folk with worse problems than hers.

The derivoo singer, face and hands whitened, stood straight beneath her spotlight and sang songs of sorrow. Betrayal, shattered hearts, death, violence, accident, suicide, horror—the derivoo's palate was cast entirely in dark colors. The point was not so much that these griefs existed as that the derivoo was still able to sing about them. Oppressed by every imaginable catastrophe, weighted down by every fearful memory, the derivoo still stood straight and broadcast a message of defiance to the universe. *I am beaten, I am bloody, but still I stand . . .*

Watching the performance was like observing an unforgiving war between passion and control. Too much passion, and the work would tip into melodrama and become absurd. Too much control, and the songs became soulless. The singer tonight was able to walk perfectly the knife-edge between fire and ice, and Sula felt her blood surge in response. She had seen the Home Fleet burn at Magaria, torn to ions by Naxid antimatter. She had brought her team out of the wreckage of the Axtattle ambush as Naxid bullets chewed the building to bits around them. She had watched her comrades die by torture.

Sula had inflicted tragedy as well as endured it. She had killed five Naxid ships at Magaria along with all their crews. "It was Sula who did this!" she had called to the Naxids at Magaria. *"Remember my name!"*

She had claimed the Sula name then, made it her own, even though Sula had not always been her name. Once, when she was very young—when her name had been Gredel—she'd pressed a pillow to the face of Caroline, Lady Sula, and afterward claimed the dead girl's name, her title, and her small fortune.

It was not clear in Sula's mind whether that was a tragedy or not. Probably it was for Caro Sula, though it wasn't likely Caro would have survived much longer anyway. She had already overdosed once, and would have again.

Whether any of this was a tragedy for her was as yet unclear to Sula. She was inclined to think not. If there were tragedy involved, she intended that it would be a tragedy for the Naxids.

She left the club feeling as if she had gained possession of some primal fact of the universe, something both despairing and joyous, and the elation carried her all the way home. Not to the apartment where she met with her team to plan assassinations and to plunder the resources of the Records Office—that was intended to be used only for meetings—but to a one-room place she'd acquired for herself.

Life on the street was fading quickly in the dim, rationed light. The last food-seller waited only to sell his last few ears of roasted maize before packing up his grill and leaving, and Sula helped him by buying an ear, enjoying its sweetness along with the smoky taste of the charcoal and the coarse sprinkling of salt.

With only a few streetlights burning, it was dark enough so that she was totally surprised by the figure that rose from the shadows next to the stairs. As her heart leaped, she stepped automatically into a strong stance, the corncob held in her fist like a knife . . .

"Is that you, beauteous lady?"

Sula recognized the voice and relaxed out of her stance. She spoke over the hammering of her heart. "One-Step? What are you doing here this late?"

One-Step replied with dignity. "You never know when someone will want to see me here in my office."

One-Step's office was the patch of pavement next to the apartment steps, and whatever business he conducted there remained obscure. Sula forgave him this and other flaws for the sake of his extraordinary black eyes, which were brilliant and liquid and beautiful, and on this night unfortunately invisible in the darkness.

One-Step's voice turned reproachful. "You haven't been home, beauteous lady. I've been desolated."

"A friend got me a bit of work in another part of town."

"Work?" His voice brightened. "What kind?"

"Inventory. But it was temporary, and now it's over."

The voice turned accusing. "You've been off spending the money, haven't you? Spending it without One-Step."

"I went to see a derivoo," Sula said.

"Derivoo!" One-Step scorned. "That's all so depressing! You should let One-Step show you a *good* time. I'll treat you like you deserve, like the highest Peer of the High City. Like a queen. You'll never regret a night with One-Step."

"Maybe some other time. I want to get some sleep tonight."

"Sleep is a treacherous object. Here's something that may keep you awake for a while."

He handed her a plastic flimsy, and she squinted at it as she held it to the dim yellow light of her apartment vestibule.

Resistance, she read.

One-Step had been trying to charm his way into her arms ever since they first met, but even so, he was probably surprised at the joyous hug and kiss.

"Beauteous lady," he said, "you'll never regret—"

"I don't," she said, backing away. "But you be careful who you give these to, all right?"

He was reproachful again. "One-Step is always careful."

Sula's heart was light as she entered the building, went up two flights, and checked her door for signs of intrusion. She entered, switched on the light, and looked at the copy of *Resistance,* properly printed on perfectly decent plastic. There was no indication where or how it had been printed, and no watermark. *"A loyal friend has suggested that we send this to you . . ."* Ah, lovely.

Thank you, One-Step, loyal friend.

The apartment smelled of heat and disuse. She went to the little alcove by the window and put the issue of *Resistance* on the broad ledge, pinning it with the pot that waited there. She opened the window to clear out the heat of the day, checked to make certain her guns and grenades were in the hidden compartments where she'd put them, then sat cross-legged on her sleeping pallet and admired the pot and news sheet together, the way the pale plastic was reflected in the blue-green crackle of the age-old pot.

The pot was *ju yao* ware of Earth's ancient Song Dynasty, an object so valuable that if her neighbors knew of it, they would have bludgeoned each other with crowbars to be the first to break into the apartment and steal it. Just before the Naxids arrived, when sad, dead Caro's whole inheritance finally came into her possession, Sula bought the pot for fourteen thousand zeniths, a little more than half the total legacy, and much less than it was worth.

Porcelain was one of her passions. She had never owned a valuable piece before, but she'd decided that, given that she was going to throw her life away on what was probably a futile effort to resist the Naxids, she might as well indulge herself in this one small thing.

The rest she had invested more practically.

She gazed with pleasure at the pot for a few luxurious moments, then went to the bathroom to wash and prepare herself for bed. Then, because she couldn't stand the merest hint of untidiness, she cleaned away the thin, soft layer of dust that lay over the room. After she used a duster to brush the dust reverently from the *ju yao* pot, she retired to her bed.

In the morning *Resistance* was everywhere: pasted to lampposts, sitting on tables at cafés, weighed down on doorsteps with scraps of iron or bits of crumbled old brick. She had a sweet red bean bun at a pastry shop and filled her mug of tea from the samovar that the customers used in common. Two women in line for the samovar were talking about the copy of *Resistance* they'd seen.

"*Now* I know what to do with that nasty Mr. Klarvash and his requests for data," one said.

Exulting, Sula walked the short distance to the larger apartment, and saw that the pot in the window had been moved to the position that meant *Someone's here, and it's all clear*. Even so, she entered via the back stairs, moving cautiously through the kitchen until she saw Spence sitting on the floor behind the little table, with the parts of the bomb spread out before her. Spence was staring at the video wall, and tears coursed unhindered down her cheeks.

Sula froze. "What's wrong?" she said.

Spence turned her streaming eyes to Sula. "They're shooting hostages. Fifty-five, eleven from each species. Because subversive literature was being distributed. And they're shooting anyone they catch, and they say they've caught a number by now." She reached for a handkerchief. *"And it's our fault!"* she cried.

Get a grip, Sula wanted to suggest. *What do you think that bomb you're building is for?*

Instead she stepped into the room and made soothing noises. "It's not our fault. That's all the enemy. It's *their* fault, not ours. *We're* not shooting hostages."

The video wall showed a group of Daimong being herded onto the execution ground. *And if we're lucky,* Sula thought, *if we're really really lucky, the Naxids won't stop shooting hostages anytime soon.*

FIVE

"I have always found tragedy to be the most human of the arts," said Senior Captain Lord Gomberg Fletcher. "Other species simply don't have a feeling for it."

"There's Lakaj Trallin's *The Messenger*," said Fulvia Kazakov, the first lieutenant.

"The choral parts are magnificent, as one might expect with the Daimong," the captain admitted, "but I find the psychology of Lord Ganmir and Lady Oppoda underdeveloped."

Captain Fletcher's dinner stretched the length of the ship's long afternoon. Every plate, saucer, cup, goblet, and salt cellar on the long table was blazoned with the captain's crest, and the table itself sat in the midst of painted revelry. The walls were covered with murals of banquets and banqueters: ancient Terrans wearing sheets and eating on couches; humanoid creatures with horns and hairy, cloven-hoofed legs roistering with wine cups and bunches of grapes; a tall, commanding youth, crowned with leaves, surrounded by women carrying phallic staves. Statues stood in the corners, graceful seminude women bearing cups. A solid gold centerpiece crowned the table, armored warriors mysteriously standing guard over piles of brilliant metal fruits and nuts.

The captain was a renowned patron of the arts, and as an offspring of the eminent and preposterously rich Gomberg and Fletcher clans, he had the money to indulge himself. He had ornamented *Illustrious* with a lavish hand, sparing no expense to create a masterpiece that would be the envy of the Fleet. The hull had been painted in a complex geometric pattern of brilliant white, pale green, and pink. The interior was filled with more geometric patterns broken by fantastic landscapes, trompes l'oeil, scenes of hunting and dancing, forests and vines, whimsical architecture and wind-tossed seascapes. Most of these works had been created in a graphics program, run off on long sheets, then mounted like wallpaper, but in the captain's own quarters the murals had been painted on, and were subsequently maintained, by a pudgy, graying, rather disheveled artist named Montemar Jukes, who Fletcher had brought aboard as a servant and promptly rated Rigger First Class.

Jukes dined in the petty officers' lounge: no one present at the captain's dinner was anything less than an officer and a Peer. All glittered in their full dress uniforms, as the captain's long-established custom was that all meals aboard *Illustrious* be formal, whether they were a special occasion or not.

He had established his rule before Martinez joined the ship, but Martinez had added his own unexpected contribution to the ritual. Since the dinners were, after all, full dress, he had worn his decorations—or, in the case of one particular decoration, carried it.

The award in question was the Golden Orb, a baton on which was mounted a transparent globe filled with swirling gold liquid. It happened to be the highest award in the empire, given Martinez for stealing the *Corona* from under Naxid noses at Magaria, and every officer and crew, every lord convocate or government employee, was required to salute it.

So the first time Martinez had arrived for one of the captain's dinners, Captain Lord Gomberg Fletcher was obliged to jump up and salute him; and this had happened on every occasion since. The captain had been gracious about it—he was never less than gracious—but there was something in the set of the long, handsome face that suggested he had discovered a flaw in the arrangement of the universe. No Fletcher had ever before in history saluted a Martinez, and he resented the fact that he should be the first.

Tonight, Lady Michi, the guest of honor, sat at the head of the table, with the rest below in order of precedence. Fletcher and Martinez sat beneath Lady Michi, and below Fletcher was the first lieutenant, Fulvia Kazakov, her dark hair braided and tied into an elaborate knot behind her head, then transfixed with a pair of gold-embroidered chopsticks of camphor wood.

On Martinez's elbow was Chandra Prasad, her knee pressed familiarly to his. Below them were ranked the other four lieutenants, the ship's doctor, and the cadets. At the far end of the table was the one non-Terran aboard *Illustrious,* a Daimong cadet who had commanded a pinnace at the Battle of Protipanu and been absent from his ship, the frigate *Beacon,* when it was destroyed with all aboard.

Like the other cadets, the Daimong maintained an intimidated silence in the presence of his superiors, so his views on the psychology of Lord Ganmir and Lady Oppoda went unrecorded.

"There's Go-tul's *New Dynasty,*" Michi said. "A very moving tragedy, I've always thought."

"I consider it flawed," said Captain Fletcher. He was a thin-faced man with ice-blue eyes that glittered from deep sockets, and silvery hair set in unnaturally perfect waves. His manner combined the Fleet's assumption of unquestioned authority with the flawless ease of the high-caste Peer.

He was a complete autocrat, but perfectly relaxed about it.

"*New Dynasty* concerns a provincial Peer who travels to Zanshaa and comes within an ace of taking her place in elite society," Fletcher continued. "But she fails, and in the end has to return home. She ends the story in her proper place." He gave Lady Michi a questioning look. "How is that tragic? Genuine tragedy is the fall of someone born into the highest place and then falling from it."

Chandra's hand, under the table, dropped onto Martinez's thigh and gave it a ferocious squeeze. Martinez tried not to jump.

"Which is more tragic, Lord Captain," Chandra asked, her voice a little high. "A provincial who rises above her station and fails, or a provincial who rises and *succeeds*?"

Fletcher gave her a sharp look, and then his expression regained its accustomed poise. "The latter, I think," he said.

Chandra dug her claws once more into Martinez's thigh. Anger vibrated in her. The other officers stiffened, their eyes on the drama being played out between Chandra and the captain. They were all aware that she and Fletcher were lovers, and they all could see that the relationship might explode right at this moment, in front of them all.

The moment appalling, Martinez thought. It was like watching an accident: you couldn't stop it, but you couldn't turn away.

"So provincials shouldn't try to rise in the world?" Chandra asked. "Provincials should stay on their home worlds and let the High City families deal with affairs? The same families that nearly lost the empire to the rebels?" She looked at Martinez. "Where would the Fleet be if Captain Martinez had followed that advice?"

Though Martinez had to agree that the Fleet was improved by his presence, he preferred not to be used as an example. He knew that despite his success, the captain considered him a freak of nature, something on a par with a bearded lady or a talking dog.

He knew, but he didn't particularly feel like rehashing it all at Michi Chen's birthday dinner, particularly since nothing he said or did would ever alter the captain's mind.

"How much worse would our situation be without Captain Martinez, I'd like to know," Chandra insisted.

"Captain Martinez," said Fletcher easily, "isn't a tragic

hero, so far as I know. We're discussing theater, not real life." He gave a graceful inclination of his head toward Martinez. "Were a figure like Captain Martinez to appear onstage, it would be a tale of high adventure, surely, not the fall of the great."

Chandra gave Fletcher a smoldering glare. "The great have abandoned Zanshaa and are running like hell from the enemy right now," she said. "Do you think there'll ever be a tragedy about that?" Her lip curled. "Or will it be a *farce*?"

"I think—" Michi began firmly, with the obvious intention of ending the discussion, when a chime from her sleeve display interrupted her. The officers fell silent as she answered: they knew no one would have interrupted the squadron commander's dinner without good reason.

From his position at Michi's elbow, Martinez saw the chameleon-weave fabric on her left forearm resolve itself into the image of the warrant officer who guided *Illustrious* from Command.

"My lady, I have received a reply from the governor of Termaine," she said.

"I'll see it," Michi said.

"It's text only. It reads: 'In view of the local superiority of your pirate forces, and the millions murdered at Bai-do by your command, I have no option but to comply with your unjust and tyrannical demands.' Signed, Fleet Commander Jakseth, Military Governor."

Michi listened to the insults with a wry smile, and when the governor's name was spoken, burst into a delighted laugh. "So Jakseth's a *Fleet Commander* now?" she said. "He's been on the captain's list since I was at the academy!"

Martinez sensed the tension drain from the company, and felt a burst of gratitude for the war that had distracted them from the combat between Chandra and the captain.

"Reply to the governor," Michi said. "In text, since that's how he wants it. 'Congratulations to the Fleet Commander on his promotion. May he have all the success he enjoyed as captain of the *Champion*.'"

There was laughter from Fletcher at this. Martinez waited for Michi to end her communication, and then spoke.

"I'm sorry, Lady Squadcom, but I don't understand your answer."

"*Champion* was Jakseth's last command," she said. "He managed to cause a collision when he docked at Comador—millions in damage, and all his fault. Family influence helped him evade a court-martial, but he hasn't been allowed to fly so much as a pinnace since." She looked pleased. "And now he has a whole planet! The rebels were his only hope for promotion."

Fletcher lifted a hand to signal his wine steward. "Perhaps we should toast the fleetcom's good luck."

Wineglasses were recharged and raised in facetious toast to the captain of the *Champion.* Servants cleared plates and brought another course, mayfish in some kind of sweet berry sauce, with a seaweed garnish.

There was a respectful knock on the door. Martinez looked to see a detachment of the cruiser's senior petty officers clustered in the doorway.

"We beg your pardon, my Lady Squadcom," said Master Weaponer Gulik. "We would like to make a presentation on the occasion of your birthday, if we may."

"I would be honored, Master Weaponer," Michi said.

Gulik—a small, dour, rat-faced man—squeezed into the room past one of the cup-bearing statues and approached Michi's seat. He was followed by Master Engineer Thuc, a massive, muscled, slab-sided Terran with the goatee and curling mustachios worn by many senior petty officers. Behind these came the senior machinist, electrician, signaler, and the other petty officers in charge of the ship's departments.

"We wish to present you with this memento of your time aboard *Illustrious,* my lady," Gulik said.

The memento was a scale model of the *Illustrious,* with the green, pink, and white of Fletcher's paint scheme minutely and exactly detailed. The model was mounted on a brass base built in the cruiser's workshop.

Michi thanked the deputation, and led the officers in a toast to the department heads. The deputation left, and the dinner resumed, one course after another, each reflecting the genius of Fletcher's personal chef, each course marked by toasts and compliments.

Martinez was aware of Chandra smoldering next to him, her leg jigging up and down with impatience.

"You might have stood up for yourself," she told Martinez as he walked to his cabin after the feast.

"No one was attacking me," Martinez said. "The worst anyone said was that I wasn't a tragic hero, and I hope to hell that's true."

"Fletcher's said a *lot* of things about you," Chandra said.

"Yes," Martinez said. He opened his cabin door, then turned to her. "But I'm not supposed to know that, am I? Because I'm not supposed to be on intimate terms with the captain's girlfriend, am I?"

He closed the door on Chandra's mask of thwarted fury, made his way to his desk and sat down. He put the Golden Orb down on the desk's deep black surface and then opened the buttons on his dress tunic.

After the four-hour formal meal, he felt like a bird stuffed and trussed for roasting.

The winged children on the walls looked at him hungrily.

Next day, Martinez was in the Flag Officer Station briefly as *Illustrious* launched a pair of pinnaces, one of them piloted by the lone Daimong survivor of the *Beacon*. These would race past Termaine, their powerful cameras and other sensors trained on the Termaine ring to make certain that Lady Michi's orders were obeyed, that all docking and construction bays were open to the vacuum and that all ships, including those under construction, had been cast off. *Illustrious* would recover the pinnaces on the far side of the system.

At Bai-do, the Naxids had opened fire on the pinnaces as they passed, killing the cadets who flew them, and Lady Michi had retaliated for this defiance by destroying the ring. Billions died in exchange for two cadets, making a point that it was hoped the Naxid high command would respect.

This time the pinnaces would have an escort. Each pinnace would fly surrounded by a cloud of twenty-four antimatter missiles, all under command of the pinnace pilots themselves. The missiles could either be used offensively or to counter missiles launched from the ring. The missiles, like the pinnaces, could be recovered after the completion of their mission, or diverted to other targets, like the merchant vessels that were accelerating madly in an effort to clear the system before Chenforce destroyed them.

Martinez watched as the missiles were flung from the tubes, as chemical rockets ignited to carry them a safe distance from the cruiser before the antihydrogen engines started. The pinnaces followed shortly thereafter, engines firing to take them on a long curve that would carry them on either side of Termaine.

The Flag Officer Station stood down once the pinnaces and the missile barrages were on their way, and Martinez tucked his helmet under his arm and made his way to his cabin, where his orderly, Khalid Alikhan, helped him out of his vac suit.

Alikhan was a thirty-year veteran of the Fleet who had retired with the rank of Master Weaponer, and who still proudly wore the goatee and curling mustachios of the senior petty officer. Alikhan was a fountain of vivid anecdotes, technical arcana, and knowledge of the devious paths one might take to circumvent the formalities and custom of the Fleet, and Martinez had employed him with the intention of taking advantage of those thirty years' experience in the weapons bays.

Alikhan hung the vac suit in its locker and served Martinez coffee from the vacuum pot that waited on a sideboard in the office.

"I was wondering, my lord, if I might trouble you for an advance on my pay," he said as he placed the cup on Martinez's desk.

Martinez paused in surprise, the cup halfway to his lips. Alikhan had never before asked for an advance.

"Yes," he said. "Yes, of course." He rose from his chair, opened his office safe, and handed Alikhan five zeniths. "Will that be enough?"

"That's more than sufficient, my lord. Thank you."

Martinez closed the safe. "Is the petty officers' club doing something special?" he asked. He couldn't think what it could be. With the ship's canteen running low after months away from port, the nearest place to spend money was Termaine.

"No, my lord," Alikhan said. His stern face hardened into an expression of vexation. "I was unlucky at cards."

Martinez looked at him, surprised again. "I didn't know you gambled," he said.

"I venture now and again, my lord."

Alikhan braced, which indicated that he hoped the conversation was over. Martinez decided it might well be.

"Carry on, then," he said, and Alikhan made his way out.

Martinez sat at his desk and sipped his coffee, then checked the tactical display.

The rebels at Termaine were obeying orders, so far as he could tell. Termaine was now surrounded by a small cloud of vessels that had been cast adrift, ready to be destroyed by Chenforce as it swept past.

Martinez didn't find the sight completely assuring.

Bai-do too had complied with Michi's demands, right up to the point where they opened fire.

SIX

The bomb was disassembled and brought up to the High City in pieces, hidden in Team 491's toolboxes and then stowed in PJ Ngeni's guest cottage behind the Ngeni Palace. The explosive itself, which might have triggered the sniffers at the funicular, was brewed in PJ's kitchen out of components purchased from hardware stores and cleaning supply houses.

As the bomb reached final assembly, PJ hovered above the table in the study, torn between anxiety and an eerie delight. Eventually he became a distraction, and Sula had to take him to his study and pour several drinks down him before he calmed down.

Sula had at one point expressed doubts about smuggling arms past the detectors on the funicular, and PJ promptly volunteered the Ngeni clan's collection of sporting weapons. Sula was about to decline—the guns were registered, and if they had to be left behind would point straight at PJ—when she hesitated and went to the nearest comm terminal.

Checking in at the Records Office, she found the arms registry and erased anything connected to anyone named Ngeni.

The police would have ballistics and forensics information regarding any legally purchased firearm, but they would be useless for an old weapon that had been fired many times. Sula made certain to equip her team with weapons that were centuries old.

On the day of the operation, Zanshaa's viridian sky was clear and sunny, which made it more likely that Lord Makish would be walking home. This was desirable from Sula's point of view, but less desirable was the probability that other Naxids, who preferred their weather hot, would be on the streets.

If they die, they die. She certainly didn't intend to risk herself in order to spare a few stray Naxids.

Shortly after noon, Spence went off to Garden of Scents to stand lookout. Sula and Macnamara strapped their toolboxes onto the back of his two-wheeler at the Ngeni Palace, got aboard, and hummed away through half-empty streets. They traveled along Lapis Street, which paralleled the Boulevard of the Praxis to the north, and parked in the lane to one side of the Urghoder Palace, the empty building next to Judge Makish's residence.

Sula tucked her hair into a bandanna, and over this put a worker's lightweight cap; then, with Macnamara following, she carried her toolbox around the corner, past the inscribed entrance to the Urghoder Palace, and to Makish's elaborate wrought-silver-alloy gate. She entered, approached the front door—whose form echoed the artichoke shape of the towers—and pressed a button that caused a clacking noise in the interior, similar to the sound of the *aejai*.

Behind her, Macnamara hovered near the gate, as though uncertain. He'd already put one of his toolboxes down behind some bushes near the path.

The liveried servant who answered the door reared back, in loathing or surprise, and stood as tall as her short-legged centauroid form permitted, on tiptoe reaching Sula's shoulder.

"You should have come to the back entrance!" she declared in a voice that rose nearly to a screech.

"Beg pardon," Sula said, "but we were told to work on the garden. If this is the Urghoder Palace, that is."

"The Urghoder Palace is next door!" the servant said. "Be away!"

"We were told wrong, then," Sula said cheerfully. "Thanks anyway!"

"Away!" the servant repeated.

Hope we blow your ass to the ring, Sula thought. Under the servant's black-on-red eyes she and Macnamara left the garden and neatly closed the gleaming alloy gate behind her. While the servant continued to watch, the two made their way to the Urghoder Palace and entered the over-grown, disused front garden, where—behind the ivy-crusted flanking wall of yellow sandstone—they were out of sight of the Makish front door.

They opened their boxes and readied their tools. Sula and Macnamara each inserted a receiver in one ear, clipped a tiny microphone to their collars, and did a brief commu-nications check with Spence. For the rest of the afternoon they worked steadily in the garden a task that Sula found more taxing than she'd expected. She had been raised in cities and grown up in ships and barracks: her experience with domestic plants was limited. Macnamara, fortunately, was from the country, and had lived so bucolic a childhood he'd actually worked as a shepherd. Under his guidance Sula pruned and hacked at the overgrown foliage and thought herself lucky that no actual sheep were involved. Macnamara assisted when a bough or a root needed more muscle than Sula possessed, but was otherwise busy in a secluded corner of the garden, digging a slit trench with a portable pick.

Sula wanted someplace for them to hide when the bomb actually went off. They had debated whether they truly needed to be anywhere in the vicinity—possibly a real pro-fessional saboteur, certain in her luck and in the technol-ogy of remote-controlled detonators, wouldn't need to be anywhere closer than the Garden of Scents—but Sula lacked that confidence. If one of the Makish servants found the toolbox hidden in the garden, she wanted to be close enough to claim it before anyone opened the box to find the bomb.

Plus the bomb might not quite do the job: Sula wanted to be on hand in case Makish needed to be finished off, and if she was to be nearby, she wanted a safe hiding place.

Macnamara sweated great stains in his coveralls as he swung his pick and cursed the roots that got in his way, and perspiration poured down Sula's face as she gasped in air heavily perfumed by sweet blossoms while she hacked at chuchuberry bushes and tried to avoid impaling herself on the diabolic swordlike thorns of pyrocantha. At least her labors kept at bay her nagging suspicion, the silent voice in her ear that told her she was an amateur, that her plan was idiotic and that when this went wrong she was going to share the fate of her superiors.

Her training in building bombs and other items of sabotage had been thorough. How and when to use them hadn't been a part of the course. Perhaps, she thought, her superiors hadn't known either.

She and Macnamara had broken out their water bottles, picked some overripe chuchuberries, and were taking a break from their exertions when Spence's voice whispered in Sula's ear that Makish and his guards were coming on foot.

It was four hours past noon. Surveillance had shown that the High Court did not keep burdensome hours, which was why Sula had decided to spend all afternoon waiting.

"Comm: acknowledge," Sula replied. "Comm: send."

At her command, the message was encoded and sent in a brief burst transmission, lasting a hard-to-detect fraction of a second. The communications protocols were an echo of those used at the disastrous Axtattle action, and at the memory, Sula felt a shimmer of unease pass along her nerves. A fresh sheen of sweat broke out as she and Macnamara tossed their tools in a corner, took refuge behind some bushes, and dug weapons out of their toolboxes.

"I believe this is yours!" came a shrill voice. Sula's heart gave a leap. She hastily stuffed her pistol into a thigh pocket, parted the branches of a chuchuberry bush, and saw Lord Makish's servant thrusting a toolbox at them, balancing it on top of the low wall that stood between the sidewalk and the Urghoder garden.

"You careless people left this in the Makish garden!" the servant cried.

"Take cover," Spence said in Sula's ear. "Less than half a minute now."

"Thank you," Sula said as she rushed forward, arms outstretched for the box and its bomb.

Leaning against the wall on the garden side, she observed, was a saw, a sharp-toothed blade fixed in a metal frame and equipped with a pistol grip.

"Who do you work for?" the servant demanded as Sula claimed the toolbox and lowered it carefully to the ground. "I shall contact your employers with a complaint."

"Please don't do that, miss," Sula said as—her eyes scanning the street—she reached for the pistol grip of the saw.

"Twenty-five seconds," Spence reported—a quarter minute, more or less.

"You are impudent and careless with your employer's property," the servant said as she leaned intently over the wall. "You have—"

Sula slashed her across the throat with the saw. The Naxid reared back as she had when she'd first seen Sula, hands scrabbling for her neck.

"Comm: abort! Stand by!" Sula said. "Comm: send!"

"Abort" and "Stand by" were actually two different orders, but Sula didn't have time to sort them out. With any luck, Spence would take her binoculars off Makish and see what was happening at the Urghoder Palace.

The Naxid fell to the sidewalk in a tangle of elaborate livery, her polished shoes kicking. Sula peered over the wall and looked down the Boulevard of the Praxis: she saw Judge Makish and his guards, and accompanying them an officer in the viridian green of the Fleet. Badges of high rank glittered on the officer's shoulders and medals gleamed on his chest.

"Standing by," came Spence's reply. Sula was aware of Macnamara emerging from cover, a pistol held warily behind his leg.

She picked up the bomb and vaulted the wall. The servant gasped and sputtered at her feet, black scales flashing red in what Sula hoped were unreadable patterns. Sula turned toward Makish and his group and advanced at a trot.

"Sir!" she called, waving. "My lords!"

The bodyguards swept to the front, alert, hands reaching for weapons. "Your servant is ill!" Sula said. "She needs help!"

The entire group increased speed, bodies weaving as the foremost pair of limbs dropped and began to be used as legs. Sula had to leap out of the way. Surprise swirled through her head as she looked at four receding Naxid backs, at black scales glittering in the brilliant light of Shaamah. Sula put the bomb down and followed the Naxids, her hand reaching into her thigh pocket for her pistol. The two guards—trained in first aid, no doubt—bent over the wounded servant, hands plucking at her livery.

The flat Naxid head served only as a platform for sensory organs: a Naxid's brain was in the center of its humanoid torso, with the heart and other vital organs being in the lower, four-legged body. Sula would prefer to have shot the guards first, but Makish and the Fleet officer—a junior fleet commander, no less—stood between her and the military constables, so she chose the more dangerous of the two and put a pair of shots into the center of the fleetcom's back.

As she shifted her aim, a long series of shots rang out, and her startled nerves gave a leap with each angry crack. Had the bodyguards got to their weapons *that fast*? she wondered. She shot Makish, her body braced for the impact of enemy bullets that didn't come, and then she realized that the other shooter was Macnamara, firing over the stone wall and catching the enemy in a cross fire.

There was a pause in which the only thing Sula heard was the singing in her ears caused by the shots' concussion. The pistols PJ had given them proved rather noisy. There were Naxid bodies sprawled on the sidewalk and a lot of deep purple Naxid blood.

"Run!" Sula said, the idea occurring to her suddenly; and she sprang over the Naxid bodies, the pistol still in her fist. Behind, Macnamara vaulted the wall and pelted in her wake.

"Comm: stand by! Any second now! Comm: send!"

The bomb was now redundant as an assassination device, but it could still serve as a propaganda weapon. The government might deny a pair of assassins with pistols, but they couldn't deny a big explosion on the Boulevard of the Praxis, right in the middle of the High City.

A file of Naxid children approached, neatly attired in school uniforms, their bodies snaking from side to side in the wake of an adult supervisor.

Sula preferred not to murder children, not even if they were Naxids, but fate had not consulted her, and she wasn't about to slow down and explain things. "Run!" she said as she dashed past. "Bad things!"

"Wait!" the supervisor said, her black-on-yellow eyes going wide. Sula didn't spare her a backward glance.

She skated around the side of the Urghoder Palace and into the narrow lane that ran down its side. The cool shade of the lane was welcome after the afternoon sun. Sula slowed to a trot, and Macnamara slowed in her wake, pausing to pull an emergency flare from his pocket, strike it on the cool sandstone wall, and toss it behind them. Their retreat would be covered by billowing red smoke.

Sula gasped for breath, her hand trailing on the palace wall for balance, and she wondered how much time to give the Naxid schoolchildren to get out of the way. She counted to ten, then spoke.

"Comm: detonate. Comm: send."

A scant second later the sandstone wall punched her fingers with surprising strength and the ground lurched beneath her feet. She didn't feel the explosion so much with her ears as with her insides, an uneasy stirring as the shock wave passed through each organ. The red smoke at the end of the lane was blown over them in a thin scarlet fog; and suddenly they were in a rain of rubble and trash blown off the Urghoder Palace roof. Sula tried to knock the stuff off her cap and shoulders as she ran.

She unfastened the gray jumpsuit as soon as she made her way out of the cloud, and when they got to Macnamara's two-wheeler, they both peeled out of their suits and took off their headgear, revealing richer clothing beneath. The workers' costumes were shoved into the two-wheeler's panniers, and with Macnamara driving, the vehicle moved out into traffic, the two passengers to all appearances a pair of upper-middle-class youth on a summer joy ride. Anyone looking closely would have seen that the clothing was soaked through with sweat, but the gyroscopically stabilized two-wheeler was moving too fast for that, weaving through the traffic, darting into lanes and alleys.

Behind them the gray cloud of debris towered over the High City like an omen foretelling dark events to come.

"The plan was too elaborate," Sula said, blinking against the setting sun. "It would have been safer to plant the bomb somewhere along the route or pull up alongside Makish in a car and gun him down."

"You wanted something noisy," Spence pointed out.

"The big boom was the only thing the plan had going for it. The rest was fucking stupid." She looked at Macnamara. "If you hadn't known exactly what to do at the critical moment, we would have been neck-deep in the shit."

The flaws in the plan seemed so obvious now: she only wished at least a few of them had occurred to her at the planning stage.

Action Team 491 stood in the shade of an ammat tree on

the broad terrace of the Ngeni Palace, looking down the cliff at the Naxid checkpoint at the base of the road that zigzagged up the acropolis to the High City. The Naxids had shut down traffic entirely, and the long line of vehicles on the switchback road hadn't moved in some time.

Probably the funicular wasn't moving either. The High City was being sealed off while the search went on for the assassins.

"Cocktails?" PJ Ngeni said as he arrived with a tray.

Sula took a Citrine Fling from the tray and raised the other hand to lightly fluff the damp hair at the back of her neck. On arrival at the Ngeni Palace, she'd first insisted on a bath and a change of clothes before conducting her debriefing. The tub PJ had offered her was large enough for a troop, and once she'd applied a lavender-scented bath oil to the steaming water, she remained in the tub till her toes wrinkled.

Macnamara and Spence took their cocktails, sipped, and made gratified noises. PJ smiled.

"Any news, my lord?" Spence asked.

"No, Miss Ardelion." Using the code name. "There hasn't been a word on any of the news channels."

"They haven't made up their minds how to report it," Sula said. "They can't deny the explosion, and they can't deny closing all the exits to the High City."

"What are they going to do?" Spence's dark eyes looked worried. "Search the High City for us?"

"I don't think they've got enough personnel. The High City's big, and they don't have that many people here." With the ring and its elevators destroyed, the Naxids had been forced to bring their forces to the surface using shuttles propelled by chemical rockets, shuttles of which they had a limited supply. The actual numbers of those brought down from orbit were still fairly small, and the new arrivals depended for order on Naxids already on the planet when they arrived.

"They could bring in Naxid police from outside the city," Spence said.

Sula looked down at the road with its traffic frozen in

place. "We'll see them from here if they do. But I don't think they will." She sipped her Fling and gave a cold smile. "With all access to the High City cut off, the Naxids are essentially besieging themselves up here. I don't think they can afford to keep it up for long."

Team 491 and their host had a pleasant cocktail hour on the terrace, after which they adjourned to the sitting room to watch the news and await the arrival of the caterer. The last light of Shaamah gleamed a greenish pink on the window panes when the Naxid announcer said that a truck containing volatile chemicals had overturned on the Boulevard of the Praxis, causing an explosion and the unfortunate death of Lord Makish, Judge of the High Court, and his companion, Junior Fleet Commander Lord Renzak.

Sula broke out in laughter. "They denied it!" she said. "Perfect!"

No mention was made of a platoon of Naxid schoolchildren being wiped out, so Sula assumed they had weathered the bomb without many serious injuries.

With a hand comm, she entered the Records Office computer on Administrator Rashtag's passwords. It took a few minutes to update the text file she had already composed, and with a verbal command she sent it into the world.

Resistance

DEATH OF A TRAITOR

Lord Makish, Judge of the High Court, was executed this afternoon by loyalist forces operating in the High City of Zanshaa. The sentence was imposed on Lord Makish by a tribunal of the secret government after Lord Makish was found guilty of signing the death warrants of Lord Governor Pahn-ko and other loyal citizens.

Executed along with Lord Makish was the traitorous Fleet officer Lord Renzak.

The sentence was carried out by loyal Fleet elements using a bomb. These Fleet personnel have now reached safety and have been debriefed by their superiors.

Though the rebel government claims that the deaths were the result of an accident with a truck carrying a volatile chemical—and whoever heard of such a truck on the Boulevard of the Praxis?—all the thousands of loyal citizens who heard or witnessed the explosion now have proof that loyalist forces operate at will even in the High City.

Those rebels who heard the explosion should know that the tribunals are waiting. Those who murder loyal citizens will be noted, and their victims will be avenged.

Who Are We?

Resistance is the official newsletter of the loyalist government-in-exile. A loyal friend has suggested that we send this to you . . .

At the end, Sula appended a copy of the first edition of *Resistance,* for any who hadn't seen it.

Because most of the Records Office personnel had gone home at the close of the business day, Sula sent out *Resistance* in smaller packets of a few thousand each so as not to tie up the broadcast node too conspicuously. As before, fifty thousand were sent. As before, they were sent randomly to inhabitants of Zanshaa who were not Naxids.

PJ's comm chimed as these operations were under way. He answered, then reported. "My smoking club. They're going to be closed for a few days, till the damage is repaired."

"Anyone hurt?" Sula asked.

"Cuts from flying glass, a couple of sprained ankles, and one broken collarbone."

Sula sent another two thousand copies of *Resistance* on their way. "Did you ask what was happening at the Makish Palace?"

PJ looked stricken. "I didn't think to." He turned to go back to the comm.

"Don't worry about it," Sula said quickly. "It's not that important. When they reopen I'm sure you'll get the story."

The caterer arrived with a glorious meal for four, crisp duck served with a creamy eswod concoction and a tart sauce of taswa fruit. PJ offered the best of the Ngeni clan's cellars to Spence and Macnamara, and afterward produced cigars.

"This reminds me," Sula said. "What is your club doing for tobacco now that the ring's gone?"

PJ gave an unhappy shrug. "Make do with the local variety, I suppose."

The climate of Zanshaa, for some reason, did not produce first-rate tobacco. Or cocoa. Or coffee. Sula, as it happens, had used half her inheritance to purchase quantities of the best of each of these before the ring was destroyed, and had them shipped to the surface, where they waited now in warehouses.

"I might be able to help them out," she said. "But no thank you, I don't smoke."

Afterward, Action Team 491 reluctantly left the Ngeni Palace for whatever lodgings they could find. They were supposed to be workers caught in the High City when the exits were closed, and it would be logical for them to look for a hostel to stay in—and Sula told her team to make certain they got receipts, in order that their stories be all the more convincing.

Lodgings were indeed hard to find—there were plenty of genuine workers wandering from one place to the next, with their IDs scanned by police patrols every few blocks. Sula finally found a place by paying more than she suspected a worker could afford. There, she enjoyed another bath, to wash away the odor of PJ's cigars, then slept on the broad, faintly scented mattress.

In the middle of the night she heard the creak of a floorboard, then felt the pillow press down hard on her nose and mouth. She gasped for breath, but there was no air. She tried to claw the pillow off her face, but her hands were pinned.

She sat up with a cry half strangled in her throat, her hands clutching at her neck. Her pulse thundered in her ears like a series of gunshots. She stared blindly out into the dark, trying to see the shadow that was her attacker.

"Lights!" she called, and the lights flashed on.

She was alone in her room.

She spent the rest of the night with the lights on and the video wall showing a harmless romantic drama that Spence would probably have adored.

In the morning she rose and found that the road and the funicular had been reopened. Showing her identification and her receipt for a night's lodging, she left the High City for the Lower Town. As she took a cab to Riverside, she saw a few copies of *Resistance* pasted to lampposts, each surrounded by clumps of readers.

Buying breakfast from a vendor near the communal apartment, she learned that the Naxids had ordered their remaining hostages shot, then sent the police out onto the streets to find more.

SEVEN

Chandra walked into Martinez's office in the middle of the afternoon watch and slid the door closed behind her. She looked at the game of hypertourney he was playing on the desktop and said, "Well, I'm free of the bastard at last."

Martinez looked up at her, his mind still filled with the game's intricacies of velocities and spacial relationships. "Congratulations," he said.

The color was high on Chandra's cheeks and her eyes burned with fury. She paced back and forth in front of the desk like a tigress whose feeding had arrived half an hour late.

"I finally asked him!" she proclaimed. "I asked him if he'd get me promoted—and he said he wouldn't!"

"I'm sorry," Martinez said. The words came reluctantly. "Captains can't promote lieutenants," he added.

"This one can," Chandra said savagely. "You know how those High City officers stick together. All he'd have to do is trade a favor with one of his cousin's—Fletcher promotes the cousin's cadet nephew in exchange for me getting my step."

Martinez knew that was true enough—Fletcher could have traded a favor with someone. That was how the high-caste Peers kept everything in their small circle.

"Bastard wants me to stay in my place," Chandra said fiercely as she paced. "Well, I *won't*. I just *won't*."

"I didn't understand how you got together with Fletcher in the first place."

Chandra stopped pacing. Her eyes glared with contempt into time, gazing at her own past. "I'm the only officer on the ship who wasn't Fletcher's choice," she said. "He had someone else picked for my place but he didn't get to Harzapid before the war happened. When the squadron shipped out, I got sent aboard. I didn't know anyone and—" She shrugged. "I tried to make myself agreeable to my captain." Her mouth drew up in a sneer. "I'd never met anyone like him. I thought he had an interesting mind." She barked out a laugh. "*Interesting mind!* He's as dull as a rusty spoon."

They looked at each other for a few brief seconds. Then Chandra took a half step closer to the desk, her fingertips drifting over the black surface, cutting through the holographic display of the hypertourney game.

"I could really use your help, Gare," she said.

"I can't promote you either. You know that."

An intense fire burned in her eyes. "But your relatives can," she said. "Your father-in-law is on the Fleet Control Board and Michi Chen is his sister. Between the two of them they should be able to work an overdue promotion for a lieutenant."

"I've told you before," Martinez said, "I can't do anything out here."

She looked at him levelly. "Someday," she said, "you're going to need a friend in the service, and I'm going to *be* that friend. I'm going to be the best and most loyal friend an officer ever had."

Martinez considered that Chandra's friendship might come at a very high price.

Though, professionally speaking, he could think of no reason why she shouldn't be promoted. Other than her erratic and impulsive behavior, of course, and her chaotic love life.

But how bad was that, really? he asked himself. Compared with some of the captains he'd known, Chandra was practically a paragon.

Misunderstanding his silence, she leaned forward and took his hand. Her fingers were warm in his palm. The hologram gleamed on her tunic. "Please, Gareth," she said. "I really need you now."

"I'll speak to Lady Michi," Martinez said. "I don't know how much credit I've got with her, but I'll try."

"Thank you, Gareth." She rested her hip on the desk and leaned across to kiss his cheek. Her scent flared in his senses. He stood, and dropped her hand.

"That won't be necessary, Lieutenant," he said.

She looked at him for a moment out of her long eyes, and her look hardened. She straightened. "As you wish, Captain," she said, her pointed chin held high. "With the captain's permission?"

"You are dismissed," Martinez said. His mouth was dry.

She went to the door and slid it open. "I meant what I said," she said, "about being your friend."

Then she was gone, leaving the door open behind her. Lord Shane Coen, Michi's red-haired signals lieutenant, walked past and cast a curious glance into the room.

Martinez nodded at him in what he hoped was a brisk, military fashion, then sat down at the desk again and hypertourney.

It was a while before he could get his mind on the game.

WHO KILLED THE HOSTAGES?

The Naxids would have you believe that the deaths of over five hundred hostages are an inevitable result of actions by loyalist forces. But who rounded them up? Who ordered them shot? Who fired their weapons? Whose bullets struck them down?

The agents of an illegitimate government!

Sula paused with her stylus poised over her desk. Frustration pounded in her temples. She had the sense that her proper argument was evading her.

Worse, she could imagine Naxid counterarguments. It wasn't as if the legitimate government, as embodied by the Shaa who founded the empire, had hesitated to take hostages. The Shaa had held entire *planets* hostage. And furthermore they hadn't hesitated to act: cities had been bombarded with antimatter weapons, and on one occasion an entire planet was wiped out in retaliation for the conspiracy of only a few people. The only legitimacy the empire had ever known was the threat of massive force.

Nor was the present war any different. Planets surrendered to one side or the other under fear of bombardment and destruction. Martinez had told her that the entire Hone Reach had almost gone over to the enemy out of sheer terror, without a shot fired, and that only the arrival of Faqforce—with their own missiles and promised destruction—prevented the defection.

Five hundred hostages were insignificant against such a history, let alone against the casualties of the war so far.

Sula continued her essay. She pointed out that the Naxids killed hostages because they couldn't locate their enemies, whereas the secret government had gone after specific targets and killed them. She promised more and greater retribution to come.

She went over her text again, making small changes, and wished she were better at debate. Her verbal gifts, as both she and others had cause to regret, were more in the direction of sarcasm, and sarcasm seemed inappropriate as a tribute to five hundred butchered citizens.

The sad fact was that the Makish assassination might be Team 491's last operation. The secret government and its operatives amounted only to three people, and if they kept risking themselves, they would be caught.

She knew that Team 491 had to recruit other operatives,

which meant trusting other people, some of whom by their nature would be untrustworthy. Others would be captured and give up everything they knew under torture.

It might make more sense to cease all activity and wait for the Fleet to drive the Naxids away.

But Sula didn't want to quit. Even as she looked at the piece of propaganda designed to take advantage of the deaths of the hostages, her blood simmered with anger against the Naxid executioners.

She rose from her desk and ordered the video wall to switch on and turn to the channel reserved for punishments. It took a long time to kill five hundred people, and the executions were still ongoing. The Torminel, Terrans, Cree, Daimong, and Lai-own were herded against the blank wall of a prison, followed by the long hammering volleys of automatic weapons, the spray of blood, the fall of bodies.

The executioners were clear in the video: the grim-faced, helmeted figures behind the tripod-mounted machine guns; the others, in their lawn-green uniforms so much brighter than the somber green of the Fleet, herding the captives with stun batons and placing them against the wall; and before them all, the thin-faced officer who gave the order to fire, a man with the consciousness of high duty blazing from his eyes.

All the executioners were Terran. The Naxids hadn't even had to do their own dirty work; they'd found others more than happy to do the job for them.

The executioners were nervous or blank-faced or merely dutiful, but the officer seemed different. His eyes glittered and his voice was pitched high, with odd hysterical overtones. Sula realized he was in a state of exaltation. This was his defining moment, the chance to commit slaughter in front of a planetwide audience. His eyes betrayed him by occasionally flicking to the camera, as if he was assuring himself that his time of glory was not yet over.

After the machine guns rattled, the officer walked slowly amid the bodies, finishing off the survivors with his pistol. His chest was inflated as he walked, a self-important spectacle, conscious of his starring role.

Pervert, Sula thought. The things people would do to get on video.

The door opened and Spence entered just as the machine guns fired again. She winced and passed through the room with her eyes turned away from the video.

"You've heard about the hostages?" Sula said.

"Yes. It's everywhere."

"Any trouble getting down from the High City?"

"No." She stiffened as the officer shouted out commands to throw the bodies on a truck. Her mouth tightened in a line. "We're going to get that bastard, aren't we, my lady?"

"Yes," Sula said, her mind made up at that moment.

Fuck caution.

A wild sensation of liberation began to sing in her heart. In a lifetime full of risks, this would be the most insane thing she'd ever done.

She didn't know the officer's name or where the executions were taking place. All she knew was that it had to be a prison on the planet of Zanshaa. She focused on the video, watched it intently, and was eventually rewarded with a glimpse, over the prison wall, of the baroque ornamentation of the Apszipar Tower, which would place the action somewhere in the southwest quadrant of Zanshaa City.

The Records Office computer had the maps that showed the only prison in that part of town, a place called the Blue Hatches, and also a list of personnel assigned to that prison.

The officer in charge was a Major Commandant Laurajean, and the picture appended to his ID showed that he was the thin-faced officer who, even now, was grinning his intense joy as a crowd of Torminel were killed on his orders. Laurajean, who was forty-six years old, had been married for the last eighteen to a plump, pleasant-looking wife, an elementary school teacher, with whom he'd had three children and lived a middle-class life in a middle-class part of the Lower Town.

Some people, Sula thought, just needed killing.

Macnamara entered as Sula—having looked up Laura-jean's address—was calling up the plans of the building, just in case she needed them. He dropped his bag of cheap iarogüt on her desk and looked over her shoulder at the three-dimensional image of Laurajean rotating in a corner of the display, next to the architects' schematics.

"He's our next?" Macnamara asked.

"Yes."

His answer was to the point. "Good." He picked up the bottles and walked to the kitchen.

Does the Major Commandant take public transport home? Sula wondered. *Or does he have an auto?* Waiting at his local tram stop and shooting him as he stepped off would be a prosaic but efficient way to accomplish his demise.

Laurajean had an auto, the records showed, a mauve-colored Delvin sedan suitable for his entire family. Sula wondered if he drove it to work or left it at home. His wife didn't have a driving permit, she found, and Laurajean himself had been granted a parking permit for use at the Blue Hatches facility.

She rose from her desk, stretched her limbs, and walked to the kitchen, where Spence and Macnamara chatted while pouring iarogüt down the sink, flooding the small room with the sinus-stinging herbal scent.

"We'll take him today," she said. "Before they decide to put guards on him."

They looked at her in surprise, then Macnamara laughed. There was a wild look in Spence's eyes. They'd caught Sula's mad, defiant spirit.

Fuck caution.

Because the arrangement had worked the first time, they decided that Sula and Macnamara would be the shooters and Spence the lookout. Macnamara got weapons out of storage and cleaned, assembled, and loaded them, while Spence rented a small, gray six-wheeled cargo van under a backup identity. Sula polished her essay one more time, sent out the third edition of *Resistance* while public indignation was at its height, then began researching the Blue Hatches prison and its immediate environs, maps of which were in the Records Office computer.

A problem existed with the rented van, the workings of which contained computers that regularly reported their location to the Office of the Censor. When a crime was reported, any vehicles in the area could be pinpointed.

When it had originally been equipped, Team 491 was given a Hunhao sedan with the ability to switch this feature off. The Hunhao was an ideal getaway vehicle, and Sula wanted to use it for the escape, not for the assassination itself.

All put on gloves so as not to leave fingerprints. Spence turned the van over to Macnamara, the best driver, and herself drove the Hunhao down the main artery beneath the Apszipar Tower, where she parked four streets away from the prison. She then jumped into the van—Sula was in the back, with the weapons—and the van headed for the prison secure behind its azure ceramic walls.

Team 491 had been tense during the Makish killing. Now they were casual almost to the point of mirth. Sula's fey spirit had spread to them all. Two killings in the period of a day—why not? The first had been overplanned, and now the second wouldn't be planned at all. They were throwing their months of training to the winds, and the relaxation of discipline was like wine in their veins.

There was chaos outside the prison, with swarms of grieving next-of-kin milling in a anxious mass, waiting for the chance to claim their relations. Sula noted the big main gate, the large garage attached to the administration block by a ramp. The van edged through the crowd and dropped Spence off at the fringes, where she wouldn't stand out amid the mourners. Macnamara swung the van through a series of turns and parked so they were ready to intercept Laurajean on his way home. He and Sula sat in the front, the windows open, and waited through the long hot afternoon.

They were in a Lai-own neighborhood. The tall, long-limbed flightless birds went about their business, too busy or too hot to pay attention to strangers. A pungent scent drifted toward them from a nearby restaurant—the Lai-own protein sauce heated in the great iron pans and ready to cook meat and vegetables.

A young male Lai-own strolled to the door of an apartment across the street, urinated copiously on the doorjamb, then adjusted his clothing as he walked away.

"Ah, young love," Sula said. Macnamara gave a snicker.

No volleys echoed over the prison's featureless wall. Sula turned her hand comm to the punishment channel and found that it was showing the executions all over again.

"This is the fate that the wicked saboteurs and assassins have brought to the people of Zanshaa," the narrator intoned. Sula snorted. Hadn't he read the third edition of *Resistance*?

Whose bullets struck them down?

There was a roar from the front of the prison, hundreds of throats together. Spence reported that an announcement had just been made that the first twenty families could enter to identify and claim the bodies of their kin, and the bereaved were crowding together by the gates.

"It's him!" Spence said, in sudden surprise. "He's in his car, with a couple of his pals. Heading your way!"

Laurajean had taken advantage of the crowd clumped around the main gate to leave unmolested through the garage exit. Macnamara pressed the throttle lever and the van's electric motors surged, bringing the vehicle silently into traffic. Sula slipped into the cargo compartment, crouched on the black composite floor as she first readied her weapon, then placed Macnamara's gun on the passenger seat where he could reach it.

"There he is!" Macnamara called, and Sula knew her luck was in. She'd been *right* to follow this wild impulse. A feral joy filled her heart at the certainty that nothing could go wrong for her today.

Just in case, for caution's sake, she called Spence to ask if there were any sign of another vehicle following, perhaps with guards.

No. The Naxids had left their killer without protection.

Sula readied her rifle. "You've got to catch him before he gets to the expressway," she told Macnamara. Vehicles on the expressways were required to surrender control to a centralized computer system, which would never let them get close.

"Easy," Macnamara said, and power surged to the motors. "They'll be on the left side." His window powered open and he shifted his stubby machine pistol to his lap.

The van swerved, then swerved again. The motors surged once more, then braked back.

"Now," Macnamara said. Sula touched controls, and silent motors rolled the big side door open. Hair whipped across her face in a sudden blast of hot wind. The mauve-colored Delvin was right there, almost close enough to touch.

There were three Terrans in the car—two women and Laurajean—all in lawn-green uniform tunics. Laurajean was driving. They were laughing at some joke, and Laurajean was gesturing expansively with one slim hand. Exhilaration still radiated from his face.

He was still rejoicing in his unexpected celebrity, unaware that his starring role on the punishment channel was about to be canceled. He glanced to his right just as Sula put the rifle to her shoulder, and his puzzled squint showed he hadn't quite worked out what he was seeing when she fired.

The rifle used caseless ammunition that was nearly recoilless, and cycled it very fast. Sula put over a hundred rounds into the car in less than two seconds. Macnamara, firing through the window, emptied his own smaller magazine.

There was the sound of a score of hammers beating metal. Parts of Laurajean's car seemed to dissolve, the glass spraying outward in crystal fountains that glimmered in the sun, the resinous composite body simply disintegrating. The Delvin swerved, and Macnamara quickly dropped his gun into his lap in order to concentrate on his driving. Sula pressed the control that slid the side door shut.

Peering out the back window, she saw the Delvin slowly cross three lanes of traffic and come to rest on the sidewalk, narrowly missing a startled Daimong pedestrian.

Macnamara made a few turns, then found a legal place to park. By then, Sula had the weapons broken down and in their cases. The two quietly left the van, walked down a baking street, turned a corner and met Spence, who had paralleled their route in the Hunhao.

In a few hours they would call the rental company from a suitably anonymous location and tell them where they could pick up their van. If its transponder hadn't happened to report within a few minutes of the assassination, there would be nothing to connect it to the killing.

To the team's strange spirit of impulse and madness was now added another dimension—that of relief. They babbled with frantic good spirits as they left the Apszipar Tower behind. They were as cheerful, Sula realized, as Laurajean had been with his two colleagues. Like children who had gotten away with something naughty.

"Who ordered them shot?" Sula asked.

"Lady Sula!" the others chanted.

"Who fired her weapon?"

"Lady Sula!"

"Whose bullets struck them down?"

"Lady Sula!" they cried, and all three broke into laughter.

This must stop, she told herself. They couldn't go on this recklessly.

But still, it would be good to put out another edition of *Resistance,* with the heading "Death of a Traitor."

Sula bought Team 491 a first-class dinner that evening at Seven Pages, a restaurant with silent, dignified waitrons and a wine list that scrolled along the display hundreds of lines. The meal went on for hours, little plates arriving every ten minutes with some small, ambrosial treat, each displayed with perfection on a plate of near-translucent Vigo hard-paste. Sula could tell that Spence and Macnamara had never been in such a place before.

Not that she had, or at least not often. Not since she was a girl named Gredel, and the real Lady Sula had paid.

"Would you care for a sweet?" the waitron asked. "We have everything on our list except the Chocolate Fancy and the Mocha Gyre."

"Why not?"

The waitron shook his glossy shaved head. "I regret there is no cocoa of a suitable quality. May I recommend the Peaches Flambé?"

"Hm." Sula looked at Macnamara and Spence, both deeply relaxed after consuming two bottles of wine, and smiled. "I hate life without Chocolate Fancy in it," she said. "Perhaps we could arrange something."

She spoke with the chef before they left and asked how much she would offer for top quality cocoa.

The chef frowned and tugged at her lower lip. "Business isn't so good, you know. Not since *they* came."

"Think how much better business would be if you had good chocolate again."

Her eyes narrowed. "How good?"

"Kabila's. We have sixty-five percent cocoa and eighty percent. Imported from Preowin."

The chef tried unsuccessfully to conceal the flare of greed that burned briefly in her eyes. "How much do you have?" she asked.

"How much do you want?"

They settled on a price, seven times what Sula had paid for the cocoa when it sat in a warehouse complex on the ring.

"I'll deliver tomorrow," she said. "I'll want payment in cash."

The chef acted as if this arrangement weren't unusual. Perhaps it wasn't.

"I wish I knew how you did that," Spence said as they walked away.

"Did what?"

"Change your accent like that. You have the voice you use back in Riverside, and the Lady Sula voice, and you used a completely different voice with the waitron and the chef."

Sula cast her mind back to the restaurant. "I don't remember doing that," she said. "I was probably just imitating them." Neither the chef nor the waitron had spoken with the drawling speech of the Peers of the High City, but a comfortably middle-class approximation.

"Wish I could do that," Spence said again.

"You've been out having fun," One-Step said later that night as Sula returned to her apartment. "You've been having fun without One-Step."

"That's right," she said cheerfully. She sprang up the stair and reached for the door, the thin plastic key in her hand.

One-Step stepped into the light that poured down from one of the first-floor apartments, and Sula paused a moment to bask in the dark light of his liquid black eyes.

"One-Step could show you a wonderful evening, better than you had tonight," he said. "You only have to give One-Step a chance."

Sula wondered how to explain her position in this matter. *I don't go out with boys who refer to themselves in the third person?*

"Maybe when you get a job," Sula said. "I'd hate to take your last few zeniths."

"I'd spend my last minim to make you happy."

She rewarded the use of the personal pronoun with a smile. "So what do you hear?" she asked.

"Riot at the Blue Hatches, the place where they were shooting people," One-Step said. "A crowd of mourners got arrested for killing a prison officer."

Sula paused a moment, thinking. "Was it on the news?"

"No. One-Step heard it from a . . . colleague."

Street rumor would spread fast, Sula knew, though what it gained in speed it lost in accuracy.

"Anyone killed?" she asked.

"My friend didn't know. Probably there were deaths, though. There's a lot of killing going around."

He stepped forward and held out something that shone yellow-white in the light that spilled from the apartment window. *Resistance.*

"I've seen it."

The plastic flimsy vanished. "You be careful," One-Step said. There was a surprising earnest quality in his voice. "You step out into the street, you look for police first. Look for police at the train, at the market. Always make sure you have an escape route."

Sula looked at him. "Do *you* have an escape route, One-Step?"

His black eyes shone in the light as again he silently held out the pale sheet of plastic.

Resistance.

Sula turned. "Good night, One-Step." She slid her key into the door lock, and alloy bolts drew back.

"Good night, miss. Keep well."

He's going to die, she thought as she walked slowly up the stair. *They'll be shooting at me, but they'll hit him.*

Plenty of bullets had been aimed at her earlier in the day, after all, but killed nearly five hundred other people instead.

EIGHT

Three watches ticked by with nothing for Martinez to do but spend his time at hypertourney, check the tactical display to see if anything had changed, and stare at Terza's picture in the surface of his desk. No one invited him to dine. He considered having the lieutenants to an evening in *Daffodil*—the ex-civilian yacht that had brought him to *Illustrious,* and which he had turned into kind of an informal club, an alternative to the full-dress dinners Fletcher had imposed on the cruiser—but then he reflected that he'd have to invite Chandra and decided against it.

No one was in a mood for amusement anyway. Not with Termaine coming closer and closer, and the memory of Bai-do fresh in everyone's mind.

After breakfast the next morning, Martinez occupied himself with the list of Authorized Names. When the Shaa made a conquest, they produced lists with names authorized for children. Names with subversive content—Freedom, Prince—were forbidden, along with names relating to superstition or other irrational beliefs contrary to the Praxis.

Since the conquest thousands of years ago, humanity had changed in countless ways, but the names had stayed the same.

Not that this was a particular hardship: there were still thousands of names to choose from, all sanitized by higher authority. Martinez liked the long list, because he could spend hours at it, and he could think about his unborn child the entire time.

Perhaps his child could be called Pandora, "All Gifts." Or Roderick, "Renowned Ruler." Or Esmé, "Beloved."

If male, he could be named after Terza's father, Maurice, or his own, Marcus, except that he didn't quite understand what the names meant. "Moor" and "Of Mars," all right, but what were Moors and Mars?

If she were a girl, she would surely be beautiful, and therefore could be named Kyla, or Linette, or Damalis.

Pity that he couldn't simply name his child "Genius," because surely that would apply better than anything.

Martinez glanced up at the sound of purposeful footsteps, and looked up to see Captain Lord Gomberg Fletcher standing in the door of his office. Fletcher wore his full dress uniform, with white gloves and the ceremonial sickle-shaped knife at his waist.

Martinez jumped to his feet and braced. "Lord Captain!" he said.

Fletcher looked at him from his deep-set eyes. "I'd be obliged if you'd join me, Captain Martinez."

"Certainly, my lord." Martinez began to walk around the desk, then hesitated. "Should I change into full dress, my lord?"

"That won't be necessary, Lord Captain. Come along, if you please."

Martinez left his office and joined the captain, who was accompanied also by Lord Sabir Mersenne, the fourth lieutenant, and Marsden, the captain's short, bald secretary, both also in full dress. Without another word, Fletcher turned and began walking down the corridor, the others following. Martinez wondered if he should have worn full dress when eating breakfast by himself, or at least should be embarrassed that he hadn't.

Fletcher's silver-embossed scabbard clanked faintly on the end of its chain. Martinez had never seen the captain wear his knife, not even at his very formal dinners.

The party went down two decks, leaving behind officers' country and the haunts of the enlisted. The captain marched to a hatch and knocked with a gloved hand.

The hatch was opened by Master Engineer Thuc, whose towering figure nearly filled the doorway before he stepped back to reveal the engine control room. Beneath panels showing strong-thewed characters working with huge levers and winches on some impossibly antique machinery, the control room crew were lined up, braced, and spotlessly turned out.

Apparently Captain Fletcher was conducting him on one of his frequent inspections. The captain was a demon for inspections and musters, and usually inspected some part of the ship every day that *Illustrious* wasn't engaged in some other crucial business. Today was the engine division's turn, but Martinez could not imagine why he had been invited along. He wasn't a line officer, but staff, and not in Fletcher's chain of command—the state of *Illustrious*'s engines was none of his business.

So while he watched Fletcher and his two subordinates crawl over the engine control room, passing white-gloved fingers over the glossy surfaces, Martinez wondered why he had been summoned to observe this ritual, and paranoia soon began to scuttle through his mind on chitinous insect legs. Surely this had to do with Chandra Prasad. Surely Fletcher suspected him of being her lover, and the inspection was part of an elaborate revenge plot.

The captain found flaws—a suspicious creak in an acceleration cage that indicated a worn part, a scratch on the transparent cover of a gauge, an emergency radiation suit carelessly stowed—and then the party went on to look at the engine department's storage lockers, at the heavily shielded antihydrogen compartments, and—after donning ear protection—at the massive reactor that powered the ship and the huge turbopumps that operated the thermal exchange system.

Martinez knew that in the reactor room the noise was

hellish, but his earphones automatically pulsed out sound waves that canceled that of the pumps, and all he heard in his ears was a distant white noise. But his *body* reacted to the sound: he could feel the vibration in his bones and in his soft organs, and when he touched a wall or pipe.

Fletcher stroked the pumps with white-gloved fingers, found them clean, and then returned to the engine control room so that his questions might be heard. Thuc followed the captain in docile silence, his muscular body looming over Fletcher's shoulder except when he darted forward to open a hatch or a locker door.

"You've changed the filters on the main pump recently?"

"Just after Protipanu, my lord," Thuc said. "We aren't due for another change for two months."

"Very good. And the pump itself?"

"We'll swap it out in another . . ." Thuc considered his answer, his eyes focused somewhere above the captain's left shoulder. ". . . thirty-eight days, my lord."

"Very well." The captain tugged his white gloves over his wrists and smoothed the fine kidskin over his fingers. "I'll just inspect your crew then."

He marched down the line of engine crew, stopping to make an occasional comment about dress or deportment. At the end of the line he encountered Thuc again, marched about him, then nodded.

"Very good, Thuc," he said. "Excellent marks, as always."

"Thank you, Lord Captain." A hint of a smile touched his lips.

When Fletcher moved, he was so fast that Martinez failed to see it properly and could only reconstruct the action later, out of fragments of memory. The sickle-shaped blade sang from the sheath, whistled through the air, and buried itself in Thuc's throat. A crescent of arterial blood splattered the mural behind Thuc's head.

Thuc was too large a man to fall all at once. First his shoulders dropped, and then his knees gave way. His barrel chest sank, his stomach sagged, and then—as Fletcher's knife cleared his throat—Thuc's head lolled down. It was only then that he fell like a tower of wooden blocks kicked by a careless child.

Martinez's heart began to beat again, roaring in his ears. He looked at Fletcher in shock.

Fletcher looked expressionlessly at the body with his ice-blue eyes, and took a step away from the spreading pool of red. He flicked scarlet from his blade with a movement of his wrist.

The smell of blood hit Martinez's senses, and he bit down hard on the stomach that was trying to quease its way past his throat.

"Marsden," Fletcher said, "call the doctor to examine the body, and have him bring a stretcher party to carry it away. Cho," to a staring petty officer, "you are now in charge of the engineering department. Once the doctor is done, call the off-duty watch to help you police this . . . untidiness. In the meantime, I'd appreciate a cleaning cloth."

Cho nearly ran to one of the storage lockers, returned with a cloth, and handed it with bloodless fingers to the captain. Fletcher used it to clean the knife blade and mop some of the red off his tunic, then threw the cloth to the deck.

A pale-faced young recruit swayed, then toppled to the floor in a dead faint. Fletcher ignored him and turned again to Cho.

"Cho," he said, "I trust you will maintain Engineer Thuc's high standards." He nodded to the control room crew, then turned and made his way out.

Martinez followed, his nerves leaping. He wanted to flee Fletcher's company, to barricade himself in his quarters with a pistol and several bottles of brandy, the first for protection and the second for comfort.

He looked left and right at Marsden and Mersenne, and saw their expressions mirroring his own thoughts.

"Captain Martinez," Fletcher said. The words made Martinez start.

"Yes, Lord Captain?" He was moderately surprised that

he managed three whole words without stumbling, screaming, or falling into dumb silence.

Fletcher reached the companionway that led to the deck above and turned to Martinez.

"Do you know why I invited you along this morning?"

"No, my lord."

He had managed another three words. He was making real progress. Soon he might be walking on his own and tying his own shoelaces.

Martinez found himself very aware of the captain's right hand, the hand that would reach across his body to draw the knife. He found his own hands ready to lurch forward and seize Fletcher's forearm if the hand approached the hilt.

He hoped that Fletcher did not see that he was so aware of his right hand. He tried not to stare at it.

"I asked you along so that you could report to Squadron Commander Chen," Fletcher said, "and tell her exactly what just occurred."

"Yes, Lord Captain."

"I don't want her hearing a rumor, or getting a distorted version."

Distorted version. As if there was a version that would make this at all understandable.

Martinez searched his numbed mind and found a question, but the question required more than three words and he took a second or two to organize his thoughts.

"My lord," he asked, "do you wish me to give Lady Michi the reason for your . . . your action?"

The captain straightened slightly. A superior smile touched his lips.

"Only that it was my privilege," he said.

A chill shimmered up Martinez's spine.

"Very good, Lord Captain," he said.

Fletcher turned and led up the companionway. At the top he met the ship's doctor, Lord Yuntai Xi, who was going down, followed by his assistant carrying his bag.

"The engine control room, Lord Doctor," Fletcher said. "A fatality."

The doctor gave him a curious look and nodded.

"Thank you, Lord Captain. Can you tell me—"

"Best you see for yourself, Lord Doctor. I won't detain you."

Xi stroked his little white beard, then nodded and began his descent. Fletcher led the party up three decks, to the deck he shared with the squadron commander, then turned to face the two lieutenants. "Thank you, my lords," he said. "I won't be needing you any further." He turned to his secretary. "Marsden, I'll need you to enter the death in the log."

Martinez walked with Mersenne to the squadcom's door. He felt a tingling in his back, as if he were expecting the captain to draw his knife and lunge at him. He didn't quite dare look at the lieutenant, and he had a feeling that Mersenne wasn't looking at him either.

He came to the squadcom's door, and without saying anything to Lord Mersenne, stopped and knocked.

Lady Michi's orderly, Vandervalk, opened the door, and Martinez asked to see the squadcom. Vandervalk said she'd check and left him waiting, then returned a few minutes later to say that the lady squadcom would meet Martinez in her office.

Lady Michi arrived a few minutes later, carrying her morning tea in a gold-rimmed cup with the Chen family crest. Martinez jumped from his chair and braced. The breath of air on his exposed throat gave him a sudden shiver.

"As you were," Michi said. Her tone was abstracted, her gaze focused on papers that waited on her desk. She sat in her straight-backed chair.

"How can I help you, Captain?"

"Lord Captain Fletcher—" Martinez began, and then his voice failed him. He cleared his throat and tried again.

"Lord Captain Fletcher asked that I inform you that he's just executed Master Engineer Thuc."

Suddenly he had the squadcom's full attention. She placed her cup very carefully on a felt coaster, then looked up. "Executed? How?"

"With his top-trimmer. During an inspection. It was . . . very sudden."

He realized now that Fletcher must have rehearsed the move. You couldn't cut a throat that efficiently unless you practiced.

He imagined Fletcher alone in his cabin, drawing the knife over and over as he slashed an imaginary throat, the cold blue eyes glittering, the superior smile on his lips.

Michi's gaze intensified. Her fingers drummed thoughtfully on the desktop. "Did Captain Fletcher give a reason?"

"No, my lady. He said only that it was his privilege."

Michi softly drew in her breath. "I see," she said.

Fletcher was technically correct: any officer had the authority to execute any subordinate at any time, for any reason. There were practical reasons why this didn't happen very often, including lawsuits in civil court from the victim's patron clan; and usually when such a thing happened, the officer produced an elaborate justification.

Fletcher very simply stood on his privilege. That had to be very, very rare.

Michi turned her eyes deliberately away and took a deliberate sip of her tea. "Do you have anything to add?" she said.

"Just that the captain planned it in advance. He wanted me there to witness it and to report to you."

"Nothing in the inspection could have provoked it?"

"No, my lady. The captain complimented Thuc on his department before killing him."

Again Michi drew in her breath. Her eyes grew thoughtful. "You can think of no reason?"

Martinez hesitated. "The captain and Lieutenant

Prasad . . . ended . . . their relationship yesterday. But if he was going to kill anyone over it, I don't know why it would be Thuc."

Maybe Thuc was handy, he thought.

Michi considered this a moment. "Thank you, Captain," she said finally. "I appreciate your informing me."

There was a clear tone of dismissal in her words, and Martinez wanted to protest. He wanted Michi to ask him to stay so they could work out some kind of theory about what had just happened and why, and then decide on a course of action. But Michi left him no choice but to stand, brace, and make his way out.

Martinez had to pass Fletcher's quarters on his way to his own. The captain's door was closed. As he walked past, he strained his senses to detect anything that might be happening inside.

Like what? he thought. *A burst of maniacal laughter? A pool of blood creeping from under the door?*

There was nothing.

He entered his own office and left the door open in the event that someone might want to talk to him.

No one did.

NINE

The fourth edition of *Resistance* flew into the world on wings of electrons, carrying with it the announcement that Laurajean and his two colleagues had been killed as a result of the sentence of a tribunal of the secret government. Sula identified Laurajean's two friends as well, having gotten the names from the death certificates filed electronically in the Records Office.

The tribunal has passed other sentences, and execution is now pending, Sula wrote.

That should put a scare into them.

The previous three editions had been sent out with the forged security heading claiming they'd originated at the broadcast node of the Naxid-occupied Hotel Spartex. Sula decided that the Spartex had probably suffered as much as it was likely to from the Naxid security services, so she looked through some of Rashtag's mail, found the code for the broadcast node at the Fleet Commandery, and used that instead.

Now the Naxid security services would have to investigate the Naxid Fleet. The Fleet, she thought, was just going to *love* that.

Sula munched a pastry filled with sweet red bean paste as she sent out the usual fifty thousand copies of *Resistance,* then licked her fingers, closed her connection to the Records Office computer, and turned to where Spence and Macnamara waited, playing a puzzle that Spence had just bought from a street vendor. It was an intricate tangle of wire, with beads that moved from one intersection to the next, and could sometimes jump from one connection to another.

Sitting cross-legged on the floor in front of the puzzle, Sula looked at it with her chin propped on her fists. "What's the point of it, exactly?" she said.

Spence gave a puzzled frown. "I'm not sure. When the vendor demonstrated the thing, it all seemed pretty clear. But now . . ."

Sula moved a bead along the wire to the next intersection, but it failed to move any farther. She moved it in the other direction, and with a sudden clang the entire puzzle fell apart into a jangling snarl of wires and beads.

She drew back her finger and looked at the others. "Was that *supposed* to happen?" she asked.

Spence blinked. "I don't think so."

Sula stood up. "Maybe we should try something a little less challenging."

Spence looked up at her. "Yes?"

"Win the war."

"Right." Spence rose reluctantly to her feet.

"And in the meantime we need to deliver some cocoa."

It was Macnamara who rented the truck this time, after which the three drove to one of the warehouses where Sula was keeping her cocoa, coffee, and tobacco, all in boxes labeled to discourage theft and marked USED MACHINE PARTS, FOR RECYCLING.

"We can't keep doing the fighting ourselves," Sula said as she drove alongside one of the slow, greenish canals that cut the Lower Town near the acropolis. "We need an army. And the problem is, we haven't got one."

The plan that Sula and Martinez had originally developed involved raising an armed force to hold Zanshaa City against the Naxids, confident that while the enemy would murder any other population without compunction, they would never dare destroy the capital and all the legitimacy that it symbolized. But the government had decided against that part of the plan, and instead settled for training Sula and Eshruq's action teams, most of whom were now ash drifting along the streets of the Lower Town.

The original plan would have worked much better, Sula thought.

"We can try recruiting," Macnamara said. "Ardelion and I can each can put together another cell."

Cells consisted of three people, like Sula's action team. Each cell leader would know only the members of his own cell and a single member of the cell above, the better to preserve security. Everyone would be known by code names only, to reduce the chances for betrayal. Contact between cells would be through cutouts and letter drops, to prevent anyone from listening to electronic communication.

"Right," Sula said, "we can recruit. And I can start by training PJ."

Macnamara gave a snort of laughter. Sula shook her head. "No, it's too slow. By the time we had the first lot trained, and they each trained a few others, and so on until we had an entire network, we'd all have gray hair and the Naxids will have— Oh, damn."

They came to a halt behind a truck offloading produce from a canal boat. Sula craned her neck, but she couldn't see whether there was enough clearance between the produce truck on one side and a Lai-own clothing emporium on the other.

"Stick your head out," Sula told Macnamara. "See if we've got room here."

Macnamara opened the window, and the rotting-flesh stench of the Daimong laborers floated into the vehicle along with the scent of green vegetables and the iodine smell of the canal. At the taste of the air, a shudder of memory trembled up Sula's spine. "The hell with it," she decided.

She shifted the truck to all-wheel-steering and crabbed into the gap. A metal rack of Lai-own clothing was run against a brick wall and slightly buckled, and Macnamara gave a wince as he drew in his head and closed the window to the sudden yelps of the Lai-own shopkeeper. Sula accelerated and kept on going.

"May need a little more practice in the driving department, boss," Macnamara said.

"Too slow," Sula said. "We can't train them in time. They've got to train themselves."

There was a moment, and then Spence nodded. "*Resistance*," she said.

"Exactly."

They delivered the cocoa to Seven Pages, and as the chef counted out the money, she asked, "You heard they shot more hostages?"

"Yes?" Sula asked.

"Thirty. And they were all relatives of the people who were shot yesterday."

"Ten hostages shot for each Terran," Sula said. "And nearly five hundred for a Naxid." Her mind had already outlined another editorial on the subject for *Resistance*.

The chef gave a sour nod. "Exactly. I'd say that's a good advertisement for how things are going to be."

"Do we get a free dessert?" Spence asked.

"Not this early, you don't. Be off, I've got work to do."

The door to the cargo compartment hummed shut on electric motors. Macnamara made certain the cargo door was locked and joined Sula and Spence in the cab.

"Lots of cocoa left," he told Sula. "What's it for?"

"Samples," Sula said. "We'll be spending the day visiting other restaurants. Some in the High City."

A good place to gather information, she thought. And they'd contact coffee shops and tobacco clubs as well.

Spence, tucked in the cab between Sula and Macnamara, turned to Sula. "Lucy," she said, "are you still 'Lucy' when we're on these deliveries? If we use that name in front of people we don't know, that's a clue to your cover identity. Gavin and I can fall back on our code names and go by

Starling and Ardelion, but *your* code name is four-nine-one, after our team. We can't call you that."

"No, you can't." Sula glanced over the street, the people moving in the shade of the gemel trees that were bright with their white summer blossoms. From the shadows she heard the echo of a name, and she smiled.

"Call me Gredel," she said.

That night, with the reflected rays of Shaamah glowing on the *ju yao* pot and One-Step quietly passing copies of *Resistance* on the pavement outside, she wrote with her stylus on the modestly intelligent, glowing surface of her table, producing an essay on how to organize a loyalist network into cells. She threw in every security procedure she could think of, from code names to letter drop procedures.

She realized that she had done part of her job already. Copies of *Resistance* were being passed from hand to hand along spontaneously formed, informal networks. For her purposes the networks already existed: all she had to do was professionalize them.

The unsuccessful networks would be caught and killed, she thought. All taking bullets meant for her.

The successful networks she would hope to contact later—so they could be killed by other bullets when she needed them.

TEN

Martinez set the wall video to the tactical display, but he didn't pay a lot of attention to it. He couldn't stay in his seat: he was compelled to pace, and march, and conduct imaginary conversations with every officer on the ship.

By the time Alikhan came in with his dinner, he'd worked himself into a near frenzy. "What's happening?" he demanded the instant Alikhan entered. "What are people saying?"

With a series of deliberate gestures Alikhan put the covered plate in front of Martinez and arranged his napkin and silverware. Then he straightened and said, "May I close the door, my lord?"

"Yes." It was all Martinez could do to avoid shouting the word.

Alikhan quietly closed the door and said, "Lady Michi asked Dr. Xi to report to her. He did so. Then she asked for Captain Fletcher, and he reported to her as well."

"Any notion of what was said?"

"No, my lord."

Martinez found himself grinding his teeth. He very much wanted to know what Fletcher said to the squadcom.

"How are the petty officers taking it?" he asked.

"They're huddling with one another, talking quietly."

"What are they saying?"

Alikhan straightened with quiet dignity. "They're not speaking much to me, my lord. I've not been aboard very long. They're talking only to people they know they can trust."

Martinez drummed his fingers on his thighs in frustration. Alikhan quietly uncovered Martinez's plate, revealing a rehydrated filet drizzled with one of Perry's elaborate sauces. Martinez looked up at him.

"Do they think the captain's mad?" he said.

Alikhan considered the question for a moment before answering. "They don't understand the captain, my lord. They never have. But mad? I don't know what a doctor would say, but I don't think the captain fits any definition of madness a petty officer would recognize, my lord."

"Yes," Martinez said. The answer depressed him. "Thank you, Alikhan."

Alikhan withdrew. A few moments later Martinez looked at his plate and discovered that his food was gone. Apparently he'd eaten it, though he couldn't remember doing so.

He thought about inviting the lieutenants for an informal meeting aboard *Daffodil*. Or the premiere lieutenant, Kazakov, to a dinner. To talk, and perhaps to plan for eventualities.

But no. That might call Fletcher's attention to his lieutenants. Because of his position on Michi Chen's staff, Martinez was one of the few people aboard *Illustrious* that Fletcher couldn't legally kill. The lieutenants weren't so lucky. If Fletcher suspected Kazakov of plotting with Martinez, then Kazakov might be in jeopardy.

Martinez sipped his glass of water, flat and tasteless from its trip through the recyclers, and then called Alikhan to clear the table. Just as Alikhan was leaving, Martinez's sleeve comm chimed.

"Martinez," he answered, and his heart leaped to see the squadcom's face on the display.

Now, he thought, Michi would call him to a conference, and the two of them would work out something to do about Fletcher.

"Lord Captain," the squadcom said, "I'd be obliged if you'd arrange a squadron maneuver—an experiment, rather—in three days, after we pass Termaine."

Martinez fought down his surprise. "Yes, my lady. Do you want any kind of experiment in particular?"

"Just make sure it lasts at least a watch," Michi said. "We don't want the squadron to get rusty."

"No, my lady." He paused for a moment in hopes Michi would open the subject of the killing, and when nothing was said, he hopefully asked, "Do you have any other requests, my lady?"

Michi's tone was final. "No, my lord. Thank you. End transmission."

Martinez gazed for a moment at the orange end-stamp on his sleeve, then blanked the display.

Chenforce hadn't had a maneuver since before Bai-do, so it was probably time to shine the squadron's collective skills. The ships would be linked by communications laser into a virtual environment and fight a battle against an enemy force, or split into two divisions and battle one another.

Maneuvers in the Fleet, traditionally, were highly scripted, with the outcome determined in advance and the ships and their crews rated on how well they performed the tasks they were assigned. Michi, however, had requested an "experiment," a type of maneuver that Martinez and Squadron Commander Do-faq had developed after the Battle of Hone-bar. In an experiment, the outcome of the maneuver was not determined in advance, and the ships and their commanders were free to improvise and experiment with tactics. It was a measure of Michi's generosity that she was willing to permit this: most commanders would have insisted on knowing they were going to win ahead of time.

What was perhaps more important under the current circumstances was that while the maneuver was going on, Fletcher would not be conducting inspections, and thereby not be tempted to execute subordinates in passing.

Nor could Fletcher conduct an inspection while Chenforce flew by Termaine in two days. Everyone would be at general quarters for ten or twelve hours while they waited to see if Termaine would attempt resistance.

That left tomorrow, still a routine day in which the captain was free, if he desired, to conduct an inspection. Martinez wondered why Michi hadn't ordered a maneuver then as well as three days hence.

Perhaps, he thought, Michi was giving Fletcher a test. One more dead petty officer and she'd know what steps to take.

He looked at the naked winged children that had been painted on his office walls, and he wondered at the mind that could both commission such art and plan a cold-blooded killing.

Martinez threw himself into planning the experiment. He altered the composition of the forces several times and modified the fine details obsessively. It was a way to avoid thinking about Fletcher, or remember Thuc falling with a fan of scarlet spraying from his throat.

That night, he wore a virtual headset and projected the starscape from outside *Illustrious* into his mind, hoping it would aid his sleeping mind in achieving a tranquility that had eluded him all day. It seemed to work, until he came awake with his heart pounding and, in his mind, the black emptiness of space turned to the color of blood.

Breakfast was another meal eaten without noticing the contents of his plate. He dreaded hearing the businesslike sound of heels on the deck, Fletcher and Marsden and Mersenne, marching to his door to summon him to another inspection.

Even though he half expected the sound, his nerves gave a surprised, jangled leap when he heard it. He was on his feet and already half braced when Fletcher appeared in his open door, wearing full dress, white gloves, and the knife in its curved, gleaming scabbard.

"Captain Martinez, I'd be obliged if you'd join us."

Cold dread settled over Martinez like a rain-saturated cloak.

"Yes, my lord," he said.

As he walked to the door, he felt light-headed, possessed by the notion that everything from this point was predestined, that he was fated to be a witness to another inexplicable tragedy without being able to intervene, that within an hour or two he would again be reporting to Michi Chen while somewhere in the ship crew scrubbed blood from the deck.

Once again the captain wanted him as a witness. He wished Fletcher had just brought a camera instead.

Again Fletcher's party consisted of himself and two others. One was Marsden, the secretary, but Mersenne had been replaced by Lord Ahmad Husayn, the weapons officer. That told Martinez where the party was going, and he wasn't surprised when Fletcher took a turn two bulkheads down and headed through a hatch into Missile Battery 3.

Gulik, the rat-faced little master weaponer, stood there braced along with his crew. Once more Martinez watched as Fletcher conducted a detailed inspection, including not just the launchers and loaders, but the elevator systems used to move personnel along the battery, the large spider-shaped damage-control robots used for repairs during high-gee, when the crew themselves would be strapped in their acceleration couches and barely able to breathe or think, let alone move. Fletcher checked the hydraulic reservoirs of the robots, inspected the radiation-hardened bunker where the weaponers would shelter in combat, and then had two missiles drawn from their tubes. The missiles were painted the same green, pink, and white pattern as the exterior of the ship, and looked less like weapons of war than strange examples of design, art objects commissioned by an eccentric patron, or perhaps colorful candies intended for the children of giants. The captain dusted them with his white-gloved fingers—he expected missiles in their tubes to be as clean as his own dinner table—then had them reinserted and asked Gulik when the loaders had last been overhauled.

At last Fletcher inspected the weaponers themselves, the line of immaculately dressed pulpies, arranged in order of rank with the petty officers at the end.

Martinez felt his perceptions expanding through the battery, sensing every last cable, every last switch. He seemed hyperaware of everything that occurred within that enclosed space, from the scent of oil on the elevator cables to the nervous way Husayn flexed his hands when the captain wasn't looking to the sheen of sweat on Master Weaponer Gulik's upper lip.

Gulik stood at the end of the line, properly braced. Fletcher moved with cold deliberation up the line, his practiced eyes noting a worn seam on a coverall, a tool inserted in its loop the wrong way around, a laundry tag visible above a shirt collar.

Martinez's nerves flashed hot and cold. Fletcher paused in front of Gulik and gazed at the man for a long, searching moment with his deep blue eyes.

"Very good, Gulik," Fletcher said. "You're keeping up your standards."

And then Fletcher, incredibly, turned and walked away, his brisk footsteps sounding on the deck, his knife clanking faintly on the end of its chain. Martinez, head swimming, followed dumbly with the rest of the captain's party.

Out of the corner of his eye, as he stepped over the hatch sill, he saw Gulik sag with relief.

Fletcher led up two companionways, then turned to Martinez.

"Thank you, Captain," he said. The superior smile twitched again at the corners of his mouth. "I appreciate your indulging my fancies."

"Yes, my lord," Martinez said, because *You're welcome* wasn't quite the effect he was after.

Martinez went to his office, sat behind his desk and thought about what he'd just seen. Fletcher had called him to witness an inspection at which nothing unusual had occurred.

Fletcher makes scores of inspections every year, Martinez thought. But he's only killed *one* petty officer. So how eccentric was that?

An hour or so later Lieutenant Coen, Michi's red-haired signals officer, arrived with an invitation to join the squadcom for dinner. Martinez accepted, and over a cup of cold green melon soup informed Michi that nothing out of the ordinary had occurred at the morning's inspection.

Michi didn't comment, but instead asked about the experiment in two days' time. Martinez outlined his plans while frustration bubbled at the base of his spine.

What are you going to do? he wanted to ask. But Michi only spoke about the war game, and then of the flight past Termaine the following day.

At the end of the meal he was more baffled than ever.

That night he came awake out of a disordered dream to find himself floating. He glanced at the amber numerals of the chronometer that glowed in a corner of the wall display and saw that it was time for a course reorientation around one of the Termaine system's gas giants, a final slingshot that would send Chenforce racing past the enemy-held planet.

Martinez watched the seconds tick past, and then the engines fired and his mattress rose to meet him.

Two hours later Alikhan woke him with a breakfast of coffee, salt mayfish, and one of Perry's fresh brioche. Afterward, Alikhan began assisting him into his vac suit in preparation for the walk to the Flag Officer Station.

Everyone on the ship knew the hour at which general quarters would be called, and most were now struggling into their vac suits, or would be shortly.

The suit checked its own systems and displayed the result on its sleeve display: all was well. Martinez took a last sip of coffee, then took his helmet from Alikhan and dismissed him to go to quarters, where he'd don his own suit with the aid of another weaponer.

Martinez clomped down the corridor, awkward in the suit, and dropped down two decks to the Flag Officer Station. Michi was already present, along with her aides Li and Coen. Michi stood with her back to him, her helmet off, her hair tucked into the cap that held her earphones and the projectors of the virtual array. The unfixed chin strap dangled on her shoulder. Her head was bent and one hand was pressed over an ear as if to hear better.

Even in the bulky suit Martinez could see the tension in her stance. "Stand by," she said, and swung around to him, her face a mask of furious calculation. He braced.

"My lady."

"I need you to take command of *Illustrious* immediately. Something's happened to Captain Fletcher."

"Has he—" Martinez began. *Run amuck with a kitchen knife, perhaps?* He couldn't seem to find a way to phrase the question tactfully.

Michi's words were clipped and curt, nearly savage. "There's a report he's dead," she said. "Now get to Command and take charge before things go completely to hell."

ELEVEN

Martinez marched into Command with his helmet under his arm and confusion warring with frustration in his heart.

"I am in command!" he said, loud enough for everyone to hear. "Per the squadcom's orders!"

Heads turned, faces peering at him from over the collars of their vac suits. Chandra Prasad looked at him from the command cage. A lock of her auburn hair curled across her forehead from under her sensor cap.

"Captain Martinez is in command!" she agreed.

Martinez stepped toward her. "Lieutenant," he said, "do you wish to confirm with the squadcom?"

Amusement touched the corners of her mouth. "I just got off the comm with her, Lord Captain. She told me you were coming."

Martinez sensed the drama that had marched in with him begin to deflate.

"Very well," he said.

Chandra tipped her couch forward and rose to her feet. "Course two-two-five by zero-zero-one absolute," she reported. "Accelerating at one gravity, and are currently moving at .341c. Our closest approach to Termaine will occur in approximately a hundred and ten minutes. We are not yet at general quarters."

"Sound general quarters then," Martinez said.

"General quarters!" Chandra called.

The alarm began to chime. The command crew reached into the net bags attached to their couches, pulled out their helmets, and began to lock them onto the connecting rings of their collars.

Chandra paused with her helmet halfway over her head. "My position at quarters is normally at signals," she said.

"Take your position then, Lady Chandra."

"Yes, my lord." As she walked by him she lowered her voice and said, "Your luck's holding, Captain."

Martinez shot her a murderous glance, but she'd already passed. He took his seat, the couch swinging with his weight as he webbed himself in. He reached above his head for the command display and locked it down in front of him.

He donned his helmet, and at once *Illustrious* turned more distant. All the noise in Command faded—the creak of the acceleration cages, the bleating of displays trying to call for attention, the distant rumble of the ship's engines. More apparent was the hiss of the air inlet and the polyamide scent of the suit seals. Martinez turned on his suit microphone and tuned to the channel he shared with the signals station. "Comm," he said. "Test, test."

"I hear you, Lord Captain."

He looked over Command. The murals Fletcher had installed were antique military scenes, horsebacked officers who looked like bolsters in odd, overstuffed clothes, all leading bodies of men who carried firearms that featured nasty long knives on the ends. Below the officers' bland gaze Martinez saw only the backs of the helmets of the crew sitting at their stations. If *Illustrious* had been his own command, he would have known their names by now: as it was, he knew only the three lieutenants and a handful of the others.

He wondered how much they knew about why he was here. It was a certainty that whatever they knew or didn't, they were probably boiling with questions.

Martinez shifted to the channel that allowed him to address everyone in Command, then paused to collect his thoughts. It was difficult to pass on information that he did not himself possess. He decided to keep it as simple as possible.

"This is Captain Martinez," he said. "I wished to inform you that the lady squadcom instructed me to take command of *Illustrious,* as Captain Fletcher has been reported ill. I don't know any details, but I'm sure that Captain Fletcher will return to command as soon as circumstances permit."

Well, he thought, *that* was as bland an announcement as he could possibly imagine. He doubted it went very far toward softening the curiosity of the watch.

Martinez then called Michi to let her know that he'd arrived in Command. The call was taken by Michi's aide, Lady Ida Li, who presumably passed it on.

He called up the tactical display and familiarized himself with the situation: Chenforce on its way to pass by Termaine, the two pinnaces and their squadrons of missiles ahead, Termaine surrounded by a cloud of ships that had been cast off and abandoned. If Fleet Commander Jakseth was preparing any act of defiance, he had yet to launch it.

"Lord Captain?" The voice was familiar, and a glance at his display showed that it belonged to Husayn, the weapons officer.

"Yes, Lieutenant?" Martinez answered.

"I was wondering if I'm likely to have to light the weapons board."

Which was very tactful of Husayn, and Martinez mentally awarded him a few points. At the moment neither he, Husayn, or anyone else aboard *Illustrious* could fire its population-crushing array of weaponry. No single officer could do that, not until certain conditions were met.

Three officers—either the captain and two lieutenants or three lieutenants on their own—would have to turn their keys to unlock the weapons board, and at least two of those keys would have to be turned in different parts of the ship.

Martinez's key was useless for the task—it wasn't configured for a line officer in the correct chain of command. He would have to organize three of the lieutenants.

"Very good, Lord Lieutenant," he said. He called the first lieutenant, Fulvia Kazakov, who was stationed in Auxiliary Command, ready to take charge of *Illustrious* if Command and all senior officers were blown to bits, and had her insert her key along with Husayn and Chandra Prasad.

"Turn on my mark," Martinez said. "This is not a drill. Three, two, one, mark."

Husayn's display brightened as all weapons went live.

"Thank you," Martinez said. "Stand by."

Lighting the weapons board was the most dramatic thing that happened until it was time to darken the weapons board again. The day crawled by like an arthritic animal looking for a hole to die in. Every so often one of the icons on the tactical display would move very slightly in one direction or another, and then everything would be still once more.

The pinnaces flashed past Termaine, cameras and sensors sweeping the planet's ring for hidden weapons or warships and feeding the data to the sensor operators in Command and Auxiliary Command. Lieutenant Kazakov correlated the data and informed Termaine that Fleet Commander Jakseth was to all appearances obeying Lady Michi's commands. The Naxids had been building no less than six warships on Termaine's ring, but none were completed and all had been cast adrift.

Martinez wasn't asked to kill a few billion people. Instead, in a voice that breathed relief with every syllable, he targeted each of the abandoned ships cast off from the ring, warships and civilian craft both, and sent missiles on their way to destroy them. He divided the missiles equally among the ships of Chenforce so that no one ship's magazines would be depleted too quickly.

He watched the missile bursts blossom in the display, as the expanding, overlapping spheres of superheated plasma momentarily obscured Termaine and its ring. When the plasma cooled and dissipated, the ring was still there, presumably much to the relief of Fleet Commander Jakseth.

Martinez watched the tactical situation crawl along for another half hour, then called Michi to ask for permission to secure from general quarters. This time he spoke to her personally.

"Permission granted," she said.

"How is Captain Fletcher?"

"He's dead. I'll need you and Lieutenant Kazakov to meet in my office as soon as we secure from quarters."

"Yes, my lady." He paused in hopes that Lady Michi would volunteer more information, but once again she remained silent.

"May I ask how the captain died?" he said finally. He was prepared to wager that Fletcher had hanged himself.

Michi's tone turned resentful. "Fell and hit his head on a corner of his desk, apparently. We don't know any more than that because we went to quarters soon after the body was discovered. Dr. Xi had the body moved to sick bay and then had to go to quarters himself, so there hasn't been an examination."

"Would you like me to make an announcement to the ship's crew?"

"No. I'll do that myself. For now, I want to see you in my office."

"Very good, my lady."

Michi ended the communication, and Martinez shifted to the channel that enabled him to speak with others in Command.

"Secure from general quarters," he ordered. "Well done, everyone."

He took off his helmet and took a breath of air free off the smell of suit seals. As the tone to secure from quarters buzzed through the ship, he unwebbed and stood.

"Who's normally standing watch at this hour?" he asked.

Chandra pulled the helmet off her head and wiped a bit of sweat off her forehead with a gloved hand. "The premiere, Lord Captain," she said.

"Lieutenant Kazakov is called elsewhere. If you're not too tired, Lieutenant Prasad, I'd be obliged if you'd take the premiere's watch."

Chandra nodded. "Very good, my lord."

"Lieutenant Prasad has the watch!" Martinez said, loud enough for anyone to hear.

"I have the watch!" Chandra agreed loudly.

Martinez stalked out of the room. The horsebacked officers on the walls watched with unfriendly, calculating eyes.

"I'm appointing you to command *Illustrious,*" Michi said. "You're the only captain we've got."

Martinez wished she had phrased it so he didn't sound so much like a desperate last resort, but the warm, exuberant pleasure of having a command again soon erased any discomfort.

"Yes, my lady," he said, glowing.

"Give me your captain's key," she said. He took his key from the elastic around his neck and handed it to her, and she slipped it into the slot on her desk and tapped codes into the desk.

"Your thumbprint, please?"

Martinez provided it. Michi returned the key to him, and he reattached it to the elastic and tucked it again into his uniform tunic.

"Congratulations, my lord," said Fulvia Kazakov. She sat next to Martinez, across the desk from the squadcom. Her dark hair was knotted as usual behind her head, but she'd changed hurriedly after *Illustrious* secured from quarters, and hadn't had time to stick the usual pair of inlaid chopsticks through the knot.

"Thank you," Martinez said, then realized he should try not to beam quite so much. "A shame it had to happen after such a tragedy," he added.

"Quite," Michi said. She touched her comm panel. "Is Garcia there yet?"

"Yes, my lady." The voice of her orderly Vandervalk.

"Send him in."

Rigger First Class Garcia entered and braced. Under the loose supervision of the military constable officer, Garcia was the head of the ship's Constabulary, all three of them, and was a youngish man, a little plump, wearing a mustache. He had never been in the flag officer's office before, at least to judge by the way his eyes kept turning to the ornamental fluted bronzed pillars, the bronze statues of naked Terran women holding baskets of fruit, and the murals filled with poised human figures sharing a landscape with fantastic beasts.

"You've finished your investigation?" Michi said.

"I've interviewed Captain Fletcher's staff," Garcia said. "I wasn't able to see them all personally, but I was able to speak to them through comm when we were at quarters."

"Report then."

Garcia looked at his sleeve display, where he'd obviously stored the particulars. "The captain worked with Warrant Officer Marsden on ship's business till about 2501 yesterday," he said. "His orderly, Narbonne, was the last person to see him. He helped the captain undress, took his uniform to be brushed and his shoes to be polished. That was about 2526."

Garcia gave a polite cough that indicated his willingness to be interrupted by a question, and when there was none, continued.

"Narbonne returned at 0526 this morning to wake the captain, bring him his uniform, and help him dress, but when he entered the captain's room he saw that the captain wasn't in his bed. He assumed Captain Fletcher was working in his office, so he hung the uniform by the bed and returned to the orderly room and waited to be called.

"A few minutes later the captain's cook, Baca, brought Captain Fletcher's breakfast into the dining room. The captain wasn't there, but that wasn't unusual, and Baca also withdrew."

"Neither of them looked in the office?" Michi asked.

"No. The captain doesn't—didn't—like to be disturbed when working."

"Continue."

"About 0601 Baca returned and saw the captain's breakfast hadn't been touched. He knew we'd be going to quarters shortly, so he paged Captain Fletcher to see if he'd be wanting anything at all to eat, and when there was no answer, he went into the office and found the captain dead."

Again Garcia coughed politely to provide a convenient break in his narrative, and this time Michi obliged him.

"What did Baca do then?"

"He paged Narbonne. Then he and Narbonne put their heads together and paged me."

"You?" Martinez was startled. "Why did they page the Constabulary? Did they suspect foul play?"

Garcia seemed embarrassed. "I think they were afraid they might be blamed for the captain's death. They wanted me there so I could . . . assure them they wouldn't be held responsible."

Martinez supposed that was plausible.

"I arrived on the scene at 0614," Garcia continued. "The captain was cold and had clearly been dead for some time. I paged the doctor and a stretcher party, and then called Lady Michi." His eyes turned to the squadcom. "You ordered me to conduct an investigation. I told Narbonne and Baca to return to the orderly room, and then waited for the doctor. Once the doctor and stretcher party arrived, Dr. Xi pronounced the captain dead and took the body to sick bay. I looked over the office and . . . well, it was obvious what happened."

"And what happened was?" Michi prompted.

"Captain Fletcher got out of bed sometime during the night, went into his office, fell and hit his head. There was an obvious wound on his right temple, and the corner of his desk had some blood, hair, and a bit of skin adhering." For some reason, Garcia had trouble pronouncing the word "adhering," but he managed it on the third try.

"My suspicion is that the captain got caught off-balance during the course change early this morning. There was one at 0346. There was a moment of weightlessness, and then when acceleration resumed he was caught wrong-footed. Or maybe he was floating weightless in the room and resumption of gravity caught him by surprise. Dr. Xi might be able to confirm the timing."

Michi saw his surprised look out of the corner of her eye. "Captain Martinez?" she said. "Did you have a question?"

Martinez was startled. "No, my lady," he said quickly. "I just remembered that I woke during that course change. I wonder . . . if I heard something."

He groped through his memory, but failed to grasp whatever it was that had brought him awake.

"It was most likely the zero-gravity alarm that woke you up," Kazakov said.

"Very possible, my lady."

Michi returned her attention to Garcia. "Was the captain dressed?" she asked.

"No, my lady. He wore pajamas, a dressing gown, and slippers."

"I have no more questions," Michi said. She glanced at Martinez and Kazakov. "Is there anything else?"

"I have a question," Martinez said. "Did you take any notice of what the captain was working on?"

"Working?"

"If he was in his office, I'd suppose he'd be working."

"He wasn't working at anything. The display wasn't turned on, and there were no papers on the desk."

"Where was his captain's key?"

Garcia opened his mouth, closed it, and opened it again. "I don't know, my lord."

"Was it slotted into the desk?"

"I don't think so."

Martinez looked at Michi. "That's all," he said. "I think."

Michi turned to the petty officer. "Thank you, Garcia," she said.

He braced and made his way out. Michi gave Martinez a look. "That was good thinking, about the captain's key. It's got access to practically everything." She turned to her desk and began entering codes. "I'll cancel the key's privileges."

This proved to be unnecessary, as the next to report was Dr. Xi, who put Captain Fletcher's key on the desk in front of the squadron commander. The strip of plastic was on an elastic band.

"I found this around his wrist," Xi said.

Lord Yuntai Xi was a small man with a well-tended white beard, salt-and-pepper hair that hung over his collar, and a little potbelly. The Xi clan were clients of the Gombergs, and he had known the captain from boyhood. He spoke in a steady tenor voice, but there was sadness in his brown eyes.

"Because we've spent most of the last several hours at general quarters, I've been able to conduct only a superficial investigation. There is a substantial depression on the right side of the skull, and the skin is torn, and skull fracture is the obvious cause of death. There are no other wounds. I made a small incision under the ribs on the right side and inserted a thermometer into the liver, and from that I calculate that the time of death was 0401, plus or minus half an hour."

Martinez noted that 0401 was only seven minutes after the change of course that might have caused the captain's stumble and death.

"Thank you, Lord Doctor," Michi said. "I think in view of the questions that will inevitably be raised, an autopsy will be required."

Xi closed his eyes and sighed. "Very well, my lady."

After Xi left, Michi took up Fletcher's key and held the thin plastic strip thoughtfully in her hand.

"Do you wish me to make an announcement to the ship's company?" Martinez asked.

"No. I'll do it." She tossed the key into the rubbish. "That's a bad coincidence," she said.

"Yes, my lady," said Kazakov. Her expression was thoughtful.

"Coincidence?" Martinez repeated.

"First Kosinic," Kazakov explained, "and then Captain Fletcher."

Kosinic had been Lady Michi's first tactical officer. He had died early in Chenforce's journey from Harzapid to Zanshaa, and his death provided an opening on the staff that Martinez—a recent addition to the Chen family—had jumped to fill.

"Coincidence?" Martinez said again. "I don't understand what you mean. I thought Lieutenant Kosinic died from wounds received at Harzapid."

"No." Michi's glare was savage. "He fell and hit his head."

Martinez returned to his cabin to find that Alikhan, assisted by his other orderlies, Espinosa and Ayutano, were packing his belongings.

Alikhan turned to him as he paused in the doorway. "I presume we will be moving to the captain's cabin, my lord," he said.

"I suppose we will." Martinez hadn't actually gotten that far in his thinking.

Nor was there any point in wondering how Alikhan knew of the vacancy in the captain's quarters. Even though no announcement had been made, everyone on the ship must know by now that Fletcher was dead.

"We've removed the staff tabs from all your tunics except for what you're wearing now," Alikhan said. "If you'd care to give me your jacket, my lord?"

Martinez unbuttoned his collar and stepped into his sleeping cabin. Alikhan and his mates had nearly finished the job, remarkably efficient considering the amount of gear an officer was supposed to carry with him from one posting to the next.

"Are the captain's belongings also being packed?" he asked.

"Everything but what was in his office," said Alikhan. "There's a constable on guard there."

"Right," Martinez said. He turned, left his cabin, buttoned his collar again, and marched down the corridor to Fletcher's office. The Constable there braced as he entered.

"Come with me, Constable," he told her, and walked through the office, deliberately averting his eyes from the desk with the blood and the scrapings of Fletcher's scalp. He entered Fletcher's sleeping cabin, stopped in the doorway and gaped.

Something Chandra said had led him to conclude that he'd find erotica on Fletcher's walls, but Fletcher hadn't adorned his private room with anything so ordinary. In place of the bright tile work or classically balanced frescoes Fletcher had placed elsewhere on his *Illustrious,* the walls in the sleeping cabin were paneled in ancient dark wood. The wood was rough-hewn and scarred and had never been painted or polished. Presumably it had been fireproofed as Fleet regulations required, but otherwise it looked to have been acquired from some timeworn ruin of a house, a timbered hulk from a desolate dark age. The ceiling panels were perhaps equally old but were in a different style, dark wood again and roughly hewn, but polished to a mellow glow. On the floor were mud-colored tiles with geometrical patterns in faded yellow. Lights were recessed into crude hand-beaten copper sconces. Small dark old pictures sat on the walls in metal frames that winked dully of gold or silver.

Dominating the far wall was the life-sized figure of a man, cast apparently in porcelain. The man had been savagely tortured and then hung on a tree to die. Cuts and blood and the marks of burning tongs were vivid in the translucent porcelain flesh and rendered in immaculate detail by the artist. Despite the many wounds and the agonized posture, the clean-shaven face of the man was serene and unearthly, with unnaturally large dark eyes that wrapped partly around the sides of the head. His hair had been braided in long ringlets that hung to his shoulders. As Martinez took a step closer, he saw that the figure had been lashed by metal bands to what appeared to be a chunk of a perfectly genuine tree.

He looked in amazement from the object on the wall to the two servants who stood braced by open trunks half filled with the captain's belongings.

"What is *that*?" he couldn't stop himself from asking.

"Part of Captain Fletcher's collection, my lord."

The answer came from the older of the two, a gray-haired man with a long nose and a moist, mobile mouth.

"You're Narbonne?" Martinez asked.

"Yes, my lord."

"Stand by a moment."

Martinez paged Marsden, the captain's secretary. When he arrived, Martinez turned to him.

"I want a complete inventory taken of all Captain Fletcher's belongings," he said. "I want that signed by you and witnessed by everyone here, including—" He nodded toward the guard. "Your name?"

"Huang, my lord."

"Including Huang."

Marsden nodded his bald head. "Yes, my lord."

"I'll try to access the captain's safe so we can inventory the contents as well."

"Very good, my lord."

Getting into the captain's safe proved more difficult than Martinez expected. A combination in records was available to the captain, but Fletcher had changed the numbers at least once since he'd taken command, and the old combination was no longer valid. Martinez got Fletcher's captain's key from Michi, but that didn't serve either. In the end he had to call Master Machinist Gawbyan. The machinist, who had a truly spectacular pair of mustachios that curled so broad and high they nearly met his eyebrows, arrived with an assistant and a bag of tools. When the safe was finally open, the contents were uninteresting: some money, a beautifully made custom pistol with a box of ammunition, some bank records, notes on investments, and a pair of small boxes. One box contained a small, frail old book written in some incomprehensibly ancient alphabet. The other box held a carved white jade statue of a nearly naked six-armed woman dancing atop a skull, a sight that wasn't very shocking after the sight of the tortured man lashed to the tree.

Martinez supposed the book and the statue were valuable, so he decided to keep them in his own safe once Gawbyan finished repairing the damage he'd just inflicted. "Make a note," Martinez told Marsden, "that I've kept in my own possession a small book and a small statue of a woman."

"Very good, my lord," Marsden said, and wrote on his datapad.

He took the objects to the safe in his own office, and on his return encountered Dr. Xi coming up the companion, climbing amid the faint scent of disinfectant. Xi braced apologetically, then said, "I was on my way to report to Lady Michi."

"Yes?"

His sad eyes contemplated Martinez for a moment, then grew hard. "Join me if you like."

They were shown into Michi's office, and Xi offered another unpracticed salute.

"I've performed the autopsy," he said, "but it was hardly necessary, since it was obviously murder nearly from the start."

Michi pressed her lips together in a thin line, then said, "Obvious? How?"

"I put a sensor net around the lord captain's head and got a three-dimensional image of the skull. Captain Fletcher's right temple was struck by three separate blows, grouped closely together—the multiple blows weren't obvious from the superficial examination I was able to conduct this morning, but on the three-dimensional image they were very clear."

"His head was driven into the desk three times?" Michi asked.

"Or hit with a blunt object twice, then slammed into the desk to make it look like an accident."

Michi spoke to her desk. "Page Rigger First Class Garcia to the squadcom's office." She looked at Martinez. "Who's military constabulary officer?"

"Corbigny, my lady."

Michi turned to her desk again. "Page Lieutenant Corbigny as well."

Martinez turned to Xi. "I don't suppose Lieutenant Kosinic's body is still on the ship."

Xi looked at him. "As a matter of fact, the body's in a freezer compartment. We didn't cremate."

"Perhaps you ought to take a look at it."

Xi turned away, his gaze directed at the wall over Michi's head. His lips pursed out, then in. "I should," he said. "I wish I had when he died."

"Why didn't you?"

Michi answered for him. "Because the cause of death seemed so obvious. In the fighting at Harzapid, Kosinic suffered broken bones and head injuries. When he came on board, he insisted he was fit, but his report from the hospital stated he was subject to blinding headaches, vertigo, and fainting spells. When he was found dead, it seemed obvious that he'd fainted and hit his head."

"Where was he found?"

"In the Flag Officer Station."

Martinez was surprised. "What was he doing there alone?"

Michi hesitated. "Li and Coen told me he sometimes worked there by himself. It was less distracting than the wardroom."

"Was he working on anything in particular?"

"He was tactical officer. I'd had him plan a full schedule of squadron maneuvers, concentrating on the defense of Zanshaa."

Martinez turned at the sound of someone entering. Rigger Garcia came into the room and braced.

"Rigger/First Garcia reporting, my lady."

"Thank you. Stand at ease, and take notes if you need to."

Corbigny arrived a few seconds later, and seemed intimidated by the presence of the squadron commander. The slim, dark-haired young woman was the most junior lieutenant on the ship, and therefore got the jobs none of the other officers wanted. One of these was Military Constabulary Officer, which put her in theoretical charge of the ship's police. If nothing else, supervising the Constabulary would give Corbigny a rapid education in the varieties of vice, depravity, and violence available to the average Fleet crouchback, an education desirable and probably necessary for her further development as an officer.

Garcia adjusted his sleeve display. "I'm recording, my lady."

Michi spoke in quick, clipped phrases, as if she wanted to get it over quickly. "The lord doctor's autopsy showed that Captain Fletcher was murdered. You'll be taking charge of the investigation."

Garcia's eyes went wide at this, and Corbigny turned pale. When Garcia began to speak, Michi's words continued without hesitation.

"Captain Fletcher's office should be sealed off and subject to a minute examination. Look for fingerprints, traces of fabric or hair, anything that may have been carelessly dropped. Take particular care—"

"My lady!" Garcia said almost desperately.

Michi paused. "Garcia?"

"Fingerprints—hair analysis—I don't know how to do any of that!" he said. "The Investigative Service is trained for that sort of thing, not the Constabulary!"

Martinez looked at the man in sudden sympathy. The Military Constabulary investigated cases of vandalism or petty theft, broke up brawls, or arrested crouchbacks drunk on wine brewed up in plastic bags they'd hidden in their lockers. Any technical investigation was well outside their strengths.

Michi's lips thinned to a line. Her fingers drummed on her desktop a few times, and then she relaxed. "Perhaps I've been watching too many *Doctor An-ku* dramas," she said. "I thought there were professionals who handled this kind of thing."

"There are, my lady," Garcia said. "But none on this ship, I guess."

Michi rubbed her forehead under her straight bangs. "I still want the office examined very carefully," she said.

Dr. Xi had a smile behind his little white beard. He turned to Garcia. "I might be able to create some fingerprint powder out of materials I have in the pharmacy," he said. "I'll do the research and see what I can manage."

"Good," Michi said. "Why don't you do that now, my lord?"

"Certainly." Xi straightened his slouch slightly in salute and turned to leave. He hesitated, seeming to remember something, then reached into his pocket and took out a clear plastic box, the sort in which he probably kept samples.

"I took the captain's jewelry from his body," he said. "To whom should I give it?"

"I'm having an inventory made of the captain's belongings," Martinez said. "I'll take the box, if you like."

Martinez took it and looked through the plastic lid. Inside were a pair of rings, a heavy signet of enameled gold with the Fletcher and Gomberg crests interlinked, a smaller ring made of a kind of silver mesh, wonderfully intricate, and a pendant on a chain. He held the box to the light and saw that the pendant formed the figure of an ayaca tree in full flower and shimmered with fine diamonds, rubies, and emeralds.

"We should try to make a list of where everyone was during the critical hour," Michi continued. "And if anyone was seen moving about."

Again Garcia looked as if despair had him by the throat. "There are over three hundred people aboard *Illustrious,* my lady," he said. "And I only have two staff."

"Most of the crew would be asleep," Michi said. "We'll have the department heads make the reports, so you don't have to interview everyone personally."

"I'll send the department heads instructions later today," Martinez added.

Michi gave Garcia a level look. "Start now with a careful examination of the scene," she said.

"Very good, my lady."

He braced in salute and left, clearly relieved to have made his escape. Michi watched him go, then turned to Martinez. There was irony in the set of her smile.

"Any thoughts, Captain?"

"Three deaths," Martinez said, "and I don't see the connection. It would be better if there were only two."

Her eyebrows rose. "How do you mean?"

"If it were only Kosinic and Fletcher killed," Martinez said, "then I'd say the killer was someone with a grudge against officers. If it were only Thuc and Fletcher, I'd say that Fletcher had been killed by someone wanting revenge for Thuc. But with all three I don't see anything to link them."

"Perhaps there *is* no connection."

Martinez considered this notion. "I'd rather not believe that," he decided.

Michi slumped in her chair and looked sidelong at the serene bronze seminude woman that Fletcher had installed in the corner, the one offering a bowl of fruit. Apparently she found no answers there, so she turned back to Martinez.

"I don't know what else to do, so I'm going to have a cocktail," she said. "Would you care to join me?"

Martinez began to accept, then hesitated. "Perhaps I'd better supervise Garcia in his efforts."

"Perhaps." Michi shrugged. "Let me know if you find anything."

Martinez braced in salute, turned to leave, and then saw Sub-Lieutenant Corbigny, who had stood without speaking for the entire interview.

"Any questions, Lieutenant?" he asked.

Her eyes widened. "No, my lord."

"You may leave," Michi said. Corbigny braced and fled.

Martinez turned to leave again, then turned back. "Are we still doing an experiment tomorrow?" he asked.

"Postpone."

"Very good, my lady."

Very little was found in Fletcher's office: Narbonne and the other servants simply kept it too clean. Crawling on hands and knees, Garcia and Martinez found several hairs that were placed in specimen flasks sent them by Dr. Xi. When Xi turned up with a squeeze bottle of his homemade fingerprint powder, they blanketed every solid surface and produced a few dozen prints, most of them of sufficient quality to be read by an ordinary fingerprint reader they procured from Marsden's desk.

While they worked, Michi Chen made an announcement to the ship's company, confirming that Captain Fletcher had died and that Martinez had been appointed to fill his place. Martinez, on his knees peering at an eyelash he'd just picked up with tweezers, failed somehow to be overcome by the sudden majesty of command that had just officially dropped onto his shoulders.

"I regret to inform *Illustrious*," Michi continued, "that Captain Fletcher's death was the result of foul play. I ask any crew with knowledge of this event to report to the Constabulary or to an officer. As the lord captain was murdered between 0301 and 0501, the testimony of anyone with knowledge of unusual movement or activity around that time would be very useful."

A new firmness, almost a ferocity, entered Michi's voice. "The squadron is alone, moving deep in enemy territory. We are too vulnerable to the enemy to permit any kind of disorder and lawlessness in our own ranks. Any weakness on our part only makes the enemy stronger. I am *determined*"—the word was almost a shout—"*determined* that the killer or killers of Captain Fletcher will be found and punished.

"Once again," more subdued now, "I ask anyone with information to come forward before any more crimes are committed. This is Squadron Commander Chen, in the name of the Praxis."

Martinez was impressed. The drinks had done her good, he decided.

Before long he began to envy Michi her cocktails. If anything were going to be solved this way, with fingerprint comparison and hair and fiber analysis, it would be through long and tedious work, and he had no time for that.

He had a warship to command.

When the job was finished, Martinez rose to his feet and looked at the office, the fine tile and elegant paneling, the martial statues of men in plate armor, and the glass cabinets holding objects of beauty, all of it smudged with fingerprints and covered with powder. If he'd set out deliberately to disfigure all the grace and perfection with which Fletcher had filled his life, he could scarcely have done a better job.

"Lord Captain," Xi said. "May I have the codes to the ship's fingerprint file?"

"Yes. As soon as I can find them."

"I'll return to my office," Xi said, "and proceed as best as I can."

Martinez thought again about Michi's cocktails. "May I offer you a drink first?"

Xi accepted. Martinez paged Alikhan and told him to serve Xi in his old office. "I have a brief errand," he told the doctor. "I'll be with you in a few minutes."

Martinez got a signed copy of the inventory from Marsden, then had the captain's possessions transferred to a locker under his own key and password. He dismissed Fletcher's servants to clean the captain's office, a task he did not envy them, and went to his own cabin to find Xi sitting comfortably amid the *putti,* his forensic samples on the desk, and a glass of whisky in his hand.

Alikhan had thoughtfully left a tray on the desk with another glass, a beaker of whisky, and another beaker of chilled water, its flanks covered with glittering gems of condensation. Martinez poured his own drink and settled into his chair.

"Interesting whisky, my lord," Xi said. "Very smoky."

"From Laredo," Martinez said, "my birthplace." His father sent him cases of Laredo's best, in hopes exposure would boost the export market.

"What it lacks in subtlety," Xi said, "is more than regained in vigor."

Martinez inhaled the fumes lovingly, then raised his glass. "Here's to vigor," he said, and drank.

The whisky blazed a trail of fire down his throat. He looked at the smoky fluid through the prisms of the crystal glass and contemplated his long, singular day.

"My lord," he said, "do you have any idea? Any idea at all?"

Xi seemed to understand the point of this vague question. "Who's responsible, you mean? No. Not the slightest."

"Or why?"

"Nor that either."

Martinez swirled whisky in his glass. "You've known Captain Fletcher for a long time."

"Since he was a boy, yes."

Martinez put the glass down and looked at the white-bearded man across his desk. "Tell me about him," he said.

Xi didn't answer right away. His thumbs pressed hard against his whisky glass, pressed until they turned white. Then the thumbs relaxed.

"Lord Gomberg Fletcher," he said, "was exceptionally well-born, and exceptionally wealthy. Most people born to wealth and high status assume that their condition isn't simply luck, but a result of some kind of perfect cosmic justice—that is, that any person as fine and virtuous as themselves should naturally take an exalted place in society." His brows knit. "I would guess that Captain Fletcher found his position more of a burden than a source of pleasure."

Martinez was surprised. "That—That was hardly my impression," he said.

"Living up to the worlds' expectations is a difficult job," Xi said, "and I think he worked very hard at it. He made a very good job of it. But I don't think it made him happy."

Martinez looked at the pink-cheeked winged children who fluttered around his office wall. "The art collection?" he asked. "All this?" He waved a hand vaguely at the flying children. "That didn't make him happy?"

"There are a limited number of roles suitable for someone of his status," Xi said. "That of aesthete was perhaps the most interesting available." He frowned, a narrow X forming between his brows. "Aestheticism took up the part of his life that wasn't taken up by the military. Between the two of them, he didn't have time to think about being happy or unhappy, or to think about much at all." He looked up at Martinez.

"Did you wonder about all those inspections, those musters?" Xi continued. "All the rituals—dressing formally for every meal, sending notes to people he could as easily have called on the comm? If you ask me, it was all to keep him from thought."

He's as dull as a rusty spoon. Chandra's words echoed in Martinez's head.

Martinez took another sip of whisky while he tried to make sense of Xi's words. "You're saying," he said carefully, "that Captain Fletcher was a kind of imitation human being."

"People realize themselves in adversity," Xi said, "or by

encountering opposition, or through the negative consequences of their decisions. For Fletcher there was no opposition or adversity or negative consequences. He was given
a part and he played it, more or less convincingly." Xi lowered his head and contemplated the whisky glass that
rested on his potbelly. "He never questioned his role. I often wish that he had."

Martinez put his glass on the table. It made more noise
than he intended, and Xi gave a start.

"There were no negative consequences for Fletcher," he
said, "until he killed Engineer Thuc."

Xi said nothing.

"Was that something he did to fill his empty hours?"
Martinez asked. "Cut a man's throat?"

Xi peered at Martinez from under his white eyebrows,
his dark eyes glittering. "I asked him, you know. The day it
happened, at Lady Michi's request. I believe she was hoping I could find Captain Fletcher insane and she could remove him from command." He made the pursing
movement of his lips. "I disappointed her, I'm afraid. Captain Fletcher was perfectly rational."

Martinez tried to avoid shouting. "So why did he kill
Thuc?" he demanded.

Xi licked his lips quickly. "He said that he killed Engineer
Thuc because the honor of the *Illustrious* demanded it."

Martinez stared at him. Words died on his tongue. He took
a drink. "What did he mean by that?" he managed finally.

Xi shrugged.

"Were you his friend?"

Xi shook his head. "Gomberg didn't have any friends
aboard. He was very dutiful in the way he kept to his
sphere, and he expected others to keep to theirs."

"But you followed him."

Xi smiled lightly and rubbed his thigh with his hand.
"The job has its compensations. My practice on Sandama
was successful but dull, and it turned me so dull that my

wife left me for another man. The children were nearly grown. When young Gomberg got his first command and made his offer, I realized I hadn't ever seen Zanshaa, or the Maw, or Harzapid Grand Market. Now I've seen all those things, and a lot more besides."

Martinez felt a sudden flash of anger. All these questions had done nothing but draw him further into the riddle that was Lord Gomberg Fletcher, and the only thing he really cared about the captain was who had killed him. He didn't even care why, he just wanted to find out who'd done it, and deal with that as efficiently as possible.

"What is that thing in Fletcher's sleeping cabin?" Martinez asked. "The man tied to the tree?"

A half-smile played on Xi's lips. "A part of his collection that could not be shown to the public. Captain Fletcher had a special license from the Office of the Censor to collect cult art."

Martinez was speechless. Cults were banned for the public good, and were defined in the Praxis as any belief or sect that made irrational or unverifiable claims about the universe. Banned as well were any art such cults had managed to inspire. Generally such work could only be seen in the Museums of Superstition that had been erected in the major cities of the empire.

Of course, there were also private collectors and scholars, those considered reliable enough to deal regularly with such explosive material. That one such might be aboard *Illustrious,* and might have part of his collection aboard, was beyond all credence.

"Was he interested in any cult in particular?" Martinez finally asked.

"Those that produced good paintings and sculpture," Xi said. "I don't know if you know anything about ancient Terran art—"

"I don't," Martinez said shortly.

"A lot of it, particularly in the early days, was the product of one cult or another. Of course most of those cults now have no followers, and the art is now seen in ordinary museums."

"Really." Martinez drummed his fingers on the table. "Do you have any idea why Captain Fletcher put that—that thing—on his wall, where it was the last thing he'd see before going to sleep?"

Xi's expression was frank. "I don't know. I'd like to know the answer myself, Lord Captain."

"It wasn't part of some kind of erotic game, was it?"

Xi was amused. "I doubt very much that Gomberg was interested in homoerotic flagellation." He shrugged. "But human variety is infinite, isn't it?"

Thwarted again. Martinez found his anger simmering once more. "If you say so."

Xi returned his empty glass to the tray. "I thank you for the drink, Lord Captain. I wish I could have been more useful."

Martinez looked pointedly at the samples. "*Those* are what's going to be useful, I think."

"I hope so." Xi rose and collected the little plastic boxes. "I'll get to my investigations, with your permission."

Martinez sighed. "Carry on, Lord Doctor."

Xi slouched out without bothering to salute. Martinez looked after him for a moment, then paged Alikhan.

"Tell Perry he can bring in supper if he's ready," Martinez said. "Also, I won't be moving into the captain's quarters till tomorrow—unpack just enough to get me through breakfast."

"Very good, my lord." Alikhan leaned over the desk to freshen Martinez's drink. "Anything else, my lord?"

Martinez looked at him. "What are they saying?"

Alikhan's tone was regretful. "I've been here all day, my lord, packing and so on. I haven't had a chance to speak to anyone outside the household."

"Right," Martinez muttered. "Thanks."

Alikhan withdrew. Martinez looked through the files

newly unlocked by his captain's key and thumbprint, and sent Xi access to the fingerprint file. Perry arrived a few minutes afterward with his supper. Martinez ate left-handed, while his right hand worked with his stylus on the desktop, drawing up one list after another.

All things he needed to do or think about as he assumed command.

After Perry carried the dishes away, Martinez sent messages to all the senior petty officers, the heads of departments, ordering them to account for the movements of all their juniors for the critical hours of the morning. He thought it a job best done soon, while memories were still fresh. This done, he called Fulvia Kazakov, the first lieutenant.

"Are you on watch at the moment, Lieutenant?"

"No, my lord." She seemed surprised at the question.

"I'd be obliged if you'd stop by my office then."

"Of course, my lord." She hesitated, then said, "Which office would that be, my lord?"

Martinez smiled. "My old office. And yours too."

When he'd come aboard, as the third-ranking officer on the ship, he'd taken the third-best cabin, which turned out to be that of the first lieutenant. Kazakov had then displaced the lieutenant next junior to her, and each lieutenant shifted in turn, with the most junior having to bunk with the cadets. Tomorrow, he supposed, would be a relief for them all, with everyone restored to his proper place.

Except, of course, for Captain Fletcher, whose body was slowly crystallizing in one of the *Illustrious* freezers.

Kazakov arrived wafting a cloud of metallic perfume. She wore full dress, and the tall collar emphasized the long neck below the heart-shaped face. Mother-of-pearl inlay gleamed on the handles of the chopsticks she'd thrust through the knot at the back of her head.

"Sit down, my lady," Martinez said as she braced. "Would you care for wine? Or something else, perhaps?"

"Whatever you're having, my lord, thank you."

He poured from the bottle of wine that Perry had opened for his supper. She took the glass and sipped politely, then returned it to the desk.

"I am a very different person from Captain Fletcher," Martinez began.

Kazakov was unsurprised by this analysis. "Yes, my lord," she said.

"But," Martinez said, "I'm going to try very hard to *be* Captain Fletcher, at least for a while."

Kazakov gave a thoughtful nod. "I understand, my lord."

Continuity was essential. Fletcher had commanded *Illustrious* for years, and his habits and idiosyncracies had become a part of the ship's routine. To change that suddenly was to risk disturbing the equilibrium of the vast organic network that was the ship's crew, and that network had been disturbed enough already by events of the last few days.

"I intend to continue Captain Fletcher's rigorous series of inspections," Martinez said. "Can you tell me if he inspected the different departments on a regular rotation, or if he chose them randomly?"

"Randomly, I think. I didn't see a pattern. But he'd call the department head before he left the office to let them know he was coming. He wanted the inspections to be reasonably spontaneous, but he didn't want to interrupt anyone in the middle of some critical work."

"I see. Thank you."

He took a sip of his wine. It tasted vinegary to him— Terza had shipped the best stuff to him from Clan Chen's cellars in the High City, but he didn't see what was so special about it.

"Can you give me a report about the state of the ship?" Martinez asked. "Informally, I mean—I don't need all the figures."

Kazakov smiled and triggered her sleeve display. "I actually have the figures if you want them," she said.

"Not right now. Just a verbal summary, if you please."

The state of *Illustrious,* not surprisingly, was good. It had suffered no damage in the mutiny at Harzapid or the Battle of Protipanu. Food, water, and fuel stocks were more than adequate for the projected length of the voyage. Missile stocks, however, were down: between battle and the enemy shipping destroyed so far on the raid, the cruiser's magazines were depleted by two-fifths.

Which was going to be a problem if Chenforce were ever obliged to fight an enemy either more numerous or less cooperative than the Naxid squadron at Protipanu.

"Thank you, Lady Fulvia," Martinez said. "Can you give me a report on the officers? I know them socially, but I've never worked with them."

Kazakov smiled. "I'm happy to say that we have an excellent set of officers aboard. All but one of us were chosen by Captain Fletcher. Some of us were friends before this posting. We work together exceptionally well."

Being chosen by Fletcher wasn't necessarily a recommendation in Martinez's opinion, but he nodded. "And the one who wasn't chosen?" he asked.

Kazakov thought a moment before she replied. "There's no problem with the way she performs her duties," she said. "She's very efficient."

Martinez gave no indication that he understood this as a less than wholehearted endorsement. He liked the fact that Kazakov felt sufficient loyalty to the other officers not to put a knife into Chandra's back when she had the chance.

"Let's take the lieutenants one by one," he said.

From Kazakov's report, Martinez gathered that three of the lieutenants were Gomberg or Fletcher clients, following in their patron's wake up the ladder of Fleet hierarchy. Two, Husayn and Kazakov herself, had benefited from those complex trades of favor and patronage so common among the Peers: Fletcher had agreed to look after their in-

terests in exchange for their own families aiding some of
Fletcher's friends or dependents.

It occurred to Martinez that perhaps Kazakov thought
that this genealogy of relationships and obligations was all
that was required to explain the lieutenants to her new captain, or perhaps she was looking into the future and letting
him know that her relations were ready to assist his friends
in the same sort of arrangement they'd had with Fletcher.
He was gratified, but insisted on knowing how well the officers did their jobs.

According to Kazakov, they did their jobs very well.
Lord Phillips and Corbigny, the two most junior, were inexperienced but promising; and the others were all talented. Martinez had no reason to doubt her judgments.

"It's a happy wardroom?" Martinez asked.

"Yes." Kazakov's answer came without hesitation. "Unusually so."

"Lady Michi's lieutenants are fitting in? Coen and Li?"

"Yes. They're amiable people."

"How about Kosinic? Was he a happy member of the
wardroom mess?"

Kazakov blinked in surprise. "Kosinic? He wasn't
aboard for very long and—I suppose he agreed well
enough with the others, given the circumstances."

Martinez raised his eyebrows. "Circumstances?"

"Well, he was a commoner. Not," Kazakov was quick to
add, aware perhaps that she'd put a foot wrong, "not that
being a commoner was a problem, I don't say anything
against *that,* but his family had no money, and he had to
live off his pay. So Kosinic had to take an advance on his
pay in order to pay his wardroom dues, and he really
couldn't afford to club together with the other lieutenants
to buy food stores and liquor and so on. The rest of us were
perfectly happy to pay his allotment, but I think he was
perhaps a little sensitive about it, and he severely limited
his wine and liquor consumption, and avoided eating some
of the more expensive food items. And he couldn't afford

to gamble—not," she added, catching herself again, "that there's high play in the wardroom—nothing like it—but there's often a friendly game going on, for what we'd consider pocket money, and Kosinic couldn't afford a place at the table."

Kazakov reached for her wine and took a sip. "And then of course the mutiny happened, and Kosinic got wounded. I think perhaps the head injury changed his personality a little, because he became sullen and angry. Sometimes he'd just be sitting in a chair and you'd look up and see him in a complete fury—his jaw would be working and his neck muscles all taut like cables and his eyes on fire. It was a little frightening. This is extremely good wine, my lord."

"I'm glad you like it. Do you have any idea what made Kosinic angry?"

"No, my lord. I don't think the wardroom conversation was any more inane than usual." She smiled at her own joke, and then the smile faded. "I always thought getting blown up by the Naxids was reason enough for anger. But whatever the cause, Kosinic became a lot less sociable after he was wounded, and he spent most of his time in his cabin or in the Flag Officer Station, working."

Martinez sipped his own wine. He thought he understood Kosinic fairly well.

He himself was a Peer, and blessed with a large allowance from his wealthy family. But he was a provincial, and marked as a provincial by his accent. He knew very well the way high-caste Peers could condescend to their inferiors, or deliberately humiliate them, or treat them as servants, or simply ignore them. Even if the other officers intended no disparagement, a sensitive, intelligent commoner might well detect slights where none existed.

"Do you happen to know how Lady Michi came to take Kosinic on her staff?" Martinez asked.

"I believe Kosinic served as a cadet in a previous command. He impressed her and she took him along when he passed his lieutenant exams."

Which was unusually broad-minded of Michi, Martinez thought. She could as easily have associated herself only with her own clients and the clients of powerful families with whom she wished to curry favor, as had Fletcher. Instead, though she came from a clan at least as ancient and noble as the Gombergs or Fletchers, she'd chosen to give one of her valuable staff jobs to a poor commoner.

Though it had to be admitted, in retrospect, that Michi's experiment in social mobility hadn't been very successful.

"Was Kosinic a good tactical officer?" Martinez asked.

"Yes. Absolutely. Of course, he didn't bring in a new tactical system, the way you did."

Martinez sipped his wine again. In spite of Kazakov's praise, it still tasted vinegary to him. "And the warrant officers?" he asked.

Kazakov explained that Fletcher had his pick of warrant and petty officers, and had chosen only the most experienced. The number of trainees was kept to a minimum, and the result was a hard core of professionals in charge of all the ship's departments, all of whom were of exemplary efficiency.

"But Captain Fletcher," Martinez said, "chose to execute one of those professionals he had personally chosen."

Kazakov's expression turned guarded. "Yes, my lord."

"Do you have any idea why?"

Kazakov shook her head. "No, my lord. Engineer Thuc was one of the most efficient department heads on the ship."

"Captain Fletcher had never in your hearing expressed any . . . violent intentions?"

She seemed startled by the question. "No. Not at all, my lord." Her brows knit. "Though you might ask . . ." She shook her head. "No, that's ridiculous."

"Tell me."

The guarded look had returned to her face. "You might ask Lieutenant Prasad." She spoke quickly, as if she wanted to speed through the distasteful topic as quickly as she could. "As you probably heard, she and the captain were intimates. He may have said things to her that he wouldn't have . . ." She sighed, having finally gotten through it. ". . . to any of the rest of us."

"Thank you," Martinez said. "I'll interview each of the lieutenants in turn."

Though he couldn't imagine Fletcher murmuring plans for homicide along with his endearments, assuming he was the sort of man who murmured endearments at all. Neither could he imagine Chandra keeping such an announcement secret, especially in those furious moments after she and Fletcher had their final quarrel.

"Thank you for your candor," Martinez said, though he knew perfectly well that Kazakov hadn't been candid throughout. On the whole he approved of the moments when she'd chosen to be discreet, and he thought he could work with her very well.

They ended the interview discussing Kazakov's plans for her future. Her career had been planned to minimize any possible intervention by fortune: in another one of those trades so common among Peers, a friend of her family would have given her command of the frigate *Storm Fury,* a plan that had been detailed when both the friend and the frigate were captured by the Naxids on the first day of the mutiny.

"Well," Martinez said, "if I'm ever in a position to do something for you, I'll do my best."

Kazakov brightened. "Thank you, my lord."

The Kazakovs seemed a useful sort of clan to have in one's debt.

After the premiere left, Martinez stoppered the wine bottle and gulped whatever was left in his glass. With his captain's key, he opened the personnel files, intending to look at the lieutenants' records. Then the idea struck him that Fletcher might have made a note in Thuc's file explaining why the engineer had been executed, and Martinez went straight to Thuc's file and opened it.

There was nothing. Thuc had been in the Fleet for twenty-two years, had passed the exam for Master Engineer eight years ago, and was aboard *Illustrious* for five of those years. Fletcher's comments in Thuc's efficiency report were brief but favorable.

Martinez read the files of the other senior petty officers and then went on to the lieutenants, looking through the files more or less at random. Kazakov, he discovered, had been fairly accurate in describing their accomplishments. What she hadn't known, of course, were the contents of the efficiency reports Fletcher had made personally. For the most part they were dry, terse, and favorable, as if Fletcher was too grand to dole out much praise, but instead dribbled it out tastefully, like a rich sauce over dessert. About Kazakov he had written, "This officer has served as an efficient executive officer and has demonstrated proficiency in every technical aspect of her profession. There is nothing that stands in the way of her further promotion and command of a ship in the Fleet."

A note that "nothing stands in the way" was not quite the same as Fletcher's endorsement that Kazakov would be a credit to the service or would do a fine job in command of her own ship; but carefully guarded enthusiasm seemed to be Fletcher's consistent style. Perhaps he hadn't thought that praise was necessary, given that his officers were so well-connected that their steps to command had been arranged ahead of time.

After the dry asperity of Fletcher's views of the other officers, Chandra's report came like a thunderbolt. "Though this officer has not demonstrated any technical incompetence that has reached her captain's attention, her chaotic and impulsive behavior has thoroughly befouled the atmosphere of the ship. Her level of emotional maturity is not in any way consistent with the high standards of the Fleet. Promotion is not indicated."

The curiously worded first sentence managed to insert the word "incompetence" without justifying its inclusion, and the rest was pure poison. Martinez stared at this for a long moment, then looked at the log to check the date at which Fletcher had last accessed the file. It had been at 2721 hours the previous evening, a mere six hours before he was killed.

His mouth went dry. Chandra had ripped apart her relationship with Fletcher, and after thinking about it for two days, Fletcher fired a rocket at Chandra with every intention of blowing up her career.

After which, some hours later, Fletcher was killed.

Martinez thought the sequence through carefully. For this to be anything other than a coincidence, Chandra would have had to know that Fletcher put a bomb in her efficiency report. He checked Fletcher's comm logs for the evening and found that he'd made only one call, to Command, possibly for a situation report before going to bed. Martinez checked the watch list and discovered that it hadn't been Chandra on watch at the time, but the sixth lieutenant, Lady Juliette Corbigny.

So there was no evidence that Chandra would have known the contents of her efficiency report. Not unless Fletcher had made a point of looking for her and telling her in person.

Or unless Chandra had some kind of access to documents sealed under Fletcher's key. She was the signals officer, after all, and she was clever.

Martinez decided that this theory had too much whisky and wine in it to make any sense, and he failed in any case to successfully imagine Chandra wrestling the fully grown Fletcher to his knees and then banging his head repeatedly on his desk.

He rose and stretched, then looked at the chronometer: 2721. At this exact time, Fletcher had made his last cold-blooded alterations to Chandra's fitness report.

The coincidence chilled him. He left his office and took a brief march along the decks, circling back to his own door. He passed the door of the captain's cabin, which was closed, then found himself turning back to it. It opened to his key. He stepped in and called for light.

Fletcher's office had been returned to its pristine state, the fingerprint powder dusted away, the desk dark and gleaming. There was a scent of furniture polish. The bronze statues were impassive in their armor.

The safe sat silvery in its niche. Apparently, Gawbyan had repaired it after his break-in.

Martinez passed into the sleeping cabin and stared at the bloody porcelain figure with its unnaturally broad eyes. He looked at the pictures on the wall and saw a long-haired Terran with blue skin playing a flute, a bearded man dead or swooning in the arms of a blue-clad woman, a monstrous being—or possibly it was a Torminel with unnaturally orange fur—snarling out of the frame, its extended tongue pierced by a jagged spear.

Lovely stuff to see at bedtime, he thought. The view dismaying.

The only picture of any interest showed a young woman bathing, but what might have been an attractive scene was spoiled by the creepy presence of elderly men in turbans who watched her from concealment.

"Comm," he said, "page Montemar Jukes to the captain's office."

Fletcher's pet artist ambled into the office wearing nonregulation coveralls and braced halfheartedly, in a way that would have earned a ferocious rebuke from any petty officer. To judge from Jukes and Xi, Fletcher was willing to tolerate a certain amount of unmilitary slackness among his personal following.

Jukes was a stocky man with disordered gray hair and rheumy blue eyes. His cheeks were unnaturally ruddy and his breath smelled of sherry. Martinez gave him what he intended to be a disapproving scowl, then turned to lead into Fletcher's bedroom.

"Come with me, Mr. Jukes."

Jukes followed in silence, then stopped in the doorway,

leaning back slightly to contemplate the great porcelain figure strapped to the tree.

"What *is* this, Mr. Jukes?"

"Narayanguru," Jukes said. "The Shaa tied him to a tree and tortured him to death. He's all-seeing, that's why his eyes wrap around like that."

"All-seeing? Funny he didn't see what the Shaa were going to do to him."

Jukes showed yellow teeth. "Yes," he said. "Funny."

"Why's he here?"

"You mean why did Captain Fletcher hang Narayanguru in his sleeping cabin?" Jukes shrugged. "I don't know. He collected cult art, and he couldn't show it to the public. Maybe this is the only place he could put it."

"Was Captain Fletcher a cultist?"

Jukes was taken aback by the question. "Possibly," he said, "but which cult?" He walked into the room and pointed at the snarling beast. "That's Tranomakoi, a personification of their storm spirit." He indicated the blue-skinned man. "That's Krishna, who I believe is a Hindu deity." His hand drifted across the scarred paneling to indicate the swooning man. "That's a pieta, that's Christian. Another god killed in some picturesque way by the Shaa."

"Christian?" Martinez was intrigued. "We have Christians on Laredo—on my home world. On certain days of the year they dress in white robes and pointed hoods, don chains, and flog each other."

Jukes was startled. "Why do they do that?"

"I have no idea. It's said they sometimes pick one of their number to be their god and nail him to a cross."

Jukes scratched his scalp in wonderment. "Jolly sort of cult, isn't it?"

"It's a great honor. Most of them live."

"And the authorities don't do anything?"

Martinez shrugged. "The cultists only hurt each other. And Laredo is very far from Zanshaa."

"Apparently."

Martinez looked at Narayanguru with his bloody translucent flesh. "In any case," he said, "I'm neither a cultist nor an aesthete, and I have no intention of sleeping beneath that gory object for a single night."

The other man grinned. "I don't blame you."

Martinez turned to Jukes. "Can you . . . rearrange . . . the captain's collection?" he asked. "Store Narayanguru where he won't disturb anyone's sleep, and put something more pleasant in his place?"

"Yes, my lord." Jukes gave him an appraising look. "Or perhaps you'd like me to create something for you? I can print something off and frame it easily enough, if you'll tell me the sort of thing you'd like."

Martinez had never been asked the sort of art he'd liked before and had no ready answer, so he asked, "Are you looking for a new patron, Mr. Jukes?"

"Always," Jukes said with his yellow-toothed smile. "Bear in mind that you'll probably retain command of *Illustrious* for years, Fletcher's collection will go to his family, and you don't want to keep the original tiles and murals on the walls. This is a warship, not a haunted palace."

Martinez looked at him. "Didn't you create all the designs on the ship? You don't mind if I rip out all the tiles and paint over the murals?"

A sherry-tinged jauntiness floated from Jukes. "Not at all. The designs are all safe in my computer, and quite frankly it's not my best work anyway."

Martinez frowned. "Wasn't Fletcher paying for your best?"

"The work's all his taste, not mine. All balanced and classical and dull. I've done a lot better work in the past, much more interesting, but no one's paying for it, and so . . ." He shrugged. "Here I am, on a warship. It's not what I expected when I first started working with a graphics program, believe me."

Martinez found himself amused. "What did Fletcher rate you, anyway?"

"Rigger First Class."

"You don't know anything about a rigger's duties, do you?"

The artist shook his head. "Not a damn thing, my lord. That's why I need a new patron."

"Well." Martinez looked at the blue-skinned flute player. "Start by removing all this gloomy stuff and putting something more cheerful in its place. We can talk about any . . . commissions later."

Jukes brightened. "Shall I start now, my lord?"

"After breakfast will be fine."

Jukes brightened still further. "Very good, my lord. I've got an inventory of what items of his collection Fletcher brought aboard, and I'll peruse it tonight."

Martinez was amused by the word *"peruse."* "Very good, Mr. Jukes. You're dismissed."

"Yes, my lord." This time Jukes managed a halfway creditable salute, and marched away. Martinez left Fletcher's quarters and locked the door behind him.

The interview had cheered him. He went to his own cabin and was startled to find that one of his servants, Rigger Espinosa, had laid cushions on the floor of his office and was stretched out on them fully clothed.

"What are you doing there?" Martinez asked.

Espinosa jumped to his feet and braced. He was a young man, muscular and trim, with heavy-knuckled hands that hung by his sides.

"Mr. Alikhan sent me, my lord," he said.

Martinez stared at him. "But why?"

Espinosa's face was frank. "Someone's killing captains, my lord. I'm to keep that from happening again."

Killing captains. He hadn't thought of it that way.

"Very well," Martinez said. "As you were."

He went into his sleeping cabin, where Alikhan had laid

out his night things. He picked up his toothbrush, moistened it in his sink, and looked at himself in the mirror.

Captain of the *Illustrious,* he thought.

In spite of the deaths, in spite of Narayanguru hanging on his tree and the unexplained deaths and the unknown killer stalking the ship, he couldn't help but smile.

TWELVE

After breakfast Martinez put on his full dress uniform with the silver braid and the tall collar, now without the red staff tabs that Alikhan had removed overnight. He drew on his white gloves and called for Marsden and Fulvia Kazakov to join him. While waiting, he had Alikhan fetch the Golden Orb from its case.

He hadn't even considered strapping on the curved ceremonial knife. The situation would be tense enough without that.

Marsden and Kazakov arrived, each wearing full dress. "My lady," Martinez said to the premiere, "please let Master Machinist Gawbyan know that we are about to inspect his department."

Kazakov made the call as Martinez led the procession to the machine shop, where Gawbyan, breathless because he'd rushed from the petty officers' mess just ahead of them, braced at the door.

Martinez gave the machine shop a thorough inspection, questioned the machinists on their work, and made note of carelessness in the matter of waste disposal. If the ship had to make a course change, cease acceleration, or otherwise go weightless, the trash would float all over the shop.

Gawbyan, his theatrical mustachios quivering, accepted the criticism with a grim set to his fleshy features that suggested that he was going to fall on one of his recruits like an avalanche the second Martinez was out of the room.

When the inspection was over, Martinez found that he'd

taken up very little of his morning, and so he called a second inspection, this time of Missile Battery 2. This review lasted longer, with time spent examining missile loaders and watching damage control robots maneuver under the command of their operators. Despite the presence of officers and the stress of the inspection, the mood of the crew was nearly cheerful, and Martinez couldn't help but compare it with the foreboding and terror that drenched the atmosphere during Fletcher's inspection two days earlier.

Seeing their sunny spirits, he wondered if the crew might be taking him too lightly. He wanted them to view him seriously, and if they weren't, he was prepared to become a complete bastard until they did. Intuition suggested, however, that this wasn't necessary. The holejumpers just seemed pleased to have him in charge.

He was a winner, after all. He'd masterminded both of the Fleet's victories over the Naxids. The crew understood a winner better than they understood whatever Fletcher was.

"I'd like to see the lieutenants after supper," Martinez told Kazakov as they left the battery. "We'll have an informal meeting in *Daffodil*. Please arrange for a qualified warrant officer or cadet to take the watch."

"Yes, my lord."

"Feel free to move into your old quarters. I thank your hospitality, involuntary though it was."

She returned his smile. "Yes, my lord."

He went into his old office, opened the safe, removed its contents, and left the door of the safe open for Kazakov. He cast a farewell glance over the *putti,* hoping he would never see their sweet faces again, and then went into the captain's office—*his* office—and looked at the statues, still stolid and arrogant in their armor, and the display cabinets, and the murals of elegant figures writing with quills or reading aloud from open scrolls to a rapt audience. Martinez opened his new safe, changed the combination, and put his papers in it along with Fletcher's book and the little statue of the woman dancing on the skull.

In the sleeping cabin he found a welcome change. The gruesome Narayanguru was gone, as was the pieta, the snarling beast, and the bathing woman. The blue-skinned flute player remained, though he'd been shifted to a brighter-lit area. Next to him a seascape showed a ground-effect vehicle thundering over a white-topped swell in a blast of spume. Over the dressing table was a landscape, snow-topped mountains standing over a village of shaggy Yormaks and their shaggier cattle.

Pride of place went to a dark old picture that showed mostly murky empty space. The composition was unusual: a sort of frame had been painted around the edges; or perhaps it was meant to be the proscenium of a stage, since a painted curtain rod stretched over the whole scene, with a painted red curtain pulled open to the right. Against the darkness on the left were the small figures of a young mother and the infant she had just taken from her cradle. The woman's dress, though hardly contemporary, nevertheless gave the impression of being comfortably middle-class. The infant wore red pajamas. Neither were paying much attention to the little cat that squatted next to a small open fire at the center of the picture. The cat bore a sullen expression and was looking at a red bowl, which had something in it that didn't seem to please him.

Martinez was struck by the contrast between the elaborate presentation, the painted frame and red curtain, with the ordinary domesticity of the scene. The red curtain, the red bowl, the red pajamas. The young mother's round face. The sulky cat with its ears pinned back. The odd little fire in the middle of the room, presumably on an earthen floor. He kept looking at the picture while wondering why it seemed so worth looking at.

There was a movement in the corner of his eye, and he turned to see Perry in the door.

"Your dinner's ready, my lord," he said, "whenever you're ready."

"I'll eat now," Martinez said, and with a last glance at

the painting, made his way to the dining room, where he ate alone at Fletcher's grand table with its golden centerpiece and its long double row of empty places.

After dinner he reported to Michi for a report on the status of the investigation. Kazakov was there already, still in full dress, sitting next to Xi, who looked even more rumpled and abstracted in comparison. Garcia arrived a few minutes later with a datapad and his notes.

Xi began with a report on the fingerprints found in Fletcher's office. "Most belonged to the captain," he said. "The rest were those of Marsden, the secretary, and the captain's servants Narbonne and Buckle, who had cleaned and tidied the room the previous day. Three prints belonged to Constable Garcia and were presumably left in the course of his investigation."

Xi's face screwed into an expression that probably intended to express wry amusement.

"Five stray prints belonged to me. And four prints, the fingers of the left hand, were found pressed under the rim of the desktop at the front of the desk." He made a movement with his hand, palm up, in the direction of Michi's desk to show how this could happen.

"The prints belonged to Lieutenant Prasad. Of course they could have left at any time, since the servants wouldn't necessarily polish daily under the rim of the desk."

Or, Martinez thought, *the prints could have been made when Chandra held onto the desk with her left hand while slamming Captain Fletcher's head into it with her right.*

Michi betrayed no evidence that this idea might have occurred to her. "Make anything of the hair or fiber evidence?"

"I haven't had time, but it's not going to prove anything unless we already have a suspect."

Michi turned to Garcia. "Any information on the movements of the crew?"

Garcia consulted his datapad, an unnecessary gesture

considering the contents of his report. "My lady, aside from the few on watch, most of the crew were asleep. Those on watch in Command or Engineering vouch for each other. Of those in bed, the only people who admit moving at all say they were visiting the toilet."

"No reports of anyone moving outside the crew compartments? None at all?"

"No, my lady." Garcia's tongue flicked anxiously over his lips. "Of course, we only have their word for it, and that's all we're going to get . . ." He cleared his throat. ". . . unless we find an informant."

Michi's eyes hardened. Her fingers drummed on the desktop. She turned to Kazakov. "Lieutenant?"

Kazakov's tone was faintly apologetic. "It's the same situation with the lieutenants and warrant officers, my lady. Those on duty vouch for one another, and those asleep were"—Kazakov began to shrug, then stopped herself—"asleep. I have no information that contradicts their stories."

"*Damn!*" Michi's right hand made a petulant clawing motion in the air. She glared at each of them in turn. "We can't leave it at this," she said. "There's got to be something else we can do." She gave a snarl. "What would Dr. An-ku do?" She didn't mean it as a joke.

"We can search the ship," Martinez said. "And search the crew."

Michi frowned at him.

"There was a little blood," Martinez continued. "Not much, but some. It just occurred to me that the killer might have got some on a shirt cuff or a trouser leg. Or he might have wiped blood off his hands with a handkerchief. He might have used a weapon on the captain and only slammed the captain's head into the desk afterward, and the weapon might be found. Or the killer might have taken a souvenir from the captain's room and hidden it."

"The captain might have fought," Garcia said, "at least a little. He might have marked someone."

"Alert the people in the laundry," Kazakov said. "They need to check every item."

Michi stood very suddenly. She looked at the others as if surprised to find them still in their seats.

"What are we waiting for?" she said. "We should have done this yesterday."

Searching *Illustrious* and its crew was the work of a long afternoon. Martinez and Kazakov called all off-duty crew into their sleeping quarters, organized the officers and petty officers into gangs, and subjected everyone to a meticulous inspection. Lockers and storage areas were searched for anything that might have been taken from the captain's quarters. Lastly, the officers were searched, by each other. Martinez stood in the corridor outside the wardroom with Lady Michi and waited for the results.

Michi had been growing more irritable as the afternoon progressed and the hoped-for evidence failed to appear. She stood with her hands clenching into fists and a scowl on her face, rising on her toes quickly and then dropping, over and over again.

Martinez decided to distract her before the jerky movement drove him mad.

"This is going to upset the crew," he said. "We should settle them down as soon as possible. Perhaps tomorrow we could schedule the maneuver that was postponed today."

Her heels stayed on the floor as she gave him a thoughtful look. "Very good. We'll do it." Another thought struck her, and she frowned. "What am I going to do for a new tactical officer?"

"You don't want to use Coen or Li?"

She shook her head. "Not seasoned enough. All their experience is in communications."

A vague sense of obligation compelled Martinez to make a suggestion. "There's Chandra Prasad."

Michi looked at him suspiciously. "Why Prasad?"

"Because she's the senior lieutenant after Kazakov, and I can't spare Kazakov. Not now."

Which certainly sounded better than, *She wrung a promise out of me to help her,* and much, much better than, *If she did kill Fletcher, we could try being very nice to her and hope she doesn't kill us.*

Michi frowned. "I'll ask her to design one experiment. I'll ask the other lieutenants too. We'll see if any of them have a talent for it."

When Kazakov and Husayn came to report that no evidence had been found in the wardroom or the lieutenants' quarters, Michi accepted the news without comment and then turned to Martinez.

"You're next, Lord Captain."

"Next?" Martinez said through his surprise.

"You're a suspect, after all," Michi said. "You're the one who benefited most from Fletcher's death."

He hadn't looked at the situation in that light. He supposed that, objectively, she had a point.

"I wasn't even aboard when Kosinic died," he pointed out.

"I know," Michi said. "What difference does that make?"

None, apparently. Martinez submitted without protest as a committee of male officers—Husayn, Mersenne, and Lord Phillips—searched his quarters and his belongings. Alikhan watched the inspection from the doorway, his body stiffened in outrage, watching every movement with glowering eyes as if he suspected the three Peers might pocket valuable items in the course of their search.

The long, useless afternoon delayed supper, and consequently Martinez's meeting with the lieutenants in the informal circumstances of *Daffodil,* the requisitioned luxury yacht that had brought him to his new assignment as Michi's tactical officer.

The party wasn't a success. Everyone was tired after having spent the day pawing so uselessly through others' belongings, and also the officers didn't quite know how the new relationship with Martinez was supposed to work. During previous get-togethers on *Daffodil*, Martinez had been a staff officer playing host to the line officers in a setting more congenial than the starchy dinners and receptions given by the captain. Though Martinez had outranked them, he wasn't in their chain of command, and the lieutenants had felt far less inhibited than they would have been in the company of a direct superior. But now the relationship had changed, and they were more on their guard. Martinez was generous with liquor, but for most of the officers the alcohol seemed only to act as a depressant.

The one exception was Chandra Prasad, who chattered and laughed all evening in loud, high spirits, oblivious to how much it irritated the others. Perhaps, he thought, she felt she had no reason to feel on guard around him because they shared a special relationship.

Martinez hoped she was wrong.

Finally he called an end to the dismal evening, and by way of good-night told everyone there would be a maneuver during the forenoon watch.

Alikhan was waiting in his cabin to take his trousers, shoes, and uniform tunic for their nightly rehabilitation. "What are they saying in the petty officers' lounge?" Martinez asked.

"Well, my lord," Alikhan said, with a kind of finality, "they're saying you'll do."

Martinez suppressed a grin. "What are they saying about Fletcher?"

"They aren't saying anything at all about the late captain."

Martinez felt irritation. "I wish they were." He handed Alikhan his tunic. "You don't think they know more than they're saying?"

Alikhan spoke with the utmost complacency. "They're long-serving petty officers, my lord. They *always* know more than they tell."

Martinez sourly parted the seals on his shoes, removed

them, and handed them to Alikhan. "You'll tell me if they say anything vital? Such as who killed the captain?"

Alikhan dropped the shoes into their little carrying bag. "I'll do my best to keep you informed, my lord," he said. He sealed the bag and looked up. "By the way, my lord. There is the matter of Captain Fletcher's servants."

"Ah."

Each officer of captain's rank was allowed four servants, whom he could take with him from one posting to the next. Martinez had his four, and so had Fletcher; but now with only one captain remaining, that left four servants too many.

"Are Fletcher's people good for anything?" Martinez asked. "Anything besides being servants, I mean?"

Alikhan's lip curled slightly, the long-serving Fleet professional passing judgment on his inferiors.

"Narbonne was a valet in civilian life," he said. "Baca a chef. Jukes is an artist, and Buckle is a hairdresser, manicurist, and cosmetologist."

"Well," Martinez said dubiously, "I suppose Baca could be sent to the enlisted mess."

"Not if Master Cook Yau has anything to say about it," said Alikhan. "He won't want that fat pudding of a man taking up space in his kitchen and fussing with his sauces."

"Alikhan." Martinez examined himself in the mirror over his sink. "Do you think I need a cosmetologist?"

Alikhan curled his lip again. "You're too young, my lord."

Martinez smiled. "I was hoping you'd say that."

Alikhan draped trousers over his arm, and then the jacket over the trousers. Martinez nodded in the direction of the door that led to his office.

"Do you have someone sleeping out there again?" he asked.

"Ayutano, my lord."

"Right. If the killers come by way of the dining room instead, I'll try to shout and let him know."

"I'm sure he'd appreciate it, my lord." Deftly, with the hand that wasn't holding Martinez's clothing, Alikhan opened a silver vacuum flask of hot cocoa and poured.

"Thank you, Alikhan. Sleep well."

"And yourself, my lord."

Alikhan left through the door that led to the dining room. Martinez changed into pajamas and sat on his bed while he drank the cocoa and looked at the old dark painting. The young mother held her infant and the little fire glowed and the cat crouched with his ears pinned back, and it all took place inside a painted frame or maybe a stage.

He kept seeing the painting for a long time after he turned out the light.

In the morning Martinez printed a series of supper invitations on Fletcher's special bond paper, and sent them via Alikhan to all the senior petty officers. He didn't know whether Fletcher would have invited the enlisted to supper—he suspected not—and he was certain Fletcher wouldn't have used the fancy bond invitations.

He didn't care. It wasn't his bond paper anyway.

The experiment began shortly afterward. The ships of Chenforce were linked by communications laser into a virtual environment, and while the ships themselves continued on their way, a virtual Chenforce maneuvered against a virtual enemy squadron of superior force, a squadron that was meeting them head-on at Osser, the system into which Chenforce would pass after Termaine. The system was largely uninhabited, with a pair of wormhole relay stations and some small mining colonies on some mineral-rich moons, but nothing else, nothing that would complicate an engagement between two forces.

Chenforce deployed the dispersed tactics that had been created by Martinez and Caroline Sula and the officers of Martinez's old frigate, *Corona*. The ships were widely separated, maneuvering in ways that seemed absolutely random but were in fact dictated by a complex mathematical formula devised by Sula, the ships riding along the convex hull of a chaotic dynamical system.

The opposing force utilized the classic, formal tactics of the empire, tactics in which the ships were shepherded in a rigid formation so their commander could retain control of them till the last possible moment.

Tungsten-jacketed antimatter missiles exploded between the converging squadrons in glowing fireballs and hellish blasts of radiation. Lasers and antiproton beams lanced out to destroy incoming missiles, and the missiles jinked and dodged to avoid destruction. Ships died under waves of fast neutrons and blasts of heat.

Chenforce didn't come through the battle unscathed: out of seven ships, three were destroyed and one severely damaged. Of the Naxid force, all ten were wiped out.

For the first time, Martinez commanded a heavy cruiser in combat, albeit a combat that took place only in simulation. The crew in Command were disciplined and well-trained, long practiced at their jobs and at working with one another, and they obeyed his orders with perfect understanding and efficiency.

Martinez ended the experiment pleased with himself and with his ship. The pleased feeling lasted until he returned to his office, where Marsden presented him with a vast number of documents, all requiring his attention, or his judgment, or at the very least his signature.

He ate his dinner at his desk while he worked his way through the documents, and sent Marsden to his own meal.

Chandra Prasad arrived half a minute after his dinner, as if she were waiting for him to be alone. He looked up at her knock, lowered his stylus to the desk and told her to come in. As she approached, he wondered in a curiously offhand way whether she'd come to murder him, but decided against it. The sunny smile on her face would have been too incongruous.

"Lieutenant?" he said, raising his eyebrows.

"The lady squadcom just told me that I was the new tactical officer," Chandra said. "I guessed you had something to do with that, so I thought I'd come by and thank you."

"I mentioned your name," Martinez said. "But last I heard it was a temporary appointment. I think she's going to try a series of people."

"But I'll be first," Chandra said. "If I impress her, she won't need the others."

Martinez smiled encouragingly. "Good luck."

"I'll need more than luck." Chandra bit her lower lip. "Can you give me a hint about how best to impress the squadcom?"

"I wouldn't know," Martinez said. "I don't think I've managed it lately."

She looked at him with narrowed eyes, as if trying to decide whether to get angry.

He picked up his stylus and said, "Come to dinner tomorrow. We'll discuss your ambitions then."

Calculation entered her long eyes. "Very good, Captain."

She braced, and he sent her away and went back to reviewing his paperwork, and nibbling on his dinner in between paragraphs. He had no sooner finished both papers and the meal when Kazakov arrived with a new series of documents that, as executive officer, she was passing to him for review.

It was mid-afternoon before he finished all that, and went into the personnel files to acquaint himself with the petty officers he would be having to supper. They were as Kazakov had said: long-serving professionals, with high scores on their masters' exams and good efficiency reports from past superiors. All received high marks from Fletcher—including Thuc, the man he'd executed.

Martinez then checked the documentary evidence that should have corroborated Fletcher's good opinions, and almost immediately found something that appalled him.

His supper, he thought darkly, would be more than social.

He opened the supper with the traditional toast to the Praxis, then gave a preamble to the effect that he was counting on his guests to maintain continuity in a ship that had just suffered a series of shocks, and he knew from their records and their efficiency reports that they were all more than capable of giving all that was required.

He looked from one of the eight department heads to the next—from round-faced Gawbyan to rat-faced Gulik, from Master Rigger Francis with her brawny arms and formidable jowls to Cho, Thuc's gangly replacement—and he saw pleased satisfaction in their faces.

The satisfaction stayed there for the entire supper, as Perry brought in each course and as Martinez questioned each of his guests about the state of their department. From Master Data Specialist Amelia Zhang he learned the condition and the capacities of the ship's computers. From Master Rigger Francis he received myriad details, from the stowage of the holds to the state of the air scrubbers. From Master Signaler Nyamugali he had an informative discussion on the new military ciphers introduced since the beginning of the war, a critical task since both sides had started with the same ciphers and the same coding programs.

It was a pleasurable, instructive meal, and the satisfaction on the faces of the department heads had only increased by the time Perry brought in the coffee.

"In the last days I've come to see how well-managed a ship we have in *Illustrious*," Martinez said as the scent of the coffee wafted to his nostrils. "And I had no doubt that much of that excellent management was due to the quality of the senior petty officers here on the ship."

He took a slow, deliberate sip of coffee, then put his cup down in the saucer. "That's what I thought, anyway," he added, "at least until I saw the state of the 77-12s."

The satisfaction on the petty officers' faces took a long, astounded moment to fade.

"Well, my lord . . ." Gawbyan began.

"Well," said Gulik.

"The 77-12s aren't even remotely current," Martinez

said. "I don't see a single department that can give me the information I need in order to know the status of my ship."

The department heads looked across the long table at one another. Martinez read chagrin, exasperation, embarrassment.

And well they should be mortified, he thought.

The 77-12s were maintenance logs supposed to be kept by every department. The petty officers and their crews were supposed to make note of all routine maintenance, cleaning, replacing, lubricating, checking the status of filters, seals, fluids, the airtight gaskets in the bulkheads and airlocks, and the stocks of replacement parts. Every item on *Illustrious* was designed to a certain tolerance— overdesigned, some would have thought—and each was supposed to be replaced or maintained well before that tolerance was ever reached. Every part inspection, every replacement, every routine maintenance, was supposed to be recorded in a department's 77-12.

Keeping the records current was an enormous inconvenience for those responsible, and they all hated it and tried to avoid the duty whenever possible. But the 77-12s, properly maintained, were the most effective way for a superior to know the condition of his ship, and to a newly appointed captain, they were a necessity. If a piece of equipment failed, the 77-12 could tell the captain whether the failure had been due to inadequate maintenance, human error, or some other cause. Without the record, the cause of a failure would be anyone's guess, and finding out the correct reason would take time and could distract an entire department.

In wartime, Martinez felt that *Illustrious* couldn't afford the time and distraction of tracking the cause of any failure of a critical piece of equipment, not when lives were potentially in the balance. And he simply *detested* not knowing the condition of his command.

"Well, my lord . . ." Gulik began again. There was a nervous look in his sad eyes, and Martinez remembered the sweat on his upper lip as he stood at the end of the line of weaponers, all passing under Fletcher's gaze. "Well, it all has to do with the way Captain Fletcher ran the ship."

"It's all the inspections, my lord," said Master Rigger Francis. She was a brawny woman, with broken veins in her cheeks and hair that had once been red. "You saw how thoroughly Captain Fletcher conducted an inspection. He'd pick a piece of equipment and ask about its maintenance, and we'd have to know the answers. We wouldn't have a chance to look it up in the records, we'd have to *know* it."

Master Cook Yau leaned his thin arms on the table and peered around Francis's broad body. "We don't have to write the information down, my lord, because we had it all in our heads."

"I understand." Martinez gave a grave nod. "If you have it all in your heads," he added, "then it should be no trouble to put it all in the 77-12s. You should be able to give me a complete report in, say—two days?"

Martinez found himself delighted by the bleak and downcast looks the department heads gave one another. *Yes,* he thought, *yes, it's absolutely time you found out I was a bastard.*

"So what's today, then?" he asked cheerfully. "The nineteenth? Have the 77-12s to me by the morning of the twenty-second."

He'd have to continue the inspections, he thought, because he'd have to check everything against the 77-12s to make sure the forms weren't pure fiction. "Yarning the logs," as it was called, was another time-honored custom of the service.

One way or another, Martinez swore he would learn *Illustrious* and its workings, human and machine both.

He let them drink their coffee in the sudden somber silence, bade them farewell, and went to his sleeping cabin intending to sleep the sleep of the just.

"How did I do, Alikhan?" he asked in the morning, as his orderly brought in his full dress uniform.

"The petty officers who aren't cursing your name are

frightened," Alikhan reported. "Some were up half the night working on their 77-12s, and kept recruits running from one compartment to the next confirming what they thought they remembered."

Martinez grinned. "Do they still think I'll do?" he asked.

Alikhan looked at him with a tight little smile beneath his curling mustachios. "*I* think you'll do, my lord," he said.

As Martinez was eating breakfast, he received a written invitation from the warrant officer's mess for dinner. He read the invitation and smiled. The warrant officers had learned something from the petty officers. They weren't going to wait for their invitation to dine with him and find out all the things he thought were wrong with them, they were going to bring him onto their home ground and then take it on the chin if they had to.

Good for them.

He accepted with pleasure, then sent a message to Chandra saying he would have to postpone their dinner for a day. He knew the message would not make her happy. He followed this with a message that none of the lieutenants would find to their liking: his request that all up-to-date 77-12s be filed in two days.

He then called for Marsden and the fifth lieutenant, whose title was Lord Phillips and whose personal name was Palermo.

Sub-Lieutenant Palermo, Lord Phillips was a tiny man whose head didn't even reach Martinez's shoulder. His arms and legs were thin, his body slender, almost frail. His small hands were beautifully proportioned and his face was pale, darkened slightly by a feeble mustache. His voice was a quiet murmur.

Phillips commanded the division that embraced the ship's electronics, from the power cables and generators to the computers that navigated the ship and controlled its engines, so Martinez started by inspecting the workshop of Master Data Specialist Zhang. The shadowy little room with its glowing screens was kept in immaculate order.

Martinez asked Zhang if she had made any progress at her 77-12, and she showed him the work she'd managed since the previous evening. He checked two items randomly and found that they'd been logged correctly.

"Excellent work, Zhang," he said, and marched with his party to the domain of Master Electrician Strode.

Strode was a little below average height but broad-shouldered and heavily muscled, with symbols of his sexual prowess tattooed on his biceps. His hair was brown and cut in a bowl haircut, with his nape shaved and pale hairless patches around the ears. His mustachios were impressive but not nearly as sensational as Gawbyan's. Martinez expected to find his department in spotless condition, since Strode would have had warning that the captain was on the prowl since he'd arrived in Zhang's domain. He wasn't disappointed.

"Have you made any progress with your 77-12?" Martinez asked.

"I have, my lord."

Strode called up the log on one of his displays. Martinez copied it to his sleeve display and asked Strode to accompany him on a brief tour to a lower deck. He paused by one of the deck access panels, marked by a trompe l'oeil niche on the wall, with Jukes's painting of a graceful one-handled vase. Martinez looked again at the annotation in the 77-12.

"According to your log," Martinez said, "you've replaced the transformer under Main Access 8-14. Open the access, please."

Not looking the least bit pleased, Strode tapped codes into the access locks and the floor panel rose on its pneumatics. An electric hum shivered up through the deck. The scent of grease and ozone rose from the utility compartment, and lights came on automatically.

Martinez turned to Lord Phillips. "My lord," he said, "would you be so kind as to go into the compartment and read me the serial number on the transformer."

Without offering a word, Phillips slid through the deck access. Crouched in the narrow space, he found the serial number and read it off.

The number wasn't the same as in Strode's 77-12.

"Thank you, Lord Lieutenant," Martinez said, staring hard into Strode's fixed, angry face. "You can come up now."

Phillips rose and brushed grime off his dress trousers.

"Close the access, please," Martinez said.

Strode did so.

"Strode," Martinez said, "you are reprimanded for yarning your log. I *will* check the 77-12s, and from this point forward I will check yours in particular."

Sullen anger still burned in Strode's eyes. "My lord," he said, "the serial number was . . . provisional. I hadn't had the chance to check the correct number."

"See that your logs are less provisional in the future," Martinez said. "I'd rather have no information at all than information that's misleading. You are dismissed."

He walked off while Marsden was still noting the reprimand on his datapad. Phillips followed.

"You'll have to check those logs yourself, Lieutenant," Martinez told him. "Those forms are going to be full of yarns otherwise."

"Yes, my lord," Phillips murmured.

"Come to my office for coffee," Martinez said.

The coffee break was not a success. Martinez knew that Phillips was one of Fletcher's protégés, that the Phillips clan were clients to the Gombergs, and that Phillips, like Fletcher, had been born on Sandama, though like the captain, he'd spent most of his life on Zanshaa. Martinez hoped to discuss Fletcher, but Phillips's responses were barely audible, and so terse and monosyllabic that Martinez gave up the task as hopeless and sent Phillips about his business.

He would have to be satisfied with sending a pair of signals, the first to the petty officers, that he was serious about

CONVENTIONS OF WAR • 171

the 77-12s, the second to the lieutenants, that they had better supervise the department heads very closely.

Dinner with the warrant officers was much more cheerful, and the table was well provided, thanks to Warrant Officer/First Toutou, who headed the commissary. The warrant officers were specialists, pilots or navigators, supply officers or sensor technicians, or the commissary, and didn't run large departments like the senior petty officers. Their own 77-12s would be much easier to complete.

Some didn't have to fill 77-12s at all, as was attested by Toutou's broad smile and laughing demeanor.

The mess orderly was pouring little glasses of a sweet trellinberry liqueur at the end of the meal when Martinez's sleeve display gave a chime. He answered.

"Captain, I need you in my office." Michi's voice told him that she would brook no delay.

"Right away, my lady," Martinez said. He rose from his chair, and before he could stop them, the others rose too.

"Be seated," he told them. "And many thanks for your hospitality. I'll return it someday."

Dr. Xi waited with Michi in her office. Martinez looked for Garcia and didn't find him.

"Tell him," Michi said, without bothering to tell Martinez to relax his salute.

Xi turned his mild eyes to Martinez. "When I was looking through my references for methods of lifting fingerprints, it mentioned that prints left on skin can fluoresce under laser light. So I asked Machinist Strode to provide a suitable laser, and he had one of his minions assemble one for me."

Martinez, still braced with his chin lifted, looked at Xi from the corner of his eye. "You found fingerprints on the captain?" he asked.

Michi looked up, and an expression of annoyance crossed her face. "For all's sake, Martinez," she said, "relax and have a seat, will you?"

"Yes, my lady."

Xi politely waited for Martinez to take a chair, then continued as if there had been no interruption. "There were fingerprints on the captain, yes. Mine, and Garcia's, and those of my orderlies. No others that I could find."

Martinez had no reply to this.

"I then got Lieutenant Kosinic's body out of the cooler, and I put a sensor net over his head and got a three-dimensional map of his injuries. He died from a single blow to the head, perfectly consistent with losing his balance, falling, and hitting his head on the rim of the hatch."

One fewer murder, anyway, Martinez thought.

"When I looked for fingerprints with the laser," Xi continued, "I found my own and my assistants'. And I also found one large thumbprint on the underside of the jaw on the right side." He pressed his own thumb to the point. "Right where a thumb might rest if a person were grabbing Kosinic's head and slamming it into the hatch rim."

He gave a little grin. "It was quite a job to read that print properly," he said. "I couldn't use a normal print reader, and so I had to take several close-up photographs while the print was fluorescing, and then convert the format to—"

"Skip that part," Michi instructed.

Xi seemed disappointed that he was not getting the chance to fully reveal the scope of his cleverness. He licked his lips and went on.

"The thumbprint was that of Master Engineer Thuc," he said.

Martinez realized his mouth was open, and he closed it. "I'll be damned," he said.

Thuc was enormous and covered with muscle, and certainly strong enough to smash Kosinic's head on the first try. He looked at Michi.

"So Thuc killed Kosinic," he said. "And Fletcher found out about it somehow and executed Thuc."

She nodded. "That seems likely."

"He said he killed Thuc for the honor of the ship," Martinez said. "He was very sensitive on points of rank and dignity, and maybe he thought it would be an affront to his own pride to order a formal inquiry to reveal the fact that one of his enlisted personnel killed an officer, and so he decided to handle it himself."

Michi nodded again. "Go on."

"But if that's true," Martinez said, "then who the hell killed *Fletcher*?"

Michi gave him an odd, searching look. "Who benefits?" she said.

Irritation rasped along Martinez's nerves. "If you're expecting me to break down and confess," he said, "you're going to be disappointed."

"Others may benefit besides you," Michi pointed out. "For example, someone who knew that Fletcher would never favor her ambitions, but who thought you might."

Martinez suspected that Michi's choice of pronoun was not accidental. "Thuc might have had an accomplice," he suggested. "An accomplice who thought he was next on Fletcher's list."

"Did you know," Michi said, "that Lieutenant Prasad excelled in Torminel-style wrestling at the Doria Academy?"

"No," Martinez said, "I didn't. I haven't had time to review her file."

Even if Torminel wrestling didn't quite allow bashing an opponent's head in, Martinez knew it was an aggressive style that included strangulation and all sorts of unpleasant, painful joint manipulation and pressure point attacks. He could now see Chandra immobilizing Fletcher long enough to hustle him to his desk and slam his head against its sharp edge, in the process leaving her fingerprints on the underlip.

"I also see," Michi said, "that you and Lieutenant Prasad shared a communications course some years ago."

"That's true. While she was there, she didn't murder anyone that I know of."

Michi's lips twitched in a grim smile. "I'll take your enthusiastic character reference under advisement. Did you notice that Captain Fletcher gave Prasad a venomous efficiency report?"

"I saw that, yes. But I know of no evidence that she was aware of it."

"Perhaps she wanted to prevent it from being written, but was too late." Michi tapped her fingers on her desktop. "I'd like you to inquire, as discreetly as possible, about Prasad's movements during the watch in which Captain Fletcher was killed."

"I can't possibly be discreet with such an inquiry," Martinez said. "And besides, Garcia already accounted for everyone on the ship."

"Garcia is an enlisted man and experiences a natural diffidence when interrogating officers. An officer is best for these things."

Martinez decided he might as well concede. He no longer knew why he was defending Chandra in any case.

"Well," he said, "I'm interviewing the lieutenants one by one anyway. I'll ask them about that night, but I don't think any will give me a story different from anything they've already told Garcia."

"I mess in the wardroom," Xi said. "I could make a few inquiries as well."

"We *must* find an answer," Michi said.

On his way to his office, Martinez contemplated Michi's choice of words: she had said *an* answer, not *the* answer.

He wondered if Michi was willing to sacrifice *the* answer—the *real* answer—in favor of *any* answer. An answer that would end the doubts and questions on the ship, that would help to unify *Illustrious* under its new captain, that would put the entire incident to bed and let *Illustrious,* and the entire squadron, get on with their job of fighting Naxids.

It was a solution that would sacrifice an officer, that was true, but an officer who was an outsider, a provincial Peer from a provincial clan, isolated from the others who had all been handpicked by Fletcher. An officer who no one seemed to like very much anyway.

An officer who was very much like the officer he himself had been just a year ago.

He didn't like Michi's solution on these grounds, and on others as well. There had been three deaths, and he thought Michi was too quick to consider the first two solved. He had a sense that the deaths all had to be related in some way, though he couldn't guess at what might connect them.

In his office he found Marsden waiting patiently with the day's reports. Martinez called for a pot of coffee and worked steadily for an hour, until a knock on the door interrupted him. He looked up and saw Chandra in the doorway.

He tried not to envision a target symbol pinned to her chest as she stepped into the room and braced.

"Yes, Lieutenant?" he said.

"It was unfortunate that we couldn't discuss . . ." Her eyes cut to Marsden, whose bald head was bent over his datapad. ". . . that matter we wanted to talk about at dinner today."

"We can talk about it tomorrow," Martinez said.

"It would be a little late." Her hands clenched and unclenched at her sides. "The lady squadcom had asked me to conduct my experiment tomorrow."

She wants to find out how much you're worth before deciding on your arrest. The bitter thought rose in Martinez's mind before he could stop it.

He sighed. "I don't know how I can help you, Lieutenant." She opened her mouth to speak, but he held up his hand. "In order for this to be what you want, it can't be anything standard. Either *my* standard or *their* standard, if you see what I mean. It has to be something that's completely yours, and something that hadn't been done before, or at least not recently."

Her hands clenched into fists, and this time did not unclench. "I understand, my lord." From the sound, her teeth were clenched too.

"It's not easy, I know." Martinez made a conciliatory gesture. "I'm sorry, but I have no useful ideas for you." He mentally reviewed the last few days. "I don't have useful ideas for anyone, it seems."

Her fists still clenched, Chandra braced, executed a military turn, and marched away.

Martinez looked after her, and in a morbid part of his mind he wondered if Chandra was angry enough to kill him.

THIRTEEN

Martinez was killed the next morning, during Chandra's maneuver. He was walking off his breakfast with a tour around the deck when Chandra's voice echoed down the corridor from the speakers at each end. "This is a drill. General quarters. This is a drill. Now general quarters."

Martinez responded to the call with a brisk walk to his quarters, where Alikhan helped him into his vac suit. If it hadn't been a drill, he would have headed straight to Command at a dead run and hoped that Alikhan and the vac suit caught up with him later.

When he arrived in Command with his helmet tucked under his arm, the officer of the watch—Mersenne—stepped aside from the captain's cage and settled himself into his usual place at the engines station. Martinez swung into his couch and called for a status report, all the while looking at his display as the various stations reported themselves ready.

The last symbol flashed, and Martinez reported to Michi that *Illustrious* was at quarters. After a modest delay, caused presumably by waiting for other ships to report themselves ready, Chandra's voice sounded in his earphones. Martinez then passed command of the ship to Kazakov in Auxiliary Command so his crew in Command could devote themselves entirely to the maneuver.

"The experiment assumes that we are six hours into the Osser system," Chandra reported.

Osser again, Martinez thought. It was almost as if Chandra were repeating his last maneuver, not a good sign if she wanted to impress Squadron Commander Chen.

"Chenforce has entered hot, and we've been able to search the system a little more than three light-hours out. No enemy force has been detected. Are there any questions?"

Apparently there were none, because Chandra went on. "The exercise will commence on my mark. Three, two, one, mark."

A new system blossomed on the navigation displays.

"My lord," said Warrant Officer Pan, one of the sensor operators, "we're being painted by a tracking laser."

"Where?"

"Dead ahead, more or less. A rather weak signal—I don't think it's anywhere near— *My lord! Missiles!*" Pan's voice jumped half an octave in pitch.

"Power all point-defense lasers!" Martinez said. "Power antiproton beams!"

But by that point they were all dead, and within seconds Chenforce was a glowing cloud of radioactive parties spreading itself into the cold infinity of space, and Martinez's heart was thumping to a belated charge of adrenaline.

Naxid missiles, Martinez realized, accelerated to relativistic velocities outside the system, then fired through the wormhole along the route they knew Chenforce had to take. The reflection of a tracking laser fired from somewhere in the system provided last-instant course corrections.

Through his shock he managed a grim laugh. Chandra had impressed the squadcom, all right.

He looked at the recording of the attack, slowing the record at the critical moment. Two of the attacking missiles had been destroyed by the squadron's automated laser defenses. Only a few of the squadron's lasers had been powered, because lasers kept powered required greatly increased maintenance and replacement of key components.

Martinez keyed open the channel he shared with the Flag Officer Station. "Request permission to run that exercise again," he said. "I'd like to begin with the antimissile weapons already powered."

"Stand by," said Michi's aide, Ida Li.

Permission was granted a few moments later. Chenforce began the exercise with all antimissile weapons powered, but it didn't make a difference. Two more missiles were killed on the way in, but the entire squadron was still vaporized twelve seconds after the exercise began.

Michi's voice came into Martinez's earphones. "Let's give the experiment to the people in Auxiliary Control. I want to see how *they* handle it."

Kazakov and her coequals on the other ships did no better, which gave Martinez small comfort.

"I'll want all officers in my quarters for dinner at fifteen and one," Michi ordered. "Captain Martinez, can you improvise an exercise to take up the rest of our time?"

"I'll try, my lady." Martinez looked over Command, then said, "Choy, Bevins, please lie down on the deck."

The two warrant officers looked at each other in surprise, then rose grinning from their seats and sprawled between the cages.

"Comm," Martinez said. "Page the sick bay and tell them to send stretcher parties to Command. We have two casualties."

He made the next call himself, to Master Rigger Francis. "Decompression in Compartment Seven. Power is down. Send a party at once to rescue any survivors from the Flag Officer Station, which is not responding to any communication. Because the power is down the hatch and will have to be opened manually."

He thought it might amuse Michi Chen to be rescued by a damage control party.

The next call went to Master Electrician Strode. "All breakers on Main Bus Two broken due to radiation attack. Send a party to replace all breakers, and in the meantime reroute power through Auxiliary Bus One."

Which risked blacking out parts of the ship, but Martinez judged the risk worthwhile to find out if Strode was actually good at his job.

"Weaponer Gulik," Martinez called. "A missile in Tube Three of Battery One is running hot in the tube. The outside hatch is jammed and hot gases have disabled the automatic loader. The missile must be unloaded before the antimatter container is breached."

And so the morning went, as Martinez devised one catastrophe or another to test the crew. Due to a failure somewhere in the chain of command, the stretcher party turned up without their stretchers, but otherwise the crew behaved very well. Strode did not black out any parts of the ship, and the missile was unloaded by a damage control robot before it could detonate. Other crises were dealt with, and Michi sounded pleased at being rescued—it appeared Francis had sent an exceptionally good-looking rigger to head the damage control team.

An hour before the scheduled dinner, permission was given to Martinez to secure from quarters. He walked to his quarters, was assisted out of his vac suit by Alikhan, and showered to remove the scent of the suit seals.

The damage control exercise had cheered him, but now that he had time to think, he grew somber again, remembering the result of Chandra's experiment, the shock he'd felt as he watched all Chenforce die. He tried to work out ways to prevent the catastrophe happening in reality, and couldn't think of much.

The mood at dinner was even more sober. The officers looked as if they'd been beaten flat by hours of high-gravity acceleration.

The meals that had been prepared in the wardroom and in the captain's and squadcom's kitchens were combined—casseroles mostly, which could cook quietly away in the ovens while everyone was at quarters. Michi had several bottles of wine opened and shoved them across the table at her guests, as if she expected the company simply to swill them down.

"I should like the tactical officer to comment on this morning's experiment," she said.

The tactical officer. Triumph glimmered in Chandra's long eyes as she rose.

"The attack was something I'd been worried about all along. I know that we were following standard Fleet doctrine for a squadron in enemy territory, but I wondered how useful that doctrine was in reality." She shrugged. "I guess we found out."

She turned on the wall display and revealed that in her simulation she'd launched thirty missiles from Arkhan-Dohg, the next system after Osser.

"It was possible to make a reasonable calculation of when we'd enter the Osser system. Since our course would be straight from Wormhole One to Wormhole Two, the missiles' track was obvious. Our course and acceleration could be checked by wormhole relay stations, and any necessary corrections sent to the missiles en route. All the Naxids would need would be a targeting laser or a radar signal to give the missiles' own guidance systems last-second course corrections." She shrugged. "And if our course and speed are very predictable, they won't need even that."

"Obviously," Michi said, "we need to make our course and acceleration less predictable." She looked at the assembled officers. "My lords, if you have any other suggestions, please offer them now."

"Keep the antimissile defenses powered at all times," Husayn said. His voice betrayed a degree of embarrassment. The tactic hadn't worked well in simulation.

"My lady," Chandra said, "I had thought we might keep our own targeting lasers sweeping dead ahead and between the squadron and any wormholes. If they pick up anything incoming, we might gain a few extra seconds."

"Decoys," Martinez said. "Have a squadron of decoys flying ahead of us. The missiles might target them instead of us, particularly since they'll have only a few seconds to pick their targets."

Decoys were missiles that could be fired from the squadron's ordinary missile tubes, but were configured to give as large a radar signature as a warship. They were less convincing whom as an observer had more time to view them, but with a relativistic missile having only a second or two to decide, that was hardly a problem.

Michi seemed dubious. "How large a cloud of decoys are we going to need?"

Martinez tried to make a mental calculation and failed. "As many as it takes," he said finally.

Michi turned to Chandra. "I want you to try all these tactics in simulation."

"Yes, my lady."

"Give me regular reports."

"Of course, my lady." Chandra turned to the others. "The danger signal will be entering a system where the radars are still operating, or where we're painted by a targeting laser from what will probably be a distant source."

Ever since Chenforce had plunged into enemy space, the Naxids had been turning off all radars and other navigation aids in any system the loyalists had entered, so Chandra was right to say that radar would be a danger signal.

Michi poured a glass of amber wine and contemplated it while she tapped her fingers on the tabletop. "The best way to prevent this kind of attack is to blow up every wormhole station we come across," she said. "That way they can't relay course corrections to any incoming missiles. I'd hate to blow those stations; it's uncivilized. But to preserve my command I'll kill anything on the enemy side of the line if I have to."

Martinez thought of the Bai-do ring burning as it fell into the planet's atmosphere.

Michi reached out a hand and picked up her glass of wine. "Isn't anyone drinking but me?" she asked.

Martinez poured himself a glass of wine and raised it in silent toast to Chandra. She had just made herself too valuable to be blamed for Fletcher's death.

* * *

Chandra and Martinez finally had their long-postponed dinner the following day. Martinez thought it was probably no longer necessary to Chandra's plans, but in any case he instructed Alikhan not to leave them alone together for too long.

Chandra entered the dining room looking splendid in her full dress uniform, the silver braid glowing softly on the dark green tunic and trousers. Her auburn hair brushed the tall collar that now bore the red triangular tabs worn by Michi's staff.

"Congratulations, Lieutenant," Martinez said.

"Thank you, Captain," Chandra said. "And my congratulations on *your* new appointment as well." She smiled. "Your luck is surprisingly consistent, you know. People get killed, and you do well out of it."

A number of replies floated uneasily in Martinez's mind. *Only lately* was one of them. The last thing he wanted was to work out exactly how many people had to die in order for him to become captain of the *Illustrious*.

"Here we are then," he said. "A couple of suspects."

"That's right," Chandra said, then brightened. "Let's conspire!"

The conspiracy was low-key. Martinez sat at the head of the table, with Chandra on his right. While Alikhan poured wine and delivered plates of nuts and pickled vegetables, they discussed which cadet could best be promoted to take Chandra's place. While they spoke, Martinez debated whether to tell Chandra how close she had come to being sacrificed to Michi's search for a killer, and decided against it.

"How are you faring with the 77-12s?" Chandra asked. "Other than scaring the hell out of the department heads, that is."

"The revised logs were delivered this morning," Martinez said. "I've been going over them ever since. Some are even complete."

At least the department heads had learned not to yarn the logs: when they didn't have the information, they admitted it. "Data pending" was the phrase they'd all decided to put in the blank spaces, probably because it looked better than nothing at all.

"Signaler Nyamugali sent a complete log, didn't she?" Chandra said.

"Yes." Martinez smiled. "Your former division did well." He signaled to Alikhan for the first course. "Of course I'll still have to check the log to confirm it hasn't been yarned."

"You won't find any mistakes," Chandra said. "I kept the signalers on their toes."

"Nyamugali had an easier job than most of the others. Francis is going to have to account for every air pump, ventilation fan, and heat exchange system on the ship."

Chandra was skeptical. "You're feeling sorry for them now?"

"No, not very."

Alikhan arrived with a warm, creamy pumpkin soup, fragrant with the scent of cinnamon. Chandra tasted it and said, "Your cook has it all over the wardroom chef, good as he is."

"I'll tell him you said so."

"That was one of the small compensations of being with Fletcher," Chandra said. "He'd always give me a good meal before boring me to death."

Martinez considered this as he sampled the soup, and decided that Chandra could at least pretend to be a little more stricken by the death of an ex-lover.

"What did he bore you with?" Martinez asked.

"Other than the sex, you mean?" When Martinez didn't smile at her joke, she shrugged and went on. "He talked about everything, really. The food we were eating, the wine we were drinking, the exciting personnel reports he'd signed that day. He talked about his art. He had a way of making everything dull." A mischievous light came into her eyes. "What did you think of what he had hanging in his sleeping cabin? Did it give you sweet dreams?"

"I got rid of it," Martinez said. "Jukes found some less depressing stuff." He looked at her. "Why did Fletcher have Narayanguru there? What did he get out of it?"

Chandra gave an elaborate sigh. "You're not going to make me repeat his theories, are you?"

"Why not?"

"Well," she said, "he said that if he ever joined any cult, it would be the Narayanists, because they were the only cult that was truly civilized."

"How so?"

"Let me try to remember. I was trying not to listen by that point." She pursed her full lips. "I think it was because the Narayanists recognized that all life was suffering. They say that the only real things were perfect and beautiful and eternal and outside our world, and that we could get closer to these real things by contemplating beautiful objects in this world."

"Suffering," Martinez repeated. "Gomberg Fletcher, who was filthy rich and born into most privileged caste of Peers, believed that life was suffering. That *his* life was suffering."

Chandra shook her head. "I didn't understand that part either. If he ever suffered, he didn't do it when I was looking." A curl of disdain touched her lip. "Of course, he felt he was more refined than the rest of us, so he probably thought his suffering was so elevated that the rest of us didn't understand it."

"I can see why the Shaa killed Narayanguru, anyway," Martinez said. "If you maintain that there's another world, which you can't prove exists, where things are somehow better and more real than *this* world, which we *can* prove exists, you're going to run afoul of the Praxis for sure, and the Legion of Diligence is going to have you hanging off a tree before you can spit."

"Oh, there was more to it than the invisible world business. Miracles and so on. The dead tree that Narayanguru was hung on was supposed to have burst into flower after they took him down."

"I can see where the Legion of Diligence would take a dim view of those stories too."

That night, sitting on his bed while he drank his cocoa and looked at the picture of the woman, her child, and the cat, Martinez thought about Fletcher sitting in the same place, contemplating the ghastly figure of Narayanguru and thinking about human suffering. He wondered what Fletcher, a prominent member of two of the hundred most prominent Terran families in the empire, had ever suffered, and what comfort he received by looking at the bloody figure strung on the tree.

Dr. Xi had said Fletcher found his position a burden, that he worked dutifully to fulfill what was expected of him. He wasn't an arrogant snob, according to Xi, he was just playing the *part* of an arrogant snob.

Fletcher had been empty, Martinez thought, filling his hours with formal ritual and aesthetic pleasure. He hadn't created anything; he hadn't ever made a statue or a painting, he just collected them. He hadn't done anything new or original with his command, he'd just polished his ship's personnel and routines the same way he might polish a newly acquired silver figurine.

Yet he had suffered, apparently. Perhaps he had known all along how hollow his life had become.

Fletcher had sat where he was now sitting, and contemplated objects that other people considered holy.

Martinez decided he wasn't going to figure Fletcher out tonight. He put the cocoa aside, brushed his teeth, and rolled beneath the covers.

FOURTEEN

Resistance, with instructions on building a partisan cell network, was distributed to the citizens of Zanshaa, and was shortly followed by essays on the manufacture of fire-bombs and plastic explosives, which was easy, and detonators, which were not.

"If you're going to tell people to mess with stuff like picric acid," Spence warned, "you're going to have them blowing their fingers off."

Sula shrugged. "I'll tell them to be careful," she said. It's not as if she could look over their shoulders and tell them how to do it right.

She just wished she was enough of an engineer to provide diagrams of how to build firearms.

The Naxids had published sketches of the two Terrans observed fleeing from the scene of Lord Makish's assassination. The pictures were composites generated by witnesses, and Sula suspected the Naxid school supervisor as the prime contributor.

Both images were male. Neither resembled Sula or Macnamara to any degree.

Sula wondered how badly she ought to be insulted. Her figure was slim but hardly boyish. Even in a worker's overalls it should be clear enough that she was female.

She concluded that the Naxids were no better at telling Terrans apart than the Terrans were at distinguishing individual Naxids.

As she was sending the newsletter out in batches of a few thousand, she heard shouts and a crash on the street outside and stepped to the window. A black-haired Terran man had run through the street vendors in an attempt to evade police, but the police had caught him. They were Terran as well. As the man was marched away, Sula wondered if he was a criminal, a new-made hostage, or a loyalist bound for execution.

Others on the street watched as well, and as they watched with carefully controlled expressions, Sula could see the same question floating behind their hooded eyes. A new tension had entered the world. An arrest had once been something comparatively simple, and now it was fraught with a thousand new, dangerous implications, particularly if the authorities needed hostages in a hurry.

People in Riverside, when they weren't working or sleeping, lived mostly on the streets because their prefabricated apartments were too cramped for themselves and their families. Their normal life had now become a calculation, necessitating a calculation of risks, whether a breath of fresh summer air was worth the chance of being round up and shot.

Everyone under the Naxids, she thought, was making that calculation now.

Within days Team 491 was making regular deliveries of cocoa, tobacco, and coffee to restaurants and clubs throughout the city. Aside from profit, the deliveries provided opportunities for gossip with the restaurant staff, and the staff overheard a great deal from their customers.

The operation promised enough money so that Sula's company was able to buy their own delivery vehicle. It was a bubble-shaped truck with chameleon panels on the sides, and since advertising that drew electricity from the grid had been forbidden since the destruction of the ring, she was able to rent out the chameleon panels for advertising and turn even more profit.

Though their chances of overthrowing the Naxid regime

seemed remote, Sula supposed that Team 491 could take justified pride in becoming highly successful entrepreneurs.

The team took no more action against the Naxids, though Sula found herself staring narrow-eyed at possible targets from the cab of the truck. We should do *something,* she found herself thinking.

Others acted without her. A group of students at the Grandview Preparatory School staged an unsuccessful ambush of a Naxid Fleet officer returning home on a train. Details were scarce in the official reports, but possibly they intended to beat the officer senseless and steal his firearm. A couple of the attackers were killed outright and the rest captured. Under interrogation, they confessed to being members of an "anarchist cell," and apparently they named others, both fellow students and teachers, because there were a series of arrests.

The Grandview school was purged. The alleged anarchists were tortured to death on the punishment channel, and the students' families shot.

Resistance mourned them as martyrs to true government and the Praxis.

A Cree delivering fish to a Grandview restaurant told Sula of a Naxid being killed by a mob, all this supposedly happening in a Torminel neighborhood called the Old Third. The Naxid had been chased down at night by a mob of nocturnal Torminel, and the next morning Naxid police surrounded the area, charged in, and shot down the inhabitants at random. Hundreds, according to the Cree, had been killed.

"Why haven't I heard of this?" she asked. Sensational news like that should have spread through the city like a storm wind.

"They wouldn't put it on the news." The Cree's musical, burbling accents were far too cheerful for his subject matter.

"Sensational news like that, it should be over the city in hours."

The Cree turned his light-sensitive patches toward her.

Sula could feel her internal organs pulsing to the subsonic throbs of his sonar.

"Perhaps it will be, inquisitive one," the Cree said, "but the incident occurred only this morning. I heard the killing from my window."

Heard, not saw. The Cree's light-patches probably wouldn't have made much sense of something going on at such a distance, but his broad, tall ears would have given him a clear enough idea of what was happening.

The Old Third was some distance away, on the other side of the city, but the restricted, computer-guided highways managed the distance in less than an hour. The truck approached through the Cree neighborhood adjoining, and there were pockmarks of bullets on the buildings, along with shattered windows and splashes of blood on the pavement. Sula decided it wasn't a good idea to get any closer.

The rest she learned later, as death certificates were filed in the Records Office computer. The Naxid who had been killed by the mob was a sanitation worker who finished her shift in the wrong neighborhood. The police hadn't killed hundreds, but around sixty.

The Naxids had next turned their attention to the local hospital, where they shot anyone they found in the emergency wards on the assumption that they'd been wounded in the earlier police action. It was a bad day for anyone to break a leg. Another thirty-eight were killed.

In the next issue of *Resistance,* Sula provided a partial casualty list—she couldn't produce a full list without giving away her access to the Records Office. Melodramatic details spilled from her imagination: the parent who died in an unsuccessful attempt to shield her children, the angry shopkeeper holding the police off with a broom until riddled with bullets, the panicked civilians herded into a blind alley and gunned down, the bloody claw marks on the bricks.

She knew the inadequacy of her words even as she wrote them. Whatever pathos she invented for her readers couldn't equal the horror and tragedy of the reality. The helpless terror of the victims, the rattle of guns, the moans of the dying and shrieks of the wounded . . .

She remembered all that from the Axtattle fight. Her atrocity fictions were a pleasant fantasy compared to the memories that swam before her gaze.

More death coming, she thought. *Human warmth not my specialty.*

As usual, she wrote in Resistance, *the Naxids were unable to find their true enemies, and settled for killing whoever they could find.* She added:

Our chief criticism of the Torminel was that they killed the wrong Naxid. Nearly a hundred deaths in exchange for a sewer worker shows a sad ignorance of mathematics.

Next time, citizens, find an official, a police officer, a warder, a supervisor, a department head or a judge. And make sure the body isn't found in your neighborhood.

Then, two days later, an elderly retiree—a Torminel— blew herself up in her own apartment with a homemade bomb. It must have been an incendiary, Sula concluded, because half the building went up in flames.

The Naxids tracked down the bomber's children and shot them.

It was while searching the Records Office death certificates in search of details of the Torminel and her family that Sula discovered that Naxid was killed in a bomb explosion ascribed to "anarchists and saboteurs." The Naxid, a minor official in the Ministry of Revenue, was likely killed on account of his vulnerability: he wasn't important enough to rate guards. The bomb was a small one, explosive packed with nails.

The next issue of *Resistance* mourned the old Torminel as a stern loyalist outraged by the deaths in the Old Third,

and made the dead tax officer a villain condemned by secret trial and executed by members of the Octavius Hong
wing of the secret loyalist army.

A hundred and one hostages were shot in retaliation; the
Naxids, as usual, inflicting death by prime numbers. It was
interesting, she thought, that the hostages hadn't been shot
in response to the bombing, but to the public revelations of
the bombing. It appeared that the Naxids weren't killing
hostages because they were being attacked, but in retaliation for the loss of face when the attack was revealed to the
public. It was something, she thought, that she might be
able to use.

Searching death certificates for other revelations, Sula
discovered a great many geriatric cases sprinkled with a
few bizarre accidents. She wondered if she could use that
too, perhaps turn some of those accidents into incidents of
sabotage, then wondered if her imagination wasn't running
away with her.

If so, she wasn't the only one. The Naxid media announced the arrest and execution of the Octavius Hong
wing of the loyalist army, along with their families.

But I invented them! Sula protested to herself.

When she checked the Records Office computer, however, she discovered that the death certificates were real.

The streets steamed after a summer shower, and the
truck's wheels splashed water over the walkway as Team
491 drew up to a café bar on the Avenue of Commerce, in
Zanshaa's business district. Macnamara touched the lever
that opened the cargo hatch, then bounded from behind the
controls to the hatch as it rose, rainwater dripping from its
lower edge. Sula climbed out to blink in the bright sun and
inhale the aroma of the overripe ammat blossoms, fallen in
the storm, mingled with the scent of fresh rain.

"I smell money on the air," she said to Spence.

Spence lifted her pug nose to the wind. "I hope you're
right," she said.

Inside, Sula collected her cash from the proprietor, a thin man with a turned-down smile and a crisp white apron, then signaled Macnamara to carry in the hermetically sealed crate of Onamaka coffee beans from Harzapid, which he laid with care behind the bar.

"Thanks," the proprietor said. He looked critically at Macnamara's wet footprints on his glossy tile floor. "By the way, a couple gents want to see you."

Sula turned as the two men rose from their small marble-topped table. "Good coffee," the first said, and Sula's nerves sang a warning. He was a large man, wearing a jacket bright with flower patterns and trousers pegged nearly to his armpits. The trouser legs belled out around heavy boots. He wore a heavy silver necklace splattered with thumb-sized artificial rubies, and a matching bracelet on one thick wrist.

"Very good coffee," his partner agreed. The second man was smaller but had the deep chest and thick arms of a bodybuilder, and hair that was razored into a perfect narcissistic ruff that shadowed his forehead like a cockscomb.

"The question is," said the first man, "do you have a permit to be in the coffee business?"

Sula sensed Macnamara stepping protectively to her shoulder, and she slid one foot back into a balanced stance as Spence, understanding that something was wrong, bustled forward with a worried expression.

Sula looked narrowly at the first man. "Who are you, exactly?" she asked.

His hand lashed out, probably a slap intended to rock her on her heels and teach her not to ask imprudent questions. But he was dealing with someone who had been through the Fleet personal combat course. Sula blocked his arm and raked her fist along his radial nerve, pulling him forward and exposing his throat. She hacked at his larynx with the edge of her hand, and as he bent to clutch at his neck, stuck her two thumbs in his eye sockets. After which she simply grabbed his head in her hands and pulled it into a rising knee.

His nose broke with a satisfying crunch. Since he was bent over, choking, it was easy for her to drop her elbow onto the back of his neck, which put him on the ground.

Macnamara had already launched himself at the second man, the bodybuilder. Blows and kicks were exchanged, and the two were about even until Spence hurled a pot of hot coffee into the bodybuilder's face, then broke his knee with a stomping kick launched from the flank.

After that, all three members of Action Team 491 swarmed the bodybuilder and kicked him till he lay still.

Macnamara searched the two men for weapons and produced a pair of pistols they had been too busy to draw. The café's only two customers watched in wide-eyed alarm and looked uncertainly at their sleeve displays as if with the thought of calling the police. Sula took two steps behind the counter and grabbed the proprietor by the hair. She dragged him across his counter and said, "Who are these people you sold us to?"

"They're Virtue Street," the man said, eyes wide. "I pay them tribute."

Sula clenched her teeth. "I don't think I'm going to sell you any more coffee."

She picked up her Onamaka coffee and carried it to the truck, anger and adrenaline rendering the box as light as a pillow.

"Fuck!" she said, furious at herself as they drove away. "Fuck! Fuck!" She beat a fist on the arm of her chair.

"We came out of it all right," Macnamara said, fingering a scrape on his cheek where the bodybuilder's rings had marked him.

"That's not what I mean," Sula snarled. "I forgot about the tax! Fuck!" She slapped herself on the forehead. "I should have *known*!" She pounded the seat again. "Damn it all anyway!"

She canceled the morning's remaining deliveries and raged her way home, spitting anger all the way. At the sight of One-Step, crouched on the pavement in the shade of her building's porch, she felt the fury fade. One-Step straightened his long shanks and rose, a white smile brilliant on his face.

"Beauteous lady!" he declaimed. "Here you come, glorious as the sun and delicate as a flower!"

"I need to know something," Sula said.

"Anything!" One-Step threw out an arm. "Anything, beauteous lady!"

"Tell me about the Virtue Street gang."

The delight faded from One-Step's face. "Are you messing with them, lovely one?"

"They're messing with the company I work for."

Suddenly he was interested. "You have work? Real work?"

"I deliver things. But tell me about the Virtue Street people."

One-Step threw out his hands. "What can I say? They're one of the cliques here in the city. They collect the tribute on both sides of Virtue Street."

"Just in that area?"

"More or less."

Virtue Street, fortunately, was in a fairly distant part of the city. Sula felt her anxiety ease. "Who collects the tribute in Riverside?" she asked.

One-Step gave her a cautious look. "You want to stay away from them, lovely one."

"Just for my information."

His face turned stony. "The Riverside Clique. They don't go in for fancy names. I have to buy things from them, just so I can stay in business."

"Are the Riversides worse than the others?" she asked. "Better?"

The sound of pneumatic hammers rang down the street from Sim's Boatyard. One-Step gave an uneasy shrug. "Depends on who you deal with."

"If I wanted to start a business, who would I talk to?"

A suspicious look crossed One-Step's face. "What kind of business?"

"I don't want to drive trucks all my life," Sula said.

"For a loan, beauteous lady, you go to your clan's patron."

Sula gave a laugh. "My clan's patron ran like hell when the Naxids came. So did *his* patron, and so on up the line."

"War is no time to start a new business."

"Depends on the business."

She looked at him until he shifted uneasily and broke the silence. "You could talk to Casimir," he grudged. "He's not as bad as the others."

"Casimir? Casimir who?"

"They call him Little Casimir, because there was another Casimir who was older. But Big Casimir got executed."

Sula felt amusement touch the corners of her lips. "So I knock on his door and ask for Little Casimir?"

"Casimir Massoud," One-Step said. "He has an office in the Kalpeia Building on Cat Street, in that club they've got there, but he's got good reason for not spending a lot of time in his office."

"Yes?"

One-Step glanced left and right before answering in a lower voice. "The police get an order to take a certain number of hostages, right? They get shot if they don't obey the Naxids, but everyone hates them if they succeed. So when they get the order they make a little calculation about who the neighborhood won't miss, right? They take the people already in jail, and arrest all the bad sorts they can find—and with them they arrest the crazy people, and the ones living on the street—and that way they figure people won't hate them so much."

Sula remembered the man arrested outside her window, and wondered if he was a clique bagman carried away in front of the people he dunned for protection.

"But don't people like Casimir buy protection from the police?" she asked.

One-Step smiled and nodded. "You understand these things, beauteous lady," he said. "Yes, there is protection for the leaders of the cliques, so the police arrest the lower-ranking members. The thieves, the hijackers, the collectors. But when that happens, money stops flowing. Eventually Casimir won't be able to pay off the police any longer, and then he gets carried off to the Blue Hatches to be shot next time someone in the secret army sets off a bomb."

Fat, hot raindrops began to plummet from the sky. One-Step winced as one struck him in the eye. Sula ignored the rain as she thought hard.

She had something Casimir wanted, she realized. There were a great many possibilities here, if she played him right.

Sula needed the appropriate documents for her demonstration, so it was two days before she could approach Casimir. During that time there were a pair of bombings in different parts of the city, causing no fatalities though each explosion was big enough so that the Naxids felt they couldn't suppress the news. Fifty-three hostages were shot.

While she waited, she went to the Cat Street club with Spence and Macnamara—it was a huge place, with one dance band in the main room and another on the lower level, glass-walled courts for ball games, a long curved bar made of black ceramic and silver alloy, and a wide selection of computerized entertainments. Women in low-slung pantalettes, bottles in holsters on their hips, wandered from table to table pouring drinks straight into the open mouths of the clientele. Smoking was permitted, and a permanent fog of tobacco and hashish hung below the high ceiling.

Sula confined her debauchery to sparkling water, but she found herself smiling as she glanced over the club. Gredel had spent a great many nights in places like this with her lover, Lamey, who had done much the same sort of work as Casimir. On Zanshaa they might be called clique members, but on Spannan they were linkboys. They were young, because few lived to be old before encountering the work farm or the garotte. Gredel's father had been a linkboy who fled ahead of an indictment, and her mother spent years on an agricultural commune paying for her man's misstep.

Gredel had grown up in an environment where she was going to meet certain people and make certain decisions. She tried not to make the mistakes her mother had made, and instead invented mistakes all her own.

The sound of the club, the music and laughter and electronic cries, rose around her. Sula had only just reached her majority at twenty-three, but somehow to her the Cat Street club seemed a younger person's idea of fun. The club was a straightforward appeal to the flesh, to desire for sex or rhythm or companionship or oblivion. For a terrorist, who plotted death by gun or bomb, it was perhaps a little tame.

One-Step looked at her reproachfully as Sula walked home reeking of other people's vices. "One-Step would show you a better time," he said.

"One-Step—" Sula began, then sneezed. She wasn't used to being around tobacco, and vowed she would wash her hair before bed, and stuff her clothing in an airtight laundry bag where she couldn't smell it.

"One-Step needs a job," she said through her stuffed nose. "You get your money from Casimir, maybe you'll give One-Step some work."

"Maybe," Sula smiled.

The idea, she admitted, had a certain wayward appeal.

"More hostages taken today," One-Step said. "I need to get off the street."

Good point, Sula thought. "I'll see what I can do," she told him.

Whatever else you could say about One-Step, he had better people skills than she did.

Sula dressed in fine Riverside low style for her meeting with Casimir. The wide, floppy collar of her blouse overhung a bright tight-waisted jacket with fractal patterns. Pants belled out around platform shoes. Cheap colorful plastic and ceramic jewelry. A tall velvet hat, crushed just so, with one side of the brim held up by a gold pin with an artificial diamond the size of a walnut.

Riverside was still, and the pavement radiated the heat of the day as if exhaling a long, hot breath. Between bars of light, the long shadows of buildings striped the street like prison bars. Sula saw no sign of Naxid or police patrols.

The night was young and the Cat Street club was nearly deserted, inhabited only by a few people knocking back drinks on their way home from or to work. The hostess said that Casimir wasn't in yet. Sula sat at a back table, ordered sparkling water, and transformed the tabletop into a video screen so she could watch a news program—the usual expressionless Daimong announcer with the usual bland tidings, all about the happy, content people of many species who worked productively for a peaceful future beneath the Naxids.

She didn't see Casimir come in: the hostess told her that he had arrived then escorted her to the back of the club, up a staircase of black iron, and to a door glossy with polished black ceramic. Sula looked at her reflection in the door's lustrous surface and adjusted the tilt of her hat.

Inside, she saw a pair of Torminel guards, fierce in their gray fur and white fangs, and concluded that Casimir must be nervous. Lamey had never gone around with guards, not until the very end, when the Legion of Diligence was after him.

The guards patted her down—she'd left her pistol at home—and scanned her with a matte-black polycarbon wand intended to detect any listening devices. Then they waved her through another polished door.

She entered a large suite decorated in black and white, from the diamond-shaped floor tiles to the onyx pillars that supported a series of white marble romanesque arches, impressive but nonstructural, intended purely for decoration.

The chairs featured cushions so soft they might tempt a sitter to sprawl. There was a video wall that enabled Casimir to watch the interior of the club, and several different scenes played there in silence. Sula saw that one of the cameras was focused on the table she'd just left.

Casimir came around his desk to greet her. He was a plain-featured young man a few years older than Sula, with longish dark hair combed across his forehead and tangled down his collar behind. He wore a charcoal-gray velvet jacket over a purple silk shirt, with gleaming black boots beneath fashionably wide-bottomed trousers. His hands were long and pale and delicate, with fragile-seeming wrists; the hands were posed self-consciously in front of his chest, the fingers tangled in a kind of knot.

"Were you watching me?" she asked, referring to the surveillance camera.

"I hadn't seen you around," he said, his voice surprisingly deep and full of gravel, like a sudden flood over stony land. "I was curious."

She felt the heat of his dark eyes and knew at once that danger smoldered there, possibly for her, possibly for Casimir himself, possibly for the whole world. Possibly he didn't know; he might strike out at first one, then the other, as the mood struck him.

The chord of danger chimed deep in her nerves, and it was all she could do to keep her blood from thundering an answer.

"I'm new," she said. "I came down from the ring a few months ago."

"Are you looking for work?" He tilted his head and affected to consider her. "For someone as attractive as you, I suppose something could be found."

"I already have work," she said. "What I'd like is steady pay." She took from an inner pocket of her vest a pair of identity cards and offered them.

"What's this?" Casimir approached and took the cards.

His eyes widened as he saw his own picture on both, each of which identified him as "Michael Saltillo."

"One's the primary identity," Sula said, "and the other's the special card that gets you up to the High City."

Casimir frowned, took the cards back to his desk and held them up to the light. "Good work," he said. "Did you do these?"

"The government did them," Sula said. "They're genuine."

He pursed his lips and nodded. "You work in the Records Office?"

"No. But I know someone who does."

He gave her a heavy-lidded look. "You'll have to tell me who that is."

Sula shook her head. "No. I can't."

He glided toward her. Menace flowed off him like an inky rain. "I'll need that name," he said.

She looked up at him and willed her muscles not to tremble beneath the tide of adrenaline that flooded her veins. "First," she said, speaking softly to keep a tremor from her voice, "she wouldn't work with you. Second—"

"I'm *very persuasive,*" Casimir said. The deep, grating words seemed to rise from the earth. His humid breath warmed her cheek.

"Second," Sula continued, as calmly as she could, "she doesn't live in Zanshaa, and if you turn up on her doorstep she'll call the police and turn you in. You don't have any protection where she is, no leverage at all."

A muscle pulsed in one half-lowered eyelid: Casimir didn't like being contradicted. Sula prepared herself for violence and wondered how she would deal with the Torminel.

But first she'd have to figure out what to do with her platform shoes. They might be fashionable but they weren't exactly intended for combat.

"I don't believe I got your name," Casimir said.

She looked into the half-lidded eyes. "Gredel," she said.

He turned, took a step away, then swung back and with an abrupt motion thrust out the identity cards.

"Take these," he said. "I'm not going to have them off someone I don't know. I could be killed for having them in my office."

Sula made certain her fingers weren't trembling before she took the cards. "You'll need them sooner or later," she said, "the way things are going under the Naxids."

She could see that he didn't like hearing that either. He walked to the far side of his desk and stood there with his head down, his long fingers tidying papers. "There's nothing I can do about the Naxids," he said.

"You can kill them," she replied, "before they kill you."

He kept his eyes on his papers, but a smile touched his lips. "There are a lot more Naxids than there are of me."

"Start at the top and work your way down," Sula advised. "Sooner or later you'll reach equilibrium."

The smile still played about his lips. "You're quite the provocateur, aren't you?" he said.

"It's fifty for primary ID. Two hundred for the special pass to the High City."

He looked up at her in surprise. "*Two* hundred?"

"Most people won't need it. But the ones who'll need it will really need it."

His lips gave a sardonic twist. "Who would want to go to the High City now?"

"People who want to work for Naxids. Or steal from Naxids. Or kill Naxids." She smiled. "Actually, that last category gets the cards free."

He turned his head to hide a grin. "You're a pistol, aren't you?"

Sula said nothing. Casimir stood for a moment in thought, then suddenly threw himself into his chair in a whoof of deflating cushions and surprised hydraulics, then he put his feet on the desk, one gleaming boot crossed over the other.

"Can I see you again?" he said.

"To do what? Talk business? We can talk business *now*."

"Business, certainly," he said with an nod. "But I was thinking we could mainly entertain ourselves."

"Do you still think I'm a provocateur?"

He grinned and shook his head. "The police under the Naxids don't have to bother with evidence anymore. Provocateurs are looking for work like everyone else."

"Yes," Sula said.

He blinked. "Yes what?"

"Yes. You can see me."

His grin broadened. He had even teeth, brilliantly white. Sula thought his dentist was to be congratulated.

"I'll give you my comm code. Set your display to receive."

They activated their sleeve displays, and Sula broadcast her electronic address. It was one she'd created strictly for this meeting, along with another of what were proving to be a dizzying series of false identities.

"See you then." She walked toward the door, then stopped. "By the way," she said. "I'm also in the delivery business. If you need something moved from one place to another, let me know." She permitted herself a smile. "We have very good documents," she said. "We can move things wherever you need them."

She left then, before glee got the better of her.

Outside, in the facing light, she spotted Macnamara loitering across the street and raised a hand to scratch her neck, the signal that all had gone well.

Even so, she used evasion procedures to make certain she wasn't followed home.

Casimir called after midnight. Sula groped her way from her bed to where she'd hung her blouse and told the sleeve to answer.

The chameleon fabric showed him with a slapdash grin pasted to his face. There was blaring music in the background and the sound of laughter.

"Hey Gredel!" he said. "Come have some fun!"

Sula swiped sleep from her eyes. "I'm asleep. Call me tomorrow."

"Wake up! It's still early!"

"I work for a living! Call me tomorrow!"

As she told the sleeve to end her transmission and made her way back to the bed, she reflected that she'd done a good job setting the hook.

FIFTEEN

Sula had some morning deliveries on the High City and thought she might as well collect some club gossip from PJ while she was on the acropolis. Having some idea of his indolent habits, she waited till the sun was high in Zanshaa's viridian sky before she called him on a public terminal. Since she trusted his intentions but not his intelligence, she'd made certain that he had no way to contact her, nothing he could betray to the enemy—he would have to wait for *her* to initiate contact.

"Yes?" he mumbled as he answered. His eyes were blurry, his thinning hair awry—either she'd awakened him or he was just out of bed.

"Hi, PJ!" she called brightly. "How's the lad this morning?"

Recognizing her voice, his eyes came into sudden bright focus as he stared at her image on the comm display. "Oh!" he said. "Oh! Things are, ah, excellent. Just excellent."

If he'd said *first-rate* instead of *excellent,* that would have meant the Naxids had nabbed him and she should ignore everything he said, particularly any attempt to set up a meeting.

"I say," PJ said, "Lady—I mean, miss—there's someone I need you to meet. Right away."

"Half an hour from now?"

"Yes! Yes!" He made a strange, thoughtful face, pulling at his jaw. "If you'll come by the palace, we'll go to his . . . place of business."

"Be cautious about, ah . . ." *About my being the secret government.*

"Of course." He gave a wink. "No problem there. He doesn't even know we're coming."

Oh dear, Sula thought as she broke the connection. PJ had contracted an enthusiasm.

She hoped he wasn't planning on blowing anything up without her advice.

Team 491 delivered its last cargo of cigars and vacuum-packed coffee beans, collected some inconsequential information from club workers, then drove to the Ngeni Palace, where PJ had already opened the service drive gate. He waited before the massive root systems of the ancient banyan tree that overshadowed his cottage, standing with his usual languid ease in the shade while he smoked a cigarette.

"Miss Ardelion! Mr. Starling!" He greeted Spence and Macnamara with great energy, then turned to Sula. "Lady, ah, Miss Lucy."

"What's up?" Sula asked.

He brightened. "Wait till you see what Sidney's got in his shop! You'll jump for joy!"

He stubbed out his cigarette, led them back down the drive, coding shut the gate behind them, then on a roughly diagonal course across the High City. PJ was practically skipping in his excitement. The streets were half empty, and vehicles full of military constables were parked at some of the intersections. As their dark Naxid eyes swept over her, Sula looked away, exceptionally conscious of the pistol tucked into her waistband under her jacket. Then she thought she shouldn't have looked away, she was acting suspiciously. But then she thought no, probably *no one* looks at them. Everyone was suspicious equally.

She walked past the Naxids and they made no move to stop her.

The sound of the *aejai* seemed to echo from half the shops in the city. There wasn't a hint of a breeze to cool the burning day, and they were all glossy with sweat by the time they arrived at their destination, a narrow shop in a pedestrian lane lined with other specialty shops, offering antiques or quality meats, tailored uniforms or Daimong delicacies, or . . .

SIDNEY'S SUPERIOR FIREARMS, said the sign. And across the door was a banner: *CLOSED BY ORDER OF LORD UMMIR, MINISTER OF POLICE.*

Sula felt an electric hum in her nerves. Brilliant, she thought.

She would try to remember to give PJ something very nice on his birthday.

"I found out at the club that Sidney was closing," PJ said as he took them down an alley behind the building. "I stopped by yesterday to chat with Sidney and reconnoiter, and since then I've been waiting for you."

PJ stopped by a door of greenish metal and banged on it. Sula stood for a moment in the hot silence and gazed at the fragrant corpse of a kanamid, probably killed by a cat, that lay between two gray resin waste bins with its six limbs pointing crookedly to the sky.

The metal door rolled open with a subdued electric hum. She shaded her sun-dazzled eyes to see the man standing in shadow on the far side of the door: he was white-haired and thin and had a goatee with a waxed, curled mustache, much like those worn by petty officers of the Fleet. Sula tasted a smoky scent that drifted from the open door.

"My lord," the man said. His voice was grainy. "These are your friends?"

"Yes, Mr. Sidney." PJ's tone was a little smug. "This is Miss Lucy, Miss Ardelion, and Mr. Starling."

The man's eyes, pupils broad as the barrels of a shotgun, scanned Sula and her companions. "Come in then," he said, and stood back.

The back of the shop was a marvelously compact work-room, computer-guided lathes, tools gleaming in their racks, magnifiers and manipulators on shelves, racks of ex-otic, cured woods and ivories, gun barrels gleaming on shelves. Sula's heart warmed to the meticulous orderliness of it all.

The heavy scent of hashish, however, made her less cer-tain, as did the curl of smoke from a gleaming metal pipe that Sidney picked up from one of the workbenches as he passed.

"Let me take you up front," he said. They passed through a door into the shop's narrow front. Weapons gleamed softly in the racks on the walls, in polished wood cabinets. Sidney stopped before a coal-black metal carrying case that held a long-barreled hunting weapon. He picked it up, held it in the air. The barrel was a damascened concoction of contrasting metals beautifully wrought together, silver and black chasing each other down its length like serpents. The stock was a deep red wood polished and inlaid with a floral pattern in ebony. There was a magnifying scope with a deep amber display that would prove easy on the eye at night, and iron sights for the classically inclined.

"I built this for Lord Richard Li," he said, speaking around the pipe clenched between his teeth.

Sula gave a start at the name. Lord Richard had been her captain, killed bringing his *Dauntless* into action at Maga-ria. He had been engaged to Terza Chen, the woman—no, the *conniving bitch*—who had married Martinez.

She fought her way back through the curtain of memory that had draped across her mind. "The Naxids have shut you down?" she asked.

Not the brightest thing she could have said, admittedly, but at least she'd gotten the words out.

"I'm surprised it's taken them this long," Sidney said. "I suppose they've had other things to think about, being a new government. I wouldn't know." He replaced the rifle in its case and took a meditative sip on his pipe. "I could apply to reopen the business if I agreed to sell exclusively to Naxids, but I don't want to think about those bastards using one of my guns to kill hostages, and all the weapons configured for other species are still unsellable no matter what I do."

He locked the rifle case and turned around. His eyes were hard. "The thing is, I can't sell these weapons. But there's nothing in the new regulations about my *giving* them away."

Sula stared at Sidney in stunned surprise. A self-conscious look crossed his face, and he took his pipe from his mouth. "I've been remiss," he said. "Would any of you care for a smoke?"

"Umm," PJ began, on the verge of accepting, but Sula answered for them all.

"Not right now, thanks," she said. She looked at Sidney. "You're going to *give* us all these guns?"

He gave her a hard look. "If you'll make *good use* of them."

Sula's mouth went dry. "That's . . . very generous."

Sidney shrugged. "They're worthless now. I can't return them to the manufacturers—the makers have been forbidden to do business too. I'll have to break my lease; I can't afford to keep this place and I can't afford to store the weapons. I could sit here waiting for the government to confiscate them, but why?" He shrugged again. "I'd rather see them put to use." He began to say something, then shook his head and clamped the pipe between his teeth again. "Not that I want to know what you're going to use them for, of course." He turned again and laid a hand on the metal case beside him on the counter. "There are only a few pieces I can't let go—the true custom work. If any of them were found after a . . . misadventure, the trail would lead straight to me."

He stepped back a pace and swept a hand along the glass of the counter, indicating a row of gleaming pistols, each adapted to the Lai-own hand. "All sporting weapons, of course," he said. "Of limited use for military purposes. But in the right hands . . ."

He sipped on his pipe, and exhaled a dense cloud of smoke. Sula made the mistake of inhaling, and burst out coughing.

"Sorry," Sidney said politely.

After the coughing ceased, Sula made an effort to collect her thoughts from the mist that swirled through her head. She knew she was going to need fresh air very soon.

"Mr. Sidney," she managed, "do I understand that you *design guns*?"

"That's right," Sidney said. He puffed another cloud of smoke, and Sula took a step back.

"Perhaps you can help me," she said, and had to cough again. Tears dazzled her eyes as she recovered her voice. "I've been looking for a particular kind of firearm."

Interest glittered in Sidney's eyes. "Yes?"

"Not at all the kind of work you usually do. The opposite, in fact. Something that could be put together without great expense out of components that could be acquired very easily."

Sidney gave a snort of amusement, then affected to consider the problem. "Computer-operated lathes can do some amazing things, given the right programming."

"Let's just say that my own lathe-programming skills are limited."

Sidney smiled. "I seem to have a lot of free time at present. Let me put my mind to it, then, Miss . . . Lucy, was it?"

"Lucy. Yes."

"Well," Sidney said. "If you'll give me a call in a few days, perhaps I'll have something for you."

"Fantastic!" Spence said as they took the first of several truckloads of firearms from Sidney's place, on their way to store them in PJ's basement. "I can't believe he's giving us all this stuff! And the ammunition too!"

"He's quite brave, isn't he?" PJ asked. His smile was sillier than usual after an hour of hauling crates through Sidney's smoke cloud.

"He's not brave," Sula said. "He's suicidal."

The silly smile faded from PJ's face. "My lady?" he said. "I mean, my Lucy. I mean—" His mouth opened fishlike for words but failed to find any.

"Do you think the manufacturers haven't kept a record of the serial numbers of all these weapons?" Sula asked. "Not to mention the ballistics tests they're required to do before the weapons even leave the factory? The first time we use one of these, they'll track it to Sidney and tear his ribs out trying to find out who he gave them to. And that would lead to *you,* PJ."

PJ turned pale. "Oh," he said.

"Maybe Sidney hopes he'll take a few Naxids with him when he goes. Maybe he doesn't care about himself *or* about you. Or maybe he thinks he'll be able to hide. But until we know what he means to do, we're going to store these guns in your basement and never use them, not unless we know Sidney is safe." She contemplated the road and the overcareful driving undertaken by Macnamara, who was no less affected by hashish fumes than anyone else.

"Besides," Sula said, "I've got other plans for our Mr. Sidney, and they'd be spoiled by his committing suicide."

By the end of the day, she'd talked Sidney into reopening his gun shop exclusive to a Naxid clientele. "Only the elite can afford your guns anyway," she told him. The tax of one hundred zeniths on every firearm sale—half a year's wages for the ordinary person—raised them entirely out of the range of the ordinary consumer. "When you deliver the guns to their new owners, you'll get through their security."

Sidney gave a grim smile. "You see me as an assassin?" he asked.

"No," Sula said. "We have *other* people for that." *She hoped.* "Instead I need you to take careful notes on access, on what guards are stationed where. On any routines that might be useful."

"I can do that," Sidney said. "How do I contact you?"

Sula hesitated. She had declined to give PJ a way of communicating with her on the grounds that he might accidentally give himself—or her—away. For her to give Sidney such a means while PJ was present might offend PJ. And while she didn't much care if PJ's feelings were hurt, she didn't want him made despondent or careless.

"We'll have to let you know about that later," she said. "In the meantime, we'll have to contact you."

For the present, she gave him the simple communications code she'd given PJ, to use the phrase "first-rate" if he were ever compromised by the Naxids. He nodded with what appeared to be sage comprehension, though considering how much hashish he'd smoked over the course of the day, Sula wondered that he could stand upright, let alone understand instructions.

She supposed she'd find out.

Now, returning to the communal apartment, she checked Gredel's comm unit and discovered that Casimir had logged three calls asking her out for the night. She took a long, delicious bath in lilac-scented water while considering an answer, then turned off the camera that would transmit her image before she picked up the hand comm to call him back.

"Why not?" she said at the sullen face that answered. "Unless you've made other plans, of course."

The sulky look vanished as Casimir peered into his sleeve display in a failed search for an image. "Is this Gredel?" he asked. "Why can't I see you?"

"I'm in the tub."

A sly look crossed his features. "I could use a wash myself. How about I join you?"

"I'll meet you at the club," she said. "Just tell me what time."

He told her. She would have time to luxuriate in her bath

for a while longer and then to nap for a couple hours before joining him.

"How should I dress?" she asked.

"What you're wearing now is fine."

"Ha ha. Will I be all right in the sort of thing I wore last night?"

"Yes. That'll do."

"See you then."

She ended the call, then ordered the hot water tap to open. The bathroom audio pickup wasn't reliable and she had to lean forward to open the tap manually. As the water raced from the tap and the steam rose, she sank into the tub and closed her eyes, allowing herself to slowly relax, to let the scent of lilacs rise in her senses.

Clean porcelain surfaces floated through her mind. Celadon, faience, rose Pompadour. Her fingers tingled to the remembered crackle of her *ju yao* pot.

The day had started well. She thought it would only get better.

Sula adjusted her jacket as she gazed out the window of the communal apartment. The last of the vendors were closing their stalls or driving away in their little three-wheeled vehicles with their businesses packed on the back. The near-blackout imposed by the Naxids—not to mention the hostage-taking—had severely impacted them, and there weren't enough people on the streets after dark to keep them at their work.

"I should be with you," Macnamara argued.

"On a *date*?" Sula laughed.

He pushed out his lips like a pouting child. "You know what he is," he said. "It's not safe."

She fluffed her black-dyed hair with her fingers. "He's a necessary evil. I know how to deal with him."

Macnamara made a scornful sound in his throat. Sula looked at Spence, who sat on the sofa and was doing her best to look as if she weren't listening.

"He's a criminal," Macnamara said. "He may be a killer, for all you know."

He probably hasn't killed nearly as many people as I have. Sula remembered five Naxid ships turning to sheets of brilliant white eye-piercing light at Magaria, and decided not to remind Macnamara of this.

She turned from the window and faced him. "Say that you want to start a business," she said, "and you don't have the money. What do you do?"

His face filled with suspicion, as if he knew she was luring him into a trap. "Go to my clan head," he said.

"And if your clan head won't help you?"

"I go to someone in his patron clan. A Peer or somebody."

Sula nodded. "What if the Peer's nephew is engaged in the same business and doesn't want the competition?"

Macnamara made the pouting face again. "I wouldn't go to Little Casimir, that's for sure."

"Maybe you wouldn't. But a lot of people *do* go to people like Casimir, and they get their business started, and Casimir offers protection against retaliation by the Peer's nephew and his clan. And in return Casimir gets fifty or a hundred percent interest on his money and a client who will maybe do him other favors."

Macnamara looked as if he'd bitten into a lemon. "And if they don't pay the hundred percent interest they get killed."

Sula considered this. "Probably not," she judged, "not unless they try to cheat Casimir in some way. Most likely Casimir just takes over the business and every minim of assets and hands it over to another client to run, leaving the borrower on the streets and loaded with debt." Macnamara was about to argue, and Sula held out her hands. "I'm not saying he's a pillar of virtue. He's in it for the money and the power. He hurts people, I'm sure. But in a system like ours—where the Peers have all the money and all the law on their side—people like the Riverside Clique are necessary."

"I don't get it," he said. "You're a Peer yourself, but you talk against the Peers."

"Oh." She shrugged. "There are Peers who make Casimir look like a blundering amateur."

The late Lord and Lady Sula, for two.

She told the video wall to turn on its camera and examined herself in its screen. She put on the crumpled velvet hat and adjusted it to the proper angle.

There. That was raffish enough, if you ignored the searching, critical look in the eyes.

"I'm going with you," Macnamara insisted. "The streets aren't safe."

Sula sighed and decided she might as well concede. "Very well," she said. "You can follow me to the club a hundred paces behind, but once I go in the door, I don't want to see you for the rest of the evening."

"Yes," he said, and then added, "my lady."

She wondered if Macnamara's protectiveness was actually possessiveness, if there was something emotional or sexual in the way he related to her.

She supposed there was. There was with most men in her experience, so why not Macnamara?

She hoped she wouldn't have to get stern with him.

He followed her like an obedient, heavily armed ghost down the darkened streets to the Cat Street club. Yellow light spilled out of the doors, along with music and laughter and the smell of tobacco. She cast a look over her shoulder at Macnamara, one that warned him to come no farther, and then she hopped up the step onto the black and silver tiles and swept through the doors, nodding to the two bouncers.

Casimir waited in his office, along with two others. He wore an iron-gray silk shirt with a standing collar that wrapped his throat with layers of dark material and gave a proud jut to his chin, heavy boots that gleamed, and an ankle-length coat of some soft black material inset with little triangular mirrors. In one pale, long-fingered hand he carried an ebony walking stick that came up to his breast-bone and was topped by a silver claw that held a globe of rock crystal.

He laughed and gave an elaborate bow as she entered. The walking stick added to the odd courtly effect. Sula looked at his outfit and hesitated.

"Very original," she decided.

"Chesko," Casimir said. "This time next year, she's go-ing to be dressing everybody." He turned to his two com-panions. "These are Julien and Veronika. They'll be joining us tonight, if you don't mind." Julien was a younger man with a pointed face, and Veronika was a tinkly blonde who wore brocade and an anklet with stones that glittered.

Interesting, Sula thought, for Casimir to include another couple. Perhaps it was to put her at ease, to assure her that she wouldn't be at close quarters with some predator all night.

"Pleased to meet you," she said. "I'm Gredel."

Casimir gave two snaps of his fingers and a tiled panel slid open in the wall, revealing a well-equipped bar, bottles full of amber, green, and crimson liquids in curiously shaped bottles. "Shall we start with drinks before supper?" he asked.

"I don't drink," Sula said, "but the rest of you go ahead."

Casimir, on his way to the bar, was brought up short. "Is there anything else you'd like? Hashish or—"

"Sparkling water will be fine," she said.

Casimir hesitated again. "Right," he said finally, and handed her a heavy cut-crystal goblet that he'd filled from a silver spigot.

He mixed drinks for himself and the others, and every-one sat on the broad, oversoft chairs. Sula tried not to oversplay.

The discussion was about music, songwriters, and musi-cians she didn't know. Casimir told the room to play vari-ous audio selections. He liked his music jagged, with angry overtones.

"What do you like?" Julien asked Sula.

"Derivoo," she said.

Veronika gave a little giggle. Julien made a face. "Too intellectual for me," he said.

"It's not intellectual at all," Sula protested. "It's pure emotion."

"It's all about death," Veronika said.

"Why shouldn't it be?" Sula said. "Death is the universal constant. All people suffer and die. Derivoo doesn't try to hide that."

There was a moment of silence in which Sula realized that the inevitability of misery and death was perhaps not the most appropriate topic to bring up on first acquaintance with this group; and then she looked at Casimir and saw a glimmer of wicked amusement in his dark eyes. He seized his walking stick and rose.

"Let's go. Take your drinks if you haven't finished them."

Casimir's huge Victory limousine was built along the lines of a pumpkin seed, and painted and upholstered in no less than eleven shades of apricot. The two Torminel guards sat in front, their huge, night-adapted eyes perfectly at home on the darkened streets. The restaurant was paneled in old, dark wood, the linen was crisp and closewoven, and the fixtures were brass that gleamed finely in the subdued light. Through an elaborate, carved wooden screen Sula could see another dining room with a few Laiown sitting in the special chairs that cradled their long breastbones.

Casimir suggested items from the menu, and the elderly waitron, whose stolid, disapproving old face suggested he had seen many like Casimir come and go, suggested others. Sula followed one of Casimir's suggestions, and found her ostrich steak tender and full of savor; the krek-tubers, mashed with bits of truffle, were slightly oily but full of complex flavors that lingered long on her palate.

Casimir and Julien ordered elaborate drinks, a variety of

starters, and a broad selection of desserts, and competed with each other for throwing money away. Half what they ordered was never eaten or drunk. Julien was exuberant and brash, and Casimir displayed sparks of sardonic wit. Veronika popped her wide eyes open like a perpetually astonished child and giggled a great deal.

From the restaurant they motored to a club, a place atop a tall building in Grandview, the neighborhood where Sula had once lived until she had to blow up her apartment with a group of Naxid police inside. The broad granite dome of the Great Refuge, the highest point of the High City, brooded down on them through the tall glass walls above the bar. Casimir and Julien flung more money away on drinks and tips to waitrons, bartenders, and musicians. If the Naxid occupation was hurting their business, it wasn't showing.

Sula knew she was supposed to be impressed by this. But even years ago, when she was Lamey's girl, she hadn't been impressed by the money he and his crowd threw away. She knew too well where the money came from.

She was more impressed by Casimir once he took her onto the dance floor. His long-fingered hands embraced her gently, but behind the gentleness she sensed the solidity of muscle and bone and mass, the calculation of his mind. His attention in the dance was entirely on her, his somber dark eyes intense as they gazed into her face while his body reacted to her weight and motion.

This one thinks! she thought in surprise.

That might make things easy or make them hard. At any rate, it made the calculation more difficult.

"Where are you from?" he asked her after they'd sat down. "How come I haven't seen you before?" Julien and Veronika were still on the dance floor, Veronika swirling with expert grace around Julien's enthusiastic clumsiness.

"I lived on the ring," Sula said. "Before they blew it up."

"What did you do there?"

"I was a math teacher."

His eyes widened.

"Give me a math problem and try me," Sula urged, but he didn't reply. She wondered if her phony occupation had shocked him.

"When I was in school," he said, "I didn't have math teachers like you."

"You didn't think teachers went to clubs?" she said.

A slow thought crossed his face. He leaned closer and his eyes narrowed. "What I don't understand," he said, "is why, when you're from the ring, you talk like you've spent your life in Riverside."

Sula's nerves sang a warning. She laughed. "Did I say I've spent my whole life on the ring?" she asked. "I don't think so."

"I could check your documents," his eyes hardening, "but of course you sell false documents, so that wouldn't help."

The tension between them was like a coiled serpent ready to strike. She raised an eyebrow. "You still think I'm a provocateur?" she asked. "I haven't asked you to do a single illegal thing all night."

One index finger tapped a slow rhythm on the matte surface of the table before them. "I think you're dangerous," he said.

Sula looked at him and held his gaze. "You're right," she said.

Casimir gave a huff of breath and drew back. Cushions of aesa leather received him. "Why don't you drink?" he asked.

"I grew up around drunks," she said. "I don't want to be like that, not ever."

Which was true, and perhaps Casimir sensed it, because he nodded. "And you lived in Riverside."

"I lived in Zanshaa City till my parents were executed."

His glance was sharp. "For what?"

She shrugged. "For lots of things, I guess. I was little, and I didn't ask."

He cast an uneasy look at the dancers. "My father was executed, too. Strangled."

Sula nodded. "I thought you knew what I meant when I talked about derivoo."

"I knew." Eyes still scanning the dance floor. "But I still think derivoo's depressing."

She found a grin spreading across her face. "We should dance now."

"Yes." His grin answered hers. "We should."

They danced till they were both breathless, and then Casimir moved the party to another club, in the Hotel of Many Blessings, where there was more dancing, more drinking, more money spread around. After which he said they should take a breather, and he took them into an elevator lined with what looked like mother-of-pearl and bade it rise to the penthouse.

The door opened to Casimir's thumbprint. The room was swathed in shiny draperies, and the furniture was low and comfortable. A table was laid with a cold supper, meats and cheeses and flat wroncho bread, pickles, chutneys, elaborate tarts and cakes, and bottles lying in a tray of shaved ice. It had obviously been intended all along that the evening end here.

Sula put together an open-faced sandwich—nice Vigo plates, she noticed, a clean modern design—then began to rehearse her exit. Surely it was not coincidental that a pair of bedrooms were very handy.

I've got to work in the morning. It certainly sounded more plausible than *I've got to go organize a counterrebellion.*

Casimir put his walking stick in a rack that had probably been made for it specially and reached for a pair of small packages, each with glossy wrapping and a brilliant scarlet ribbon. He presented one each to Sula and Veronika. "With thanks for a wonderful evening."

The gift proved to be perfume, a crystal bottle containing Sengra, made with the musk of the rare and reclusive atauba tree-crawlers of Paycahp. The small vial in her hand might have set Casimir back twenty zeniths or more— probably more, since Sengra was exactly the sort of thing that wouldn't be coming down from orbit for years, not with the ring gone.

Veronika opened her package and popped her eyes open wide—that gesture was going to look silly on her when she was fifty, Sula thought—and gave a squeal of delight. She opted for a more moderate response and kissed Casimir's cheek.

There was the sting of stubble against her lips. He looked at her with calculation. There was a very male scent to him.

She was about to bring up the work she had to do in the morning when there was a chime from Casimir's sleeve display. He gave a scowl of annoyance and answered.

"Casimir," came a strange voice. "We've got a situation."

"Wait," he said, left the room and closed the door behind him. Sula munched a pickle while the others waited in silence.

Casimir returned with the scowl still firm on his face. Without a trace of apology, he looked at Sula and Veronika and said, "Sorry, but the evening's over. Something's come up."

Veronika pouted and reached for her jacket. Casimir reached for Sula's arm to draw her to the door. She looked at him. "What's just happened?"

He gave her an impatient, insolent look—it was none of her business, after all—then thought better of it and shrugged. "Not what's happened, but what's going to happen in a few hours. The Naxids are declaring food rationing."

"They're *what*?" Sula's first reaction was outrage. Casimir opened the door for her, and she hesitated there, thinking. He quivered with impatience.

"Congratulations," she said finally. "The Naxids have just made you very rich."

"I'll call you," he said.

"I'll be rich too," she said. "Ration cards will cost you a hundred apiece."

"A *hundred*?" For a moment it was Casimir's turn to be outraged.

"Think about it," Sula said. "Think how much they'll be worth to you."

They held each other's eyes for a moment, then both broke into laughter. "We'll talk price later," Casimir said, and hustled her into the vestibule along with Veronika, who showed Sula a five-zenith coin.

"Julien gave it to me for the cab," she said triumphantly. "And we get to keep the change!"

"You'd better hope the cab *has* change for a fiver," Sula said, and Veronika thought for a moment.

"We'll get change in the lobby."

A Daimong night clerk gave them change, and Veronika's nose wrinkled at his corpse scent. On the way to her apartment Sula learned that Veronika was a former model and now an occasional club hostess.

"I'm an unemployed math teacher," Sula said.

Veronika's eyes went wide again. "Wow," she said.

After letting Veronika off, Sula had the Torminel driver take her within two streets of the communal Riverside apartment, after which she walked the distance to the building by the light of the stars. Overhead, the broken arcs of the ring were a curved line of black against the faintly glowing sky. Outside the apartment she gazed up for a long moment until she discerned the pale gleam of the white ceramic pot in the front window. It was in the position that meant *Someone is in the apartment and it is safe.*

The lock on the building's front door, the one that read her fingerprint, worked only erratically, but this time she caught it by surprise and the door opened. She went up the stair, then used her key on the apartment lock.

Macnamara was asleep on the couch, with a pair of pistols on the table in front of him, along with a grenade.

"Hi, Dad," Sula said as he blinked awake. "Junior brought me home safe, just like he said he would."

Macnamara looked embarrassed. Sula gave him a grin.

"What were you planning on doing with a *grenade*?" she asked.

He didn't reply. Sula took off her jacket and called up the computer that resided in the desk. "I've got work to do," she said. "You'd better get some sleep, because I've got a job for you first thing in the morning."

"What's that?" He rose from the couch, scratching his sleep-tousled hair.

"The market opens at 0727, right?"

"Yes."

Sula sat herself at the desk. "I need you to buy as much food as you can carry. Canned, dried, bottled, freeze-dried. Get the biggest sack of flour they have, and another sack of beans. Condensed milk would be good. Get Spence to help you carry it all."

"What's going on?" Macnamara was bewildered.

"Food rationing."

"What?" Sula could hear the outrage in his voice as she called up a text program.

"Two reasons for it I can think of," she said. "First, issuing everyone a ration card will be a way of reprocessing every ID on the planet . . . help them weed out troublemakers and saboteurs. Second . . ." She held up one hand and made the universal gesture of tossing a coin in her palm. "Artificial scarcities are going to make some Naxids very, very rich."

"Damn them," Macnamara breathed.

"We'll do very well," Sula pointed out. "We'll quadruple our prices on everything on the ration—you don't suppose they'd be good enough to ration *tobacco,* would you?—and we'll make a fortune."

"Damn them," Macnamara said again.

Sula gave him a pointed look. "Good night," she said. "Dad."

He flushed and shambled to bed. Sula turned to her work.

"What if they ration *alcohol*?" she said aloud as the thought struck her. There would be stills in half the bathrooms in Zanshaa, processing potatoes, taswa peels, apple cores, whatever they could find.

In the next few hours she roughed out an essay for *Resistance* denouncing the food ration. Her previous job, before she'd volunteered to get herself killed with partisan forces, had been with the Logistics Consolidation Executive, which had been deeply involved with cataloging and deployment of resources. She knew that, as the Praxis demanded, the planet of Zanshaa was self-sufficient in foodstuffs, and that from the practical point of view of providing food to the population, the ration was nonsense. She quoted numerous statistics from memory, and was able to get the rest out of public data sources.

By the time she finished, dawn was greening in the east. She took a shower to wash the tobacco smell out of her hair and collapsed into bed just as she heard Macnamara's alarm go off.

She rose after noon, the apartment already hot with the brilliant sun of summer. As she rubbed her swollen eyelids and blinked in the sunlight flooding the front room, she began to remember what it was like to be a clique member's girlfriend.

And then she had another thought. Thus far Action Team 491 had been selling her own property out of the back of a truck, a business that was irregular but legal. But once the ration came into effect, selling cocoa and coffee off the ration would be against the law. The team wouldn't just be participating in informal economic activity, they'd be committing a *crime*.

People who committed crimes needed protection. Casimir was going to be more necessary than ever.

"*Damn* it," she said.

SIXTEEN

Macnamara failed to procure a large stash of food. Police were already in force at the market, and foodsellers had been told not to sell large quantities to any one person. He wisely decided to avoid attracting attention and bought only quantities that might be considered reasonable for a family of three.

The announcement of rationing had been made while Sula slept and the food marts were packed. Tobacco had not been included, but Sula couldn't hope for everything. Citizens were given twenty days to report to their local police station in order to apply for a ration card. The reason given by the government for the imposition of rationing was the destruction of the ring and the decline in food imports.

The news reports announced that certain well-established Naxid clans, out of pure civic spirit, had agreed to spare the government any expense, and would instead use their own means to manage the planet's food supplies. The Jagirin clan, whose head had been temporary interior minister during the changeover from the old government to the new, the Ummir clan, whose head happened to be the Minister of Police, the Ushgays, the Kulukrafs . . . people who, even if some of them hadn't been with the rebellion from the beginning, clearly found it in their interest to support it now.

Sula reworked her *Resistance* essay to include a list of the cooperating clans, along with a suggestion that anyone working for the ration authority was a legitimate target of war.

The Naxids, she thought, had just created a whole new class of target.

Naxids were placed in every police station to monitor the process of acquiring ration cards, and the Naxids wore the black uniform of the Legion of Diligence, the organization that investigated crimes against the Praxis. All members of the Legion had been evacuated from Zanshaa before the arrival of the Naxid fleet, so apparently the new government had reformed the Legion, probably with personnel from the Naxid police.

Another class of target, Sula thought.

She then sent out the usual fifty thousand copies through the Records Office broadcast node. The next few days were spent making deliveries, arguing with restaurant and club managers about her increased prices, and watching resentment build among the city's population. Fury against the Naxids was now quite open, and even solid, prosperous citizens felt free to vent their rage publicly.

She wondered how people like One-Step would fare at acquiring their ration card. What, for instance, would One-Step claim as an occupation?

Sula kept a watch on the death certificates filed in the Records Office and discovered that a minor member of the Ushgay clan had died in a bomb explosion, and a Naxid police officer had been run over by his own car. The death certificate gave no indication how the officer had managed this, but she decided that the next number of *Resistance* would claim the incident as an action of the Lord Richard Li wing of the secret army.

Sula bypassed the local police and the Legion of Diligence and acquired her team's ration cards directly from the Records Office, splicing into the record the signatures and testaments of perfectly legitimate police officers and members of the Legion. She acquired a card for each of the team's many backup identities and had each mailed to the communal Riverside apartment. She later changed the address in the records so it wouldn't seem odd that so many people were sharing the same address.

She also acquired a card in the name of Michael Saltillo, the identity she'd established for Casimir. It might come in handy at some point.

Three days after the announcement about rationing, Sula was making deliveries in the High City, and called Sidney. He said that progress had been made and invited her to visit the shop.

Because she didn't know Sidney well enough to assess whether it was safe, she left Spence and Macnamara in the truck, parked inconspicuously down the street. "If I'm ambushed," she said, "try to pull me out. But if you can't, make sure one of your bullets finishes me."

Spence looked as if she weren't listening. In Macnamara she saw horror, then acceptance. He nodded and said nothing.

This time she was able to go in the front door. The shop had been reopened, and the display cases and racks showed only weapons suitable to Naxid anatomy.

Sidney waited behind a tall ceramic desk, his mustachios newly waxed and elaborately curled. "That was fast," he said in his ruined voice.

"Efficiency is my motto."

From his desk, Sidney locked the front door and reprogrammed the sign out front to announce that the shop would reopen in an hour. "Come along," he said, and took her to the back room.

The room was the same model of neatness and regularity it had been a few days earlier, though the smell of hashish was more subdued than on Sula's first visit. On the immaculate surface of a workbench she saw a short rifle. Sidney turned on a lamp, picked it up and held it to the light.

"The Sidney Mark One, if you like," he said. "I went for a simple firearm—nothing requiring a heavy battery pack or elaborate technology."

Light gleamed on the rifle's matte-black surfaces. It was obviously crude, with a stock made of pieces of carbon-fiber rod, a barrel that might have originally been a resinous pipe fitting, a receiver of metal, and iron sights.

"That was fast," Sula said.

"Simple firearms are easy, if you don't want elegance," Sidney said. "It helped that the gun's completely illegal—I didn't have to add the unlocking code and thumbprint-recognition pad required by law. Computer-assisted lathes did the work. The hard part was the ammunition."

He reached into a drawer, withdrew a tubelike magazine, and snapped it into place. "I wanted a traditional propel-lant, one that carries its own oxidant. I wanted it caseless so people wouldn't have to worry about making car-tridges." He rooted around in the drawer and came up with some small yellow cylinders, like cigarette filters. "The propellant wasn't hard," he said. "It's standard Fleet issue DD6 and will fire on a planet's surface, in the vacuum of space, and underwater. Its ingredients are readily obtain-able, and you can mix the stuff on your kitchen table and bake it in an oven." He handed a few of the cylinders to Sula. They felt dry and grainy. She pictured grandmotherly types turning them out on cookie sheets and smiled.

"You can cast the bullets out of metal or hard plastic, then stick them to the propellant with epoxide," Sidney said. "Unfortunately, neither bullet type will penetrate standard police armor, but they'll be useful against softer targets."

Sula examined the propellant cylinders again. "What do you use for a detonator?" she asked.

Sidney gave a grim smile. "I didn't want people messing around with mercury fulminate and the like. Blow their own fingers off."

"That's the problem we've been having with our bombs."

"Maybe I can help you with that. DD6, you see, will ig-nite at high temperature, so I built a standard laser-emitting diode into the breech." A few competent movements of his hands broke down the weapon and held the part to the light. "This is the most critical piece of the gun, and it can be scavenged from practically every piece of communications equipment made. Comm units, music and video players . . . there's no way the Naxids can prevent people from acquiring as many of these as they like. It will run off a little micro battery you can acquire anywhere. The operator will have to replace the diode every few hundred rounds, but it's a quick job and you can do it in the field."

Sidney reassembled the gun. "Breaks down easily," he said, "and reassembles without fuss. The parts are machined to a fairly low tolerance, which means there's a lot of slop in the movement and parts will wear out quickly, but it'll stand hard handling without jamming. There's no real safety, but you can lock the bolt back—so. This lever"—Flicking it— "switches from single shot to full automatic."

"May I handle it?"

He smiled. "Of course."

The gun was clean and cool in Sula's hands. She raised it to her shoulder and felt the balance. The tubular butt was padded against recoil with scraps of foam and shiny tape, and it felt like a toy.

"Want to fire it?" Sidney asked.

Sula looked at him in surprise. "We can do that *here*?"

In answer, Sidney spoke a few words into the air. There was a hum of machinery, and a slab of the floor lifted on hinges as a small elevator rose.

"I use it to move some of the heavier merchandise," he said. He stepped onto the elevator, and Sula lay the rifle carefully against her shoulder and joined him. Sidney spoke another few words and the elevator descended.

Below the shop there was a darkened room that smelled of must and metal. Sidney turned on lights and Sula saw a storage area—largely empty—and a pair of wide epoxide sewer pipes that ran the length of the shop in the direction

of the street, forming a firing range with targets at the far
end. Sidney gestured at the far wall, where a target already
lay waiting. He reached for a pair of ear protectors from a
rack and placed them comfortably on his head. "Be my
guest," he said.

Sula got ear protection, braced the rifle on her hip and
flicked the bolt with her thumb to let it slam forward. She
put the rifle against her shoulder, gazed through the simple
iron sights, took a calming breath, let it out, and squeezed
the trigger. The bang was very loud in the small space, and
there was very little recoil, which was normal with caseless
ammunition. A hole appeared in the filmy plastic surface
of the target, a hand's breadth off center.

"Not bad," Sidney said. "This gun's strong point isn't
accuracy."

Sula fired a few more rounds to get the feel of the
weapon, then clicked to full automatic. She half expected
the smooth, continuous roar of the weapons she'd trained
with, the rifles that could cycle at over a hundred rounds
per second, but instead there was a reliable chug-chug-
chug action, slow enough so she could keep the weapon on
target.

She fired several bursts, and then the magazine was
empty. She lowered the rifle, and Sidney reached over her
shoulder to press the keypad that would bring the target
swaying on its cable to her. She'd riddled the center section.

"Not very slick, is it?" Sidney said. "It won't match police or Fleet weapons in a stand-up fight. But in a surprise
attack or an assassination, it should do the job."

Sula removed the magazine and looked at the weapon.
"Show me how to break it down."

"Certainly. And while I do that, tell me how many other
people are in this insurrection of yours."

She looked at him. "Sorry. Even if I knew, I couldn't
tell you."

His look was somber. "You can't have very many. Otherwise you wouldn't need me to design your weapons for you." He smiled. "And you *really* wouldn't need PJ Ngeni."

Sula suppressed a burst of laughter. "Well," she said, "let's just say that the Naxids cut down our numbers after the Axtattle ambush."

Sidney's eyes were intent. "Yes. So there's really no secret government to report to, is there?"

Sula hesitated, then said, "I'd appreciate it if you didn't tell anyone that. PJ in particular."

He flashed another smile. "He *does* enjoy being a secret agent, doesn't he?"

Sula felt a warning tingle run up her spine. "How much does he enjoy it, exactly?"

Sidney caught her meaning at once. "I don't think he's being indiscreet," he said. "But he comes over here and babbles. I think he's very happy that he finally has someone to talk to about all this." He shook his head. "And the girl threw him over too, didn't she?"

"Yes. She did."

He looked down at the floor. "The things people do for love."

She frowned at him. "Why are *you* doing this?"

He glanced up, and there was a flash of teeth beneath the curling mustachios, a kind of snarl. "Because I hate the bastards, that's why."

Love and hate, Sula thought. That kept things basic.

She had wondered why she herself was in this fight. The secret government was gone, and Lady Sula was officially dead: she could sit in some quiet part of town, sell chocolate and tobacco, and wait in comfort for the war to end.

And so she could, if it weren't for love and hate. She hated the Naxids, and she loved Martinez and hated him. She hated the whole shambling, sick edifice that was the empire, and a part of her would rejoice in its ruin. She loved the part of a leader, the exhilaration of action, the sweetness of savagery and the satisfaction of a plan well-forged and well-executed. She hated herself but loved the parts she played, the masks she donned, one convincing falsehood after another. She loved the game of it, the way it could take the form of one of her mathematical puzzles, a complex equation with one variable after another, Casimir and the Records Office, deliveries and assassinations, *Resistance* and PJ and the Sidney Mark One rifle . . .

Sidney had the gun apart, and he was looking at her with frank interest. Sula collected herself, reassembled the rifle, then took it apart again.

He began to clean the weapon. "Can you take it home with you?" he asked.

She looked up at him. "I don't need it—my group's pretty well armed."

"Yes, but I've got the whole design ready to download, and once you put the data in *Resistance,* I imagine my place will be searched, along with that of anyone who designs guns for a living. I don't want any part of it here."

"I suppose."

"You can take it disassembled into the Lower Town easily enough," Sidney added. "I've noticed they don't search people *leaving* the High City."

"And they don't search us going up much either," Sula said. "The guards have got to recognize our truck, and they know we're just delivering food and such."

"That'll change when rationing starts."

Oh. She hadn't considered that.

She would have to get herself the proper vouchers when she went through the checkpoints. Another job for Casimir, damn it.

Sidney packed the rifle in a case, then took Sula to his workroom again to give her all the remaining ammunition and several spare laser diodes. "Perhaps you'd better leave by the back way," he suggested. "Any Naxids might be interested in a Terran leaving a gun shop with a case."

"I'll do that."

Sidney pulled up the schematics of the rifle on his computer, then beamed them to Sula's arm display. "I've included a design for a sound suppressor," he said. "You screw it onto the barrel, and it should be good for the first dozen shots or so before things get noisy again. I didn't have time to actually build it." He opened a drawer, pulled out a pipe, and loaded it with a large chunk of hashish from a green leather box.

Sula looked down at two photo cubes attached to the wall above Sidney's desk. They showed a young man and young woman in the uniform of the Fleet.

"Your children?" he asked.

Sidney reached for his lighter. His tones were unnaturally even, as if he was suppressing every possible emotion. "Sonia died retaking the *Destiny,* on Zanshaa's ring the first day of the mutiny. Johannes was killed at Magaria on *The Glory of the Praxis.*"

"I'm sorry," Sula said. "And your wife?"

He took a deep breath of smoke before he answered. "She left me years ago, before I had my accident and had to leave the Fleet. I was just getting to know the children again before—" He waved his pipe. "Before all this started."

Love and hate. He had given all his guns away to her group, not caring if they could be traced to him. Now she knew why.

Sula hoped she could give him a new job that he could love, something that would keep him alive and useful. All she had to do was promise to fulfill his hatred.

"Mr. Sidney," she said, "shall we go to PJ's and cadge a lunch?"

He exhaled a deep blue cloud of smoke and nodded.

"Why not?" he said. "The caterers will be out of work when the rationing comes. We may as well let PJ give them some money."

SEVENTEEN

A shimmering layer of afternoon heat stretched across the pavement like a layer of molasses, thick enough to distort the colorful canopies and displays of the Textile Market that set up in Sula's street every five days. Early in the morning vendors motored up with their trailers or their three-wheelers with the sheds built onto the back, and at dawn the sheds opened, canopies went up, and the merchandise went on sale. After sunset, as the heat began to dissipate and the purple shadows crept between the stalls, the vendors would break down their displays and motor away, to set up the next day in another part of the city.

As Sula walked past on her way to her apartment, the rifle in its case under one arm, vendors called her attention to cheap women's clothing, baby clothes, shoes, stockings, scarves, rubbery Bogo toys, inexpensive dolls, cheap puzzles and games. There were bolts of fabric, foils of music and entertainment, sun lotion and sun hats, and knit items—unseasonable in the heat—alleged to be made from the fleece of Yormak cattle, and sold at a surprisingly low price.

Despite the heat, the market was thronged. Tired and hot, Sula elbowed her way impatiently through the crowd to her doorstep. A glance to one side showed that One-Step wasn't in his accustomed place. She entered the building, then heard the chime of a hand comm through her apartment door and made haste to enter. She put the rifle case down, snatched up the comm from the table and answered, panting.

Casimir surveyed her from the display. She could watch his eyes travel insolently over her image as far as the frame would permit.

"Too bad," he said. "I was hoping to catch you in the bath again."

"Better luck next time." Sula switched on the room coolers, and somewhere in the building a tired compressor began to wheeze and faint currents of air to stir. She dropped into a chair near the *ju yao* pot, and holding the comm in one hand, began to loosen her boots with the other.

"I want to see you tonight," Casimir said. "I'll pick you up at 2101, all right?"

"Why don't I meet you at the club?"

"Nothing happens at the club that early." He frowned. "Don't you want me to know where you live?"

"I don't have a place of my own," Sula lied cheerfully. "I sort of bounce between friends."

"Well." Grudgingly. "I'll see you at the club then."

She had time to bathe, get a bite to eat, and work for a while on the next issue of *Resistance,* the one with the schematics for Sidney's do-it-yourself rifle. Then she dressed, dabbed Sengra on her throat, and trotted out of the apartment, the rifle case still under her arm. The sun was low in the viridian sky and the heat rose in waves, but the Textile Market was still thronged. People felt safe in such numbers, she thought, even though if she were a Naxid looking for hostages, she'd think of a park or an open-air market first thing.

One-Step stood in his usual place, wearing baggy shorts and a scarred leather vest. "Hey One-Step," Sula said.

A brilliant smile blossomed on his face. "Hello, beauteous lady. How are you this lovely evening?"

He smelled as if he hadn't bathed for a few long hot

summer days, a fact she did her best to ignore. "Do you know a man named Julien? A friend of Casimir's?"

The smile vanished at once. "One-Step advises you to stay away from such people, lovely one."

"If I'm supposed to stay away from him, you'd better tell me why."

One-Step scowled. "Julien's the son of Sergius Bakshi. And Sergius is the boss of the Riverside Clique. You don't get any worse than Sergius."

Sula nodded, impressed. Sergius was not only a clique leader, he'd cheated the executioner long enough to have a grown son. Few of his kind stayed alive that long.

"Thanks, One-Step."

One-Step looked bleak. "You're not going to follow One-Step's advice, are you? You're going out with Julien tonight."

"He's not the one who asked me out. Good night, One-Step! Thanks!"

"You're making a mistake," One-Step said darkly.

Sula negotiated the crowds at the Textile Market, then ducked down a sun-blasted side street, trying to keep on the shady side. The heat still took her breath away. She made another turn, then entered the delightfully cool air of a block-shaped storage building built in the shadow of the even larger Riverside Crematorium. She showed her false ID to the Cree at the desk, then took the elevator upstairs and opened one of Team 491's storage caches. There, she stowed the rifle case alongside the other rifle cases, the cases of ammunition and grenades and explosives and body armor.

For a moment she hesitated. Then she opened one of the cases, withdrew a small item and pocketed it.

Casimir waited by his car in front of the Cat Street club with an impatient scowl on his face and his walking stick in his hand. He wore a soft white shirt covered with minutely stitched braid. As she appeared, he stabbed the door button, and the glossy apricot-colored door rolled up into the car roof. "I *hate* being kept waiting," he growled in his deep voice, and took her arm roughly to stuff her into the passenger compartment.

This too, Sula remembered, was what it was like to be a clique member's girlfriend.

Sula settled herself on apricot-colored plush across from Julien and Veronika, the latter in fluttery garb and a cloud of Sengra. Casimir thudded into the seat next to her and rolled down the door, Sula called up the chronometer on her sleeve display.

"I'm three minutes early," she said primly, in what she trusted was a math teacher's voice. "I'm sorry if I spoiled your evening."

Casimir gave an unsociable grunt. Veronika popped her blue eyes wide and said, "The boys are taking us shopping!"

Sula remembered that too.

"Where?" she said.

"It's a surprise," Julien said, and slid open the door on the vehicle's bar. "Anyone want something to drink?"

The Torminel behind the controls slipped the car smoothly from the curb on its six tires. Sula had a Citrine Fling while the rest drank Kyowan. The vehicle passed through Grandview to the Petty Mount, a district in the shadow of the High City, beneath the Couch of Eternity where the ashes of the Shaa masters waited in their niches for the end of time. The area was lively, filled with boutiques, bars, cafés, and eccentric shops that sold folk crafts or antiques or old jewelry. Sula saw Cree and Lai-own on the streets as well as Terrans.

The car pulled to a smooth stop before a shop called Raiment by Chesko, and the apricot-colored doors rolled open. They stepped from the vehicle and were greeted at the door by a female Daimong whose gray body was wrapped in a kind of satin sheath that looked strangely at-

tractive on her angular body with its matchstick arms. In a
chiming voice she greeted Casimir by name.

"Gredel, this is Miss Chesko," Casimir told Sula in a
voice that suggested both her importance and his own.

"Pleased to meet you," Sula said.

The shop was a three-level fantasy filled with sumptuous
fabrics in brilliant colors, all set against neutral-colored
walls of a translucent resinous substance that let in the fading light of the sun. Gossamer Cree music floated tastefully in the air.

A Daimong who designed clothes for Terrans was something new in Sula's experience. The shop must have had
excellent air circulation, or Chesko wore something that
suppressed the odor of her rotting flesh, because Sula
didn't scent her even once.

Casimir's mood changed the instant he entered the shop.
He walked from one rack to the next and heaved out clothing for Sula or Veronika to try on. He held garments critically to the light and ran his hands over the glossy, rich
fabrics. Veronika's were soft and bright and shimmered;
Sula's were satiny and tended to the darker shades, with
light accents in the form of a scarf, lapel, or collar.

He's dressing me as a woman of mystery, Sula thought.

His antennae were rather acute.

Sula looked at herself in the full-length video display
and suspected his tastes were fairly good as well—though
she was forced to admit that she couldn't be certain herself; her own dress sense was so undeveloped that she
wasn't sure of her judgment.

She found that she enjoyed herself playing model, dis-
playing one rich garment after another. Casimir offered informed comment as she changed outfits, twitched the
clothing to a better drape, and sorted the clothing into piles
of yesses, maybes, rejects. Chesko made respectful suggestions in her bell-like tones. Shop assistants ran back and
forth with mountains of clothing in their arms.

It hadn't been like this with Lamey, Sula remembered.

When he walked into a shop with Gredel, the assistants knew to bring out their flashiest, most expensive clothing, and he'd buy them with a wave of his hand and a pocket of cash.

Casimir wasn't doing this to impress anyone, or at least not in the way Lamey had. He was demonstrating his taste, not his power and money.

"You should have Chesko's job," she told him.

"Maybe. I seem to have got the wrong training though."

"Your mama didn't give you enough dolls to play with," Julien said. He sat in a chair in a corner, out of everyone's way. He had a tolerant smile on his pointed face and a glass of mig brandy, brought by the staff, in one hand.

"I'm hungry," Julien said after an hour and a half.

Casimir looked a little put out, but he shrugged and then looked again through the piles of clothing, making a final sorting. Julien rose from his chair, put down his glass and addressed one of the assistants.

"*That* pile," he said. "Total it up."

Veronika gave a whoop of joy and ran to embrace him. "Better add this," Casimir said, adding a vest to the yes pile. He picked up an embroidered jacket from another heap and held it out to Sula. "What do you think of this?" he asked. "Should I add it to your pile?"

Sula considered the jacket. "I think you should pick out the single very nicest thing out of the stack and give it to me."

His dark eyes flashed and his gravel voice was suddenly full of anger. "You don't want my presents?" he asked.

Sula was aware that Veronika was staring at her as if she were insane.

"I'll take *a* present," Sula said. "You don't know me well enough to buy me a whole wardrobe."

For a moment she sensed thwarted rage boiling off of him, and then he thought about it and decided to be amused. His mouth twisted in a tight-lipped smile. "Very well," he said. He considered the pile for a moment, then reached in and pulled out a suit, velvet black, with satin braid and silver beadwork on the lapels and down the seams of the loose trousers.

"Will this do?" he said.

"It's very nice. Thank you." Sula noted that it wasn't the most expensive item in the pile, and that fact pleased her. If he wasn't buying her expensive trash, it probably meant he didn't think she was trash either.

"Will you wear it tonight?" He hesitated, then looked at Chesko. "It didn't need fitting, did it?"

"No, sir." Her pale, expressionless Daimong face, set in a permanent caricature of wide-eyed alarm, gave no sign of disappointment in losing sales worth hundreds of zeniths.

"Happy to," Sula said. She took the suit to the changing room, changed, and looked at herself in the old-fashioned silver-backed mirrors. The suit probably *was* the nicest thing in the pile.

Her old clothes were wrapped in a package, and she stepped out to a look of appreciation from Julien and the more critical gaze of Casimir. He gestured with a finger as if stirring a pot.

"Turn around," he said.

She made a pirouette, and he nodded, more to himself than to anyone else. "That works," he said. The deep voice sounded pleased.

"Can we eat now?" Julien asked.

Outside, the white marble of the Couch of Eternity glowed a pale green in twilight. The streets exhaled summer heat into the sky like an overtaxed athlete panting at the end of his run.

They ate in a café, a place of bright red and white tiles and shiny chrome. The café was packed and noisy, as if people wanted to pack in as much food and good times as possible before rationing began. Casimir and Julien were in a lighthearted mood, chattering and laughing, but every so often Sula caught Casimir looking at her with a thoughtful expression, as if he was approving his choice of outfit.

He had made her into something he admired.

Afterward they went to a bar, equally crowded, with a live band and dancing. The other night Casimir had danced with a kind of gravity, but now he was exuberant, laughing as he led her into athletic kicks, spins, and twirls. Before, he had been pleasing himself with a show of his power and control, but now it was as if he wanted all Zanshaa to share his joy.

He was taking me for granted the other night, Sula thought. *Now he's not.*

It was well past midnight when they left the bar. Outside, in the starlit darkness, a pair of odd colossi moved in the night. Leather creaked. A strange barnyard smell floated to Sula's nostrils.

Casimir gave a laugh. "Right," he said. "Get in."

He launched himself into some kind of box that, dimly perceived, seemed to float above the street. There was a creak, a shuffle, more barnyard smell. His long pale hand appeared out of the night.

"Come on," he said.

Sula took the hand and let him draw her forward. A step, a box, a seat. She seated herself next to him before she understood where she was, and amazement flooded her.

"Is this a pai-car chariot?" she asked.

"That's right!" Casimir let a laugh float off into the night. "We hired a pair for tonight." He thumped the leather-padded rim of the cockpit and called to the driver, "Let's go!"

There was a hiss from the driver, a flap of reins, and the carriage lurched into movement. The vehicle was pulled by a pai-car, a tall flightless bird, a carnivorous, unintelligent cousin to the Lai-own driver that perched on the front of the carriage. There were two big silver alloy wheels, ornamented with cutouts, and a boat-shaped body made out of leather, boiled, treated, sculpted, and ornamented with bright metal badges of a pattern unique to each driver. Mounted on either side were some cell-powered lamps, not very powerful, which the driver now switched on.

The car swayed down off the Petty Mount and into the flat cityscape below. Sula relaxed against Casimir's shoulder. Darkened buildings loomed up on either side like valley walls. The slap of the pai-car's feet and its huffing breath echoed off the structures on either side. There seemed to be no other traffic at all, nothing but the limousine, with its Torminel guards, which followed them at a distance, the driver able to navigate perfectly well with his huge nocturnal eyes.

"Is this legal?" Sula wondered.

Casimir's bright white teeth flashed in the starlight. "Of course not. These carriages aren't permitted outside the parks."

"You don't expect police?"

His grin broadened. "The police are bogged down processing millions of ration card applications. The streets are ours for the next month."

Veronika's laughter tinkled through the night. Sula heard the slap of another pair of feet, and saw the savage saw-toothed face of another pai-car loom up on the left, followed soon by the driver and Julien and Veronika. Julien leaned out of the carriage, hands waving drunkenly in the air. "A hundred says I beat you to Medicine Street!"

Sula felt Casimir's body grow taut as Julien's face vanished into the gloom ahead. He called to the driver: "Faster!" The driver gave a hiss and a flap of the reins. The carriage creaked and swayed as the pace increased.

Veronika's laughter taunted them from ahead. Casimir growled and leaned forward. "Faster!" he called. Sula's nerves tingled to the awareness of danger.

A few lights shone high in office buildings where the staff were cleaning. A rare functioning street lamp revealed two Torminel, in the brown uniforms of the civil service, having what seemed to be a disagreement. The two fell silent and stared with their big eyes as the carriages raced past, their silver wheels a blur.

The side-lamps of Julien's carriage ahead loomed closer. "Faster!" Casimir called, and he turned to Sula, a laugh rumbling from deep in his chest. Sula felt an answering grin tear at her lips. *This is mad,* she thought. *Absolutely mad.*

She heard Julien's voice calling for greater speed. The wheels threw up sparks as they skidded through a turn. Sula was thrown against Casimir. He put an arm around her protectively.

"Faster!"

Veronika's laughter tinkled from ahead, closer this time. Casimir ducked left and right, peering around the driver for a better view of the carriage they were pursuing. They passed through an intersection and both carriages glared white in the startled headlamps of a huge street-cleaning machine. Sula blinked the dazzle from her eyes. The night air was cool on her cheeks. She could feel her heart beating high in her throat.

She heard Julien curse as they drew even. Then they were in another turn, metal wheels sliding, and Julien's carriage loomed close as it skidded toward them. Their driver was forced into a wider turn to avoid collision, and Julien pulled ahead.

"Damn!" Casimir jumped from his seat and leaped to join the driver on the box. One pale hand dug in a pocket. "Twenty zeniths if you beat him!" he called, and slapped a coin down on the box. Twenty zeniths would buy the chariot, the pai-car, and the driver twice over.

The driver responded with a frantic hiss. The pai-car seemed to have caught the fey mood of the passengers and gave a determined cry as it accelerated.

The road narrowed as it crossed a canal, and Casimir's coach was on the heels of Julien's as they crossed the bridge. Sula caught a whiff of sour canal water, heard the startled exclamation of someone on the quay, and then the coach hit a bump and she was tossed in the car like a pea in a bottle. Then they were in another turn, and she was pressed to one side, the leather bending slightly under her weight.

She gave a laugh at the realization that her whole life's adventure could end here, that she could die in a ridiculous carriage accident or find herself under arrest, that her work—*Resistance,* the war against the Naxids, Team 491—all could be destroyed in a reckless, demented instant . . .

Serve me right, she thought.

The labored breathing of the pai-car echoed between the buildings. "Twenty more!" Casimir slapped another coin on the box.

The carriage swayed alongside that of Julien. He was standing in the car, urging his driver on, but his pai-car looked dead in his harness. Then there was a sudden glare of headlights, the clatter of a vehicle collision alarm, and Julien's driver gave an urgent tug on the reins, cutting his bird's speed and swerving behind Casimir's carriage to avoid a crash with a taxi taking home a singing chorus of Cree.

Sula heard Julien's yelp of protest. Casimir laughed in triumph as the singers disappeared in their wake.

They had passed through the silent business district and into a more lively area of Grandview. Sula saw people on the street, cabs parked by the curb waiting for customers. Ahead she saw an intersection, a traffic signal flashing a command to stop.

"Keep going!" Casimir cried, and slapped down another coin. The driver gave Casimir a wild, gold-eyed stare, but obeyed.

Sula heard a rumble ahead, saw a white light. The traffic signal blazed in the darkness. Her heart leaped into her throat.

The carriage dashed into the intersection. Casimir's laughter rang in her ears. There was a brilliant white light, a blaring collision alarm, the wail of tires. Sula threw her arms protectively over her head as the pai-car gave a wail of terror.

The padded leather edge of the chariot body bit her ribs as the carriage was slammed sideways. A side-lamp exploded into bits of flying crystal. One large silver wheel went bounding down the road ahead of the truck that had torn it away, and the carriage fell heavily onto the torn axle. Sparks arced in the night as the panicked bird tried to drag the tilted carriage from the scene.

The axle grated near Sula's ear. She blinked into the night just in time to see Casimir lose his balance on the box and fall toward her, arms thrashing in air. She made a desperate lunge for the high side of the coach and managed to avoid being crushed as he fell heavily onto the seat.

Clinging to the high side of the coach, she turned to him. Casimir was helpless with laughter, a deep base sound that echoed the grinding of the axle on pavement. Sula allowed herself to slide down the seat onto him, wrapped him in her arms and stopped his laughter with a kiss.

The panting pai-car came to a halt. Sula heard its snarls of frustration as it turned in the traces and tried to savage the driver with its razor teeth, then heard the driver expertly divert its striking head with slaps. She could hear the truck reversing, the other pai-car padding to a halt, the sound of running footsteps as people ran to the scene.

She could hear Casimir's heart pounding in his chest.

"I conceive that no one is injured," said the burbling voice of a Cree.

This time it was Sula who was helpless with laughter. She and Casimir crawled from the wreckage of the carriage as the apricot-colored limousine rolled silently to a stop, the Torminel guards appearing in time to prevent a very angry Daimong truck driver from bludgeoning someone. Julien and Casimir passed around enough money to leave everyone happy, the chariot drivers in particular, and then the party piled into the limousine for the ride to the Hotel of Many Blessings.

Sula sat in Casimir's lap and kissed him for the entire ride.

He wasn't anything like Martinez. Maybe that was the most attractive thing about him.

She insisted on taking a shower before joining him in bed. Then she insisted that he take a shower as well.

"We could have showered *together*," Casimir grumbled.

"You could use a shave too," Sula pointed out.

He grumbled toward the shower and left her wrapped in the luxurious velvet dressing gown that he'd loaned her. Being alone was a mistake, because she had nothing to do but think, and once she began to think, she began to fear.

All night she had been playing a part—by now Gredel was no less a role than Sula—but she couldn't play a part in bed. She wasn't experienced enough that way. With Lamey she'd been too young, and with Martinez . . . well, with Martinez the experience had been too singular.

In a few minutes Casimir would encounter a young, unsophisticated bed partner, caught without the assured, arrogant persona she'd worn all night.

Sula considered putting on her clothes and leaving, and then she thought about the consequences of that. Then she remembered Casimir's grating laugh as the wrecked pai-car chariot was dragged along the street, and his scent as her arms went around him, the pulse of adrenaline in her ears.

She dimmed the lights to almost nothing. Perhaps in the dark he wouldn't notice the change in her.

The bathroom door opened and Casimir stood framed in the spill of yellow light. Sula's blood surged. Before she could change her mind, she stepped toward him and pulled him to the bed. He was showered and shaved and scented with taswa-blossom soap.

His long-fingered hands began to touch her. He wasn't anything like Martinez, Sula discovered with relief. Martinez had been patient and giving, and Casimir was impatient and greedy.

That was all right, because it gave her permission to be impatient and greedy too.

"Hey!" he said in surprise. "You're really a blond!"

She gave a slow laugh. "That's the least of my mysteries."

The fear had gone. That surprised her because in the past fear had always been an element. Perhaps Martinez had liberated her from that.

Or perhaps she was unafraid because she still knew some things that Casimir didn't. She still had some cards to play. She was still in charge, whether he knew it or not.

An hour or so later she decided to play a card or two, and told the room light to go on. Casimir gave a start and shielded his eyes. Sula crawled out of bed and looked for the package that held the clothing she'd worn at the beginning of the evening.

"Gredel, what are you *doing*?" Casimir complained.

"I have something to show you." She put on her jacket and triggered the sleeve display. She activated the video wall and beamed the jacket's memory to the wall. "Look at this."

Casimir blinked uncertainly at the schematics of the Sidney Mark One. He screwed up his face. "What *is* that, anyway?"

"Tomorrow's edition of *Resistance*."

"*Tomorrow's?* What are you—" He looked at her, and as comprehension entered his eyes, his mouth opened in shock.

Sula dug in an inner pocket and removed the item she'd taken from the storage locker earlier in the evening. She opened the slim plastic case and showed Casimir her Fleet ID.

"I'm Caroline, Lady Sula," she said. "I represent the secret army."

There was a moment of silence. Casimir squeezed his eyes shut for a long moment, as if in disbelief, and then opened them.

"Shit," he said.

"Do you still want to buy me a new wardrobe?" Sula smiled at him. "You can if you like."

EIGHTEEN

The meeting with Julien's father occurred three days after the madcap carriage race, on an afternoon dark with racing clouds. Sula dressed for it with care. In order that she look more like the person in the Fleet ID, she left off her contact lenses and bought a shoulder-length wig in something like her natural shade of blond. She wore a military-style jacket in a tone of green that wasn't quite the viridian of a Fleet uniform but that she hoped suggested it. She brought Macnamara as an aide, or perhaps a bodyguard, and bought him a similar jacket. She reminded herself to walk with the straight-backed, braced posture of the Fleet officer and not the less formal slouch she'd adopted as Gredel.

She wore a pistol stuck down her waistband in back. Macnamara had a sidearm in a shoulder holster.

These were less for defense than to shoot themselves, or each other, in the event things went wrong.

There was a lot of shooting going on these days. The Naxids had shot sixty-odd people for distributing the latest copy of *Resistance*—apparently the plans for the Sidney Mark One had made them more than usually homicidal. Someone had firebombed a Motor Patrol vehicle in the Old Third, where resentment had obviously not died since the massacre, and eleven Torminel were shot and more rounded up.

The meeting took place in a private club called Silk Winds on the second floor of an office building in a Lai-own neighborhood. Casimir met her on the pavement out front, dressed in his long coat and carrying his walking stick. His eyes went wide as he saw her, and then he grinned and gave one of his elaborate bows. From his bent position he looked up at her.

"You still don't look much like a math teacher," he said.

"Good thing then," she said in her drawling Peer voice. His eyebrows lifted in surprise and he straightened.

"Now *that's* not the voice I heard in bed the other night."

From over her shoulder Sula heard Macnamara's intake of breath. Great, Sula thought, now she'd have a scandalized and sulking team member.

"Don't be vulgar," she admonished, still in her Peer voice.

Casimir bowed again. "Apologies, my lady."

He led her into the building. The lobby was cavernous, brilliant with polished copper, and featured a twice-life-size bronze statue of a Lai-own holding, for some allegorical reason beyond Sula's comprehension, a large tetrahedron. Uniformed Lai-own security guards in blue jackets and tall pointed shakos gave them searching looks but did not approach. A moving stair took Sula to the second floor and the polished copper door of the club, on which had been placed a card informing them that the club had been closed for a private function.

Casimir swung the door open and led her and Macnamara into the shadow-filled club. Faint sunlight from the darkened sky gleamed fitfully off copper fittings and polished wood. Lai-own security—this time without the silly hats—appeared from the gloom and checked everyone thoroughly for listening devices. They found the sidearms but didn't touch them. Apparently they discounted the possibility that Sula and her party might be assassins.

Casimir, adjusting his long coat after the search, led them to a back room. He knocked on a nondescript door.

Sula smoothed the lapel of her jacket, straightened her shoulders and reminded herself to act like a senior fleet commander inspecting a motley group of dock workers.

She couldn't give orders to these people: she had to use a different kind of authority. Being a Peer and a Fleet officer were the only cards she had left to play. She had to be the embodiment of the Fleet and the legitimate government and the whole body of Peers, and she would have to carry them all along through the sheer weight of her own expectation.

Julien opened the door and his eyes went wide when he saw Sula. Suddenly nervous, he backed hastily from the door.

Sula walked into the room, her spine straight, hands clasped behind her. I *own* this room, she told herself, but then she saw the eyes of her audience and her heart gave a lurch.

Two Terrans, a Lai-own, and a Daimong sat in the shadowy, dark-paneled room, facing her from behind a table that looked like a slab of pavement torn from the street. Nature had made the Daimong expressionless, but the others were so blank-faced they might have all been carved from the same block of granite.

She heard Macnamara stamp to a halt behind her right shoulder, a welcome support. Casimir stepped around them and stood to one side of the room.

"Gentlemen," he said, and again made his elaborate bow. "May I present Lieutenant the Lady Sula."

"I'm Sergius Bakshi," said one of the Terrans. He looked nothing like his son Julien: he had a round face and a razor-cut mustache and the round, unfeeling eyes of a great predator fish. He turned to the Lai-own. "This is Am Tan-dau, who has very kindly arranged for us to meet here."

Tan-dau did not look kind. He slumped in the padded chair that cradled his keel-like breastbone, his bright, fashionable clothes wrinkled on him as they might on a sack of feathers. His skin was dull, and nictating membranes were half deployed across his eyes. He looked a hundred years old, but Sula could tell from the dark feathery hair on each side of his head that he was still young in years.

Bakshi continued. "These are friends who may be interested in any proposition you may have for us." He nodded at the Terran. "This is Mr. Patel." A young man with glossy hair that curled over the back of his collar, Patel didn't even blink in response when Sula offered him a small nod.

The Daimong's name was Sagas. His gray-white face had been permanently set by nature into a look of howling anguish.

Sula knew, through Casimir, that the four were a kind of informal commission that regulated illegal activities on the south end of Zanshaa City. Bakshi's word carried the most weight, if only because he'd managed to reach middle age without being killed.

"Gentlemen," Sula drawled in her Peer voice. "May I present my aide, Mr. Macnamara."

Four pairs of eyes flicked to Macnamara, then back to Sula. Her throat was suddenly dry, and she resisted the impulse to reveal her nervousness by clearing it.

Bakshi folded large, doughy hands on the table in front of him and spoke. "What may we do for you, Lady Sula?"

Sula's answer was swift. "Help me kill Naxids."

Even that request, which Sula hoped might startle them, failed to provoke a reaction.

Bakshi deliberately folded his hands on the table before him. His eyes never left her. "Assuming for the sake of argument that this is remotely possible," he said, "why should we agree to attack a group so formidable that even the Fleet has failed to defeat them?"

Sula looked down at him. If he wanted a staring contest, she thought, then she'd give him one.

"The Fleet isn't done with the Naxids," she said. "Not by a long shot. I don't know whether you have the means to verify this or not, but I know that even now the Fleet is raiding deep into Naxid territory. The Fleet is ripping the guts out of the rebellion while the main Naxid force is stuck here guarding the capital."

Bakshi gave a subtle movement of his shoulders that

might have been a strangled shrug. "Possibly," he said. "But that doesn't alter the fact that the Naxids are *here*."

"How do we know?" Tan-dau's voice was a mumble. "How do we know that she is not sent by the Naxids to provoke us?"

It was difficult to be certain to whom Tan-dau addressed the question, but Sula decided to intercept it. "I killed a couple thousand Naxids at Magaria," Sula said. "You may remember that I received a decoration for it. I don't think they'd let me switch sides even if I wanted to."

"Lady Sula is supposed to be dead," Tan-dau said, to no one in particular.

"Well." Sula permitted herself a slight smile. "You know how accurate the Naxids have been about everything else."

"How do we know she is the real . . ." Tan-dau's sentence drifted away before he could finish it. Sula waited until it was clear that no more words were coming and then answered.

"You can't know," Sula said. She brought her Fleet ID out of her jacket. "You're welcome to examine my identification, but of course the Naxids could have faked it. But I think you know . . ." She gazed at them all in turn. ". . . if the Naxids wanted to target you, they wouldn't need me. They've declared martial law; they'd just send their people after you, and no one would ever see you alive again."

They absorbed this in expressionless silence. "Why then," Sergius Bakshi said finally, "should we act so as to bring this upon us?"

Sula'd had three days to prepare what came next. She had to restrain herself from babbling it out all at once, to urge herself to remain calm and to make her points slowly and with proper emphasis.

"You want to be on the winning side, for one thing," she said. "That brings its own rewards. Second, the secret government is prepared to offer pardons and amnesties for anyone who aids us."

It was like talking to a blank wall. She wanted to stride

about, to gesture, to declaim, all in desperate hope of getting at least one of the group to show some response. But she forced herself to be still, to keep her hands clasped behind her, to stand in an attitude of superiority. She had to project command and authority: if she showed weakness, she was finished.

"What," said Sagas, speaking for the first time in his beautiful chiming Daimong voice, "makes you think that we need pardons and amnesties?"

"A pardon," Sula said, "means that any investigations, any complaints, any inquiries, any proceedings come to a complete and permanent end. Not only for yourself, but for any of your friends, clients, and associates who may wish to aid the government. You may not need any amnesties yourself, but perhaps some of your friends aren't so lucky."

She scanned her audience again. Once again no response.

"My last point," she said, "is that you are all prominent, successful individuals. People know your names. You have earned the respect of the population, and people are wary of your power. But you're not loved."

For the first time she'd managed to provoke a response. Surprise widened Sergius Bakshi's pupils, and even the expressionless Sagas gave a jerk of his head.

"If you lead the fight against the Naxids, you'll be heroes," Sula said. "Maybe for the first time, people will think of you as agents of virtue. You'll be loved, because everyone will see you on the right side, standing between them and the Naxids."

Patel gave a sudden laugh. "Fight the Naxids for love!" he said. "That's a *good* one! I'm *for* it!" He slapped the table with a hand, and looked up at Sula with his teeth flashing in a broad grin. "I'm with you, princess! For love, and for no other reason!"

Sula ventured a glance at Casimir. He gave her a wry, amused look, not quite encouragement but not dispirited either.

Bakshi gave an impatient motion of his hand, and Patel

fell silent, his hilarity gone in an instant, leaving a hollow silence behind. "What exactly," Bakshi began, "would the secret government want us to do . . ." Chill irony entered his voice. ". . . for the people's love."

"There are cells of resisters forming all over the city," Sula said, "but they have no way to communicate or coordinate with each other." Again she looked at them all in turn. "You *already* have a paramilitary structure. You *already* have means of communication that the government doesn't control. What we'd like you to do is to coordinate these groups. Pass information up the chain of command, pass orders downward, make certain equipment gets where it's needed . . . that sort of thing."

There was another moment of silence. Then Bakshi extruded one index finger from a big, pale hand and tapped the table. In a man so silent and restrained, the gesture seemed as dramatic as a pistol shot. "I should like to know one thing," Bakshi said. "Lord Governor Pahn-ko has been captured and executed. Who is it, exactly, who runs the secret government?"

Sula clenched her teeth to avoid a wail of despair. This was the one question she'd dreaded.

She had decided that she could lie to anyone else as circumstances demanded, but that she would never lie to the people at the table before her. The consequences of lying to them were simply too dire.

"I am the senior officer remaining," she said.

Surprise widened Patel's eyes. His mouth dropped open, but he didn't say anything. Tan-dau gave Bakshi a sidelong glance.

"You are a lieutenant," Bakshi said, "and young, and recently promoted at that."

"That is true," Sula said. She could feel sweat collecting under the blond wig. "But I am also a Peer of ancient name, and a noted killer of Naxids."

"It seems to me," Tan-dau said, again seeming to address no one in particular, "that she wishes us to organize and fight her war for her. I wonder what it is that *she* will contribute?"

Defiant despair rose in Sula. "My training, my name, and my skill at killing Naxids," she answered.

Bakshi looked at her. "I'm sure your skill and courage are up to the task," he said. "But of course you are a soldier." He looked at the folk on either side of him and spread his hands. "We, on the other hand, are men of commerce and of peace. We have our businesses and our families to consider. If we join your resistance to the Naxids, we put all we have worked for in jeopardy."

Sula opened her mouth to speak, but Bakshi held up a hand for silence. "You have assured us that the loyalist Fleet will return and that Zanshaa will be freed from Naxid rule. If that is the case, there is no need for an army here on the ground. But if you are wrong, and the Naxids aren't driven out, then any resisters here in the capital are doomed." He gave a slow shake of his head. "We wish you the best, but I don't understand why we should involve ourselves. The risk is too great."

Another heavy silence rose. A leaden hopelessness beating through her veins, Sula looked at the others. "Do you all agree?" she asked.

Tan-dau and Sagas said nothing. Patel gave a rueful grin. "Sorry the love thing didn't work out, princess," he said. "It could have been fun."

"The Naxids are already nibbling at your businesses," Sula said. "When rationing starts and you go into the food business, you'll be competing directly with the clans the Naxids have set in power. It's then that you'll be challenging them directly, and they'll have to destroy you."

Bakshi gave her another of his dead-eyed looks. "What makes you think we'll involve ourselves in illegal foodstuffs?"

"A market in illegal foodstuffs is inevitable," Sula said.

"If you don't put yourselves at the head of it, you'll lose control to the people who do."

There was another long silence. Bakshi spread his hands. "There's nothing we can do, my lady." He turned to Casimir and gave him a deliberate stone-eyed look. "Our associates can do nothing either."

"Of course not, Sergius," Casimir murmured.

Sula looked down her nose at them each in turn, but none offered anything more. Her hands clenched behind her back, the nails scoring her palms. She wanted to offer more arguments, weaker ones even, but knew it would be useless and did not.

"I thank you then, for agreeing to hear me," she said, and turned to Tan-dau. "I appreciate your offering this place for the meeting."

"Fortune attend you, my lady," Tan-dau said formally.

Fortune was precisely what had just deserted her. She gave a brisk military nod to the room in general and made a proper military turn.

Macnamara anticipated her and stepped to the rear of the room, holding the door for her. She marched out with her shoulders still squared, her blond head high.

Bastards, she thought.

There was a thud behind her as Macnamara tried to close the door just as Casimir tried to walk through the doorway. Macnamara glared at Casimir as he shouldered his way out and fell into step alongside Sula.

"That went better than I'd expected," he said.

She gave him a look. "I don't need irony right now."

"Not irony," he said pleasantly. "That could have gone a *lot* worse."

"I don't see how."

"Oh, I knew they wouldn't agree with you this time around. But they listened to you. You gave them things to think about. Everything you said will be a part of their calculations from now on." He looked at her, amused appreciation glittering in his eyes. "You're damned impressive, I must say. Standing there all alone staring at those people as if they'd just come up from the sewer smelling of shit." He shook his head. "And I have no idea how you do that thing with your voice. I could have sworn when I met you that you were born in Riverside."

"There's a reason I got picked for this job," Sula said.

And her ability to do accents wasn't it. She and Martinez had just blown apart and she'd thought that killing people or getting killed herself would be a welcome distraction from her miseries. Her idiot superiors had taken her, and now here she was.

There was a moment of silence as they all negotiated the front door of the club. This time, at least, Macnamara didn't try to slam the door on Casimir. Score one, she thought, for civility.

The delay at the door gave Julien time to catch up. He caught his breath in the copper-plated corridor outside, then turned to Sula. "Sorry about that," he said. "Better luck next time, hey?"

"I'm sure you did your best," Sula said. It was all she could do not to snarl.

"Tan-dau got wounded in an assassination attempt last year, and he's not game for new adventures," Julien said. "Sagas isn't a Daimong to take chances. And Pops," he gave a rueful smile, and shook his head, "Pops didn't get where he is by sticking his neck out."

"And Patel?" Sula asked.

Julien laughed. "He'd have followed you, you heard him. He'd like to fight the Naxids just for the love, like he said. But the commission's rulings are always unanimous, and he had to fall in line."

They descended the moving stairs. Sula marched to the doors and walked out onto the street. The pavement was wet, and a fresh smell was in the air: there had been a brief storm while she was conducting her interview.

"Where's a cab rank?" Sula asked.

"Around the corner," said Julien, pointing. He hesitated.

"Say—I'm sorry about today, you know. I'd like to make it up to you."

Can you raise an army? Sula thought savagely. But she turned to him and said, "That would be very nice."

"Tomorrow night?" Julien said. "Come to my restaurant for dinner? It's called Two Sticks, and it's off Harmony Square. The cook's a Cree and he's brilliant."

Sula had to wonder if the Cree chef thought it was his own restaurant, not Julien's, but this was no time to ask questions of that kind. She agreed to join Julien for dinner at 2401.

"Shall I pick you up?" Casimir said. "Or are you still in transit from one place to another?"

"I'm *always* in transit," Sula lied, "and now you know why. I'll meet you at the club."

"Care to go out tonight?"

Sula decided she was too angry to play a cliqueman's girl. "Not tonight," she said. "I've got to assassinate a judge."

Casimir was taken aback. "Good luck with that," he said.

She kissed him. "See you tomorrow."

She walked with Macnamara to the cab rank and got a cab. He sat next to her in the seat, arms crossed, staring straight forward. One muscle in his jaw worked continually.

"So what's *your* problem?" Sula demanded.

"Nothing," he said. "My lady."

"Good!" she said. "Because if there's anything I don't need, it's *more fucking problems.*"

They sat in stony silence. Sula had the cab let her off two streets from her apartment. Rain had started again, and she had to sprint, her jacket pulled over her head. One-Step, sharing a vendor's awning with a few others caught in the downpour, did a double take as she ran past, her blond hair flying.

Inside, she tossed the wet wig onto the back of her chair and combed her short, dyed hair. She considered checking the news, but decided against it, knowing the news would only further irritate her.

In the end she decided a long bath was in order. Followed by her latest book of mathematical puzzles, and possibly a book she'd acquired at a stall two days ago, *The Diplomatic History of Napoleonic Europe,* something obviously printed by a history student for his own use, bound cheaply, then discarded. It was just the sort of page-turner she most enjoyed.

She took the book into the bath with her and found it an ambiguous comfort. Compared with the likes of Paul II or Godoy, her own superiors seemed positively . . . *brilliant.*

After her bath, she wrapped herself in a robe and went to the front room. The rain was still pouring down. For a long moment she watched her *ju yao* pot as the crackled glaze reflected the beads of water that snaked down the window.

While watching the pot an idea occurred to her.

"Ah. Hah," she said. The idea seemed an attractive one. She examined it carefully, probing it with her mind like a tongue examining the gap left by a missing tooth.

The idea began to seem better and better. She got a fresh piece of paper and a pen and outlined it, along with all possible ramifications.

There wasn't a problem that she could see. Nor a way it could be traced to her.

Perhaps she could credit the influence of Metternich or Castlereagh or Talleyrand for the idea. Perhaps the afternoon of staring into Sergius Bakshi's predator-fish eyes and wondering what was going on behind them.

Or perhaps the scheme came entirely from her own mind, from the mind that floated with the reflection of the raindrops on the window. In which case, she really had to admire her brain.

She destroyed the paper, leaving no evidence of her scheme. She looked at her right thumb, the thick pad of scar tissue where her print had once been.

It was very important that she not leave her fingerprints on this one.

NINETEEN

In the morning, Sula made deliveries with Macnamara and Spence. Macnamara was a little stiff but at least he wasn't sulking too visibly.

In the afternoon, she went to the Petty Mount for a shopping expedition, and wore the result to meet Casimir at the Cat Street club. She was late, and as she approached the club with her large shoulder bag banging her hip with every stride, she found Casimir pacing the pavement next to the apricot-colored car. He was scowling down at the ground, his coat floating behind him like a cloak.

He looked up at her and relief flooded his face. Then he saw how she was dressed, in a long coat, black covered with shiny six-pointed particolored stars, like a rainbow snowfall.

"You got a coat like mine," he said, surprised.

"Yes. We need to talk."

"We can talk in the car." He gestured toward the door.

"No. I need more privacy than that. Let's try your office."

Petulance tugged at his lip. "We're already late."

"Julien will be all right. His chef is brilliant."

He nodded as if this remark made sense and followed her through the club. There were few patrons at this early hour, mostly quiet drinkers at the bar or workers who hadn't managed to get home in time for dinner.

Sula bounded up the metal stairs leading to Casimir's office. "How did the judge thing go?" he asked.

She had to search her mind for a moment to recall the story.

"Postponed," she said.

He let her into his office. "Is that what you need to talk about? Because even though Sergius said I wasn't supposed to help you, there are a few things I can do that Sergius doesn't need to know about. Because— Oh, damn."

They had entered his office, the spotless black-and-white room, and Sula had thrown her bag on a sofa and opened her coat to reveal that she wore nothing underneath it but stockings and her shoes.

"Damn," Casimir repeated. His eyes traveled over her. "Damn, you're beautiful."

"Don't just stand there," Sula said.

It was the first time she had set out to please a man so totally and for so long. She moved Casimir over the room from one piece of furniture to the other. She took full advantage of the large, oversoft chairs. She used lips and tongue and fingertips, skin and scent, whispers and laughter. She would never have dared try this with Martinez— with him, she lacked this brand of confidence. There was something whorish about it, she supposed, though her own violent, mercifully brief encounter with whoring had been far more sordid and unpleasant than this.

She kept Casimir busy for an hour and a half, until the chiming of his comm grew far too insistent. He rose from one of the sofas, where he was sprawled with Sula on top of him, and made his way to his desk.

"Audio only," he told the comm. "Answer. Yes, what is it?"

"Julien's arrested," said an unknown voice.

Sula sat up, an expression of concern on her face.

"When?" Casimir barked. "Where?"

"A few minutes ago, at the Two Sticks. He was there with Veronika."

Calculation burned in Casimir's gaze. "Was it the police or the Fleet?"

The voice shifted to a higher, more urgent register. "It was the *Legion*. They took *everybody*."

Casimir stared intently at the far wall as if it held a puzzle he needed badly to put together. Sula rose and quietly walked to where her large shoulder bag waited. She opened it and began to withdraw clothing.

"Does Sergius know?" Casimir asked.

"He's not at his office. That's the only number I have for him."

"Right. Thanks. I'll call him myself."

Casimir knew he couldn't get away with a video-suppressed call to Sergius Bakshi, so he put on a shirt and combed his hair. He spoke in low tones and Sula heard little of what was said. She finished dressing, took a pistol from her bag and stuck it in her waistband behind her back.

Casimir finished his phone call. He looked at her with somber eyes.

"You'd better make yourself scarce," Sula said. "They might be going after all of you."

"That's what Sergius told me," he said.

"Or maybe," Sula's eyes narrowed, "they're after *you*, and they went to the Two Sticks thinking you'd be there."

"Or they might be after *you*," Casimir said, "and Julien and I are both incidental."

"That hadn't occurred to me," she said.

Casimir began to draw on his clothing. "This looks bad," he said. "But maybe you'll get what you want."

She looked at him.

"War," he explained, "between us and the Naxids."

"That *had* occurred to me," she said.

It had occurred to her the previous night, in fact, while she gazed at reflections of raindrops in her *ju yao* pot. Which was why, that morning, she'd gone to a public comm unit. She wore a worker's coveralls and the blond wig and a wide-brimmed hat pulled down over her face, and she'd taken the hat off her head and put it over the unit's camera before she manually punched in the code that would connect her to the Legion of Diligence informer line.

"I want to give some information," she said. "An anarchist cell is meeting tonight in a restaurant called the Two Sticks, off Harmony Square. They are planning sabotage. The meeting is set for twenty-four and one, in a private room. Don't tell the local police, because they're corrupt and would warn the saboteurs."

She'd used the Earth accent that had once amused Caro Sula. She walked away from the comm without removing her hat from the camera pickup.

She must have been convincing because Julien was now under arrest.

"How shall I contact you?" Sula asked Casimir.

He adjusted his trousers, then gave her a code.

Sula nodded. "Got it."

He gave her a quizzical look. "You don't need to write it down?"

"I compose a mental algorithm that will allow me to remember the number," she said. "It's what I do with everyone's numbers."

He blinked. "Clever trick," he said.

She kissed him. "Yes," she said. "A very clever trick."

The next day the Naxids went berserk. Someone with a rifle went onto a building overlooking the Axtattle Parkway, the main highway that connected Zanshaa City with the Naxids' landing field at Wi-hun. The sniper waited for a convoy of Naxid vehicles to go by, then shot the driver of the first vehicle. Because the vehicles were using the automated lanes, the vehicle cruised on under computer control with a dead driver behind the controls. Then the sniper shot the next driver, and the next.

By the time the Naxids got things sorted out, at least eight Naxids were dead, and more wounded. The sniper, who was clearly using a weapon much better than the Sidney Mark One, made a clean getaway.

The Naxids decided to shoot fifty-one hostages for every dead Naxid. Sula had no idea how they decided on fifty-one. It wasn't even a prime number.

Maybe whoever gave the order didn't know that.

Casimir, who heard the news before anyone else, called Sula shortly after dawn to tell her to stay off the streets. She called the other members of Team 491 and told them to stay where they were, then stuck her head out the door and told One-Step to make himself scarce.

She spent the morning in her apartment with her book of diplomatic history and her mathematical puzzles. At midday her comm chimed with a message that Rashtag, the head of security for the Records Office, had changed his password for the Records Office computer. The new password was included in the message, so she contacted the Records Office computer and found that the Naxids had worked out how *Resistance* was being distributed.

Rashtag was ordered to change the passwords of everyone in the office and to watch the office's broadcast node for signs of unusual activity. Neither of these worried Sula: she would always get Rashtag's new password when he changed it; and when she distributed *Resistance,* she always turned off the logging on the broadcast node, so there would be no record of the node being used. It would require some fairly high-level coordination to detect her, and she saw no sign of that as yet.

It was only a matter of time, however.

Casimir called again after nightfall. "Can we meet?" he asked.

"Is it safe to go out?"

"The police have finished rounding up new hostages to replace the ones they shot today, and they're back to processing ration cards. But just in case I'll send a car."

She told him to pick her up at the local train stop. He gave her a time. The car was a dark Hunhao sedan with one of the Torminel bodyguards at the controls. He took her to a small residential street on the edge of a Cree neighborhood—she saw Cree males on the streets exercising their quadruped females, who bounded about them like large puppies.

Casimir was in the apartment of a smiling, elderly couple who apparently did very well for themselves renting out their spare room as a safe house. The room was roomy and comfortable, with flower pots on the windowsills, fringed throw rugs, the scent of potpourri, family pictures on the walls, and a macramé border around the wall video. The remains of Casimir's dinner sat on a tray along with a half-empty bottle of sparkling wine.

Sula kissed him hello and put her arms around him. His flesh was warm. His cologne had a pleasant earthy scent.

"I think we've got a false alarm," Casimir said. "The Legion doesn't seem to be after me. Or Sergius, or anyone but Julien. There haven't been any raids. No inquiries. Nobody's been seen doing surveillance."

"That may change if Julien talks," Sula said.

Casimir drew back. His face hardened. It was as if she'd just challenged the manhood of the whole Riverside Clique.

"Julien won't talk," he said. "He's a good boy."

"You don't know what they're going to do to him. The Naxids are serious. We can't count on anything."

Casimir's lips gave a scornful twitch. "Julien grew up with Sergius Bakshi beating the crap out of him twice a week—and not for any reason either, just for the sheer hell of it. You think Julien's going to be scared of the Naxids after *that*?"

Sula considered Sergius Bakshi's dead predator eyes and large pale listless hands and thought that Casimir had a point. "So they won't get a confession from Julien. There's still Veronika."

Casimir shook his head. "Veronika doesn't know anything." He gave her a pointed look. "She doesn't know about *you*."

"But she knows Julien was expecting the two of us for

dinner. And the Naxids will have seen that Julien was sitting at a table set for four."

Casimir shrugged. "They'll have my name and half of yours. They'll have a file on me and nothing on you. You're not in any danger."

"It's not me I'm worried about," Sula said.

He looked at her for a moment, then softened. "I'm being careful," he said in a subdued voice. He glanced around the room. "I'm here, aren't I? In this little room, running my criminal empire by remote control."

Sula grinned at him. He grinned back.

"Would you like something to eat or drink?" he asked.

"Whatever kind of soft drink they have would be fine."

He carried out his dinner tray. Sula toured the room, tidied a few of Casimir's belongings that had been carelessly discarded, then took off her shoes and sat on the floor. Casimir returned with two bottles of Citrine Fling. He seemed surprised to find her on the floor but joined her without comment. He handed her a bottle and touched it with his own. The resinous material made a light thud rather than a crystal ringing sound. He made a face.

"Here's to our exciting evening," he said.

"We'll have to make all the excitement ourselves," Sula said.

His eyes glittered. "Absolutely." He took a sip of his drink, then gave her a reflective look. "I know even less about Lady Sula than I do about Gredel."

She looked at him. "What do you want to know?"

There was a troubled look in his eye. "That story about your parents being executed. I suppose that was something that you said to get close to me."

Sula shook her head. "My parents were executed when I was young. Flayed."

He was surprised. "Really?"

"You can look it up if you want to. I'm in the military because it's the only job I'm permitted."

"But you're still a Peer."

"Yes. But as Peers go, I'm poor. All the family's wealth and property were confiscated." She looked at him. "You've probably got scads more money than I do."

Now he was even more surprised. "I've never met a whole lot of Peers, but you always get the impression they're rolling in it."

"I'd like to have enough to roll in." She laughed, took a sip of her Fling. "Tell me. If they don't find Julien guilty of anything, what happens to him?"

"The Legion? They'll try to scare the piss out of him, then let him go."

Sula considered this. "Are the Naxids letting *anyone* go at all? Or does everyone they pick up for any reason join the hostage population in the lockups?"

He looked at her and ran a pensive thumb down his jaw. "I hadn't thought of that."

"Plus he could be hostage for his father's good behavior." Casimir was thoughtful.

"Where would they send him?" Sula asked.

"Anywhere. The Blue Hatches, the Reservoir. Any jail or police station." He frowned. "Certain police stations he could walk right out of."

"Let's hope he gets sent to one of those then."

"Yes. Let's."

His eyes were troubled.

Good, she thought. There were certain thoughts she wanted him to dwell on for a while.

The first use of the Sidney Mark One rifle came the next morning, as a car drew up alongside two Naxid members of the Urban Patrol and gunned them down. Unfortunately, the driver failed to make a successful escape and three young Terrans were killed in a shootout that left two more members of the Patrol wounded.

Despite the fact that the assassins had been killed, the Naxids shot seventy-two hostages anyway. Why seventy-two? she wondered.

Team 491, alerted by Casimir through the Riverside Clique's contacts in the police, stayed indoors for the day.

By then Sidney had his Mark Two ready. Sula called him as the team were out making deliveries, and he said things were excellent, not first-class, and she could pick up her package.

The Mark Two was a pistol, small and useful for assassination, that used the same ammunition as the Mark One. It came complete with designs for a sound suppressor.

Sula kissed Sidney on his smoky mouth, gave him enough money to pay the next month's rent on his shop, and let PJ buy them all lunch.

Meanwhile, Julien had been cleared of suspicion by the Legion of Diligence, though he was remaining in custody as a hostage. Casimir called to tell Sula. "He's in the Reservoir prison, damn it," he said. "There's no way we can get him out of there."

Calculations shimmered through her mind. "Let me think about that," she replied.

There was a moment of silence. Then, "Should we get together and talk about it?"

Sula knew there were certain things one shouldn't say over a comm, and they were skating right along the edge. "Not yet," she said. "I've got some research to do first."

She spent some time in public databases, researching the intricacies of the Zanshaa legal system, and more time with back numbers of the *Forensic Register,* the publication of the Zanshaa Legal Association. More time was spent seeing who in the *Register* had left Zanshaa with the old government and who hadn't.

Having gathered her data, Sula called Casimir and told him she needed him to set up a meeting with Sergius. While waiting to hear back from him, she prepared the next number of *Resistance.*

In addition to including plans for the Sidney Mark Two, she praised the Axtattle sniper—"a member of the Eino Kangas wing of the secret army"—and eulogized the assassins of the Urban Patrol officers as "members of the Action Front, an organization allied with the secret government." She hoped the realization that they had *two* organizations fighting them now would drive the Naxids crazy.

When Casimir called, he told her the meeting had been arranged. Sula removed her contacts, donned her blond wig, and went to the Cat Street club to meet him.

Sergius Bakshi and Casimir had resumed their normal lives after the Legion had released Julien to the prison system, as Sula was taken to meet Sergius in his office, on the second floor of an unremarkable building in the heart of Riverside.

She and Casimir passed through an anteroom of flunkies and hulking guards, all of whom she regarded with patrician hauteur, and into Sergius's own office, where he rose to greet her. The office was as unremarkable as the building, with scuffed floors, second-hand furniture, and the musty smell of things that had been left lying too long in corners.

People with real power, Sula thought, didn't need to show it.

Sergius took her hand, and though the touch of his big hand was light, she could sense the restrained power in his grip. "What may I do for you, Lady Sula?" he asked.

"Nothing right now," she said. "Instead, I hope to be of service to you."

The ruthless eyes flicked to Casimir, who returned an expression meant to convey that he knew what Sula proposed to offer. Sergius returned his attention to her.

"I appreciate your thinking of me," he said. "Please sit down."

At least, Sula thought, she got to sit down this time. Sergius began to move behind his desk again.

"I believe I can get Julien out of the Reservoir," Sula said.

Sergius stopped moving, and for the first time, she saw emotion in his dark eyes; a glimpse into a black void of deep-seated desire that seemed all the more frightening in a man who normally appeared bereft of feeling.

Whether Sergius wanted his son back because he loved him or because Julien was a mere possession that some caprice of fate had taken from him, it was clearly a deep, burning hunger, a need as clear and primal and rapacious as that of a hungry panther for his dinner.

Sergius looked at her for a long moment, the need burning in his eyes, then straightened in his shabby chair and clasped his big pale hands on the desk in front of him. His face had again gone blank.

"That's interesting," he said.

"I want you to understand that I can't set Julien at liberty," she said. "I believe I can get him transferred to the holding cells at the Riverside police station, or to any other place that suits you. You'll have to get him out of there yourself.

"I'll provide official identification for Julien that will allow him to move freely, but of course . . ." She looked into the unreadable eyes. "He'll be a fugitive until the Naxids are removed from power."

Sergius held her gaze for a moment, then nodded. "How may I repay you for this favor?" he asked.

Sula suppressed a smile. She had her list well prepared.

"The secret government maintains a business enterprise used to transfer munitions and the like from one place to another. It's operating under the cover of a food distribution service. Since food distribution is about to become illegal, I'd like to be able to operate this enterprise under your protection, and without the usual fees."

Sula wondered if she was imagining the hint of a smile that played about Sergius Bakshi's lips. "Agreed," he said.

"I would also like ten Naxids to die."

One eyebrow gave a twitch. "Ten?"

"Ten, and of a certain quality. Naxids in the Patrol, the Fleet, or the Legion, all of officer grade; or civil servants with ranks of CN6 or higher. And it must be clear that they've been murdered—they can't seem to die in accidents."

His voice was cold. "You wish this done when?"

"It's not a precondition. The Naxids may die within any reasonable amount of time after Julien is released."

Sergius seemed to thaw a little. "You will provoke the Naxids into one massacre after another."

She gave a little shrug and tried to match with her own the glossy inhumanity of the other's eyes. "That is incidental," she said.

He gave an amused, twisted little smile. It was as out of place on his round immobile face as a bray of laughter. "I'll agree to this," he said. "But I want it clear that I'll pick the targets."

"Certainly," Sula said.

"Anything else?"

"I'd like an extraction team on hand, just in case my project doesn't go well. I don't expect we'll need them, though."

"Extraction team?" Sergius's lips formed the unaccustomed syllables, and then his face relaxed into the one he probably wore at home, which was still, in truth, frightening enough.

"I suppose you'd better tell me about this plan of yours," he said.

Sula's legal research told her that three sets of people had the authority to move prisoners from one location to another. There was the prison bureaucracy itself, which housed the prisoners, shuttled them to and from interrogations and trials, and worked them in innumerable factories and agricultural communes. All those in the bureaucracy with the authority to sign off on prisoner transfers were now Naxids. Sergius apparently hadn't yet gotten any of them on his payroll, or Julien would already have been shifted out of the Reservoir.

The second group consisted of Judges of the High Court

272 • Walter Jon Williams

and of Final Appeal, all of whom had been evacuated before the Naxid fleet arrived. The new administration had replaced them all with Naxids.

The third group were Judges of Interrogation. It was not a prestigious posting, and some had been evacuated and some hadn't. Apparently, Sergius didn't have any of these in his pocket, either.

Lady Mitsuko Inada was one of those who hadn't left Zanshaa. She lived in Green Park, a quiet, wealthy enclave on the west side of the city. The district had none of the ostentation or flamboyant architecture of the High City—probably none of the houses had more than fifteen or sixteen rooms. Those homes still occupied by their owners tried to radiate a comfortable air of wealth and security but were undermined by the untended gardens and shuttered windows of the neighboring buildings, abandoned by their owners, who had fled to another star system or, failing that, to the country.

Lady Mitsuko's dwelling was on the west side of the park, which was the least expensive and least fashionable. It was built of gray fieldstone, with a green alloy roof, an onion dome of greenish copper, and two ennobling sets of chimney pots. The garden in front was mossy and frondy, with ponds and fountains. There were willows in the back, which suggested more ponds.

Peers constituted about two percent of the empire's population, and as a class, controlled more than ninety percent of its wealth. But there was immense variation within the order of Peers, ranging from individuals who controlled the wealth of entire systems to those who lived in genuine poverty. Lady Mitsuko was on the lower end of the scale. Her job didn't entitle her to an evacuation, and neither did her status within the Inada clan.

All Peers, even the poor ones, were guaranteed an education and jobs in the Fleet, civil service, or bar. It was possible that Lady Mitsuko had worked herself up to her current status from somewhere lower.

Sula rather hoped she had. If Lady Mitsuko had a degree of social insecurity, it might work well for Sula's plans.

Macnamara drove her to the curb in front of the house. He wore a dark suit and a brimless round cap and looked like a professional driver. He opened Sula's door from the outside, and helped her out with a hand gloved in Devajjo leather.

"Wait," she told him, though he would anyway, since that was the plan.

Neither of them looked at the van cruising along the far side of the park, packed with heavily armed Riverside Clique gunmen.

Sula straightened her shoulders—she was Fleet again, in her blond wig—and marched up the walk and over the ornamental bridge to the house door. With gloved fingers, to hide fingerprints, she reached for the grotesque ornamental bronze head near the door and touched the shiny spot that would alert anyone inside to the presence of a visitor. She heard chiming within, removed her uniform cap from under her arm and put it on her head. She had visited one of Team 491's storage lockers, and now wore her full dress uniform of viridian green, with her lieutenant's shoulder boards, glossy shoes, and her two medals—the Medal of Merit, Second Class, for her part in the Blitsharts rescue, and the Nebula Medal, with Diamonds, for wiping out a Naxid squadron at Magaria.

Her sidearm was a weight against one hip.

To avoid being overconspicuous, she wore a nondescript overcoat, which she removed as soon as she heard footsteps in the hall. She held it over the pistol and its holster.

The singing tension in her nerves kept her back straight, her chin high. She had to remember that she was a Peer. Not a Peer looking down her nose at cliquemen, but a Peer interacting with another of her class.

That had always been hardest—to pretend that she was born to this.

A female servant opened the door, a middle-aged Terran. She wasn't in livery, but in neat, subdued civilian clothes.

Lady Mitsuko, Sula concluded, possessed little in the way of social pretension.

Sula walked past the surprised servant and into the hall-way. The walls had been plastered beige, with little works of art in ornate frames, and her shoes clacked on deep gray tile.

"Lady Caroline to see Lady Mitsuko, please," she said, and took off her cap.

The maidservant closed the door and held out her hands for the cap and overcoat. Sula looked at her. "Go along, now," she said.

The servant looked doubtful, then gave a little bow and trotted into the interior of the house. Sula examined herself in a hall mirror of polished nickel asteroid material, ad-justed the tilt of one of her medals, and waited.

Lady Mitsuko appeared, walking quickly. She was younger than Sula had expected, in her early thirties, and very tall. Her body was angular and she had a thin slash of a mouth and a determined jaw that suggested that, as a Judge of Interrogation, she was disinclined to let prisoners get away with much. Her light brown hair was worn long and caught in a tail behind, and she wore casual clothes. She dabbed with a napkin at a food spot on her blouse.

"Lady Caroline?" she said. "I'm sorry. I was just giving the twins their supper." She held out her hand, but there was a puzzled frown on her face as she wondered whether she had met Sula before.

Sula startled her by bracing in salute, her chin high. "Lady Magistrate," she said. "I come on official business. Is there somewhere we may speak privately?"

"Yes," Lady Mitsuko replied, her hand still outheld. "Certainly."

She took Sula to her office, a small room that still had the slight aroma of the varnish used on the shelves and fur-niture of light-colored wood.

"Will you take a seat, my lady?" Mitsuko said as she closed the door. "Shall I call for refreshment?"

"That won't be necessary," Sula said. "I won't be here long." She stood before a chair but didn't sit, and waited until Lady Mitsuko stepped behind her desk before she spoke again.

"You have my name slightly wrong," Sula said. "I'm not Lady Caroline, but rather Caroline, Lady Sula."

Lady Mitsuko's eyes darted to her and she froze with one hand on the back of her office chair, her mouth parted in surprise.

"Do you recognize me?" Sula prompted.

"I . . . don't know." Mitsuko pronounced the words as if speaking a foreign language.

Sula reached into a pocket and produced her Fleet ID. "You may examine my identification if you wish," she said. "I'm on a mission for the secret government."

Lady Mitsuko pressed the napkin to her heart. The other hand reached for Sula's identification. "The secret government . . ." she said softly, as if to herself.

She sank slowly into her hair, her eyes on the ID as Sula sat down too, with her overcoat and cap in her lap. She waited for Lady Mitsuko's eyes to lift from the ID, then said, "We require your cooperation."

Mitsuko slowly extended her arm, returning Sula's identification. "What do you—what does the secret government want?" she asked.

Sula leaned forward and took her ID. "The government requires you to transfer twelve hostages from the Reservoir Prison to the holding cells at the Riverside police station. I have a list ready—will you set your comm to receive?"

Speaking slowly, as if in a daze, Lady Mitsuko readied her comm. Sula triggered her sleeve display to send to the desk comm the names of Julien, Veronika, nine prisoners chosen at random from the official posted list of hostages, and—just because she was feeling mischievous when she made the list—the Two Sticks' Cree cook.

"We expect the order to be sent tomorrow," Sula said. She cleared her throat in a businesslike way. "I am authorized to say that after the return of the legitimate government, your loyalty will be rewarded. On the other hand, if the prisoner transfer does not take place, you will be assassinated."

Mitsuko's look was scandalized. She stared at Sula for a blank second, then seemed to notice for the first time the holstered pistol at Sula's hip. Her eyes jumped away and she made a visible effort to collect herself.

"What reason shall I give for the transfer?" she said.

"Whatever seems best to you. Perhaps they need to be interrogated in regard to certain crimes. I'm sure you can come up with a good reason." Sula rose from her chair. "I shan't keep you."

And best regards to the twins. Sula considered adding that, a clear malicious threat to the children, but decided it was unnecessary.

She rather thought that she and Lady Mitsuko had reached an understanding.

Mitsuko escorted her to the door, lost in thought, her movements disconnected, as if her nervous system hadn't quite caught up with events. At least she didn't look as if she'd panic and run for the comm as soon as the door closed.

Sula threw the overcoat over her shoulders. "Allow me to wish you a good evening, Lady Magistrate," she said.

"Um . . . good evening, Lady Sula," Lady Mitsuko replied.

Macnamara waited in the car, and leaped out to open the door as soon as Sula appeared. She tried not to run over the ornamental bridge and down the path, and instead managed a brisk, military clip.

The car hummed away from the curb as fast as its four electric engines permitted, and made the first possible turn. By the time the vehicle had gone two streets, Sula had squirmed out of her military tunic and silver-braided trousers. The blouse she'd worn beneath the tunic was suitable as casual summer ware, and she jammed her legs into a pair of bright summery pantaloons. The military kit and the blond wig went into a laundry bag. The holster shifted to the small of her back.

The van carrying the extraction team roared up behind, and both vehicles pulled to a stop: Sula and Macnamara transferred to the van, along with the laundry bag. Another driver hopped into the car—he would drive it to the parking stand of the local train, where it could be retrieved at leisure.

As Sula jumped through the van's clamshell door, she saw the extraction team, Spence, Casimir, and four burly men from Julien's crew, all bulky with armor and with weapons resting in their laps. Another pair sat in front. The interior of the van was blue with tobacco smoke. Laughter burst from her at their grim look.

"Put the guns away," she said. "We won't be needing them."

Triumph blazed through her veins. She pulled Macnamara into the van, and then, because there were no more seats, dropped onto Casimir's lap. As the door hummed shut and the van pulled away, she put her arms around Casimir's neck and kissed him.

She knew that Sergius and the whole Riverside Clique couldn't have managed what she'd just done. They could have sniffed around the halls of justice for someone to bribe, and probably already had without success; but none of them could have convinced a Peer and a judge to sign a transfer order of her own free will. If they'd approached Lady Michiko, she would have brushed them off; if they'd threatened her, she would have ordered their arrest.

It took a Peer to unlock a Peer's cooperation—and not with a bribe, but with an appeal to legitimacy and class solidarity.

Casimir's lips were warm, his breath sweet. Macnamara, without a seat, crouched on the floor behind the driver and looked anywhere but at Sula sitting on Casimir's lap. The cliquemen nudged each other and grinned. Spence watched with frank interest: Peer and criminal was probably a pairing she hadn't seen on her romantic videos.

The driver kept off the limited-access expressways, taking the smaller streets. Even so, he managed to get stuck in traffic. The van inched forward as the minutes ticked by, and then the driver cursed.

"Damn! Roadblock ahead!"

In an instant Sula was off Casimir's lap and peering forward. She could see Naxids in the black-and-yellow uniforms of the Motor Patrol. Their four-legged bodies snaked eerily from side to side as they moved up and down the line of vehicles, peering at the drivers. One vehicle was stopped while the patrol rummaged through its cargo compartment. Their van was on a one-way street, its two lanes choked with traffic; it was impossible to turn around.

Her heart was thundering as it never had when confronting Sergius or Lady Mitsuko. Ideas flung themselves at her mind and burst from her lips in not quite complete sentences. "Place to park?" she said urgently. "Garage? Pretend to make a delivery?"

The answer was no. Parking was illegal, there was no garage to turn into, and all the businesses on the street were closed at this hour.

Casimir's shoulder clashed with hers as he came forward to scan the scene before them. "How many?"

"I can see seven," Sula said. "My guess is, there are two or three more we can't see from here. Say ten." She pointed ahead, to an open-topped vehicle partly on the sidewalk, with a machine gun mounted on the top and a Naxid standing behind it, the sun gleaming off his black-beaded scales.

"Starling," she said to Macnamara. "That gun's your target."

Macnamara had been one of the best shots on the training course, and his task was critical since the gunner had to be taken out first. The Naxid didn't even have to touch his weapon, just put the reticule of his targeting system on the van and press the *Go* button: the gun itself would handle the rest, and riddle the vehicle with a couple thousand rounds.

And then the driver of the Naxid vehicle would have to be killed, because he could operate the gun from his own station.

A spare rifle had been brought for Sula, and she reached for it. There was no spare suit of armor, and she suddenly felt the hollow in her chest where bullets would strike.

"We've got two police coming down the line toward us. One on either side. You two"—she indicated the driver and the other man in the front of the van—"pop them right at the start. The rest of us will exit the rear of the vehicle— Starling first, to give him time to set up on the gunner. The rest of you keep advancing—you're as well-armed as the patrol, and you've got surprise. If things don't work out, we'll split up into small groups—Starling and Ardelion, you're with me. We'll hijack vehicles in nearby streets and get out as well as we can."

Her mouth was dry by the time she finished, and she licked her lips with a sandpaper tongue. Casimir was grinning at her.

"Nice plan," he said.

Total fuckup, she thought, but gave what she hoped was an encouraging nod. She crouched on the rubberized floor of the van and readied her rifle.

"Better turn the transponder on," Casimir said, and the driver gave a code phrase to the van's comm unit.

Every vehicle in the empire was wired to report its location at regular intervals to a central data store. The cliquemen's van had been altered to make this an option rather than a requirement, and the function had been turned off while the van was on its mission to Green Park. An unresponsive vehicle, however, was bound to be suspicious in the eyes of the patrol.

"Good thought," Sula breathed.

"Here they come." Casimir ducked down behind the seat. He gave Sula a glance—his cheeks flushed with color, his eyes glittering like diamonds. His grin was brilliant.

Sula felt her heart surge in response. She answered his grin, but that wasn't enough, and lunged across the distance between them to kiss him hard.

Live or die, she thought. Whatever came, she was ready.

"They're pinging us," the driver growled. One of the patrol had raised a hand comm and activated the transponder.

The van coasted forward, then halted. Sula heard the front windows whining open to make it easier to shoot the police on either side.

The van had a throat-tickling odor of tobacco and terror. From her position on the floor she could see the driver holding a pistol alongside his seat. His knuckles were white on the grip. Her heart sped like a turbine in her chest. Tactical patterns played themselves out in her mind.

She heard the footfalls of one of the patrol, walking close, and kept her eyes on the driver's pistol. The second it moved, she would act.

Then the driver gave a startled grunt and the van surged forward. The knuckles relaxed on the pistol.

"She waved us through," the driver said.

There was a moment of disbelieving silence, then the rustle and shift of ten tense, frightened, heavily armed people all relaxing at once.

The van accelerated. Sula's breath sighed slowly from her lungs and she put her rifle carefully down on the floor of the vehicle. She turned to the others, saw at least six cigarettes being lit, laughed and sat heavily on the floor.

Casimir turned to her, his expression filled with savage wonder. "That was lucky," he said.

She didn't answer. She only looked at him, at the pulse throbbing in his neck, the slight glisten of sweat at the base of his throat, the fine mad glitter in his eyes. She had never wanted anything so much.

"Lucky," he said again.

In Riverside, when the van pulled up outside the Hotel of Many Blessings, she was careful not to touch him as she followed Casimir out of the van—the others would store the weapons—and then went with him to his suite, keeping half a pace apart on the elevator.

He turned to her then, and she reached forward and tore open his shirt so she could lick the burning adrenaline from his skin.

His frenzy equaled hers. Their blood smoked with the excitement of shared danger, and the only way to relieve the heat was to spend it on each other.

They laughed. They shrieked. They snarled. They tumbled over each other like lion cubs, claws only half sheathed. They pressed skin to skin so hard that it seemed they were trying to climb into one another.

The fury spent itself sometime after midnight. Casimir called room service for something to eat. Sula craved chocolate, but there was none to be had. For a moment she considered breaking into her own warehouse to satisfy her hunger.

"For once," he said, as he cut his omelette with a fork and slid half of it onto Sula's plate, "for once you didn't sound like you came from Riverside."

"Yes?" She raised an eyebrow.

"And you didn't sound like Lady Sula either. You had some other accent, one I'd never heard before."

"It's an accent I'll use only with you," she said.

The accent of the Fabs, on Spannan. The voice of Gredel.

Lady Mitsuko signed the transfer order that morning. Transport wasn't arranged till the afternoon, so Julien and the other eleven prisoners arrived at the Riverside station late in the afternoon, about six.

Sergius Bakshi had a longstanding arrangement with the captain of the Riverside station. Julien's freedom cost two hundred zeniths. Veronika cost fifty, and the Cree cook a mere fifteen.

Julien would have been on his way by seven, but it was necessary to wait for the Naxid supervisor, the one who approved all the ration cards, to leave.

Still suffering from his interrogation, Julien limped to liberty on the night that the Naxids announced that the Committee to Save the Praxis, their own government, was already on its way from Naxas to take up residence in the High City of Zanshaa. A new Convocation would be assembled, composed both of Naxids and other races, to be the supreme governing body of their empire.

"Here's hoping we can give them a hot landing," Sula said. She was among the guests at Sergius's welcome-home dinner, along with Julien's mother, a tall, gaunt woman, forbidding as a statue, who burst into tears at the sight of him.

Veronika was not present. Interrogation had broken a cheekbone and the orbit of one eye: Julien had called a surgeon, and in the meantime provided painkillers.

"*I'll* give them a welcome," Julien said grimly, through lips that had been bruised and cut. "I'll rip the bastards to bits."

Sula looked across the table at Sergius and silently mimed the word "ten" at him. He smiled at her, and when he looked at Julien, the smile turned hard.

"Ten," he said. "Why stop there?"

Sula returned the smile. At last she had her army. Her own team of three plus a tough, disciplined order of killers who had decided, after all—and after a proper show of resistance—to be loved.

TWENTY

Time passed. Martinez dined with Husayn and Mersenne on successive days, and the next day spent eight hours in Command, taking *Illustrious* through the wormhole to Osser. Squadrons of decoys were echeloned ahead of the squadron, in hopes of attracting any incoming missiles. Pinnaces flew along with the decoys, painting the vacuum ahead with their laser range finders. Every antimissile weapon was charged and pointed dead ahead.

Chenforce made some final-hour maneuvers before passing the wormhole, checking their speed and entering the wormhole at a slightly different angle, so as to appear in the Osser system on a course that wouldn't take them straight on to Arkhan-Dohg, the next system, but slightly out of the direct path.

Martinez lay on his acceleration couch, trying not to gnaw his nails as he stared at the sensor displays, waiting for the brief flash that would let him know that missiles were incoming. His tension gradually eased as the returning radar and laser signals revealed more of the Osser system, and then a new worry began to possess him.

The Naxids would have to wonder why Chenforce had changed its tactics, particularly when they hadn't met any genuine opposition since Protipanu, at the very beginning of their raid. If the Naxids analyzed the raiders' maneuvers, then reasoned backward to find what the tactics were intended to prevent, they would be able to see that Michi

Chen and her squadron was concerned about a missile barrage fired at relativistic velocities.

If the tactic hadn't yet occurred to the Naxids, Chenforce might now be handing them the idea.

But that was a worry for another day. For the present it was enough to see that the ranging lasers were finding nothing, that more and more of the system was being revealed without an enemy being found, and that Chenforce was as safe from attack as it was ever going to be.

Eight hours after they entered the new system, Martinez finally asked permission from Michi to secure from general quarters, and *Illustrious* dropped to a lower level of alert. He returned to his paperwork, but it was all he could do to avoid calling the officer of the watch every few minutes to make certain the squadron wasn't flying into jeopardy.

Days passed. Martinez conducted regular inspections to learn his ship and crew and to confirm the information reported on the 77-12s. He dined in rotation with Lord Phillips, who was scarcely more talkative than at their previous meeting; with Lieutenant Lady Juliette Corbigny, whose nervous chatter was a contrast to her silence in the presence of the squadcom; and with Acting Lieutenant Lord Themba Mokgatle, who had been promoted to the vacancy left as Chandra shuttled to Michi's staff.

Late one day, as Martinez sipped his cocoa and gazed at the painting of the woman, child, and cat, he realized that there was another figure, a man who sat on a bed opposite the fire from the woman and her baby. He hadn't noticed him because the painting was dark and needed cleaning, and the man wasn't illuminated by the fire. One moment he wasn't there, and the next Martinez suddenly saw him, head bent with a stick or staff in his hands, appearing like a ghost from behind the painted red curtain.

He couldn't have been more surprised if the cat had jumped from the picture into his lap.

The dim figure on the canvas was the only discovery Martinez managed during that period. The killer or killers of Captain Fletcher remained no more than a phantom. Michi grew ever more irritable, and snapped at him and Garcia both. Sometimes Martinez caught a look in her eye that seemed to say, *If you weren't family . . .*

In time, after the first breathless rush of taking command was over, he was reminded that there were too many captains' servants on the ship. He had Garcia take Rigger Espinosa and Machinist Ayutano into the Constabulary, with the particular duty of patrolling the decks on which the officers were quartered. Buckle the hair stylist was sent to aid the ship's barber. Narbonne was taken onto Martinez's service as an assistant to Alikhan, a demotion that Narbonne seemed to resent.

That left Baca, the fat, redundant cook that no one seemed to want, and Jukes. Baca was eventually taken on as an assistant to Michi's cook, a post he wasn't happy about either, and that left Martinez with his own personal artist.

Martinez called Jukes into his office to give him the news, and the man turned up in Fleet-issued undress and managed to brace rather professionally in salute. Martinez decided that tonight he must have gotten to Jukes before Jukes got to the sherry.

"I've been playing with a design for *Illustrious,*" Jukes said. "Based on folk motifs from Laredo. Would you like to see it?"

Martinez said he would. Jukes downloaded from his sleeve to the wall display, and revealed a three-dimensional model of an *Illustrious,* covered with large, jagged geometric designs in violent shades of red, yellow, and black. Nothing more unlike Fletcher's subtle, intricate pattern of pink, white, and pale green could be imagined.

Martinez looked in surprise at the cruiser, which was rotating in the display, and managed to say, "That's very different."

"That's the point. Anyone looking at *Illustrious* is going to know that Captain Martinez is on station, and that he's a bold skipper who's not afraid to stand out from the common run of officers."

Martinez suspected that he already stood out more than was good for him. He knew that Lord Tork, head of the Fleet Control Board, was not about to forgive him for achieving such prominence so quickly, not when the Fleet's whole style was based on letting family connections quietly work behind the scenes to further elevate those who had been already elevated from birth. As far as the board was concerned, any further glory won by Martinez would only be at the expense of more deserving Peers, that he should have taken his promotion and decoration and been happy to return to the obscurity from whence he'd come.

Flying that gaudy red and yellow design anywhere within Tork's domain would shriek his presence aloud in the ears of a superior who never wanted to hear his voice again. It would be like buying media time to advertise himself.

But Tork was already a lost cause, Martinez thought. A little advertising wasn't going to change anything. So why not?

"Have you considered interiors?" he asked.

Jukes had. Martinez looked at designs for the office and dining room, both as brazen as the exterior designs, one dominated by verdant jungle green and the other by dark reds and yellows that suggested sandstone cliffs standing over a desert.

"Keep working along these lines," Martinez said. "And if another theme occurs to you, feel free to work it out. We've got a lot of time." It would be ages before *Illustrious* saw a dock or underwent a refit—the raid into Naxid space would last at least another couple months, and then the Fleet would have to reunite to retake Zanshaa.

There was a whole war between *Illustrious* and any new paint job.

Still, Martinez saw no reason not to plan for a grand triumph and its aftermath, in which he could decorate *Illustrious* as if it were his private yacht. For the odds were that either he would experience a grand triumph or be blown to atoms, and for his part, he'd rather assume the former.

"I should mention at this point, my lord," Jukes said, "that Captain Fletcher was paying me sixty zeniths per month."

"I looked up the captain's accounts, and he paid you twenty," Martinez said. "For my part, I propose to pay you fifteen."

As Martinez spoke, Jukes's expressions went from smug confidence to chagrin to horror. He stared at Martinez as if he'd just turned into a creature with scales and fangs. Martinez tried not to laugh.

"I don't *need* a personal artist," he explained. "I'd rather have a rigger first class, but I don't expect I'll get one."

Jukes swallowed hard. "Yes, my lord."

"And I was thinking," Martinez said, "that when things become a little less busy, you might begin a portrait."

"A portrait," Jukes repeated dully. He didn't seem to be thinking very well through his shock, because he asked, "Whose portrait, my lord?"

"The portrait of a bold skipper not afraid to stand above the common run of officers," Martinez said. "I should look romantic and dashing and very much in charge. I shall be carrying the Golden Orb, and *Corona* and *Illustrious* should be in the picture too. Any other details I leave to you."

Jukes blinked several times, as if he'd had to reprogram part of his mind and the blinks were elements of his internal code.

"Very good, my lord," he said.

Martinez decided he might as well pay Jukes a compliment and take his mind off his misfortunes. "Thank you for changing the pictures in my cabin," he said. "The view is now a considerable improvement."

"You're welcome." Jukes took a breath and made a visible effort to reengage with the person sitting before him. "Was there a piece you particularly liked? I could locate other works in that style."

"The one with the woman and the cat," Martinez said. "Though I don't think I've seen any painting quite in that style anywhere."

Jukes smiled. "It's not precisely typical of the painter's work. That's a very old Northern European piece."

Martinez looked at him. "And North Europe is where, exactly?"

"Terra, my lord. The painting dates from before the Shaa conquest. Though I should say the *original* painting, because this may be a copy. It's hard to say, because all the documentation is in languages no one speaks anymore, and hardly anyone reads them."

"It *looks* old enough."

"It wants cleaning." Jukes gave a thoughtful pause. "You've got a good eye, my lord. Captain Fletcher bought the painting some years ago, but decided he didn't like it because it didn't seem one thing or another, and he put it in storage." His mouth gave a little twitch of disapproval. "I don't know why he took it to war with him. It's not as if the painting could be replaced if we got blown up. Maybe he wanted it with him since it was so valuable, I don't know."

"Valuable?" Martinez asked. "How valuable?"

"I think he paid something like eighty thousand for it."

Martinez whistled.

"You could probably buy it, my lord, from the captain's estate."

"Not at those prices, I can't."

Jukes shrugged. "It would depend on whether you could get a license for cult art anyway."

Martinez was startled. "Cult art. *That's* cult art?"

"*The Holy Family with a Cat,* by Rembrandt. You wouldn't know it was cultish except for the title."

Martinez considered the painting through his haze of surprise. The cult art he remembered from his visits to the

Museums of Superstition, and the other pieces he'd seen on Fletcher's cabin walls, made its subjects look elevated, or grand or noble or at the very least uncannily serene, but the plain-faced mother, the cat, and the child in red pajamas merely looked comfortably middle-class.

"The cat isn't normally seen with the Holy Family?"

A smile twitched at Jukes's lips. "No. Not the cat."

"Or the frame? The red curtain?"

"That's the contribution of the artist."

"The red pajamas?"

Jukes laughed. "No, that's just to echo the red of the curtain."

"Could the title be in error?"

Jukes shook his head. "Unlikely, my lord, though possible."

"So what makes it cult art?"

"The Holy Family is a fairly common subject, though usually the Virgin's in a blue robe, and the child is usually naked, and there are usually attendants, with some of them, ah . . ." He reached for a word. ". . . floating. This particular treatment is unconventional, but then there were no hard and fast rules for this sort of thing. Narayanguru, for example, is usually portrayed on an ayaca tree, I suppose because the green and red blossoms are so attractive, but Captain Fletcher's Narayanguru is mounted on a real tree, and it's a vel-trip, not an ayaca."

A very faint chord echoed in Martinez's mind. He sat up, lifting his head.

". . . and Da Vinci, of course, in his *Virgin of the Rocks,* did a—"

Martinez raised a hand to cut off Jukes's distracting voice. Jukes fell silent, staring at him.

"An ayaca tree," Martinez murmured. Jukes wisely did not answer.

Martinez thought furiously, trying to reach into his own head. Mention of the ayaca tree had set off a train of associations, then conclusions, but in an instant, without him having to think through a single step. He now had to consciously and carefully work backward from his conclusions through the long process to make certain that it all held together, and to find out where it had started.

Without speaking, he rose from his desk and walked to his safe. He opened a tunic button and drew out his captain's key on its elastic, inserted the key into his safe and pressed the combination. Seals popped as the door swung open, and Martinez caught a whiff of stale air. He took out the clear plastic box in which Dr. Xi had placed Fletcher's jewelry, opened it and separated the signet ring and the silver mesh ring from the gold pendant on its chain. Holding the chain up to the light, he saw the tree-shaped pendant dangling, emeralds and rubies glittering against the gold.

"An ayaca tree like this?" he asked.

Jukes squinted as he looked at the dangling pendant. "Yes," he said, "that's typical."

"Would you say that this pendant is particularly rare or unusually beautiful or stands out in any way?"

Jukes blinked at him, then frowned. "It's very well made and moderately expensive, but there's nothing extraordinary about it."

Martinez flipped the pendant into his hand and returned to his desk. "Comm," he said, "page Lieutenant Prasad."

A shadow fell across his door, and he looked up to see Marsden, the ship's secretary, with his datapad.

"My lord, if you're busy—"

"No. Come in."

"Lord Captain." Chandra's face appeared in the depths of Martinez's desk. "You paged me?"

"I have a question," Martinez said. "Did Captain Fletcher wear a pendant in the shape of a tree?"

Chandra was taken aback. "He did, yes."

"Did he wear it all the time?"

Her look grew more curious. "Yes, so far as I know he did, though he took it off when he, ah, went to bed."

Martinez raised his fist into view of the pickups on the

desk and let the pendant fall from his grasp so it dangled on the end of its chain. "This is the pendant?"

Chandra squinted, and her face distorted in the camera pickups as she stared into her sleeve display. "Looks like it, my lord."

"Thank you, Lieutenant. End transmission."

Chandra's startled face faded from the display. Martinez looked at the pendant for a long moment as excitement hummed in his nerves, and then became aware of the silence in his office, of Jukes and Marsden staring at him.

"Have a seat for a moment," he said. "This may take a while."

He was still reaching deep into his own head.

He called up a security manual onto his desk display, one intended for the Constabulary and Investigative Service. Included was a description of cults and the methods of recognizing them. He read:

> **Narayanism,** a cult based on the teachings of Narayanguru (Balambhoatdada Seth), condemned for a belief in a higher plane and for the founder's alleged performance of miracles. Narayanguru's teachings show a kinship to those of the Terran philosopher Schopenhauer, themselves condemned for nihilism. Though cult tradition maintains that Narayanguru was hanged on an ayaca tree, historical records show that he was tortured and executed by more conventional methods in the Year of the Praxis 5581, on Terra. Because of this false tradition, cultists sometimes recognize one another by carrying flowering branches of the ayaca on certain days, planting ayacas about the home, or by using the ayaca blossom on jewelry, pottery, etc. There are also the usual variety of hand and other signals.
>
> Narayanism is not a militant cult and its adherents are not believed to pose an active threat to the Peace of the Praxis, except insofar as they promote false

beliefs. The cult has recently been reported on Terra,
Preowin, and Sandama, where entire clans some-
times participate secretly in cult activity.

Martinez gazed up at Jukes and held out the pendant
dangling from his fist. "Why would Captain Fletcher wear
this pendant?" he asked. "It's not a particularly rare or precious form of art, is it?"

Jukes looked blank. "No, my lord."

"Suppose he was actually a believer," Martinez said.
"Suppose he was a genuine Narayanist."

A look of pure horror crossed Marsden's face. Martinez
looked at him in surprise. Marsden took a few moments to
find words, and when he spoke, his voice trembled with
what Martinez supposed was fury.

"Captain Fletcher, a cultist?" Marsden said. "Do you realize what you're saying? A member both of the Gombergs
and the Fletchers? A Peer of the highest possible pedigree,
with noble ancestors stretching back thousands of years—"

Martinez was taken aback by this rant, but was in no
mood for a pompous lecture on genealogy. "Marsden," he
said, cutting him off, "do you know where the personal
possessions of Thuc and Kosinic have been stored?"

Marsden's larynx moved in his throat as he visibly swallowed his indignation. "Yes, my lord," he said.

"Kindly bring them."

Marsden rose, put the datapad on his seat, and braced.
"At once, Lord Captain."

The secretary marched away, his legs stiff with anger.
Jukes looked after him in surprise.

"An odd man," he said. "I had no idea he was such a
snob." He turned to Martinez and raised an eyebrow. "Do
you really think Captain Fletcher was a cultist?"

Martinez looked at the pendant that still dangled from
his hand. "I don't know why else he'd wear this."

"Maybe it was a gift from someone he cared for."

"A *cultist* he cared for," Martinez muttered.

He leaned back in his chair and followed his chain of reasoning again, piece by piece. No part of it was implausible by itself, he decided, and therefore his ideas were better than any other theory that had come his way.

Much of it had to do with the way the Praxis viewed cults, and the way servants of the Praxis had interpreted their duty.

The Shaa had believed in many things, but they did not believe in the numinous. Any cult that promoted a belief in the supernatural was, by definition, a violation of the Praxis and illegal. When the Shaa conquered Terra, they had found the place swarming with cults, and acted over time to suppress them, gradually over many generations. Meeting houses of the faithful had been torn down, turned to secular use, or converted to museums. Believers were dismissed from government and teaching posts. Cult literature was confiscated and its reproduction forbidden. Cult organizations were disbanded, any professional clergy dismissed, and schools of instruction shut down.

Any believer determined on martyrdom was given ample opportunity to exercise his choice.

Cults had never vanished, of course. The Shaa, who were not without their own shrewd intelligence, might not have expected they would. But by forbidding the spread of doctrine, professional clergy and houses of worship, and the reproduction of literature and cult objects, they had turned what had been by all accounts a thriving business into a strictly amateur affair. If there were meetings, they were small and took place in private homes. If there were clergy, they had no opportunity for specialized study, and had to hold regular jobs. If there was literature, it was copied clandestinely and passed from hand to hand, and errors crept in and many texts were incomplete.

Believers were usually not harassed as long as they did not practice in public or proselytize, and in time they learned discretion. Though belief was not destroyed, its force was reduced and cults became indistinguishable from superstition—a set of arcane and irrational practices designed to achieve the intervention of who knew what against the inflexible workings of an unknowable fate.

There were certainly cults scattered through the empire, but most of them existed very quietly and often in fairly remote corners of the Shaa dominion. Cult members tended to marry within one another's families and avoid public service. Occasionally a governor or a local official would try to earn a name for himself by rooting them out, executing some and forcing others to renounce their beliefs, but for the most part they were left alone.

There was no point in persecution. Over the centuries, the supernatural had simply ceased to be a threat to the empire.

Marsden returned within a few moments, carrying a pair of gray plastic boxes. "I assumed you wanted possessions other than clothing, my lord," he said. "If you want to examine the clothing as well, may I requisition a hand truck?"

That would be for Kosinic's trunks containing the amazing number of uniforms required of an officer, plus his personal vac suit. Thuc would have had fewer uniforms, and used a vac suit from the ship's stores.

"The pockets would have been emptied, and so on?" Martinez asked.

"Yes, Lord Captain. Pockets are gone through, and other places where small items might be found, and anything discovered put in these boxes."

"I won't need the clothing then. Put the boxes on my desk."

Martinez opened Kosinic's box first. He found a ring from the Nelson Academy, from which Martinez had graduated before Kosinic arrived, and a handsome presentation stylus—brushed aluminum inlaid with unakite and jasper, and engraved "To Lieutenant Javier Kosinic, from his

CONVENTIONS OF WAR • 295

proud father." There was a shaving kit, a modestly priced cologne, and a nearly empty bottle of antibiotic spray that a doctor had probably given him for his wounds. Martinez found some fine paper, brushes, and watercolor paints, and looked at several finished watercolors, most of them planet-bound landscapes of rivers and trees, but including one recognizable impression of Fulvia Kazakov sitting at a table in the wardroom. To Martinez's unpracticed eye, none of the watercolors seemed particularly expert.

In a small pocketbook he found a series of foils, neatly labeled, that held music and other entertainments, and at the bottom of the box, a small pocket-sized datapad, which Martinez turned on. It asked for a password, but he wasn't able to provide one. He slotted his captain's key into it, but the datapad was a private one, not Fleet issue, and wouldn't recognize his authority. Martinez turned it off and returned it to the box.

The few belongings—the cologne and the academy ring and the inexpert watercolors—seemed to add up to an inadequate description of a life. Whatever had most mattered to Kosinic, Martinez thought, probably wasn't here: his passions remained locked in his brain, and had died with him. He looked again at the stylus, sent by the father who might not yet know that his son had been killed, and closed the box on Kosinic's life.

He turned to the box labeled THUC, H.C., MASTER ENGINEER (DECEASED), and found what he was looking for right on top.

A small enameled pendant in the form of a tree with green and red blossoms, hanging from a chain of bright metal links.

"I think there was a group of Narayanists on *Illustrious*," Martinez explained to Michi Chen. "I think Captain Fletcher was one of them. He wore a Narayanist symbol around his neck, and he had a huge statue of Narayanguru in his sleeping cabin. I think he adopted the pose of a collector of cult art so he could collect Narayanist artifacts legally, and he covered his activities by collecting artifacts from other cults as well."

"If you insist on that theory," Michi said, "you're going to have trouble with the Gombergs and Fletchers, maybe even a suit in civil court."

"Not if I'm right, I won't," Martinez said. "If there are Narayanists in either of those families, we won't hear a word from them."

Michi nodded silently. "Go on," she said.

He had asked Michi into his office on a confidential matter, and she was surprised on her arrival to find Marsden and Jukes present. Martinez called Perry to bring out coffee and snacks, and ordered Marsden to record the meeting and take notes.

"I think there were, perhaps still are, a number of Narayanists aboard," Martinez said. "Captain Fletcher protected them. Somehow, Kosinic found out about at least some of this, though possibly he didn't know the captain was a part of the arrangement. As Kosinic's knowledge was now a menace to the cultists, one of them—Thuc—killed him."

Michi nodded. "Very well," she said.

"It was a masterfully done murder, and we would never have found out about it if Captain Fletcher wasn't killed the same way and made us suspicious."

Perry and Alikhan arrived with coffee and little triangular pastries, and Martinez fell silent while everyone was served. He took an appreciative taste of the coffee and felt heat flush at once to the surface of his skin. He could feel his theories boiling in his skull, and he wanted to let them escape; he was so impatient that it took an effort for him to compliment Perry on the coffee. Finally, the two left the room and he was able to continue.

"We know that Thuc was a Narayanist because he too wore a Narayanist medallion. I think that once Kosinic was killed, Captain Fletcher began to realize that he was in a bad spot. All it would take would be a little indiscretion on the part of a petty officer, and he would be implicated in the death of a fellow officer—and not just *any* officer, but a member of the squadron commander's staff.

"He couldn't indict Thuc, because any public proceedings would expose his own membership in the cult. So he used his officers' privilege and executed Thuc during the course of an inspection."

Martinez gave a little shrug. "Everything from this point is completely speculative," he said. "I think Captain Fletcher was intent on eliminating every member of the cult in order to protect himself, but I can't be certain that he wasn't just after Thuc. In any case, one or more other cult members *assumed* that Fletcher was going after them, and they acted to kill him first."

Michi absorbed this quietly. "Do you have any idea who those other cult members might be?"

Martinez shook his head. "No, my lady. The only people I'm inclined to exempt from suspicion are Weaponer Gulik and the crew of Missile Battery Three. Fletcher inspected them on the day of his death and didn't execute any of them."

"That still leaves something like three hundred people."

"Though I would start with those among the crew who are from Sandama, like the lord captain, or who are Fletcher's clients. Dr. Xi, for example."

"Xi?" Michi was startled. "But he's been helpful."

"He helpfully explained away his own fingerprints that were found in Captain Fletcher's office."

"But he was the one who proved that Captain Fletcher was murdered in the first place. If he'd been part of the conspiracy, he would have kept silent."

Martinez opened his mouth, then closed it. *Dr. An-ku I'm not,* he thought. "Well," he said, "let's *not* start with Dr. Xi then."

She held his eyes for a moment, then her shoulders slumped as she seemed to deflate. "We're no better off than we were. You've got an interesting theory, but even if it's true, it doesn't help us."

Martinez took the two pendants, Fletcher's and Thuc's, in one large hand and held them dangling over his desk. "We searched the ship once, but we didn't know what we were looking for. Now we do. Now we're looking for these. We look in lockers and we look around necks."

"My lord." Martinez and Michi both turned at the sound of Marsden's flat, angry voice. "You should check me first, my lord. I'm from Sandama, and I was one of Captain Fletcher's clients. That makes me a double suspect, apparently."

Martinez gazed at the secretary and his annoyance flared. Marsden was offended on Fletcher's behalf, and apparently on behalf of the crew as well. A search of the crew's private effects was an insult to their dignity, and Marsden had taken it to heart. He was going to insist that if Martinez was going to violate his dignity, he was going to violate it personally, and right now.

"Very well," Martinez said, having no choice. "Kindly remove your tunic, open your shirt, and empty your pockets."

Marsden did so, a vein in his temple throbbing with suppressed fury. Martinez sorted through the contents of Marsden's pockets while the secretary pirouetted before him, arms held out at the shoulder to show he had nothing to hide. No cult objects were detected.

Martinez clenched his teeth. He had degraded another human being, and for nothing.

And the worst part was that he felt degraded himself for doing it.

"Thank you, Marsden," Martinez said. *You bastard,* he added silently.

Without a word, the ship's secretary turned his back on him and donned his tunic. When he had buttoned it, he resumed his seat, put his datapad on his lap, and picked up his stylus.

"The last inspection was too helter-skelter," Michi said. "And it took too long. This next has to be more efficient."

The two of them discussed it for a while, then Michi rose. The others rose and braced. "I'm going to dinner," she told Martinez. "After dinner we'll confine the crew to quarters and begin the search, starting with the officers."

"Very good, my lady."

She looked at Marsden and Jukes, who had spent the entire meeting sipping coffee and eating one pastry after another. "You'll have to dine with these two in your quarters. I don't want news of this getting out over dinner conversation in the mess."

Martinez suppressed a sigh. Marsden was not going to be the jolliest of guests.

"Yes, my lady," he said.

Michi took a step toward the door, then hesitated. She looked at Jukes, her brows knit. "Mr. Jukes," she said, "why exactly are you here?"

Martinez answered for him. "He happened to be in the room when I had my brainstorm."

Michi nodded. "I understand." She turned away for a moment, hesitated again, then returned her gaze to the artist. "There are crumbs on your front, Mr. Jukes," she said.

Jukes blinked. "Yes, my lady," he said.

The officers' quarters were searched first, by Martinez, Michi, and the three lieutenants on Michi's staff. The officers' persons were also searched, with the exception of Lord Phillips, who was officer of the watch and in Command.

"This is what you're looking for," Martinez told them, showing them the two pendants. "These are cult objects, representations of ayaca trees. They need not be worn around the neck—they could be a ring or a bracelet or any kind of jewelry, or they could be on cups or plates or picture frames or practically anything. *Everything needs to be examined.* Do you understand?"

"Yes, my lord," they chanted. Kazakov and Mersenne looked determined. Husayn and Mokgatle were uncertain. Corbigny seemed worried. None spoke.

"Let's go then."

The lieutenants, Martinez, Michi, and Michi's staff marched off in a body to inspect the warrant officers and their quarters. No ayaca trees were found, on jewelry or anyone else. Now reinforced by the warrant officers, the party moved on to the petty officers' quarters.

The petty officers stood braced in the corridor, out of the way, and did their best to keep their faces expressionless. Lady Juliette Corbigny held back as the other officers began going through lockers. Her white, even teeth gnawed at her lower lip. Martinez ghosted up to her shoulder.

"Is there a problem, Lieutenant?"

She gave a little jump at the question, as if he'd startled her out of deep reflection, and she turned to him with her brown eyes open very wide.

"May I speak to you privately, Lord Captain?"

"Of course." Corbigny followed him into the corridor outside, where he turned to her. "Yes?"

She was gnawing her nether lip again. She paused in her champing to say, uncertainly, "Is this a bad cult we're looking for?"

Martinez considered the question. "I'm not an expert on cults, good or bad. But I think the cultists are responsible for Captain Fletcher's death."

Corbigny began to gnaw on her lip some more. Impatience jabbed at Martinez's nerves, but instinct told him to remain silent and let Corbigny chew on herself for as long as she needed to.

"Well," she said finally, "I've seen a medallion like that on someone."

"Yes? Someone in your division?"

"No." Her eyes looked wide into his. "On an officer. On Lord Phillips."

Phillips? That can't be right. It was the first thing he

thought. He couldn't imagine little Palermo Phillips banging Fletcher's head against his desk with his tiny hands.

His second thought was, *Maybe he had help.*

"Are you sure?" Martinez asked.

Corbigny gave a nervous jerk of her head. "Yes, my
lord. I got a good look at it. I remember him running out of
the shower that day you paged him and inspected his division. He was in a hurry to get his tunic on, and the chain of
the pendant got caught on one of his buttons. I helped him
untangle it."

"Right," Martinez said. "Thank you. You may rejoin the
others."

Martinez collected Cadet Ankley, who was qualified to
stand watches, and Espinosa, his former servant who had
been shifted over to the military constabulary, then walked
straight to Command.

"The lord captain is in Command," Lord Phillips called
as he entered. Phillips rose from his couch to let Martinez
take his place if he so desired.

Martinez marched forward until he stood before Phillips,
who even fully braced failed to come up to his chin.

"My lord," Martinez said, "I'd be obliged if you'd open
your tunic."

"My lord?" Phillips stared up at him.

Suddenly Martinez didn't want to be there. He had begun to think the whole day had been a mistake. But here he
was, having joined the role of detective to his authority as
captain, and he could think of nothing but following the
path he'd set himself, wherever it took him.

"Open your tunic, Lieutenant," he said.

Phillips looked away, suddenly thoughtful. His hand
came slowly to the throat of his tunic and began undoing
the silver buttons. Martinez looked at the rapid pulse beating in Phillips's throat as the collar came open and he saw
the gold links of a chain.

Anger suddenly boiled in Martinez. He reached out,
took the chain, and brutally pulled until the pendant at the

bottom of its loop was revealed. It was an ayaca tree, red and green jewels glittering.

Martinez looked down at Phillips. The chain was cutting into his neck, and he was on his toes. Martinez let go of the chain.

"Please accompany me, Lieutenant," he said. "You are relieved." He turned and addressed the room at large. "Ankley is the officer of the watch!" he proclaimed.

"I am relieved, my lord!" Phillips repeated. "Ankley is the officer of the watch!"

As Ankley came forward, Martinez bent to speak in his ear. "Keep everyone here," he said. "No one is to leave Command until a party arrives to search them."

Ankley licked his lips. "Very good, my lord."

Cold foreboding settled into Martinez's bones as he marched to the ship's jail. Phillips followed in silence, buttoning his tunic, and Espinosa came last, a hand on the butt of his stun baton.

He walked through the door into the reception room of the *Illustrious* brig, and the familiar smell hit him. All jails smelled alike, sour bodies and disinfectant, boredom and despair.

"I'll need your tunic, belt, shoes, and your lieutenant's key," Martinez said when he came to the brig. "Empty your pockets here, on the table." He had been military constabulary officer on the *Corona,* and he knew the drill.

The stainless steel table rang as Phillips emptied his pockets. He rolled an elastic off his wrist, one that had his lieutenant's key on it, and handed that to Martinez.

The sense that this was all a horrible mistake continued to hang over Martinez's head like a dense gray cloud. He couldn't imagine shy, tiny Phillips committing a crime as serious as stealing a candy bar, let alone killing his captain.

But it had been his own idea that the deaths were cult related, and that cult symbols would mark the killers. He had begun this. Now Fate would finish it.

"All your jewelry, please," Martinez said.

Phillips took off his academy ring with some effort, then opened his tunic and reached for the chain with both hands. He looked at Martinez.

"May I ask what this is about?"

"Two people wearing that medallion have died," Martinez said.

Phillips gaped at him. "Two?" he said.

Martinez's sleeve comm chimed. He answered and saw Marsden's frozen face resolve on his sleeve's chameleon weave.

"The lady squadcom was wondering where you went," he said.

"I'm in the brig, and I'm about to report to her. Have there been any developments?"

"None. We're about to finish here."

"Tell Lady Michi that I'll be right there."

Martinez ended the conversation and looked at Phillips, to see bewilderment still on his face.

"I don't understand," Phillips said.

"Your jewelry, Lieutenant."

Phillips slowly took the chain from around his neck and handed it to him. Martinez issued him a pair of the soft slippers worn by prisoners and showed him to his narrow cell. The metal walls were covered with many thick layers of green paint, and the single light was in a cage overhead. The room was almost filled with the acceleration couch used for a bed, the toilet, and the small sink.

Martinez closed the heavy door with its spy hole and told Espinosa to remain on guard. He put the ayaca pendant in a clear plastic evidence box and returned to the petty officers' quarters. The cabins had all been searched, and the search party had gone on to the body search, women searching women in the petty officers' mess while men searched men in the corridor.

Nothing was found. Martinez approached Michi and handed her the box with the ayaca pendant inside. She looked up at him in silent query.

"Lord Phillips," he said.

At first Michi was surprised, and then her expression hardened. "Too bad Fletcher didn't get him first," she said.

Michi's expression didn't soften throughout the rest of the search, and Martinez could tell she was thinking hard, particularly after the search of the enlisted and those on duty in Command and Engine Control produced no cult symbols, no murder weapons, and no suspects.

"Page Dr. Xi to the brig," Michi told her sleeve display. She looked up at Martinez. "Time to interrogate Phillips," she said.

"I don't think he killed Fletcher," Martinez said.

"I don't either, but he knows who did. He knows who the other members of the cult are." Her lips drew back from her teeth in a kind of snarl. "I'm going to have the lord doctor use truth drugs to get those names out of him."

Martinez suppressed a shiver. "Truth drugs don't always produce the truth," he said. "They lower a person's defenses, but they can confuse a prisoner as well. Phillips could just babble names at random, for all we know."

"I'll know," Michi said. "Maybe not this first interrogation, but we'll keep up the interrogations day after day, and in the end I'll know. The truth always comes out in the end."

"Let's hope so," Martinez said.

"Get Corbigny here as well. I'll take her to the jail with me. You and"—with a look at Marsden—"your secretary can get back to running the ship."

Martinez was startled. "I—" he began. "Phillips is my officer, and—"

I want to watch as you use chemicals to strip away his dignity and his every last secret. Because it's my fault you're putting him through this.

"He's not your officer anymore," Michi said flatly. "He's a walking dead man. And frankly, I don't think he's going to welcome your presence." She looked at him, and her look softened. "You have a ship to run, Captain."

"Yes, my lady." Martinez braced.

He and Marsden spent the rest of the day in his office dealing with the minutiae of command. Marsden was silent and hostile, and Martinez's mind kept running into blind alleys instead of concentrating on his work.

He supped alone, drank half a bottle of wine, and went in search of the doctor.

As he approached the pharmacy, he encountered Lady Juliette Corbigny leaving. She was pale and her eyes were wider than ever.

"Beg pardon, Lord Captain," she said, and sped away, almost in flight. Martinez looked after her, then walked into the pharmacy, where he found Xi slumped over a table, his chin on one fist as he contemplated a beaker half filled with a clear liquid. The sharp scent of grain alcohol was heavy on his breath.

"I'm afraid Lieutenant Corbigny isn't well," Xi said. "I had to give her something to settle her tummy. Partway into the interrogation she threw up all over the floor." He raised the beaker and looked at it solemnly. "I fear she isn't cut out for police work."

Savage, pointless anger roiled in Martinez. "Did *anything* go well?" he asked.

"The interrogation wasn't a success, particularly," Xi said. "Phillips said he hadn't killed the captain and didn't know who did. He said he doesn't belong to a cult. He said the ayaca pendant was given to him by his sweet old nurse when he was a child, and by the way, the story can't be confirmed because she's dead. He said he had no idea that the ayaca had any significance other than being a pretty tree that a lot of people put in their gardens."

Xi slumped over his table and took a drink from the beaker.

"When the drug hit him he kept to his story until his mind got the addles, and then he started to chant. Garcia and the squadcom and Corbigny—when she wasn't spewing—tried to keep him on the subject of the captain's death, but he kept going back to the same chant. Or maybe they were different chants. It was hard to tell."

"What was he chanting?"

"I don't know. It was in some old language that nobody recognized, but we heard the word *'Narayanguru'* all right, so it's a cult ritual language, and when the Investigative Service hears the recording they'll find someone to identify it, and that will be the end of Lord Phillips. And if the I.S. is on speaking terms with the Legion that week and passes the information, the Legion will probably arrest half the Phillips clan and that will be the end of *them,* because the Legion have many more methods of interrogation than are available to us here, and doctors who are far more bad than I am and are very proud that their confession rate is nearly one hundred percent." He looked at the beaker again, then raised his head to look at Martinez.

"Captain, I have been remiss. I am a bad doctor and a bad host. Will you share my beverage of consolation?"

"No thanks, I've had enough already. And you're going to have a hell of a hangover."

Xi gave a weary grin. "No, I'm not. A dose of this, a dose of that, and I will rise a new man." His face fell. "And then the squadcom will turn me into a bad doctor again, and have me shoot chemicals into the carotid of a harmless little man who didn't hurt anybody, if you ask me—which nobody did—but who's going to die anyway, and I wish I'd kept my damn mouth shut about the captain's injuries." He poured more alcohol into his beaker. "I thought I was going to be a brilliant detective, tracking clues like the police in the videos, and instead I find myself involved in something soiled and disgusting and sordid, and frankly, I wish I could throw up like Corbigny."

"Keep this up and you will," Martinez said.

"I shall do my best," Xi said, and raised his glass. "Bottoms up."

The bitter taste of defeat soured Martinez's tongue. As

he left the pharmacy, he swore that the next time he had a brainstorm, he'd keep it to himself.

A call from Garcia brought Martinez out of bed and running to the brig while still buttoning his undress tunic over his pajamas. "There was a guard here all night, Lord Captain," Garcia said in a rapid voice as soon as Martinez entered the room. "There's no way anyone could have got to him."

Martinez walked to Lord Phillips's cell, looked inside and wished he hadn't.

Sometime over the course of the night, Phillips had torn open the acceleration couch that served as his bed, pulled out fistfuls of the foam padding, then filled his mouth with the foam and kept packing it in until he choked.

Choked to death. Phillips was half off the couch and his mouth was still full of foam and his face was black. His eyes were open and gazed overhead at the light in its cage. Bits of the foam floated in the air like motes of dust.

Dr. Xi knelt by him. He eyes were red-rimmed and his hands trembled as he made a cursory examination.

"He knew he'd crack," Michi said after she arrived. "He knew he'd give us the names sooner or later. He decided to die first to protect his friends." She shook her head. "I wouldn't have thought he had the nerve for it."

Martinez turned to her, rage poised on his tongue, and then he turned away.

"We're still no better off than we were!" Michi cried, and slammed her fist into the metal door.

Later that morning Martinez conducted vicious, mean-spirited inspections of Missile Battery 1 and the riggers' stores, but it didn't make him feel any better.

TWENTY-ONE

Lord Chen's comm unit began to make an urgent squeak. "Pardon me, Loopy," he said. He put down his cocktail and reached into the pocket of his jacket.

He stood on the seaside terrace of his friend Lord Stanley Loo, known since his school days as "Loopy." A Cree orchestra played festive music from a bandstand that looked as if it had been designed by a lacemaker. The sea breeze carried over the terrace the refreshing scent of salt and iodine, and the roar of the waves on the rocks sometimes drowned out the band. Antopone's red sky gave the waves a lurid cast.

"Chen," he said, raising his unit to his ear.

"My lord. Lord Tork requires your immediate presence aboard *Galactic*."

Lord Chen recognized the careful diction of Lord Convocate Mondi, one of the members of the Fleet Control Board, a Torminel who took special care not to lisp around his fangs.

"The meeting's not for another three days," Chen said. He reached for his cocktail with his free hand and raised it to his lips.

"My lord," Mondi said, "is this communication secure?"

A cold hand touched Chen's spine. He put down his drink and turned away from the group on the terrace. "I suppose so," he said. "No one's within listening distance."

There was a slight hesitation, and then Mondi spoke again. "The Naxids are moving from Zanshaa," he said. "It looks like they're heading for Zarafan under high acceleration."

And from Zarafan, Lord Chen knew, they could go straight on to Laredo, where the Convocation were taking up residence.

Where his daughter would land any day.

"Yes," he said, "I understand. I'll be there as soon as I can arrange transport."

And then, as the surf boomed below, he put his hand comm away and returned to the party.

"Something's come up, Loopy," he said. "Can you have someone arrange my return to the skyhook?"

"General quarters! Now general quarters! This is not a drill!"

From the panic that clawed at the amplified voice of Cadet Qing, Martinez knew from the first word this wasn't a drill. By the time the message began to repeat he had already vaulted clean over his desk and was sprinting for the companion that led to Command, leaving Marsden sitting in his chair staring after him.

Martinez sprang for the companion just as the gravity went away. The distant engine rumble ceased, leaving the corridor silent except for the sound of his heart, which was thundering louder than the general quarters alarm. Martinez had no weight but still had plenty of inertia, and he hit the companion with knees and elbows. Pain rocketed through his limbs despite the padding on the stair risers. He bounced away from the companion like an oversized rubber eraser but managed to check his momentum with a grab to the rail.

His feet began to swing out into the corridor, and that meant *Illustrious* was changing its heading. He had to get up the companion and into Command before the engines fired again. His big hand tightened on the rail so he could swing himself back to the steep stair, kick off and jump to the next deck.

No good. The engines fired suddenly and he had weight again. His arm couldn't support his entire mass and folded under him, and the rail caught him a stunning blow across the shoulder. He flopped onto his back on the stair. Risers sliced into his back.

Martinez tried to rise, but the gravities were already beginning to pile on. *Two gravities. Three . . .* Pain lanced through his wrist as he seized the rail to try to haul himself upright. The stair risers were cutting into him like knives. *Four gravities at least . . .* He gasped for breath. Eventually he realized he wasn't going to be able to climb.

He realized other things as well. He was on a hard surface. He hadn't recently taken any of the drugs that would help him survive heavy gravity. He could die if he didn't get off this companion, cut by the stairs like cheese by a slicer.

A sort of crabbing motion of his arms and legs brought him bumping down the stairs, each step a club to his back and mastoid, but once his buttocks thumped on the deck it was harder to move, and the risers were still digging into his spine. *Five gravities . . .* His vision was beginning to go dark.

Martinez crabbed with his arms and legs and managed to thump down another stair. Comets flared in his skull as his head hit the tread. He clenched his jaw muscles to force blood to his brain and dropped down another step.

It was Chandra's nightmare, he realized. Relativistic missiles were inbound *and he needed to get to Command.* It would be the height of stupidity to die here, vaporized by a missile or with his neck broken by the sharp edge of a stair.

He thumped down another stair, and that left only his head still on the companion, tilted at an angle that cramped his windpipe and strained his spine. *Six gravities . . .* His vision was totally gone. He couldn't seem to breathe. Without the drugs, Terrans could only rarely stay conscious at more than six and a half gravities. He had to get off the stair or his neck was going to be broken by the weight of his head.

With a frantic effort he tried to roll, his palms and heels fighting for traction against the tile, fighting the dead weight that was pinning him like a silver needle pinning an insect to corkboard. Vertigo swam through his skull. He fought to bring air into his lungs. He gave a heave, every muscle in his body straining.

With a crack, his head fell off the stair and banged onto the tile. Despite the pain and the stars that shot through the blackness of his vision he felt a surge of triumph.

Gravity increased. Martinez fought for consciousness.

And lost.

When he woke, he saw before him a window, and beyond the window a green countryside. Two ladies in transparent gowns gazed at the poised figure of a nearly naked man who seemed to be hovering in a startlingly blue sky. Above the man was a superior-looking eagle, and on the grass below the two ladies were a pair of animals, a dog and a small furry creature with long ears, both of whom seemed to find the floating man interesting.

It occurred to Martinez that the man in the sky wasn't alone. He, Martinez, was also floating.

His heart was thrashing in his chest like a broken steam engine. Sharp pains shot through his head and body. He blinked and wiped sweat from the sockets of his eyes.

The man still floated before him, serene and eerily calm, as if he floated every day.

It was only gradually that Martinez realized he was looking at a piece of artifice, at one of the trompe l'oeil paintings that Montemar Jukes had placed at intervals in the corridors.

The engines had shut down again. Now weightless, Martinez had drifted gently from the deck to a place before the painting.

He gave a start and looked frantically in all directions.

The companion leading to Command was two body lengths away. So far as he knew, the emergency, the battle, or whatever it was, had not ended.

He swam with his arms to reorient himself, and kicked with one foot at the floating man. He shot across the corridor, absorbed momentum with his arms—pain shot through his right wrist—and then he did a kind of handspring in the direction of the companion.

He struck the companionway feet first and folded into a crouch, which enabled him to spring again, this time through the hatch atop the companion.

From there it was a short distance to Command's heavy hatch. The door was armored against blast and radiation and would have been locked down at the beginning of the emergency. Martinez hovered before the hatch, his left hand clutching at the hand grip inset into the door frame, his right stabbing at the comm panel.

"This is the captain!" he said. "Open the door!"

"Stand by," came Mersenne's voice.

Stand by? Martinez was outraged. Who did the fourth lieutenant think he was, some snotty cadet?

"Let me into Command!" Martinez barked.

"Stand by." The irritating words were spoken in an abstract tone, as if Mersenne had many more important things on his mind than obeying his captain's orders.

Well, perhaps he did. Perhaps the emergency was occupying his full attention.

But how much attention did it take to open a damn hatch?

Martinez ground his teeth while he waited, fist clamped white-knuckled around the hand grip. Lieutenant Husayn floated up the companion and joined him. Blood floated in perfect round spheres from Husayn's nose, some of them catching on his little mustache, and there was a cut on his lip.

There hadn't been the regulation warning tone sounded

for high gee—or for no gee, for that matter. Probably there hadn't been time to give the order. Martinez wondered how many injuries Dr. Xi was coping with.

After Martinez had been waiting nearly a minute, the hatch slid open with a soft hiss. He heaved on the hand grip and gave himself impetus for the command cage.

"I have command!" he shouted.

"Captain Martinez has command!" Mersenne agreed. He sounded relieved. He was already drifting free of the command cage, heading toward his usual station at the engines display.

Martinez glanced around the room as he floated toward his acceleration cage. The watch were staring at their displays as if each expected something with claws to come bounding out of them.

"Missile attack, my lord," Mersenne said as Martinez caught his acceleration cage. The cage swung with him, and he jacknifed, then inserted his feet and legs inside. "At least thirty. I'm sorry I didn't let you into Command, but I didn't want to unseal the door until I was certain the missiles had all been dealt with—didn't want to irradiate the entire command crew if there were a near miss."

It grated, but Martinez had to admit Mersenne was right.

"Any losses?" he asked.

"No, my lord." Mersenne floated to a couch next to the warrant officer who had been handling the engines board, then webbed himself in and locked the engine displays in front of him. "We starburst as soon as we saw the missiles incoming, but when we hit eight gravities, there was an engine trip."

Martinez, in the act of webbing himself onto his couch, stopped and stared. *"Engine trip?"* he said.

"Engine number one. Automated safety procedures tripped the other two before I could override them. I'll try to get engines two and three back online, and then work out what happened to engine one."

So now he knew why he'd suddenly found himself floating. The engines had quit, apparently on their own, and in the middle of a battle.

He pulled his displays down from over his head, heard them lock, began a study of the brief fight.

The Naxids hadn't attacked in the Osser system, as Chandra's war game had predicted. They'd waited for Chenforce to proceed to the next system, Arkhan-Dohg, where the hot, humid world of Arkhan supported a population of half a billion, mostly heat-loving Naxids, and cold, glacier-ridden Dohg supported a billion more, for the most part furry Torminel.

Chenforce hadn't found anything to shoot at in Osser, and there was very little traffic in Arkhan-Dohg. The Naxids knew they were coming, and every ship that could move was being routed away from them.

Even though Chenforce was finding few targets at present, they were still creating a massive disruption in the rebel economy. The hundreds of ships fleeing Chenforce weren't carrying cargoes to the appropriate destination. Not only were cargoes being routed well out of their way, many cargoes were stalled waiting for transport, and elsewhere industries were failing for want of supply.

The Naxid attempt to swat them from the sky had occurred when the squadron was two days into the Arkhan-Dohg system. Chenforce was suddenly painted with tracking lasers. Mersenne had immediately gone to general quarters and ordered *Illustrious* to accelerate as rapidly as possible away from the other ships. Before *Illustrious* was on its new heading, the sensor operators were reporting brief flares that showed incoming missiles making last-instant course corrections.

Most of the missiles targeted the swarm of decoys cruising ahead of Chenforce, but a few got through the screen to target the squadron itself, all to be destroyed by point-defense weapons. By that time the number one engine on *Illustrious* had tripped off and the cruiser was drifting, its captain floating bruised and unconscious in the corridor outside his office.

The Battle of Arkhan-Dohg, from the first alarm to the destruction of the last incoming missile, had taken a little less than three minutes.

"One failure in the point-defense array," Husayn reported from the weapons station. "Antiproton gun three failed after one shot."

"Just like Harzapid," muttered Mersenne.

"How many decoys do we have in the tubes?" Martinez asked Husayn.

"Three, my lord."

"Fire them immediately. We want to get decoys ahead of the squadron in case the Naxids have a follow-up attack."

The Command crew looked a little hollow-eyed at this possibility.

"Decoys fired, my lord. Tubes cleared. Decoys proceeding normally under chemical rockets to safety point."

"Replace them in the tubes with another set of decoys," Martinez added.

Primary command crew were drifting through the hatch and quietly taking up their stations. Alikhan arrived lugging Martinez's vac suit by a strap. Martinez told him to report to the weapons bays after putting the suit in one of the vac suit lockers: he didn't have time to put it on right now.

"I've commenced a countdown on engines two and three," Mersenne reported. "We're at five minutes twenty-one."

"Proceed."

"My lord," Husayn said, "decoys' antimatter engines have ignited. All decoys maneuvering normally."

"My lord," said Signaler Roh, "*Judge Arslan* queries our status."

"Tell them we experienced a premature engine shutdown," Martinez said. "Tell them we expect no long-term problem."

"Yes, Lord Captain. Ah . . . Squadcom Chen wants to speak with you."

"Put her on my board."

"Yes, Lord Captain."

Martinez hadn't strapped on the close-fitting cap that held his earphones, virtual array, and medical sensors, so Michi's voice came out of the speaker on his display, and was audible to everyone in command.

"Captain Martinez," she said, "what the *hell* just happened?"

Martinez reported in as few words as possible. Michi listened with an intent, inward look on her face. "Very well," she said. "I'll order the rest of the squadron to take defensive positions around us until we're maneuverable again."

Martinez nodded. "May I recommend that you order more decoy launches?"

"Lieutenant Prasad's already taken care of that." Michi's head tilted as she looked into her display. "Captain," she said, "you look like you got run over by a herd of bison."

"Acceleration threw me down a companion."

"Are you all right? Shall I page Dr. Xi to Command?"

"I'm sure he's busy enough where he is."

She nodded. "Find out who painted us with that laser," she said, "and blow him the fuck up."

"Yes, my lady."

"And take out the wormhole stations as well. I'm not having them spotting for the enemy."

It's uncivilized, Michi had said when she'd first raised the possibility of destroying wormhole stations. She'd occasionally done it in the past, when it was necessary to preserve secrecy concerning Chenforce's movements, but for the most part she'd left them alone.

The moment defining, Martinez thought. Nothing like being shot at to rub away these refined little scruples.

The orange end-stamp came onto the display, signaling that Michi had broken the collection.

"Sensors," Martinez said, "are we still being hit by that laser?"

"No, my lord," Pan said. "They switched off as soon as the last missiles were destroyed—and because their information is limited by the speed of light, they don't *know* what happened here yet. So they must have had advanced warning concerning exactly when to light us up and when to stop."

"Did you get a bearing?"

"It would help if I could communicate with the other ships and triangulate."

"Do so." Martinez turned to Husayn. "Weapons, target Wormhole Stations One, Two, and Three. Take them all out, one missile each. Don't wait for my command, just do it."

"Yes, Lord Captain."

Martinez let himself float for a moment in his harness and considered the order he'd just given. It *was* uncivilized. The wormhole stations not only maintained communication between the worlds, they acted to stabilize the wormholes by balancing the mass moved through them in either direction. Commerce would be slowed to a crawl through wormholes that were in danger of becoming unbalanced.

Arkhan-Dohg had just effectively been blockaded. It was a blockade that would continue until new stations were both built and equipped with the massive asteroid-sized chunks of matter they used to keep the wormholes in balance. The war might be over for ages before Arkhan-Dohg saw another merchant vessel.

"One minute to engine ignition, my lord," Mersenne said.

"Hold at ten seconds." Martinez hesitated, then said, "We can proceed on two engines without trouble?"

Mersenne's tone was confident. "Yes, my lord."

"Missiles launched and proceeding on chemical rockets," Husayn said. "Tubes clear."

"Roh, put me through to the squadcom."

"Yes, my lord."

Ida Li's face appeared on Martinez's display. "You have a message for Lady Michi?"

"Just that we'll have two engines online in less than a minute. Does the lady squadcom have a heading for us?"

"Stand by."

The screen blanked, and when an image returned it was that of Chandra Prasad. "I'm sending course coordinates to your pilot's station now. Acceleration one-tenth of a gravity, until we're sure the engines don't cut out again."

"Understood. Mersenne, sound the warning for acceleration."

There were a few moments of genuine suspense waiting for the engine countdown to conclude, and then a distant rumble and a slight kick that sent the acceleration cages slowly tumbling until they settled at their deadpoints. Computers balanced the angle of thrust of the two engines to compensate for the loss of the third. Acceleration was gradually increased until one constant gravity was maintained.

"Engines performance normative," Mersenne said.

"Very good."

"My lord." It was Pan. "We've tracked the origin of that targeting laser. It was Arkhan Station Three."

Arkhan, with its relatively small population, didn't rate a full accelerator ring around the planet, but instead had three geosynchronous stations tethered to the planet's equator by elevator cables. Station 1 had a modest-sized accelerator ring grappled to it, like a gold band attached to a diamond.

"Husayn," Martinez said, "one missile to target Station Three, please."

As the missile was launched, he supposed the Naxids had no right to be surprised. Chenforce had made it clear that anything that fired on it would be destroyed, be it ship, station, or ring.

At least it wasn't Bai-do. At least he wouldn't be dropping an entire ring, with its billions of tons of mass, into the atmosphere of an inhabited world.

He hoped the Naxids had evacuated the station's thousands of civilians before putting them in a cross fire, but he suspected they hadn't. The Naxids, so far as he could tell, never had a Plan B—if Plan A didn't work, they just tried Plan A all over again, only with greater sincerity.

"My lord," said Roh. "I have a message from Rigger Jukes."

"Yes?" Martinez couldn't imagine what the artist wanted.

"He asks permission to enter your quarters and inspect the paintings for damage."

Martinez suppressed a smile. The artworks were in highly intelligent frames that should have guarded them against acceleration, but nevertheless the impulse to protect the eighty-thousand-zenith painting showed Jukes had his priorities straight.

"Permission granted," he said.

"My lord," Mersenne said after the missile went on its way. "I've tracked the origin of the engine shutdown."

"Yes?"

"It was a high pressure return pump from the number one heat exchange system. It failed, and set off a cascade of events that led to complete engine shutdown."

"Failed?" Martinez demanded. "What do you mean, failed?"

"I can't tell from this board. But for some reason when the pump failed, the valve on the backup system failed to open, and that led to the engine trip. The computer wasn't a hundred percent confident that it could keep the ship balanced with only two engines firing at all of eight gravities' acceleration, so it tripped the other engines as well."

"Right," Martinez said. "Thank you, Mersenne."

This was going to take some thought.

As soon as the ship secured from general quarters, he was going straight to the engine compartment and find out just what had happened.

"**Y**arning the logs." Martinez spoke in a cold fury. "You yarned the logs to hide the fact that you hadn't been doing scheduled replacements, and as a result the ship was driven into danger."

Master Rigger Francis stared expressionlessly at the wall behind Martinez's head and said nothing.

"Didn't I give you enough advanced warning?" Martinez asked. "Didn't you guess what would happen if I caught you at something like this?"

Rage boiled in Martinez, fueled by the murderous aches in his head and wrist. For the first time in his career he understood how an officer could actually use his top-trimmer, could draw the curved knife from its sheath and slash the throat of a subordinate.

The evidence that damned Francis was plain. The huge, sleek turbopump designed to bring return coolant from the heat exchanger to the number one engine had been partly dismantled by Francis and her riggers. The plain metal-walled room reeked of coolant, and Martinez's shoes and cuffs were wet with the stuff. The finely machined turbine that was the heart of the pump had disintegrated, sending shards downstream that jammed the emergency valve designed to shut off coolant flow in the event of a problem with the pump. With the first valve jammed open, a second valve intended to open the backup system had refused to open, and the result was an automatic shutdown for the engine.

It was difficult to understand how such a critical pump could suffer so catastrophic a failure. The pump and other pieces of crucial equipment were deliberately overdesigned, intended to survive well beyond their official lifespan. The only way a pump would crash in so terminal a fashion was because routine maintenance had been neglected.

That much was deduction. But what proved the final nail in the master rigger's coffin was the fact that the serial number on the pump and the number recorded in the 77-12 were different. So far as Martinez could tell, the number in the 77-12 was pure fiction.

"Well," Martinez said, "Rigger Second Class Francis, I suggest that you get your crew busy replacing this pump."

Francis's eyes flashed at the news of her demotion, and Martinez saw the firming of her jowls as her jaw muscles clenched.

Martinez turned to Marsden, who stood with his feet meticulously placed on a piece of dark plastic grate so as not to get coolant on his shoes.

"Who's the senior rigger now?" Martinez asked.

"Rigger/First Rao." Marsden didn't even have to consult his database for the answer.

Martinez turned back to Francis. "I will require the new department head to check every one of your entries in the 77-12. We don't want any more mysterious failures, do we?"

Francis said nothing. The humid atmosphere of the room had turned her skin moist, and droplets tracked down either side of her nose.

"You are at liberty to protest your reduction in rank," Martinez said. "But I wouldn't if I were you. If Squadron Leader Chen finds out about this, she's likely to have you strangled."

He marched out, shoes splashing in coolant, his head and wrist throbbing with every step. Marsden followed, far more fastidious about where he put his feet.

Martinez next visited the weapons bay where Gulik and Husayn were both examining the guts of the antiproton projector that had failed in the Naxid attack. The whole mechanism had been pulled from the turret and replaced, and now a postmortem was under way, parts scattered on a sterile dropcloth that had been spread on the deck.

Gulik jumped to his feet, bracing with his chin high as Martinez approached. There were dark patches under his arms and sweat poured down his face. Martinez hadn't seen him this nervous since Fletcher's final inspection, when the captain had slowly marched past Gulik and his crew with the knife rattling at his waist.

Martinez wondered if word had already passed to Gulik about what had just happened to Francis. The noncommissioned officers were wired into an unofficial communications network, and Martinez had a healthy respect for its efficiency, but he could hardly believe it worked this fast. Perhaps Gulik was always this nervous around higher officers.

Or perhaps he had a guilty conscience.

He called up Gulik's 77-12 on his sleeve display and quietly checked the serial numbers. They matched, so at least Gulik wasn't yarning his log.

"Do we know what happened?" Martinez asked.

"The electron injector's packed up, my lord," Gulik said. "It's a fairly common failure, on this model particularly."

As the antiprotons piggybacked on an electron beam, which kept the antiprotons contained until they hit the target, the electron injector was a critical component of the system.

"I'll do further tests," Gulik said, "but it's probably just a matter of tolerances. These parts are machined very precisely, and they're stuck in the turret where they're subject to extremes of temperature and cosmic rays and all knows what. The turrets are normally retracted, but we're keeping every point-defense weapon at full charge now, with the turrets deployed. Critical alignments can go wrong very easily."

Martinez remembered what someone had said in Command, and he said, "So it's not what happened at Harzapid?"

Gulik gave a start. Husayn answered for him, and firmly. "Decidedly not, my lord."

Martinez sensed that a significant moment had just slipped by, somehow, but he had no idea why the moment was significant.

"What *did* happen at Harzapid?" he asked.

There was silence as both Husayn and Gulik seemed to gaze for a moment into the past, neither of them liking what they saw there.

"It was bad, my lord," Husayn said. "The Naxids were outnumbered five to one, so they tried to bluff us into surrender. They occupied Ring Command and ordered us all to stand down. But Fleet Commander Kringan organized a party to storm Ring Command, and he ordered the loyal squadrons to prepare a fight at close range with antiproton weapons.

"None of us kept the antiprotons on our ships when we were in dock—you know how touchy they can be—so Lieutenant Kosinic was sent with a party to bring antiprotons in their containment bottles. He did, but when we hooked them up to the antimatter feeders, we discovered that the bottles were empty."

Martinez looked at him in surprise. "Empty?"

"The Naxids must have got into our storage compartment and replaced the full bottles with empty ones. The squadcom sent Kosinic out again to get bottles from *Imperious,* which was berthed next to us, but that's when the shooting started. That's when the station airlock was hit and Kosinic was wounded."

Husayn's mouth stretched in a taut, angry grimace beneath his little mustache. "The Fourth Fleet blew itself to bits in a few minutes of close-range fire. All the Naxids' ships were destroyed, but most of the loyalists were hurt too, and some ships completely wrecked. There were thousands of deaths. But *the Naxids didn't shoot at us!* They knew *Illustrious* was helpless."

Frustration crackled in Husayn's voice. Martinez could imagine the scene in Command, Fletcher calling for firepower that simply wasn't there, the weapons officer—Husayn himself—pounding his console in fury. Kosinic racing along the docking tube with a party of desperate crouchbacks and the hand carts that carried the antiproton bottles. The long moments of helpless silence as the battle started and the crew waited for the fire that would rend their ship and kill them, followed by the horrid realization of the insult that the Naxids were flinging in their teeth, that the enemy *knew* that *Illustrious* could be of no assistance to their own side, and disdained so much as to target them.

The feeling of helplessness, Martinez thought, must have been at least as frustrating and terrifying as that of the captain of a ship pinned to a stair by heavy gee while his ship fought for its life without him.

"Captain Fletcher cast off from the ring, my lord," Husayn continued, "and maneuvered as if to attack. We were hoping to draw their fire away from the others, but the Naxids still refused to respond. We hit them with our lasers, but the lasers really can't do the sort of damage antimatter can in those conditions, and . . ." He grimaced again. "Still they wouldn't attack us. We watched the whole battle from the sidelines. Captain Fletcher was in a perfect rage—I'd never seen him like that, never saw him show emotion before."

"Where was Squadron Commander Chen?"

"On the planet, my lord. Dinner party."

Martinez couldn't imagine Michi being happy about what had happened to *Illustrious* either.

"We were very glad to finally get a swat at the Naxids at Protipanu, my lord," Husayn said. "It was good to pay them back."

"Yes," Martinez said. "*Illustrious* did very well at Protipanu. You all did very well."

He looked from Husayn to Gulik, who was still standing rigid, the sweat pouring down his face, his eyes staring into some internal horror.

No wonder they hadn't talked about it, Martinez thought. He'd thought *Illustrious* had won a hard-fought victory alongside the other loyalists of the Fourth Fleet, and assumed the cruiser had just been lucky not to suffer any damage. He hadn't known that *Illustrious* and its crew hadn't been a part of the fighting at all, except for Kosinic and his little party who had been caught out of their ship.

"Very good," Martinez said softly. "I think we might institute a series of test firings and inspections to make sure the point-defense weapons won't fail when we need them."

"Yes, my lord."

"Carry on then."

As he left, Martinez felt Gulik's wide-eyed stare boring into his neck, and wondered what it was that Gulik was really looking at.

His next stop was the sick bay, where he received Dr. Xi's report on the twenty-two crew with broken bones and the twenty-six more with bad sprains or concussions, all as a result of the unexpected high accelerations. The failure of engine number one had probably saved the ship from more casualties, and very possibly from fatalities.

Xi examined the back of Martinez's head and prescribed painkillers, and a muscle relaxant before bed. He scanned the wrist and found a minor fracture of the right pisiform carpal. He taped the wrist and gave Martinez a shot of fast-healer hormones, then gave him a med injector with more fast-healers.

"Three times a day till you run out," he said. "It should be healed in a week or so."

Martinez toured the sick bay, speaking to each of the injured crouchbacks, then returned to his office to find Jukes waiting, happy to report that the artworks had survived the accelerations without damage. Martinez sent Jukes on his way, then made official his demotion of Francis, added a furious couple of paragraphs to Francis's efficiency report, and had supper.

He remained awake for the countdown that started engine number one, and made certain that the new turbo-pump was performing up to specs before calling for Alikhan to bring him his nightly cocoa.

"What are they saying now, Alikhan?" Martinez asked.

Alikhan was looking with great disapproval at Martinez's shoes, spattered with engine coolant and the muck of the heat exchange room.

"Francis is furious," he said. "She was planning on retiring after the war, and now she'll have a much smaller pension."

Martinez held his cup of cocoa under his nose and inhaled the rich sweet scent. "So she's gathering sympathy then?" he asked.

Alikhan drew himself up with magisterial dignity and dropped the soiled shoes into their bag. "Fuck her," he pronounced, "she put the ship in danger. You could have cut her throat, and maybe you should have. As it is, you hit her where she hurts. With Francis it's always about money."

"Right," Martinez said, and concealed a smile. "Thank you, Alikhan."

He swallowed his muscle relaxant, then slid into bed and sipped his cocoa while he looked at the painting of the woman, child, and cat.

Day by day, *Illustrious* was becoming his ship, and less something that belonged to Fletcher, or the petty officers, or the Fourth Fleet. Today had been an important step in that process.

Another couple months, he thought pleasantly, and the cruiser would fit him like a glove.

Chenforce made a high-gravity burn around Arkhan-Dohg's sun and hurled itself for Wormhole 3, its presence marked by the radioactive dust that had been its relay station. No Naxid missiles barred their way.

On the other side of Wormhole 3 was Choiyn, a wealthy world with five billion inhabitants and considerable industry. Four uncompleted medium-sized warships, large frigates or light cruisers, were cast adrift from its ring and destroyed, along with half a dozen merchant ships that had been unable to clear the system in time.

No Naxid attack threatened, but to be safe, Michi vaporized all the wormhole stations anyway, lest they provide tracking data to the enemy.

Martinez was busy with drills, inspections, and minutiae. Rao, Francis's replacement, produced revised 77-12s that corrected Francis's elisions, and Martinez's inspections showed that Rao's data were not in error.

Cadet Ankley, who had been made Acting Lieutenant after Phillips's suicide, spectacularly lost his temper when an inspection of his division had turned up some chaotic inventory, and had to be returned to the ranks of the cadets while Cadet Qing was promoted in his place.

This failure was balanced by Chandra Prasad's success. Her exercises had Chenforce pelted by relativistic missiles from all directions, and also compelled the squadron to confront a wide variety of Naxid attacks, the enemy converging on Chenforce from various headings and with a wide variation in velocity. It was a big surprise when a virtual Naxid squadron starburst to mirror Martinez's new tactics, and Chenforce had a murderous fight on its hands that ended in mutual annihilation. The sting of this humiliation stayed with Martinez for some time, but eventually he concluded that if the war went on long enough, the Naxids were bound to adopt the new tactics or something like them, and that the Fleet should be ready with countertactics.

If only he could think of some.

After Choiyn came Kinawo, a system that featured a main-sequence yellow star orbited by a blue-white companion so furiously radioactive that the system was bereft of life except for the crews of a pair of heavily shielded wormhole stations, both of which were quickly destroyed. Chenforce would transit Kinawo in six days and then enter El-Bin, a system with two habitable planets, one heavily industrialized and the other covered with grazing, herdsmen, and their beasts.

El-Bin also had four wormholes, each of which offered a different possibility. Which meant that El-Bin was the last possible place to make a certain decision, and whatever way that decision went, it would effect the outcome of the war.

Martinez invited Lady Michi to supper the night before the squadron was to transit to El-Bin. He had Perry pull out all the stops and prepare a ham, a duck that had been preserved in its own fat, and dumplings stuffed with cheese, smoked pork, and herbs. When Michi arrived, he greeted her with cocktails, pickles, and cheese huffers. She seemed undefinably different, and more attractive. Studying her, he decided the difference was the hair. She still wore it at collar length, with straight bangs across the forehead, but somehow the style suited her more now than in the past.

"You've changed your hair," he said, "but I can't work out how."

She smiled. "Buckle. Since he doesn't belong to Captain Fletcher anymore, I thought I'd take advantage of his availability."

"He's done a splendid job. You're looking very well."

She patted her hair. "Now that Buckle's on staff, I think you'll find some more attractive crew walking about the ship."

"I'll look forward to that."

Martinez sat Michi at the place of honor in the captain's dining room and had Alikhan open a bottle of wine. The plates arrived, each served by Narbonne in its turn, and Michi was impressed by the vast quantity of food that kept rolling out of the kitchen.

"I won't keep my good looks for long if I eat all this," she remarked.

"I'd be alarmed for you if you ate everything," Martinez said, "but I can have Perry prepare a package of leftovers for you. He'd love it, I'm sure—score points against *your* cook."

"I'd rather not have my cook in a mood to poison me, thanks all the same."

Over coffee and fried ice cream they began a discussion of that morning's exercise, in which Chandra had set a pair of converging Naxid squadrons on a virtual Chenforce.

"Prasad is proving useful," Michi said. "I've completely changed my mind about her."

"Yes?"

"Before I took her on staff, I thought I disliked her. Now that I've had a chance to work with her closely, I realize that I hate her guts." She scowled, her brows meeting. "She's ambitious, she's unscrupulous, she's tactless, and she's ill-bred. But she's too good, damn it. I can't get rid of her."

Martinez didn't disagree with this estimate, and though he was pleased at having unloaded Chandra onto his superior, he felt it would be tactless to show it.

"I'm sorry she's so turbulent," he said.

"I have to wonder what Kosinic saw in her," Michi muttered.

Martinez stared at her. "Kosinic and Chandra were . . . ?"

"Yes. It began over a year ago, when Kosinic first joined my staff and Prasad had a job on Harzapid's ring. I'm not sure it continued after Kosinic was wounded, because that's when Prasad came aboard and began her relationship with the captain." She scowled. "I suppose Kosinic lacked the strength of character to resist her."

Martinez feigned a fascination with his coffee cup. *Is Chandra killing all her ex-lovers?* he wondered, and then wondered whether the one guard outside during the night watches was enough.

"Interesting," he said.

Michi raised an eyebrow. "Do you think so? I think it's squalid."

"No reason it can't be both." Surprise about Chandra and Kosinic swam through his mind, and then he wondered about Michi's reaction to the business. Perhaps she'd had a little crush on her young protégé? With an effort he pushed speculation to the side. He had other things in mind.

He looked at Michi. "I have some ideas, my lady, of a tactical nature."

A delicate smile touched her lips. "Yes? This supper isn't purely social then?"

"I hoped to show you a pleasant evening in exchange for having to listen to my ideas—well, idea, there's only one."

"The dumplings have made me generous. Go on."

Martinez took a deliberate sip of his coffee, the bitter taste welcome after the sweet dessert. He put his cup carefully in the saucer. "I'd like to make the case for an attack on Naxas."

Michi smiled. "I was wondering when you'd suggest an attack on the enemy capital. I was making little bets with myself about it."

"The Naxids have fifty warships in their fleet," Martinez said, "and we know that forty-three of them were in the fleet that took Zanshaa. That leaves seven at Magaria and Naxas combined. There was a small squadron of five ships at Naxas at the beginning of the war, and I'd bet they're still there. I'd also be willing to bet they haven't been reinforced.

"Chenforce has seven ships, though admittedly *Celestial* was damaged at Protipanu and can't fight at full efficiency. Our magazines are depleted by about a third, but we have new tactics, good morale, and a tradition of victory. One attack at Naxas can overwhelm the defenders and put the enemy government at our mercy. It might be the winning stroke."

Michi gave a long sigh. "You have no idea how tempting you make it all sound." She placed her hands flat on the table before her, fingers extended. "But we don't know that the enemy government is still on Naxas. It might well be in transit to Zanshaa."

"That's a risk," Martinez admitted.

"Plus it's not as if the Naxids don't know where we are. They may have sent reinforcements to Naxas. Even if we get there first and defeat the five ships, a rescue force may still arrive, and we'd have another fight on our hands, with magazines running empty from the previous fight."

"Yes."

"And of course they may have completed some of their new ships and sent them to Naxas. And we might not be lucky. And of course my orders specifically order me *not* to go to Naxas."

"True." Martinez nodded.

She peered at him from beneath her bangs. "You have no answer to these objections?"

Martinez felt a sigh building somewhere in his diaphragm, and he suppressed it. "I don't, my lady." Because he had considered all these points himself, and all together the objections were formidable.

Michi seemed disappointed. "I was hoping you would. Because I've been thinking about Naxas for some time."

Martinez groped for words. "I don't have logic on my side," he admitted. "All I have is the sense that we should go to Naxas. It seems to me that we could knock off five enemy ships at a fairly small risk. And then, if the Naxids don't give up, we could leave and complete our return journey."

Michi looked at her hands again. "No. Too many unknowns. We've had a very successful raid thus far. If we were unlucky at Naxas, we'd not only hand the enemy a victory—and our own side would have no way to know what happened to us—but we'd be altering the Fleet's strategic plan." She looked at him, amusement in her dark eyes. "And since you're the unacknowledged author of the Fleet's strategic plan, I presume you'll want to maintain it."

"Yes, my lady." Martinez felt a constriction in his chest as a mental calculation reached its inevitable conclusion. "In that case," he said, "I feel obliged to raise the possibility of doing to the Naxids what they tried to do to Chenforce. Accelerate some missiles to relativistic velocities and use them to hammer Naxas. We could bring the ring right down on the heads of their government."

Michi shook her head again. "That wouldn't end the war," she said. "That would just widen it. The Naxids would feel obliged to use the same tactic, and I don't want to see the rings at Harzapid and Zarafan and Felarus come down."

Martinez felt his breathing slowly ease. "That's a relief," he admitted. "I felt that the option should be mentioned, but I can't say my heart was behind the recommendation."

"Yes." Michi sipped her coffee. "If I'm going to have to destroy our civilization in that way, I'd much rather it be a result of a direct order from a superior, and not something I did on my own."

Martinez smiled, but he wondered exactly how readily Michi would obey such an order. She'd been ruthless enough in other areas.

Uncomfortable with this line of thought, he allowed further calculation to spin through his mind. "Well," he said, "if we're not going to the Naxid home world, it seems to me that we should do our best to convince the enemy that Naxas is *exactly* where we're going."

"You have a suggestion, I take it?"

"There are four wormholes in El-Bin. We'll be entering the system through Wormhole One. If we exit the system by way of Wormhole Two, we'd be on the direct route for Naxas, and Wormhole Three takes us eventually to Seizho by way of Felarus, which is a *very* long route. We actually want to take Wormhole Four, which will begin our loop to rejoin the Home Fleet.

"At present, our course takes us directly from Wormhole One to Wormhole Four, minus a bit of dodging to avoid hypothetical missiles. But if instead we loop around El-Bin's sun, it might look to the enemy as if we're intending to slingshot for Wormhole Two and Naxas. And if they're indeed sending reinforcements to their home world, that'll keep them heading for home under high gees just at the moment when Naxas is no longer under threat."

"Wrong-foot them a few days more," Michi murmured. "Yes, I'll do that."

After that the conversation descended into trivialities, and eventually Michi yawned and rose and thanked him for dinner. He walked with her to the door and she surprised him by putting an arm around his waist and resting her head on his shoulder.

"If you weren't married to my niece," she said in his ear, "and if I didn't actually *like* her, I'd make an adulterer out of you right now."

CONVENTIONS OF WAR • 333

Martinez tried not to let his mouth fall open. "I'm sure it would be delightful," he said finally, "but on Terza's behalf I thank you."

She gave him a smile from under one cocked eyebrow and made her way out. Martinez waited for the door to close, then walked to the nearest chair and sat down heavily.

We have all been on this ship too long, he thought.

The voyage continued. Chenforce entered El-Bin and made its deceptive swing about its star, all crew strapped into their couches and unconscious through a ten-gee deceleration. Whether the maneuver fooled the Naxid command into diverting ships wasn't apparent until two systems later, in Anicha, where Chenforce stumbled on a host of merchant ships, all in desperate flight. Anicha, it turned out, was where the Naxids had diverted their merchant ships, getting them out of the way of the presumed showdown at Naxas.

Chenforce destroyed 131 ships at Anicha and more in the next system, where some had managed to flee.

The great ship slaughter at Anicha was an exception: for the most part, *Illustrious* settled into a routine, inspections and drills and musters. The officers invited one another to dinner parties, but behind the gaiety was a kind of weariness. It was clear that everyone had been on the ship too long.

Martinez now found the 77-12s perfectly reliable. Because they gave him ways of knowing his ship, and because *Illustrious* was performing so well in the squadron exercises, he reduced the number of inspections and hoped the crew were grateful. He also sometimes abandoned the full-dress formality: on occasion he arrived at an inspection in Fleet-issue coveralls and crawled into conduits and access tunnels, places where Fletcher would never have gone lest he soil his silver braid.

Fletcher had polished *Illustrious* to a high gloss but

hadn't really known his ship. Even with his frequent inspections, he could only guess at the real status of the ship's plant and systems. He saw only the surface, and never knew what rot might be concealed by a thick layer of polish.

Martinez was learning his ship from the inside out. He would inspect every pump, every launcher, every conduit. He would make *Illustrious* his own.

He worked hard. His wrist healed. He still sometimes woke to the phantom scent of Caroline Sula on his pillow.

Every so often he met with Jukes to discuss the new designs for *Illustrious*. He was beginning to get used to the idea of his ship as a gaudy personal banner, as far away from Fletcher's concept as possible.

In the meantime, Jukes painted his portrait. The artist had wanted to create the portrait electronically and print it, but Martinez desired a proper portrait, with paint on canvas, and Jukes complied with weary grace. He put an easel in Martinez's office and worked there, preferring more obscure hours.

His portrait was romantic and lofty, Martinez in full dress, the Orb in one hand, his gaze directed somewhere over the viewer's right shoulder. The other hand rested on a tabletop, next to a model of *Corona*. Behind him would be a picture-within-a-picture, a portrait of *Illustrious* blazing into battle. Jukes seemed to think the picture-within-a-picture device was clever. Martinez didn't understand why exactly, but saw no reason to contradict the other's professional judgment.

There was some discussion whether the portrait of *Illustrious* should portray the ship in its current form, with Fletcher's abstract color scheme of pink, white, and green, or in the bolder style they planned for *Illustrious* after the war.

Martinez put off making the decision, but eventually decided to use Fletcher's color scheme. Should he win any glory in the war, it would be with *Illustrious* in its current appearance, and that would be what he wanted to commemorate.

Besides, he thought, there was no reason to stop at just one portrait. The redesigned *Illustrious* could be immortalized another time.

Martinez began to notice at musters and inspections that the crew looked obscurely more attractive. Kazakov came to dine one day with her hair down rather than knotted behind her head, and Martinez was struck by how good-looking she was.

Buckle, it seemed, was working his magic as a hair stylist and cosmetician. Even Electrician Strode's bowl haircut seemed more shapely. Martinez called Buckle to his cabin for a haircut, and had to admit that the result was an improvement.

He made Jukes repaint the portrait to include the more attractive hair style.

There were more disciplinary problems among the crew now, fights and occasional drunkenness. They also had too little to occupy their time. It would have taken only thirty-odd people to con the ship from one place to another, and another thirty weaponers to manage the fighting. The rest were partly for redundancy's sake, in the event of casualties, and many of the crew were intended to support the dignity of the officers, acting as their servants; but mainly crew were needed for damage control. In an emergency, hundreds of pairs of well-trained hands might be needed to keep the ship alive. The rest of the time the officers had to invent work for them, cleaning and spit-polishing, playing parts in rituals and ceremonies, and performing and reperforming routine maintenance.

Everyone, officers and crew alike, were growing tired of it all.

Still, beneath the weariness, Martinez began to sense an undercurrent of optimism. Chenforce was returning to the Home Fleet, and once there, would move on the enemy at Zanshaa and retake the capital. The crew were anticipating the war coming to its conclusion, and with it, the end of all the monotony.

Even the danger of a merciless enemy had begun to seem preferable to the endless repetition and routine.

One night, Martinez sipped his cocoa and looked at the mother and the cat and the infant in his red pajamas. It seemed to him that the Holy Family, whoever they were, had things pretty easy. They had their fire, their beds, their comfortable middle-class clothing, a child that was well-fed and well-clothed, enough food so they could spare some for their cat.

There was no indication that they had to worry about unknown killers skulking outside their ornate painted frame, or coping with a sudden relativistic barrage of antimatter missiles, or whether reports given them by others had been yarned.

By the time he finished his cocoa, Martinez began to feel envy for the lives of the people in the painting. They were simple, they were Holy, they were carefree.

They were everything a captain wasn't.

TWENTY-TWO

Perhaps, Martinez thought, it was the boredom induced by the long days of the ship's routine that had led him to think about the killings again. After mulling it over for several days, he asked Chandra to come to his office in the middle of one long, dull afternoon.

"Drink?" he asked as she braced. "By which I mean coffee."

"Yes, my lord."

"Sit down." He pushed a cup and saucer across his desk, then poured from the flask that Alikhan habitually left on his desk.

A rich coffee scent floated into the room. Chandra sat expectant, eyes bright beneath the auburn hair.

"I wanted to ask you about Kosinic," Martinez said.

Chandra, reaching for the coffee, pulled back her hand and blinked in surprise. "May I ask why?"

"Because it occurred to me that all our thinking about the killings has been exactly wrong. We've been looking at Captain Fletcher's death and trying to reason backward about what might have motivated it. But Kosinic's death was the first—*he* was the anomaly. Thuc's death followed from his, and I think Fletcher's followed as well. So if we can just work out why Kosinic was murdered, everything else will fall into place."

Chandra frowned as she considered this reasoning, then gave him a searching look. "You don't think it's all down to Phillips and the cultists?"

"Do you?"

She was silent.

"You knew Kosinic best," Martinez said. "Tell me about him."

She accepted the remark without comment, then reached for the coffee and considered her words while she fiddled with the powdered creamer; *Illustrious* had long ago run out of fresh dairy. She took a sip, frowned, and took another.

"Javier was bright," Chandra said finally, "good-looking, young, and probably a little more ambitious than was sensible for someone in his position. He had two problems: he was a commoner and he had no money. Peers will mingle with commoners if they've got enough money to keep up socially; and they'll tolerate Peers who have no money for the sake of their name. But a commoner with no money is going to be buried in a succession of anonymous desk jobs, and if he gets a command, it's going to be a barge to nowhere, an assignment that no Peer would touch."

She took another sip of her coffee. "But Javier got lucky—Squadron Commander Chen was impressed by a report on systems interopability that happened to cross her desk, and she took him on staff. Javier wasn't about to let an opportunity like that slide—he knew she could promote him all the way to Captain if he impressed her enough. So he set out to be the perfect bright staff officer for her, and right at that moment war broke out and he was wounded."

She sighed. "They shouldn't have let him out of the hospital. He wasn't fit. But he knew that as long as he stayed on Chen's staff he could have a chance to do important war work right under the nose of an important patron—and of course by then he was in a perfect rage to kill Naxids, like all of us, but more so."

"He had head injuries," Martinez said. "I've heard his personality changed."

"He was angry all the time," Chandra said. "It was sad, really. He insisted that what had happened to *Illustrious* at

Harzapid was the result of a treacherous Naxid plot—
which of course was true—but he became obsessed with
rooting out the plotters. That made no sense at all, because
by that point the Naxids at Harzapid were all dead, so what
did it matter which of them did what?"

Martinez sipped his own coffee and considered this. "*Illustrious* was the only ship that wasn't able to participate in
the battle," he said. "Was that what Kosinic was obsessing
about?"

"Yes. He took it personally that his load of antiproton
bottles were duds, and of course he was wounded when he
went back for more, so that made it even more personal."

"The antiproton bottles were stored in a dedicated storage area?"

"Yes."

A ship in dock was usually assigned a secure storage
area where supplies, replacement parts, and other items
were stockpiled—it was easier to stow them there, where
they could be worked with, rather than have the riggers
find space for them in the holds, where they wouldn't be as
accessible when needed. Those ships equipped with antiproton weapons generally stored their antiproton bottles
there, in a secure locked facility, as antiprotons were trick-
ier to handle than the more stable antihydrogen used for
engine and missile fuel. An antiproton bottle was something you didn't want a clumsy crouchback dropping on
his foot.

"The Naxids had to have gained the codes for both the
storage area and the secure antiproton storage," Chandra
said. "I don't see how we'll ever find out how they did it,
and I don't see why it matters at this point. But Javier
thought it *did* matter, and if anyone disagreed with him,
he'd just turn red and shout and make a scene." Sadness
softened the long lines of her eyes. "It was hard to watch.
He'd been so bright and interesting, but after he was
wounded, he turned into a shouter. People didn't want to be
around him. But fortunately, he didn't like people much ei-

ther, so he spent most of his time in his quarters or in Auxiliary Control."

"He sounds a bit delusional," Martinez said. "But suppose, when he was digging around, he found a genuine plot? Not to help the Naxids, but something else."

Chandra seemed surprised. "But any plot would have to be something Thuc was involved in, because it was Thuc who killed him, yes?"

"Yes."

"But Thuc was an *engineer.* Javier was a staff officer. Where would they ever overlap?"

Martinez had no answer.

Suddenly, Chandra leaned forward in her seat, her eyes brilliant with excitement. "Wait!" she said. "I remember something Mersenne once told me! Mersenne was somewhere on the lower decks, and he saw an access hatch open, with Javier just coming out from the underdeck. He asked Javier what he was doing there, and Javier said that he was running an errand for the squadcom. But I can't imagine why Lady Michi would ever have someone digging around in the guts of the ship."

"That doesn't seem to be one of her interests," Martinez murmured. "I wonder if Kosinic left a record of what he was looking for." He looked at her. "He had a civilian-model datapad I didn't have the passwords for. I don't suppose you know his passwords?"

"No, I'm afraid not." Her face grew thoughtful. "But he didn't carry that datapad around with him all the time. He spent hours in Auxiliary Control at his duty station, so if there were records of what he was looking at, it's probably still in his logs, and you can—"

His mind, leaping ahead of her, had him chanting her conclusion along with her.

"*—access that with a captain's key!*"

A quiet excitement began to hum in Martinez's nerves. He opened his collar and took out his key on its elastic. He inserted the narrow plastic key into the slot on his desk and called up the display. Chandra politely turned away as he entered his password. He called up Javier Kosinic's account and scanned the long list of files.

"May I use the wall display?" Chandra asked. "I could help you look."

The wall display was called up and the two began a combined search, each examining different files. They worked together in a silence interrupted by Martinez's call to Alikhan for more coffee.

Frustration built as Martinez examined file after file, finding only routine paperwork, squadron maneuvers that Kosinic had planned as tactical officer, and a half-finished letter to his father, dated the day before his death but filled only with mundane detail and containing none of the rage and monomania Chandra had described.

"He's hiding it from us!" he finally exploded.

His right hand clenched in a fist. The captain had hid his nature as well, but he'd finally cracked the captain's secret.

Kosinic would crack too, he swore.

"Let me check the daily logs," Chandra said. "If we look at his activity, we might be able to see some patterns."

The logs flashed on the wall screen, the automatic record of every call that Kosinic had ever made on the computer resources of the ship.

Tens of thousands of them. Martinez's gaze blurred as he looked at the long columns of data.

"Look at this," Chandra said. She moved a cursor to highlight one of Kosinic's commands. "He saved a piece of data to a file called 'Rebel Data.' Do you remember seeing that file?"

"No," Martinez said.

"It's not very large. It's supposed to be in his account, in another file called 'Personal.'" Chandra's cursor jittered over the display. "Here's another save to the same file," she said. "And another."

Though he already knew it wasn't there, Martinez

looked again at Kosinic's personal file and found nothing. "It must have been erased."

"Or moved somewhere," Chandra said. "Let me do a search."

The search through the ship's vast data store took about twelve seconds.

"If the file was moved," Chandra concluded, "it was given a new name."

Martinez had already called up the log files. "Let's find the last time anyone gave a command regarding that file."

Another five seconds sped by. Martinez stared in shock at the result. "The file was erased."

"Who by?" Chandra said. When he didn't answer, she craned her neck to read his display upside down, then gave a soft cry of surprise.

"Captain Gomberg Fletcher," she breathed.

They stared at one another for a moment.

"You can't suppose," Chandra began, "that Fletcher was somehow part of the Naxid plot, and that Javier found out about it, and Fletcher had him killed?"

Martinez considered this, then shook his head. "I can't think of anything the Naxids could offer Fletcher to make him betray his ship."

Chandra gave a little laugh. "Maybe they offered to give him a painting he really wanted."

Martinez shook his head. "No, I think Kosinic must have discovered the Narayanist cult. Or he discovered something else that got him killed, and Fletcher suppressed the information in order to protect the Narayanists." He looked at the data glowing in the depths of his desk, and his heart gave a surge as he saw the date.

"Wait a moment," he said. "Fletcher erased the file the same day he died." He looked more carefully at the date. "In fact, he seems to have erased the file around the time he was killed."

Chandra surged out of her hair and partway across his desk to confirm this. Her perfume, some kind of deep rosewood flavor with lemony highlights, floated into his senses. Glowing columns of data reflected in her eyes as she scanned for information. "The erase command came from this desk," she pointed out. "Whoever killed him sat in your chair, with the body leaking on the floor next to him, and cleaned up the evidence."

Martinez scanned along the log file. "Fletcher logged in three hours earlier, and never logged out. So he was probably looking at Kosinic's file when the killer arrived."

"What *other* files was he looking at?" Chandra slid off the desk and onto her own chair. She gave a series of rapid orders to the wall display. "That night he made entries in a file called 'Gambling.'"

Martinez looked at her in surprise. "Did Fletcher gamble?"

"Not in the time I knew him."

"Did Kosinic?"

"No. He couldn't afford it."

"Lots of people gamble who can't afford it," Martinez said.

"Not Javier. He thought it was a weakness, and he didn't think he could afford weakness." She looked at Martinez. "Why else do you think he exposed himself to hard gee when he had broken ribs and a head injury? He couldn't afford to be wounded, and he did his best to ignore the fact he should have been in the hospital." She returned her attention to the display. "The gambling file was erased at the same time as Javier's rebel file."

Martinez scanned the files that Fletcher had been accessing in the two days before his death. Reports from the department heads, statistics from the commissary, reports on the status of a damage control robot that had been taken offline due to a hydraulic fault, injury reports, reports on available stores . . . all the daily minutiae of command.

Nothing was unusual except those two files, Rebel Data and Gambling. And those had been erased by the killer.

And erased very thoroughly, as Martinez discovered.

Normally a file was erased by simply removing it from the index of files, and unless the hard space had been overwritten with some other data, it was possible to reconstitute it. But the two missing files had been zeroed out, erased by overwriting their hard space with a series of random numbers. There was no way to find what had been in those files.

"Damn it!" He entertained a brief fantasy of hurling his coffee cup across the room and letting it smash the nose of one of Fletcher's armored statues. "We got so close."

Chandra gave the wall display a bleak stare. "There's still one chance," she said. "The system makes automatic backups on a regular basis. The automatic backups go into a temporary file and are erased by the system on a schedule. The *files* aren't there any longer, but the *tracks* might be, if they haven't been written over in the meantime."

"The chances of finding those old files must be—"

"Not *quite* astronomical." She pursed her lips in calculation. "I'd be willing to undertake the search, my duties permitting, but I'm going to need more authority with the system than I've got as a member of Chen's staff."

He warmed his coffee while he considered Chandra's offer. He supposed that, as someone involved with both murder victims, she was still theoretically a suspect. But on the other hand, it was unlikely she'd offer to spend her time going through the ship's vast datafiles track by track.

Unless, of course, she was covering up her own crimes.

Martinez's thoughts were interrupted by a polite knock on the dining room door. He looked up to see his cook, Perry.

"I was wondering when you'd be wanting supper, my lord."

"Oh." He forced his mind from one track to the next. "Half an hour or so?"

"Very good, my lord." Perry braced and withdrew, closing the door behind him.

Martinez returned his attention to Chandra and realized,

belatedly, that it might have been polite to invite her to supper.

He also realized he'd made up his mind. He didn't think Chandra had killed anybody—had never believed it—and in any case he had to agree with Michi that the squadron couldn't spare her.

If she wanted to spend her spare hours hunting incriminating tracks in the cruiser's data banks and erasing them, he didn't much care.

"If you'll give me your key," he said, "I'll see if I can give you more access."

He awarded her a clearance that would enable her to examine the ship's hard data storage, then returned her key. She tucked it back into her tunic and gave him a provocative smile.

"Do you remember," she said, "when I told you that I'd be the best friend you ever had?"

Again, Martinez was suddenly aware of her rosewood perfume, of the three tunic buttons that had been undone, and of the fact that he'd been living alone on the ship for far too many months.

"Yes," he said.

"Well, I've proved it." She closed the buttons, one by one. "One day the squadcom talked to me about whether you could have killed Fletcher, and I talked her out of the idea."

Martinez was speechless.

"You shouldn't count too much on the fact that you married Lord Chen's daughter," Chandra went on. "The impression I received was that if you died out here, it might solve any number of Lord Chen's problems. He'd have a marriageable daughter again, for one thing."

Martinez considered this, and found it disturbingly plausible. Lord Chen hadn't wanted to give up his daughter, not even in exchange for the millions the Martinez clan were paying him, and his brother Roland had practically marched Lord Chen to the wedding in a hammerlock. If

Martinez could be executed of a crime—and furthermore, a crime against both the Gombergs and the Fletchers—then he couldn't imagine Lord Chen shedding many tears.

"Interesting," he managed to say.

Chandra rose and leaned over his desk. "But," she said, "I pointed out to Lady Michi that you'd played an important part in winning our side's only victories against the Naxids, and that we really couldn't spare you even if you *were* a killer."

The phrasing brought a smile to Martinez's lips. "You might have given me the benefit of the doubt," he said. "I might *not* have killed Fletcher, after all."

"I don't think Lady Michi was interested in the truth by that point. She just wanted to be able to close the file." She perched on his desk and brushed its glossy surface with her fingertips. A triumphant light danced in her eyes. "So am I your friend, Gareth?" she asked.

"You are." He looked up at her and answered her smile. "And I'm yours, because when Lady Michi was trying to pin the murder on you—with far more reason, I thought—I talked her out of it by using much the same argument."

He saw the shock roll through Chandra like a slow tide. Her lips formed several words that she never actually spoke, and then she said, "She's a ruthless one, isn't she?"

"She's a Chen," Martinez said.

Chandra slowly rose to her feet, then braced. "Thank you, my lord," she said.

"You're welcome, Lieutenant."

He watched her leave, a little unsteadily, and then paged Mersenne. When the plump lieutenant arrived, Martinez invited him to sit.

"Some time ago," Martinez said, "before I joined the squadron, you found Lieutenant Kosinic leaving an access hatch on one of the lower decks. Do you happen to remember which one?"

Mersenne blinked in utter surprise. "I haven't thought about that in months," he said. "Let me think, my lord."

Martinez let him think, which Mersenne accomplished while pinching his lower lip between his thumb and forefinger.

"That would be Deck Eight," Mersenne said finally. "Access Four, across from the riggers' stores."

"Very good," Martinez said. "That will be all."

As Mersenne, still puzzled, rose to his feet and braced, Martinez added, "I'd be obliged if you mention my interest in this to no one."

"Yes, my lord."

Tomorrow, Martinez thought, he would announce an inspection on Deck 8, and there would be plenty of witnesses to anything he might find.

After breakfast, Martinez staged an inspection in which Access 4 on Deck 8 was opened. The steady rumble of ventilation blowers rose from beneath the deckplates. He descended with Marsden's datapad, squeezed between the blowers and a coolant pipe wrapped in bright yellow insulation material, and checked the serial numbers on the blowers against the numbers on the 77-12 that had been supplied by Rigger/First Rao.

The numbers matched.

Martinez crouched in the confined space and checked the numbers again. Again they matched.

He straightened, his head and shoulders coming above deck level, and looked at Rao, who looked at him with anxious interest.

"When were these blowers last replaced?"

"Just before the war started, my lord. They're not due for replacement for another four months."

So these were the same blowers that Kosinic had seen when he'd gone down the same access. If it wasn't the serial numbers, Martinez thought, what had Kosinic been looking for?

Martinez ducked down the access again and ran his hands along the pipes, the ductwork, the electric conduit, just in case something had been left here, a mysterious message or an ominous warning. He found nothing but the dust that filled his throat and left him coughing.

Perhaps Mersenne had been wrong about where he'd seen Kosinic. Martinez had several of the nearby access plates raised, and he descended into each to find again that everything was in order.

Frustration bubbled in his blood as he complimented Rao on his record-keeping, and it kept bubbling as he marched away.

Hours later, while he was eating a late supper—a ham sandwich made of leftovers from the meal he'd given Michi—a memory burst on his mind.

With Francis it's always about money.

That had been Alikhan's comment on the cruiser's former master rigger, and now, days after they'd been spoken, it came back to Martinez.

Gambling, he thought.

He carried his plate from the dining room to his desk, where he called up the display, then used the authority of his captain's key to access the commissary records and check the files of the commissary bank.

Actual cash wasn't handed to the crew during the voyage: accounts were kept electronically in the commissary bank, which was technically, a branch of the Imperial Bank, which issued the money in the first place. Crew would pay electronically for anything purchased from the commissary, and any gambling losses would be handled by direct transfer from one account to another.

The crew were paid every twenty days. Martinez looked at the account of Rigger Francis and saw that it totaled nearly nine thousand zeniths, enough to buy an estate on nearly any planet in the empire.

And this was only the money that Francis had in *this account*. She could have more in accounts in other banks, in investments, in property.

Martinez called for Alikhan. His orderly came into the dining room first, was surprised to find Martinez in his office, and approached.

"Would you like me to take your plate, my lord?"

Martinez looked in surprise at the plate he'd brought with him from the dining room. "Yes," he said. "No. Never mind that now."

Alikhan looked at him. "Yes, my lord."

"Some time ago," Martinez said, "you took an advance on your salary in order to pay a gambling debt."

Alikhan gave a cautious nod. "Yes, my lord."

"I would like to know who you were gambling *with*."

Alikhan hesitated. "My lord, I shouldn't like to—"

"Do they cheat?" Martinez asked.

Alikhan considered his answer for a long moment before speaking.

"I don't think so, my lord. I think they're very experienced players, and at least some of the time they play in concert."

"But they gamble with recruits, don't they?"

Martinez thought he saw an angry tightening of Alikhan's lips before the answer came.

"Yes, my lord. In the mess, every night."

It's always about money. Again Alikhan's words echoed in his head.

Gambling was of course against Fleet regulations, but such regulations were applied with a degree of discretion. Action was rarely taken if the petty officers played cards in their lounge, or the lieutenants wanted to play tingo in the wardroom, or the recruits rolled dice in the engine spaces. It was a minor vice, and nearly impossible to stop. Gambling games and gambling scams were almost universal in the Fleet.

But the gambling could become dangerous when it crossed lines of caste. When petty officers gambled with recruits, serious issues of abuse of power came into play. A superior officer could enforce a vicious payment schedule, and could punish recruits with extra duties or even assault. A recruit who owed money to his superior could not only lose whatever pay he happened to possess at the time, but could lose future salary either in direct losses or interest payments. The recruit might be forced to pay in other ways: gifts, sexual favors, performing the petty officers' duties, or even being forced to steal on behalf of his superior.

It had been months since Chenforce left Harzapid, and it would be months more before *Illustrious* would stop in a Fleet dockyard. A recruit in the grips of a gambling ring could lose his pay for the entire journey, possibly the entire commission.

"Who's taking part in this?" Martinez asked.

"Well, my lord," Alikhan said, "I'd rather not get anyone in trouble."

"You're not getting them in trouble," Martinez said. "They're *already* in trouble. But you can exclude those who aren't a part of it by naming those who are."

This logic took a few seconds to work its way through Alikhan's mind, but in the end he nodded.

"Very well, my lord," he said. "Francis, Gawbyan, and Gulik organize the games. And Thuc was a part of it, but he's dead."

"Very good," Martinez said. He turned to his desk, then looked back at Alikhan. "I don't want you mentioning this conversation to anyone."

"Of course n—"

"Dismissed."

Martinez was already racing on to the next problem. He called up the accounts of Francis, Gawbyan, Gulik, and Thuc, and saw that they jumped on every payday, far more than if they were being paid their salary. Nearly two-thirds of their income seemed to come in the form of direct transfers from other crew. Martinez backtracked the transfers and found no less than nine recruits who regularly transferred their entire pay to the senior petty officers. They'd been doing it for months. Others were paying less regularly, but still paying.

Anger simmered in Martinez. *You people like playing with recruits so much,* he thought, *maybe you should be recruits.*

He would break them. And he'd confiscate the money too, and turn it over to the ship's entertainment fund, or perhaps to Fleet Relief to aid distressed crew.

He checked the totals and found that Gulik was losing the money practically as fast as he was making it. Apparently the weaponer was truly devoted to gambling, and eventually lost every bit of his earnings to his friends. At the moment he had practically nothing in his accounts.

The scent of coffee wafted past his nose, and he looked up from the accounts to find that someone had placed a fresh cup of coffee by his elbow, next to a plate of newly made sandwiches. Alikhan had made the ghostly delivery and Martinez hadn't even noticed.

He ate a sandwich and drank a cup of coffee.

Always about the money, he thought.

He opened the 77-12 that he'd viewed just that morning and looked again at the serial number of the ventilation blowers. He backtracked through the record and found that Rao had corrected the serial number from the purely fictional one that Francis had originally recorded in the log.

Every item in *Illustrious,* Martinez knew, came with its own history. Every pump, every transformer, every missile launcher, every robot, every processor, and every waste recycler came with a long and complex record that included the date of manufacture or assembly, the date at which it was purchased by the Fleet, the date at which it was installed, and each date at which it was subject to maintenance or replacement.

Martinez called up the history of the air blowers on Deck 8 and discovered that, according to the records, the blowers had been destroyed with the *Quest,* a Naxid frigate involved in the mutiny at Harzapid.

Rebel Data, he thought.

He checked the history of the turbopump that had failed at Arkhan-Dohg, and found that the turbopump had been decommissioned three years earlier, replaced by a new pump fresh from the factory, and sold as scrap.

His mouth was dry. He was suddenly aware of the silence in his office, the easy throb of his pulse, the cool taste of the air.

He knew who had killed Kosinic and Fletcher, and why.

TWENTY-THREE

Once the Fleet Control Board and their staff had come aboard, *Galactic* cast off from the ring in order to build the delta vee necessary for escape in the event the Naxids came to Antopone. A few hours later the two brand-new heavy cruisers launched. Their Daimong crews were inexperienced, and the ships hadn't yet received their weapons. They couldn't fight, and so would have to flee.

A squadron of eight Naxid ships had departed the fleet guarding the Zanshaa system: they were heading for Zanshaa Wormhole 2 at a steady four gees acceleration. At that rate they could be at Zarafan in less than ten days.

From Zarafan they could continue to Laredo, normally a journey of three months, but less if they continued to tenderize themselves with heavy gravities. Or from Zarafan the Naxids could take a wormhole that could lead them eventually to Antopone and, from there, Chijimo; or alternately, they could use another wormhole to take them through a series of barren systems to Seizho, from which they could return to Zanshaa.

This last was thought unlikely. If they wanted to raid Seizho, they could go there direct from the capital.

"They've learned from us," Mondi said in his precise way. He adjusted the dark goggles he wore over his night-adapted eyes. "Our raids must be hurting them if they're launching a raid themselves."

"But is this their *only* raid?" Pezzini wondered. "This could be a probe designed to get our defenses off balance, and then they launch a larger strike elsewhere—Harzapid and what remains of the Fourth Fleet, for example."

Lord Chen contemplated mosaics on the walls, with their bright warships rocketing out of wormholes, and shook his head.

"That doesn't matter, my lords," he said. "We don't have the ships to oppose more than one raid, and in any case Laredo has to be protected."

He was just a politician, he thought, not a Fleet officer, but even he knew *that*. He could already picture in his mind the panicked series of instructions from the Convocation, demanding that the Fleet save them from the Naxids.

"Very well," said Lord Tork. "We shall order Lord Eino to move his forces in this direction, to guard the Convocation if necessary."

Tork was in the process of dictating this order to the secretary of the board when the secretary's comm unit chirped—a message from Lord Eino Kangas stating that the Home Fleet was already in motion, heading for Antopone.

Kangas had read the situation as the board had, and reached an identical conclusion.

Bulletins arrived almost hourly, so Lord Chen and the others were kept well-informed of the movements of the various players. The Naxids took ten days to reach Zarafan, a journey that normally took a month. Once there, they destroyed the few civilian ships that hadn't made their escape and demanded and received the planet's surrender. It had been hoped that the Naxids might detach ships to remain in the system—detachments could be picked off later—but instead they reduced their fierce acceleration and swung through Wormhole 3 on a course that would eventually take them to Antopone. The course of the enemy raid was now clear: Zarafan-Antopone-Chijimo, and then the return to Zanshaa. It was an unambitious raid compared to those Michi Chen and Altasz had launched into Naxid space, but perhaps it was a rehearsal for others.

Now that Kangas knew where the enemy were bound, he

increased his acceleration and headed for Antopone, his ships crossing paths with the *Galactic* and the two refugee cruisers heading the other way. Kangas wanted to arrive at Antopone ahead of the Naxids to protect the shipbuilding facilities on the planet's ring.

Kangas's ships were ready for a fight. The five survivors of the Home Fleet burned to avenge their defeat at Magaria, and Do-faq's seven ships were confident of victory, having already wiped out a Naxid squadron at the Lai-own home world of Hone-bar.

Kangas succeeded in arriving first, placing his forces between Antopone and the arriving Naxids. The raiders—seven frigates led by a light cruiser—arrived in the system to find twelve heavy cruisers driving for them head-on, with barrages of missiles already launched.

The Fleet Control Board, in their meeting room on *Galactic,* watched the battle courtesy of the amazingly detailed spectra gathered by detectors on the Antopone ring, and projected in three-dimensional holographic images above the board's long table. The illusion that they were watching in real time was perfect, and Lord Chen had to keep reminding himself that the battle had in fact occurred fifteen hours before. They saw the missiles launched at a target that had not as yet appeared through the wormhole, the Naxid squadron entering "hot" with radars and ranging lasers hammering, and then a frenzy of countermissile firings and maneuvers as the Naxid commander rearranged his formation.

"The Naxid's pissing his pants by now," Pezzini said with satisfaction.

"*No!*" Tork cried, his melodious voice edged with an uncanny shimmering quality that Lord Chen had never heard before. Chen stared at him, and then at the display.

"Starburst," Pezzini said critically. "And damned early too."

The compact bundle of ships that was Kangas's command were separating, flying apart like the casing of an exploded bomb.

"Kangas may just have lost the war!" Tork said. Anger buzzed in his voice. "He has shamed us before our ancestors!"

Chen knew that warships usually clumped together in rigid formations that enabled the commander to communicate with them, and that at some point in a battle the ships would "starburst": separate from one another in order to provide a less compact target. He also knew that his son-in-law, Captain Martinez, had devised a new tactical system based on the ships separating from one another early and engaging in maneuvers governed by some rather obscure branches of mathematics. Lord Tork and other conservative officers were bitterly opposed to these new ideas.

"Do-faq has corrupted Kangas!" Tork said. "Do-faq, who was corrupted by Martinez and has practiced these innovations! The fleetcom has fallen a victim to these dangerous new fashions!"

"The Home Fleet's advantage was in numbers," Pezzini remarked. "Kangas has thrown that all away. With his ships separated that way, each is fighting on its own."

Chen remained silent. The battle had been fought *hours* ago, he reminded himself.

The opposing forces, hurtling toward each other, closed the distance rapidly. Missiles found each other in the spaces between the contending squadrons, creating expanding spheres of hot expanding plasma and radio hash. The Naxid force disappeared from the display as the missile burst screened them from the sensors on the Antopone ring. More missiles hurled themselves into the gap between the racing squadrons, and the plasma screen broadened and thickened.

Eventually the Home Fleet flew into the screen, and vanished as if an invisible hand had wiped it from existence.

"Damn," Pezzini said, rather clinically.

No one else spoke. Even Tork could find no words.

Then the plasma screen began to cool and disperse, and gradually—winking into existence on the holographic display like a distant flight of fluorescent insects—the Home Fleet reappeared, one ship after another, their torches now pointed away from the planet, decelerating.

One, Lord Chen counted to himself, *two, three . . . five. Eight! Ten!*

Ten survivors of the Home Fleet were now narrowing their dispersed formation as they approached the wormhole that would take them in the direction of Zarafan.

Of the Naxids there was no sign.

"We wiped them out!" Lord Chen blurted. "It's a victory!"

"Damn Kangas!" Tork said. "Damn him! He's lost two ships!"

It was only a short time later that Squadron Commander Do-faq's report reached *Galactic.* The Home Fleet had wiped out eight enemy ships and lost two of their own.

And one of the casualties was the flagship. Lord Eino Kangas had died in the act of giving the Home Fleet its one and only victory.

Invitations went out in the morning, sent to all the senior petty officers. An invitation for drinks with their new captain, set for an hour before supper, was not something the customs of the service would let them decline, and decline they did not. The last affirmative reply came within minutes of the invitations being sent out.

The touchstone dramatical, Martinez thought. The scene climactic.

The petty officers entered the dining room more or less in a clump: round-faced Gawbyan with his spectacular mustachios, Strode with his bowl haircut, burly Francis, thin, nervous Cho. Some of them were surprised to find the ship's secretary Marsden waiting with his datapad in his hands.

The guests sorted themselves out in order of seniority, with the highest-ranked standing near Martinez at the head of the table. Gulik was on his right, across from Master Cook Yau, with Gawbyan and Strode the next pair down, one grand set of mustachios confronting another; and then Zhang and Nyamugali. Near the bottom of the table was the demoted Francis.

Martinez looked at them all as they stood by their chairs. Francis seemed thoughtful and preoccupied, and her eyes looked anywhere but at him. Yau looked as if he had left his kitchens only reluctantly. Strode seemed determined, as if he had a clear but not entirely pleasant duty before him; and Gulik, who had been so nervous during inspections, was now almost cheerful.

Martinez picked up his glass and raised it. Pale green wine trembled in Captain Fletcher's leaded crystal, reflecting beads of peridot-colored light over the company.

"To the Praxis," he said.

"The Praxis," they echoed, and drank.

Martinez took a gulp of his wine and sat. The others followed suit, including Marsden, who sat by himself to the side of the room and set his datapad to record. He picked up a stylus and stood ready to correct the datapad's transcription of the conversation.

"You may as well keep the wine in circulation," Martinez said, nodding to the crystal decanters set on the table. "We'll be here for a while, and I don't want you to go dry."

There were murmurs of appreciation from those farther down the table, and hands reached for the bottles.

"The reason this meeting may take some time," Martinez said, "is because like the last meeting, this is about record-keeping."

There was a collective pause from his guests, and then a resigned, collective sigh.

"You can blame it on Captain Fletcher, if you want to," Martinez said. "He ran *Illustrious* in a highly personal and distinctive way. He'd ask questions during inspections and he'd expect you to know the answers, but he never asked for any documentation. He never checked the 77-12s, and never had any of his officers do it."

Martinez looked at his wineglass and nudged it slightly

with his thumb and forefinger, putting it in alignment with some imaginary dividing line running through the room.

"The problem with a lack of documentation, though," he said, keeping his eyes on the wineglass, "is that to a certain cast of mind, it means *profit*." He sensed Yau stiffen on his left, and Gulik gave a little start.

"Because," Martinez continued, picking carefully through his thoughts, "in the end Captain Fletcher only knew what you told him. If it looked all right, and what he was told was plausible, then how would he ever find out if he'd been yarned or not?

"Particularly because Fleet standards require that equipment exceed all performance criteria. Politicians have complained for centuries that it's a waste of money, but the Control Board has always required that our ships be overbuilt, and I think the Control Board's been right.

"But what *that* meant," he said, "is that department heads could, with a little extra maintenance, keep our equipment going far longer than performance specs required." He looked up for the first time, and saw Strode watching him with a kind of thoughtful surprise, as if recalculating every conclusion about Martinez that he'd ever reached. Francis was staring straight ahead of her, her graying hair partly concealing her face. Cho seemed angry.

Gulik was pale. Martinez could see the pulse beating in his throat. When he saw Martinez studying him, he reached for his glass and took a large gulp of the wine.

"If you keep the old equipment going," Martinez said, "and if you know where to go, you can sell the replacement gear for a lot of money. Things like blowers and coolers and pumps can bring a nice profit. Everyone *likes* Fleet equipment, it's so reliable and forgiving and overbuilt. And they were getting *this* stuff new, right out of the box."

He looked at Francis's scowling profile. "I checked the turbopump that failed at Arkhan-Dohg—using the *correct* serial number, not the number that Rigger Francis tried to yarn me with—and I found out the pump was supposed to have been retired three years ago. Someone had been keeping it going long after it should have been sold as scrap."

Martinez turned to Gulik. Sweat was pouring down the weaponer's face. He looked as deadly sick as he had been on the morning of Fletcher's last inspection, as the captain stalked toward him with the knife dangling at his waist.

"I also checked the serial number of the antiproton gun that failed in the same battle, and that was supposed to have been retired thirteen months ago. I hope that whoever sold the replacement wasn't selling it to someone intending to use it as a weapon."

"It wasn't me," Gulik croaked. He wiped sweat from his upper lip. "I don't know anything about this."

"Whoever did it," Martinez said, "didn't intend to endanger the ship. We weren't at war. *Illustrious* had been docked in Harzapid for three years without so much as shifting its berth. The heavy equipment was moving on and off the ship all the time, moving through the locked storage room where substitutions could be made without anyone being the wiser."

Martinez turned to look down the line of petty officers. "In order to work this scheme," he said, "you'd need that storage room. You'd also need the services of a first-rate machinist, with access to a complete machine shop, so that the old equipment could be rehabilitated before it was reinstalled."

Strode turned to look thoughtfully at the master machinist. Gawbyan's lips had thinned to a tight line across his fleshy face. His mustachios were brandished like tusks. One large, fat-fingered hand had closed into a fist around the stem of his wineglass.

"So far, so good," Martinez said. "Our happy band of felons were making a profit. But then they took on some partners. And the partners were Naxids."

That surprised some of them. Yau and Cho stared. Strode's mouth dropped open.

"Specifically," Martinez said, "the Naxid frigate *Quest,* which was berthed next to *Illustrious* on the ring station. I expect the gang knew the Naxid petty officers informally before anyone mentioned the possibilities of mutual profit. And then they began using one another's facilities and swapping parts with one another, which is how equipment from the *Quest* ended up aboard *Illustrious*.

"Now in order to exchange parts, the codes for the storage areas had to be exchanged as well. And that didn't work out so well, because the Naxids involved somehow got the *extra* codes for the antiproton storage areas— maybe they came up with a plausible story of needing to exchange antiproton bottles, or maybe they just hid a camera where they could get a view of the lock so they could record the combination—but the result was that shortly before the Naxid rebellion, all of our antiproton bottles were exchanged for empty ones."

The *our* was deliberate, even though Martinez hadn't been there. In war there was us and them, and Martinez wanted to make it clear who was which.

"The result was that *Illustrious* was helpless to defend itself in the battle, and unable to aid our comrades. I'm sure you all remember what that was like."

They did. He watched as they relived their helplessness, as anger blotched their faces, as jaw muscles clenched at the memory of humiliation.

"The bastards," Nyamugali said. Hatred burned in her eyes. "The bastards," she repeated.

Us and *them,* Martinez thought. Very good, signaler.

"*Illustrious* survived the battle," Martinez said, "no thanks to the thieves. But the Naxid rebellion left them with a problem. Before the war, they were felons; but once shots were fired, they were *traitors*. And while the penalty for theft from the state can be dire under the Praxis, the cost of being found a traitor is much, much worse.

"The thieves' problems increased," Martinez said, "when an officer launched his own, personal investigation of how the antiproton bottles turned up empty. Maybe his injuries had turned him into an obsessive, or maybe when he was running into the storage area to fetch the bottles, he'd seen something that made him suspicious. But once Kosinic started conducting his own equipment inspections—lifting access plates and checking the machine spaces—it was clear that he was going to find the evidence that would condemn our ship's clique. So Kosinic had to die."

"It was Thuc." Gawbyan's voice came out in a half-strangled croak. "Thuc killed Kosinic because of the cult. You said so yourself."

"I was both right and wrong," Martinez said. "Thuc *did* kill Kosinic. But not because Thuc was a cultist. Kosinic was killed because Thuc was a thief, and Thuc may not have acted alone."

There was a moment of silence. Somewhere down the table, Master Data Specialist Zhang tossed back her glass of wine, then reached for a bottle and refilled it.

"Kosinic's death was ruled accidental, as it was meant to be," Martinez continued. "All continued well for the conspirators, until the worst possible thing happened. Captain Fletcher himself grew suspicious. Maybe it was his turn to wonder how only *his* antiproton bottles, of all those in the Fourth Fleet, had turned up empty; or maybe he began to realize the weakness in his own system of inspections; or maybe he grew offended when he discovered that a gambling ring composed of high-ranking petty officers was skinning a group of recruits in the mess hall every single night."

That accusation struck home, Martinez saw. Even those who weren't a part of the gambling had to know about it, and most of them had the decency to look embarrassed.

"Captain Fletcher was a proud man," Martinez said. "His pride had already been offended when his ship was disarmed in a crucial battle. That was the sort of thing that would have launched an official investigation if *Illustrious* hadn't been so badly needed in the emergency—and maybe there would have been an investigation anyway if Fletcher hadn't been so well connected, I don't know.

"That his ship had not only been humiliated at Harzapid, but was also home to a gang of traitorous thieves, was a further blow to the captain's pride. Any kind of official investigation would reveal how badly Captain Fletcher had let things get out of hand. *That* would be a black mark that neither his career or his pride would survive.

"So Captain Fletcher decided to handle the situation on his own. He executed Thuc and claimed captain's privilege. No doubt he intended to execute the rest as well."

"I wasn't a part of any ring," Gulik said suddenly. "Fletcher had the chance to execute me, and he didn't."

Martinez looked at the weaponer and slowly shook his head. "Fletcher looked at your current bank account and saw that you were broke. He didn't think you were a thief because he couldn't find the profits. But when I looked at a running total of your bank account, I saw that you were very clearly a member of the ring, but that you're also a compulsive gambler. Your money slips through your fingers almost as soon as you earn it."

Desperation shone in Gulik's eyes. There was a strange odor coming off of him, sweat and fear and alcohol ghosting out of his pores. "I never killed anybody," he said. "I didn't have anything to do with that."

"But you know who did," Martinez said.

"I—" Gulik began.

"Quiet!" Francis barked. She glared down the table at Gulik. "Don't you see what he's doing? He's trying to get us to turn on each other." Her fierce gaze looked at each of the petty officers in turn. "He's trying to divide us! He's trying to get us so frightened that we start making accusations against each other!" She looked at Martinez, and her lip curled. "We know who *really* killed Fletcher, don't we? The man who stepped into his place!"

She looked at the other department heads and snarled.

"We all know how Martinez got to be captain! Married the squadcom's homely niece, then bashed Fletcher's head in so he could have the ship. And when Phillips found out, he had Phillips arrested and murdered so Phillips wouldn't talk."

Martinez fought to control the adrenaline that surged into his veins. He pressed his hands carefully to the table-top to control any trembling. With deliberation, he looked at Francis and gave her a sweet smile.

"Nice try, Rigger Francis," he said. "You're at liberty to file that accusation if you wish. But you'd better have evidence. And you'd better have an explanation for how air blowers from the *Quest* ended up on Deck Eight, Access Four."

She stared at him for a moment, hate-filled eyes locking his, and then she turned away. "Fucking officers!" she said. "Fucking Peers!"

Martinez spoke into the ringing silence and tried to keep his voice level.

"So Fletcher had to die. And once the killers disposed of him, they must have again congratulated themselves on a narrow escape. Except that then I stepped into Fletcher's place, and I insisted on every department completing its 77-12."

Martinez permitted himself a thin smile. "The conspirators must have had a debate among themselves as how best to handle the new requirement. If the 77-12s had accurate information, it would point to obsolete equipment and the *Quest*. But if the logs were yarned, an inspection could reveal the deception."

He looked at Francis. "Rigger Francis's misadventures with the turbopump demonstrated the folly of yarning the log. So the others gave correct information and hoped that no one ever checked the hardware's history." He shrugged. "It took me a while, but I checked."

He swept the others with his eyes. "I'm going to assume that any department with equipment from the *Quest* is run by someone who's guilty. I've checked enough to see that there's machinery from the *Quest* in Thuc's old department, and in Gulik's, and in Francis's."

Francis made a contemptuous sound with her tongue and turned her head away. Gulik looked as if someone had just thrown a poisonous snake in his lap.

Martinez turned to Gawbyan. "They couldn't have done any of it without you. So you're guilty too."

Gawbyan's lips emerged from the thin line into which he'd pressed them. "Naxids," he said. "Naxid engineers could have done that work."

Martinez considered this idea and conceded that it was possible, if unlikely.

"Your account at the commissary will be examined closely," he said, "and we'll see if you share any mysterious payments with your mates. That'll be proof enough as far as I'm concerned."

A contemptuous look entered Gawbyan's eyes.

"I didn't kill anyone," Gulik said rapidly. "I didn't want to be a part of any of it but they talked me into it. They said I could earn back some of the money I'd lost at cards."

"Shut up, you rat-faced little coward," Francis said, but she said it without concern, as if she'd already lost interest in the proceedings.

"Gawbyan and Francis killed the captain!" Gulik cried. "Fletcher had already shown he wasn't going to kill me, I had no reason to want him dead!"

Francis flashed the weaponer a look of perfect disdain but said nothing. Martinez saw Gawbyan's big hands closing into fists.

If this were one of the Dr. An-ku dramas that Michi enjoyed, Martinez thought, it would have been the moment at which the killers produced weapons and made a murderous lunge for him, or taken hostages and tried to bargain their way out. But that didn't happen.

Instead Martinez called for Alikhan, and Alikhan entered from the kitchen with Garcia and four constables, including Martinez's servants Ayutano and Espinosa. All, even Alikhan, were armed with stun batons and sidearms.

"Gawbyan, Gulik, and Francis," Martinez said. "Lock them up."

All three were cuffed from behind. There was no resistance, though Francis gave Alikhan a scornful look.

"Wait, Captain!" Gulik said as he was manhandled out the door. "This isn't fair! They *made* me!"

Alikhan remained behind, hovering behind Martinez, who felt a great tension begin to ebb. He picked up his wineglass, took a long drink and put the glass back on the table.

It wasn't as if he didn't deserve a drink right now.

He looked at the remaining petty officers. "There were lines crossed on this ship," Martinez said. "Four senior petty officers conspired to rob recruits of their pay, and no one complained, no one talked, and no one did anything about it. Those same petty officers branched out into sale of Fleet property, and they put the ship in danger over and over. People died at Harzapid because of those four.

"And it wasn't just the petty officers," Martinez said. "Captain Fletcher crossed some lines too, and maybe that made others think it was acceptable."

He looked at his remaining guests and saw them staring at nothing, or perhaps looking inward. Cho and Zhang seemed angry. Nyamugali looked as if he were ready to weep.

"If any of you were involved with any of these schemes," Martinez said, "I need to know *now*. I need to know what you know. Believe me, it will go better with you if you turn yourselves in than if I find it out on my own. Right now I haven't done anything more than spot-check the logs, and I haven't looked at financial records in any kind of detailed way. But I *will*. Now that I know what to look for, I'll have that information very soon."

There was silence, and then Amelia Zhang turned to Martinez and said, "You won't find anything wrong in my department, my lord. And you can look at my finances and see I live on my pay and that most of it goes to my kids' school fees."

"My department's clean," said Strode. He brushed one of his mustachios with a knuckle. "I yarned my log, I admit that, but I didn't like those others, Thuc and Francis particularly, and whenever they talked to me about ways of making money I wouldn't listen."

Martinez nodded.

"*Illustrious* depends on you all," he said. "You're more important to this ship than the officers. You're all professionals and you're all good at what you do, and I know that's the case because Captain Fletcher wouldn't have had you aboard otherwise. But those others—they're the *enemy*. Understand?"

He had a feeling he'd made better speeches in his career. But he hoped he'd succeeded in creating a dividing line, the kind that was necessary in war, between us and them. Those he'd just labeled as *us* were people he needed very badly. *Illustrious* had been scarred, not in combat but in its heart, and the remaining petty officers were going to be a vital part in any healing. He could have had the killers arrested in their beds and dragged to the brig, but that wouldn't have had the same effect on their peers. It could have been put down to arbitrary action on the part of an officer, and that wasn't what Martinez wanted. He wanted to demonstrate in front of their peers how guilty the killers were, and exactly how long and detailed their treachery was, and how badly it had put the ship in danger. He had wanted to separate *them* from *us*.

Martinez felt a sudden weariness. He'd done everything he'd set out to do, and said far more than he'd intended to say. He pushed back his chair and rose. Chairs scraped as they were pushed back, and the others jumped to their feet and braced.

Martinez reached for his glass and raised it. "To the Praxis," he said, and the others echoed him.

He drained his glass, and the others drained theirs.

"I won't keep you," he said. "I'll talk to the new department heads tomorrow morning."

He watched them file out, and when they were gone, he reached for a bottle and refilled his glass. He drained half of it in one long swallow, then he turned to Alikhan.

"Tell Perry I'll have supper in my office after I report to the squadcom."

"Very good, my lord."

Alikhan turned and marched, adjusting the belt with its sidearm and baton. Martinez looked at Marsden.

"Did you get all that?"

"Yes, my lord."

"Turn off your record function, please."

Marsden did so, and stood bald and impassive, waiting for Martinez's next order.

"I'm sorry about Phillips," Martinez said.

Surprise fluttered in the other man's eyes. He turned to Martinez. "My lord?"

"I know you would have saved him if you could."

There was an instant of surprise on Marsden's face, and then he mastered it and his face was impassive again.

"I'm sure, my lord, I don't know what you mean."

"You people have hand signals and so on, don't you?" Martinez asked. "You would have given Phillips a warning if he hadn't happened to be on watch in Command." He took in a breath and sighed it out. "I wish you had."

Marsden looked at him with intense brown eyes but said nothing.

"I worked out a while ago," Martinez said, "that Thuc may have been a killer, but he wasn't a Narayanist. The tree pendant was found in Thuc's belongings because you put it there, Marsden, when I sent you to collect his things. You knew that I was about to launch an investigation into cult affiliations, and you wanted to get rid of the evidence. So you took the pendant from around your own neck and put it in with Thuc's jewelry."

Marsden's neck muscles twitched. He looked stonily at Martinez.

"My lord," he said, "that's pure speculation."

"I couldn't work out why you were behaving so strangely," Martinez said. "You were very angry when I first mentioned Narayanists—and then you denounced me for daring to insult the Gomberg and Fletcher clans. You forced me to search you right then and there, though of course that was after you'd ditched your pendant. I thought you were some extreme kind of snob. What I didn't realize was that I'd just insulted your most deeply held beliefs.

"The problem is, that pendant helped to condemn Phillips. You didn't know that one of Thuc's fingerprints was found on Kosinic's body. That linked murder and Narayanism in my mind, and I charged off on a campaign to find cult killers. That's the way cultists are always portrayed in video dramas—killing people and sacrificing children to false gods. I was misled by a lifetime of watching that sort of drama. I forgot that Narayanism isn't a killing sort of belief."

"I wouldn't know, my lord." Marsden spoke with great care.

Martinez shrugged. "I wanted you to know I was sorry about the way I handled things. You won't forgive me, I'm sure, but I hope you'll understand." He took a long drink of his wine. "That's all, Marsden. If you can copy me that recording, and append a transcription as soon as you can, I'd be very much obliged."

Marsden braced. "Yes, my lord."

"You are dismissed."

Marsden turned and walked away, his back straight, his head facing rigidly forward. Martinez watched the door close behind him.

Apology not accepted, he thought.

He took another long drink of his wine, and then he walked to his office, put the wineglass on his desk, and walked out into the corridor.

It was time to report to Lady Michi.

TWENTY-FOUR

Anxiety over the Naxid raid had not improved Tork's appearance. His flesh was dying faster than ever, and dry twists of skin hung from his hands and gray, expressionless face. Decay came off him in great gusts. But however frail his body seemed, his mind remained firm and inflexible as ever.

"There is only one possible solution," he said, "and that is for this board to appoint me commander of the Home Fleet."

Lady Seekin's eyes were huge beneath her dark goggles. "But aren't you retired, my lord?"

Resignation tinged Lord Tork's voice. "This board has the power to restore me to active service. I will accept, of course, with regret. I had hoped that those days were long past."

Lord Chen doubted that Tork's regret could possibly be greater than his own.

"I don't understand, my lord," he ventured. "You've been entrusted with the direction of the entire Fleet establishment, not just ships, but ring stations and everything on the ground as well. You're crucial to our hopes of victory. Can you possibly forsake this trust for the command of only one element?"

Chen had been afraid his words might provoke another diatribe from Tork, but the chairman's chiming voice remained level.

"There is no one else. Consider—the Home Fleet must be led by someone of suitable rank. Most of the active officers of fleet command rank died at Magaria, and the rest are too distant from the scene of action. Kringan is three months away, at Harzapid with the Fourth Fleet. Pel-to is at Felarus, with Naxid-held systems in the way. Trepatai is at Seizho, but her health broke down early in the war, and she hasn't left her bed for months. Lord Ivan Snow has suitable rank, but has spent most of his career with the Investigative Service, has never commanded a large formation, and is in any case three months away at Laredo, where he reports to the Convocation. Whereas I . . ."

There was a moment of silence. Lord Chen closed his throat against the sickly waft of dying flesh that floated to his nostrils.

"I am available," Tork said. "I will hold suitable rank once I am restored to the active list. I am a Daimong, and could join the two new Antopone cruisers, which are adapted for Daimong crews and could take me aboard without difficulty."

"Couldn't we *promote* someone into the position?" Lady Seekin asked. "Lord Pa Do-faq is a victorious commander. We couldn't find a more experienced officer."

Chen closed his eyes and wished he could close his ears as well, against the sonic storm that was bound to peal from Tork at Lady Seekin's sensible but naive sentiments. Again he was surprised, for Tork said nothing, while the question was answered by Pezzini.

"Do-faq's an advocate of the innovations that got Kangas killed," he said. "We can't put the Home Fleet under him—he'd just kill more good officers, and probably lose Zanshaa all over again. The Fleet needs to be under a strong disciplinarian and an advocate of orthodox tactics." He nodded at Tork. "The lord chairman fits the description."

"I am no longer young," Tork said, "but my health remains good. And in any case I need retain my vigor only a few more months."

After that there was no choice. Tork and his loyalists would block any attempt to promote Do-faq or anyone else.

Lord Chen raised his hand with the others when the vote was called, and Lord Tork was appointed unanimously to command the Home Fleet, charged with the reconquest of Zanshaa and the defeat of the rebels.

Tork threw himself into the work with his usual dedication. He didn't transfer himself to the Daimong ships right away, but stayed where he had sufficient support staff to keep himself informed of the status of the Fleet throughout the empire.

The Daimong ships continued to Chijimo, where they would dock and receive their weapons. Tork made certain all necessary equipment was shipped from Antopone. The Home Fleet under Do-faq decelerated all the way to Zarafan, then swung around its sun and whipped back to Chijimo.

Reinforcements were on their way. Three ships from the Fourth Fleet that had finished repairs after the battle at Harzapid. Three brand-new frigates, built with astounding efficiency by the Martinez yards at Laredo, were undergoing trials; and the Convocation, mightily impressed, commissioned five frigates more. Thirty-one more ships were nearing completion elsewhere in friendly space, and construction had begun on another sixty.

Fleet Commander Kringan, at Harzapid, apparently heard the call of the trumpets once the news of Kangas's death reached him. Within three days he'd placed himself aboard a frigate, one that hadn't yet finished repair, and launched himself for Chijimo with repair crews still aboard. Clearly he was hoping to arrive in time to be appointed commander of the Home Fleet, but unfortunately no one else was hearing the same trumpets, because by the time the frigate left Harzapid's system, Tork had already received the supreme command.

Lord Chen would be grateful for Kringan's presence, however. It would be good to have another high-ranking officer on hand in case Tork worked himself into a stroke.

But Tork showed no sign of flagging. He grew leaner and he shed skin at a fantastic rate, but he burned with a fever that his age could not quench. Lord Chen had to admit that no other officer could possibly have been more dedicated.

The Naxids launched no more raids.

"They've learned not to make detachments," Lord Mondi said as they relaxed one evening in *Galactic*'s lounge. "Every time they send a force out on its own, they lose it. Hone-bar, Protipanu, and now Antopone—and since there have been no Naxid survivors, they have no idea what's doing it to them."

"So it all comes down to one big battle then," said Pezzini. "It all comes down to Zanshaa."

The three traitors were executed two days after their arrest. The Convocation, in the hours following the start of the rebellion, had decreed that the penalty for treason was torture followed by hurling the condemned from a great height. Martinez managed to talk Michi out of the torture on the grounds that the squadron had no professional torturers and that amateurs were bound to make a mess of it. He couldn't tell whether Michi was relieved by her decision or not.

There were no heights to throw the condemned men from, but Michi managed an approximation. *Illustrious* was decelerating at one gravity, to swing around the blue giant Alekas and on to another wormhole, so she decided to eject the traitors from an airlock. Once free of the ship, the traitors would no longer be decelerating and would fall into the ship's burning antimatter tail.

And they would be ejected without vac suits. "Damned if I'll waste vac suits on them!" Michi snarled. The vacuum might well kill them before they were torn to atoms by the antimatter blast. Martinez didn't know which death would be worse.

Gawbyan was stoic in the moments leading up to his execution. Francis was contemptuous, and Gulik, who had condemned himself and the others repeatedly during his interrogation, sagged in a kind of bewilderment. He seemed to suggest that it was unfair to execute him. He'd cooperated and freely confessed, and he didn't understand why he didn't get a prize from a grateful empire.

They died with ceremony. A party waited at the airlock, Martinez, Michi with her staff, and all the lieutenants except Corbigny, who was on watch. All glittered in full dress. There was a guard, witnesses from each of the prisoners' departments, and the ship's band, which played the low, mournful "Death Without Honor" as the prisoners shuffled from the brig in their coveralls.

Constable Garcia stripped from the condemned their badges of rank and seniority. Guards tied their ankles together with white mourning tape, and their arms were taped to their sides. They were then taken into the airlock and loaded onto an apparatus designed to eject the bodies of crew who had died in accident or as a result of enemy action. The apparatus hadn't ever been used on live crew, so far as Martinez knew, but he imagined the principle remained the same.

The inner airlock door closed smoothly. Garcia stepped to the airlock controls. The band halted at the end of the phrase, and the drummer began a slow, throbbing pulse on the hourglass-shaped drum.

"Evacuate the airlock, Mr. Garcia," Martinez said.

"Evacuate the airlock, my lord." Garcia turned to the controls. If there was a sound, a hiss or the throb of pumps, it was covered by the sound of the drum.

If he were one of the condemned, Martinez thought, he'd try to hold his breath and hope to give himself a quick embolism.

Garcia turned back to him. "Airlock evacuated, my lord."

"Open outer airlock doors, Mr. Garcia."

The drum thudded on. Martinez was suddenly aware of a furious itch below his right shoulder blade.

"Outer doors opened, my lord."

"Proceed, Mr. Garcia."

Ejecting the condemned into space was the matter of pressing a keypad. Martinez hoped they were already dead. Garcia looked into the airlock through the little window, then turned back to Martinez.

"Airlock's clear, my lord."

"Close the outer door and repressurize. Lieutenant Mokgatle?"

Acting Lieutenant Mokgatle, who was blessed with an impressive reading voice, stepped forward from the ranks of the officers and read from the service from the dead.

"Life is brief, but the Praxis is eternal," Mokgatle concluded. "Let us all take comfort and security in the wisdom that all that is important is known."

He took a neat step back into ranks.

By now the condemned were stripped ions floating on the void. Martinez felt a moment of stillness building around him. The prisoners had been condemned according to law and executed with all the majesty that the traditions of the Fleet could provide. Their comrades had been present, either in person or mustered to observe by video from the mess or from duty stations in the ship. They were witnesses to the fact that the executions had been conducted properly, just as they'd been witnesses to the larceny that had begun the series of deaths.

Mute witnesses, in both cases. The recruits hadn't been consulted when their own department heads had conspired to rob them, and they hadn't been consulted when Martinez had proved their guilt and Michi ordered their executions.

Maybe it was time they were taken into their superiors' calculations.

Lady Michi cleared her throat in a deliberate way, suggesting that she was tired of waiting for something to happen.

Martinez took a step forward and turned to look at the camera that was recording the ceremony.

"The three condemned," he said, "and their partner Engineer Thuc, operated a gambling ring for months, preying openly on the crew of *Illustrious*. There is no record that any notice was taken of this, or that anyone registered a complaint. Their activity led by degrees to theft, treason, and the murder of two officers, including the captain of this ship."

He looked into the camera and tried to imagine the scene in the mess, the crew standing braced behind their tables, watching the proceedings on the video walls. The mess, where the gamblers had plundered their comrades every night.

"All the deaths could have been prevented," Martinez said, "if a proper report of their activities had been made, and action taken. For some reason, everyone, even the victims, chose to keep silence.

"Perhaps the crew has not been properly encouraged to report wrongdoing to their officers. I would like to change that."

He took a deep breath. "I want to assure the ship's company that my door is now open to any reports the crew may wish to make. Any crew will be admitted to see their captain, on any matter they consider important." He glanced at the line of officers behind and to one side of him. "I trust that my officers will be similarly receptive." They shifted uneasily in their line.

He faced the camera again. "When Captain Fletcher executed Engineer Thuc, he said it was for the honor of the ship. He was right. Our ship's honor was being daily dragged through the mud by a criminal gang. *Illustrious*'s honor is far from restored, but I'll be *damned* if I see it degraded any further."

Martinez paused, wondering if he hadn't said enough, or if he'd said too much.

He took his eyes off the camera, then looked at the crew

standing shoulder-to-shoulder in the corridor outside the airlock.

"Dismissed," he said.

The crew broke ranks and shuffled away as the band began a slow, dirgelike rendition of "Our Thoughts Are Ever Guided by the Praxis," normally a brisk marching tune. Michi stepped up to him, drawing her gloves off her fingers.

"You've let yourself in for it," she said.

"I hope not," Martinez said.

"Every recruit coming to you with his problems. Every slacker on the ship asking you for money or time off." She shook her head. "You'll be buried in them."

"Maybe, but I'll share," Martinez said, with another glance at his officers. Michi grinned and marched away. Chandra, standing behind her, began to follow, then hesitated and approached Martinez.

"You just made the ship yours," she said. "Treat her well."

At the words, Martinez felt, somewhere behind his breastbone, a slow unfolding of pride.

"Thank you." He glanced around him, then leaned closer to Chandra. "I enjoyed your exercise in creative writing, by the way."

She didn't look the least embarrassed. "I thought I caught his style rather well."

"Too many adverbs," Martinez said. "I pruned them back."

The night before, he'd looked at the prisoners' personnel files and brought them up to date. While he had the files open, he'd decided to go into Chandra's file and remove the poisonous fitness report that Fletcher had written for her.

In the end Martinez had decided the report simply wasn't worthy of Fletcher. He didn't want Fletcher's last act to be the slagging of an officer against whom he'd had a grudge.

Opening the file, Martinez was surprised to find that someone else had already rewritten the report. The report now emphasized Chandra's mastery of all aspects of her profession and the captain's admiration for her talents and personality. Where Fletcher's conclusion had read, "Promotion is not indicated," the line was now "Promotion is enthusiastically indicated."

Martinez had removed the word "enthusiastically." And then he'd removed the extra user privileges he'd given Chandra before she got it into her head to rewrite anything else.

The Naxids took their parting shot at Chenforce the next day, four hundred missiles tearing into the system on their tail.

Because Michi had destroyed the wormhole stations that would have tracked Chenforce, the missiles weren't able to make last second corrections and had to do their own searching. Because targeting took time, the missiles weren't able to fly as fast as they had at Arkhan-Dohg. From the instant Chenforce first felt the touch of the targeting lasers, the squadron had nearly twenty-six minutes to prepare their response. Batteries of countermissiles were launched and every defensive weapon was deployed.

Chenforce performed flawlessly. Countermissiles destroyed most of the incoming warheads on the approach, and the rest were targeted by lasers and antiproton beams before they could close with the squadron. The closest was killed nearly two minutes out. The mood in Command throughout the combat was clinical. Even the applause at the destruction of the last incoming missile was restrained.

That was the last Chenforce heard from the Naxids. The squadron passed through one more enemy-controlled system without finding anything to shoot at, and then entered the nearly barren Enan-dal system through Wormhole 1.

Last they heard, both the station at Enan-dal Wormhole 1 and the station at Wormhole 2 were still controlled by the loyalists.

Martinez, suited and watching his displays, sat in Command while communications lasers pulsed queries to each station.

Wormhole Station 1 did not reply, which argued that the Naxids had occupied it. Michi sent a message informing them that they would be destroyed if they didn't respond, and as if in answer, a lifeboat, presumably with the station crew aboard, broke from the station and began a high-gravity sprint toward the wormhole. Michi ordered both the station and the lifeboat destroyed, as either could conceivably track the squadron for a barrage of missiles.

It would take ten hours for Michi's message to reach Station 2, and nearly ten hours for any response to return. After the first few hours, when it was clear that no Naxid force was lurking behind the system's swollen red sun, Michi reduced the squadron to a lower level of alert, and Martinez left Command with suspense still humming in his nerves.

The squadron had been out of communication for nearly four months, and during that time the cause for which they fought could have died. The Naxids could have won a crushing victory over the remnants of the Home Fleet, or the loyalist cause simply collapsed in the wake of the fall of Zanshaa. It was a matter of conjecture whether Chenforce would have a home to return to.

Martinez was in Command at the earliest possible hour that he could expect a reply from Wormhole Station 2. It was early in the morning, before his usual hour for rising, and he clutched a cup of coffee in one hand, sipping as he listened to the routine chatter.

"Message from Station Two, my lord!" The joy in Acting Lieutenant Qing's voice was answered by a leap of Martinez's heart. "The message is in the proper code for the day. Decoding now . . ."

A pale Daimong face, set in a frozen expression of horrified surprise, appeared on Martinez's displays.

"Welcome to Enan-dal, Lady Michi," the Daimong said. "I am Warrant Officer Kassup of the Exploration Service.

We have been told to await you. Word of your arrival has already been sent to the Fleet. I am sending a digest of the latest news, and I will forward your mail and any instructions from the Fleet as soon as they arrive."

Martinez felt the easing of a tension he didn't know he had. He half listened to Michi's polite reply, then waited for a moment to see if she had any orders for him. She didn't.

Michi finished the report of her raid, with its account of the battles at Protipanu, Arkhan-Dohg, and Alekas, its lists of casualties, the status of her seven ships, the totals of enemy ships destroyed, the description of the ring's destruction at Bai-do, plus the details of the deaths of Captain Fletcher, two lieutenants, and four petty officers. The report was wrapped in several layers of cipher and sent to the Fleet Control Board by way of Station 2.

An instant later the crew's personal messages, already in the queue, were sent, and with these went Martinez's long serial letter to his wife Terza and shorter letters to his father, his mother, to his father-in-law Lord Chen, and to the two sisters who were still speaking to him. He also sent his father a scan of his portrait.

Martinez wasn't needed. He returned command of the ship to Qing, went to his bed, and slept dreamlessly for many hours, well past his normal time for waking.

Alikhan, wisely, let him sleep.

Four days later Chenforce sped through Enan-dal Wormhole 2, and half a day later received its mail. Martinez gave the entire crew two hours free time to catch up with the news from home.

He took advantage of his own offer and retired to his office and shut the door. He opened his desk display and scanned the long list of mail. There was no communication from Caroline Sula. He hadn't expected anything, but managed to notice its absence anyway.

He wondered where she was and what she was doing.

Martinez looked for the very last item by date, sent

eleven days earlier. It was a video file from Terza, and he opened it.

Lady Terza Chen was quite visibly pregnant now—nearly seven months, he calculated. She stood in the camera's range, draped in a long dark violet gown that emphasized the paler beauty of her face and of the hands that rested lightly on her pregnant belly. Her hair was long and black and worn in a pair of long tails, threaded with ribbon, that fell past her shoulders. Her lovely face bore the serenity that had always seemed slightly unreal to Martinez and had led to uneasy thoughts concerning what exactly was happening behind the tranquil mask.

With a shock he recognized where she was standing. It was a study in his family's palace on Laredo, the long, elegant building of white and chocolate marble that stood in the center of the capital. He recognized the hulking, scarred old shelves of dark wood, the equally battered light fixtures.

The room had once been his. The half-open door behind Terza led to the bedroom in which he'd slept until he left for the academy at the age of seventeen, the room to which he had never returned. His parents must have put Terza in his old room—it was just the sort of sentimental gesture that would have appealed to his mother.

Martinez hoped she wasn't too appalled by the old furniture, so badly knocked about by a houseful of active children.

And he maintained a devout wish that Terza would not discover the nude pictures of an old girlfriend, Lord Dalmas's daughter, that he'd hidden in the back of the wardrobe that summer before he left for the academy.

"Hello," Terza said. She turned to give a profile to the camera and smoothed the folds of her gown over the outline of her pregnant belly. "I thought I'd send a video so you could have an update on the status of your son."

Son. Martinez felt his heart give a lurch. That the child was a boy hadn't been clear when Chenforce had departed for its raid.

"He's becoming rather an active child," Terza said, "and is growing fond of exploration. We've been considering names, and in light of his conduct and in the absence of any instructions from the father, we've decided we rather like Gareth." She turned to face the camera, a slight smile on her face. "I hope you approve."

"As long as they don't called him Junior," Martinez found himself saying aloud, but he felt a warm surge of pride flush through his blood.

Terza drew back a chair from the battered old desk, rearranged her gown again, and sat. The camera, which was not without its own intelligence, followed her.

"As you can see," she said, "I'm still on Laredo. Your parents and Roland" —the brother Martinez wasn't speaking to, at least not when he could help it— "are dealing with, ah, a great many important guests, who are going to be feted and celebrated and generally fussed over until they give Roland and your father what they want."

The very important guests, Martinez knew, were the members of the Convocation, which had fled Zanshaa for a world as far away from the Naxids as they could find. Their location was a state secret—though presumably everyone on Laredo knew—and Terza couldn't mention them by name without triggering one of the algorithms at the Office of the Censor, which might have stopped the correspondence dead.

In any case, the Convocation was now completely in the hands of Lord Martinez, Roland, and the rest of the family. If their incompetence hadn't caused the war in the first place, Martinez would have felt sorry for them.

"I've been playing my part as a kind of auxiliary hostess," Terza said, "which is less tiresome than you'd think, and gives me something to do other than languish in the nursery. I've known many of these guests all my life. And since my father isn't here, I'm handling Chen business as well as representing *you*, though it's hard to say at this point how any of that's going."

Martinez paused the video and wondered why Lord Chen wasn't present along with the rest of the Convocation. Terza wasn't in mourning, and she didn't seem sorrowful when she spoke of him, so he wasn't dead or somehow disgraced.

Perhaps he was on a mission of some sort.

Probably that information was on one of the communiqués he'd skipped. Martinez triggered the video again.

Terza gave him a significant look. "I obviously can't go into details," she continued, "but I've been around some important people, and I've seen some interesting reports. The material side of the war is encouraging, and time is not on the Naxids' side."

She raised a hand. "I hope you're raising a lot of mischief but otherwise staying out of trouble. Come back to me and young Gareth as soon as you can."

The orange end-stamp appeared on the screen. Martinez stared at it, his mind swimming.

She had decided to name their son after him. Perhaps that meant she was thinking of remaining in the marriage even after her father and his enterprises ceased to require a massive Martinez subsidy.

Perhaps the woman his family had bought for him, and with whom he'd spent all of seven days before being parted by the war, had decided to remain a fixture in his life.

His sleeve comm chimed. He answered, and saw the chameleon weave on his sleeve resolve into Michi's image.

"Yes, my lady?"

"I thought I'd let you know that we've just received orders to head for Chijimo. That's where we were told to rendezvous with the Home Fleet in our original orders."

"Things can't have changed much in our absence then," Martinez said.

Michi hesitated. "I'm not sure. Our orders were signed by Senior Fleet Commander Tork, Supreme Commander of something called the Righteous and Orthodox Fleet of Vengeance."

Martinez took a moment to absorb this. "Tork?" he said. "Not Kangas?"

"No, not Kangas. And I don't know what that means either."

"Tork hates me," Martinez said. "You told me so yourself."

She raised her eyebrows and said nothing. After a while Martinez sighed.

"Terza sends her love," he said, speaking on the assumption that love would be sent somewhere in Terza's messages, even if it hadn't been on the one video he'd had a chance to view so far.

"How is she?"

"Doing very well, apparently. Maintaining Chen interests on Laredo in the absence of her father."

"Maurice isn't on Laredo?" It was Michi's turn to be surprised.

"Maybe he's with Kangas."

"I have letters from Maurice that I haven't had a chance to view," Michi said. "Perhaps he'll enlighten me."

"Let me know if—" He realized he might be trespassing on Chen family business. "—if it's relevant to our situation," he finished.

"Comm," Michi said, "end transmission."

The orange end-stamp appeared in Martinez's sleeve display. He blanked it, then looked at the long list of mail that waited for him.

He decided to go to the top of the list and work his way right through to the end.

And then he would review the highlights.

A son, he thought, and smiled.

And then he thought, *Tork hates me. And now he's something called the Supreme Commander.*

TWENTY-FIVE

Once Sergius Bakshi allied himself with the secret government, everything began to fall into place. Groups who had been fighting Naxids, or who wanted to fight Naxids, or who were merely thinking about fighting Naxids, were brought into contact, and—at least theoretically—placed under Sula's orders. A table of organization, if anyone had been unwise enough to assemble one, would have been much less neat than the ideal assembly of three-person cells arrayed in tiers. Whole gangs of friends joined at once, and even if organized into cells, knew each other's identities. The result could be a security catastrophe, but Sula did her best to make sure such groups were as isolated from the rest of her army as possible.

Messages began to move along the clandestine communication network already employed by the cliquemen. The cliquemen, hardened to violence and death, provided a stiffening that the secret army otherwise would have lacked, a stoic, practical approach to killing that the new recruits would have taken months to learn, if ever. The cliquemen might not have earned love, but they were certainly earning respect.

Sergius killed the ten Naxids that Sula had demanded of him, and did it with remarkable efficiency, and all outside his own territory. Each assassination provoked retaliation by the Naxids, and each hostage shot created more potential recruits, and tension between the Naxids and the local cliquemen.

The high sun of summer blazed down on shootings, on bombings, on hijackings, on secret deliveries. Much of the action was directed against the ration authority, both the most visible and the most vulnerable symbol of the Naxid regime. The Naxid police who came into local police stations to oversee distribution of the ration cards were favorite targets. After five were killed and three more wounded, they began traveling in armored vehicles with guards. Since this was about the time that Sidney developed a rocket launcher, the Naxid precautions only let the assassins bag more enemy at once. More cliques were drawn into the war to profit from control of food—as Sula had suggested, the cliques dared not surrender control of the market to anyone else, which included Naxid clans that aimed at controlling the legitimate market.

Sidney was going through a period of remarkable creativity. From his workshop came designs for small, concealable pistols, for snipers' rifles far more accurate than the Mark One, for bombs, and for his crude but surprisingly effective rockets. All plans were distributed in issues of *Resistance*. All, in time, were put to use.

Sula traveled continuously through the city, for the most part coordinating groups of cliquemen, or talking them into joining the cause, or judging disputes over bits of profitable territory. The visit to Green Park had shown the folly of traveling with an armed group of guards, and so often as not she went riding behind Macnamara on his two-wheeler, a vehicle agile enough to avoid roadblocks or other inconveniences. Sometimes she went alone, or with Casimir in his apricot-colored car. She was expected to appear as Lady Sula, and over the course of the long summer the blond wig grew hot and unpleasant. Her own hair grew out somewhat, and finally she had it cut into her old style and turned more or less her own shade again. The enemy weren't looking for Lady Sula anyway.

Nobody seemed to be looking for Julien either. There was a warrant out for him, but no one appeared interested in serving it. Perhaps the Legion of Diligence thought he was still in prison somewhere; and Sergius Bakshi's influence was enough to keep the ordinary police from pursuing any leads.

Sula's delivery company quietly expanded, a fleet of anonymous vehicles quietly delivering contraband from one part of the city to another. One-Step was taken on as an assistant driver. Sula began to miss his presence on the pavement in front of her apartment.

Not that she often saw her apartment. She whirled through the long summer nights with Casimir, a sequence of dark, close rooms filled with dangerous young men, sweaty dance floors, and clean cool sheets. Late at night, tangled with one another in some grand hotel suite, they laid plots against the Naxids, chose targets, deployed fighters, discussed strategy.

Casimir and Julien had quietly assembled a group of young, deadly cliquemen, along with other volunteers recruited by Patel, the young cliqueman who had first volunteered to fight the Naxids for love. They called themselves the Bogo Boys, after a practically indestructible toy.

The Bogo Boys were sent against more difficult objectives. Two judges were killed, one of them an Ushgay returning to the city from his country house. A warehouse of Jagirin foodstuffs was burned. Three mid-level executives with the rationing board—a Jagirin and two Kulukrafs— were assassinated along with their bodyguards.

Sula took part in none of these operations. "You're a general now," Casimir reminded her, "it's not your job to fight in the streets with the troops." She devoted herself instead to obsessive planning, making certain that escape routes were properly laid and that no one would be left behind.

When the rebel government finally arrived from Naxas, Sula resisted Julien's arguments to attack them as they paraded up Axtattle Boulevard to the High City. The enemy would be ready for that; and events proved her right, as thousands of Naxid police brought in from the countryside saturated the area, occupied the roofs of buildings, and lined the boulevard itself.

Instead she ordered the entire secret army go on the attack in other districts of the city. The targets didn't matter, she emphasized, so much as explosions and fire. Cars and trucks were blown up, abandoned buildings put to the torch, flammables piled in streets or public parks and set alight. Security was concentrated on the approach route, so there was little force available to stop the attacks. The Committee for the Salvation of the Praxis moved to the High City surrounded by pillars of smoke and with the sound of explosions echoing between the buildings.

The committee and their pathetic undersized Convocation—the delegates they'd convinced or coerced into representing their home worlds—took their places in the Hall of the Convocation to take their oaths of allegiance to the new government. From that vantage point they could look through the great glass walls to the Lower Town beyond and see the tall rising columns of smoke; like the bars of a prison they had entered of their own free will.

The Naxids then grew more serious about roadblocks and searches, putting more police on the streets, importing them from other towns and barracking them in local hotels. As far as Sula was concerned, more Naxids on the streets simply meant more targets, though it also meant that attacks and escape routes had to be more carefully arranged.

Since the "official" objectives were now more difficult, the attackers shifted to softer targets. Any Naxid in the brown uniform of the civil service became a target, and eventually any Naxid at all. As a result, Naxids were a lot more scarce in parks, squares, and public concourses. They stayed in their own neighborhoods except while in transit from home to work and back again.

The Naxids wandered free only in the High City. Sula hadn't managed a successful operation there since the assassination of Judge Makish. The security presence was too heavy, the escape routes limited, and there were too few non-Naxids living there. An armored blockhouse now guarded the one road to the summit, and both the road and the funicular railway were under the sights of antiproton guns mounted in the High City.

She rode regularly to the High City in trucks carrying luxury goods meant for the new ruling caste. From what she could see, the luxuries had become the entire point of Naxid rule. The High City was being transformed into a fortress guarding the wealth that was sticking to Naxid fingers. Her own transport company was constantly moving glittering furniture to the High City, or carpets, or ornaments, or paintings, or statues. More of the old palaces were being confiscated by the new regime and refitted to suit Naxid tastes.

Even the signs in the High City had begun to reflect the Naxid occupation. Naxid eyes embraced a different spectrum than that of Terrans: they couldn't see red, but could see into the ultraviolet, and unlike most Terrans, they could distinguish between blue and indigo. Thus, many of the new shops and restaurants in the High City had signs that looked like blobs of gray on other blobs of gray to Sula, or one subtly different shade of blue laid on another. They might as well have read *"Naxids Only."*

Elsewhere, the loyalists were making fifty attacks per day throughout the city. Then seventy. Then eighty. Spence was occupied full-time running a bomb factory in Riverside, custom-building packages that were distributed throughout the city. The Naxid officer who ran the ration card system at the police station in that district was assassinated so often that the ration desk was moved to another station in another neighborhood.

But the news wasn't all good. The secret army continued to lose members to arrest, to operations that went wrong, or simply to bad luck. And Naxid reprisals remained savage. Hostages died in droves.

To respond to the increased attacks upon them, the Naxids set up mobile forces to quickly catch attackers before they could withdraw. The mobile forces caught a number of loyalist units, and some fighters were killed and others captured. Still other fighters had to be hidden, along with their families, before the captured fighters could give them up.

Sula decided to teach the Naxids a lesson. She chose a conveniently located police station in a Torminel neighborhood, with mostly Torminel police, and killed the Naxid assigned as ration control officer as she arrived for work. The assassins—an entire action group of thirty-nine fighters—didn't withdraw after the killing, but instead laid siege to the station, firing at it from cover and hitting the parking garage with rockets. The police called for help, and two of the Naxids' mobile squads raced to the rescue.

The topography of the city told Sula which roads would be used, and she'd arranged ambushes along each beforehand. Trucks drawn across the road at the last second stopped one mobile squad on a broad street in a business district, and fighters on the surrounding buildings created a kill zone that left the entire Naxid force dead, lying in their yellow and black uniforms on the pavement next to their burning vehicles. Sula was on one of the buildings with Macnamara and Spence, pouring fire down on the trapped enemy and screaming in joyous rage as they died.

The other route to the beleaguered Torminel neighborhood was on a major highway, and Casimir and the Bogo Boys, driving big trucks in line abreast, managed to occupy all available lanes ahead of the Naxids. The trucks slowed and their rear doors cycled open, revealing tripod-mounted machine guns taken from Team 491's storage area near the Riverside Crematorium.

The Naxid vehicles were armored, but not against such a storm of fire. The Bogo Boys sped away, leaving burning wreckage in their wake.

The action group besieging the Torminel station quietly faded away. The Torminel, sensibly, did not emerge from their station to conduct a pursuit.

The fury that possessed Sula in the fight did not spend itself till later, when she and Casimir were alone in the Hotel of Many Blessings and they made a kind of war on one another's flesh. They were young, and fierce, and triumph sang in their veins. Neither expected to live long, but for now the victory was sweet.

The Daimong clique run by Sagas scored another, if less violent, coup: they managed to hijack a convoy of foodstuffs from one of the Kulukrafs' warehouses and drive it into their own neighborhood, where they left the vehicles open for the entire district to plunder over the course of a long night.

Resistance celebrated these victories, and the heroes and martyrs of the secret army. Though Sula, as usual, transmitted only fifty thousand copies from the Records Office broadcast node, paper likenesses were now nearly ubiquitous: stuck on lampposts, sitting on tables in restaurants, piled in drifts in doorways. People read them openly on trams, at their desks at work, or while eating breakfast in cafés while the official video news nattered away over their heads.

It didn't take the Naxids long to realize that cliques were directing operations, and they struck suddenly, intending to decapitate the entire leadership in one coordinated operation. But they hadn't reckoned with the cliques' cozy relationship with some of the higher figures in the police and judiciary.

All clique leaders were warned well in advance, and when the Urban Patrol and the Legion of Diligence smashed down the door of Sergius Bakshi's shabby little office, they found no one there and all computer data logs zeroed out. In fact, the only person the Naxids managed to arrest was the captain of a Virtue Street crew who had been too drunk to check his messages and didn't know the Naxids were after him.

Casimir was flattered when his own arrest warrant was issued—he hadn't thought he was important enough. He didn't mind having to shift again into a series of safe houses, but was vexed at having to give up his Chesko clothing and his apricot-colored car. He wasn't used to being inconspicuous, and he didn't enjoy it at all.

Sula, in contrast, had grown used to being inconspicuous, and so was jolted to discover her own face on the wall video as she bought take-out coffee and pastry one morning. She felt the blood burning her face as she ducked her chin into her collar and hustled back to the safe house, casting nervous glances over her shoulder.

Casimir was barely awake, his arms and legs draped over the edges of the narrow bed when she walked in. She dropped their breakfast on the table and ordered the wall video on, changing channels until she found her face again.

It was a picture taken from an earlier news item, showing her being decorated after the Battle of Magaria. She was in full dress, standing braced as Fleet Commander Tork put the medal around her neck.

"A reward of three thousand zeniths," the news reader said in a chiming Daimong voice, "is offered for the false Lady Sula."

Her heart gave a sudden lurch, and she sat down heavily on the bed as her knees gave way.

The *false* Lady Sula? she thought. How could they possibly have found out about Caro?

"False?" came Casimir's deep voice. He laughed. "They can't admit they've made a mistake, can they?"

"A mistake?" Sula put a hand over her hammering heart, then felt a flash of anger as Casimir laughed again. She glared at him in rage.

"They think you're an imposter!" Casimir explained. "They've been saying all along that the real Lady Sula died in an explosion, right? So *you've* got to be a phony!"

Sula stared at him. Stars flashed in her vision, and she realized she'd forgotten to breathe. She filled her lungs and turned back to the screen, her mind whirling.

Caro could stay dead, she thought. She hadn't risen from the Sola River, sediment dripping from her golden hair, to strike her down. The deadly secret of her past would stay locked away.

Casimir leaned forward and put his arms around her. "Don't worry," he said in her ear. "It's not so bad, living underground. I'll be able to keep you company."

She managed an edgy laugh. "I've *been* living underground," she said. "I've been dodging for months." *If not years . . .*

She knew she would have to abandon her little apartment. Too many people there knew her. She would have to retrieve the *ju yao* pot and the various munitions she'd secreted in the furniture . . . in fact, it would be best to send one of her own trucks, with a false bill of lading, to pick up everything, in case her apartment was already staked out. And a heavily armed extraction team, in the event anyone tried to intervene.

The communal apartment would have to be abandoned as well, she realized, and she was about to message Macnamara and Spence to tell them they had to leave. Then an idea burst in her mind like a missile flaring in the void.

"We can't let them get away with this," she said, thinking aloud. "We've got to respond."

Casimir was amused. "What do you want to do? Bomb the broadcast station?"

"Not a bad idea," she replied. "But no—I'm thinking of something more public even than that."

She had to argue them into it. Macnamara was appalled, but he was her subordinate, someone to whom she could give orders. Casimir needed more work, but eventually Sula managed to appeal to the impish rebel in him, and he began to think her idea a vastly amusing one.

Thus, two days after the reward money had been put on her head—wearing her undress uniform, with the medals pinned over her heart—Sula walked into the Textile Market in Riverside to distribute the latest edition of *Resistance* to the startled vendors and their customers. She also brandished a printout of the previous morning's *Salvation,* an official government broadsheet that prominently featured her face.

It was all for the benefit of the video camera carried by Casimir, who walked backward ahead of her, grinning hugely as he captured her morning walk. Carrying the news sheet with her picture put a firm date on the video, showed that even with a price on her head, she could walk safely and openly through a crowded street.

Though she was unarmed, Casimir's squad of killers orbited her just outside camera range, walking in grim silence with guns displayed openly to prevent anyone from doing anything foolish to collect their three thousand zenith reward. Still, she had to force herself to walk slowly, to stop and smile at the vendors, to exchange a few words with the shoppers. She bought a vanilla drink from a beverage seller and refused to accept her change. She examined a bolt of silk, or something the vendor claimed was silk. She chucked a baby under the chin.

At the far end of the market, she turned, waved, and dived into a waiting sedan. She was eight minutes clear before the first of the Naxid squads arrived.

The next day's edition of *Resistance* came with brief video clips, plus a number of stills, that documented Sula's stroll. The faces of anyone she met or had spoken to were carefully blacked out.

We own the streets. That was the message *Resistance* was sending.

Three days later the Naxids did their best to prove *Resistance* wrong.

The antimatter missile struck a little past noon, shortly after people had left work for their midday break. As she passed between buildings, riding behind Macnamara on his two-wheeler, Sula caught the flash, felt a touch of heat on her cheek even through the faceplate of her helmet.

The sky had turned in an instant to the color of milk. People on the street stood pale over stark black shadows. Sula gave Macnamara an urgent punch in the ribs.

"Stop! Pull over! Get into one of the buildings!"

People on the street were staring at the sky. The two-wheeler swerved through stunned, slowing traffic, raced between two parked vehicles, bounced hard over the curb, and weaved between pedestrians. Macnamara pulled to a stop before a pair of bright brass doors. Sula saw the reflection of her own startled face in the polished red marble of the building's wall.

She slapped up her faceplate. "Take cover!" she shouted to anyone within earshot. "Take cover *now!*"

The two-wheeler's gyroscopic stabilizers kept it upright as the two passengers sprang for the doors. They found themselves in a quiet haberdashery aimed at the Lai-own trade. Tall, well-dressed avians stared at them as the intruders barged into the showroom, eyes scanning for a place to hide free of flying glass.

"Take cover!" Sula kept shouting. "Take cover!"

So many bombs had exploded in the city that by now the Lai-own had the reflexes of veterans. Regardless of their fine clothing, they were down behind counters or under tables within seconds. Sula and Macnamara crouched on either side of the doors, their backs to the thick walls. Sula slapped her faceplate closed again.

People came running in from the street, looked wildly for cover, and ran into the store. There was a crash as someone stumbled over the two-wheeler; the two-wheeler remained upright, the pedestrian didn't. The brilliant light outside had begun to fade.

Sula heard the shock wave coming, a rising rumble felt through the steel, concrete, and marble pressed against her back. She ducked her head between her knees and clasped her hands over the helmet.

The blast blew the brass doors open. The sound was a cosmic shout she could feel as a shiver in her bones and a slap of pressure against her ears, followed then by an absence of pressure that sent vertigo shimmering through her skull. Someone stumbled and fell across the doorway. There was a whirl of dust, and clothing on the racks swayed angrily. Objects tumbled from counters to the ground, the sound buried beneath the booming fury of the atmosphere.

Sula's ears rang. She blinked up at the room. No glass had broken. There was a strange scent of heat and dust.

She thought it was over until she sensed something else rushing toward her and braced again. This time the shock came up through the floor, the wave moving through her viscera.

The slower moving ground wave, she thought.

The brass doors tried softly to close, but sprang back as they encountered the figure that had sprawled across the doorway. Sula reached for the fallen figure, a male Cree, took him by the arm and helped him crawl out of the doorway and get his back to the wall.

"Stay in cover!" she called. "There might be another one!"

The Cree's big ears turned toward the sound of her voice. Odd little muscles trembled beneath his deep purple skin. But otherwise he remained in position, back against the wall, his breath coming fast.

Sula reached for her hand comm and turned it to a news channel.

"The Committee for the Salvation of the Praxis," she heard, "has decreed that the city of Remba was to be destroyed for multiple acts of rebellion against the Peace of the Praxis. A single missile has been fired by the Fleet as it passed close to Zanshaa. No more attacks are contemplated. The population of surrounding areas are urged to return to work and to act normally."

Remba . . . Sula's head whirled. Remba was a smallish

city on the outskirts of the greater Zanshaa area. There was no significant resistance to the Shaa there that she knew about. In fact, because she didn't know if other cities on the planet shared Zanshaa City's immunity, she had discouraged assassinations and bombings outside of the capital, and told recruits there to confine themselves to intelligence gathering and nonlethal forms of sabotage.

Sula put her hand comm away and rose to her feet. "It's over," she told Macnamara. "Let's get out of here."

The Cree began unsteadily to rise to his feet. Sula helped him. He turned to her, the big ears pricked forward. Sula felt a strange throbbing in her bones as the Cree gave out a subsonic sonar cry.

"You are she," the Cree said, his voice intent.

"If you say so," Sula said.

The Cree leaned closer. "You are the White Ghost," he said. His voice was a fierce whisper.

Sula felt an eerie thrill run up her spine at the unfathomable words. Her thoughts seemed jumbled and she couldn't manage a response.

She turned to Macnamara. "Let's go."

They brushed dust off the standing two-wheeler, rolled it off the sidewalk, and moved through the stunned and slow-moving traffic. The Cree stood in the doorway without speaking and sent sonar throbs after her.

White Ghost, she thought.

She met with Casimir and Julien that night, in a room off the kitchen of a restaurant in Riverside. With its cheap furniture and plastic tablecloths, it was a place set aside for employees to eat, and it smelled of garlic and rancid cooking oil. Despite the owner's proven loyalty, Sula swore she'd never eat there again.

"It was a warning," Julien said. He gave a wolfish smile. "They didn't dare hit Zanshaa, but they hit a city close enough so that everyone here could see it and feel the fear."

"They're trying to terrorize us," Casimir said. He looked at Sula. "Do we feel terrorized?"

Sula didn't bother to answer. The Naxids had struck at the city's population of six hundred thousand, and used a missile without the usual tungsten jacket so there was no fireball—the shock wave had caused some damage, but almost all the casualties were from the radiation attack. There were radiation treatments available, but the guards had been ordered to turn people away from the hospitals.

"They're going to have a depopulated city they can give to their clients," Julien said. "That'll buy a lot of friends."

"I want the ratfucks who did this," Sula said.

Casimir laced his long pale fingers together. "We all do," he said. "But they could all be in orbit for all we know."

Sula's eyes shifted to a picture on the wall. Behind decades of dirt and cooking grease was a heavily retouched shot of the High City, the sky too brilliant a green for reality, the buildings too bright.

"The Naxid Fleet wouldn't do this on its own," she said. "It was their damn committee that ordered this. And *they're* where we can get them."

"All of them?" Casimir raised an eyebrow. He reached for a glass of the cheap sorghum wine the landlord had poured for them. "We can get at a few, I suppose. Our contacts in the High City can provide their location. But they're all well-guarded, and any escape route is going to be—"

"All of them," Sula said. Her mind had been caught up in the whirlwind of the idea. "And I'm not talking about knocking them off one by one. Let's make a clean sweep of them. Get some antimatter and blow them right off their rock."

Julien was amused. "Where are we going to get antimatter?" he asked. Only the military and the power authorities had antimatter, and in each case it was heavily guarded.

"And how are we going to put together a delivery system?" Casimir asked. "This is outside Sidney's area of expertise."

So they discussed other possibilities. Truck bombs, if

they could get one close enough. Catapults hurling bags of fertilizer explosive. "We could build a cannon," Sula said at one point. "We won't need the carriage or anything, just the barrel. We build it on the roof of a building, under a shed or something so it's not obvious. Then we bore-sight it on the room where their committee meets, and blow them to bits with one shell."

By then the others had drunk enough sorghum wine to make this seem both plausible and hilarious. They discussed the idea for an hour before breaking up.

By the time Sula and Casimir reached their safe house, her mood had sobered. When he came into the room from the shower—she always made him shower before bed—he found her sitting on a chair holding the *ju yao* pot that she'd rescued from her old apartment. She looked at her dark, distorted reflection in the crackled surface, and her fingers slid blindly over its contours.

Casimir stepped up behind her and put his long hands on her shoulders. She put the pot on a scarred old table, took one of his hands in her own and brushed against the knuckles with her cheek.

"Do we really know what we're doing?" she said. "Those people in Remba—they died because of what *we* did. Tens of thousands of them. And tonight we met to plan more trouble, and for all we know, another city will be destroyed as a result."

His fingers clasped hers. "The Fleet will come soon," he said.

"In that case," Sula said, "what's the point of what we're doing? The war will be decided off the planet."

"We're killing Naxids. I thought that's what you wanted." One long pale hand caressed her hair. "I never expected to live as long as Sergius," he said. "I always thought it would be torture and the garotte before I was thirty. If you and I die together in this war, it doesn't change anything for me. It's better than dying alone."

Tears burned her eyes. She rose from the chair and

400 • Walter Jon Williams

pressed herself against him, inhaling the scent of soap and
his wine-scented breath. His arms came around her.

"Don't be sad," he said. "The Naxids are afraid of us.
That's why they hit Remba."

Her hands formed fists behind his back. "I want it to
mean something," she said. "I want to do something the
Fleet can't do even if they bring a million ships to Zanshaa."

"Build your cannon." There was laughter in his voice.
"We'll blast their committee and their Convocation
halfway to the ring."

His words brought a rising sense of steadiness to stand
against her confusion. She leaned on him as if he were a
wall and wiped the tears from her eyes.

Fighting the hot swelling that had lodged in her throat,
she said, "The original plan called for an army to hold Zanshaa. The government decided not to build an army, but
we've built one now. Let's do something with it. Let's take
the High City."

Again he seemed vastly amused. "Take the High City?
Why not?"

Angered flashed through her at the laughter that danced
behind his word. "Don't condescend," she said.

"Condescend?" He pulled away, and she saw an answering anger that smoldered in his eyes. "We'll take the High
City. Fine. Or we'll build a cannon. Fine. Or we'll do
something else. I don't care. But whatever we do, let's *do* it
and stop asking ourselves questions."

She looked into the dark eyes for a long moment, then
pressed her mouth to his.

A strange, unexpected happiness pulsed through her
blood. I am home, she thought, home after all this time.

Home amid the war, with its chaos and instability, its
danger and terror. Home in this safe house, with its old,
dingy furniture. Home in Casimir's arms.

She tore her lips away from the kiss. Calculations were
already spinning through her mind.

"Yes," she said, "we'll take the rock, and kill them all."

TWENTY-SIX

Chenforce flashed through the wormhole to join the Righteous and Orthodox Fleet of Vengeance in their orbit around Chijimo's star, and were promptly met by a massive flight of missiles, roaring toward them like a hellish blood tide bent on slaughter—and then the missiles reversed, decelerated, and hovered alongside the newcomers like sheep dogs escorting the flock to their pen. Chenforce recovered them all to fill their depleted magazines.

Six days later Chenforce joined the Fleet proper, slotting into the loose formation between the flag squadron and the next astern, and were met by tenders sent out from Chijimo with supplies of fresh food, liquor, and delicacies for the officers. Even the antimatter stores were topped up, though the ships could still run for years on the antihydrogen already in their fuel reservoirs.

With the arrival of Chenforce, the Orthodox Fleet now constituted twenty-eight ships, half of them newly built and crewed. It was the largest collection of loyalist ships since the Home Fleet had launched for Magaria.

After a few hours in which the crew of Chenforce luxuriated in reasonably fresh fruit and vegetables only partially compressed by acceleration, Supreme Commander Tork ordered Michi Chen, all captains, and all first lieutenants, aboard his flagship, the *Judge Urhug*.

Martinez and the others spangled themselves in dress uniforms and then visited Dr. Xi for spray bottles of a concoction that would deaden their senses of taste and smell—

an entire ship crowded with Daimong was a formidable terror to the senses.

The party waited in *Daffodil* till the last plausible minute before casting off and making their way to the flagship. Martinez noticed that the other Terran and Torminel captains had likewise delayed their arrival.

At the airlock, a Daimong chorus cried out a song of joyous welcome. The sound was both deafening and magnificent, but a disturbing odor of decay was already clawing its way up the back of Martinez's throat. One of Tork's staff lieutenants took the new arrivals along corridors strung with wire and conduits to Tork's suite, where everyone from Tork on down braced to salute Martinez's Orb.

The table was a clear plastic over a metal framework, and the chairs were plastic too, curved for the comfort of the Daimong anatomy. The metal walls were painted a bilious shade that Martinez could only think of as government green, and ornamented with photos of Tork ancestors, framed degrees and certificates that Tork had been awarded at various points along his career path, and pictures of ships that Tork had commanded.

It was a far cry from the luxurious flagships of the recent past, with their parquet floors, custom artwork commissioned by well-known painters and designers, and exquisite hand-made furniture. *Judge Urhug* had been built quickly, sprayed with the cheapest paint available, and filled with mass-produced furniture just intelligent enough to hang onto the floor in the event of weightlessness. The urgency of war permitted little else.

"Take your seats, my lords," Tork said. Strips of dead flesh dangled from his face. His fixed expression seemed fierce, but his voice was a mellow chiming, like distant bells.

Martinez laid the Golden Orb on the table before him and perched gingerly on a chair more suited to the narrower Daimong frame. The ghastly smell was now clogging the back of his throat. He cleared it and took a sip of the water that had been provided in each place.

"I have reviewed Squadron Commander Chen's report," Tork said, "as well as reports filed by the individual captains. I am compelled to observe that the record of Chenforce is like no other I have ever encountered."

At these words Martinez felt a certain optimism rise. Perhaps Tork had mellowed in the last months. Perhaps the success of the raid had convinced him to look on Chenforce as an example to the rest of the Fleet.

"Chenforce has destroyed many of the wormhole relay stations on which our civilization depends," Tork said. "It has destroyed a planetary accelerator ring and killed many, perhaps most, of the inhabitants of Bai-do. Aboard the flagship we find officers—including the captain!—killed by the crew, murderers who were permitted to run free and to continue their vicious activities for months before paying for their crime. These same enlisted crew were involved in a continuous string of felonies, extortions, and a treasonous partnership with Naxid rebels. We even have evidence of cult activity aboard the ship, sure evidence that the officers did not properly indoctrinate the crew in their responsibilities to the Fleet and to the Praxis."

Tork's voice began in as a melodious chiming but built to a furious abrasive monotone, a harrying strident tone that grated on Martinez's nerves and raised the hairs on the back of his neck. Anger flared like a raging fire under his high collar.

"I have to ask myself," Tork continued, "if these are proper acts of war. Certainly a *pirate* might boast of wormhole stations destroyed, of the annihilation of a planet, of murder and his allegiance to cults. But are these proper activities for a Peer and an officer?"

He moved his pale bald head to stare at the officers before him.

"I make no judgments," he said. "I was not at the scene.

I tell you only that no such activities will be permitted in the Righteous and Orthodox Fleet of Vengeance. We do not attack planets. We do not attack helpless crew in relay stations. We exist for one purpose only, and that purpose is to engage the enemy fleet in battle—in *proper* battle—and by destroying them, to end the war that divides the empire. No deviations from this single task will be contemplated or permitted."

He jabbed at the transparent surface of the table with his long fingers.

"We will engage the enemy and beat him by using the formations and methods that were bequeathed to us by our ancestors, ancestors beside whose greatness we exist as mere shadows. None of the deviant tactics that killed Fleet Commander Kangas will be permitted. The Fleet will exercise proper tactics, properly applied, and these tactics will guarantee victory."

He leveled a finger along the table, pointing at each officer in turn. "There will be no premature starbursts, my lords! Any formation wishing to starburst must receive the permission of the Supreme Commander before executing the maneuver."

Again the voice rose to a nerve-scraping pitch.

"All that is important is known! All that is perfect is contained in the Praxis! All innovation is deviation from the Supreme Law! *No deviation is permitted!*"

"I never expected to be called a pirate by my own side," Michi said as *Daffodil* left *Judge Urhug*'s airlock.

"He makes no judgments," Martinez said.

And, he thought, Tork might at least have mentioned that they'd vaporized over two hundred enemy merchant vessels, putting a permanent crimp in the Naxid economy, and finished the twenty or more warships that, the Fleet, wouldn't have to fight at Zanshaa.

"Well," Martinez said, "we can at least practice the new tactics on our own. We don't have to tell Tork everything we do."

But that wasn't the case. The next day, Tork broke up Chenforce. The light cruiser *Celestial,* damaged at Protipanu, was sent to the yards at Antopone for repair. The other light cruiser and the frigate were sent to a newly created light squadron. The two Torminel cruisers were made part of an all-Torminel division, and the two remaining Terran ships became the nucleus of the spanking new Cruiser Squadron 9, to which were added the three survivors of the Home Fleet, also crewed by Terrans, three new-built Terran ships that had not yet arrived at Chijimo, and the *Bombardment of Delhi,* a badly damaged Magaria survivor under repair since the battle.

The lone Daimong cadet—the survivor of the *Beacon,* lost at Protipanu—who had been haunting *Illustrious* since the battle, was brought aboard Tork's flagship; probably, Martinez thought, to be debriefed about any deviations that might have been practiced on Michi's flagship during his time aboard.

At least Michi commanded the new squadron, so *Illustrious* remained the flagship.

It was impossible to practice any new tactical system for the simple reason that Michi and Martinez could not trust their subordinates not to rat them out to Tork. Chenforce had been a highly cohesive force, united by victory and by a faith in their commander. Michi could have run forbidden exercises within her old command and stood a reasonable chance that none of her subordinates would inform Tork of their activities. But no such trust existed within Cruiser Squadron 9. Neither Michi nor Martinez dared to suggest any prohibited experiments to the new arrivals.

"Tork's doing this deliberately," Michi told Martinez. "He's trying to isolate everyone he feels he can't trust, and surround them with strangers."

"Let's hope he's not isolating contagion, but spreading the virus instead," Martinez replied.

Tork kept his new formations busy with daily exercises, all drawn from the old playbook. Martinez thought Tork's staff must have been working twenty-nine hours per day planning out the scripts. Every move was planned in advance; every maneuver, every missile fired, every casualty. Ships were judged not on how well they did against an enemy, but on how well they obeyed instructions.

For anyone who had experienced the new-style, free-form experiments that Martinez, Michi, and Do-faq had created, Tork's maneuvers were agonies of frustration. Anyone who had ever been in an actual battle, Martinez thought, would have observed that real combat didn't follow anybody's script, and seen what a useless waste of time Tork's maneuvers were.

But Tork hadn't ever been in an actual battle, or in one of Martinez's experiments. The maneuvers continued, one after another, all dreadfully familiar. Martinez could only hope that Tork had an intellectual equal on the Naxid side.

He had to admit, however, that the maneuvers were at-least giving the new ships practice at basic maneuvers. Their quality, marked by hastily trained crews under newly minted officers, was in general wretched. Even he, as a brand-new skipper aboard the newly crewed *Corona,* hadn't been as hapless as these officers.

Light Squadron 14 under Squadron Commander Altasz, which had been on a raid similar to that of Chenforce, arrived three days after Chenforce was broken up. Martinez had once commanded the squadron, and he looked at his old command on the tactical display with a mixture of nostalgia and resignation. None of the old crews were aboard, none of those with whom he'd shared danger from Magaria to Hone-bar. The ships were old friends, but the crew in them were strangers.

Michi wanted to know how Squadron 14 had avoided danger from relativistic Naxid missiles, and queried Altasz in private. Altasz replied that he'd simply blown up every single relay station he'd come across.

"Tork will get another chance to use the word *'pirate,'*"

Michi predicted, and later found out that her forecast came true.

Routine in Tork's command wasn't all drill and discipline. There was a great deal of visiting back and forth among the officers, and a round of dinners, parties, and receptions. As new-minted ships joined, old acquaintances arrived or sent their greetings. Lady Elissa Dalkeith, Martinez's first officer on *Corona,* invited him to a handsome dinner on her new frigate *Courage.* Small, blond Vonderheydte, who Martinez had promoted to Lieutenant on *Corona*'s flight from Magaria, invited him to a dinner in the wardroom of his cruiser, where *Corona*'s escape was recounted in detail to a fascinated group of officers. Ari Abacha arrived aboard *Illustrious* to drink a bottle of Chen wine and complain languidly about the amount of work he had to do as second officer of the *Gallant.* Dour Master Engineer Maheshwari, his flamboyant mustachios still dyed a highly industrial shade of red, sent respectful greetings and congratulations from Engine Control of his new frigate. Squadron Commander Do-faq, who had won the Battle of Hone-bar by following Martinez's advice, made him guest of honor at a large reception, and there he met Cadet Kelly, with whom Martinez had shared a carnal romp after they had narrowly escaped annihilation at the hands of the Naxids, and who stood out of the crowd, with her broad grin blazing.

A letter or video from Terza arrived almost every day. Martinez watched the growing pregnancy with a mixture of awe, desire, and frustration.

One video showed his portrait, which his proud father had printed and set in the foyer of the palace.

There was no word or sign of Caroline Sula. Martinez wondered where she was.

The rounds of social contact made it easier for him to promote his tactical system in casual settings. There were hundreds of officers in the Orthodox Fleet who had never seen battle, some of them of senior rank, and most were eager to hear from those who had. Martinez refought Honebar and Protipanu dozens of times at dinners and receptions, and always made a point of mentioning the tactical lessons learned. He was describing the mathematics of the new system to a newly arrived captain from Harzapid, a self-important man with ginger whiskers, and found that the man understood him.

"Oh yes," he said. "The convex hull of a dynamical system. That's the Foote Formula."

Martinez raised his eyebrows. "I'm sorry?"

"The Foote Formula—the system developed by one of the bright young lads assigned to the Fourth Fleet at Harzapid, Lord Jeremy Foote. He was promoting the system among his friends when he was still on his way to the Fourth Fleet from Zanshaa, and once he arrived, he acquainted everyone he could. He's made quite a number of converts among the younger officers. A pity Lord Tork isn't keen on it."

Martinez couldn't believe his ears. He remembered Foote well, a big, blond cadet with all the drawling arrogance of the elite Peerage, a man who, despite his inferior military rank, did his best to make him feel his social inferiority at every meeting.

"Do you really think Lord Jeremy understands the math?" he said.

The captain seemed surprised. "He devised it, didn't he?"

"Well, no actually." Resentment simmered beneath Martinez's words. "When I was working out the system, I consulted with other officers, among them Lady Sula—the hero of Magaria, if you remember."

The captain was trying to follow this. "You consulted with Lord Jeremy then?"

"No." Martinez felt an angry smile draw itself across his face. "Lord Jeremy was the censor aboard Lady Sula's ship. He had a complete record of the correspondence, and apparently he's been passing it off as the Foote Formula among his friends at the Fourth Fleet."

The captain processed this, then turned stern. "Surely not," he said stoutly. "I knew Lord Jeremy's father—a worthy heir to the most impeccable ancestors. I can't imagine anyone in the family doing such a thing."

Martinez felt his savage grin return. "I'll be sure to ask him when I see him."

He was able to do so ten days later, at a reception for the officers of the newly arrived *Splendid*. The cruiser was aptly named, being one of the flying palaces of the old Fourth Fleet, heavily damaged on the day of the mutiny but now repaired and returned to duty, and with Foote among its junior officers.

Martinez waited until late in the reception, when Sub-Lieutenant Foote was relaxed and talking to a group of his cronies, and then approached. Since the reception was formal and Martinez was carrying the Golden Orb, Foote and his friend were compelled to brace in salute.

"Foote!" Martinez cried with pleasure. "How long has it been?" He transferred the Orb to his left hand and held out his right. Foote, taken aback, took his hand.

"Very pleased to see you, Captain," he said. He tried to withdraw his hand, and Martinez clamped hard and stepped close.

Yes, it was the same Foote. Large and handsome, with a blond cowlick on the right side of his head and an expression of arrogant disdain that had probably settled onto his face in the cradle.

"Everyone has been telling me about the Foote Formula!" Martinez said. "You absolutely *must* explain it to me!"

Foote's heavy face flushed. Again he tried to withdraw his hand, and again Martinez held him close.

"*I* never called it that," he said.

"You're too modest!" Martinez said. He turned to the other officers, the young high-caste Peers whom Foote counted among his equals.

"Lord Jeremy," he said, "you absolutely must explain to your friends where you first encountered the formula!"

Martinez saw rapid calculation reflected in the pale eyes, and then Foote drew himself up to his considerable height. When he spoke, there was light amusement in his drawl.

"I encountered the formula, of course," he said, "when I had the duty of censoring Lady Sula's correspondence with you, my lord. I was struck by the formula's adroitness in coping with the tactical problems revealed by the Battle of Magaria, and I decided to show it to as many officers as I could."

Martinez had to give Foote credit for finding the most graceful way out of his situation. Foote had realized that claiming authorship of the formula would only lead to his humiliation; instead he claimed only the role of popularizer.

Martinez gave a broad grin. "You know," he said, still grinning, still pumping Foote's hand, "you *should* have mentioned the real authors of the formula. It would have been more thoughtful."

Foote's reply was smooth. "I would have," he said, "if I'd known for certain who the authors were. I knew that you were involved, and Lady Sula, but the correspondence indicated that other officers had contributed, and I didn't know their names. And besides . . ." He glanced over his shoulder, as if in fear of being overheard. ". . . I recognized the controversial nature of the work. Anyone whose name was associated with the formula was bound to get on the wrong side of certain senior officers."

"How considerate of you to leave my name out of it!" Martinez exclaimed, with what he hoped was an expression of transparently false bonhomie. "But you needn't in the future—I'm sure you couldn't change Lord Tork's opinion of me in the least."

Foote only lifted one supercilious eyebrow. Martinez turned to look at Foote's companions, who were watching the two with expressions ranging from wariness to thoughtful surprise.

"I won't keep you from your friends any longer," he said, and released Foote's hand. Foote flexed the hand and massaged it with the other. Martinez looked from one face to the next.

"Take care with your formulas, now," he said, "or you may find Foote giving them to all sorts of people."

Then, with another smile and a wave of the Orb, he turned and walked away.

Given the wide social rounds of the officers, he knew that their exchange would circulate throughout the Orthodox Fleet in days.

Revenge might at best be a petty emotion, he thought, but at times it was a strangely satisfying one. And in something called the Orthodox Fleet of Vengeance, it seemed to have the blessing of higher authority.

The funicular creaked as the strain came on its cable, and Sula's seat swayed on its gimbals. As the train rose, it passed between the gun emplacements—turrets of heavy, near-impenetrable plastic—that had been placed on the terraces on either side of the terminus. The barrels of antiproton guns thrust from the turrets, ready to turn any attacker into a scattering of subatomic particles.

Sula left the car at the upper terminus and stepped out onto the flagstone terrace. A blast of wind scoured her face. One of the turrets squatted, featureless and ugly, on the terrace before her. It was barely large enough to contain the gun, its crew, and the rotating mechanism. Stubby little ventilators protruded from the top, along with periscopes and antennae. There was a low Naxid-sized door in the back, and it was closed.

Naxid guards dashed about, legs churning, or stood in the lee of the turret, sheltering from the wind. Sula pretended to adjust her long scarf, then took her shopping bag and headed into the city.

Satchel charges, she thought. Deliver enough kinetic energy to the turrets and anything inside was going to get scrambled whether the turrets were breached or not. Unfortunately, the sensitive antiproton ammunition might get scrambled as well, and the result would be an explosion that . . . well, whatever else it might do, it would at least solve her problem.

Still, it would be nice if they could *use* those guns.

She wondered when the gun crews got their meals. Surely the doors would open then.

But even if the antiproton guns were disabled or captured, there was no practical way to get a large force up that slope. It was too steep, and her people could climb only slowly and be exhausted by the time they arrived. Plus, any defenders at the upper terminal of the funicular could hold off an army with small arms.

Any large force would have to come up the switchback road on the other side of the acropolis, a route that had its own problems, not the least being that it would be under fire every step of the way.

These calculations spun through her mind as she walked across the High City, emerging by the Gate of the Exalted, marked by the two pillars where the switchback road entered the plateau, a place guarded by another pair of antiproton guns in turrets. Looking to the other side, she recognized the large barrel-vaulted edifice of the Ngeni Palace, with the terrace behind and the banyan that overshadowed PJ's cottage.

From PJ's, she thought, she might be able to view the defenses, see when the guard changed and when meals arrived.

Besides, she was freezing.

PJ brightened when she arrived on his doorstep, and he offered her tea and soup.

"I wish I could contribute more," he said as he watched her eat. "I'm not giving you much information these days. My clubs are almost empty—more servants than members. Everyone who could leave has gone."

"You're still very well placed here," Sula said. "Any information you provide is valuable." Her attempts to boost PJ's morale had become so standardized that she could practically recite the lines in her sleep. "I'm counting on you," she added, "to stay in the High City and keep your ear to the ground."

"I'm a good shot," PJ said hopefully. "I could move into the Lower Town and become an assassin."

Sula mopped the last of her soup with her bread. The soup was flavored with lemon and saffron both, an unusual but in this case successful combination.

"You're useful here," she said.

"For what?" PJ said darkly. "You can buy soup in a restaurant."

"You have binoculars, I assume."

"Yes. Naturally."

"I want you to keep an eye on those antiproton guns at the Gate of the Exalted. Check regularly. Find out when the crews are changed, when they're fed. When the doors in the turrets are open or closed."

PJ's look was intense. "You're thinking of attacking them?"

"I'm thinking I'd like to have a pair of antiproton guns, yes. Or at least the ammunition."

Her action team had been trained on the weapons, and the stay-behind force under Fleetcom Eshruq had some in inventory, but Sula hadn't known where, and presumably they'd been captured by the Naxids.

Perhaps the four guns on the High City were the ones that the secret government had once owned. It was only right to take them back.

"Oh, PJ, another thing," Sula said. "You don't happen to know any expert mountaineers, do you?"

PJ's first report was astoundingly detailed. It seemed to Sula that he must have been checking the batteries every half hour, and stayed up all night to make observations. He'd caught the shift changes, mealtimes, the number of guards, the number of officers, and the type of transport that moved them to and from their barracks.

Sula had begun visiting the High City regularly to observe the two turrets overlooking the funicular, but her data only confirmed PJ's, and in the end she saved herself the commute and assumed the two gun batteries were on the same schedule.

When the cold wind finally spent its last strength howling around the eaves of the High City, she found the answer to the question of when the turret doors were opened—in good weather. The turrets were small and cramped, and the crews much preferred being out of doors, at least when an autumn wind wasn't blustering around the gray granite battlements of the acropolis.

"So we set the attack on a nice day," Sula said at a planning meeting. "All we need is to glance at the long-range forecast."

"We can probably manage that, princess," said Patel with an easy smile. "It's climbing that damned rock I'm worried about."

They were holding the meeting in Patel's hotel suite, sitting around an elegant chrome-rimmed table that seemed strangely at home with the fussy laquered cabinets, the collected bric-a-brac, and the bright bouquets of fragrant flowers. The room, with its oddities and perfumes, appeared to be a perfectly suitable environment for a man who had offered to fight for love.

"I wish we could rehearse the climb somehow," Julien said. "We've not only got to get ourselves up that cliff, but our gear." He gave a tight, uncomfortable grin. "And I don't much like heights."

It was clear that no frontal assault on the acropolis could possibly succeed. The positions that controlled the two gateways to the High City—the funicular and the switchback road—could only be taken from behind, and that meant first sneaking a force onto the acropolis.

Getting an army up the cliff was a task that would have been impossible in peacetime, when the long granite bulk of the High City was illuminated by brilliant floodlights that would have pinned any climber to the cliff. After the destruction of the ring, the electricity shortage had turned the floodlights off. Even most of the streetlights on the High City were dark, so the area was full of shadows.

The Ngeni Palace was very large, enough to hide two entire action groups until it was time for them to move out.

"We can have them practice on a real cliff," Macnamara suggested. "Take them out to the country and send them up an escarpment."

Julien looked at him in something like shock. He was a city boy, and the very idea of countryside was alien to him.

"Can't we do it in town somewhere?" he said. "Climb a building or something?"

Sula smiled "That might attract attention." She looked up at Macnamara. "You'll work out the training schedule for the trips to the country and the climbs. I want everyone to ascend at least twice."

Julien was dismayed. "Won't there be snakes and things?" he asked.

Casimir grinned at him. "Yes. Big nasty poison ones too."

Macnamara sniffed and made a note on his datapad. He had never learned to like the cliquemen, and he wasn't able to hide it. The Bogo Boys responded with a good-natured condescension that suggested they were hated by a lot more interesting people than Macnamara.

Sula took a sip of her sparkling water and looked at her agenda. "My worry is security," she said. "This is a big operation. Any leaks and most of us die."

"Keep the inner circle small," Casimir said. "Only a few of us should know the actual objective."

Spence tapped cigarette ash into one of Patel's elegant ashtrays—hanging around cliquemen, along with a delivery job that delivered tobacco in large quantities, had taught her to smoke.

"I've been thinking about that," she said. "What we should do is hide one big operation under *another* big operation. We tell them to prepare for one thing, and then— on the day—they all get new orders."

Sula looked at her in surprise. "What's bigger than taking the High City?"

"Attacking Wi-hun," Spence suggested, naming the airfield the Naxids used as a base for their shuttlecraft. "That might draw security forces out into the countryside."

"No," Casimir said. "We tell everyone we're taking the prisons and liberating all the hostages."

Sula looked at him in admiration. "Very nice," she said. "Storming the prisons will require a lot of the same skills as storming the High City, so we can explain any training exercises. And we'll put a watch on the prisons, have people take notes about the number of guards, shift changes, and so on, so that if the Naxids find out about it, the data will seem to support the cover story."

"The security forces will be drawn out of the High City," Spence said. "There aren't any prisons in the city center."

"I'd like to completely isolate the High City if we can," Sula said. "The High City has all the political and military leadership in their palaces. The mid-level leadership stays in requisitioned hotels on the acropolis, particularly the Great Destiny, and most of the rankers sleep in those hotels in the Lower Town, at the foot of the funicular. If we can keep the officers from their troops, they're going to have to overcome their own leadership deficit before they can do anything else."

"Princess," Patel said, "can't we kill those officers, somehow, while they're asleep?"

"I wanted to take out the Great Destiny Hotel early on, with a truck bomb," Sula said, "but Hong wanted to concentrate on the Axtattle Parkway attack first." Which had been the end of Hong and the secret army, all but Team 491.

"Can't we use a truck bomb now?" Patel asked.

"They have barricades all around the hotel. We couldn't get a truck up to it."

"Barricades can be knocked down," said Spence, the practical engineer.

"We'd need heavy equipment to do it," Sula said. "And how are we going to get that up on the rock?"

Spence flicked her cigarette in the ashtray and shrugged. "All sorts of ways. They have building projects on the High City that can provide us cover, I assume."

"You'll handle the arrangements then?"

Another shrug. "Sure."

"And any truck bombs?"

"Of course." She smiled. "The bombs are more in my line, really."

Patel looked at Spence and smiled. "I know just where I can get the equipment we need. A government storage facility, near one of my enterprises. I don't even think it's even guarded at night."

"Let me run up to the High City first and see exactly what's required."

Julien looked from one person at the table to the next. "You know," he said, "I'm beginning to think we're actually going to do this."

Casimir looked at Sula and gave one of his rumbling laughs. His eyes were sparkling. "With the White Ghost leading us," he said, "how can we fail?"

Autumn came quickly on the heels of the Naxid missile. A blast of frigid wind blew in from the northwest, howling around the corners of the buildings like mourners crying their anguish at the death of Remba. The wind blew cold for days. Leaves turned brown and crisp and were blown from the trees before they could display their glories of orange and yellow.

Sula, wearing a windbreaker and with a scarf wrapped around her blond hair, traveled over the High City, confirming the information given by PJ, Sidney, and other informants. She took note of defenses and dispositions, as well as the location of police patrols and the hotels and palaces where security forces slept.

The project began to develop its own astounding plausibility. Naxid defenses in the High City were surprisingly thin. Most of the security forces weren't barracked on the High City at all, but in the complex of hotels around the train station at the base of the funicular. If the secret army attacked at night and could hold the two routes to the crest of the acropolis, they might have a chance of maintaining a grip on the High City, at least for a while.

Sula didn't want to refer to her scheme directly; she thought it might tempt fate. Instead she called it Project Daliang, after a campaign fought by Sun Pin, the general of Qi. When Wei attacked Zhao, Zhao appealed for help to Qi. Sun Pin was expected to march into Zhao to help drive off the invaders, but instead marched straight for Daliang, the Wei capital, which forced Wei to abandon its campaign and retreat in disorder.

Sula never explained the significance of the name to anyone. That too might tempt fate.

As the cold wind died and a crisp autumn cooled the high spirits of summer, as explosions and rifle fire continued to shake the windows of the capital, she began to look seriously at her order of battle and to make plans.

With the Naxids weaker than expected, her problems were entirely with her own forces. Her soldiers had never trained for a real battle, and she had no idea whether they could ever fight one. Security was another problem—she knew there had to be informers in her ranks, and so the large massing of the action groups, and the elaborate plans necessary, were going to be hard to keep secret.

While she pondered these difficulties, she made two more appearances in uniform, one in a secret clinic where survivors of the Remba disaster were treated with stolen antiradiation drugs, and again in public during the Harvest Festival—a dispirited business under rationing—where she arrived in the Old Third with a convoy of stolen food, handed out a few copies of *Resistance* to the startled

Torminel survivors of the police massacre, and vanished before the police could reappear.

Again she heard the words "White Ghost," lisped from a fanged Torminel mouth at the moment when she swung herself out of the cab of the lead truck and into the crowd.

Each appearance was celebrated in editions of *Resistance*. She began to see graffiti around the city: *Long live the White Ghost! For the White Ghost and the Praxis! Down with the Naxids, up with the White Ghost!*

The mysterious Axtattle sniper continued to make appearances, not always on the Axtattle Parkway, but always attacking military convoys from a height. Sula found out who he was on his sixth excursion, when he was wounded by counterfire and his family brought him into one of the secret clinics.

The sniper was a semiretired Daimong named Fer Tuga, a hunting guide from the Ambramas Reserve, half a continent away. On his periodic visit to Zanshaa to visit his daughter, he'd take the hunting rifle he left in her apartment and use it to kill Naxids.

The last occasion had gone wrong when the Naxid convoy returned a torrent of accurate fire within a few seconds of his firing his first round. He'd barely escaped with his life.

"The Naxids have got to have something new," Tuga reported. "Either they saw me behind a darkened window or they saw the bullet in flight."

It turned out to be the latter. A small mobile phased-array radar system linked by a cleverly programmed computer to automatic weapons platforms.

Sniper tactics at once became much less profitable. Bomb use increased by way of compensation. Bombs began getting larger and more sophisticated, and adapted to different targets.

The Naxids moved more security forces into the capital, which just created new targets.

* * *

There were plenty of ways for Project Daliang to fail, and Sula tried to work them all out in advance. She spent long hours with maps of the city and with timetables, trying to arrange for proper rendezvous. Two light earth-moving machines were abstracted from government stores. Prisons were put under observation. Word was passed along the entire unwieldy apparatus of the secret army that action was imminent, and that it would involve taking and holding buildings. Bombs, grenades, and rockets were manufactured and stored in secret depots. Grannies were set to work baking ammunition for the Sidney rifles.

Sula went up to the High City on a day when chill drizzle had turned the funicular's flagstone terrace dark and wet. She wanted to inspect the empty Ngeni Palace and make certain it was adequate for hiding the Bogo Boys and the other strike troops who were scheduled to come up the cliff.

PJ seemed more cheerful than usual. "I'm happy to show you the old place," he said, "but when are you going to need it?"

Sula hesitated, sensing something behind his words. "What do you mean?"

"I've been evicted. Some Naxid clan has requisitioned the property. I got the notice two days ago, and they gave me ten days to get myself and my belongings out." He gave her a brilliant smile. "I can be useful now. I don't have to live in the High City. I can move to the Lower Town and become a soldier in the secret army."

Already calculations were flooding through her mind. "Can we check the weather report?" she asked.

He led her to a desk, and with a few commands she discovered that the cold drizzle would last for another two days, then be pushed away by a high pressure front from the southwest. There would be at least four days of beautiful, sunny, summery weather.

There's our window, she thought. She hoped six days would be enough.

She straightened and looked at him. "I hope you'll employ our trucking firm to move your belongings to your new lodgings."

He shrugged. "I don't have any belongings to speak of. Not since my father lost all our money."

"You've forgotten the pile of weaponry that Sidney gave us, and that's still in storage."

"Oh." PJ's eyes widened.

"And surely Clan Ngeni doesn't want all their furniture and other possessions to go to the Naxids? Or have the Naxids insisted that everything remain?"

PJ looked as if he hadn't considered this. "No," he said. "I suppose I can take anything."

"Then we'll remove your clan's stuff for you. And I'll need to look at the palace after all—assuming, of course, that you don't mind if we use the place for one last operation."

"Certainly. Of course." Anxiety crossed PJ's expression. "But I really can join the secret army after I've left the High City?"

She looked at him. "PJ," she said, "you've *always* been in the secret army. You were my first recruit."

He was flustered and, she thought, pleased. "Well yes. Thank you. But I mean a real soldier."

"You've always been a real soldier."

Surprised delight flushed PJ's cheeks. "I've only wanted to be . . . to be worthy."

"You're more than worthy," Sula said. "And as far as I'm concerned, better off without her."

Her words brought an uncomfortable sadness to PJ's long face. "Oh, I don't know," he said. "She was so bright and lively, and I . . ." He fell silent.

Something he'd said came to Sula's mind.

"PJ," she said, "you mentioned that your father lost your family's money."

"Yes. Gambling, and—" He sighed. "—other sorts of gambling too—unwise investments. Stocks and futures and debentures, whatever those are. My father hid the losses for a long time, and I had a very pleasant life for a while, with cars and clothes and entertainments and . . ." He groped for words. ". . . the usual. But it was all borrowed money. So I turned thirty-five and then . . ." He threw out his hands. "Then it was all gone."

Sula was surprised. She had always assumed PJ lost his money in debauchery. Instead he'd lived a perfectly normal life for a member of his class, oblivious to everything around him, until suddenly his life wasn't there any longer, and he became the object of pity and contempt that his relatives had tried to sell to Clan Martinez, only to have him rejected by the woman he loved and bundled into marriage with someone else.

Perhaps, she thought, her own life had been easier, since she'd never had any money to begin with.

"I'm sorry, PJ," she said.

The expression on his face was hopeless. "I know the marriage to Sempronia was supposed to be all about money," he said. "But I was too useless and ridiculous to take seriously, and—" His eyes were starry with tears. He turned away. "Let's look at the palace, shall we? I have the key right here."

Sula followed him across the court and through the cavernous, empty house, filled with silence and ghosts, and gathering dust. She wanted to comfort him, but knew she was the wrong woman for the job.

He was another casualty of Martinez's ambitions. As was she.

Three days of frenzied work followed, and the long-limbed, stumbling, uncoordinated giant that was the secret army began to pull itself free from the muck in which it hid itself and prepare to take its first great strides. Trucks rolled up to the High City, carrying away Ngeni furniture, replacing it with paint, canvas, medical supplies, and mountaineering gear. Sula rode the trucks along the streets of the High City, making notes on a map of which palaces had guards, and therefore held someone worth guarding. She wondered what would happen to the guards during an emergency, whether they'd stick at their posts or rush to the fighting. She supposed she'd find out on the day.

Storage cabinets were opened and Team 491's formidable arsenal removed and placed in willing hands. Friends on the police opened a warehouse and over four hundred modern automatic rifles, an equal number of sidearms, ammunition, sets of body armor, and grenades and their launchers became the possession of the secret army. The police didn't even have to be bribed.

A pair of the scouts watching the prisons were captured, and apparently provided to the Naxids the false information with which they'd been primed. Through the friendly contacts the cliques maintained with agents of law enforcement, Sula learned that the prison guards had been quietly reinforced and that police and Fleet personnel were shifted out of the city center to react to any mass breakout attempts.

The Naxids were apparently satisfied that they were about to spring a trap. So was the White Ghost. Time would tell which of them was right.

At last there came a moment when the last message had been sent, the last weapon readied, the last plan made, revised, and remade. Then, as the sun touched the horizon, Sula walked into the safe house she shared with Casimir and found him dressed in his long Chesko coat with the triangular mirrors, the shining boots, the long walking stick with its glittering globe of rock crystal.

The room had a strange scent of lavender, and she paused in the door in astonishment. He turned to her, the skirts of his coat swirling, and made an elaborate bow.

"Welcome, Lady Sula," he said. "We're going out tonight."

"You're mad," Sula said. "Do you realize how much—"

"Everything's taken care of," Casimir said. "The soldiers are doing all the work, and the general can relax." He took a step to one side and revealed the green moiré gown that he'd draped on the bed. "I've provided more suitable clothing for an evening out."

Sula closed the door behind her and took a few dazed steps into the room. "Casimir," she said, "I'm a complete *wreck*. I haven't slept in days. I'm keeping myself going on coffee and sugar. I can't do *anything* like this."

"I have drawn a relaxing bath," he said. He made an elaborate show of looking at his sleeve display. "Our car will pick us up in half an hour."

Wondering, Sula walked into the bathroom, shed her clothing, and stepped into the lavender-scented bath. She lay back in the lukewarm water and commanded the hot water tap to open. She added hot water until steam was rising from the surface of the water, then lay back and closed her eyes. It was only an instant before she jerked awake to Casimir's knock.

"The car will be here in ten minutes," he said.

She busied herself quickly with the soap, then dried, brushed her hair, applied cosmetic and scent. She stepped naked into the front room to put on the gown, and Casimir watched from a corner chair, a connoisseur's smile on his face. The gown fit perfectly. He rose from his chair and bent to kiss one of her bare shoulders, a brush of lips on her clavicle that sent a shimmer of pleasure along her nerves.

The car was a long sedan, driven by Casimir's two Torminel bodyguards. It was the first time she had seen the guards since Casimir went underground, when their conspicuousness necessitated shifting them to other duties.

The car eased its way through the growing shadows and delivered them to the side entrance of a club on the Petty Mount. The place was dark, with a few spotlights here and there, on a table beneath an immaculate crisp white tablecloth, on the gleaming dance floor, on the empty bandstand. A tall Lai-own waitron stood in reflected light by the table.

"Sir," he said. "Madam."

The Lai-own poured champagne for Casimir and sparkling water for Sula, then vanished into the darkness. Sula turned to Casimir.

"You've done this just for us?" she asked.

"Not entirely for us alone," he said, and then she heard Veronika's laugh.

She came in with Julien, both dressed well and expensively, if not with Casimir's flair for style. Veronika wore her glittering anklet. Sula hadn't seen her since her exit from jail. Veronika looked at her as she approached, and her eyes went wide.

"They tell me you're a Peer!" she said. "They say you're the White Ghost, in command of the secret army!" She waved a hand dismissively. "I tell everyone that I knew you when you were just a math teacher!"

The waitron brought more drinks and their meal. When they finished eating and were served coffee, a four-piece Cree band came in and began setting up their instruments. A shiver of apprehension wafted up Sula's spine as she remembered the Cree in the haberdashery, the one who had first addressed her as the White Ghost. *You are she,* he had said.

The Cree with his wonderfully acute hearing must have recognized her voice from the brief video clips in *Resistance.* Now she wondered if she dared speak in front of the band.

She touched Casimir's thigh and leaned next to him.

"Are you sure we're safe here?" she asked.

He grinned. "I have two extraction teams waiting outside," he said. "Anybody comes, they're in for a fight." He nuzzled close to drop a kiss on her earlobe. "And I've got the escape route planned. Just like you taught me."

"After the war," she said, "the Riverside Clique will be

found to have acquired a very dangerous collection of skill sets."

The band began to play. The two couples stepped onto the dance floor and Sula's nervousness faded. In the slow dances, she clung to Casimir, her head on his shoulder, her eyes closed, existing happily in a world of sensation: the music that beat in time to her heart, the sway of Casimir's weight against hers, the deep musky scent of his warm body. In the faster dances, she was content to let him guide her, as he had all evening, a responsibility he accepted with silent gravity. He was focused entirely on her, his face composed in an expression of solemn regard, his dark eyes rarely leaving her face.

The band fell silent. The dancers' applause was swallowed in the huge empty room. Casimir took her hand and led her to the table.

"This next act is just for you," he said.

A Terran woman stepped onto the stage in a rustling flounce of skirts, her face and hands powdered white except for round rouged spots high on each cheek. She carried herself like a warrior, her chin high, imperious pride glittering from her eyes.

A derivoo. Sula's heart surged, and she pressed Casimir's hand.

"Thank you," she whispered.

Julien raised an eyebrow. "I hope you realize what a sacrifice the rest of us are making," he said.

The derivoo stood in a spotlight, one of the Cree played a single chord, and the derivoo began to sing. The single strong voice rang in the air, proclaiming a passionate love fated to become anguish, a lover once adoring now turned to stone. Each syllable raked Sula's nerves; each word seared. The singer proclaimed the confrontation of one lone heart with the Void, pure in the knowledge that the victory of the Void was foreordained.

For the next half hour the lone brave voice faced every horror: sadness, isolation, death, lost love, violence, terror.

There was no pity in the world of the derivoo, but neither was there surrender. The derivoo walked proudly into the realm of death, and died with scorn and defiance on her tongue.

The performance was brilliant. Sula stared in silent rapture throughout, except for the moments when she burned her hands with furious applause.

It was the most perfect thing she could imagine, to hear these songs just before making a desperate gamble with her own life. It was good to be reminded that her own existence was just a spark in the darkness, so brief that it scarcely mattered whether it ended now or later.

At the end of her performance, the derivoo held for a moment a pose of pure defiance, then turned and vanished into the darkness. Sula applauded and shouted, but the singer scorned the very idea of an encore.

Sula turned to Casimir. "That was wonderful," she breathed.

"Yes, it was." He took her hand. "I watched you the whole time. I've never seen an expression like that on your face."

"Sing like that," she said, "and you'll see it again." She turned to Julien and Veronika. "What did you think?" she asked.

Veronika's eyes were wide. "I had no *idea*," she said. "I've never seen derivoo live before."

Julien loosened his collar. "For me, it was a little intense," he said, "but she's a terrific performer, I'll hand you that."

The two couples parted. Casimir and Sula returned to the long car with the Torminel bodyguards and followed the vehicles of the extraction team out of the area. When they were alone in the apartment, which still smelled of the lavender bath oil, Sula put her arms around Casimir and gave him a long, grateful kiss.

"That was the most perfect evening I can imagine," she said.

His body was warm against hers. "I wanted to give you one special night to remember," he said, "before our time together ends."

Her nerves gave a leap at his words. She looked at him.

"What do you mean?"

There seemed an extra measure of gravel in Casimir's deep voice, as if there were an obstruction in his throat, but there was perfect logic in his words.

"Project Daliang will either succeed or not," he said. "If it fails, we won't have much to worry about, because it's likely one or both of us will be dead. But if it succeeds, then you become Lady Sula again, and I stay who I am. Lady Sula lives in a whole different world from me." He attempted a defiant grin. "But that's all right. It's as it should be. I have no right to complain, being what I am."

Her mind whirled, but she managed to assemble a protest. "That doesn't have to be true."

Casimir laughed. "What are you going to do?" he said. "Introduce me to your Peer friends? And what will I be to *them*? An exotic pet."

Sula took a step away from him. She felt her face harden into anger. "That is simply not true," she said.

There was a touch of scorn in his voice. "Of course it is. I'm a cliqueman. The only way I can get into the High City is to fight my way in with an army."

Angry words boiled up from her heart, but she caught them at the last minute. *Don't destroy this,* she thought. She had smashed perfect evenings in the past, and she would smash this one if she wasn't careful.

"I'm fighting my way in too," she said.

"Yes. And I know how much it must have cost you to get where you are now."

Her mind staggered under the certainty that Casimir somehow knew about Caro Sula. How *could* he? she thought wildly.

"What do you mean?" she said in a whisper.

"The night that Julien was arrested," Casimir said. "That

performance you put on in my office, showing up naked under your coat. I was completely boggled by what you did that night." He reached out a cool hand and drew a long finger along her bare shoulder. "You haven't acted like that since, but then you haven't had to. You got what you wanted—me clear of Julien's arrest, which you'd arranged so you could get old Sergius on your side in the war."

Her nerves turned to ice. "Who else knows?" she said.

"I figured it out, but that's because I was there to see that very impressive show you put on for my benefit. Julien will never guess, but I wouldn't put it past Sergius to work it out eventually."

Sula let out a long breath. Her head swam.

"Yes," she said. "I manipulated you at first." A nervous laugh rasped past her throat. "Why not? I didn't know you." She looked at him. "But I know you now. You're not someone I can simply use any longer."

His brows came together. "What accent is that?"

She could only stare. "What?"

"You're speaking in a different accent now. Not Riverside, not High City."

Sula cast her thoughts back and reformed the words in her mind. "Spannan," she said. "The Fabs. Where I was b— I mean, where I grew up."

"You were on Spannan long enough to pick up the voice, but you left and became Lady Sula, with the swank accent. And that's what you'll do again, once we win the war." He turned away, his fingers pressed to his forehead. "I'm sorry," he said. "I've upset you. I shouldn't have brought this up tonight, not before we make our move on the High City. You need to be focused on that, not on anything I say."

She watched him, despair rising like a flood to drown her heart. "Look," she said, "I'm dreadful at being Lady Sula. I'm an absolutely awful Peer." She followed him, touched his arm. "I'm much better at being Gredel. At being the White Ghost."

Casimir looked at her hand on his arm. A bitter smile

twisted his lips. "You may hate being Lady Sula, but that's who you are. That's who you'll have to be, if we win. And I'll still be Casimir Massoud, the cliqueman from Riverside. Where does that leave me, when all the Peers come back to run things?"

I am not *Lady Sula!* she thought desperately. But it wasn't something she could say aloud, and even if she did, it wouldn't make any difference.

Sula dropped her hand and straightened, as defiant in her despair as any derivoo.

"It leaves you Lord Sula," she said, "if you want to be."

His jaw dropped in astonishment and he turned to face her. "You can't mean it."

"Why not?" she said. "You couldn't be any worse a Peer than I am."

A trace of scorn crossed his face. "They'll laugh," he said. "I'll be a freak—a cliqueman in a High City palace. Until someone finds out some of the things I've done, and then I'll be tried and strangled."

"Wrong." Urgency sent the words spilling in a cascade from her lips. "You don't remember that I've promised amnesties. Once you get your amnesty, you don't have to go back to your old life. You're an honored businessman, probably with a medal and the thanks of the empire."

He gave her a skeptical look. "And what happens then? I sit in a palace and rot?"

"No. You make money." A hysterical laugh bubbled from deep within her. "You don't get it, do you? How the Peers made their money? They *stole* it." She laughed again. "Only they did it legally! If you have the right connections, if you have the right name, you can wedge yourself into legitimate business and collect your dues forever. It's not called protection, it's not called extortion, it's a *patron-client relationship*! You just need to learn the right *vocabulary*!"

Sula couldn't stand still any longer. She walked the two paces to the outside wall, then walked back again, then repeated the circuit. "There are two ways to take the High

City," she said as she walked. "One is with guns, and we'll do that in two days. The other way is with the right name, and Sula is one of the right names. You have *no idea* how ripe the empire is for plunder. The whole place is tottering, and not just because the Naxids have got greedy. I say we turn pirate and leave the place in smoking ruins. What do *you* say?"

She stopped her pacing and grinned up at him. Astonishment and confusion and chagrin and reluctant understanding worked their way across his face, each in its turn.

"I think you could do it," he said in a voice of soft surprise.

"*We* could do it," Sula said. "I'd need help. I told you I'm lousy at being a Peer."

"Life is such a strange adventure," Casimir remarked, and shook his head. He held out his arms. "How can I say no to becoming a lord?"

She stepped into his arms and felt them close tight around her.

There was a little problem with the Peers' Gene Bank that she would have to resolve, the drop of blood she was required to contribute if she ever married and which could prove her an imposter. The drop of blood that had come between her and Martinez.

But the gene bank was in the High City, and if she won her battle in the next few days, the genetic records of the Sula clan could vanish in the aftermath. Any barrier to marriage would vanish with them.

It wasn't just the cliquemen, she thought, who were now fighting for love.

TWENTY-SEVEN

The Righteous and Orthodox Fleet of Vengeance grew to thirty ships, then thirty-five, then forty. The Naxids at Magaria were known to have thirty-five ships, and many Fleet officers wanted to launch at once for immediate battle, but Tork continued his orbit of Chijimo and his drills. Martinez had to concede that Tork was probably right—if he was going to use the stodgy old tactics against a fleet that had already won a colossal victory against just those tactics, it was best to have a massive advantage in numbers.

The Naxids were reinforced to thirty-seven, the Orthodox Fleet to forty-six. Still Tork didn't move. Still he continued to drill his squadrons and hector his officers with demands for obedience and conformity. Still he bombarded the Convocation with demands for a vast new wave of ship construction, not simply warships, but support vessels, shuttles for landing troops, and the troops to be landed from the shuttles.

Then intelligence reports indicated that the Naxids numbered forty-two, which—since it happened to be the total number of ships they were absolutely known to possess—conceivably meant that the entire Naxid fleet might be at Zanshaa. The Orthodox Fleet had grown to fifty-two by then. Martinez found himself begin to itch for action. Engage *now,* he thought, before the Naxids could replace those unfinished ships destroyed at the shipyards by Chenforce and Squadron 14.

Tork was apparently immune to such itches. The Naxids were reinforced to forty-eight, which meant they had shipyards producing warships in places that neither raiding squadron had reached, probably including Naxas and Magaria. Tork then gained four new frigates and four heavy cruisers of the new *Obedience* class, *Obedience, Conformance, Compliance,* and *Submission.*

From the tenor of the lineup, Martinez suspected that Tork now had a hand in the naming of ships. "Logically," Martinez told Michi, "the next in the sequence will be 'Surrender.' "

Despite the reinforcements, Tork still declined to launch for Zanshaa. Martinez began to receive hints from Michi Chen—which had apparently originated with her brother—that both the government and the Fleet Control Board had lost patience with Tork and were on the verge of taking action—if, that is, they could make up their minds whether the action would be to replace Tork with Kringan, formerly of the Fourth Fleet and now Tork's second in command, or simply to order Tork to attack.

Possibly Tork heard these same hints, because he announced that he would move as soon as he had been reinforced by another three frigates from Laredo, ships that were already on their way. By the time that happened, the Naxids had received five ships, and Tork's advantage in numbers had fallen from twelve to ten.

Tork delayed for another four days after the Laredo frigates arrived—long enough, Martinez observed, for a query to be sent to the Control Board on Antopone, and for the return of an adamantine response. At this point Tork finally committed himself. Orders were sent to his squadron commanders, to individual ships, and to other Fleet elements in other systems.

The Righteous and Orthodox Fleet of Vengeance kindled its mighty antimatter torches, echeloned its squadrons, took a last high-gee swing around Chijimo, and hurled itself for Chijimo Wormhole 1 and the foe that waited at Zanshaa.

Sula rode the first of several trucks into the High City and took the Ngeni Palace for her headquarters. Maps and equipment were spread out on the dining room table. Portraits of Ngeni ancestors looked down in shock.

In the palace courtyard, screened by trees and shrubbery and statues of more ancestors, the trucks were repainted in Fleet colors. A pair of earth-moving vehicles with huge plow blades and wheels taller than a Terran already waited on their trailers. Members of Sula's advance team began fitting sheets of improvised plastic armor around the drivers' compartments.

Shawna Spence and a pair of assistants ripped out the interiors of a pair of cars that she would later pack with explosive. An entire truck bomb, her calculations suggested, would be redundant for the jobs intended—the cars would do perfectly well.

PJ Ngeni wandered around trying to be useful and generally getting in the way.

Elsewhere in the great city, combat teams were assembling. Or so Sula had to hope.

The sun sank slowly into a pool of hemoglobin red, signaling the end of a perfect autumn day. The fragments of the Zanshaa ring glowed in the darkening sky. The scents of the city rose on the still air: uncollected trash, dying flowers, cooking. Sula had her people gather on the terrace behind PJ's cottage and assemble the mountaineering gear, the long lines laid out in coils, the harnesses and ascendors that would carry people and gear up the cliff face.

Before the escalade began, Sula made a scan in either direction with light-enhancing binoculars. None of the Naxid guards at the Gate of the Exalted seemed interested in anything going on below.

Her sleeve comm gave a chirp. She looked at the display

and saw a text message: WANT TO MEET TOMORROW AT THE BAKERY?

The party at the foot of the cliff was ready.

Sula sent a return message—WHAT TIME?—then gave the command to hurl the long ropes over the parapet. Each rope ended in a bundle that included a climbing harness and the end of a safety line that would be belayed by one of the advance team on the terrace.

The reply was: 1301. Which meant that all three ropes had hit the ground without being hung up on snags or brush. Less than three minutes later Sula heard the soft whine of an electric motor, and a few seconds afterward the first head crested the terrace wall. A white grin split the dark face.

"Hi, princess," Patel said, and two of the advance team rushed forward to take him under the arms and lift him onto the terrace flagstones. His harness was efficiently stripped and sent back down under its own power. Patel loosened the strap of the rifle he'd been carrying and lowered his heavy pack. Sula pointed at the Ngeni Palace.

"Go through the courtyard to the big house. We have some food there."

"Thanks, princess."

More electric whines announced the arrival of two more climbers. The high-torque ascendor motors carried them up the rope at a walking pace, which meant the ascent required little skill except for staying in the harness, fending off the cliff with their feet, and hanging onto their gear.

The first group of thirty-nine were all Bogo Boys, an entire action group. Among them was Casimir, who reached for Sula with one hand and gave her a fierce kiss.

"Julien's with the rear guard," he said. "I think it's because he just doesn't want to come up this cliff."

"I can see his point," she said.

Fuel packs on the ascendors were replaced. The next deliveries sent up the static lines were equipment: weapons, ammunition, explosive, and detonators, all the gear they despaired of getting past the chemical sniffers at the foot of the High City's one access road. Spence and her engineering team hustled the packs of explosive to her stripped vehicles. A chill wind began to float between the spires of the High City, and Sula shivered in her coverall.

Casimir faded into the darkness, then returned a few moments later carrying a long coat that he wrapped around her shoulders.

"From PJ's closet," he murmured into her ear.

"Thank you," she whispered, and kissed him again.

She kept peering into the night with her binoculars, particularly at the Naxid installation at the Gate of the Exalted. She saw lookouts there, but their attention seemed occupied mainly with the traffic far below on the switchback road.

The last of the supplies whined up the static lines, and then the ascendors began delivering Sula's soldiers once again, the Lord Commander Eshruq Wing of the Secret Army—fighters, mostly Torminel, recruited mainly from the Zanshaa Academy of Design. The undergraduate industrial designers had become ruthless bombers and assassins, perhaps because of their youth and flexibility, or possibly because of their carnivore Torminel heritage. Now they would prove useful on account of their huge night-adapted eyes.

After the Eshruq Wing came another group of Bogo Boys, followed at last by Julien. He required three assistants to haul him, pale and shivering, over the parapet. With trembling hands he lit a cigarette, then shook his head and said, "I'm never getting in one of those harnesses again. Never again."

"If this goes right," Sula said, "you won't have to."

She made a brief inspection of her army, most of whom were lying on the beds, tables, and carpets of the Ngeni Palace that hadn't yet been taken to storage. Many were ritually cleaning and readying their weapons. Some

were gambling. Sidney sat in an antique hooded armchair, the hood filled with a cloud of hashish smoke. Fer
Tuga, the Axtattle sniper, limped from room to room,
looking at the fighters in apparent surprise. He had fought
all his battles alone till now, and the number of his allies
on this mission was a revelation to him.

Sula found PJ in his drawing room, looking far from the
stylish Peer. He wore durable baggy trousers with a leather
seat, as she'd sometimes see horsemen wear, and a ragged
brown pullover. He had two weapons disassembled on the
glossy Dwell-period table in front of him, a long hunting
rifle with a butt inlaid with ivory and chased with silver,
and a small pistol. He was cleaning the weapons with care
and great fussiness, and he didn't look up as she paused in
the doorway.

She wanted to tell PJ to leave the guns and get into bed
and wait for the war to be over, so he could dress in one of
his lovely tailored suits and drift down the road to one of
his clubs. She wanted to tell him that he had proved his
worth a thousand ways, that dying in a street fight wasn't
going to make Sempronia Martinez love him. She wanted
to tell him to head down the funicular to some bar or
restaurant in the Lower Town, find some pliable girl, and
fuck Sempronia out of his mind.

She wanted to say these things, but didn't. She just looked
at him for a moment and walked on without speaking.

Nothing she said would have made any difference anyway.

Sula lay for a few hours in Casimir's arms, the both of
them fully clothed and stretched on an old sofa in one of the
cottage's upstairs room. She supposed she might have slept.
She was up before dawn, however, to make certain that the
action groups received a meal, to conduct a last minute inspection of the vehicles, and to see that the group and team
leaders understood what they were expected to do.

She went onto the terrace as dawn broke over the capi-

tal, the sun rising into the green sky out of a pool of blood-
red that mirrored the one it had fallen behind the night before. Her binoculars were turned on the Naxid installation.
Nothing seemed to have changed since the previous evening.

The Naxids shift changed at 0736, with most of the Fleet
personnel coming up the funicular to join their officers
who barracked in hotels in the High City. Sula wanted to
keep any newcomers off the acropolis, and so had scheduled her attack to begin at 0701, half an hour before shift
change and a little more than twenty minutes after sunrise.

The High City was slowly coming to life, and she could
hear the calls of morning birds and an occasional vehicle
on the road outside. The Lower Town remained largely in
darkness, though many lit vehicles moved on the streets,
ghosting through the gaps between buildings. She passed
among the waiting fighters and gave the command to move
onto the vehicles.

The action groups climbed in silence onto their transport. Sula watched Casimir march up the ramp of one of
the trucks, awkward in the armor with which he'd never
had a chance to familiarize himself, and he turned, a half-
wistful, half-ironic smile rising onto his face as he saw her.
He raised a hand and gave her a mocking salute, fingers
flicking at his forehead, then stepped into the truck and sat
with a group of Bogo Boys.

Sula wanted to hurl herself onto the truck with the others, but she didn't move. She was a general, not a soldier.
As she watched the ramp rise, she felt a fist clamp on her
throat.

Fortune attend you, she thought uselessly. Ultimately,
luck was all she had to count on.

Electric motors provided traction to the big wheels, and
the vehicles slid away on their various errands. She wondered what anyone on the road outside might think, seeing
the Ngeni Palace service gate disgorging Fleet military

transport, a few civilian sedans, and the two earth-moving machines on their trailers.

The vehicle gate closed with a whir. Torminel guards armed with Sidneys stood behind the gate out of sight, while others quietly fortified the Ngeni Palace against any attack. His balding head bowed, PJ marched with his rifle at port arms in the shadow of the palace, awaiting his moment of glory.

In the cottage, Sula donned her cuirass and helmet, not because she expected to be shot at, but because it held her secure communications equipment and battery packs. She opened the visor, took her binoculars, and left the cottage for the shadow of one of the trees, where she could watch the Naxid guards without giving herself away.

Eskatars, scaly four-legged birds from Naxas, rained down angry cries from above her head, as if warning their distant kin of mischief afoot. Dead leaves and twigs pattered down on her shoulders.

The teams maintained radio silence on the approach. Then Sula heard a pair of signals.

"Four-nine-one, Thunder ready." Spence's voice, a little loud, a little excited.

"Four-nine-one, Rain ready." Macnamara's voice.

"Four-nine-one, Wind ready." Sula's heart gave a lurch at the sound of Casimir's grating tones.

Her mouth was dry. She summoned saliva to moisten her sandpaper tongue and gave the orders.

"Comm: to Rain. Launch Rain. Comm: send.

"Comm: to Wind. Launch Wind. Comm: send."

Rain and Wind, the seizure of the two entrances to the High City. Sula's words were coded, compressed into microsecond bursts, and fired into the city at the speed of light. Brief acknowledgments sang in her headphones.

There was a moment of stillness, and she could swear that, in the morning stillness, even with the headphones and the helmet over her head, she could hear the distant sound of a pair of trucks pulling around a corner and heading toward the Naxids at the Gate of the Exalted.

Her pulse sang in her veins. Her forehead ached where the padded rim of the binoculars were pressed against it.

These were trucks painted in the viridian green of the Fleet, the same model of Sun Ray the Fleet used, and they would arrive just ahead of the time the Naxids would expect a pair of trucks bringing their relief. The Naxids moved casually toward the vehicles as they rolled onto the broad terrace, expecting to see their own emerge as the rear ramps began to come down and the side doors to roll up.

What emerged were a swarm of Bogo Boys spitting bullets and hurling grenades. Though surprised, the Naxids managed to fight back, and they were well-armored and tenacious, but were badly placed and in the end simply mowed down. Any Naxids that come near the open doors of the antiproton gun turrets were killed by Fer Tuga, the Axtattle sniper, who had crept up on the Naxid position in a chameleon-weave cape capable of projecting active camouflage, rendering him nearly invisible against his background.

The snap of rifles stunned the Eskatars into silence. It was as if they knew their side had just lost.

"Rain has secured its objective," Macnamara said. His voice was a little breathless.

"Comm: to Rain. Can you use the antimatter guns? Comm: send."

"I'm checking that now."

The distant sound of fire reached Sula's ears. The fight over the funicular terminal was still going on. Casimir was leading that fight, with Sidney as the group's sniper.

There was the far-off crack of a grenade, and then the fading echoes of the explosion reverberating off the buildings of the High City and the great sprawl below. Then silence. Then, finally, Casimir's deep voice.

"This is Wind. We've taken the funicular. We're having

the operator move the train to the High City terminus, and we'll lock it here."

A flood of joy filled Sula's heart. She wanted to send Casimir a torrent of love, but instead made a brief acknowledgment and ran to the parapet as she sent another message.

"Launch Thunder. Repeat, launch Thunder."

Thunder was the attack on the Great Destiny and the Imperial hotels. At Sula's command, Spence launched the two big plows off their trailers, to hurl themselves with lowered blades to knock away the barriers placed around the buildings.

Sula turned her binoculars to the scene at the foot of the granite acropolis, where the Naxids stationed at the two blockhouses guarding the switchback road were reacting to the firefight overhead. It was clear they heard the shots, but it seemed they weren't sure where the sound had come from. Some were crouching with raised weapons, others had stopped all traffic approaching the High City. Probably the rest were in their bunkers.

While Sula gazed down at the Naxids, she heard a breathless commentary from Spence, little excited bursts of prose that she sent when she remembered to, and when she had nothing more important to do.

"The plow's hit the barrier! Wa— Did you *hear* that? The first barrier just went down! . . . Nothing left but bits of concrete and twisted rebar . . . Backing up to start again . . . heard a crash from the second plow . . . guards reacting . . . *Keep those guards pinned down!*"

Sula turned her binoculars on the Gate of the Exalted once more. Macnamara's action group was taking up positions in the buildings behind the gate, ready to repel any counterattack aimed at retaking the position from behind. Spence's one-sided comments continued, her voice a shout over the rattling sound of fire.

"*The second barrier's down! The guards are running!* . . . Send in the car *now*! . . . Go! Go! . . . She's *in*!

She's got the car *right in the lobby of the hotel!* . . . I'm hearing shooting from the Imperial. It's hard to see what's happening there . . . *Suppressive fire! Suppressive fire!* . . . The driver's away, she's gotten out! She's jumped up behind the plow blade and she's using it for cover . . . *Stand by, everybody! Fall back! . . .*"

Sula lowered her binoculars and wondered if she should take cover herself, if, as far as she was from the Great Destiny Hotel, she was in any danger, standing on the open terrace.

The explosion came in three stages, a very fast one-two-three, first a massive bang that seemed to stun the world into brief silence, then a great percussion that Sula felt as a blast of wind against her face, then the great shivering roar that came up from the High City's granite heart. A huge plume of debris and dust jetted high above the acropolis, glittering as it rose into the brilliant dawn.

Well *that* should wake the Naxids up, she thought.

"Success!" Spence's excited voice was faint against the continuous noise that still dinned Sula's ears. "We've taken out the Great Destiny Hotel!"

And with it some six hundred mid-level Naxids, Sula knew. Naxid fleet officers, police officials, officers in the Legion of Diligence, bureaucratic functionaries in the government ministries . . .

When planning the operation, she and Casimir had joked that the Naxid government might well run more efficiently once their mid-level bureaucrats were eliminated, but she knew that the middle layer were exactly those with the technical skills to keep the Naxid government running. Many of their superiors had been promoted on the basis of family or political connections, and the middle layers were the people who actually kept things functioning.

"Comm: to Thunder. Good work! What's happening at the Imperial Hotel?"

"I'm not sure," came the reply. "We're in a huge dust

cloud. So are they, probably. The reports I got were confusing, and I can't seem to contact the plow operator."

Gradually reports came in. The other half of Thunder wasn't going well. The plow had got hung up on a barrier, and while trying to maneuver clear, the operator had apparently been shot. At any rate, he wasn't replying and had ceased to maneuver the plow. Spence sent the Great Destiny plow to provide backup, but the huge machine had to detour around the vast pile of rubble that was the wrecked hotel and got lost in the dust cloud. The explosive car following the plow had been badly shot up by the hotel's guards, and when the dust cloud rolled up from the Great Destiny Hotel, the driver had taken the opportunity to abandon the vehicle and run for it.

In the end Spence had her crews take cover and detonated the car anyway. The explosion itself was spectacular, but the damage to the Imperial was superficial. The building was scarred and all the windows were blown out, but there were presumed to be relatively few enemy casualties. The debris cloud paled before the magnificent pall of the Great Destiny Hotel.

Sula ordered Spence to keep the hotel under fire. It might at least keep the Naxids pinned down and unable to take up their posts in the emergency.

"Four-nine-one, this is Rain." Macnamara's voice came calmly into Sula's stunned ears. "I found both antiproton guns already activated. The ammunition was locked, but I opened the boxes with the officers' keys, and now antiproton bottles have been loaded into both guns. We're ready to fire."

"Brilliant!" Sula told him. "Let's open the floodgates."

She trained her binoculars downward again, at the blockhouses guarding the foot of the switchback road, and saw the guards all staring upward at the huge, brilliant dust cloud that had been their comrades. Then there was a loud *bang,* and part of the nearest blockhouse disintegrated in a sizzling flash, hurling the nearby guards to the ground.

444 • Walter Jon Williams

Sula remembered that there were lots of very fast neutrons and gamma particles involved, and she faded back from the parapet and only heard the follow-up shots that Macnamara placed around the installation, turning it and the Naxid guards to subatomic particles and blazing hot slag. A wild triumph filled her heart as she realized the last barrier to the success of Project Daliang had just fallen.

"Comm: to all units," she called. "Launch Flood! Launch Flood! Repeat, launch Flood! Comm: send."

She stepped back to the parapet again, and had only a few minutes to wait before a convoy of trucks and automobiles rolled out of the Lower Town and toward the wrecked roadblock, bringing the first of the combat teams who had been briefed to prepare for storming prisons and were carefully assembled and guided during the night to locations beneath the High City. Now the guides told the drivers their true destination, and the convoys were heading up the long narrow trail toward the Gates of the Exalted.

Sula watched the first few convoys climbing the acropolis, each marked by brilliant headlight beams, and then ran back to the cottage to send out a message to the world.

Resistance

This is a message from the White Ghost.

Today is the day we retake our city!

For months we have been waiting for the inevitable return of the Fleet to Zanshaa, to drive away the Naxid invaders and restore proper government to our world.

Though that day will still come, there is no longer any need to wait. For months we have been building our strength, gathering weapons, and training in secret. We no longer need the Fleet. We can do the job ourselves.

All action teams, all cells, and all groups are now called to the fight. Strike the rebels wherever you can find them!

Attack their officials, strike down their guards, sabotage their equipment!

If you have ever contemplated action against the rebels, the time for action is now. If you have a gun, use it! If you can wreck a piece of enemy equipment, wreck it! If you have a rock, throw it! The city of Zanshaa can be ours in only a few hours!

If you are a member of the security services, we have this note of caution for you. Be careful how you behave this day. Note will be taken of which side you join. Make certain that it's the right one.

Maximum chaos, Sula thought. Not every enemy of the Naxids belonged to the secret army, or were under her control, or had quite dared to volunteer. She wanted them all to cut loose at once. The more emergencies buzzing around the Naxids' ears, the better.

And if anyone was actually unwise enough to follow her advice and throw rocks at Naxids, the bullets the Naxids fired in retaliation at least were bullets that weren't being fired at her and her comrades.

They needed all the help they could get. She figured there were between six and seven thousand loyalists in the secret army, and there were slightly in excess of 800 million Naxids on the planet. Whatever extra forces she could bring were desperately needed, if only to prevent the odds from looking more absurd than necessary.

Instead of her usual fifty thousand copies, she sent a million through the Records Office node. She suspected that anyone on duty in the Records Office now had many more urgent things to do than to keep a close watch on what the broadcast node was doing.

And as usual she'd turned off the node's logging, so there would be no record of her messages having been sent. And as usual she'd appended the address of a false node as the message's point of origin.

The false node was that of the Great Refuge, the massive domed structure at one end of the High City from which the Shaa had ruled their empire.

It was as if the Shaa themselves had returned from the dead to denounce the Naxids.

She had now added the Great Masters to the bewildering array of identities that she'd inhabited the last few months: Lady Sula, the White Ghost, Lucy Daubrac, Jill Durmanov, Gredel, and the team leader known only as 491. It was useless to ask which of these was the real personality.

The point was that all of them killed Naxids.

When it was time to stop killing, perhaps she'd ask herself who she really was.

She waited as PJ's desk console confirmed that *Resistance* had been sent, then logged out of the Records Office computer and returned to the terrace. The cloud of dust and debris was dispersing on the light morning breeze. A stream of vehicles was climbing up the switchback road, each filled with fighters preparing to seize the High City.

She went to the dining room of the Ngeni Palace, where her maps had been set out on the table. The groups coming up the switchback road were arriving in no particular order. The first groups were ordered to help secure the two bridgeheads at the funicular and the Gates of the Exalted. The next groups went to reinforce Spence's force, who were still laying a very precarious siege to the Imperial Hotel and the Naxid officials trapped inside, Naxids who outnumbered their attackers twenty to one.

The reinforcements were just in time. Spence's position had gone critical very fast. Whoever was in charge of the Naxid security forces on the acropolis must have been receiving a lot of confusing information, but one thing was clear: the hundreds of Naxids at the Imperial Hotel were calling for help, and they were calling with one voice.

Help was duly sent, in the form of two companies of Legion of Diligence paramilitaries, wearing black armor over their black uniforms, driving their special black vehicles, and carrying matte-black weapons. These were reinforced by whatever Motor and District Patrol were available. They punched easily through Spence's thinly held lines and reached the hotel, where they commenced organizing an evacuation.

Fortunately, this occurred just as Sula had reinforcements available. They were put into place around the hotel, hardening Spence's defenses just as the Naxid commander on the scene realized that he was facing a dilemma.

The Naxids didn't have enough transport to get everyone in the hotel away, and under the circumstances, they could hardly call for a city bus. They decided to open a corridor leading to the far end of the High City, beneath the dome of the Great Refuge where the government ministries were clustered. It wasn't clear whether they then intended to shuttle their charges out on their vehicles or march them briskly to safety, because the Naxid plan failed at the outset. When the feared Legion of Diligence rolled out of the hotel, they were met by a blistering fire from every building along their path. Grenades, rockets, and bombs rained down on their vehicles. Their retreat was much faster and more confused than their onset, and they left three vehicles behind, burning in the street.

After twenty minutes the Naxids tried again in another direction. Again they were sent scurrying back to the hotel.

Sula decided things were going rather well. She liked the Legion's force right where it was, stuck in the Imperial Hotel instead of defending the ministries and the Convocation. She decided it was time to open another front, and the next groups through the Gates of the Exalted were told to report to the Ngeni Palace.

There were certain targets that had to be taken in order for Project Daliang to be considered a success. The Ministry of Wisdom, which headquartered the principal broadcast media. The Office of the Censor, which scanned every message sent on all of Zanshaa for content hostile to the Naxids. The Commandery of the Naxid Fleet, which contained the apparatus that controlled the Naxid military, and the Ministry of Right and Dominion, which supervised the Commandery and the Fleet. The Ministry of Police. The Ministry for the Defense of the Praxis, which controlled the Legion of Diligence.

And of course the Convocation itself, where the Committee to Save the Praxis, the supreme body of the Naxid rebellion, met with its tame legislature.

All these crucial government departments were clumped in one area, beneath the shadow of the Great Refuge and its granite dome. This was the area that Sula determined to seize.

She called for group and team leaders to meet her in the dining room. With a series of questions, she tried to determine the levels of experience available and the state of each group's equipment. The most capable she reserved for her assault on the government departments. Others she sent to seize the Glory of Hygiene Hospital, so her wounded fighters would have medical care. To the least useful she provided addresses, and sent them to scour the homes of high-ranking Naxids and bring as many officials of the rebellion as possible under her control.

"I want them alive, understand?" she said. "They're hostages for the other Naxids' good behavior. We need *them* to keep *us* alive."

The action teams raced off on their errand of abduction, to which she knew they would very likely add vandalism and pillage. The remaining captains she brought close around her maps on the table, to plan a multipronged attack up each street leading to the Great Refuge.

"I want a line of fighters going up each side of the street," she said. "Vehicles should lag behind, but should be ready to rush forward and support. Understand? Any questions?"

One young Lai-own raised a hand. "Are you the real Lady Sula?" she asked. "Or a fake, like they say?"

She grinned. "I'm as real as you," she said. "Are *you* a fake?"

She sent them off and told them to begin their assault at 0826. She would hope that at least one column would do well, and that she could support that attack with reserves. Her army's amateur nature was a severe handicap: the attack on a broad front was necessary because she had no way of scouting the enemy, she could only attack everywhere and hope someone got lucky. And she had to organize the entire assault herself, with communications limited to those who were similarly equipped with headsets, and for those who weren't, to a hand comm. She badly needed a staff, but didn't have one. Spence and Macnamara might have filled that role, but they had vital assignments of their own that she didn't dare trust to anyone else.

While the new assault forces moved into position, she was given a running commentary from Casimir concerning events at the funicular. The Naxid security forces in the Lower Town hotels had finally organized themselves and paged the funicular operator to send the train to pick them up. The operator—an elderly Daimong who had held his job for decades—told the Naxids that he had strict orders to keep the funicular at the upper terminal. The Naxid repeated their demands. The Daimong repeated his explanation.

The Naxids then contacted someone in the Ministry of Works to order the Daimong to lower the funicular. The Daimong refused on the grounds that it was the military who had ordered him to keep the funicular at the terminus. The Naxids then contacted the Commandery, and a senior captain of the Naxid Fleet contacted the terminus and countermanded the order. The Daimong replied that the order hadn't come from the Fleet, so the Fleet couldn't countermand it. The Daimong was asked what service had given the order, and the Daimong said he didn't know.

Successive calls came from the District Patrol, the Motor Patrol, and the Legion of Diligence. In all cases, the Daimong replied that they couldn't countermand his order since it hadn't come from that service.

"What officer gave the order?" the Naxid finally demanded.

"The one right here," the Daimong finally said.

"Let me speak to him!"

The Daimong stepped aside to let Casimir step to the comm unit, wearing his Fleet-issue armor and carrying his rifle. The Naxid stared speechlessly while his scales flashed red, unreadable patterns.

"What do *you* want?" Casimir asked.

The Naxid overcame his surprise enough to manage a command. "You must lower the train at once."

Casimir looked straight into the camera pickup. "Piss on you," he said. "I work for the White Ghost."

Sula laughed when she heard this from Casimir. He and the cooperative Daimong operator had kept the Naxids stuck at the lower terminus for over half an hour, during which they couldn't interfere in the battle of the High City.

Now, however, the Naxids came up the railway, a whole swarm marching up the steep track and the maintenance paths on either side. Most of Casimir's teams, in good positions in palaces overlooking the Lower Town, opened fire and sent them tumbling down the slope again. Casimir reported that he was having a hard time getting some of the teams to stop shooting once they'd started and that he was worried about poor fire discipline eating up his ammunition supply.

The Naxids took a few minutes to reorganize, and then Casimir reported that he could hear them all shouting slogans in unison: *Death to anarchists! Long live our leaders! On to the High City!*

On they came, better organized this time, with Fleet security forces in the lead in viridian armor, scuttling up the steep slope as fast as their four legs could carry them. Casimir's fighters met them with a blast of fire that cut them down by rows but the Naxids charged on, trampling the wounded and dying. Then the two antimatter cannons began to fire, and the head of the long column faltered and turned back. Those at the rear still drove them forward, however, and the collision sent Naxids flying off the track and tumbling down sheer granite slabs to lie broken at the bottom of the acropolis. The survivors pulled back into cover.

"They're bound to get smarter about this," Casimir told her.

Sula was concerned that, failing the attack up the funicular, the enemy would try to scale the High City at some other point along its lengthy perimeter. Naxids weren't exactly built for mountaineering, but it could be done, and at the moment there was no one to stop them. She sent action teams as lookouts to various points on the city's cliffside to make certain that no Naxids were turning mountain goat.

Reports came in to her that the Glory of Hygiene Hospital had been taken. It was guarded, but hospital security were private and non-Naxid and stood aside. Some of them had joined the loyalists, which would have been more encouraging had they been armed with anything more effective than sidearms and stun batons.

A growing crackle of fire, heard through the open windows of the dining room, told Sula that the coordinated offensive on the government complex had gone forward on schedule. The firing rose to a tremendous din, died away to a continual crackle, then diminished still further, to what sounded like desultory sniping. Sula was in a near frenzy to contact her units to find out what had gone wrong. It seemed that all groups had run into resistance, gone to cover, and were now awaiting further developments.

"Get your people moving!" she told one group leader over her comm unit. He was a youngish Terran with a receding, unshaven chin and a startled expression, as if he hadn't ever expected to be in this situation.

Perhaps he hadn't. Few of her army had ever been in actual combat before. The teams that had been passing information and copies of *Resistance,* firebombing Naxid homes and vehicles, or sniping at the enemy from a reasonably safe distance were now discovering what a genuine battle was like, one where the enemy fought back.

"Well," the leader said, "getting the people moving is going to be hard. We were advancing up the road, see, and when the Naxids opened fire, everybody jumped into these offices and shops. They're all kind of scattered out now. I don't know how I'm going to get them all going again or—"

"Just get out there and round them up!" Sula demanded.

"Well, see," the man said, "I'd have to get out on the street to do that, and they've got machine guns, you know."

"Bring up the vehicles to give you covering fire!"

"Well," he answered, "those cars don't want to come any closer, see. They'd get shot up, and they don't have armor or anything."

"Get those people moving, you cowardly son of a bitch!" Sula shrieked, *"or I'll come up there and personally shoot you in the fucking head!"*

The young man's startled face took on an expression of deep indignation. "If you're going to talk like that," he said, "I don't see why I should continue this conversation."

Sula stared open-mouthed as the orange end-stamp filled the screen. *"The bastard!"* she shouted, and cocked her arm to throw her comm unit through the open window. Then she thought better of it and lowered her arm.

She called more units and received promises that they would try to move forward. Firing briefly increased, then died away again. The fierce hammering of machine guns sounded clear in the morning air. She knew that those guns were programmable to fire at any movement detected within a certain defined area. It would be hard to move fighters in against them as long as their ammunition supply held out.

She considered sending in her reserves, but was afraid they would get pinned down as well. There was no one she could trust to scout the enemy who didn't have another vital job. It was a job, she realized, that she was going to have to do herself.

She rolled up her maps and left the palace, passing the Torminel guards at the gate. Several groups of fighters, just arrived, had parked in the street, waiting for orders.

"I need someone to give me a ride," she said.

A Lai-own rose to open the door of his long violet-colored car, but a familiar voice spoke.

"That would be me, beauteous lady."

Sula grinned. "One-Step!"

The onetime vagrant of Riverside was dressed in clean coveralls and heavy boots. A Sidney Mark One was slung over his shoulder, and there were strands of cheap glass beads around his neck.

She ran to his truck and gave him a hug. "One-Step hasn't seen you," he said reproachfully. "The lovely lady's been too busy for One-Step."

"I'm about to get busier," Sula said.

"Here." He took off a strand of beads and put them around Sula's neck. "These will keep you safe."

She blinked. "Thanks." *Whatever works,* she thought.

She jumped into the passenger seat of his truck, and One-Step pushed the throttle forward and eased it into the crowded street.

For the next twenty minutes she viewed the areas where the attack had gone in, and saw where wrecked vehicles and scattered bodies signaled the high-water mark of the advance. The long straight streets provided ideal fields of fire for enemy heavy weapons. The Naxids dominated the streets from the far end and were hardening their positions. Something, she thought, would have to break things loose.

As she was finishing her survey, she heard a torrent of fire from somewhere else in the city. She paused and waited for a communication.

"Four-nine-one," came Casimir's voice in her helmet, "this is Wind. The Naxids are up to something. We're getting a lot of fire from positions in those hotels down there. It's obviously meant to make us keep our heads down. I can hear them starting to shout again, so they'll be charging again fairly soon."

Sula asked if he thought he was in any trouble.

"We're just fine, lover," he said. "You do what you need to do, and don't worry about us."

She asked if he could spare Sidney.

"Sidney? Sure. Where do you want him sent?"

She had him brought to Ashbar Square, where she had collected her reserves. There, amid the scent of blossoming ayaca trees, she unrolled her maps on a marble bench beneath the statue of Enlightenment Bringing Joy to the People. Sidney arrived just as the firing at the funicular grew to a vast roar.

"You live on the High City," she asked him. "How do we get around those Naxid positions?"

In addition to the long, straight streets in the High City, there were also small pedestrian lanes lined with small shops, and alleys and little squares behind the shops intended for service vehicles. Sula had first entered Sidney's shop through just such an alley. They were marked on her maps, but it was difficult to tell from the maps exactly how to enter the lanes and what could be found there.

Sidney pointed out the byways he knew and explained how to access them. Sula called several of her commanders and gave them instructions.

"Stay off the main roads," she said. "Leave your vehicles behind and move up through the alleys. We can expect that the Naxids will have guards here, but they won't be in commanding positions, they'll be close, where you can reach them. Keep moving and you'll get behind those heavy gun positions and can take them out." She looked at Sidney. "You can lead one group, can't you?"

"Of course, my lady."

She sent them on their way and turned to the reserve units that were clustered around the square. The din at the funicular was dying away.

"Those were police in the lead this time," Casimir reported. "Urban Patrol. I think they're running out of Fleet landing groups." He gave a laugh that sounded like shale sliding down a slope. "It may be the Motor Patrol charging next."

Cheered, Sula left the fountain, went to an area where a number of vehicles were parked and jumped onto the flat bed of a truck. "Gather around!" she called, and took off her helmet. She shook out her blond hair and gazed out over her fighters. There were three or four hundred, and she had never laid eyes on most of them before. They included the tall Lai-own with their feathery hair, the shorter Torminel with their large nocturnal eyes shaded by goggles or dark glasses, the pale expressionless Daimong with their gaping mouths and round, hollow, startled-looking eyes, the Cree with their huge ears and dark purple flesh, and the Terrans, who looked more like curious schoolchildren than determined soldiers.

Sula took a long, drawn-out breath, the air sweet with the scent of morning blossoms, and then shouted out into the morning.

"Which of you is the bravest?"

There was a moment of surprise, and then a half-articulate shout went up and she saw a sudden forest of pumping fists and waving rifles.

"Right," she said, and began to point. *"You,* and *you,* and you there . . ."* Then she looked down at the man with the beads dangling around his neck. "Not you, One-Step," she said. "I've got other plans for you."

When she had her dozen chosen, she brought them up to the hydraulic tailgate of the truck: five Torminel, two Daimong, three Terrans, and a pair of Lai-own so nearly identical that they might have been twins.

"I need the bravest," she said, "because I need you to drive like hell right up the Boulevard of the Praxis and the Street of Righteous Peace. I need you to drive until your vehicles are so shot up they can't move any longer."

The Naxids' computer-controlled heavy weapons were programmed to fire at movement, and would shoot at the nearest targets first. Her plan was to provide targets that would suck up all those enemy rounds, targets behind which the rest of her force could advance.

"You'll all be in trucks," she told her dozen. "And you'll be charging in reverse, so that the rear of the trucks will take most of the damage and you won't be committing suicide." *At least not so blatantly.*

Sula activated the record function on her sleeve display. "I want your names," she said, "so that when they write the histories of this battle, you'll be in them."

Pride sang in their voices when they spoke their names.

She made her assignments, then gave orders to the rest of the reserves. They were to fill their vehicles with fighters and charge up the streets behind the dozen of the advance group. They weren't to stop and take cover until all the advance group were stopped dead or until their own vehicles were hit.

"Move when you hear the horn blasts," Sula said. "Now go!"

She turned to One-Step. "I need you to go back to the Ngeni Palace," she said, "and bring all the groups waiting there to the square."

She knew she might have to repeat this trick more than once, with fresh cannon fodder.

Firing began at the funicular once more as she waited on the Boulevard of the Praxis while her army got into position. Casimir reported that it was the same Naxid tactic as before—covering fire for an attack that hadn't started yet.

"Do you suppose all that shouting is meant to draw our attention away from something else?" he wondered.

She'd been thinking much the same thing. She tried to contact the teams she'd placed around the perimeter, but they reported nothing. Then she put on her headset and tried Macnamara.

"Nothing's happening here, my lady," he said. "There's no sign of the Naxids at all. A few action groups are still coming up the road. We've blocked the gate with trucks and won't let them pass until they identify themselves, and then we send them on to the Ngeni Palace as you ordered."

She told Macnamara to send them to Ashbar Square instead.

"Very good, my lady."

"What is the status of the antimatter guns?" she asked. "Can you remove them from the emplacements?"

"Yes, my lady," he replied. "They're the same guns we trained on, and we can take them out of the turrets. We'll have to remove and then reattach the big antiradiation shield, but all it will take is time."

"Good. Pull one out and put it on the back of a truck. Let me know when you're ready," she concluded.

She had been worried about the antiproton guns—they were an invincible weapon right up to the moment when the Naxids brought up antiproton guns of their own and blew them to radioactive dust. Getting the weapons out of the conspicuous turrets and putting them in a more camouflaged location might be the best way of preserving them.

There was a sudden burst of fire up ahead. Sula couldn't see where it was coming from, and had to assume that one of the groups she'd sent into the lanes and alleys had run into the enemy. She didn't want the Naxids to think of sending reinforcements there, so she decided it was time to launch her next attack.

"Blow your horns!" she shouted. "Let's go!"

The cars, vans, and trucks began honking their horns, each producing anything from a saucy little blip to a bass organ roar. Her suicide squads rolled ahead, driving very large vehicles in reverse. Even in reverse they managed a good pace, though some were clearly better drivers than others. She hoped the swerving would help keep them alive.

When the advance wave hit the Naxid guns' preprogrammed defense area, the air suddenly filled with hammering that began to shred the trucks. The driving grew more erratic as pieces flew off and clattered in the street.

There were at least three machine guns, she thought, because at least three of the trucks were getting hit at once.

The rest of the reserves followed in a dense swarm, firearms thrusting out the windows, some spraying the buildings ahead. Sula followed at a run, dashing up one of the walks until she encountered the first scattered bodies, then she ducked into a shop where bullets had marred the neat window displays.

Five Torminel looked at her in surprise from amid a collection of pens and stationery. "Move up!" she shouted. "We need your unit to move ahead and leapfrog the forces I've just sent in!"

The Torminel seemed to see the point of this, and they ran out of the shop, beating on doors and windows as they advanced and calling out to their comrades to join them.

Ahead, the street was noisy chaos. The smell of burning caught at the back of her throat. Bullets cracked overhead. Sula sprinted across the boulevard and jumped over a dead body that lay sprawled in the doorway of a vegetable market.

Something about the body made her stop before she entered the store. She braced her back against the solid doorway and saw that it was PJ Ngeni.

He had been hit in the chest and had fallen backward to the pavement. His elaborate hunting rifle lay across his body. His face bore an expression of wistful surprise.

Sula felt as if a soft pillow were pressed on her face, and she forced herself to breathe.

She had liked PJ. She had liked his amiable goodwill, and his foolish bravery, and the accuracy of his social sense. He had been everything that was fond and silly in the old order, and everything that the war had doomed.

A bullet glanced off the pavement nearby. She opened the door and stepped into the vegetable store.

Three Terrans looked at her. One was the surprised-looking man with the receding chin who had refused her orders to advance. Another was a young woman with greasy hair, and a third a teenage boy with bad skin, his lips stained with berry juice. Apparently they'd been having a feast of food gathered off the ration.

"Get your people together," Sula told them. "Get up the street. You're going to leapfrog the units that just went in."

"Well," the man said, "that's going to be hard because—"

"I don't *care* how hard it is!" Sula said. "Just get out there and *do* it."

"Well," the young man said, "we were *supposed* to be attacking a prison. I don't even know what we're *doing* up here on the hill."

Rage flared in Sula's veins. "What we're *doing*," she said, "is winning the war, you incompetent fuck! Now get *out* there!"

He nodded, as if acknowledging a minor rhetorical point. "You know," he said, "I don't think this thing is very well thought out, because—"

Sula remembered that she'd left her rifle behind at the Ngeni Palace. She reached for her pistol, pulled it out of the holster, touched the activation stud and pointed it at the group leader.

"Brave soldiers are dying for every second you hide in here," she said. "Now are you going to show some leadership, or am I going to shoot you like I promised in our *last* conversation?"

The woman and the boy gaped at the sight of the pistol. A stubborn expression crossed the leader's face. "Not till I have my say," he said, "because—"

Sula shot him in the head. The woman gave a little shriek as blood and brains spattered her. The boy took a step back and knocked over a crate of pomegranates. The little purple-red fruits bounced as they rolled along the floor.

Sula saw Caro Sula lying dead on the cart, her translucent skin paper-white. She saw Caro vanish into the river, her hair a flash of gold.

For a moment, as she looked down at the body, she saw Caro Sula's face staring back at her.

The coppery smell of blood swamped her senses and she clamped down hard as her stomach tried to quease its way past her throat. The pistol swayed in her hand. "Get out onto the street!" she told the other two. "And do it *now*! And if you head anywhere but toward the battle, I'll shoot the both of you, I swear."

They edged around her, their weapons held in their hands as if they'd never seen them before. "Get up the road!" Sula shouted. The two reached the doorway, stepped gingerly over PJ Ngeni, and broke into a trot as they jogged up the street, toward the fighting.

Sula followed. She picked up PJ's rifle and looked at its display. It hadn't fired a single shot.

She slung it over her shoulder and moved up the street, pounding on doors and windows as she went.

"Come out of there," she called, "you cowardly sacks of shit! Get moving! Move, you useless ass-wipes!"

Fighters emerged from their hiding places, and she sent them into the firestorm ahead. All of the vehicles had pulled off the road or been destroyed. Gunfire was roaring nonstop.

Having dug out as many fighters as she could, she trudged back to Ashbar Square, where new units were beginning to arrive. If the current attack failed, she decided, she'd pull the trick with the suicide trucks again.

It wasn't necessary. Sidney and the other infiltrators had worked their way through the maze of lanes and alleys and gotten behind the Naxid positions. They attacked seized some of the heavy weapons positions and turned the weapons on the other hardened positions. The fighters trying to move up the street suddenly surged forward as the Naxid defense disintegrated.

The Naxids had no reserves to speak of, and their positions had no depth. Once their line was breached, they had to pull back everywhere to avoid being cut off. Most were overrun before they could retreat. Sula's fighters seized the Ministry of Right and Dominion, the Ministry of Police, the Ministry for the Defense of the Praxis, and the High Court with its admirable view of the surrounding terrain.

Mad triumph raged in her veins. She called Casimir.

"We've thrown down another attack," Julien replied. "We're just slaughtering them. I don't know why they keep on coming."

"Julien?" Sula said in surprise. "Where's Casimir?" Then she remembered communications protocols and repeated the question using the proper form.

"He's gone to sort out some of the units with poor fire control," Julien said. "They keep wasting ammunition. He gave me his comm protocols while he's running his errand."

Sula sagged with relief. "Comm: to Wind," she said. "Tell him that I love him madly. Tell him that it looks like we're taking all the government buildings on this end. Comm: send."

"We figured you would," came the answer.

She spoke too soon. When the army tried to move on to the Commandery, they ran into serious trouble.

"They've installed one of those units they've been using against snipers," Sula was told. "Fire one bullet across their perimeter, and a whole series of automated weapons blast the hell out of you."

Fortunately, Macnamara reported that he'd pulled an antiproton gun out of its turret and mounted it on the back of a truck. Sula ordered it to the Commandery.

The automated defense system could pinpoint any bullet or rocket aimed in its direction. But it wasn't capable of spotting a minute charge of antiprotons traveling along an electron beam at one-third the speed of light.

Macnamara demolished the Commandery's defenses with ten minutes of careful fire. The loyalists charged forward with a great roar, chasing the remaining guards through the maze of corridors and capturing the entire Naxid Fleet staff in the situation room.

The Ministry of Wisdom was taken without a fight. The Naxid security forces tried to make a stand in the courtyard of the Hall of the Convocation but were swarmed from all sides and massacred.

Forty of the rebels' tame Convocation were captured hiding in various parts of the building. Lady Kushdai, who chaired the Committee for the Salvation of the Praxis, was captured in the quarters formerly belonging to the Lord Senior of the Convocation.

Sula had launched the only ground battle fought in the empire's history, and won it.

Zanshaa High City was now hers, and so was the government.

TWENTY-EIGHT

The technicians at the Ministry of Wisdom were mostly non-Naxids, and happy to cooperate with the forces that had stormed their workplace. Thus it was that an expressionless Daimong news reader, droning through the statistics of the northern hemisphere's most recent spelt harvest, interrupted his recital to announce a special proclamation.

The image then switched to Sula, who had occupied a desk in the next studio. She was still wearing her cuirass, and despite the last minute attention of a cosmetician on the department staff, her hair was stringy and still bore the impressions of her helmet liner. One-Step's necklace hung over her armor plate. Her helmet and PJ's rifle lay on the desk in front of her.

The image went out on every video channel on the planet. Audio channels carried it as well.

Sula looked at the nearest camera and lifted her chin. She tried to remember how she had acted and spoken when she first met Sergius Bakshi, how Lady Sula had looked down her nose at the assembled cliquemen and demanded their allegiance.

"I am Caroline, Lady Sula," she said in her best High City accent. "I serve the empire as Military Governor of Zanshaa and commander of the secret army. This morning forces under my command took the High City of Zanshaa and captured the rebel Naxid government. Lady Kushdai surrendered to me shortly thereafter, on behalf of the Committee for the Salvation of the Praxis."

She paused for dramatic effect, and let an arrogant curve develop along her upper lip. "As Lady Governor," she said, "I decree the following:

"All hostages and political prisoners taken by the rebel government are to be released immediately.

"All Naxids in the military and police forces are to surrender their weapons at once to units of the secret army, or to any captain of the Urban Patrol or Motor Patrol provided that he is not a Naxid. Naxid forces will then return to their barracks and await further orders. Those with families on the planet may return home.

"All promotions in the civil service, judiciary, and military made since the arrival of the Naxid rebels are canceled. Those placed in positions of authority by the previous administration may return to work at their old jobs and at their old rates of pay.

"All units of the secret army are ordered to cease offensive action against any rebel force that is in obedience to my instructions. Those who disobey may still be attacked. Units of the secret army are to hold themselves ready for further orders."

She paused again, and tried to glare into the cameras as if it were an enemy.

"Disobedience of my orders will be met with the highest possible penalty. The cooperation of all citizens in the restoration of legitimate and orderly government will be required. Further announcements will be made as necessary.

"This is Caroline, Lady Sula. This announcement is at an end."

We now return you to spelt prices, she thought, and had a hard time containing a sudden eruption of laughter until one of the techs signaled her that they'd cut back to the Daimong announcer.

Presumably, Naxids on other parts of the planet would be acting to cut off the broadcasts in their own areas, so Sula and her crew acted to get as much information into the hands of the public while it was still possible.

The announcers and staff at the ministry were ordered to repeat her announcement regularly, along with any news or analysis they cared to add that was favorable to the point of view of the loyalists. They were professionals, and had spent their careers cleaving to one ideological line or another, and they all understood their instructions. Camera crews were sent out to take pictures of the fighters standing around the various public buildings and monuments and wandering through the Convocation and the Commandery.

Sula realized that her claim that Lady Kushdai had surrendered to her would be considerably bolstered if Lady Kushdai actually *did* surrender to her, so she had the elderly Naxid brought from the bloodstained courtyard of the Convocation, where prisoners were being held, into the hall itself and onto the speaker's platform. Behind Sula was the huge glass wall that looked out onto the Lower Town, where towers of rising smoke marked the acts of sabotage that she had called for in that morning's edition of *Resistance*.

Lady Kushdai was escorted to the platform and presented with the formal articles of surrender, written by Sula herself a few minutes earlier.

"No flashing your scales, now," Sula said. The red flashes could be used to send messages to other Naxids, messages that other species found it difficult to translate. Kushdai obeyed, and scratched her signature onto the sheet of paper that Sula had cribbed from one of the convocates' desks.

She looked up at Sula from her black-on-red eyes. "I hope you will provide me with the means to kill myself," she said.

"I don't think so," Sula replied. "You're too valuable to throw away."

The circumstances of her death, Sula suspected, would be a good deal more imaginative than any official act Lady Kushdai had attempted during her term on Zanshaa.

She picked up a pen and signed, just the single title "Sula."

A camera crew from the Ministry of Wisdom recorded the event, and the recording was broadcast immediately on all video stations, along with the text of the surrender message, calling for all Naxid forces throughout the empire to surrender unconditionally.

It occurred to Sula that she was pressing her luck with such a demand, but she thought it wouldn't hurt to ask.

She decided to make the Ministry of Wisdom her headquarters. Unlike the Commandery, where all the comm techs had been Naxids, now dead or imprisoned, the ministry was stuffed with communications equipment, and with techs who knew how to use it. She walked across the road to the ministry just as another burst of fire broke out to the west.

Spence at the Imperial Hotel and Julien at the funicular told her what was happening. The Naxids had made an attempt to break out of the Imperial Hotel in the direction of the funicular, an attack coordinated with another charge from the base of the incline railway. Sula sent some groups to the area as reinforcements, but they weren't needed. Though both attacks were pressed with great determination, they were driven back with slaughter.

She wondered why the Naxids were so persistent in their hopeless attacks up the funicular. Possibly, she thought, they were responding to orders: their superiors were trapped in the Imperial, were demanding immediate rescue, and weren't willing to tolerate delay or excuses.

She supposed she should be grateful that the Naxid officers weren't giving their subordinates time to come up with anything clever.

"To: Wind. Where's Casimir?" she asked Julien after the fighting had died down. "Is he still trying to kick some discipline into those fighters? Comm: send."

The silence that followed was long enough that cold dread began to seep into the pit of her stomach.

"I'm sorry, Gredel," the answer finally came. "He made

me promise not to tell you till we'd won the battle. I guess we've won now, haven't we?"

There was another silence in which Sula felt a scream building deep in her chest, a howl of pain and rage that she bottled inside only because she couldn't yet be sure that Julien's next words would be what she feared.

"Casimir was wounded earlier this morning," he said. "It was the suppressive fire from those hotels down below. He's been sent to the hospital. He was awake and talking when we sent him away, and like I said, he made me promise not to tell . . . He didn't want you distracted when you had a battle to fight."

"I need a car!" Sula shouted to the people around her. "I need a car *now*!" People began to bustle.

And then she used proper communications protocols to respond to Julien.

"Comm: to Rain. Where in the hospital is he? Have you heard from him? Comm: send."

"I sent two of the boys with him," Julien replied. "One came back and said he was getting treatment and that it looked as if he'd be all right. The other's still with him. I'll call him and get right back to you with as much information as I can."

Sula left Macnamara in charge of the headquarters and referred all immediate problems to him. One-Step shuttled her and a pair of walking wounded to the hospital. The wheels threw up clouds of choking dust, the drifting remains of the New Destiny Hotel. By the time she arrived, Sula knew which hospital ward Casimir was in and learned that he'd been through an operation and was still alive. The wounds were minor, the report said, and he was resting peacefully in his bed.

The hospital was a nightmare. Beneath the barrel-vaulted ceilings, with their mosaics of medical personnel flying to the aid of gracefully injured citizens, hundreds of wounded jammed the corridors, most of them High City residents caught in a cross fire. They were waiting for treatment because the secret army's wounded, who had guns, demanded to be treated first. There was a small pile of dead Naxids in front of the building, mostly security forces who had come for treatment and then been dealt summary justice by the loyalist army. Some of the dead were medical personnel who had displeased the fighters one way or another. Others were civilians who had simply been in the wrong place.

The very fact that she had to observe any of this while she was on an urgent errand drove Sula into fury. She was barking angry orders as soon as she stepped out of One-Step's truck, demanding that all group and team leaders meet her in Casimir's ward.

The place smelled of blood, panic, and despair. The corridors were tracked with the rust-brown debris of the New Destiny Hotel that no one had time to clear. Fighters swaggered along the corridors brandishing weapons, and insolently supervised the work of the medical personnel. The wounded moaned, screamed, or cried for help as Sula passed. She pictured Casimir lying on the floor in some dingy, blood-soaked ward and hurried onward.

Her heart surged with relief as she saw him lying, as the report had indicated, on a bed in one of the wards. His eyes were open and she could hear the deep croak of his voice even over the continuous murmur of the other wounded in the ward.

She rushed toward him. His chest and one shoulder were bandaged and a pastel blue sheet was drawn up to his waist. An intravenous tube ran from a plastic bag on a rack to one arm. The ward was crowded, and the bed had been shoved in among a group of injured, many of whom did not have beds, only cushions and thin mattresses. Casimir's guard—one of his Torminel—stood by the head of the bed, rifle propped on his hip and a stolid expression on his furry face.

Casimir's dark eyes turned to her as she approached, and

his face lit with surprise and weary delight. She pressed herself to him and kissed his cheek. His flesh was cold. She drew back and touched his cheek, feeling the stubble against her fingertips.

His eyes were somber, though there remained the shadow of a smile on his face. "I thought I wouldn't see you again," he rumbled. "I've been making my will."

"Wh-What?" she said, the word stumbling across her tongue.

"I'm leaving everything to you. I'm trying to remember the passwords to the hidden safes."

She touched his chest, his arm. He was bloodless and cold. She looked at the Torminel. "Why's he saying that?"

Uncertainty edged the Torminel's voice. "The doctor said he'd be all right. He said the wounds weren't serious and that he got all the shrapnel out. But the boss has this idea he's dying, and so I'm recording his will on my sleeve display." He gave an indifferent flip of one hand. "I mean, why not? He'll laugh over it later."

Casimir's eyelids drooped over his solemn eyes. "Something went wrong. I can feel it."

Sula looked at the bed displays and saw that none of them were lit. "Why isn't the bed working?" she asked.

The Torminel looked at the displays as if seeing them for the first time. "The bed?" he said.

The bed wasn't connected to the power supply, apparently because there were too many beds in the room. Someone else's bed had to be disconnected before Casimir's could be jacked into a wall socket. Casimir watched without interest as the displays over his head brightened as Sula told the bed that its contents was a male Terran.

Alarms began chirping immediately. Casimir's blood pressure was dangerously low.

"I told you something was wrong," he said. He spoke without apparent interest.

"Get a doctor!" Sula shouted at the Torminel. He raced for the door.

Sula turned back to Casimir and took his hand. He squeezed her fingers. His grip was still powerful.

"You're going to need the money, after this," he said. "I'm sorry I won't be Lord Sula and help you loot the High City."

His attitude outraged her. She had known him angry, known him convulsed with laughter, known him shocked and surprised. She had known his charm, known him filled with murderous fury. She had known him as a lover, boyish and a little greedy. She had known him cunning, planning the death of Naxids. She had known the way he tried to dominate almost every situation in which he found himself.

She had never before seen this passivity. It made her furious.

"You are *not* going to die!" she commanded. "You are going to be Lord Sula."

He looked at her through half-closed lids, and his lips quirked in a rueful smile. "I hope so," he said, and then his eyes rolled back and he passed out. The bed chirped its alarm.

Casimir recovered somewhat as orderlies dashed to his bed. His eyes opened slightly and he surveyed without emotion the fuss going on around him. Then his eyes lighted on Sula, and he smiled again, his strong hand tightening on her fingers.

With her free hand Sula took from around her neck the beads One-Step had given her and put them in his hand.

"These will keep you safe," she said.

His hand closed on the beads, and behind his heavy eyelids was a glow of pleasure.

A Daimong doctor arrived, dignified in sterile robes colored an elegant mauve, and he stared at the bed display for a long moment.

"I got every bit of shrapnel," he said, as if offended by Casimir's obstinate refusal to be well. "I don't understand what's wrong."

Sula wanted to shriek at him, but instead caught a whiff of his dying flesh and felt her insides give a lurch.

Casimir passed out again. The doctor ordered the bed wheeled away for further tests. Sula tried to follow, but the doctor was strict.

"You'll only be in the way," he said. His unwinking eyes looked her up and down. "And you aren't sterile." Sula glanced down at herself, saw the spatters of blood and decided that the doctor was right.

Besides, the team and group leaders she'd ordered here were beginning to arrive.

"This place is a mess," she told them after Casimir and the doctor had left. "You need to get it under control, and you need to get your people under control too."

She assigned two of the groups to guard duty: Torminel and Lai-own, to alternate night and day. The rest she assigned to cleanup.

"From this point on," she said, "and unless you're needed for fighting, all your people are to be considered auxiliaries to the medical personnel. If an orderly asks one of your people for help, you'll provide it. If a corridor needs cleaning, your people will clean it—and they'll ask damn politely for the cleaning supplies too.

"And I want that pile of bodies at the entrance taken away. We want to keep this place sanitary, for all's sake. If the morgue won't hold the corpses, put them on a truck and take them to someplace that will."

Something in her manner—possibly the rage and the spatters of blood—convinced them to obey without comment. At any rate, she didn't have to shoot any more of her own command. It was only a few moments later that she saw some Terran fighters march past the door with their weapons slung over their backs and their hands busy with mops and buckets.

A whiff of dead flesh preceded the return of the Daimong doctor. He had an oversized datapad with a digitalized cross section of Casimir's insides.

"I understand the problem now," he said. "The young gentleman was hit by shrapnel from a rocket. The case was straightforward. All the scanners were in use, but with shrapnel we might as well use X ray, so that's what we did. I located every bit of shrapnel and removed it."

He showed Sula the display. Garish false color swam before her eyes.

"The problem is, the gentleman was wearing armor when he was wounded. A piece of the armor was driven into his body, and the armor is some kind of hard plastic that happens to be radiolucent, so the X rays didn't see it. A full-body scan revealed the fragment, however, and here it is."

Sula could make no sense of the display. She forced sound past the fist that had clamped on her throat.

"Tell me what's happening," she said.

The chiming Daimong voice took on a sonorous, practiced note of sympathy.

"The fragment of armor is in his liver. We can't put fluids into him fast enough to counteract the bleeding. I'll be operating as soon as the gentleman is prepped, but it's bound to be a mess."

She looked at him. "Get him fixed," she said.

Superiority rang in the doctor's voice. "I'll do what's possible, but please consider how hard it is to reassemble a Terran liver once it's been cut up."

The doctor floated out of the room, leaving Sula with the unsettling image in her mind. She knew it would be a while before she heard anything of Casimir, and she didn't want to wait while acid chewed on her insides, so she made an impromptu inspection of the hospital, followed in silence by One-Step and Casimir's Torminel bodyguard. Progress was being made, but the place was still in chaos, and more qualified personnel were clearly needed. She called Macnamara to tell him to have all broadcast stations put out a call for medical personnel and volunteers to report to the Glory of Hygeine Hospital.

"Immediately, my lady," Macnamara said. There was a pause while he gave orders, after which Sula asked him for a report.

"The Naxids made another try at the funicular," Macnamara said, "and it didn't go any better than last time. Other than that, I've just been trying to get an idea of where our units actually *are*. A lot of them seem to have just disappeared." There was a pause, and then he added, "It's lunchtime. Maybe they'll report when they've eaten."

Sula told him to start putting together a staff.

"But *who*?"

A lot of what he needed was communication, and the Ministry of Wisdom was full of communications specialists. Then he needed runners to make certain that units were doing what he'd told them to, and someone to keep track of supplies. Sula suggested starting with Sidney.

"I'll do what I can, my lady," Macnamara said.

She needed to be there, she thought, in her headquarters, building a staff herself, but found she couldn't tear herself away. She walked back to Casimir's ward, stopping every so often to talk to the casualties who were still lying in the corridors. Most were lightly wounded, in good spirits, and inclined to blame the Naxids for their trouble. Sula began to feel a faint stirring of optimism.

A Terran waited in Casimir's ward, clad in the sterile robes of a surgical assistant, with the muffler lowered only partly from her face. Sula saw her, saw the concern and sympathy in her eyes, and felt her hope die.

"I'm sorry," the woman said. "He died before we could finish prepping him. The doctor did his best for the next half hour but by that point there was really no chance."

"Where's the doctor?" Sula said. She wanted to hear it directly, from the motionless chiming lips.

"Still in surgery. He went on to the next patient."

Bitter laughter rang in her mind. No point in interrupting the doctor before he had the chance to kill another wounded man.

"His name was Massoud," Sula said. "Casimir Massoud. Make a note of that."

"Yes, my lady."

"I'd like to see him."

Because all pallets and stretchers were required for the wounded, Casimir lay in the morgue on cold floor tiles. He wore only the bandages from his first operation and the twisted blue pastel sheet. The small holes on the right side, where the doctor's equipment went in, had been neatly sealed by circles of pink plastic that looked like a child's toy suction cups.

One-Step's beads were wrapped around his hand.

Sula knelt by the body and looked down at the heavy-lidded eyes fallen shut for the last time. A vast storm of sheer feeling boiled through her, emotions rising strong and unbounded to the surface only to fall again before she could identify them.

I would have made you a lord, she thought. We would have gone through the High City like an angry wind, and if you had died then, it would have been because everyone was afraid of you, and of me.

I don't know if I have the strength to do it on my own.

I don't know if I'll want to.

She bent to kiss the cold lips and to breathe his scent for the last time, but Casimir didn't smell like himself anymore. It was this that brought the tears to her eyes.

Sula rose abruptly and turned to the surgeon's assistant. "I'll claim the body later," she said. "Right now I have a war to direct."

"Yes, my lady."

One way or another she would be with Casimir again. Either she would come for the body and bring it to a glorious funeral—a cliqueman's extravagance with a greenhouse's worth of flowers and a Daimong chorus and a hearse drawn by white horses—or she would lie bloodless with him here on the cold tiles.

At the moment she didn't care which.

One-Step and the Torminel bodyguard followed her out of the morgue. She turned to the Torminel.

"What's your name?"

"Turgal, my lady."

"You're working for me now, Turgal."

"Yes, my lady."

"Where's your partner?"

"Dead, my lady."

Sula hesitated. "Sorry," she said.

"My lady," the Torminel said, "I have Mr. Massoud's will."

She made the adjustment to her sleeve display. "I'm set to receive," she said.

You're going to need the money, he'd said, knowing he was dying. He wanted her to cut a figure in the High City once the war was over.

Maybe she would. Or maybe she'd convert it all to precious stones and hurl them off the High City to the people below.

Macnamara's voice came to her headset as she was walking down the steps at the front of the hospital.

"My lady." There was a strange urgency in his voice. "I know you want to be at the hospital, but I really think you should head for the Commandery."

Sula told him that she was on her way, and asked him why.

"We didn't have the expertise to handle the equipment in the Commandery once the Naxids were gone," Macnamara explained. "But some of the techs from the ministry have been over there, and it looks as if there's something going on. Something in space.

"It looks as if the Fleet is coming."

TWENTY-NINE

The Battle of Zanshaa was preceded by skirmishes on a number of fronts. On seizing Zanshaa, the Naxids had also occupied all eight of its wormhole relay stations. They then hopped armed teams through the wormholes to seize the stations on the other side, giving them a view of all systems, friendly and enemy, that surrounded Zanshaa.

Since possession of these stations would also give them a splendid view of the Righteous and Orthodox Fleet as it burned toward Zanshaa, and allow them to estimate its course, velocity, numbers, wormhole through which it would pass, and its approximate arrival time, Supreme Commander Tork decided to take the wormhole stations back before they could supply information to the enemy.

Accordingly, before the Orthodox Fleet had even left Chijimo's system, attack craft carrying highly trained and motivated assault teams launched for the five wormhole stations leading into systems still loyal to the Convocation. The teams were intended not simply to capture the relay stations on the friendly side of the wormholes, but to move through them and capture the stations on the Zanshaa side, thus providing Tork and the Orthodox Fleet with fresh intelligence concerning the numbers and location of the Naxid enemy.

The assault teams were equipped with the latest in zero-gravity weaponry designed to minimize damage to the stations—plastic bullets that would deform before punching through station walls, projectors to flood an area with fast-hardening foam to trap any enemy and render him immobile and incapable of resistance and flèchettes to penetrate gaps in body armor and inject a neurotoxin fatal to Naxids but somewhat less lethal to other species. The teams wore heavily armored vacuum suits with maneuvering rigs for maximum tactical advantage in a zero-gravity environment. They flew assault craft with specially designed airlock access doors that would override any internal airlock control, or could burn through station walls to create a new airlock if necessary.

If a station was damaged, the assault craft were equipped with repair facilities and enough bottled air to resupply the station in the event of decompression. The assault team members were cross-trained not only in zero-gravity assault, seizure, and other forms of mayhem, but in repair and in the operation of a wormhole station once it was emancipated from Naxid control.

The assault teams were the finest the Fleet could provide—dedicated, intelligent, and indoctrinated fully in obedience to the Praxis. Their officers were level-headed, capable, and flexible. They were packed into their assault craft already in their armor, injected with drugs to aid them in high-gee, high-stress situations, and sent racing for the wormhole stations at accelerations of nine gravities or more.

It was expected that the Naxids in the wormhole stations would see them coming. When in fact they did, they reported the blazing deceleration torches to their superiors. In response, the Naxid fleet at Zanshaa fired missiles that sped through the wormholes at ever-growing velocities, located the assault craft, intercepted and vaporized them.

So it was that Tork's approach to Zanshaa Wormhole 8 was observed by the Naxids after all. Perhaps Tork had expected it and thought the high-stakes gamble with the assault teams worth the risk. His approach showed his commanders that he had at least learned a few of the lessons taught by Chenforce. The Orthodox Fleet was screened by over two hundred decoys, all resembling real ships, all ready to intercept any enemy missiles flung through Zanshaa's wormhole at relativistic speeds.

Hundreds of other decoys appeared in other systems at the same time, all vectoring for the wormhole gates to Zanshaa. To Naxid observers, it would look as if five Orthodox Fleets were racing toward them on a mission of vengeance and annihilation.

The Naxids had nearly five days to work out which fleet was the real one, and though they might have, no relativistic missiles were fired.

They were saving their missiles for battle.

The first loyalist elements in the system were its own relativistic missiles, a long stream fired days earlier from the ring stations at Zarafan, Chijimo, and Antopone. They flashed through Zanshaa's neighboring systems without having to make a single correction burn, thus assuring that they would arrive at Zanshaa undetected. They weren't intended to destroy enemy ships, but to saturate Zanshaa's system with furiously blue-shifted radar and laser bursts, their echoes revealing enemy formations to the Orthodox Fleet as soon as they arrived in-system.

Tork's command burst through Wormhole 8 at the same hour that the decoy fleets from four other systems arrived through their own wormholes. The Naxids had been expecting them and their radars were turned off. No antimatter torches were visible—apparently, the enemy were moving in zero gravity, hiding somewhere in the system with their engines off. No ranging laser painted the Orthodox Fleet as it arrived, but there was no need—the Naxids knew perfectly well where they were.

But because of the relativistic sensor missiles that had been swarming into the system for the last ten hours, it wasn't just the Naxids who possessed the latest tactical information. Updates began appearing on the displays of loyalist warships within seconds of their arrival.

Martinez sat in his captain's chair in *Illustrious,* his eyes fixed on the tactical display. Cruiser Squadron 9 was still astern of Tork's flag squadron, arranged in a clump carefully calculated so the ships would be able to stay clear of one another's antimatter tails during maneuver, but still close enough so they could react instantly to orders.

It took several minutes before laser echoes resolved the location of the Naxid fleet. There were fifty-two warships surrounded by clouds of a couple hundred decoys, having just made a slingshot turn around the Stendis gas giant on a course for Zanshaa itself, a course that would gently converge with that of the Orthodox Fleet in slightly over four days. In fact, the point where the tracks of the ships would cross would be Zanshaa, and the final moments of the battle that would decide the fate of the empire might be fought above the capital itself.

The courses of the two fleets were converging on a track ideal for the kind of battle Tork had in mind. The fleets would draw closer to one another slowly, allowing each side to hammer the other with flight after flight of missiles, a battle of attrition that would favor the side with the most ships. One side would be annihilated, and the other would lose heavily even in victory.

Tork must have known where they were, Martinez thought. It was too much of a coincidence to believe that the Orthodox Fleet would jump into the system and find the enemy right where Tork needed them to be. He must have had spies in the Zanshaa system who were able to tell him exactly where the Naxids were, and he had adjusted the timing of his own attack to conform to enemy movements.

Martinez breathed his first free breath in several days. The fighting wouldn't start for another three days at least. He removed his helmet, scratched his whiskered chin, and called to Alikhan for sandwiches and coffee.

Ten hours later, as he caught a few hours' sleep in his cabin, he was called to Command by an urgent message from Kazakov. One glance at the tactical display showed him that something entirely unanticipated had happened.

The Naxid ships, instead of continuing on their course to encounter the Orthodox Fleet in three days' time, had suddenly accelerated. They were racing toward Zanshaa at five gravities, as if planning on beating Tork to the capital.

Or as if they were running away.

Martinez began pulling on his vac suit. He could anticipate what would happen next.

He was proved correct. Tork ordered the Orthodox Fleet to accelerate and match the enemy's velocity.

The problem was, Tork couldn't catch up. The Naxids had nine hours' head start before the light of their torches reached the Orthodox Fleet. And Tork couldn't accelerate as fast as the enemy, because the Lai-own, with their hollow bones, would not stand accelerations of greater than two and a half gees. Tork would either fall behind or would have to leave his Lai-own formations behind.

Martinez, locked into his suit with the scent of suit sealant and the stink of his own body, watched from his captain's chair as the enemy pulled ahead. Tork would never be able to bring about his decisive, orthodox battle. Instead he'd fall into the Naxids' wake as he swung around Zanshaa, and even then could only fight an engagement if the Naxids' reduced acceleration and permitted Tork to overhaul them.

Martinez couldn't imagine why the Naxids were racing for Zanshaa with such urgency.

The reason was revealed when a radio message, sent in the clear, arrived from Zanshaa. He heard Master Signaler Nyamugali's surprised intake of breath as she viewed the message, and then a chuckle.

"You'd better view this, Lord Captain."

Martinez himself gave a gasp of surprise as the image resolved on his display and he saw Caroline Sula in all her brilliant beauty. Blood flashed hot in his veins as he viewed the pale skin, the flashing green eyes, and the familiar curl of sardonic amusement at the corner of one lip.

"This is Lady Sula, Governor of Zanshaa," she said, "to

the commander of the loyalist fleet. What took you so long?"

Martinez was able to listen in on Sula's conversation with Tork because her communications were in the clear—she didn't *possess* a code, not even a simple one. So he learned early on that Sula, commanding something called the secret army, had seized the High City of Zanshaa and the entire Naxid government. The report was buttressed by video feed of Lady Kushdai signing articles of surrender in the Hall of the Convocation, and of some dubious-looking fighters lounging around public buildings.

That was *my* idea, Martinez thought. He had originally submitted a proposal to raise an army to hold Zanshaa until the Fleet could come to the city's rescue, but he supposed that raising an army after the city was captured by the enemy counted as the next best thing.

Tork, whose response was of necessity also in the clear, was brusque.

"This is Lord Tork, Supreme Commander of the Righteous and Orthodox Fleet of Vengeance. Lady Sula, you will execute all traitorous rebels immediately by hurling them from the High City. Otherwise, hold the city and stand by for further orders."

Martinez thought about this for a moment, then contacted Chandra Prasad in the Flag Officer Station.

"Does it strike you," he said, "that Tork was griped to discover that Sula jumped the gun and won a battle on her own before the Orthodox Fleet could fire a single weapon at the enemy?"

"She may have won the only battle anyone's going to fight for Zanshaa," Chandra responded. "If you ask me, I think the enemy's running for it."

Which was exactly what the Naxids were doing. Three and a half days later the enemy raced past Zanshaa without firing a missile at Sula or anyone else, and accelerated on a path for the Vandrith gas giant. Once there, they could slingshot on to Wormhole 3 and away to Magaria—or, conceivably, whip around Vandrith to race past a number of other gas giants and back into the system again. The rationale for this last seemed scant.

Tork made an effort to catch the Naxids before it was too late. All non–Lai-own warships were ordered into punishing accelerations, charging in to engage the Naxids even with inferior numbers, but the Naxids just pushed their own accelerations in order to stay ahead. Both sides fired missiles at long range, to no effect.

Martinez spent the accelerations on his couch with gravities lying on him like a pyramid of wrestlers, all elbows and hard muscles; and though he tried to concentrate on the dull facts represented by his tactical display, the image of Sula kept rising in his mind. Her reappearance had been so startling, so dazzling, so unforgettable, and it seemed to have burned itself into his mind like a laser stitching a picture on his retinas. Over and again he conjured the emerald eyes, the hint of mischief in the corners of the lips, the silver-gold hair. Other images floated to the surface of his thoughts: Sula in bed, a flush of excitement mantling the pale skin; Sula at the breakfast table, licking jam from her lips; Sula on the dark street by the canal, walking away from him, her heels rapping on the pavement as she left him standing helpless in the scorched ruins of his love.

A startling fact overshadowed it all. His brilliant lover had somehow made herself Queen of Zanshaa, put the Naxids to flight, and upstaged the Supreme Commander and the entire empire.

With regret, he realized that this meant she was hardly likely to beg his forgiveness.

Eventually Tork gave up the pursuit. He ordered the entire Fleet to decelerate prior to a slingshot around Vandrith that would put them in a wide orbit around Zanshaa's sun, then broadcast a general message to all flag officers and captains.

Tork's flesh was a more sickly gray even than usual.

Strips of skin hung from his brow and chin. He clearly hadn't been holding up well under acceleration.

"My lords," he declared, "the primary mission of the Righteous and Orthodox Fleet of Vengeance has been completed. We have driven the Naxid rebels from Zanshaa. Unfortunately we have been unable to bring their fleet to battle—that inevitable triumph will have to wait for another day.

"Certain officers have suggested that we pursue the Naxids until we can engage them."

Martinez raised an eyebrow—*he* hadn't been one of those officers. He preferred to delay any pursuit, and hope in the meantime that Tork would drop dead or be replaced.

"The Naxids are retreating onto their supports," Tork continued, "just as we did when we withdrew from Zanshaa. The farther the Naxids retreat into rebel-controlled space, the greater the number of reinforcements will be able to join them. I do not wish to commit this fleet to a pursuit deep into enemy territory, to an engagement where, at an unknown location, against an unknown number of enemy, our own reinforcements will be unable to locate us and in the meantime to leave the capital without defenders."

A tone of finality came into Tork's voice. He knew perfectly well that he was speaking for history as well as to his officers, and his voice rang like bells tolling down the long line of generations. Martinez could only admire the effect.

"Legitimate government will be restored to the capital," Tork went on, "and the rebel leadership punished. The Orthodox Fleet will be reinforced to even greater numbers, and then will advance on the enemy. Our victory is assured. *The truth of the Praxis will prevail!*"

Depressed rather than inspired by the Supreme Commander's words, Martinez climbed out of his vac suit and dragged himself to his cabin for a cup of coffee and a quick meal. The crew, he thought, would not be pleased—they had been ready for the final battle, had steeled themselves for victory or death, and now would discover that both triumph and annihilation had been indefinitely postponed and that they would have to stay in orbit around another damned star, going in dreary circles for months while waiting for the war to start again . . .

He knew he wouldn't enjoy it either. His son would be born on distant Laredo before *Illustrious* would leave Zanshaa, and might well have spoken his first words before he ever laid eyes on the child that had been named for him.

Plus there would be bruising decelerations for the next few days, as the Orthodox Fleet prepared to swing around Vandrith for the defense of the system.

No one was listening to his advice.

It seemed like Sula was having all the fun.

After sending her first message to the arriving loyalist Fleet, Sula shouldered PJ's rifle and left the Commandery for the Ministry of Wisdom. It would be hours before the new arrivals received her message, and hours again before a reply would arrive, and there were many things she needed to do.

And she knew she *needed* to occupy herself. The more things that occupied her, the less time she would have to think of Casimir lying bloodless on the cold tile floor of the morgue.

As she crossed the boulevard to her headquarters, she could smell the dust of the New Destiny Hotel that covered every surface and formed little drifts in the gutters. She heard the snap of fire, and over it the sound of turbines. She looked up. A coleopter was floating over the High City, moving very slowly from east to west.

So far as she knew, the Naxids didn't have any flying warcraft—since no one had fought a terrestrial battle in thousands of years, there had been no need to build any—but improvisations were possible, and at least one person on the Naxid side was thinking in the right direction.

Contemplating antiaircraft defense, she hopped up the

steps of the ministry and passed beneath an ornate bronze portal into her headquarters. As she entered her improvised command center—she'd taken a large meeting room, with onyx walls and a brilliant mirrored ceiling— Macnamara and Sidney leaped to their feet and braced. Others stared at them, then at Sula. She looked back expectantly. Eventually they shambled into something resembling a proper salute.

"As you were," she said finally. "Try to remember you're in an army."

"My lady," Macnamara said, "may I introduce the staff."

Macnamara seemed to have chosen well. The majority were communications techs, and many were very familiar with the High City. Sidney had called some people he knew, people who ran businesses and understood how to organize small groups, and set about molding all the newcomers into something resembling a proper staff.

Sula's first priority was to announce to the world at large that the loyalist fleet had arrived and would shortly be demolishing the Naxid ships on which the rebels relied for their protection. The announcement, she hoped, might serve to moderate any Naxid response.

Her next task was to assemble an order of battle and to locate the parts of her army that had disappeared. To that end, she sent people out into the city to find units and tell them to report in.

The next task was to make certain that all possible avenues into the city were covered, including all possible routes by which an enemy could climb the cliffs. The coleopter was scouting the city for a reason, and Sula was determined that it would find no unguarded area.

She placed units as well as she could, working with her maps, but knew she would have to make a personal inspection later. She looked down at her map, at the Gates of the Exalted, where the turrets of the antimatter guns were marked on the map in pencil.

"I want to get the antimatter guns out of those turrets,"

486 • Walter Jon Williams

she told Macnamara. "The rebels must have other antimatter guns, and the turrets are just targets waiting to be blown up."

"You want me to do that now?"

"Yes."

"I could put other guns in the turrets. Some of the machine guns we captured."

"Good idea. Do that."

Her comm chimed with a report from Julien. The Naxids were charging up the funicular again, and being wiped out again.

She knew they must have been reinforced substantially, because this time they came in greater numbers and with greater determination. This didn't get them any farther, however, it just left them with larger piles of corpses.

As the assault faded away in blood and failure, Sula looked up to find a young Lai-own in the brown uniform of the civil service knocking politely at the door.

"Yes?"

The Lai-own came in and braced. "Enda Far-eyn, my lady," she said. "I work in the Office of the Censor. I have a report to make."

Sula looked up at the Lai-own and wondered why the guards passed a censor to see her. "Go ahead," she said.

"At the Office of the Censor we receive a copy of every electronic transmission made on nonmilitary channels, my lady," Far-eyn said. "Including those made by the Naxids."

"Ah. Hah." Sula cursed herself for an idiot. "I can use that."

Indeed she could. Naxid officials on the High City had been calling for help ever since the battle began, and since most of them were at home or in a hotel when the action started, few if any had access to dedicated, encrypted military communications systems. They were calling on the regular state comm system, and the censor's office had not only logged all the calls, but with the press of a few touch screens was usually able to pinpoint the comm unit from which the message had been sent.

Once the Naxid officials had been located, Sula sent out units to take them prisoner and add them to the growing collection of enemies in the courtyard of the Convocation. A few escaped capture, but when confronted, none resisted.

Far-eyn also managed to locate the official who had been ordering the suicidal assaults up the funicular. He was the assistant commander general of the police, and he was holed up in the Imperial Hotel.

"Let's not cut his communications," Sula said. "I *like* the orders he's giving."

Macnamara returned to report that he'd succeeded in swapping out the remaining antimatter guns. Two were now mounted on trucks, to use as a reserve, and two were emplaced in palaces overlooking the funicular and the Gates of the Exalted.

"I've hidden them well, my lady," he reported. "The Naxids shouldn't be able to see them the way they can spot the turrets."

Which didn't mean they couldn't be destroyed, just that the Naxids would have to go to greater effort.

"Is the coleopter still scouting us?" Sula asked.

"It flew away."

"If it comes back, try to knock it down with the antimatter guns."

"My lady!" One of the staff, a young Torminel with sharp, fierce fangs, looked up from the comm display in the room's large table. "It's the Commandery! They say the Naxid fleet has begun to accelerate!"

The Naxids, Sula found, were piling on the gees, heading for Zanshaa at a bruising speed. Since they didn't need to change velocity in order to fire missiles at Zanshaa, Sula suspected they were in fact fleeing the system.

"That's what we'll tell the world, anyway," she decided.

The announcement was duly made on every video and

audio network. Sula wondered how many of the announcements were getting through to the outside world, how many relays the Naxids had succeeded in shutting down. It might be that only the city of Zanshaa was receiving the broadcasts by now.

She didn't sleep that night, instead making inspections of her units and shuffling reserves around. A good thing, she thought. Any sleep would be filled with Casimir and Caro and blood.

Lord Tork's reply to her greeting arrived two hours before dawn, and Sula considered the Supreme Commander's terse order to execute her prisoners. The hostages were her only guarantee of good Naxid behavior—not that it seemed to be working—and she'd hoped to interrogate them, a task for which up till now she had no time, and for that matter no interrogators but her own amateur army.

"Right," she said. "Pick three minor functionaries out of that pack and chuck them off the rock at first light. Make sure it gets video coverage. We'll point out on the broadcast that if the Naxids are naughty, more members of their government are going to get a chance to find out whether or not they can fly."

First light, however, provided other distractions. The Naxids had been planning another major attack up the funicular, the plans for which were overheard by Far-eyn in the Office of the Censor; and this attack was supposed to be preceded by an attack by the "air element." Sula alerted her reserves and moved the two mobile antimatter guns to cover the funicular.

The air element arrived first, cargo craft with machine guns mounted in the cargo doors. These made slow passes over the south cliff of the acropolis, the guns hammering the area around the funicular. After a number of misses, antimatter guns shot down two of the craft and the rest withdrew.

The attack itself was the usual bloody failure.

After the firing died away, Sula summoned a camera

crew and walked to the Convocation, where two Naxid convocates and a captain of the Naxid fleet, previously chosen by Macnamara, were bound and thrown over the terrace to shatter on the stones below.

"Executions will continue as long as the rebels refuse to honor the instrument of surrender signed by Lady Kushdai," Sula told the camera, and then dismissed the camera crew and took a walk along the terrace. The metal furniture was adapted to the Naxid physique, and the umbrellas were bright against the gray stone of the Great Refuge. The air was crisp and cool, and the sky had turned its usual deep green. Most of the columns of smoke that had been rising from the city the previous afternoon were gone. The city was very still.

Sula put a hand on the smooth, cool surface of the granite terrace wall and looked out over the rooftops. The streets between the buildings were deep, shadowed canyons, and as far as she could see, were absolutely empty. People were keeping their heads down, or watching their video walls for the latest bulletin, or both.

If there were Naxids keeping watch on this part of the cliff, they were hidden.

She knew they had to be down there somewhere. Naxid police were probably arriving by the thousand at the train stations, and sooner or later they were going to think of something more imaginative to do than charge up the funicular.

She considered this and decided that it probably didn't matter. Her forces and reserves were sufficient to contain any threat to her perimeter. All she had to do was hold out long enough for the Naxid fleet to flee the system, and she suspected the High City contained enough food to keep the army eating for that length of time.

She would have liked to stay on the terrace awhile, perhaps with a sweetened, syrupy tea and a cream-filled brioche, but the Convocation's food service seemed to have been disrupted. She returned to the Ministry of Wisdom and was told that she'd just had a call from the Commissioner of Kaidabal, who wanted to negotiate his surrender.

"He said that the rebels appointed him to the position against his will," Macnamara said. "He said he's a loyal subject of the empire."

"What did you tell him?" Sula asked.

"We said you'd call him back."

"Ah. Hah," she said, and felt a slow smile break out on her face.

She'd won.

THIRTY

Sula had thought fighting a war was hard. She discovered that running a planet was harder.

Worse, she had to be Lady Sula all the time. As Gredel, she'd been able to follow her own instincts, to fall into old patterns. Caroline Sula's skin was more difficult to inhabit. It was artificial rather than natural, a personality she had deliberately created, an artifice she had to carefully assemble every day.

She wore Lady's Sula's uniform. She kept the High City accent on her lips and held her spine straight and military, and she kept her head rigidly erect and looked levelly at others from beneath the brim of her uniform cap.

Lady Sula was *born* to run planets. She kept telling herself that.

She called as many old civil servants to the colors as she could, to staff the ministries and keep services running. Naxid security forces were disarmed and either sent to the barracks or to their homes, if they had any. Naxid police were permitted to patrol their own neighborhoods, though without firearms. The Naxids in the Imperial Hotel surrendered, and about a third were arrested and the rest told to find lodging off the High City and report their whereabouts to the local police.

An advisory council was formed, with people from the ministries, with Macnamara and Spence as representatives of the secret army, and with Julien and Sergius Bakshi to add a dose of grim realism.

She ordered no more arrests, except for a few of the more spectacularly brutal officers of the security services. She wasn't surprised to hear that most of them didn't survive the trip to the jails.

Nor was she surprised to hear of a spasm of revenge killings as people settled old scores. She ordered the members of the secret army to have nothing to do with it, but had her doubts about whether the orders were obeyed.

Tork kept urging her to greater bloodshed.

"All who served the enemy deserve death!" he said. "Let their heads be mounted on every street corner!"

All who served the enemy? she wondered. Every tram conductor, every sewer worker, every usher in the Convocation?

She settled for tossing a few more bureaucrats off the High City.

The city's professional interrogators had reported to work after the surrender, the same professionals who for the last months had been flaying and murdering members of the secret army. Now they were set to work on the senior members of the rebel government. Computer passwords were disgorged, and the records of the Naxid administration were laid bare.

All of them.

Sula discovered the disposition of the Naxid fleet, the five ships at Magaria, the two guarding Naxas, the eighteen under construction in one corner or another of the Naxid dominions. She sent the information to Tork, and received more harassment in return.

"You have failed to conduct the executions that I ordered!" he said. "I want lists of those who cooperated with the Naxids forwarded to my staff, and arrests made at once!"

By then, contact between her office and the Supreme Commander had been regularized. With the passwords to the powerful communications centers of the Commandery, Sula had been able to use the dedicated lasers mounted on the roof to send Tork a code through which they could communicate. It didn't make his demands any less aggravating.

"I fully intend that those responsible for the rebellion should die for their crimes," she responded. The Supreme Commander was on the other side of Shaamah at present, and the message wouldn't reach him for eleven hours or thereabouts. "But I intend in the meantime to serve the empire by extracting every bit of information from the prisoners before throwing them off the rock. I wouldn't have been able to send you the enemy order of battle unless I had pried it out of their Fleet personnel first."

She began assembling lists. Lists of Bogo Boys and other cliquemen, so she could grant the amnesties she'd promised; and a list of the secret army, with real names replacing the code names used till now. She wanted to know who had enlisted and who didn't, because after the war, many would falsely claim to have been on the High City on the day of the battle, and she would have the evidence to refute that. She also wanted to recommend awards and medals to the Fleet and to the Convocation, and for that she needed documentation.

She also demobilized certain elements of the secret army—certainly those who raced up and down the boulevards of the High City in stolen vehicles, firing guns into the air and looting palaces. They were sent home, and as much of their loot confiscated as possible. Julien acted as her enforcer. The rest of the secret army were put on the government payroll.

She slept a few hours each night, but badly.

Her more immediate problem had to do with food rationing. Most of the foodstuffs on the planet was in the hands of the ration authority. The population assumed that rationing would end along with the Naxid occupation. Sula was tempted to simply abolish the authority, but Sergius Bakshi warned her against it.

"You abolish rationing," he said, "and food will disappear from every market on Zanshaa. The ration authority was run as a private concern, and if you abolish the bureaucracy, that still leaves all the food in the hands of the Naxid clans who were put in charge. They'll keep food off the market till prices go sky-high—or they'll sell it to speculators who will do the same thing—and you'll get the blame."

He turned his dead-fish eyes to her. "It's what *I'd* do in their place," he said.

Sula considered this. "Perhaps we could limit prices," she said.

Sergius flapped his listless hands. "That won't make them sell," he said. "They'll just hang onto the food and sell illegally, to people like me."

Sula chose her words carefully. "You could make a lot of money yourself off this scenario. I have to commend your sense of public spirit."

Sergius's expression didn't so much as flicker. "I've already made money off this situation," he said. "The best way of preserving what I've made is to make certain that once we're in power, things improve for the ordinary population."

Sula suspected that Sergius had an angle, that whatever happened, he was going to make himself a vast profit, but on reflection she didn't care.

There was probably a very sophisticated macroeconomic solution to the problem, but she couldn't think of one, and neither could anyone else. She abolished rationing for ordinary citizens, and imposed price controls on basic staples like grains, legumes, and the types of meat that the Torminel preferred for their carnivore diet. The prices were slightly below the prewar market levels, and Sula took pleasure in the thought of the Ushgays, Kulukrafs, Ummirs, and the others seeing a slight loss on every sale.

There was no point in controlling vegetables and fruit because if anyone tried to hoard them, they would spoil. Luxuries she simply didn't care about.

Those clan heads in her custody were released, though ordered to remain on the High City. Then, to make certain they got the point, Sula called each and told them the new arrangement.

"As long as staples are plentiful in the markets," she said, "I will take no action against you, and I will note your civic spirit. If there are any shortages, then I'll have you killed and appoint a new clan head."

She probably *would* have to kill a number of them, she thought.

In the end she had to kill only one, Lady Jagirin, whom she ordered arrested and beheaded following the appearance of spot shortages in the southern hemisphere. Since the Naxid head contained no vital organs and only sensory apparatus, the body staggered around, arms and legs flailing, for quite some time before Jagirin finally died of shock and blood loss.

Sula made certain the video of the execution was sent to the other clans on the ration board. There was no further trouble. The new Lord Jagirin was particularly cooperative.

"We'll continue price controls until the harvest from the southern hemisphere is in," she told the council. "After that, we'll remove controls from certain items and see what happens. If the results are positive, we'll lift controls gradually from then on."

It was difficult to be certain, but she thought, as she spoke, that she caught a glint of approval in Sergius Bakshi's cold eye.

Casimir got the extravagant funeral that Sula had promised him. It took place six days after the surrender, in one of the cemeteries on the fringes of the city. In one of the gestures that seemed natural to the absolute ruler of a world, she confiscated an elaborate marble tomb that had originally belonged to a family of Daimong who had either become extinct or left Zanshaa. The original inhabitants of the tomb were removed to one of the city's ossuaries and the memorial plaque outside replaced with one that featured Casimir's name, dates, and engraved image.

He was buried wearing one of his Chesko outfits, strips of leather and velvet ornamented with beads and mirrors, and polished boots. His long pale hands were folded over his crystal-topped walking stick. The cliquemen had emptied half the flower shops in the city: the coffin was carried between tombs along a lane made of fragrant blossoms that wafted gusts of perfume to the mourners.

Sula led the procession in formal parade dress, with the cloak that fell to her ankles, the heavy shako with its silver plate, the polished jackboots, the curved knife at her waist. Winter had clamped down firmly on the city: the skies were a mass of gray, and wind kept whipping the cloak off her shoulders. Occasional drizzle moistened her face. Behind her, Julien and Sergius and other cliquemen carried the coffin; and behind them the Masquers of Sorrow performed their ritual dance.

Cameras were present—anything the lady governor did was news—but had been told to keep their distance.

A Daimong chorus chanted Ornarak's arrangement of the Fleet burial service, ending with the deep bass rumble, "Take comfort in the fact that all that is important is known." As the harmonies faded among the tombs, Sula bent to kiss the polished surface of the coffin, and looked down to see her own distorted, reflected face, its expression carefully painted on that morning lest the features beneath dissolve into turmoil and grief.

She was expected to say something, and could think of no words. Casimir had thrived in a life of crime and glamour and violence, a happy, amoral carnivore, and died, with many others, fighting to replace a vicious tyranny with another tyranny that at least possessed the grace of being inept. He and Gredel, as Lord and Lady Sula, could have burrowed into the darker corners of the High City and emerged gorged with loot, content and sleek as a pair of handsome young animals. The House of Sula would have been built on a foundation of plunder.

Casimir's lack of compunction was a part of his dangerous glamour. He took what he wanted and simply didn't care what happened later. Sula had taught him that patience, at least occasionally, paid; but it was only out of his strange sense of courtesy that he deferred to her—courtesy, and perhaps love, and perhaps curiosity to find out what she would do next. Perhaps she and Casimir had been more in love with adrenaline and their own mortality than with each other. Whatever the case, she knew that each had taken from the other what they wanted.

None of this was anything Lady Sula could say in public, or anywhere else.

She stood by the coffin and looked out over the crowd—the fighters, the cliquemen, Spence and Macnamara in viridian green, the Masquers in their strange white costumes with their tufted ears. A gust of wind brought an overwhelming waft of the flowers' scent, and she felt her stomach turn. She moistened her lips and began.

"Casimir Massoud was one of my commanders, and a friend," she said. "He died in the act of bringing the Naxid dominion to an end.

"Like everyone else in the secret army, Casimir had other choices—he didn't have to be a fighter. He was very successful at his work, and he could have kept his head down for the remainder of the war and come out of it with wealth and credit and"—for a moment her tongue stumbled—"and his life," she finished.

She looked at the coffin, at the expectant faces ranked behind it, and felt a tremor in her knees. She anchored herself on the concrete beneath her feet and spoke over the heads of the people in front of her, into the wet cold sky.

"And his life," she repeated.

"I would like to be present at every memorial for every

victim of the Naxids," she said, "but I can't. Let this service represent them all. Let the record state that Casimir was brave, that he was very smart, that he was as loyal to his friends as he was deadly to the enemy. That he chose to fight when he didn't have to, and that he never regretted his choice, not even when he was dying in the hospital."

Her voice faltered again, and she managed through an act of will to make a gesture of finality.

"May the Peace of the Praxis be with you all."

The Bogo Boys stepped forward, raised rifles, and fired volleys into the air. The Masquers went into their ancient pantomime as the pallbearers lifted the coffin and carried it into the tomb.

As the tomb was sealed and the monument placed in front of the door, Sula felt dropping upon her the horrendous weight of being Lady Sula, of living every minute with the consequence of a reckless, angry decision taken years ago, of living forever behind the mask she had painted that morning on her face, and living alone . . .

She and One-Step and Turgal traveled then through Riverside and the other neighborhoods in the Lower Town and carried out the instructions given by Casimir in his will. One safe after another was opened and emptied, and the proceeds of Casimir's businesses dumped into pillowcases. In similar fashion, Sula acquired the profits of her shipping company from their hiding places and the *ju-yao* pot from her last safe house. She then went to a bank, opened an account, and deposited it all.

A hundred and ninety-five thousand zeniths, more or less. Hardly a sum to compare with the great fortunes of the High City, but enough to keep her in luxury to the end of her days.

The money was spare comfort. Perhaps she would throw it all off the terraces of the High City after all.

She held the pot between her hands as One-Step drove her back to the Commandery, and as her fingers blindly traced the smooth, cool crackle, she thought that perhaps she, as well as the pot, had outlived her proper time.

* * *

"I have received the recommendations for awards and decorations that you have forwarded to me." The image of Tork had been recorded seven hours earlier and spent the intervening hours in transit. Sula had made a point of finishing her luncheon before viewing it, as she knew it was bound to sour her digestion.

"I believe that on further review you will wish to reconsider some of the recommendations," Tork said. "You have recommended commoners for awards that are customarily given only to Peers. A lower grade of decoration is surely more appropriate."

A buzzing disharmony entered the Supreme Commander's chiming voice.

"And as for the amnesties that you have proclaimed for various citizens, I must question them. To fight bravely for the Praxis is no more than one's duty, and hardly excuses any criminal offenses that might have been committed earlier in life. I shall keep these for a careful review. And now . . ."

Tork's voice filled with clashing discord, a sound that raised the hackles on Sula's neck. She could imagine that the sound was intimidating at close range—even at the range of seven light-hours it was unpleasant enough.

"I must strongly disapprove," Tork said, "of your appearance at the funeral of someone who seems to have led an—irregular—life. This is consistent neither with the dignity nor the gravity of an official of high rank. Nor did the—the 'soldiers' at the funeral"—Sula could hear the quotes in Tork's voice—"display appropriate military discipline. I trust that there will be no repetition of this kind of disgraceful exhibition."

The orange end-stamp appeared on the screen before Sula could hurl at it the obscenities she held pent-up in her lungs.

And then she thought, *How does he know?*

The funeral had been broadcast on Zanshaa, but how had Tork heard of it light-hours away? No one was beaming news video from Zanshaa to the fleet.

Someone, Sula thought, had been sending Tork messages. She wondered who it was.

These speculations moderated the tone of her reply, though not by much.

She replied from the private quarters of the commander of the Home Fleet, with the polished silver symbol of the Fleet on the paneled wall behind her, and seated behind the commander's massive kesselwood desk.

The *ju yao* pot stood on a corner of the desk, just in pickup range.

"I would love to have rewarded Peers for their bravery, my lord," she said, "but unfortunately most of them had already fled Zanshaa as fast as their yachts could carry them, and the ones that didn't seemed to have kept away from anyplace where bullets were likely to fly. So far as I know, there were only two Peers in the entire secret army, and I was one of them. The other, PJ Ngeni, you'll note I recommend for the Medal of Valor, First Class.

"The fact is, my lord," she went on, gazing straight into the camera pickups, "the commoners have been far braver in this war than the Peers, and they know it. If we Peers want any credit at all, we should at least recognize the courage that these people displayed. All of my recommendations stand—and in fact they will be proclaimed publicly by the time you have a chance to view this."

She offered the camera her most pleasant smile.

"Because the Peers and the political leadership fled, and because my own superiors were captured by the Naxids within days of their arrival, in order to carry on the war I was forced to make deals with individuals who hold . . . local power. One of the promises I made them was that of amnesty for any *'irregularities,'* to use your term, they may have committed prior to their joining the army. If the word of a Peer is to mean anything . . ."

Anything more, she thought, *than the word of the Peers,*

Lord Tork among them, who swore to defend Zanshaa to their dying breath and then ran like dogs.

"If the word of a Peer is to mean anything at all, I repeat, then these amnesties should stand. This list too will be made publicly available within the hour."

She took a breath and leaned slightly forward. "As for the discipline of the army," she said, "they were so busy killing Naxids that they didn't have a chance to learn to march properly." *Perhaps in your own command,* she thought, *the reverse is true.* "I'll do my best to teach them the necessary skills, however.

"End communication."

Sula sent the message before she had the opportunity to change her mind, then arranged for the Ministry of Wisdom to make public the list of decorations and amnesties. It was then that she received a message from the guard on the Commandery's main entrance saying that she was needed there urgently.

She arrived to find a group waiting at the front door in a drizzling rain. In the lead was a tall Torminel in the undress uniform of the Fleet, followed by others similarly clothed. Sula looked at the rank badges and saw that the leader was a lieutenant captain, and the rest petty officers.

The next thing she checked was to see if they were armed. No weapons were visible. She signed for the door to be opened.

"Yes?" she said. "Who the hell are you?"

The leader gave her a surprised look, the fur tufting up above her dark goggles. "I would expect a salute," she said, "from a lieutenant."

"From a military governor," Sula said, "you get nothing till you tell me who you are."

"Lieutenant Captain Lady Trani Creel, Action Group 569." She reached in her pocket and produced a Fleet ID.

Sula looked at the picture now dotted with tiny drops of rain. Everything seemed in order.

"Ah. Hah," she said. There had been Torminel missing from the Naxid roundup following the Axtattle battle, and now she knew where they were, all—she counted—thirteen of them.

It also occurred to her that she now knew who had been sending Tork reports of her activities.

Lady Trani licked her fangs delicately. "I would appreciate a report, Lieutenant," she lisped.

Sula looked at her. "To what end?" she asked.

"So that I understand what's happening in my command. I gather that I'm the senior officer present."

A burst of laughter erupted from Sula. "You can't be serious!" she said.

Again that surprised look. "Of course I'm serious. May I please come in out of the rain?"

"Why not?" Sula laughed again, and stepped back from the door. Lady Trani moved into shelter, brushing rain off her shoulders. Drops of water glittered like rhinestones on her goggles. The other Torminel crowded in behind her. The air began to smell of wet fur.

"Do you really expect to take command of my army?" Sula said.

"Of course. And the government as well, until a proper governor arrives from the Convocation." Sula could see her reflection in the Torminel's dark eyeshades. "I'm still awaiting a salute."

"You'll wait a long time if you expect a salute from the army," Sula said. "May I ask where you've spent the war?"

"Kaidabal," Lady Trani said, naming a city south of Zanshaa. "We ran there after we heard that everyone was being arrested. We stayed with a client of ours, a wealthy businessman."

"And what did you do there?"

"Hid. We had no other options, because we had to abandon all our equipment in Zanshaa." Lady Trani sighed. "There were such problems. We couldn't get ration cards, you see."

"I see." Sula looked Trani up and down and saw little evidence of starvation. Her fur was glossy and her bottom was no less plump than that of most Torminel.

"Lady Trani," Sula said, "may we speak privately?"

"Of course."

Sula took Trani's arm and led her to the room where important visitors had once been asked to wait while their escorts were found. The place still had its thick carpeting and expensive paneling, but the original furniture was gone, and had been replaced by some cheap sofas on which the guard took their breaks.

"My lady," Sula said, "please believe I have your best interests at heart. I ask that you not make yourself ridiculous."

"Ridiculous?" Again that surprised look. "Whatever do you mean, Lady Sula?"

"You can't expect my army to respect a commander who spent the war hiding in Kaidabal when they were fighting and dying here in Zanshaa. And the government—I proclaimed myself Governor on the day of the victory and no one has disputed it."

"But I'm the senior officer," Lady Trani said, her lisping voice quite mild. "One doesn't salute the person; one salutes the rank—and obeys it too. You keep referring to 'my' army, but it doesn't belong to you, it belongs to the empire, and I am the senior imperial officer present. I don't dispute that you're the military governor, just as I don't expect you to dispute the fact that I'm about to succeed you."

"They'll laugh at you," Sula said. Her own laughter had faded, to be replaced by a growing foreboding.

"As long as they laugh in private," Trani said, her voice level. "If they laugh in public, or disobey, I shall be forced to cut their throats."

Sula refrained from taking a step back, and reminded herself that Lady Trani was unarmed.

"I think," she said, "that we should refer this matter to higher authority."

The delay was mainly to allow herself time to think.

Lady Trani no longer seemed a figure of fun. She was going to be a serious problem, and worse for the fact that Fleet law, custom, and the Praxis were all behind her.

Furthermore, the only person to whom Sula could appeal was Tork. He was exactly the sort of person who would find Lady Trani's simplicities appealing; and in any case, Sula very much doubted that Tork, on the heels of receiving her last message, would feel much in sympathy with her.

"While I don't dispute that Lady Trani outranks me," Sula said in her message to Tork, "I am nevertheless concerned whether someone who spent the war in hiding, after abandoning her equipment, is going to receive the respect of the army and other institutions here in the High City. I don't want to push myself forward, but if the disparity in rank is truly a problem, you could solve the problem by promoting me. I'm already doing the work, after all."

As Sula expected, Tork's reply, received some fifteen hours later, ignored this suggestion.

"It has long concerned me that a lieutenant of such youth and of only a few months' seniority held such a critical post," he said in a message addressed to Lady Trani Creel. "It is meant as no offense to Lady Sula to say that she has suffered from her inexperience. Lady Trani, I am pleased to confirm you as Military Governor of Zanshaa. I hope you will rule with firmness, and consider it your first duty to kill the traitors who have caused our people so much suffering."

Lady Trani turned from the screen to where Sula sat, in the office of the Home Fleet commander with its huge curved glass window.

"I believe I'll take that salute now, Lady Sula," Trani said.

"Yes, my lady." With grave deliberation Sula rose from her desk and braced.

"Thank you very much," Trani said. She ambled across the office to join Sula behind her desk. She looked through the great curved window at the morning light shining over the Lower Town, the kingdom she had just conquered without firing so much as a shot.

"I'll need your access codes," she said. "I trust you will remain on hand for the duration of the transition, after which I will find you a posting suitable to your station. And of course I'll recommend you for a nice decoration for all you've done here."

Sula tried not to show the savage amusement she felt. No doubt Trani was trying to be kind.

"Thank you, my lady," she said.

She'd had nearly fifteen hours to make herself ready for this moment.

Lady Trani looked down at the desk. "I'll also need to meet with your council, or cabinet, or whatever they're called."

"I don't believe they have a name," Sula said. "But I'll call them."

"No," Lady Trani said firmly. "*I'll* call them. If you'll provide me with contact information."

"Very well."

Sula had to admire Lady Trani's composure. She knew so very clearly what she wanted, what was proper, and what was her due.

Whether anyone else could be brought to agree with her was another problem.

"I've been reviewing the communications between the governor's office and Supreme Commander Tork," Lady Trani told the meeting later. "The Supreme Commander has several areas of concern.

"First, the matter of punishments. We simply haven't been killing enough traitors. It's my understanding," she said, turning to Sula, "that we have something like a thousand prisoners?"

"They're being debriefed," Sula explained. "Once the interrogators are done with them—"

"Lord Tork said just to kill them," Trani said. "It seems to me that we could do it all at once, with machine guns."

"The penalty for treason," Sula reminded, "is to be thrown from a height."

"Blast. I forgot." A shiver of annoyance crossed Trani's furry face. "Well, can't we machine-gun them first, then chuck them?"

The governing council gazed at her from their places. They used the room in the Commandery, all subdued lighting and polished wood, that had been used by the Fleet Control Board before the evacuation. Overhead glowed a wormhole map of the empire, Zanshaa a burning red jewel with its eight wormhole gates. The council sat at a U-shaped table, with the new lady governor at its center.

"The High City lacks the necessary open spaces for a mass execution in that style," Sula said. "Besides, the custom is for the victim to be alive when he's tipped over the side."

"Blast," Trani said. "Well, see that it's done as quickly as possible."

"Yes, my lady," Sula said.

Her reluctance to kill the Naxid prisoners had nothing to do with compassion. They had killed tens of thousands, and she wished them nothing but years of torment. She just didn't want them to die until their last brain cell had been stripped of any useful content.

Lady Trani paused to light a cigarette, which she placed in a holder that clipped to one of her fangs, allowing her to talk and smoke without using her hands. Sula wondered idly if the cigarette was one that, at some point, she'd had in one of her warehouses.

Trani looked at the others. "Smoke if you please, my lor— I mean, ladies and gentlemen."

Julien reached in a pocket for a cigarette. Sergius, seated next to him, stared expressionlessly at the lady governor, his thoughts well hidden behind his dead eyes.

"Another item," Lady Trani said, "concerns the matter

of awards and decorations. I shall personally review any recommendations to make certain they are appropriate.

"And the third," she said, looking up, "concerns the matter of amnesties promised by Lady Sula for offenses committed prior to the war. I will review these on a case-by-case basis. The Supreme Commander sees no reason why doing one's duty in fighting the enemy should excuse criminal activity in the past."

Julien snickered behind his cloud of cigarette smoke. Sergius Bakshi maintained his expressionless stare. Sula gave a cough as a whiff of tobacco hit the back of her throat.

"Lady Commissioner . . ." Lady Trani spoke to the senior police officer present. "I would appreciate your assistance in locating police files."

"Yes, my lady."

Julien snickered again. The Lai-own commissioner was a friend of the Bakshis, and had a long, financially profitable relationship with them. It was likely that quite a number of files would turn up missing.

Trani received reports on antimatter and power supplies, on economic and security matters. Sula made notes on the data screen set into the table in front of her.

Certain of the notes were sent to a desk at the Ministry of Wisdom. While Lady Trani received the reports of the council, the ministry broadcast the news of Sula's supercession, along with capsule biographies of Sula and the new lady governor. It was made clear that Trani had spent the Naxid occupation in hiding.

It also mentioned that amnesties were being questioned, and that the army was going to have its medals taken away by someone who had spent the war skulking in Kaidabal.

Nothing could have served to make the new governor less popular with her citizens.

That would be a useful lesson, Sula thought. If she had the time and energy, she could teach Lady Trani quite a lot with lessons like these, and very possibly Trani would find herself seeing Sula's point of view.

But she didn't have the time, and she certainly didn't have the energy. The lesson, therefore, would have to be for the benefit of someone else.

As the meeting broke up, Sula found herself walking next to Julien. "You'll take care of this, won't you?" she said.

Julien gave her a cold little smile. "Leave it to me," he said.

"My lord," Sula sent to Tork, "your new governor lasted all of two days before she got herself killed in a riot. Exactly what happened is a little vague at this point, but it appears that during the course of a public address, she saw fit to threaten the crowd—told them that if any of them had ever cooperated with Naxids, they were going to be punished. It was the wrong sort of crowd to threaten, I'm afraid."

She looked into the camera pickup and suppressed her instinct to shrug.

"I will of course launch a thorough investigation. The official video record of the proceedings seems to have been destroyed, but maybe something will turn up."

She had returned to the office of the commander of the Home Fleet, with its magnificent view of the Lower Town. Techs were in the process of changing the passwords to all the computer files. The *ju yao* pot was back in its place on her desk.

"I have been reviewing your correspondence with Lady Trani," Sula said, "and I have come to agree with you that the task of military governor is unsuitable to someone with the permanent rank of lieutenant."

She couldn't quite hide the smile that she felt twitching at the corners of her mouth.

"I believe I should like to be promoted Captain, at least," she said. "I'm going to need all the advantages of rank in dealing with this situation. The people here have overthrown two governments that didn't suit them, and I don't want them to get into the habit."

Not unless it suits me *as well,* she thought.

After concluding her message, with the little threat at the tail like the sting of a scorpion, Sula reached for the cup of tea that waited on the desk and turned her swivel chair to view the Lower Town below. The scent of cardamom rose from the tea, and she'd sweetened it with condensed milk, just as she liked it.

Not caring helps, she thought. She could bet everything on a single throw of the dice because the results didn't matter to her.

Perhaps she'd be accused of conspiring to murder Lady Trani.

Perhaps Lady Trani was but the first governor of Zanshaa she'd have to kill.

Perhaps she'd even be promoted to Captain. She was open to that sort of surprise.

Tork showed that he'd learned Sula's lesson, and promoted her to Captain, though he couldn't bring himself to do it in person—the message came from a staff officer. Sula sent to her tailor for new uniforms.

Her mastery of the Records Office computers proved a bonus. Fictional killers were created, their names proclaimed to the public at large, and police sent after them.

She decided to keep the back door into the Records Office after her term as governor ended. It was proving too useful.

She now was surprised to discover the existence of another loyalist force that had remained behind, one that she'd never guessed at.

There were small stay-behind intelligence teams in the fragments of Zanshaa's demolished ring, floating weightless for months, listening to electronic communications and forwarding it to the Convocation and the Fleet, relaying it through stealthy, uncharted satellites placed on the far sides of the wormholes. Sula surmised that they must have been providing Lord Tork with very detailed knowledge of the Naxid Fleet throughout the enemy occupation of Zanshaa.

The teams asked Sula for relief. She wanted to oblige—particularly since the highest-ranking of them was a warrant officer and there was no danger of them trying to supplant her—but the only way she had of relieving them was to pick them up with shuttles, and since the only shuttles she had on the planet were configured for Naxid crews, she had to tell them to wait.

Perhaps, she thought, she'd overestimated Lady Trani. She hadn't been reporting behind her back to Lord Tork, it had been the intelligence teams on the ring.

Two days after Lady Trani's death, as frozen sleet pounded the High City, regular communication was opened between the empire and Zanshaa. Another wave of Tork's commandos had been launched at the relay stations, and this time there was no Naxid fleet to vaporize them.

After months of silence, massive amounts of information began to flood into Zanshaa. Messages, held in some remote electronic buffers for ages, now poured into the private files of Zanshaa's citizens: information about relatives and loved ones, births and deaths, money and markets. The capital went mad with rejoicing.

Sula received very little personal mail. A kind note from Lord Durward Li, a former client of the Sula clan whose son, Sula's captain, had died at Magaria. A formal change of address notice from Morgen, who had been the senior surviving lieutenant of the *Delhi,* and who had been promoted to Lieutenant Captain.

Two queries from Lady Terza Chen, Martinez's wife, asking where she was and how she was faring. Terza also happened to mention that she was pregnant with Martinez's child.

Hatred exploded in Sula's breast. She erased the messages and hoped that, through some kind of sympathetic magic, Terza would be erased along with them.

Among the news items was the information that the

Convocation had appointed a new governor of Zanshaa, Lord Eldey, who had been in transit from Laredo to Zanshaa for nearly two months and would arrive in something like twenty days. Sula checked the capital's copious data banks and found that the head of the Eldey clan was a sixty-one-year-old Torminel and had chaired the Power, Antimatter, and Ring Committee in the Convocation. Between that connection to extraplanetary matters and a nephew who was a captain in the Fleet, perhaps he would have a more sympathetic view of an upstart young officer than someone like Tork.

It seemed worth a try anyway. Sula sent him a complete report of the state of Zanshaa, along with a brief history of her activities and those of the secret army. She also enclosed advice on how to treat the army and the various interests that it represented.

The report, minus the advice, also went to the Convocation and to the Fleet Control Board. She wanted them to see her own words and her own achievements without being filtered through Tork.

To her immense surprise, a reply came from Eldey two days later. The camera showed him in an elaborate acceleration couch, brown leather and silver mountings, and he was dressed informally, in the simple vest that Torminel often wore to keep from overheating in their fur. His voice was very soft, with a bit of a hesitation. His fur was thinning with age. He looked like a slightly worn, much beloved stuffed toy.

"I take your point in regard to the army," he said, "and I quite agree with your solutions. I will confirm all amnesties and awards under my own authority. I think you have done an extraordinary thing, and I will recommend to the Fleet Control Board that you be decorated. I can't help but think you have a remarkable career ahead of you."

This might have been flattery mixed with a careful politician's appreciation of the possibilities for his own survival—perhaps he meant none of it at all—but at least the words were the right ones. Sula began to think the Convocation might have made a good choice.

If she'd known a few days earlier that someone like Eldey was on his way, perhaps Lady Trani wouldn't have died. Perhaps the planet could have endured Trani's presence for twenty-odd days.

On the scale of Sula's regrets, however, Trani's fate didn't rate very high.

Since it appeared she wasn't about to be killed on orders of higher authority, she began to consider her own future. She went to a pharmacy, donated a drop of blood, and had her genetic code read. Then, with the nonchalance she was developing as an absolute ruler, she marched into the Peers' Gene Bank, an ornate building of brown stone squeezed between two government offices, and asked for a tour. A flustered Lai-own clerk showed her how the genetic records of every Peer on Zanshaa were collected when that Peer applied for a marriage license, and how these were recorded in the gene banks that went back to the founding of the empire. She showed Sula how the scanned genetic material would be compared for points of coincidence to determine ancestry, if there were ever a question about a given person's genetic heritage.

"Is there a backup?" Sula asked.

"Yes. In the safe downstairs."

Sula tried to suppress her amusement. The priceless genetic record of the Peerage and its only copy were kept in the same building, and could be subjected to the same accidents, a fact that revealed a confidence that the High City, and the empire, would stand forever.

"Let me see the backup," Sula said.

The clerk took her to a room in the basement and opened the safe. Sula had pictured a small, perhaps antique safe, but in fact the safe was huge and magnificent, all gleaming, polished metal. She watched her distorted reflection ooze across the door as it swung open. She and the clerk stepped inside. The interior of the safe smelled faintly of lubricating oil.

The data store, and its operation, were identical to those of the primary computer on the ground floor.

"Show me how it works," Sula said.

The clerk obeyed.

"Very good," Sula said. "Now clear out."

The clerk stared at her with wide golden eyes. "My lady?"

"Leave. Take an early lunch, and take everyone else with you. I need to extract genetic information on some wanted Naxid fugitives, murderous officials who are escaping punishment for their crimes."

The clerk's muzzle dropped open in shock. "My lady. We can do that for you."

"No, you can't. I can't allow you to know their names. It's a military secret."

"But my lady—"

"You know," Sula said, "I could save a lot of money for the administration just by shutting this place down. It's not like any Peers have been getting married lately."

There was a scurrying for overcoats and hats, and the clerks fled into the slate-gray winter day. Sula locked the front door and sat at the control station. After a pause to savor the moment, she deleted all Caro Sula's ancestors going back some 3,500 years, replaced them all with herself, then shut down the terminal.

She did the same for the backup.

Perhaps, she thought, that would finally put Caro to rest.

Sula and Lord Eldey developed a cordial relationship in the days that followed their first exchange. He confirmed all her appointments, her amnesties, and recommended to the Fleet Control Board that they confirm the awards she had given to the army. She told him of the shortages Zanshaa was experiencing in antimatter for power generation, and he told her that the shortage had been anticipated and shipments of antihydrogen were on the way. She told him of the various conflicts that were appearing between loyalist factions that had stepped into power in various cities, and Eldey offered suggestions for handling them.

"I have to compliment you on your firmness in dealing with the Naxids in charge of the food ration," he added. "But you might have accomplished your task much easier by announcing a stiff tax on food, to go into effect in, say, six months."

Sula grinned. There really *was* a macroeconomic solution to the problem.

"What truly surprises me is the Naxids," Sula said. "They've been very quiet and cooperative, even the captives. I understand that the prisoners may be cooperating so we won't go after their relatives, but there's no way to tell if there's some Naxid out there working from my playbook, and that any day we're going to start seeing assassinations and bombings."

The answer, when it arrived a day later, startled her.

"I think that after their defeat, the Naxids will become good and loyal citizens," Eldey said. "When the revolt first happened, I couldn't understand it—why would some of the most prominent people in the empire, Peers who already held vast amounts of wealth and power, risk so much?"

He bobbed his venerable head. "I think the Naxids' revolt should be read through their species psychology—they are pack animals, and will follow a clear leader. The Shaa were the head of the pack that was the empire, and when their replacement was a committee of equals, it must have made the Naxids uneasy. The situation was too ambiguous. They couldn't be certain where they stood in relation to all the other members of the pack.

"When the war is over, and it's clear that the Naxids have been thoroughly beaten and are driven to the absolute bottom of our society, I think they will be content with that. Once they know for certain where they are in the hierarchy, they will be happier than they would be otherwise. They will excel in their particular niche."

Sula considered this through a haze of surprise, and decided that though the theory was interesting, she'd better continue to be ready for a Naxid counterattack. This thought occupied her sufficiently that Eldey's next statement caught her unprepared.

"What we should perhaps begin to concern ourselves with," he said gently, "is sending the army back to their normal lives. I will welcome your suggestions."

Well, Sula thought, that was the crux of the matter, wasn't it? Her own position on Zanshaa depended on the army, and the army was small, imperfectly trained and equipped, and already longing for their own beds. Someone like Lady Trani, a latecomer of little understanding and deserving no respect, could be dealt with. Tork, confined to running circles around the Zanshaa system and unable to unleash his formidable weaponry on his own capital, could be kept at arm's length.

Lord Eldey, intelligent and credible and with the authority of the Convocation and the empire behind him, was something else. Once he landed, Sula realized she became not simply redundant, but a potential embarrassment. What exactly could she do, in command of an army that was no longer needed? If she rebelled, who would it be against?

For a moment she entertained the thought of returning to her underground life and becoming Bandit Queen of Zanshaa, but common sense reasserted itself before she developed this fantasy very far. It was a role without a future, and it could only bring jeopardy to people she cared about.

There were many roles available to her now, but the only plausible one was that of Captain Sula, a high-ranking Peer of the empire. At least she'd wangled command rank out of Tork—it would have been difficult to be reduced in rank to Lieutenant after so absolutely ruling an entire planet.

Besides, the only thing she was absolutely good at—besides being unlucky with men—was killing things.

Time to threaten Tork again, she thought.

She sent the message in text rather than video because she didn't want Tork to see the smirk on her face:

Lord Commander, I am pleased to report to your excellency that within a few days I will welcome Lord Eldey to his new posting in Zanshaa High City. As my presence in the city afterward may prove at best a distraction and at worst a focus of discontent, I should like to request an immediate posting. As I desire nothing so much as to once more lead loyal citizens into action against the Naxids, I request command of a warship in the Righteous and Orthodox Fleet of Vengeance.

It wasn't quite *Give me a job or we'll have civil war,* but it would do.

She copied the message to Eldey and to the Fleet Control Board, and made certain this was plainly indicated on the message before she ordered it coded and sent. That way Tork couldn't order her to a remote posting on Harzapid or into the Hone Reach without the others noticing.

What remained now, alas, was to tell the army.

She told her friends first, in a dinner in the eight-hundred-year-old New Bridge restaurant. She had once been part of a drunken celebration there, rejoicing at Jeremy Foote's promotion to lieutenant, and had topped her evening by threatening to set one of Foote's friends on fire.

The current setting was a lot more sedate. She had rented one of the private dining rooms upstairs, with ancient roof-beams of a deep amber gold, a fireplace of soot-scarred red brick, and a balcony with a wrought-iron rail topped by polished bronze. Thick snowflakes, so heavy and majestic they might have been created by a firm specializing in high-quality atmospheric effects, fell in silent grandeur outside, building a rich, cold carpet on the balcony.

Logs crackled and roared in the fireplace. An antique

spring-loaded mechanism, with chains and cogs of black iron, roasted a Hone-bar phoenix on the slowly rotating spit. The odors of cooking filled the room. Patel and Julien drank hot toddies from a punch bowl placed on a heavy wooden table, and Sula had tea sweetened with cane sugar.

"I should make the rounds of the guard posts before I turn in," Julien said. "A night like this, the guards are probably all hiding indoors."

Sula smiled. Julien was turning into a martinet, and his newfound rigor saved her a good deal of disciplinary work.

"Eldey," Sula said, "suggested we should begin to think about disbanding the army."

Julien gave a contemptuous laugh. "What does Eldey have to say about it? He's one of those that ran and left us here with the Naxids."

Patel, however, was looking carefully at Sula. "You're going to do it," he said. "Aren't you, princess?"

"Yes. I've requested a posting with the Fleet." And to Julien's shocked look, she said, "Once they're back—the real government—we become a danger to them. And we can't beat them."

Julien flushed with anger, all but the thin white scars he'd received in the Naxid interrogation. "You're giving up!" he said.

"I'm getting on with fighting Naxids. That's what I'm good at." She looked at him. "We've got to quit while we're ahead. Before we make too many enemies. Ask your father—he'll agree."

Julien turned his pointed face to the fire. He raised his cup of punch to his lips, then lowered it. "I *like* being in the army," he said. "It's going to be hard going back to the old life after this."

"You don't have to go back to the old life," Sula said. "That's what the amnesties are about."

"I don't have that option." He gave her a look. "Pop's taking the amnesty route, but he wants me to step into his place."

"I'm sorry," she said, "if that's not what you want."

Julien shrugged. "It's not a bad life," he said. "I'll have money and any other damn thing that takes my fancy, and this time I'll be boss."

Patel watched the two of them with soft dark eyes. "The thing is, princess," he said, "we all got used to being loved."

Sula smiled. "That was the best part, wasn't it?"

Being loved. Finding the words *"Long live the White Ghost!"* sprayed on some apartment wall, seeing people stepping off trams reading copies of *Resistance,* watching the look on the faces of others when she appeared in public, walking through the Textile Market in her uniform or delivering stolen food to the Old Third. Being folded in Casimir's arms, his musky scent filling her senses. She had been at the center of something magnificent, and knew that she would never matter that much again.

She turned to Patel. "And you?"

His lips quirked in something like a smile. "Oh, I'm going back to the old life. How else can I afford my vices?"

She raised her teacup. "To new adventures," she said.

The others raised their glasses and drank. Julien looked gloomily into the fire.

"It won't be as much fun without Casimir," he said.

Sula followed Julien's gaze into the flames as regret wafted through her heart.

"That's true," she said.

He was Martinez, but somehow not Martinez—he had the lantern jaw and the heavy brows, but there was something different in the set of his face, and his hair was black and straight instead of brown and wavy. He and Sula stood in the front room of Sula's old apartment, the one behind the old Shelley Palace.

The not-quite-Martinez wore the silver-braided captain's uniform, and he held out a Guraware vase filled with gladioli. "You gave this to my father for his wedding," he said. "I thought I would give it to you for yours."

Sula stared in shocked silence as she realized that this wasn't Martinez, but his son by Terza Chen.

"It only makes sense that our clans be united," said the future Lord Chen. "If you've solved that little problem, that is."

Sula managed to speak. "What problem?" she asked.

The young man gave her a pitying look. "That was Gredel's voice," he said. "You're slipping."

Sula adopted her High City voice. "What problem?" she demanded.

"We only need to take a drop of blood. It's for the gene bank."

Chen put down the vase and reached out to take Sula's hands. She stared at her own hands in horror, at the blood that poured from little lakes of red in her palms. The scent of blood flowed over her like a wave. Chen looked down at the blood pooling on the floor and spattering on his polished shoes, and a look of compassion crossed his features.

"That won't do," he said. He released her hands. "There won't be any wedding until we deal with this situation."

He stepped to the ugly Sevigny sofa and picked up a pillow. Little gold tassels dangled from each corner. He approached her, the pillow held firmly in the large, familiar hands.

"It's the only way, I'm afraid," he said, in Terza's soft tones, and pressed the pillow over her face.

She fought, of course, but he was far too strong.

Sula woke with a scream bottled in her lungs and her mouth as dry as stone. She leaped out of bed, her hands lashing out blindly at any attacker. She tried to call for lights but failed to get the words past her withered tongue. Eventually she fell against the wall, groped her way to a touch pad, and hammered it with a fist till lights blazed on.

The large, silent bedroom in the Commandery glittered in the light, all mirrors, gilt, and polished white marble. No intruders menaced her. No Chens lurked behind the curtains. Her broad bed lay with its viridian spread tangled. One of her pillows had been flung partway across the room by Chen, or Martinez, or possibly someone else.

The door burst open and Spence rushed in, her straw-colored hair wild, her nightdress rucked up above her sturdy hips. She wore white underpants, had a wild look in her eye, and carried a pistol ready in her hand.

"My lady?" she said.

Sula tried to speak, failed, made a gesture of concilia-tion. Spence hesitantly lowered the pistol. Sula turned to where a beaker of water waited, poured, and rinsed out her sandpaper mouth.

"Sorry," she said. "Bad dream."

A look of compassion crossed Spence's face. "I get them too," she said. She looked at the pistol in her hand. "I wonder how smart it is to keep firearms within arm's reach. I'm always afraid I'm going to ventilate the ceiling."

Sula looked back at her bed, at the sidearm she'd placed carefully by the comm unit.

"I forgot I had a gun," she said.

Spence put her gun on one of the gilt and marble tables and twisted the hem of her nightdress to let it fall to her knees. She stepped close and put a warm hand on Sula's shoulder. "Are you all right now? Would you like me to get you something?"

"I'm fine now," Sula said. "Thanks." Her heart was still crashing in her chest.

"Would you like me to sit up with you for a bit?"

Sula wanted to laugh. She put an arm around Spence and hugged her close. Spence's hair smelled of tobacco, with just the faintest whiff of gun oil.

"Thank you," Sula said, "but I'm fine."

Spence took her pistol and left. Sula put her glass of wa-ter on the bedside table and straightened the covers. She got into the bed and told the room to dim the lights, leaving just enough illumination to be certain no nightmares lurked in the corners.

She lay back on her pillow and wondered what sort of nightmares made Spence keep a pistol within arm's reach.

She was glad she had someone on her staff who made human warmth her specialty.

Tork took three days to answer Sula's suggestion concerning a posting. Perhaps he'd spent the intervening time in conference with the Fleet Control Board and Lord Eldey, or had taken that long to work himself into the right state.

As with all good news from Tork, Sula's appointment came through a staff officer. After Lord Eldey took his post as governor, the order stated, Captain Sula was to proceed to take command of the frigate *Confidence,* where she would replace Lieutenant Captain Ohta, who had no doubt to his own vast surprise been appointed military aide to the new governor.

Sula took a long moment to savor her triumph, then began preparing her departure.

She still had prodigious stores of cocoa, tobacco, and coffee stored in crates labeled "Used Machine Parts, for Recycling." She saved a few boxes as gifts, kept some for her own use, then sold the rest in a brief auction staged between local wholesalers. Sergius Bakshi bought all the cocoa, and paid generously. Perhaps he was getting into legitimate food distribution. Perhaps he thought of it as a way of bribing her.

One of her gifts was a truck to One-Step, which she filled with commodities. With luck, he'd never have to do his business on the street again.

Even though she'd spent money to fund her army, the profit on the commodities still came to over six hundred percent. War was definitely good for her pocketbook.

She asked Macnamara and Spence if they wanted to remain with her as her personal staff or accept assignment elsewhere.

"Staying with me means a demotion," she said. "You've gotten used to running parts of an army and serving on staff; but if you stay with me, you'll be rated as captain's servants." She shrugged. "Of course, you'll have money either way," she added.

Macnamara stood straight and tall in his uniform, the light that came in the curved window of Sula's office turning his curly hair into a halo.

"Naturally I'll come with you, my lady," he said.

"Nothing for me here," Spence said. There was a mild smile on her face that made it difficult to remember that she was the woman who had blown up the Great Destiny Hotel.

Warmth kindled in Sula's heart. She wanted to embrace them but, unfortunately, this was not an option for Lady Sula and her servants. Not in her office anyway.

She promoted each to Petty Officer First Class and gave each five thousand zeniths as their share of Sula's liquidated business.

Spence's mouth dropped open. "That's . . . rather a lot," she said.

"No false modesty," Sula said. "No pretending that you don't deserve it."

Spence closed her mouth. "No, my lady," she said.

Sula grinned. "No reason," she said, "the cliquemen should be the only ones to turn a profit from this." She looked at them. "Now go hire me a cook," she said. "I gather that I'm going to need one."

Lord Eldey's shuttle landed at the Wi-hun airfield on a day of brilliant sun, flashes of gold running along the polished surface of the vehicle as it extended its great wings and sighed to a landing on the long runway. Its chemical rockets hissed as it turned and moved past the row of shuttles that had brought the Naxid administration and their support elements to Zanshaa. These were configured for Naxids and were now mere souvenirs of war until someone got around to refitting them.

The rockets flared, then died. A massed Daimong chorus sang the "Glorious Arrival" song from An-tar's *Antimony*

Sky as the main door cycled open. A grand reviewing stage, draped with bunting in red and gold, moved toward the shuttle under its own power and jockeyed up to the door. Sula stood on the stage, the silver braid glittering on her dress uniform. Spence and Macnamara stood with her.

Wearing the dark red tunic of the lords convocate, Eldey stepped out in the shuttlecraft and gazed at his domain with his huge night-adapted eyes. The recent snow had melted, except for patches of white in the darkest shadows, but the country all round the airfield was brown and dead, especially where the Naxids had torn away groves of trees to clear fields of fire for their defensive installations. The air smelled of decaying, moist vegetation and spent rocket fuel.

Sula braced. "Welcome to Zanshaa, Lord Governor."

"Thank you, Lady Sula. It's good to see a—a real world again." He inhaled deliberately, and apparently he didn't mind the smell of rocket fuel because his nose fluttered with pleasure. He turned to her. "Please stand at ease, and allow me to introduce you to my staff?"

Introductions were made. Sula presented Spence and Macnamara to the lord governor, who surprised them by shaking their hands.

"Shall we continue then?" Eldey asked. "I'm no longer young, and I believe a rather long day is planned."

"Yes, my lord," Sula said.

Everyone faced the front of the stage. Sula gave an order on her sleeve comm.

What followed was the first, last, and only grand review of Sula's army.

The action groups came marching along the landing strip in ranks under their commanders, bearing banners that identified them by the names they had proudly chosen for themselves: the Bogo Boys, the Defenders of the Praxis, the Tornados, the Academy of Design's Lord Commander Eshruq Wing, with a particularly effective banner, the Savage Seventeen, Lord Pahn-ko's Avengers . . .

Sidney and Fer Tuga, the Axtattle sniper, walked in each other's company, rifles on their shoulders. The old Daimong still limped from his wound.

They wore no uniform, but some wore Fleet or police body armor, and they all wore red and gold armbands. They all shared a common esprit, hats and caps cocked at jaunty angles, weapons carried proudly. They loped along to a Cree band, feet tramping the pavement in unison. Even Lord Tork would have had to admit that the army had learned to march very well indeed.

After the review, the army wheeled around and came back to the stage, standing motionless in ranks before the new governor. Lord Eldey, Sula, and their parties left the stage and walked onto the runway. Sula activated the list on her sleeve display and called out over the motionless heads.

"Fer Tuga!"

The sniper limped forward, and Lord Eldey presented him with the Medal of Valor, First Class. The Daimong braced, then retreated into the throng as Sula called for Sidney, who received the same decoration.

Julien and Patel wore glittering outfits that must have been designed by Chesko, and that set off their medals spectacularly. Sagas, Sergius Bakshi, and Tan-dau, dressed more conservatively, received their decorations in polite silence.

Most of the awards went for bravery—being a member of the secret army, particularly on the day of the High City battle, seemed to call for sheer courage more than anything else. Of the twelve truck drivers she'd sent charging the emplaced Naxid positions on the High City, eight had actually survived, though half the survivors had been wounded. One was still in the hospital and would receive her medal later. The other seven received their decorations from the hands of the new lord governor.

The award ceremony went on throughout the long afternoon. A cold wind ruffled Lord Eldey's fur. His staff began to fidget as they passed the decorations forward from the boxes Sula had placed on the back of the stage. The shadows of the fighters grew long as they stood on the pavement. Then lights flooded the area with a soft glow that illuminated the platform for the fighters and the cameras.

Sula now wondered how many medals had been awarded so far in this war, and if those to the secret army might in fact exceed those awarded in all other battles so far. The vast majority of decorations would have gone to Fleet officers, after all, and the number of Fleet officers who had actually participated in battle were few, and most of those hadn't survived.

Spence and Macnamara were each awarded the Medal of Valor and the Medal of Merit, both First Class. Flushed with pleasure, they followed Eldey and Sula back onto the reviewing platform, where Sula read aloud the list of those who would be decorated posthumously.

The list ended with PJ Ngeni. She let a silence fall after the name, and for a moment the image of PJ rose before her eyes, the balding head, the pleased smile, the fashionable clothes and the amiably vacant expression . . .

Eldey's words returned her to the present. "And now, Lady Sula," he said, "I have the honor to present you with the following decorations."

Sula stood in surprise as she received a Nebula Medal to match that won at Magaria, this time with Diamonds and Lightning Bolts, as well as a Medal of Valor, Grand Commander. Then Lord Eldey turned to the army, waved an arm, and said, "Three cheers for the White Ghost!"

The first cheer struck Sula almost with the force of a blow. The other two seemed to draw the air from her lungs. They left her stunned and breathless on the platform, staring in a helpless trance at the sea of shouting faces, at the forest of weapons brandished overhead by shouting, triumphant warriors.

"I believe Lady Sula would like to say a few words," El-dey said, and shuffled to the rear of the platform, leaving her alone with her army.

She had prepared a farewell address, but the cheers had blown the words clean out of her head. She took a step forward, then another. Thousands of eyes followed her. She gazed out at the ranks of the soldiers she had made and thought, *I am mad to give this away.*

She had spent all her adult life hiding—hiding her true name, her true person behind the caustic personality and immaculate uniforms of Lady Sula. But hiding from the Naxids, strangely, had freed her from all that—all that she was, all that she had been, Gredel as well as Sula, had been unleashed in the service of gathering her army and fighting the enemy. The army was an extension of her, of her mind and nerve and sinew, and to abandon it now seemed as wrong as cutting off her arm.

The fighters were still looking at her, and the words still failed to come. Sula remembered that she'd written notes for her speech and loaded them on her sleeve display, and she glanced down at her sleeve and manipulated the sleeve buttons with half-paralyzed fingers until the words flashed before her eyes.

"Friends," she began, and the army exploded in cheers again. Her mind spun like a pinwheel in the whirlwind of love and adoration.

"Friends," she began again, when control had been regained both of the army and her voice. "Together we have lived a great adventure. With no resources but our own determination and intelligence we have built this army, we have engaged the enemy, and we have brought that enemy down in humiliation and total defeat."

Another great cry went up. It was growing dark, and she had a hard time seeing the individual fighters against the dazzle of the spotlights, perceiving only the vague great mass that was her army, the organism that she had called into existence as an instrument of her will.

"None of you were required to take up arms," she said, "but you were unable to tolerate the Naxid regime, with its murders and hostage-taking and theft, and you—each of you, on your own—made up your minds to strike a blow against these crimes."

Cheers began again, but Sula shouted over them. *"You chose your own destiny! You destroyed an illegitimate regime, and you did it all on your own! By your own choice, you made the High City yours! By your own choice, you sent the Naxid fleet fleeing from the system!"*

Sula felt a wild vertigo as the cheers seemed to send her spinning like a snowflake into the sky. The dark mass of bodies and heads and weapons in front of her surged like a storm-slashed sea. The cries didn't cease until she gestured madly for order.

"I thank you from the bottom of my heart for letting me lead you," she said. "I will never forget you, or forget this moment."

She took a long breath, and spoke the words she had been dreading.

"Now I am called to further duty against the enemy, and I must leave you."

There were cries of *"No!"* from shocked fighters who hadn't yet worked this out for themselves.

"No one can take your achievements away from you," she said. "Take pride in them, and never forget your comrades, or those who gave their lives."

She raised a hand. "Fortune attend you all."

Again the cheers sounded, and they resolved into a chant, *"Su-la! Su-la! Su-la!"* Her heart raced at the sound. She stepped back and let Lord Governor Eldey step forward.

He gave a speech, and Sula heard none of it. *I am mad to give this up,* she kept thinking.

Hiding from the Naxids had given her freedom. Now that she was Lady Sula again, she was once again in hiding, but from her own side.

Afterward she joined Eldey in the vehicle that raced for the city. Overhead, multiple sonic booms announced the arrival of other shuttles that carried elements of Eldey's support staff and the thousands of personnel that the empire was bringing to the capital.

Bureaucrats to run the government, engineers to keep services going, and executioners to work their will on the vanquished. It was the way Zanshaa had always been governed.

"I wish you had not so much emphasized those people bringing down a government through choice," Eldey said. "We really can't have that sort of thing. But otherwise I think you did very well with them."

"Thank you, my lord," Sula said dully. Her mind still swam in the surge of emotion that had swept her that afternoon.

He looked at her with his large eyes. "You might have a future as a politician," he said.

"I don't have the money."

"Don't you?" Eldey said softly. "Well, there are ways."

If she hadn't been so exhausted, she might have asked what Eldey had in mind, but she just sat in the vehicle until it drew up to the Commandery, where the governor bade her good-night and continued on to his own residence.

Her sleep that night was an empty blackness filled with roaring, as if she were at the center of a huge, invisible army, all calling her name.

On Sula's last morning in Zanshaa she reported to Lord Governor Eldey, gave him the passwords for the more critical files, and then formally resigned her command of Zanshaa's military. She sent Macnamara, Spence, and her new cook, Rizal, ahead to the Wi-hun airstrip, and then had One-Step drive her to the city of the dead where Casimir lay in his stolen tomb.

A bitter wind scattered flakes of snow over the dried, brown blossoms of the flowers the cliquemen had piled on the sepulcher. The monument installed before the tomb projected a three-dimensional holographic image of Casimir, but it lacked the touch of mordant humor and the slight aura of menace that she remembered. The hologram looked more like the pale, cold face she saw on the floor of the hospital morgue.

Sula paused for a moment before the tomb, her hands in the pockets of her greatcoat, and then drew from her pocket the *ju yao* pot. She held it up to the faint light and saw Casimir's holographic image reflected irregularly in the blue-green crackle of its glaze. A sharp pain pierced her breastbone. How many deaths had the pot survived, she wondered, in the millennia since it had been carried away from Honan just ahead of a Tatar invasion? How many owners had lifted their eyes to the pot and drawn peace and strength from its timeless beauty?

Too many, she thought.

She walked around the memorial to the tomb itself, to the brushed titanium slab that sealed the doorway. Her reflection wavered uncertainly in the cold light. She raised the pot and smashed it against the slab. It crumbled to bits between her fingers. A sob broke from her throat. She stomped the fragments with her feet, and then a weakness flooded her and she leaned against the tomb for support, her head pressed to the cold metal.

You selfish bastard, she thought. *You died and left me alone.*

The cold metal was a shooting pain against her forehead. She gathered her strength and pushed herself away from the tomb, then began the walk back to the car.

Fragments of the pot crunched beneath her soles.

Everything old is dead, she thought. *Everything new begins now.*

THIRTY-ONE

Lord Eldey kindly offered Sula the use of his private yacht, the *Sivetta,* which he would not be needing for the months he served as governor. Sula understood the historical reference to the grand old Torminel monarch, and Eldey was surprised and pleased that she knew.

On the shuttle from Zanshaa to the yacht, she flew past one of the huge merchant vessels that had brought supplies and personnel to the capital. The cargo ship was a gleaming mirror-bright dome, with the engine module on the far side like the stem of a mushroom. It was far larger than any Fleet warship, with room enough aboard to carry a cargo of ten thousand citizens; and it was only one of half a dozen ships brought to the capital. Clearly, the empire was very serious about keeping hold of Zanshaa now that they'd retaken it.

Sivetta was a beautiful miniature palace, filled with elaborate mosaics of complex, interwoven geometric figures that dazzled and bewildered the eye, and managed to be more dazzling and bewildering the longer Sula looked at them. The crew was Torminel, but since Eldey had Terran aides, there were furniture and acceleration couches suitable for Terrans, and a cook who could assist her own cook, Rizal, in providing food other than raw meat served at blood temperatures. Sula had given Rizal money for food shopping before they'd left Zanshaa, and brought up as well a large collection of wine and spirits donated by the grateful merchants of the High City—an odd gift for someone who didn't drink, Sula thought, but she supposed she'd spend time entertaining, and so the wine would come in handy.

Not that she expected to spend much time enjoying the yacht's comforts. She would be enduring long periods of high gee as *Sivetta* caught up with *Confidence,* which was orbiting the Zanshaa system with the rest of the Orthodox Fleet.

Among the information sent her by Tork's staff was an order of battle for the Orthodox Fleet. Scanning it, her eye immediately lit on the flagship of Michi Chen's Cruiser Squadron 9—*Illustrious,* Captain Lord Gareth Martinez.

At the name, her heart gave a surge.

The last she'd heard of Martinez, he had become Michi Chen's tactical officer. Now he actually commanded the flagship.

She wondered how many of *Illustrious*'s people had to die or be captured by the enemy in order to accomplish that. It was how Martinez seemed to get his promotions.

Her own ship, *Confidence,* was probably the smallest vessel that Tork could have offered her, a frigate with fourteen missile launchers, and it was normally an elcap's command. Possibly, Tork had hoped she would refuse the appointment as beneath her dignity. If so, he would now be thumping the walls in chagrin.

Confidence was a part of Light Squadron 17, a formation made up of five Terran frigates and four Torminel light cruisers, all of them commanded by lieutenant captains— which meant that as a full captain, she was now senior officer of the squadron and its commander, so long as Tork made no other dispositions.

Tork, she realized, had decided not to offer a heavy cruiser, normally the province of a captain, but instead given her an entire squadron. This act of unexpected generosity struck her at first as a trap of some kind, though she couldn't imagine what it would be. Did Tork expect that she'd fail in a squadron command, when she'd been mistress of an entire world? And then it occurred to her that the assignment might simply be an oversight. Tork had a lot on his mind: maybe it had slipped his mind that he'd handed her nine ships.

But on further thought, that didn't seem likely. A master of detail like Tork would not have made such a mistake.

Maybe Lord Eldey's support, complete with the loan of his yacht, had made Tork cautious about offending any of her powerful supporters, and therefore made him generous. Or perhaps he'd simply decided to give her the benefit of the doubt. Clan Sula was one of the oldest and—at least until recently—most distinguished families of Peers. Maybe Tork assumed that her genes would bring her into line.

She gained a better idea of Tork's motivations once she contacted her new command. From *Sivetta* she sent messages to each ship, requesting a full report on their status plus the data on the latest squadron maneuvers.

The ships were in good order and, according to their officers, in an excellent state of training. Sula hadn't expected the officers to say anything else, and assumed the data from the maneuvers would give her an idea of the real situation.

The maneuvers showed ships moving in close formation, each move scripted well in advance. The side declared the victor of the maneuver had known it would win before the maneuver even started. Some of the squadron's ships were a bit late or awkward in their course changes, but there was nothing very wrong with their performance.

What was wrong was the sort of thing they had to perform in the first place.

Now she knew why Tork had given her command of a squadron. Shackled to the old tactical system, her presence as squadron commander would make little difference. The worse she could do was bungle the maneuvers of her own ship, since the rest would be locked in their standard formations.

Martinez, she thought, *can't you do* anything *right?*

You'd think he would have sold at least a few people on their new tactical system by now.

She sighed. Clearly she had to do it herself.

She took a long deep breath against the two-gravity acceleration, raised her heavy hands to the display attached to her deluxe, luxurious acceleration couch, and busied herself with *Sivetta*'s tactical computer. It was a machine as sophisticated as those used in Fleet warships, though without the proper database: she had to program in the characteristics of missiles from memory.

She contacted Lord Alan Haz, *Confidence*'s first lieutenant. "I'd like the squadron to undertake an experiment," she said. "What I intend is a free-form type of maneuver with no fixed outcome. Just do your best against the threat I've programmed into the scenario. In order to run it, you'll have to add a patch to your tactical program—I'll be sending that."

The first time Martinez had tried to run the new system in *Corona*'s computer, the tactical program had crashed. One of his officers—the one who had run off with PJ's fiancée, she recalled—had created a software patch that solved the problem.

"You'll be commanding the squadron from *Confidence*," Sula went on. "I'll expect a report when you're done, as well as the raw data. Good luck."

After sending the message, the scenario, and the software patch, she tried, in the heavy gravity, to relax onto the acceleration couch. It sent miniwaves pulsing along her back, massaging sore muscles and preventing blood from pooling.

Her reply came some hours later. Lieutenant Haz was a well-scrubbed, square-shouldered man with the look of a person who had been a popular athlete in school. He had a deep, impressive voice and a tailored uniform that looked soft and rich even on video.

"Thank you for the scenario, my lady. Lord Tork has scheduled no maneuvers for tomorrow, so we'll be able to implement it then." His look turned earnest. "I also appreciate your confidence in placing me in charge of the squadron. Thank you, my lady."

He ended the communication. Sula figured that Haz would be less thankful the next time she heard from him.

She looked at the chronometer over her head and saw that it was over an hour before the ship's acceleration decreased to one gravity.

Over an hour till the next pee break.

She would try to endure.

"It was . . . well, frankly, it was a disaster." Chagrin drew Haz's mouth into a tight line. "We were wiped out. The enemy used tactics that we didn't understand. We ran the scenario three times. The best results came when we starburst early—at least we took a few of the enemy with us that time."

Haz's distress was so evident that Sula felt something like sympathy for how she'd tricked him. She had created a computer-controlled opposition force to battle Squadron 17, and though the enemy was equal in force, she'd programmed them with the new tactics. She'd just sent her own Squadron 17 into an ambush.

"My condolences on the results of the experiment," she sent in reply. "I have another experiment I would like you to undertake as soon as your other duties permit. I will broadcast the scenario at once."

The new scenario was similar, except the enemy was approaching head-on instead of converging at an angle. The next day, Haz reported similar results, though at least Squadron 17 had succeeded at destroying half the enemy before being annihilated.

Sula had her next scenario ready, this time with Squadron 17 attempting to overtake an enemy. The enemy destroyed them.

After the third virtual catastrophe, Sula scheduled a conference with Haz and all eight of the other captains. The conversation was almost normal, as the Orthodox Fleet on its circuit about Shaamah was racing past *Sivetta* at several times its rate of speed.

Sula wore her decorations, having decided it might help to remind her underlings that she'd won battles and killed Naxids. She used a virtual reality rig to look at all her officers at once: she had their faces tiled in rows, three by three, in order of seniority, each labeled with their name and ship so she wouldn't confuse them. An anxious expression spoiled Haz's good looks. Perhaps he thought he was going to be blamed for three failures in succession.

"My lords," she began. "You've now seen what can happen when unconventional tactics are used against standard Fleet formations. My question to you is this: would you rather be on the winning side, or the other?"

There was a half-second delay in the reply.

"We desire victory, my lady, of course." This came from one of the Torminel captains.

"Do you all agree?" Sula asked.

They all murmured assent.

"The squadron can conduct experiments based on these tactics," Sula said. "But I don't want anyone to feel that I'm imposing unwanted drills, and I don't want to deal with resentment on that or any other account. If we're to conduct these new experiments, I want you all to agree that this is desirable."

There was a hesitation. Some, Sula thought, were nonplused—they were used to giving or taking orders, and hadn't encountered a situation in which they were required to express an opinion. Others seemed to be rapidly calculating the odds of their careers being sidetracked.

It was Haz, after a moment's pause, who clarified the situation.

"My lady," he said, "the Supreme Commander has forbidden us to practice unconventional tactics."

Ah. Hah. Perhaps the inadequacy of the Orthodox Fleet wasn't Martinez's fault after all.

Though, truthfully, she preferred to believe otherwise.

"Well," Sula said, as her lips drew back in a snarl, "he hasn't forbidden *me* from doing anything. I have received no orders on the subject whatsoever." She glanced over the nine heads in the virtual array before her. "I still want agreement, however. Shall we conduct these exercises or not?"

"I believe we should." The statement came from one of the Torminel, labeled in Sula's display as Captain Ayas of the light cruiser *Challenger*. "We worked with this system when *Challenger* was assigned to Chenforce, and it contributed to our victory at Protipanu."

"I agree with Captain Ayas," Haz said stoutly.

With two officers leading the way, the others fell in line, though some with hesitation. It wasn't quite the same feeling as her army chanting her name, but it would do. Sula smiled.

"Thank you, my lords," she said. "We'll begin with a security exercise. I will now censor all officers' mail, which will be sent through me for forwarding to any appropriate address. All daily situation and activity reports will be passed through me. Neither officer nor enlisted shall refer to our private exercises in any conversation or mail with any other member of the Fleet."

She saw surprise and consternation among her officers.

"It is my intention," she explained virtuously, "to avoid anything that might leave the Supreme Commander's mind anything less than easy. He has many responsibilities, and he has far more important affairs than whether or not one of his squadrons is conducting experiments."

She smiled again, and saw a few hesitant, answering smiles among the Terrans.

"Forgive me for what follows," Sula said. "I don't know you well, and I apologize in advance if you feel slighted, but I think this should be said."

She took a deep breath against the heavy gravities that pressed upon her. "Some officers may think that informing Lord Tork of our activities will be a road to his favor. Allow me to assure you that, whatever basis the Supreme Commander uses to determine promotion, performance isn't one of them."

While they chewed that over, Sula continued.

"Another consideration is that anyone unsettling the lord commander's mind is unlikely to survive. First, if the performance of this squadron is not improved, the Naxids are likely to kill that person, along with the rest of you. And second, if the Naxids don't kill you—" She took another long breath. "—*rest assured that I will.* I'll cut off your damn head and claim captain's privilege."

She took a few panting breaths while reaction rippled across the faces in her display. Shock, mostly—Peers weren't used to people talking to them this way.

"Later today I will send you a mathematical formula that is the basis behind the new tactics," she said. "I will also record a lecture concerning the formula's application."

"My lady," Ayas said, "I have a record of exercises conducted by Chenforce."

"Very good. Please forward these to me at your convenience, and to the others as well."

"Yes, my lady."

"My lords," Sula said, again looking over the faces in her display, "are there any questions?"

"Yes." One of the Terrans raised a hand, as if she were in school. "Is this the Foote Formula, or something else?"

"The *what* formula?" Sula cried.

The Terran explained, and Sula treated her officers to a display of invective so prolonged and inventive that when she finally ran out of breath, a long, stunned silence followed.

"Well," said the same hapless officer, "if it *isn't* the Foote Formula, what do we call it?"

We can call you *a useless cretin,* Sula wanted to reply, but managed to stop her tongue in time.

On reflection, she decided, the Terran captain had a point. The new tactics had no name other than "new tactics," and they needed something better. "Foote Formula" had the advantage of being brief, descriptive, memorable, but offered credit to someone who did not deserve it. A situation, she thought, that should be rectified.

"Call them Ghost Tactics," she said. "I will send the formula and its exegesis within a few hours."

That was one in the eye for Martinez, she thought, and ended the transmission with a modest glow of triumph.

Sula handed *Sivetta*'s crew generous tips for their service, then stepped through the airlock and aboard *Confidence,* followed by her servants. A recording of "Defenders of the Empire" blared out, deafening in the small space. Her lieutenants saluted; an honor guard presented arms. Sula shook Haz's hand, then was introduced—with a shout, over the crashing music—to the other two lieutenants, Lady Rebecca Giove and Lord Pavel Ikuhara.

There was no room available on the small ship for the entire crew to be assembled, so half the crouchbacks crowded into the mess and the others stood braced in the corridors and crew quarters spaces while Sula formally read her commission over the frigate's public address system.

" 'Lord Tork, Supreme Commander, Righteous and Orthodox Fleet of Vengeance,' " she said, reading the signature, and then added, with a grin, "Signed in his absence by Lieutenant Lord Eldir Mogna."

No sense in not being thorough, she thought.

She looked at the stolid faces before her, the mixture of raw recruits and gray-haired veterans called to service in the emergency. She decided they might as well get a look at her, so she stepped onto one of the mess tables. The low ceiling brushed her hair as she looked down and told them to stand at ease.

"Some of you," she said, "may wonder how someone my age is qualified to run a squadron. I'm taking this command for a very simple reason . . ." She gestured broadly with one arm. *"I know how to kill Naxids!"*

Bright surprise glittered in the eyes of the crew. She grinned at them.

"I plan to teach you everything I know about killing the enemy," she continued. "You'll be pulling a lot of extra duty, and I don't plan to be easy on any of you, but if you work with me, you'll survive the war, and we'll get along."

She paused, searching her mind for anything more profound to say, and decided there was little point in being profound. She nodded. "That's all."

She jumped off the table in the slight, surprised silence that followed, and then the officers were calling the crew to attention. Haz introduced her to the warrant and senior petty officers before Sula conducted her first inspection.

Confidence had been damaged severely in the rebellion at Harzapid, and it showed. The officers' mess and the lieutenants' quarters were dark-paneled luxury, with softly gleaming brass and the faint scent of lemon polish. The parts of the ship that had been damaged or replaced were paneled in alloy or resinous sheeting and painted gray or pale green. Wires and conduits were in plain sight rather than hidden behind discreet access doors. Supplies and equipment were stored anywhere, lashed down in gravity-resistant containers.

Sula found nothing very wrong in her inspection. She had studied plans of the ship ahead of time, and was able to impress the division heads by knowing where odd lockers or control consoles had been tucked away. She asked no questions she didn't know the answers to in advance, and trusted this would impress everyone with her intelligence.

She ended the inspection in her own quarters, a coffin-sized sleeping cabin and a small office with walls, ceiling, and floors entirely of metal sheeting painted a uniform, dismal gray.

She wasted no time mourning the beautiful paneling and splendid fixtures that had been destroyed or irradiated at Harzapid, and immediately sat down at her desk and inserted her captain's key. Haz gave her the codes that provided full access to all the ship's systems, from its planet-shattering weapons to the waste recyclers.

"Very good," she said. "Thank you."

On the wall behind her, Macnamara hung PJ Ngeni's rifle, along with the very first model of the Sidney Mark One. Then he and Spence began the considerable task of stowing her personal possessions, the uniforms and vac suit, the food and liquor.

Sula paid no attention. She was already working on a plan for the next day's maneuver.

Martinez watched Sula's ascension with considerable interest and a modest amount of envy. First she commanded the High City of Zanshaa, then the entire planet. Then there was another governor for two days, and then Sula was back, this time with a promotion. Martinez had to wonder how she'd done it.

Then, lastly, Sula was given a squadron, which to Martinez's mind was better than a planet any day. When he heard the news, he recalled with nostalgia the days he'd spent commanding Light Squadron 14, and the glory of his position of honor and prominence on Michi Chen's flagship seemed to dim.

He dreamed of her almost every night, lurid blood-burning fantasies from which he woke with a mixture of relief and regret. He called images of Terza onto the display above his bed and watched her walk gracefully through her pregnancy while his nerves cried out for another woman.

Time passed. The Orthodox Fleet continued its circuit of Zanshaa's system, waiting for reinforcements and news of the Naxids. There was suspense concerning whether the enemy would adopt the same strategy the loyalists had used after the fall of the capital, to break up into small groups and raid into loyalist territory. But there was no news of raids, and it became apparent that the Naxids were hunkered down at Magaria, presumably crying for reinforcements of their own.

For once Martinez was happy for a delay in the fighting. When he advanced on the enemy, Tork would have to detach part of the Orthodox Fleet to guard Zanshaa, which meant he'd need enough new ships both to make up for the detachments and to match any reinforcements the Naxids had procured.

Disciplinary hearings on *Illustrious* demonstrated how bored the crew had become. The officers sometimes visited from ship to ship; but the enlisted were stuck with one another, and complaints of fighting, theft, and vandalism occupied an increasing amount of Martinez's time.

He knew it wasn't as if he hadn't asked for it. He'd assured the crew that they could speak to him at any time, and though most had the good sense to leave him alone, some took full advantage. He not only found himself dealing with disciplinary issues, but advising crew on their investments and on matrimonial issues. He disclaimed any authority on these last, but in the end advised investment in Laredo Shipyards as well as wedlock. Weddings on the ship at least provided an excuse for a party and raised the crew's spirits—unlike the two cases of genuine madness, crew who were actually raving and had to be subdued and tranquilized by Dr. Xi. One recovered, but the other showed every evidence of remaining a frenzied lunatic to the end of his days. He was shipped home on a courier vessel.

The days of Terza's pregnancy slowly drew to their close. When he wrote her letters—or more properly, electronic facsimiles of letters—he found himself filled with a rising tenderness that surprised him. He hadn't thought of himself as a sentimental person, as the sort of man who would flush with remembered affection for a woman he'd known for only a few days and who carried a child he might never see. He kept viewing Terza's videos and had the latest playing silently in his desk display when he wasn't using it for business.

In his dreams, however, he still burned for Sula. Perhaps the boredom and isolation were getting to him, as well as to the crew.

The time passed when he had expected to hear of the birth of his son, and he grew fretful. He snapped at Jukes during a meeting over some of the artist's ideas for decorating *Illustrious,* and gave Toutou an angry lecture about some supplies misfiled in the commissary.

The first bulletin came from his father, a video of Lord Martinez flushed with pride and bouncing in his chair with enthusiasm. "A large, lovely boy!" he boomed. "And named after the both of us—Gareth Marcus! Terza had no trouble at all—it was as if she's been practicing in secret." A large fist smacked into a meaty palm. "The Chen heir, born on Laredo, and with our names—I expect they'll have to make him king, don't you?"

Martinez was perfectly willing for his son to be proclaimed Gareth Marcus the First. He called for a bottle of champagne and shared it with Alikhan.

For once he didn't dream of Sula. As he woke with a blurry head the next morning, he found a video from Terza waiting for him. She was propped up in bed wearing a lavender-colored nightdress buttoned to the neck. Someone had combed her hair and applied cosmetic. She held the future Lord Chen in her arms, and tilted the round face toward the camera lens. Young Gareth's eyes were squeezed shut with stubborn determination, as if he had resolved that the outside world should not exist and he refused to contemplate any evidence to the contrary.

"Well, here he is," Terza said. Her smile was weary but not without pride. "He's given no trouble at all. The doctor said it was the easiest delivery he'd ever seen. We both send our love, and we hope to see you soon."

Martinez's heart melted. He watched the video half a dozen times more, then proclaimed a holiday on the ship, the crew excused from normal duties except for watchkeeping. He ordered Toutou to open the spirit locker and share out a drink to the crew. Again he split a bottle of champagne, this time with Michi.

My *son's going to be the head of* your *clan,* he thought.

A few days later he was invited to a reception on Fleet Commander Kringan's flagship. The invitation specified undress, so he left the Golden Orb and the white gloves in his cabin. Michi used *Daffodil* to ferry all her other captains to Kringan's flagship, so they arrived a little late. The air aboard *Judge Kasapa* tasted of Torminel rather than Terrans. *Kasapa* was a sixty-year-old ship, old enough to have gained the dignity that comes with age—the allegorical bronzes in their niches were polished smooth and bright by the hands of generations, and the geometrical tiles had lost a bit of their original brilliance and faded to a more mellow shade.

The officers were grouped in the fleetcom's dining room, from which the long table had been removed to make room. Smaller buffet tables had been set on either end—lest Torminel eating habits spoil anyone's appetite, the marrow bones and bloody raw meat were across the room from the food intended for other species. Tork, busy planning his next conquest, wasn't around to spoil the party. Kringan, wearing braid-spangled viridian shorts and a vest over his gray fur, chatted amiably in his adjoining office with a group of senior officers. Martinez got a whisky from one of the orderlies and held a plate with some kind of fritter in the other hand. He was pleased to encounter a Torminel captain he had once commanded in Light Squadron 14, who had been given command of one of the new cruisers, and Martinez chatted for a moment about the new ship and its capabilities.

And then the grouping of officers shifted and a sudden awareness of Sula crawled across his skin on scuttling insect legs. She stood about five paces away, talking to a Terran elcap Martinez didn't know. She stood straight and slim in her dark green uniform, and there was a slight smile on her face. Whatever words Martinez was about to offer his former captain died on his lips.

"Yes, my lord?" the Torminel said.

From a stiffening of Sula's spine and the way the smile caught on her face, Martinez knew that she was aware of his presence. He tried to continue his conversation, but his mind was awhirl and his heart lurched in his chest.

This was impossible. He should at least try to be civil.

"Excuse me, my lord," he said, and stepped toward her, awkward with the fritter sitting like an offering on his plate.

Sula likewise disposed of her companion and turned to face him. She was so lovely that her beauty struck him like a blow. Her hair was a shade more golden than he remembered, and shorter. Her scent was something muskier than the Sandama Twilight he remembered. Her green eyes examined him with something that might be calculation, or malevolence, or contempt.

"Congratulations on your promotion," he said.

"Thank you." She cocked her head to one side and studied him. "You deserve congratulations as well, my lord," she said. "I hear your wife has spawned."

A blast of furnace anger flashed through his veins, but even in his fury he felt an icy sliver of rationality amid the flame, and he clung to it.

He could hurt her now. And she had just given him the justification.

"Yes," he said. "Terza and I are very happy. And you?"

Her mouth pressed into a firm line. Her eyes were stone. "I haven't had the leisure," she said.

"I'm sorry," Martinez said. "You seem to have made a wrong choice or two, somewhere in the recent past."

He saw a shift in her eyes as the blow struck home.

"True," she said. "I made a bad decision when I first met you, for instance."

She turned and marched away, heels clicking on the tiles, walking away from him as she had at least twice before; and Martinez felt the tension suddenly drain from him. His knees wavered.

Honors about even, he thought. But she was the one who fled.

Again.

Feeling a need for support, he went to the buffet in order to have something to lean against. There he found Michi gazing at the food without much interest. He offered her his fritter.

"May I order you something to drink, my lady?" he asked.

"I'm trying not to drink," she said. "Torminel toilets don't agree with me, and it's a long walk back to the airlock and *Daffodil.*"

Martinez could see Sula out of the slant of his eye. She was turned away from him, her back arrow-straight as she spoke to a Lai-own captain.

He bolted his whisky. Michi raised an eyebrow.

"I'll take my chances with the toilets," he said.

"**F**ucking imbecile," Sula told Lord Sori Orghoder. "Next time try following my instructions."

Lord Sori had grown accustomed to this sort of abuse by now, like the rest of Sula's captains, and his furry Torminel face was resigned.

"Apologies, my lady. I thought I was—"

"You're supposed to be following the hull of a chaotic dynamical system, not driving a runaway tram through a parking lot!"

Lord Sori's face gave a tremor, then subsided. "Yes, my lady."

Peers, Sula knew, weren't used to be talked to this way. Her savagery had at first stunned them—and then, perhaps because they had no idea of anything better to do, they had obeyed. Sula's talent for invective had produced results. Light Squadron 17, under the lash of her tongue, was becoming proficient in Ghost Tactics.

She would never have dared speak to her army this way. Volunteers could all too easily have walked away. The

546 • Walter Jon Williams

Peers who commanded her ships were stuck with her, and perhaps they were too wedded to their notions of hierarchy ever to protest a tongue-lashing from a superior.

Sula worked them hard. She called them idiots and dunces. She criticized their ancestors, their education, and their upbringing. She even censored their correspondence—which was, she learned, remarkably dull.

Without her, she decided, they were nothing. A bunch of coddled aristocrats without an idea in their collective head. But she was going to be the making of them.

"We are going to storm the Naxid citadel," she told them. "And I know we can do it, because I've done it before."

One of the advantages of not caring about anything, she had decided, was that she could decide to care about any particular thing. She had decided she was going to care about Light Squadron 17. Her command would become immortal in the eyes of the Fleet.

She was particularly vicious at the moment because of her meeting with Martinez the previous evening. She felt the encounter had shown her at her worst. Not because she'd tried to cut him down, which he thoroughly deserved, but because she'd done it out of anger and surprise. She should have slashed Martinez to ribbons coolly and dispassionately, but instead had blurted out a few feeble insults and then run for it.

She had shown that she was vulnerable. She had demonstrated that she, who cared about nothing, still cared about him.

It was her officers who paid for this discovery with their dignity.

"Have some brain food with your dinner," she told Lord Sori, "and we'll try another experiment, starting at eighteen and one."

She broke the connection with Sori—and with the other captains who had been watching with properly impassive faces—and then unwebbed herself from her acceleration couch.

"Secure from general quarters," she said. "Send the crew to their dinner."

"Yes, my lady," said Lieutenant Giove.

While Giove made the announcement to the ship's crew, Sula swung forward to put on her shoes, which she'd kicked off and dropped on the deck. The advantage of the Ghost Tactics experiments—radical tactics performed in a shared virtual environment while her actual ships soared innocently in the close formations Tork demanded—was that she didn't need to suit up. She disliked vac suits, the suits' sanitary arrangements, the helmet visors that locked her into a closed, encapsulated, smothering world. In an experiment, she could wear ordinary Fleet coveralls, kick off her shoes, and feel free to try out any outrageous strategem she pleased.

On the simplest level, each ship could simply follow the formula as she had created it, maneuvering within a series of nested fractal patterns that maximized both its defensive and offensive capabilities, and—significantly—moving in a pattern that would seem completely random to any observer.

There were more complex levels to the system, as there would be with anything involving fractals, and these had to do with the designated "center of maneuver," around which the squadron would be navigating, which could be the flagship, a point in space, or an enemy. Choosing the center of maneuver, Sula suspected, was far more an art than a science.

With all the practice, she thought she was getting very good at her art, and she was beginning to hunger for the day when she could test it against the enemy.

Martinez realized that Sula must have been charming others as she'd charmed him, because Tork announced a change in the fleet's order of battle. Light Squadron 17 was shifted into the van as the lead squadron. In the sort of battle that Tork clearly intended to fight, the van squadron would be the first to engage the enemy, and remain in action until the battle was over or until the squadron had been reduced to radiant debris.

Martinez wondered how exactly Sula made Tork so determined to sacrifice her to the necessities of war. Tork was giving the Naxids every possible chance to kill her along with most of her command.

"For once Tork's had a good idea," Martinez said aloud as he sat at his desk and reviewed the order, and then was annoyed at himself because he felt the comment lacked conviction.

He looked down at his desk, at the image of Terza holding Young Gareth, which floated at the margins of the display.

At least, he thought, he'd stopped dreaming about Sula. He could give his family that.

Bulletins came almost daily from Terza, charting Young Gareth's progress, and when Terza was busy and no message arrived, Martinez found himself missing the daily contact. He sent letters in return, and a few videos so Young Gareth could hear his voice and practice focusing his eyes on his father.

Another message, less welcome, arrived from his brother Roland. The video opened with a shot of Roland seated importantly in a hooded armchair upholstered in some kind of scaly leather that might have been Naxid skin. He had the Martinez looks, the big jaw, broad shoulders, big hands, and olive skin. He was also wearing the dark red tunic of the lords convocate.

"I have good news," Roland began.

It seemed to Martinez that Roland was trying too hard not to be smug.

"Whatever vices Lord Oda might have enjoyed in the past," Roland continued, "they seem not to have affected his fertility. Vipsania's pregnant."

Martinez's mental wheels spun a bit before they found traction, and it finally dawned that Roland's good news— the *first* bit of good news, presumably—concerned their sister, who had been married to the heir of the high-caste Yoshitoshi clan. There had been a cordial sort of blackmail involved, Martinez recalled, Roland having bought the debts that Lord Oda hoped to conceal from his family.

Not unlike the arm-twisting that had gone into his own marriage. Roland's social wrestling had paid off twice now, with Martinez babies placed, like cuckoos, in the cradles of two of the High City's most prominent clans.

And as the clan heirs, no less.

"I don't know whether you've heard," Roland said, "but it seems that PJ Ngeni died heroically in the battle for Zanshaa High City. Walpurga is now an eligible widow, and after a decent interval will find a more suitable spouse. Let me know if you encounter any candidates, will you?"

Martinez wished there were some way to engage his formidable sister to Lord Tork. That would kill the Supreme Commander faster than anything else.

"In return for his magnificent hospitality," Roland continued, "the Convocation has voted to open Chee and Parkhurst to settlement, and under Martinez patronage. So our centuries-long ambition has finally been fulfilled."

Chee and Parkhurst would be the first planets opened in hundreds of years, and both under Martinez patronage. No one could freeze the Martinez family out of the High City now.

"And of course," Roland continued, finally getting to the point, "the Convocation voted to co-opt our father into their midst. He declined, with the wish that they'd consider me instead." He spread his arms, offering a view of his wine-colored tunic. "The Convocation graciously agreed to abide by his wishes. I have volunteered for a committee that will return to Zanshaa ahead of the rest of the Convocation, to make recommendations concerning the organization of the capital. So, soon we may actually be able to communicate without these annoying delays."

Roland returned his hands to the arms of his chair.

"I trust you will continue to massacre Naxids at your

normal rate, and by the time I see you in person you'll have gained more medals and your usual dose of undying fame. I'll send you a message when I arrive in the Zanshaa system."

The orange end-stamp filled the screen. Martinez blanked it in annoyance.

Roland was up to something, and an early visit to Zanshaa was part of it. Martinez didn't know what his brother's plot entailed, but he had little to do but speculate. Roland might be plotting another marriage, his own perhaps; or scouting the High City for the location of a new Martinez Palace grand enough for the city's newest lord convocate; or working to corner some essential supply coming down from orbit.

He only hoped that he himself was not an essential element in Roland's scheme.

As it turned out, Roland wasn't the only member of his family leaving Laredo. The next video from Terza informed him that she and Young Gareth were leaving to join her father—the location was a military secret, but it was presumably closer to Zanshaa than was Laredo.

"It's time my father saw his grandson," Terza said. Her expression bore its usual serenity, and at once Martinez felt anxiety begin to gnaw at him. He wondered if Lord Chen had expressed some private disappointment in Young Gareth, and if therefore Terza was rushing the child to her father to reassure him . . . or, he thought darkly, to confirm his suspicions.

He considered forbidding the journey—he could claim that Lord Chen was too close to a possible Naxid attack— but decided against it.

He was too far away to issue his wife orders, but that was only a part of it. The fact was, the only daughter of Lord Chen outranked the second son of Lord Martinez. Young Gareth was Lord Gareth Chen, not Lord Gareth Martinez the Younger. He was the son of the Chen heir and the presumed Chen heir himself.

In other words, Terza could take the child anywhere she damn well pleased, and he had very little to say about it.

Martinez sent Terza a letter in which he wondered whether it was completely safe for her to make the journey, but otherwise made no protest. He bade her to give Lord Chen his very warmest regards.

He dared say nothing else.

From her position in the middle of the van squadron, Sula half drowsed through one of Tork's maneuvers. After the intricacies and complexities of Ghost Tactics, Tork's standard exercises were a dreary trudge toward slumberland.

"Enemy missile flares," said Warrant Officer Maitland from the sensor station. "Flares across the board. Forty—sixty—nearly seventy, my lady."

The languor in Maitland's drawling voice as he announced the launch of a host of enemy missiles aimed at the squadron showed that he too was merely going through the motions.

"Comm," Sula said. "Each ship will fire one battery counterfire. Weapons"—to Giove at the weapons station—"this is a drill. Engage the enemy barrage with Battery Two."

"This is a drill, my lady," Giove reported. "Tubes eight through thirteen have fired. We have a failure to launch from tube thirteen. Missile is running hot in the tube."

Lady Rebecca Giove—short, dark, and kinetic—was incapable of sounding bored by anything. Her sharp voice had a clear ring of urgency even when she was making the most routine report.

"Weaponers to clear the faulty missile," Sula said.

"Weaponers to clear the faulty missile, my lady."

Sula could only imagine what the scene would be like in real life—seventy enemy missiles racing for the squadron, each with its antihydrogen warhead ready to rip apart the fabric of matter, the countermissiles lashing out, the faulty missile flooding the missile bay with heat and energetic

neutrons, on the verge of destroying the ship, tension taut-
ening the nerves, the scent of rising panic in her vac
suit . . .

Nothing like that here. *Confidence* was following a
script that had been written ahead of time by Tork's staff.
The faulty missile had been planned from the beginning,
to give the weaponers practice at clearing a missile from
the tube.

Sula sat in her vac suit and recited the lines that the
script more or less demanded. She left her helmet off so
she didn't have to feel closed-in. Counterbattery fire destroyed most of the enemy missiles, and point-defense
lasers got the rest. Weaponers operating damage-control
robots cleared the defective missile from the tube. Light
Squadron 17 launched its own attack, which was duly par-
ried by the approaching—and virtual—enemy.

Confidence was annihilated early in the action, which
gave a senior surviving captain practice at commanding
the squadron until she too was destroyed. In the end Light
Squadron 17 was wiped out, along with the squadron it had
engaged.

After losing her ship, Sula had one of the cooks bring
coffee and soft drinks to Command, and she added clover
honey and condensed milk and drank in perfect content-
ment while listening to calls between ships.

Confidence had been wiped out in three of the last four
of Tork's exercises. Sula was inclined to view this as a
threat.

It had been clear from the moment Tork had ordered
Squadron 17 into the van that he was planning to eliminate
her from his long list of troubles. Sula supposed she
couldn't blame him. After all, she had spoiled his attack on
Zanshaa by capturing the place without him; she had
arranged for the elimination of his choice of governor; and
she'd blackmailed him into giving her a ship. Probably he
wished he could simply have her shot. But she was too

prominent for that, too celebrated. Instead he affected to take her at her word—*I desire nothing so much as to once more lead loyal citizens into action against the Naxids*—and put her in a place of maximum danger.

She had to admit that she admired Tork's straightforward ruthlessness.

Still, it wasn't as if she hadn't anticipated something like this. She knew she was putting herself in Tork's hands as soon as she requested duty in the Orthodox Fleet.

There only remained the question of what she was going to do about it.

From her point of view, there was only one possible response.

She would have to become a legend.

The Righteous and Orthodox Fleet of Vengeance continued its awkward orbit around Zanshaa. Reinforcements arrived, two or three or five at a time. Martinez continued to hear from old acquaintances. The arrival of the Exploration Service frigate *Scout* brought greetings from Shushanik Severin, who served as its third officer. Severin and his little lifeboat had spent months grappled to a frozen asteroid at Protipanu in order to provide last minute intelligence to Martinez and Chenforce just prior to the battle there, and as a result had been promoted lieutenant despite being born a commoner. Severin seemed cheerful and comfortable in his new status, and Martinez—who remembered the troubles the commoner Kosinic had experienced—was relieved.

He was also impressed that the down-at-heels Exploration Service had actually gotten a brand-new frigate out of the emergency. It was the first actual warship in the service for many centuries, though it would serve under Fleet command for the rest of the war.

Martinez also received greetings from Warrant Officer Amanda Taen, who arrived in command of a boat bringing supplies to the warships. She was a stunningly beautiful young woman who had shared a pleasantly carnal relationship with him before his marriage, and viewing her message sent a nostalgic charge through his groin.

Her arrival made him wonder just how many of his former lovers were serving with the Orthodox Fleet. He counted four women he had known intimately now circling Shaamah without him, and he felt depressed for the rest of the day.

Terza and Young Gareth joined Lord Chen at whatever secret location was playing host to the Fleet Control Board, driving home the fact that the location was secret to Martinez, but not to his wife. The stream of letters and videos from Terza arrived regularly. Martinez tried to find enough subjects for reply, but new topics of interest were rare on the ship. He began to send Terza word-portraits of his fellow crew, starting with Kazakov and working his way down the list in order of seniority. He wondered what she made of these descriptions of people she'd never met, but reckoned she had to at least give him credit for trying. When he ran out of people he wanted to describe, he began a description of Fletcher's paintings, beginning with *The Holy Family with a Cat*. He had a feeling that his description didn't do the work justice. He considered sending a picture instead.

Martinez saw Sula twice more, as officers visited back and forth. They kept their distance and did not speak.

Roland arrived on Zanshaa and sent him occasional messages. He was with a committee of other convocates, though what they were actually doing in the capital was obscure. Martinez was content that it remain that way.

The Orthodox Fleet grew. Seventy ships. Eight-one. Ninety-five. The last known number of enemy ships had been forty-seven. Martinez began to wonder if Tork would ever engage.

It was when the Orthodox Fleet reached the prime number of 109 that orders began raining down from Tork's staff. Censorship was tightened. Enlisted crew could send no personal messages home, but only choose from a list of messages provided by the Fleet. All of them were variations on the theme, "I am well, and send you greetings. Long live the Praxis!"

The twenty-two Lai-own ships were placed under Senior Squadron Commander Do-faq and detached to guard Zanshaa against a surprise Naxid attack. The fragile bones of their avian crew would not impede the acceleration of the Orthodox Fleet in pursuit of any enemy.

The rest of the Fleet, on its last swing around the system, participated in several final exercises to accustom them to maneuvering in their new order-of-battle, and then burned one last time around Vandrith for Zanshaa Wormhole 3, where the enemy had fled four months before.

Martinez sent one last message to Terza. If he skated the limits of the censorship, it was because he knew that Michi would be the officer censoring his mail, and that Terza would know more about Fleet activities from her father than she could ever learn from her husband.

Don't worry about me, he wrote. *We've beaten them before, and we'll do it again.*

I hope to see you and Gareth within a few months. You have no idea how much I regret this time we have spent apart.

When he signed the word *Love,* it was with perfect sincerity.

THIRTY-TWO

When Fleet Commander Jarlath advanced toward Magaria at the beginning of the rebellion, he had come in fast, racing like an arrow aimed at the heart of the enemy.

When Tork moved, he came in slowly, like the tide, and with the same inexorable force.

Magaria had a well-equipped ring and seven wormhole gates to other systems. From Magaria the enemy could threaten a third of the systems in the empire. The Naxids had to defend it or risk losing everything.

There were four wormhole jumps and three systems between Zanshaa and Magaria. The loyalist forces had managed to seize the wormhole station on the far side of Zanshaa Wormhole 3, but not the others—Tork had sent another wave of special forces, but the Naxids again wiped them out with missiles fired from another system. The loyalist forces could see into the first of those three systems but no farther.

Though the Naxid fleet was almost certainly based at Magaria, Martinez knew it was possible they wouldn't choose to fight there, but to defend their base by fighting forward of it. The Orthodox Fleet had to make every wormhole transit after the first with the assumption that they might at any point encounter the Naxids. In response, Tork repeated the tactics he had used at Zanshaa. The Orthodox Fleet was screened by hundreds of decoys. Relativistic missiles were fired into each system ahead of time, radars and ranging lasers hammering out, all timed so that when the Orthodox Fleet arrived, their sensors would be able to pick up a fairly complete picture of the system. Between wormhole jumps, the Fleet and its decoy screen performed random changes of course to baffle any relativistic missiles fired at them.

The wormholes were unusually close together, and the entire journey to Magaria took only sixteen days. The first eight were spent accelerating, and then the blazing antimatter torches were turned toward the enemy and a deceleration began. Jarlath had gone in fast with the Home Fleet and lost almost everything; Tork would go in more slowly, grapple the enemy with slow deliberation, and crush him with superior weight.

Martinez spent most of his transit time in Command gazing fretfully at the tactical display. He took his meals there and often slept on his acceleration couch. He had been caught away from Command during one attack and nearly broke his neck: he wasn't going to let that happen again.

He stared at the display and watched the slow advance of the little symbols that represented the Orthodox Fleet as they crawled across the display's vast emptiness. Decoys were shown in pink, real ships in red. At the head of the long column of red was the little clump that was Squadron 17. Martinez wondered what Sula was doing as she sat at the point of Tork's spear; if she sat in Command, as he did, and watched her ship creeping toward its destiny.

The long hours of waiting in Command produced a restlessness in Martinez that worked itself out in motion. When he wasn't watching the tactical display, he walked the corridors of *Illustrious,* wandering from one department to the next, watching his crew as they too waited for the Naxids. He knew the value of his own ship and crew by now and wasn't interested in detailed inspections; and when the crew braced to attention, he was quick to set them back to their work. He chatted informally with the department heads and sometimes with the ordinary recruits; he tried to project an air of quiet conviction in victory, the assured confidence of the veteran commander leading his crew to yet another inevitable conquest.

To his surprise, he found that the crew didn't seem to need his confidence—they had plenty of their own. They possessed a moral certainty of victory that Martinez began to find inspiring. He had hoped to cheer his crew, and instead they cheered him. It would have seemed churlish not to live up to their trust in him.

The Orthodox Fleet plunged on through the three systems that neither side could truly claim as their own. Along the way, Tork issued demands for obedience and surrender. This was fairly pointless in the case of the first two systems, which were largely barren of life save for a few mining colonies. These, having surrendered to the Naxid fleet when the enemy were heading for Zanshaa, now surrendered with equal alacrity to the loyalists heading the other way.

In the third system, Bachun, Tork demanded that he be able to broadcast to the population. The Naxid governor declined to answer. Intercepted transmissions from the planet showed joyous celebrations in honor of a record harvest and increased industrial production, all testifying to the efficiency of the new regime.

Tork fired a missile straight at Bachun's capital city. Without missing a beat, his messages began to be broadcast throughout the system. Tork recalled the missile.

To Martinez, it was beginning to look as if there would be no suspense until the Fleet reached Magaria.

He was wrong. When the alarms began to chirp, he was suited on his acceleration couch. He knew from the sound of the alarm tone what had happened before Warrant Officer Pan, the sensor operator, could cry his warning.

"We're being painted by a targeting laser!"

"Engines!" Martinez shouted over him. "Cut acceleration. Pilot, rotate to heading one-two-zero by zero-eight-zero! Weapons, all point-defense lasers on automatic! Comm, get me Lady Michi! Engines, sound warning for acceleration!"

Gravity and the distant rumble of the engines ceased. The ship began its swing to its new heading. Inside the vac suit, Martinez's heart sounded like a roll of thunder.

Michi had given the squadron standing orders for this situation. All ships would disperse without the need for an order from the flagship.

"We're still being painted, my lord," Pan said, more quietly.

The acceleration warning began to clatter. "Everyone med up," Martinez said, and reached for the med injector in its holster by the side of his couch. He pressed it to his carotid and fired into it a precise dose of the drug that would—it was hoped—keep his veins and brain supple and safe from the effects of heavy acceleration.

The others in Command took their injectors and did likewise.

The ship ceased to swing. "One-two-zero by zero-eight-zero," the pilot said.

"Engines, accelerate at six gravities."

The roar of the engines overwhelmed the feeble warning tones of the sensor board. The room became a blur as Martinez's acceleration couch dropped to its zero point.

"Captain, what's the problem?" Michi's voice, hoarse with her battle against acceleration, sounded in his earphones.

"Enemy targeting laser," Martinez said. "Are you all right?"

"I'm in my sleeping cabin. I got to my bed in time. Does—"

The squadcom's voice was drowned by a shout from Pan. "Here they come!"

"Ten gravities for one minute!" Martinez called.

He saw the flashes of white on the tactical display that

were incoming missiles, a perfect swarm of them shooting out of Bachun Wormhole 2 like a stream of water caught by a stop-action camera.

The ship shuddered and groaned under the great surge of gravity. Martinez clamped his jaw in order to force blood to his brain. His vision darkened, narrowed to a tunnel focused on the tactical display. He saw blooms of bright light flash on the display as antimatter missiles detonated. Symbols flickered, indicating that *Illustrious*'s point-defense weapons were firing. He fought for breath and consciousness, aware that control of the battle had never been his, that he would either live or die in the next few seconds and that he was helpless to make any difference . . .

The great pressure on his chest and mind eased. He had never felt he would be thankful to experience a mere six gravity acceleration.

Expanding clouds of plasma floated in the void ahead of the ship, showing where the oncoming Naxid missiles had destroyed part of the fleet's decoy screen. Silver flickers on the display indicated rapidly receding missiles that had flashed through the system so fast they failed to acquire a target. By the time they finished decelerating and had begun their return to the point of origin, the Second Battle of Magaria would be over, one way or another.

There seemed to be no new missiles coming their way.

"Reduce acceleration to one-half gravity," Martinez said.

Michi's voice sounded in his earphones. "I take it we've survived, Lord Captain?"

"No casualties in the fleet, my lady. We seem to have lost forty or so decoys."

"Message for the squadcom from the Supreme Commander," said Nyamugali at the comm station.

"Forward it to her."

Martinez heard the message secondhand, since his channel to Michi was still open when she played it.

"The lord commander," said a chiming Daimong voice,

"reminds Squadron Commander Chen that no element of the fleet is to disperse without permission of the Supreme Commander."

Tork, Martinez thought, at least had the virtue of consistency.

More decoys were launched to fill the gaps caused by the surprise attack. Tork then launched a missile to destroy the source of the ranging laser, which turned out to be Wormhole Station 2.

"The old pirate," Michi said, with feigned affection.

Illustrious suffered the expected number of sprains and broken bones during the attack. No one was incapacitated. The Naxid strike had come to nothing, but the crew of the wormhole station observed the Orthodox Fleet's reactions, and would have been able to deduce at least some of the icons on their screens that represented real ships and some that were decoys.

Perhaps that had been the whole point.

Martinez wrenched off his helmet to relieve himself of the scent of spent adrenaline that was souring his suit, then examined the spectra from the brief battle. There had been over two hundred enemy missiles, he saw. Most had missed completely. Only two squadrons had tried to starburst, his own and Sula's.

Something about the way Sula's squadron maneuvered seemed familiar, and he subjected the trajectories to analysis. They looked random, but on closer inspection they were not—they seemed to be following the hull of a chaotic system.

Somehow, Sula had taught the new tactics to her squadron, and presumably done so without Tork finding out.

Clever girl, he thought. He wished he and Michi had been as clever.

Martinez decided that he wasn't going to leave Command until the campaign was over. He ordered Narbonne to bring him coffee and settled in for the approach to Bachun Wormhole 2, now marked on the display by the glowing dust that had been its station.

The Orthodox Fleet was preceded through the wormhole by the now usual swarm of relativistic missiles equipped with laser trackers and radar, and then by hundreds of decoys. In order to avoid any theoretical host of missiles waiting for them on the other side, the fleet performed some last minute maneuvers to delay their entry into the Magaria system, a movement that only served to increase suspense.

Martinez shifted to a virtual display before the fleet made its transit. The Bachun system filled his skull, the sun a white sphere, Bachun itself a tiny blue dot surrounded by a silver ring.

The wormhole sped closer. Martinez strained his thoughts to sense whatever waited on the other side. Energy raced along his nerves. He could feel his pulse beat hard in his throat.

He knew that *Illustrious* had made its leap through the wormhole when the Bachun system vanished from his mind, replaced by complete darkness. His mind flailed without bearings, and then the sensors began picking up data from the scanning missiles that had been fired into the system ahead of time, and bit by bit Magaria's system blossomed in his mind.

When Fleet Commander Jarlath had led the Home Fleet to disaster at Magaria, the battle was influenced by two gas giants, Barbas and Rinconell, that lay between Magaria Wormhole 1 and Magaria itself. This tactical map no longer existed—Barbas and Rinconell had moved on in their orbits, and Magaria itself was on the far side of its primary. The Orthodox Fleet could skate past Magaria's sun, Magarmah, and blast straight for the enemy-held world.

Except of course for the enemy fleet, which now flashed onto Martinez's display like a distant glittering string of fireworks. The Naxids had swung around Rinconell and were themselves heading for the primary.

The two fleets were on a gently converging course, and if nothing intervened, they could begin hurling missiles at each other in about five days.

The enemy commander had given Tork exactly the battle he was looking for.

"Lord Captain," said Warrant Officer Choy at the comm station, "we have a radio signal from the Naxid commander. It's in the clear."

Martinez had to admire the enemy's timing. The message came within three minutes of the Orthodox Fleet's last squadron transiting into the Magaria system. The Naxids had known approximately when Tork would turn up, and had sent their message to arrive shortly afterward.

"Let's see it," he said. He was still scanning the tactical display, just in case the message was intended to distract the loyalist command while some kind of skulduggery went on.

The image of a Naxid appeared in a corner of Martinez's display, and he enlarged it. The Naxid was elderly, with gray patches on his head where scales had fallen off. He wore the uniform of a Senior Fleet Commander, a uniform covered with softly glowing silver braid, and his eyes glimmered a dull scarlet in his flat head.

"This is Fleet Commander Lord Dakzad." The voice was imperious. "In the name of the Praxis, I demand the immediate unconditional surrender of the disloyal, anarchist, and pirate elements that have just entered the Magaria system. You may signal your surrender by launching all missiles into interstellar space. If you fail to meet this demand, you will be destroyed by fleet elements operating under my command. I await your immediate reply."

Martinez was already looking up Dakzad in *Illustrious*'s database. The enemy commander was even older than Tork, and had in fact retired some eight years earlier. Apparently, the crisis had dragged him back into harness, to replace the hapless commander who had fled Zanshaa after the fall of the High City.

A text message from Chandra appeared in another corner of his display.

"I don't think Tork is going to like having his own surrender message preempted."

"I don't think he's going to like being called a pirate," Martinez answered.

He was right. Tork's reply—also sent in the clear, so his own subordinates could admire it—denounced the rebels as traitors before demanding their surrender. It included a video of Lady Kushdai surrendering all rebel forces to Sula, as a reminder to Dakzad that by fighting he was violating the orders of his own superiors as well as that of the government and Fleet.

Dakzad replied with a lengthy justification of the Committee for the Salvation of the Praxis, a denunciation of piracy as demonstrated by the destruction of wormhole stations and the Bai-do ring, and further demands for submission.

Tork's response was even more elaborate, with historical references to the Shaa's first Proclamation of the Praxis on Zanshaa, and repeated his original demand for capitulation.

Martinez supped at his own table that night and slept in his own bed. He didn't think there would be anything interesting happening as long as the opposing commanders were arguing ideology.

Though there was no fighting beyond the verbal sort, the days following the transit to Magaria were not entirely tranquil. There were many conferences with Michi and her staff, with Martinez's officers, with sensor operators, and with Tork's staff and analysts in other squadrons. Enemy formations were endlessly examined to find whether they were decoys or enemy warships. At one point Chandra put forward the startling possibility that they were *all* decoys, and that the real enemy were elsewhere, hiding behind Magaria's sun perhaps, racing toward them behind a pack of a few thousand missiles.

Fortunately, subsequent evidence disproved this theory. Sensor missiles probed the area behind Magaria's sun and found nothing but Magaria itself. Careful reading of laser ranging spectra suggested that there was a difference in size between at least some of the Naxid blips and others, indicating a mix of warships and decoys.

The enemy they saw before them was real.

The two great fleets gradually approached each other. The Orthodox Fleet remained on course to whip around Magaria's sun en route for the planet. The course of the Naxid fleet would intersect that of the loyalists right there, at Magarmah.

Which, Martinez reflected, was an interesting tactical problem. The two fleets would hammer at each other for several hours, and then have to form into a queue for the slingshot around the sun. Given the considerable distance between ships even in the same formation, there was no real danger of collision, but the ships of the two fleets would be intermingled in that long queue, and presumably still be hurling missiles at each other.

And after their passage around the sun, the two fleets would have to separate somehow, all the while engaged at close range.

Tork showed he wasn't totally unaware of these problems, and ordered his fleet into an acceleration to arrive at the intersection point ahead of the Naxids. He was confident he possessed superior numbers, and so ordered his lead squadrons to envelop the enemy as they came up. The Naxids increased acceleration to prevent this. This went on for the better part of a day, the crews crushed into increasingly flatter shapes, until Tork gave up and grudgingly ordered his rear squadrons to double on the enemy instead.

The problem of the intersection was still present. Martinez hoped by the time anyone neared the intersection point, the loyalists would already have won the battle.

Tork thought ahead, and took no chances. He ordered all ships, after passing Magarmah, to form on the same bearing for the passage to Magaria. Tork's bearing might be the same one the Naxid commander would choose. There was no way of knowing.

"This shows that a textbook battle is only possible if both sides cooperate," Martinez told Michi over dinner. "The Naxids knew approximately when Tork would enter the system, and they set up to receive him exactly the way the tactical manuals said to do it. If they'd done *anything* else, we'd all be improvising."

Michi gave a wry smile. "All Tork's maneuvers were practice for the real thing after all."

"In order to fight his kind of battle," Martinez said, "Tork had to find a Naxid commander who was even older and more set in his ways than he is." He thought of the two long lines of ships sailing toward their rendezvous, all more or less in the same plane.

Neither commander seemed interested in using the third dimension that was available to them. If he were in charge, Martinez thought, he would have stacked his squadrons in that third dimension and descended on the enemy like a giant flyswatter. As it was, Tork's superior force would drag into battle slowly, one element at a time. It was almost as if he was deliberately dissipating his advantage.

When battle was within three hours, Martinez turned out in full dress, complete with white gloves and the Orb, and gave *Illustrious* a complete inspection. Each division cheered him as he arrived. He found nothing out of place. The division heads' 77-12s were all up to date, but he checked a few of the items for form's sake, knowing he would find no discrepancy.

"Carry on," he said, unable to think of anything more inspiring, and the crew cheered *that* too.

He returned to his cabin and Alikhan helped him out of his uniform and into coveralls and his vac suit. He marched to his station and entered.

"I am in Command," he said.

"The captain is in Command," agreed Husayn. Martinez helped the lieutenant out of the command couch, then lowered himself into it. Husayn took his place at the weapons board. Martinez put on his helmet, locking himself in with the scent of his body and suit seals.

"Lord Captain," Pan said from the sensor board, "I'm detecting missile flares from the lead enemy ships."

The Second Battle of Magaria had begun.

Cruiser Squadron 9 was astern of the Supreme Commander's cruiser division, which was square in the middle of the fleet, and neither would be involved in the fighting for some time yet. Martinez had little to do but watch Sula's engagement at the head of the long column, and watch it with growing impatience. Apparently the lead squadrons of each fleet were to be allowed to have their battle, and then the next squadrons in line, and the next. Tork had the advantage in numbers, Martinez thought, why didn't he press the engagement? He should order the entire Orthodox Fleet to close with the enemy all along the line and hammer them till they were nothing but dust glowing on the solar wind.

Apparently this hadn't occurred to Tork, or if it had, he'd decided against it. Perhaps he was giving the fates every chance to remove Caroline Sula from his life.

Martinez found his blood burning with anger on Sula's behalf. He told himself that he would have been equally angry if it hadn't been Sula, that he was outraged at the waste of loyal officers and crew.

In the display, he saw that Sula ordered counterfire to intercept the enemy missiles, and that otherwise she did nothing. He understood her tactics. Past experience showed that long-range skirmishing was unlikely to produce results, and Sula clearly wasn't about to waste missiles when the odds didn't favor her.

The Naxids, it appeared, hadn't learned this lesson, and fired several more salvos before Sula replied with one of her own. Explosions moved closer to Light Squadron 17, providing a radio-opaque cloud behind which other missiles could advance. Fury and frustration raged in Martinez's veins. He punched the key that would connect him to the Flag Officer Station.

"May I speak with Lady Michi, please?" he asked when Coen answered.

In answer, Michi's image appeared on his display. "Yes, Lord Captain?"

"Can we prod Tork into some action?" Martinez demanded. "Do we have to let Sula fight on her own?"

She looked at him with impatience. "By *we* you mean *me,* I suppose. You should have an idea by now of how the Supreme Commander responds to prodding."

"Ask for permission to engage the enemy more closely."

Michi's tone turned frosty. "Not yet, Captain."

Martinez clenched his teeth. "Yes, my lady," he said, and ended the transmission.

He gazed at the display with burning anger. Sula was on her own.

Sula watched the Naxid squadron's latest volley of missiles get blown into perfect spheres of blazing plasma by Squadron 17's counterfire. She sat in her vac suit on her couch in Command, a gray, featureless, metal-walled space that had replaced the more sumptuous room flashed into ruin by a charge of antiprotons at Harzapid. Her neck itched where she'd applied a med patch—she felt a spasm of fear whenever she saw a carotid injector, and she refused to use them.

Her helmet sat in its mesh bag attached to her couch. She hated the damned helmet and the suffocating sensation she got while wearing it; as the captain, she didn't have to wear it if she didn't want to.

She would have preferred not to have worn the vac suit either, but supposed she might need its sanitary arrangements by the end of the day.

"Another salvo incoming, my lady," said Maitland.

"Track and destroy, Weapons," Sula said.

"Yes, my lady! Track and destroy!"

Giove's excited response rang off the metal walls. Sula wished Giove would calm down. She would have preferred a little peace in which to contemplate her options.

Tork had put her here to die, that was clear enough. The rest of the fleet wasn't maneuvering to her support, and Squadron 17 would engage an enemy of equal force on terms that implied mutual annihilation. The woman called Caroline Sula was intended to have a hero's death within the next hour or two.

The question that most interested Sula was whether Tork, in his simple way, might not have a point. The first act of her life ended with her wresting an entire planet from the claws of the Naxids and reigning over it as an absolute despot. Whatever any hypothetical second or third acts might contain, they could hardly equal the first.

Perhaps she had overstayed her welcome in the realm of existence. Perhaps the fittest trajectory of her life would be that of a meteor, blazing a brilliant trail in the heavens before annihilation.

She couldn't construct a rationale that justified her own existence, or that of anyone else either. Existence was too improbable to come supplied with a justification, like a book of instructions supplied with a complicated bit of equipment.

She couldn't work out why she was alive, and it was therefore difficult to work up a reason why she shouldn't die.

"Comm," she said. "Message to Squadron: fire in staggered salvo, fifteen seconds apart."

On the other hand, she thought, there was her pride to consider. The pride that she had instilled in her well-drilled squadron. The pride that didn't want her effort, and those of others, to go to waste. The pride that rejoiced in her superiority over the Naxids. The pride that wanted Ghost Tactics to triumph over the enemy. The pride that didn't want to hand Tork a cheap victory.

Vainglory, she wondered, or Death?

It was pride that won the argument.

"Comm," she said, "message to Squadron. Starburst Pattern Two. Execute at twelve eleven. Pilot, feed Pattern Two into the nav computer."

A few minutes later the nav computer cut the engines, and Sula's heart lifted as the ship swung in zero gravity to its new heading, the first in the sequence of bobs and weaves dictated by Pattern 2's chaos mathematics.

When Tork's furious message came, she took her time about answering.

"My lord!" This from Bevins, who was at the sensor station with Pan. "Starburst! Squadron Seventeen has starburst!"

Martinez enlarged the tactical display and saw Sula's command separating from one another, engines firing at heavy accelerations. A gust of laughter burst from his throat.

Sula was surprising them all. Defying the Supreme Commander and her own sentence of death, and setting the rest of the Orthodox Fleet an example.

Admiration kindled a flame in Martinez's breast. *O Lovely! O Brilliant!* Sula's maneuver made him want to chant poetry.

He sent a text message to Chandra. *Why can't we do that?*

Chandra didn't reply. Perhaps she was making the argument on her own.

Martinez wasn't the only one sending messages, because *Illustrious* intercepted a message from Sula to Tork. It was a reply to a message that *Illustrious* hadn't received, since Tork's message was sent by communications laser to Sula at the van of his fleet, and *Illustrious* was not in position to intercept the tight beam. But since *Illustrious* was astern of the flagship, it was in a position to catch the reply.

"*Confidence* to Flag. Unable to comply." That was the entire message.

Martinez was helpless with adoration. He was even more delighted when *Illustrious* intercepted the answer to Tork's following message.

"*Confidence* to Flag. Unable to comply." There it was *again*.

His joy faded, and a cold chill ran up Martinez's spine as he considered what Tork might do next. He could order each individual ship back into place, bypassing Sula altogether—or he could simply order one of Sula's subordinates to slit her throat and take command.

There was a silence from the Supreme Commander that lasted several minutes. Squadron 17 and the enemy continued to rain missiles at each other. The next squadrons astern had begun to fire as well.

Martinez waited, feeling unease in his inner ear for a moment as *Illustrious* went through a minor programmed course change. The warships were all swooping a bit now, dodging any theoretical beam weapons being aimed at them.

"Message from the Supreme Commander, my lord," said Choy. A text of the message flashed onto Martinez's display as Choy read it aloud.

" 'All ships rotate to bearing zero-two-five by zero-zero-one relative. Accelerate one point eight gravities at eleven twenty-three and one.' "

Martinez let out a long sigh of relief, then looked at the chronometer. He had a little less than one minute to complete the rotation.

The Orthodox Fleet was finally going to close with the enemy. Apparently, Tork had decided that Sula's maneuver compromised either his dignity or his tactics or both, and he had to retrieve the situation.

"Zero gravity warning," Martinez said. "Engines, cut engines. Pilot, rotate ship to zero-two-five by zero-zero-one relative. Stand by to accelerate on my command."

As the ship swung, as the acceleration couch swung lightly on its runners, Martinez took the opportunity to

shift again to a virtual display. His visual centers filled
with the vast emptiness of space, the distant planets and
Magaria's looming sun, the two great formations of ships
and decoys and the blazing curtain of antimatter bursts between the lead squadrons. The stars, an unnecessary distraction, weren't shown. Tucked away in an unoccupied
corner of the solar system was a softly glowing display that
would allow him to communicate with anyone else on the
ship, or call up information from any of the other displays
in Command.

"Accelerate at one point eight gee on my mark," he said.
"Three, two, one, mark."

Illustrious's great torches lit smoothly. The metal hoops
of the accelerating cage sang lightly as the weight came on.
Martinez drew a long, hard breath against the gravities that
were piling weights on his chest.

Ahead, Sula's squadron was well and truly separated
now, all the ships moving in an irregular, spasmodic fashion that seemed filled with random course and acceleration
changes. Only an appreciation of the mathematics would
show that the ships never strayed outside a mutually supporting distance, that their prearranged movement pattern
allowed them to stay in secure laser communication with
one another, that the formation could be shifted to concentrate offensive power on a group of enemy ships, or a single ship, or to form a protective screen around a damaged
comrade.

*If only Michi Chen's squadron could adopt a similar or-
ganization.*

He had every confidence that the loyalists would win the
battle. The only question was the cost. Tork would grind
the enemy down, using ships and crew as the grinder, but
the numbers used by the new tactics were mathematical,
and more flexible. Martinez wanted to tease the Naxids,
surround them, baffle them, trap them like a slow-moving
bear amid a pack of racing, snapping hounds. Using his

tactics, the loyalists would still win, but there would be many more loyalists alive to enjoy the victory.

Tork's stolid, workmanlike tactics offended him. Offended his intelligence, his professionalism, his sense of pride. The waste of lives offended him, and the waste of ships.

Tork might even waste *me,* he thought.

He reached with his hands into virtual space, called up the comm board, then once again paged Michi. When Li answered, he asked for the squadcom.

"Stand by."

It was a few moments before Michi appeared, miniature helmeted head and suited shoulders floating in the starless virtual space.

"Yes, Lord Captain?"

"May I suggest that we starburst, my lady?" Martinez said. "I realize the entire squadron doesn't have the formula, but Lieutenant Prasad, plus Kazakov and the crew in Auxiliary Command, can feed them their necessary course changes, and—"

"My lord," Michi said, her gaze stolid, "let me be plain. First, I am not about to disobey a direct order from the Supreme Commander. Second, you are not my tactical officer any more. Please confine yourself to managing the ship, and I will take care of the squadron."

Martinez stabbed at the virtual button that ended the communication. Rage pulsed in his ears.

Michi's words were all the more infuriating because they were true. *Illustrious* was his job. It really wasn't his business to suggest tactics to the squadcom.

Other commanders, he told himself, *had* followed his advice, to their benefit. Do-faq had followed his recommendations at Hone-bar, and come out of it with a bloodless victory. Michi herself, at Protipanu . . . well, he had been tactical officer then.

"Missile flares from the enemy squadron," Pan reported.

"Eighteen—thirty-six—forty-four missiles, my lord. Heading our way."

Martinez returned his attention to the display. Right, he thought. Concentrate on running *Illustrious*.

Concentrate on keeping himself and his ship alive.

And somehow manage this without tactics. He felt as if he were shackled to an iron cannonball while an angry mob pelted him with rocks.

"Keep tracking them," he said. "Weapons, alert Battery One to possible counterfire."

It would be Michi who would order any response. At this range, any missile launch was the squadcom's business.

Orders came from the Flag Officer Station a few seconds later. *Illustrious* would fire five countermissiles as part of the squadron's coordinated response.

Missiles leapt off the rails. Martinez watched as chemical rockets carried them to a safe distance so their antimatter engines could ignite, then saw the curves' trajectories as the missiles raced toward the oncoming barrage.

The two salvos encountered each other at the approximate midpoint and caused a series of expanding radio blooms that temporarily blocked Martinez's view of the squadron he was preparing to engage. He was able to view other enemy units, though, and they didn't seem to be maneuvering, so he assumed his own enemy wasn't either.

At the head of the fight, where Sula battled the enemy van, missiles were detonating in a continuous silent ripple, a ceaseless flash of brilliants against the darkness. Squadrons of decoys danced and maneuvered around the action, though without purpose—both sides had long since worked out which formations were decoys by now.

A text message from Chandra appeared on his display. "Target enemy with fifteen missiles. Immediate."

Fifteen: that was a full battery.

"Weapons," he said. "Battery Two to target the enemy. Fire when ready."

"Fire fifteen from Battery Two," Husayn replied smoothly. "Shall I fire a pinnace, my lord?"

The pinnaces were designed to race toward the enemy alongside missile barrages, to shepherd them to their targets. Martinez had worn the silver flashes of a pinnace pilot when he was a cadet, as had Sula. Pinnace pilots were dashing, and the duty was considered an entrée to the fashionable world of yachting. Peers competed with one another for the few places available.

Unfortunately, the war had been hard on pinnace pilots, with casualty rates of something like ninety percent. Sula had been the only pinnace pilot to survive the First Battle of Magaria. For some reason, Peers weren't volunteering for the duty in their usual numbers: most of the new pinnace pilots were now enlisted.

"No pinnace, Weapons," Martinez said.

"No pinnaces, my lord." There was a moment of silence, and then, "Missiles away, my lord. Tubes clear. All missiles running normally."

"Tell Battery Three to stand by for counterfire," Martinez said. Michi had used the radio blooms as cover to fire a salvo: possibly the Naxids would as well.

An idea floated into Martinez's mind, and the hairs on the back of his neck prickled. The thought of the radio-opaque wall of missile bursts between him and the Naxids had combined with Husayn's query about pinnaces to produce a fresh, bright notion that glittered in his thoughts like a precious gem.

Martinez probed the idea for a moment and found that it only glittered all the more.

"Comm," he said, "I need to speak to the pilots of Pinnaces One and Two."

"Yes, my lord," said Choy.

The two pilots reported in. One was a cadet and a Peer, the other a commoner and a recruit.

"I'm going to fire you in opposite directions, at right angles to the plane of the ecliptic," he said. "I want to use you as observation platforms, to get as many angles on the action as possible. Use passive detectors only—there will be enough radar and lasers out there. Send me all information real-time, and we'll overlay it with our picture of the battle here."

The pilots were too well-trained to show any relief at the knowledge that Martinez was not about to send them alongside flights of missiles into the hell of antimatter bursts that awaited them.

"Yes, my lord," they said.

The pinnaces were launched. They were packed with sensor equipment and transmitters, in order to detect openings in enemy defenses and order whole sheaves of missiles into course changes. They would do very well as spotters, able perhaps to see around the missile bursts and provide a new angle on the combat.

Martinez instructed Choy and Pan to coordinate the reception of the pinnaces' transmissions and their integration into the sensor picture of the battle. During the time it took to set that up, Michi ordered one more offensive barrage and another salvo of defensive missiles against incoming enemy.

Missile bursts were raging up and down the first two-thirds of the Fleet. At the head was a continuous seething blaze, like endless rippling chains of fireworks going off. So pervasive was the radio interference that Martinez had no clear picture of what was happening there, but he sensed that Sula's fight had reached some kind of climax.

His picture of the battle was beginning to get a little murky. Both fleets were now flying past or through the dispersing plasma spheres caused by the detonation of Sula's missiles, and though the bursts had cooled, they were still fuzzing the sensors.

Ahead of Squadron 9, Tork's Daimong squadron fired one volley after another. More missiles than made sense, Martinez thought. He preferred greater elegance in these matters. It was as if Tork viewed the opposing fleets as gangs of primitives armed with clubs, charging into one another and thumping away. Tork presumably took comfort in the fact that his side had more clubs.

To the rear, the loyalist squadrons were still driving toward the enemy. Tork had more ships and squadrons than the Naxids, and he had ordered his rearmost formations to double the Naxid formation, get behind it to catch the rear elements between two fires. The tactic was obvious enough, and the Naxids were clearly aware of it: their squadrons were stretching their formations to engage as many of Tork's ships as possible without permitting a clear path through their battle order.

More missiles launched, one salvo after another, all of which were destroyed to create radio-opaque walls between the approaching ships. It was as if the enemy were disappearing into thick clouds, clouds in which enemy missiles could hide. The data from *Illustrious*'s two pinnaces began to be factored into the tactical display, and they enabled Martinez to see several missile barrages being launched from behind the radio haze, and to plot his own missile intercepts. He congratulated himself that he had given himself a slight advantage over the enemy.

Considering the number of missiles racing toward him, he was going to need it.

He spared a moment for what was happening at the head of the column. He could see nothing through the plasma murk, but the intensity of fire appeared to have dropped away. Sula's fight, at least for the moment, was over.

"Course change, my lord," said Choy. "From the Supreme Commander."

Tork's new order aimed the squadron again for the original interception point, near Magaria's sun, and reduced acceleration to a standard gravity. Apparently, the Supreme Commander had looked into the flights of enemy missiles coming at him and figured he'd gotten close enough.

Martinez decided Tork was probably right. Unless Tork

was actually going to use tactics—something the Supreme Commander seemed determined to avoid—he might as well slug it out at this range as anything.

From what Martinez could see, the rear squadrons had given up trying to double the enemy. So it was just going to be hammer-hammer-hammer until the two fleets reached the intersection point, when things would turn very interesting indeed.

Data from the pinnaces was flooding in. Martinez kept shifting between the points of view of *Illustrious* and the two pinnaces, trying to spot the enemy missiles coming in, as well as approaches by which his own missiles could get nearer the enemy. He fed the data to Chandra, and at least occasionally she followed his suggestions.

The Naxid missiles came closer. Point-defense lasers and antiproton weapons lashed out. Plasma bursts were filling far too much of Martinez's field of vision. He remembered the data from First Magaria, the way the squadron defenses held up perfectly well until suddenly they collapsed and whole formations were wiped out in seconds. He began to feel as if someone had pasted a large target symbol to his chest.

"Permission to starburst?" he sent to Chandra. It was more than time.

He received his answer in text: *"Squadcom says not yet."*

Martinez clamped down on his frustration and began again the business of trying to visualize trajectories. He checked plots from the two observation pinnaces against *Illustrious*'s own spectra, plotted possible missile courses against the expanding, overlapping spheres of plasma that raged between the two fleets . . . and then, when he saw his opportunity, he almost gave voice to a cry of pure joy. Tork's Daimong squadron just ahead was heavily engaged: a dense cloud of plasma from Tork's fight was going to pass between Squadron 9 and the Naxids in five or six minutes.

If Squadron 9 fired now, the missiles could be launched behind the plasma bursts that were currently screening it from the enemy. The missiles would dash ahead and make the approach through the cooling plasma from Tork's battle. The attack would arrive from an unusual angle, and the Naxids might not see it at all—or if they did, it might be glimpsed for only a few seconds as the missiles dodged from one plasma cloud to another.

Nearly stammering in his haste, Martinez informed Chandra of this opportunity. The answer was immediate: fire a full fifteen-launcher flight following his trajectory, and then launch another full barrage straight at the enemy to keep their attention occupied.

Missiles leapt from the tubes, and this time Martinez fired Pinnace 3 along with them. The pinnace pilot couldn't accelerate with the same angry speed as the missiles, but would follow them and perhaps be able to see the enemy from a perspective useful enough to make vital last second corrections.

Another flight of missiles roared in on Squadron 9, and was destroyed by lasers and antiproton beams. Martinez felt anxiety gnaw his nerves with sharp, angry teeth. The enemy missiles were getting so close that it was difficult to launch countermissiles in time—the missiles just took too long getting clear of the ship in order to ignite their antimatter engines. He would have to depend entirely on the point-defense beams.

His head swiveled within the virtual environment as he saw ahead a horrific, violent series of flashes. The Daimong squadron vanished into overlapping blooms of plasma light. Martinez felt his heart lurch against his ribs. Very possibly Tork, his flagship, and his squadron had all been destroyed, annihilated in an instant like so many squadrons at First Magaria.

He wondered how hot the fireballs would be when *Illustrious* flew into them, in just a few minutes.

Chandra's urgent voice sounded in his ears. "All ships prepare to starburst."

About time, he thought.

"Engines," he told Mersenne, "cut engines. Pilot, swing to course two-four-five by zero-six-zero. Engines, prepare to accelerate at eight gravities."

Mersenne triggered the heavy-gravity warning.

"Starburst!" Chandra cried in Martinez's earphones. "All ships starburst!"

"Engines," Martinez said, "fire engines."

The onset of eight gravities was like being kicked in the stomach by a horse. The sound of the engines was the roar of a fire-breathing monster. The cruiser's spars and hull groaned aloud.

Martinez fought for breath. The virtual world in his head began to dim, and elements in the display flickered and faded out. The cruiser's unexpected maneuver was making it impossible for the two observation pinnaces to maintain their telemetry.

"All ships fire by salvo." Chandra's voice was a hoarse, throaty cry against gravity. Martinez repeated the command.

"Missiles . . . fired." Husayn's voice seemed to have chirped up about an octave—or perhaps, Martinez thought, heavy gravity was affecting his perceptions.

"My Lord!" Pan's shout showed no strain at all from the gravity. *"Missiles!"*

Martinez barely saw them coming before half the virtual display flared white, and then went completely dead as every sensor on that side of the ship was burned out.

"Roll ship!" Desperate urgency filled Martinez. Without sensors, the point-defense weapons couldn't see the enemy missiles coming at them.

The pilot rolled the ship, and the darkness of dead sensors exchanged places with the white of a fireball. The burst had already expanded beyond the ship, filling the vacuum with radio hash, and neither Martinez nor the sensors could see anything beyond. Martinez looked at the radiation indicators. Neutrons, gamma rays, and pions pulsed as missiles detonated nearby. The hull temperature was spiking.

The half of the universe that had gone black slowly turned white as sensors were automatically replaced.

An enormous radiation pulse blacked out half the sensors again. This was no mere missile going off. Something that big had to be the destruction of an entire ship with all its antimatter fuel and ammunition.

"Twelve gravities for two minutes!" Martinez shouted.

The engines thundered. Martinez screamed against the onset of gravity, at the darkness filling his mind. He clamped his jaw muscles and swallowed to force blood to his brain. His breath was harsh in his ears.

Oblivion was a glorious release.

He fought his way to consciousness moments later. Michi's voice rang in his ears.

"All ships fire by salvo!"

Martinez tried to speak around what seemed to be a felt-covered rubber ball in his mouth.

"Weapons, did you receive that? Fire by salvo."

Husayn didn't reply. He was probably still unconscious. Martinez was stumbling through the sequence of oral commands that would give him command of the weapons computer when he heard Husayn's muzzy voice.

"Never mind, Lord Captain, I've got that." There was a pause. "Missiles away."

Illustrious was still inside a plasma fireball, though the fireball was thinning and cooling. Martinez returned his attention to the radiation counter. The pulses were small and therefore distant. Hull temperature was beginning to drop.

Radars and ranging lasers lashed out into the radio murk. The images of a few ships nearby resolved out of the gamma ray haze, other survivors of Cruiser Squadron 9.

Three, Martinez counted, four. Five if you counted *Illustrious*.

A few minutes earlier they had been nine.

"All ships fire by salvo." It was Chandra's voice this time. Presumably she'd just regained consciousness.

Another salvo was fired at the enemy they couldn't see.

Martinez wished he could link his sensors with those of the two observation pinnaces.

The plasma fog was cooling and dispersing rapidly. A ship appeared, vaguely, ahead, proving there had been at least one survivor of Tork's Daimong squadron. Ahead of the single Daimong ship, Martinez could see the flares of missile explosions. There were many more explosions behind.

And then, within the space of a few seconds, the plasma surrounding the ship dispersed to the point where the ship's sensors were suddenly able to receive data from one end of the fleet to the other.

Martinez looked at first for the enemy squadron he had been engaging, and saw nothing but the flights of missiles he had just sent at them. He supposed the Naxids were still concealed by cooling plasma bursts.

At least no missiles seemed to be heading in his direction.

Astern, opposing squadrons were still smashing at each other. Ahead, one more Daimong cruiser had materialized, and this one was tentatively identified by the computer as the *Judge Urhug,* Tork's flagship. At any rate, it was maintaining *Urhug*'s course.

Farther ahead a battle blazed against the brightness of Magaria's sun. Martinez saw ships whirling around the action in a series of irregular curves, and his heart gave a shout as he realized that Sula's squadron was still fighting, still deploying the new tactical system.

She had destroyed the squadron she'd first engaged, apparently, and then decelerated to attack the next enemy squadron from its unengaged flank, the classic doubling maneuver that the rearmost squadrons had failed to accomplish. After destroying the second group of enemy, Sula and the second loyalist squadron were now dropping back to engage a third enemy force.

He could see at least five of Sula's ships, and their pattern of movement implied that there were more survivors that he couldn't detect. A song of relief caroled through his heart at the realization that Sula was almost certainly alive.

"My lord," said Choy. "Message from Pinnace Three. *'Attack successful. Enemy destroyed. Request orders.'* "

Martinez looked in surprise at the space that had been occupied by the enemy squadron. Even though the plasma bursts had thinned, no enemy ships had appeared. It appeared that *Illustrious* had just fired a series of missile barrages at enemies that had already been vaporized.

A burst of cold satisfaction raced through him. "Order Pinnace Three to return to the ship," he said. "Weapons, direct all remaining missiles to attack the enemy next astern. Engines, reduce acceleration to one-half gravity."

Relief akin to euphoria flowed through his sinews as the great pressure of eight gravities eased. The hull gave a series of cracks and shudders as if it were flexing vast limbs. Martinez pressed the touchpad that would connect him with Chandra.

"Request permission to decelerate and double the enemy next astern."

Chandra's answer was swift. "We've only got twenty-two minutes to our nearest approach to the sun," she said. "We'll have to wait till after our slingshot."

Martinez looked in surprise at the display and saw that she was right. He'd been paying so much attention to the battle that the range to Magarmah had escaped him. Hours had gone by since the first Naxid squadron fired its initial flight of missiles, and meanwhile the sun had been growing closer.

"All ships to form on the flag," Chandra said, this time over the general broadcast channel. "*Illustrious,* here's your course."

The cruiser altered its heading to bring it onto the course Tork had ordered for the fleet after the solar passage. Three other survivors of the battle took station near *Illustrious,* each keeping a wary distance from the flagship and each

other in order to avoid getting fried by the other ship's
blazing antimatter tails. The last survivor did not acknowledge any of Michi's transmissions, but shaped its own
course for the solar approach. It was unable to communicate though it was clearly under command, and it probably
hadn't received Michi's order. The other ships stayed clear
lest it do something unexpected.

Judge Urhug gave no orders and did not alter its course.
Its engines were unlit, and as a result Squadron 9 was
slowly closing on it. Martinez wondered if Tork's cruiser
was a ship of the dead.

Ahead of *Urhug* there was a ferocious blaze of action
and then silence. Sula's squadron broke its formation and
began heavy accelerations to line up for the passage across
Magarmah.

If they had left any Naxids alive, the enemy was hidden
by expanding plasma bursts.

Engines roared and *Illustrious* quaked as Squadron 9
burned around Magarmah. Martinez clenched his teeth in
the face of high gravity and managed to hold onto consciousness. *Illustrious* maintained heavy thrust for another
four minutes after the passage, to shape its course for Magaria, and Martinez looked ahead.

There were nothing but friendly ships between
Squadron 9 and Magaria. Sula's Squadron 17 was already
dispersing again into its whirling formation and decelerating to engage the enemy. Martinez counted seven ships remaining in her squadron, and fourteen in the other friendly
squadrons ahead.

Judge Urhug hadn't fired its engines during the solar by-
pass, and so hadn't shaped the course that Tork himself had
ordered for the fleet. The flagship was flying by itself toward the interstellar void.

"Prepare to decelerate," came Chandra's voice on the
all-ship channel. "We will double the enemy squadron to
our rear."

Martinez hung weightless as *Illustrious* rotated to its

new heading. He could only imagine what was happening on the other side of Magarmah as the two fleets approached the same point. Annihilating flights of missiles would be fired at point-blank range, as much a danger to the aggressor as the target. Possibly on account of the danger, they'd stop shooting missiles entirely, but that didn't mean they were through fighting. As the opposing squadrons fell into line ahead and astern of one another, they would be close enough to begin deploying their antiproton beams as offensive weapons, and cause the same kind of carnage that Harzapid had seen on the first day of the mutiny. The opposing forces would roar around the sun shooting great chunks out of each other, and if they didn't separate sufficiently after the transit, they'd just keep on shooting.

Martinez was at a loss as to how he'd be able to aid friendly ships if that were the case. He might not be able to fire missiles for fear of hitting his own side.

"Decelerate on my mark, at three gravities," Chandra said. "Five, four, three, two, one, mark."

Deceleration kicked Martinez in the spine. He saw that most of the other survivors began decelerating at the same moment—all but Sula's, which had been decelerating all along—and he wondered if Michi was the senior surviving officer and had given them all an order.

Two ships didn't decelerate. One was the cruiser that had been unable to communicate, which plodded along on its preset course, and the other a ship farther up the line, which might be in the same condition.

Martinez saw specks whirl around the sun, their torches flaring to bring them on track for Magaria. It was impossible to tell whether they were loyalist or Naxid, and Michi transmitted a demand that they identify themselves.

The reply flashed back at the speed of light. The new arrivals were Cruiser Squadron 20, five ships that remained of the ten that had started the battle.

The sun spat out another line of ships, tiny bright seeds

flying across the darkness. They were on a different heading from the loyalist squadrons and therefore presumed to be enemy.

"All ships fire by salvo," Chandra said. "No—wait. Stand by."

The new arrivals' course was peculiar. They weren't racing after the loyalists, and they weren't shaping a course to get between the loyalists and Magaria. In fact they didn't seem to be heading anywhere in particular, and were soaring more or less into empty space.

No, Martinez realized. Not quite empty . . .

He stabbed the virtual button to send a message to Chandra.

"They're running!" he said. "They're heading for Wormhole Five."

Which, he recalled, would eventually take them to the Naxid home world of Naxas.

"We've got to go after them!" he told Chandra. "The enemy fleet *is* the rebellion now. Magaria is nothing without them."

"Fire by salvo," Chandra said. "Stand by for course correction."

Missiles were already being launched by the enemy squadron and by the remains of Squadron 20. It was very close range, and soon the space between them was filled with detonations.

Another squadron flung itself around Magaria's sun, on track for Wormhole 5. They were already shedding missiles aimed at Cruiser Squadron 20.

"Turn to course zero-six-zero by zero-zero-one relative," Chandra said. "Accelerate to six gravities, beginning at sixteen forty-one and one."

"Engines, cut engines," Martinez told Mersenne. "Pilot, do you have the new heading?"

"Yes, my lord."

The loyalists began their pursuit of the fleeing enemy, gravity piling on their bones. The next two formations to pass the sun were loyalist, already engaged with the Naxid squadron astern of them. Antimatter burned and boiled in the space between ships.

Not all of the ships passed the sun intact. Two flew off on the trail of *Judge Urhug,* unable to make use of their engines. It was unclear whether they were friendly or Naxid. Others fell into the wake of the loyalist squadrons, but reported too much damage to continue the engagement with the enemy.

If the Naxids had similar problems, they were silent about it.

More ships were flung out of the sun's gravity well. Enemy squadrons vanished behind clouds of raging plasma. The radiation detector spiked as missiles reached fuel stores. The Naxids increased acceleration, and Michi did as well. *Illustrious* groaned to the increase in gravities. Martinez panted for breath against the leaden giant that squatted on his chest. Michi's ships fired one salvo after another. Ships reported that their magazines were beginning to run low.

Eventually Michi called off the pursuit. The opposing forces had become too separated in their slingshot around the sun—those extra four minutes of thrust had thrown the loyalists too far away. The Naxids could keep their distance by matching Michi's acceleration.

"Is Lady Michi the senior officer surviving?" Martinez asked Chandra.

"She must be," Chandra answered. "Everyone's following her orders."

Martinez scanned the display, adding up the ships. The Orthodox Fleet had come into the battle with eighty-seven ships, and something like forty had survived—the exact number depended on how many of the three silent, uncontrolled ships now drifting for the void belonged to the loyalist fleet.

The Naxids had started with seventy-two warships, and thirty were now making their escape.

Ships on both sides were damaged, but at the moment it was impossible to say how many, or how badly.

What seemed clear was that combat had taken a heavy toll of flag officers. Tork's ship was silent and drifting. Kringan's *Judge Kasapa* hadn't survived, unless it was another one of the ship-sized flotsam on course for nowhere. The third in command, Acting Junior Fleet Commander Laswip, had died with his ship.

That put Michi very definitely in charge.

"Captain Martinez." Michi's brusque voice rang in his head. "I'll need you in my quarters at once."

"Yes, my lady."

Martinez let the virtual display fade and blinked as the control room swam into his vision for the first time in hours. Ancient Terran officers on horseback gazed sternly at him from the walls, and below the feet of their horses the displays glowed in colors that seemed dull compared to the brilliance of the virtual world.

"Comm," Martinez said, "get me the premiere."

When Kazakov answered, Martinez told her she was in command of *Illustrious* while he was in conference.

"Yes, my lord." She hesitated. "Congratulations, my lord."

"Thank you."

He unwebbed and swung forward to plant his feet on the deck, then wrenched off his helmet for a breath of somewhat freer air. While he still had the microphone on, he addressed the crew in Command.

"Well done, people. Take a breather and a stretch, but don't go far. I'll try to have food brought to you."

As he stood, they turned to him, wheeling around in their acceleration cages. Mersenne raised his gloved hands and began to applaud. The others echoed him, the sound muffled by the vac suit fabric. Martinez grinned.

He *had* done rather well, he thought, considering his superiors' mistakes.

He thanked them, then stripped off the cap that held his

headphones, microphone, virtual projection net, and the diagnostic sensors that read his vital signs.

Michi had said *at once*. He supposed he didn't have time to change out of his suit.

Helmet under his arm, he left Command and trudged down the companionway to officers' quarters. Michi, Chandra, Li, and Coen were grouped around Michi's dining room, all bulky in their vac suits. Michi and Chandra were gazing at a wall display, the aides at datapads. Martinez entered and braced.

"Come in," Michi said, her eyes intent on the wall display, and then she turned to him.

"I intend to pursue the enemy," she said, "and finish them off once and for all."

"Yes, my lady," Martinez said.

Good idea, he thought.

THIRTY-THREE

"I've ordered all squadron commanders to give a complete report on the status of their ships," Michi said. "If we can build a large enough force, I'm going to swing around the far side of Magaria and head right for Wormhole Five on the tail of the enemy."

A sense of pure satisfaction sang like a Daimong chorus in Martinez's head.

"Yes, my lady," he said.

"You were right when you told Chandra that the Naxid fleet *is* the rebellion," Michi said. "Kill their ships, and the war dies." She returned her attention to the screen. "Yes, my lord," she said. "Continue."

"*Compliance* has frames broken, two bulkheads breached, and two missile batteries severely damaged by heat," reported the captain of the *Conformance*. "I doubt it'll be able to pull heavy gravities, and though a well-equipped dock might save her, it might be easier in the end to scrap the ship and build a new one. *Submission* has suffered hull breach in two places and the death of sixty-odd crew, but reports the hull damage is repairable and that repairs are ongoing. The captain reports the ship as ready for battle, though half of one missile battery has been permanently slagged. *Conformance* has suffered superficial damage, and is ready to continue the fight now, though our magazines are at two-fifths full strength."

"Don't worry about missiles," Michi said. "We'll get you more. Thank you, Lord Captain."

Don't worry about missiles. That was interesting. Perhaps Michi intended the damaged ships to donate their unfired missiles to those about to go in pursuit of the Naxids.

Chandra made notes on her sleeve display, which were reflected in another one of the wall displays that showed a list of ships, with tick marks in one of three columns.

"Sit down, Captain," Michi said. "There'll be food and coffee in a minute."

Martinez found a seat and listened to another report. More ticks went into different columns.

The next report was from Sula. Her silver-gilt hair was pinned back and revealed her delicate ears. A flush floated in the translucence of her cheeks, and defiance glittered in her green eyes. She wasn't wearing a vac suit, but wore instead her undress tunic. Martinez figured she had showered and changed before reporting.

"Light Squadron Seventeen reports the loss of *Councillor* and *Eager,*" she said. "All other ships are undamaged and prepared to engage the enemy."

Martinez stared. He didn't think he'd ever seen her so arrogant.

"Missile stores?" Michi asked.

Sula gave her precise numbers for each of her ships. She hadn't fired so prodigiously as other ships, and she'd preserved nearly half the missiles in her magazines.

"Thank you, Captain Sula," Michi said. "You've done an outstanding job."

"Yes, my lady," Sula said, and blanked the screen.

Yes, she had said. Not *Thank you.*

No humility here, Martinez thought.

Two of Michi's servants arrived with plates, silverware, and a casserole that had been quietly baking while the missiles were slashing between ships. Coffee and water arrived shortly after. The mingled scent of tomatoes and garlic rose gently into the air as dinner was dished out, and everyone began eating and working with the figures in the wall displays.

All squadrons reported in. Twenty-eight ships were capable of action. The rest would be left behind to guard Magaria's system from any Naxid counterattack—and at least some of them could receive repair at Magaria's ring, assuming that Magaria surrendered.

"Twenty-eight against thirty," Michi said thoughtfully.

"The Naxids will have a high percentage of damaged ships," Martinez said. "Ours was nearly a third, and theirs might well be higher."

"I'm worried less about that," Michi said, "than why they're retreating."

"Panic?" Martinez suggested. "Terror?"

Grim amusement glittered beneath Michi's dark bangs. "Possibly. But it bothers me that they stopped fighting when they did. I'm wondering what they're running *to*."

"Reinforcements?" Martinez said. "But wouldn't they have sent reinforcements *here*? To Magaria?"

"I'm sure they would have if it were possible. But possibly they still have ships guarding Naxas, or they have ships under construction or undergoing trials."

"There can't be that many. And if any are new construction, they'll have inexperienced crews and maybe they won't have even shaken down. We'll blow them to bits."

Michi allowed herself a smile. "I suspect you're right, Lord Captain."

"Momentum's on our side, my lady. We can finish them quickly if we don't give them a chance to catch their breath."

Michi's smile broadened. "Please remember," she said, "that this pursuit is my idea. You don't have to talk me into it."

Chandra snickered. Martinez decided this was a good moment to change the subject.

"We can have the damaged ships donate their missiles to the pursuit force," he said. "That'll help fill our magazines."

"Not necessary." Michi turned to her casserole.

"My lady?"

"Tork's insurance policy." Michi spoke around a mouthful of food. "In four days, something like two thousand missiles are going to rip into the system at relativistic speeds."

Martinez stared. Michi swallowed, then took a drink of water.

"Unless they get the right code," Michi said, "they're going to hit every ship they can find."

Insurance policy, Martinez thought.

"So just in case the Naxids won another victory here," he said, "Tork was going to do his best to destroy any Naxids remaining."

"And the Magaria ring," Michi added, "so the Naxids couldn't repair." She took another sip of water.

"He called us pirates for Bai-do," Martinez said. "Now he's going to blow up the Magaria ring?"

"Pirate is the nicest thing Tork would have been called if he'd lost this battle," Michi said. "I'm sure he knew that."

"I suppose you have the code to control the missiles," Martinez said, "otherwise we'd be piling on the gravities to escape the system by whatever wormhole is nearest."

"That's right. The right code, and all those missiles turn into our resupply. We're going to have to decelerate enough to stay in the system and recover at least some of the missiles before we go on to Wormhole Five."

"How many people know this code?"

"It was given to all flag officers."

"Three of whom seem to be dead. If you'd all been killed, it would have been hard on any survivors."

"Lucky that Altasz and I survived," Michi said equably. "Which brings me to my next point. I'm going to have to leave Altasz here to command the remnant we're leaving behind—which is easy, because his ship is damaged too. The twenty-eight ships of the attack force will divide neatly into three squadrons. I'll take one, and Sula will have another." Michi looked at him, eyebrows raised. "I don't suppose you'd care to command the third?"

Martinez took at least two seconds to bask in the radiant

joy that suddenly filled him—and then the joy came to an abrupt end as Li bent to a communication flashing on her sleeve display.

"Communication, my lady," she said, "from Lord Tork."

A sudden dark pall fell on the room like a cloud across the sun.

"Put it on the wall," Michi said, and straightened in her chair as she looked at the wall and its camera pickup. One of the wall screens filled with Tork's wide-eyed, gray, expressionless face.

"Yes, Lord Commander," Michi said. "I rejoice to see you alive."

Martinez, for his part, could barely keep from snarling. His squadron was now surely a lost cause.

"Please report, Lady Michi," Tork said.

"We have thirty-nine confirmed survivors, and two silent ships we're not sure about. I was in the process of assembling a force of our twenty-eight effectives for an immediate pursuit of the enemy."

Due to the growing distance between *Illustrious* and *Judge Urhug,* there was a pause of several seconds before Tork responded. Martinez studied his image, and saw that the Supreme Commander wasn't wearing a vac suit. His torso was encased in puffy bright orange plastic—he was wearing one of the inflatable body casts used by Fleet medics. He was a more leaden color than Martinez had ever seen him. His face was free of strips of dead skin, which argued that some medic had just cleaned him up.

"Very good, Lady Michi," Tork said. "Your pursuit is authorized."

Martinez was surprised. He'd been expecting Tork to want to orbit Magaria for another three or four months before his next advance.

"Kindly send me all information on the status of the fleet and your proposed dispositions," Tork said.

Michi did so. There was another pause while they watched Tork's wide, round eyes absorb the data. If he felt any regret at losing over half his command while winning his victory, he failed to show it.

"Acting Squadron Commander Altasz shall remain in the Magaria system to command the stay-behind force," Tork said. "You may take all the remaining heavy cruisers into Squadron Nine—no, all but *Splendid,* which will join Squadron Seventeen, and its captain will replace Lady Sula as its squadron commander. The remaining vessels may form a light squadron under . . . would it be Captain Tantu?"

Misery at losing his squadron warred in Martinez with rage on behalf of Sula. She might be murderous, insolent, and insane, but she and her squadron had performed brilliantly, losing fewer ships than any other formation and inflicting far greater harm on the enemy.

"I believe Tantu is senior, my lord," Michi said. "But wouldn't *Splendid* make a more logical member of the heavy squadron?"

"I desire that Captain Sula be superseded," Tork said. "She disobeyed my express orders and starburst early during the battle. She refused to reform when ordered to do so. I want a loyal captain in charge who will bring her to proper obedience."

Martinez could see that Michi was on the verge of offering further comment, but then decided against it.

"Yes, my lord," she said. "Do you need help? Shall I send a vessel to bring you off the *Urhug*?"

"That won't be necessary," Tork said. "I've suffered spinal damage and the doctor says I shouldn't be subjected to high accelerations. I am told that *Judge Urhug* will have one engine repaired within twenty-nine hours, and that should provide a slow deceleration that will put me on the Magaria ring station about the time that the fast-healer hormones have repaired my injuries. Now that communication has been restored, my staff and I can continue to run the Righteous and Orthodox Fleet of Vengeance from the *Urhug,* at least for the present."

Would Tork never give up? Martinez wondered. Would he never die, retire, check himself into the Fleet hospital, blow his brains out?

Would Tork never get out of Martinez's way?

"I wish you to demand the surrender of Magaria and the enemy fleet," Tork said. "Though I very much derire to issue the ultimatum myself, the fact of its coming from a near-derelict ship might reduce its impact."

Not to mention attract enemy missiles.

Martinez was cast in gloom for the rest of the conversation, and then the planning session that followed. Finally Michi dropped her coffee cup into its saucer and gave him a severe look.

"Cheer up, will you?" she said. "We're alive, we've won the battle, we'll win the next."

"Yes, my lady," Martinez agreed.

"And Tork's arrangements will last only until we pass through Wormhole Five. After that, I can arrange the fleet to my liking, and you're just the acting squadron commander who can whip our provisional light squadron into shape and teach it the tactics that will win us a victory at Naxas."

Martinez paused a moment while a carillon rang changes of joy through his head. Michi grinned.

"That's better," she said.

Sula took her supersession with equanimity. She had defied Tork, flouted his death sentence, then rubbed salt into his wounds by blowing up sixteen enemy ships at the cost of two of her own. There wasn't an officer in the fleet who hadn't seen the superiority of Ghost Tactics demonstrated on their very own tactics displays.

She hoped Tork was furious. She hoped he was raving. She hoped that every time he thought of her, he sprayed angry spittle over everyone in the Flag Officer Station.

All Tork could do in response to her defiance was put a nobody like Carmody of the *Splendid* over her. If an officer of hers had defied her the way she'd defied Tork, she would have thought of something much more interesting to do with him.

Splendid shouldered its way into Squadron 17 like a prizefighter moving through a crowd of schoolchildren. Sula was having tea in her little bare-walled office when the new squadcom called.

Or rather, his communications officer. Sula looked at the wall display and saw the handsome face of Jeremy Foote.

"Hello, Foote," she said. "How's the formula?"

He flushed. "Captain Carmody to speak with you."

Carmody appeared, a blocky-looking man with ginger whiskers. Behind him Sula saw rich arculé paneling. He was presumably calling from his quarters, which would allow her to be frank.

"Yes, my lord," Sula said. "How may I help you?"

"I wanted to speak with you personally," Carmody said. "I want you to know that I did not seek this appointment, and in fact was rather surprised by it."

"I think we all were, my lord," Sula said cheerfully.

"Ye-es." Carmody's brow furrowed, as if he had lost his place in the conversation and was trying to find it again. "I witnessed Squadron Seventeen's performance in the battle," he said after a moment, "and I hope I can perform as well."

"You won't," Sula said, "if you obey Lord Tork's orders." She took a sip of the tea, sweetened as she liked it with cane syrup, and then looked at Carmody's startled face. "Tell me, my lord, did the Supreme Commander give you any instructions regarding me?"

He blinked at her with puzzled blue eyes. "No. None. What do you mean?"

"I mean he wants me killed. I mean he sent Squadron Seventeen into combat without proper support. Surely you noticed."

Expressions danced across Carmody's face. His eyes showed surprise while his mouth showed shock. His mouth showed surprise while his eyes showed denial. Then his brow showed thought while his jaw showed resolution.

"Of course not, Captain," he said. "Why would the fleet-com do such a thing?"

"It's rather a long story," Sula said. "But I think Lord Tork feels that the empire would be better off without me. He can't get rid of me—another long story—but he thinks it would be just as well if the Naxids sent me to my reward."

Carmody visibly calmed himself. "I can assure you the Supreme Commander has implied no such thing in any communication with me. In any case, I would decline any such directive when the life of a fellow officer is at stake."

Sula found herself rather touched by this brotherly declaration.

"Thank you, my lord. I appreciate your goodwill." She took another sip of tea, and wondered if she'd just convinced Carmody that she was crazy. She put down her teacup.

"Did Lord Tork give you instructions regarding tactics to be employed against the enemy?"

"He said he would permit no innovations."

Sula gave a slow nod. "You served in a squadron that permitted no innovations, a squadron that suffered casualties so severe that it had to be broken up. I don't envy you your choices, my lord."

Carmody looked uncertain. The conversation had taken another unexpected turn.

"Ah—perhaps not." Probably not even Carmody knew what he meant by this answer.

"I was able to use Ghost Tactics because I knew that Lord Tork wanted me dead anyway. I had nothing to lose. Whereas *you*—if you act to prevent a slaughter of your own crews, you may earn the Supreme Commander's undying enmity. But if you don't use Ghost Tactics, your command could be slaughtered, and you with it."

Carmody's face did that little dance again. Sula tried to keep her smile hidden behind her eyes.

Of the many possibilities raised by her words, Carmody decided to focus on what was probably the safest.

"Ghost Tactics?" he asked.

"I'll send you the formula, and the lecture I prepared for the squadron." She smiled. "Even if you choose not to use them, at least you'll be able to understand what the other captains are talking about."

Michi demanded surrender, and Magaria gave it. The Naxid fleet, possessing more choice in the matter, did not. It wasn't clear whether the enemy commander was still Dakzad, since no one responded to Michi's ultimatum.

Probably Dakzad was dead, Martinez thought. He hadn't tried to argue ideology or give Michi orders.

Michi put Magaria in the charge of Junior Fleet Commander Jinja, who had been captured there on the first day of the rebellion and held in a prison on the surface ever since. She also ordered all Naxid military and security personnel to surrender their arms and evacuate the ring.

Martinez didn't envy Jinja his job. The only forces he had were those that were captured with him, four or five thousand military to police several million Naxids.

Altasz and the stay-behind force would help, though. Altasz, along with his missiles, to keep everyone on the planet and the ring compliant and obedient.

Martinez wondered if his old shipmates from *Corona* were well. Fahd Tarafah, his old football-crazy captain, and his premiere Koslowski, the talented goalie. And Lieutenant Garcia, the only other officer to believe that the Naxids were going to rise. At a crucial moment she had slipped him her lieutenant's key, which allowed him to enable *Corona*'s weapons and permitted his escape.

He sent messages to them all to let them know that *Corona* had survived and was in the system. There was no answer, so perhaps proper communications weren't working yet, or the old Coronas had been moved to another planet.

600 • Walter Jon Williams

He checked on his friends and lovers. Lady Elissa Dalkeith's *Courage* had been lightly damaged, and would be part of the attack force. Vonderheydte's cruiser had suffered severely and would remain in the Magaria system, but Vonderheydte had survived and seemed reasonably cheerful. Cadet Kelly, in her pinnace, had survived the strike that wiped out her shipmates, and was taken aboard Sula's *Confidence*. Martinez could only hope that Sula and Kelly didn't spend their time exchanging stories about him.

Ari Abacha's *Gallant* had done very well as part of Sula's Squadron 17. Shushanik Severin's Exploration Service frigate *Scout* had been heavily damaged and would need dockyard repairs. Severin had survived with a broken collarbone.

Illustrious sent off repair parties to aid other ships. Some of them came back shocked at the carnage they'd seen. Martinez kept busy devising exercises for the squadron that Michi had promised him.

The two derelict ships turned out to be friendly. One had lost all its engines to antiproton weapons, and its crew was taken off by the other, which was barely able to maneuver.

Tork sent off a missile carrying his official report. It would accelerate to relativistic velocities between Magaria and Zanshaa, then broadcast its coded contents to the capital.

The attack force sorted itself into its new formations and began exercises to accustom each ship to maneuvering with its new comrades.

Two thousand missiles arrived in the system and, defanged by the proper codes, began braking at speeds that would have pulped any human. The weaponers spent several harried hours recovering missiles before the fleet narrowed its trajectory to pass the wormhole.

Still in the inflatable body cast, still on the flagship that was feebly decelerating in an attempt to claw its way back toward Magaria's ring station, Tork issued a last ringing command.

"In the past, under the Shaa and the Praxis, the empire existed in a state of harmony and perfection. Your ancestors were a part of that harmony. It is your task to restore the lost perfection of the empire by cutting out the imperfect and disharmonious element.

"Prove yourselves worthy of your ancestors! Fulfill the perfection they have bequeathed to you! Purge yourself of irregularities and innovations! *Long live the Praxis!*"

The Orthodox Fleet flashed through Magaria Wormhole 5, and at that instance became Chenforce. Martinez felt his heart sing a chorus of thanksgiving. Chenforce had been lucky for him.

He had his squadron now, and Tork was far behind.

THIRTY-FOUR

A few hours after passing the wormhole, Lady Michi shifted Captain Carmody's *Splendid* to Cruiser Squadron 9, which put Sula back in charge of Squadron 17.

Martinez happened to witness Michi's communication to Carmody, and was struck by how relieved Carmody seemed to have escaped squadron command.

"Please understand," Michi said, "that this reassignment is meant as no reproach to yourself. I will put a note in your file to that effect."

"Very kind of you to say so, my lady," Carmody said. "Truth to tell, I never understood what a heavy cruiser was doing in a light squadron in the first place, and . . ."

Carmody seemed to lose track of his conversation.

"And?" Michi prompted.

Carmody blinked. "Oh. Well. Lady Sula is—quite an extraordinary person—isn't she?"

Martinez concluded that Sula had managed to bring Carmody to a state of terror in an unusually short time. He figured the only reason Tork wasn't afraid of her was that he lacked the imagination.

Martinez himself had no time to be terrified. He was shifting to Light Squadron 31 in a few hours, with the rank of Acting Squadron Commander.

He had a final breakfast with Acting Captain Fulvia Kazakov and gave her the combination to his safe. His belongings and his portrait were packed. He had Buckle give him a final haircut so he could make the best possible impression on his new officers.

In his address to the crew of *Illustrious,* he told them how privileged he felt to have commanded them in battle and how proud he was of them. He said that his current assignment was temporary and that he would be back after Lady Michi finished off the Naxid fleet once and for all.

He heard the cheers ringing down the corridors. Smiling, carrying the Golden Orb, he made a royal progress to the airlock, where he met his servants and the cadet, Falana, who would act as his signals officer. He stepped aboard *Daffodil* for the journey to Squadron 31.

As the airlock door swung shut, he heard one rigger turn to another and say, "There goes our damn luck, off to that useless undeserving set of buggers."

He stepped aboard Lieutenant Captain Lady Elissa Dalkeith's *Courage* twenty minutes later, to the usual honor guard, the silent row of officers, and a jaunty recording of "Our Thoughts Are Ever Guided by the Praxis."

Dalkeith had been his premiere on *Corona.* She was middle age and gray-haired, and had been languishing as a very senior lieutenant until Faqforce's victory at Hone-bar had put all Martinez's officers into the spotlight. She had been lucky enough to be promoted to Lieutenant Captain after the battle, when Martinez's star was at its height but before Lord Tork and his clique had decided to drag that star down by main force.

"Welcome to *Courage,* Lord Captain," she said. Martinez was surprised, for about the hundredth time, at Dalkeith's voice, the high-pitched piping lisp of a child.

"Happy to be aboard," he said.

He shook her hand and was introduced to her officers, then escorted to his quarters.

Courage was a large frigate, with twenty-four missile launchers in three batteries, and was enough like *Corona* that Martinez was surprised when he came across the occasional difference. Frigates had no quarters for flag officers aboard, since light squadrons were usually commanded by the senior captain rather than a designated squadron commander. As he had once displaced Kazakov from her quarters on *Illustrious,* he now displaced Dalkeith, who displaced her first lieutenant, and so on down the line.

More annoying was the fact that *Courage* had no Flag Officer Station. Martinez would command Squadron 31 from Auxiliary Command, from the couch normally used by Dalkeith's first lieutenant, who was supplanted—again—to one of the engine boards, where she would monitor the ship's condition from a reconfigured station. Since the premiere—whose name was Khanh—had little to do in combat other than wait for Dalkeith to die, the inconvenience was not crucial.

Nor were the sleeping arrangements going to be much of a disadvantage to anyone. Martinez knew he wouldn't have much chance to sleep in the bed he'd taken from Dalkeith—that Michi was planning a series of heavy accelerations—and suspected he'd be doing most of his sleeping on his acceleration couch.

Martinez left Alikhan and Narbonne to stow his belongings, procured a cup of coffee from the kitchen, and headed for Auxiliary Command. His new aide, Cadet Lord Ismir Falana, contacted the captains of Squadron 31 while he inhaled the coffee aroma and took his first sip.

Martinez met them in virtual, four rows of three little portraits. Of his twelve captains, four were Terran, two Daimong, four Torminel, and two were survivors from one of the Fleet's rare Cree squadrons. The Cree were not a species much tempted by the military life. Once they could be persuaded to join, they served aboard ships modified with displays that made use of their superb hearing and deemphasized their poor vision. A Terran in a Cree control room would find it a dark place filled with maddening sonic interference and white noise.

Supposedly the Cree all slept piled together in a heap,

officers in one stateroom, enlisted in heaps of their own. This was what they did at home, except at home the females were part of the piles too. The females were unintelligent quadrupeds and were rarely allowed on ships. The males were unintelligent quadrupeds for their first years of life, but then straightened and grew large brains.

Nature was odd, especially where the Cree came from.

"Welcome to you all," Martinez said. "I am Captain Lord Gareth Martinez, and I have been assigned by Lady Michi Chen to take command of this provisional squadron. I suppose some of you might be surprised to find me in charge of the squadron, and you wonder how I am qualified to command such a group of experienced officers.

"First, I'm an honors graduate of the Nelson Academy. I worked hard as a cadet and a lieutenant, and served on shipboard as well as on the staff of Fleet Commander Enderby. I won the Golden Orb by rescuing *Corona* from the Naxids.

"And then," he said, "I married your squadcom's niece."

He looked from one blank face to the next.

"You may laugh," he said.

Only the Cree seemed to find this amusing. Martinez decided he might as well surrender his career as a wit.

"I expect we'll be working very hard," he said. "I have been ordered to work up this squadron in a new system of tactics."

"We're defying the Supreme Commander's express orders?"

This from Captain Tantu, the Daimong commander of the light cruiser *Vigilant*. By virtue of his seniority, Tantu had commanded the squadron until now.

"The situation has changed, my lord," Martinez said smoothly. "The Supreme Commander is out of contact, and we're following the enemy so closely that it's unlikely a conventional battle will develop. Lady Michi feels that we should look into different tactical options—those employed at Protipanu, for instance."

What Tantu thought of this was hidden behind his expressionless Daimong face. Those faces that Martinez could read seemed intrigued.

"The wise worm learns from the worm-eater," said one of the Cree.

"And the tree rejoices in the night rains," said the other.

Martinez looked at them. "Ye-es," he said.

"My lord?"

One of the Terran captains looked at him with a question poised on her lips.

"Yes, my lady?" he said.

"Is this the Foote Formula we'll be learning?"

He smiled. "No. Something better than that."

"Ghost Tactics?" lisped one of the Torminel.

Martinez paused for a moment of surprise, in which he deduced that the White Ghost had given their tactical innovations a name that reflected glory on her and left him out of the picture.

Well, he thought. One good turn deserved another.

"Not quite," he said. "We're going to practice the Martinez Method."

Sula was pleased to have her squadron again, though she was sorry at the effort she'd wasted on Carmody. She had to wonder which way he would have jumped in the end.

Still the point of the spear, she and *Confidence* raced on the track of the enemy. The Naxids had gained something like twenty hours on their pursuers, and Michi wanted to narrow the distance.

Sula approved. Like Michi, she wondered what it was the Naxids were retreating to, and whether there were reinforcements speeding to Naxas or already there.

Whatever the Naxids planned, timing had to be a crucial element. And the faster the loyalists pursued, the more the Naxids would be forced to advance their timing, straining ships and crew and equipment. The more the enemy were stressed, the more likely they were to make mistakes.

Maybe those reinforcements—if they existed—wouldn't turn up in time.

The price of wrecking the Naxids' timing was enduring a three-gravity acceleration at least fifteen hours per day. The rest of the time was spent in drills and experiments, working the squadron's two new ships into the pattern. The only people excused from the drills were the cooks, who produced the meals that the crew gobbled at their action stations.

Michi Chen gave her ships one hour of free time each day, when the acceleration was reduced to one gee and no drills were scheduled, time that allowed people to leave their couches, stretch, and empty the waste collection bags from their vac suits. Never a pleasant job, the crowding at the toilets and waste disposers now made it worse. Sula rejoiced in her private toilet and her private shower. She wasn't prepared to share them with anyone.

She hardly had to abuse her new captains at all. They had seen what she'd done at Second Magaria, and all were now believers in Ghost Tactics.

She meet Martinez in virtual conferences with Michi and other officers. She was civil. He was civil. He reported progress with his squadron. So did she. Everyone was learning fast, under the pressure of imminent combat. Sula wanted them all to learn their moves before the constant pounding of heavy gravity made them stupid and careless.

There were three systems between Magaria and Naxas, a swollen red giant, a blue-white star boiling off angry radiation, and a neutron star surrounded by the wreckage of a planetary system it had destroyed in a great supernova. The systems were mostly barren, and when the two fleets entered them, their population doubled or tripled.

Chenforce pressed the Naxids and narrowed the distance. The Naxids didn't respond to the loyalists' increased acceleration until five hours had gone by, and then they matched their pursuers' acceleration without trying to increase their lead.

On the second day, on an hour when Chenforce had reduced its acceleration, the Naxids sent a swarm of pinnaces, shuttles, and other small craft to ferry crew away from one of their ships. Michi saw what was happening and ordered a fast, hard burn in pursuit. The Naxids finished their evacuation and raced away. When they were a safe distance from the abandoned vessel, they blew it up with a missile.

One of the damaged Naxid ships hadn't been able to stand the increased pressure that Michi Chen was applying. That left the enemy fleet with twenty-nine. Sula approved.

The pursuit went on. Sula peeled med patches off her neck and applied new ones. She ate badly and slept badly, her dreams choked with asphyxiation and blood. Casimir called to her from his pilfered tomb.

Once, she felt his warm touch on her skin. She reached to take his hand, and found that the hand wasn't Casimir's, wasn't long and thin, but broad and blunt-fingered, the hand of Martinez—and she woke, eyes wide and staring at the man who touched her, and he wasn't Martinez but the almost-Martinez, Terza's son, who gazed at her in malicious triumph from beneath his heavy brows . . . and then she woke *again*, heart lurching against her ribs, and saw the glowing pastel displays of Command and the crew drowsing at their stations while Haz in Auxiliary Command conned the ship.

Both fleets were going to have to decelerate in order to have a hope of maneuvering in the Naxas system. Until they arrived at the turnover point where the deceleration would normally start, Michi continued her accelerations. The Naxids continued to flee before them. Michi was going to wreck the Naxids' schedule past all repair.

Sula began to think that Michi should continue the accelerations regardless. Press the Naxids to the point where it was impossible for either side to maneuver in the system, only to flash through it on their way to the next wormhole. The Naxids would have to accept straight-up combat this side of their home planet in order to keep Chenforce from blasting the place en route to somewhere else.

She contacted Michi and made this suggestion. Michi said she'd take a few hours to think about it, and a few hours later sent Sula a message saying she'd decided against the idea.

"We don't know what's there," she said. "Going in slower gives us more time to work out our options."

Sula shrugged with shoulders three times their normal weight. She concluded that Michi probably had a point.

Chenforce rolled and began its deceleration. The Naxids rolled and decelerated as well. Due to the delay in rollover, gee forces were heavier than during the accelerations. Sula felt as if the big hand of the almost-Martinez had clamped on her throat. Her heart raced to erratic surges of panic. She fought against the fear. In the shower, she scrubbed herself with perfumed soap to scour off the sour odor of spent adrenaline.

The Naxids' deceleration wasn't quite as heavy as that of Chenforce. The loyalists were slowly overtaking them. Sula checked the trajectories and matched them against a current map of the Naxas system, which featured eleven planets dotted around the primary. Chenforce would overtake about halfway toward the Naxid home world, having just passed the orbits of three gas giants.

There *were* reinforcements then. Most likely they would sweep around one or more of those gas giants and burn like fury to join the Naxid fleet before the battle.

Sula messaged these speculations to Chandra Prasad. The tactical officer answered that she, Michi, and Captain Martinez had already worked it out, but thanks anyway.

Sula consoled herself with the thought that at least there were a few other keen minds in the squadron.

A swarm of Naxid missiles raced into the systems, hundreds of them. Alarms flashed along Sula's displays. The missiles decelerated, approached the Naxid ships, and were taken aboard.

The loyalists weren't the only ones to have worked out this method of resupply.

The wormhole to Naxas approached. The Naxids formed into a long line and vanished through it. Hot on their heels came loyalist missiles, racing at relativistic velocities with their lasers and radars pounding out to light up the system before Chenforce arrived.

Chenforce took its time. Michi reduced the deceleration to three-quarter gravity and gave everyone three hours' holiday. Meals were laid on the mess room tables for the first time since pursuit had begun, and the crew ate in shifts. A modest amount of alcohol was decanted, enough to produce a glow in the crew.

Alone in her cabin, Sula drank fragrant tea sweetened with clover honey, ate her dinner, then had three desserts. Every cell in her body rejoiced at the low gravities. She lay on her bed and slept in dreamless peace till Spence arrived to help her into the vac suit.

Reduction in deceleration of course meant that the fleets would meet earlier, not later. And Michi was still pushing ahead, still doing her best to demolish the Naxid timetable.

Chenforce flashed into the Naxas system with every sensor operator straining for sign of the enemy, and with Sula having switched her display to virtual. The sensor missiles that had gone into the system earlier had done their work—bits of the system flashed into her mind almost immediately, jigsawing together until she saw, like a spatter of brilliant stars against the blackness, what the Naxids had been running toward.

For a moment her heart lurched. It seemed that a vast enemy fleet lay ready in the system—but of course at this stage it would look that way, the real ships surrounded by scores of decoys that loyalist observers had not yet sifted out from the genuine warships. But even if ninety percent of the enemy force were bogus, the size of the force still surprised her.

They were right where Sula had thought they'd be, having swung in succession around a pair of the outer gas giants, and were now burning at eight or nine gees acceleration for a rendezvous with the survivors of the Magaria fleet, which was decelerating briskly in an effort to keep the rendezvous.

Those heavy gravities that were torturing the Naxids were Michi's fault, for having pressed the pursuit.

"Sensors, I want ranging lasers on those new blips," Sula said.

"Already done, my lady."

The relativistic sensor missiles were racing through the system too swiftly to keep the enemy in their sights for long. The rest of the system seemed bare, however. The Naxids had cleared away everything for this final combat.

Lady Michi, speaking in the clear, transmitted her demand for surrender. Only time would tell whether the government on Naxas was headed by someone as chatty as Dakzad had been at Magaria.

"My lady," said Maitland, "I have a preliminary analysis of the enemy. Some of those blips are . . . well, they're very large."

"I'll take a look."

She enlarged the sensor image on her display. Some of the blips *were* large—not just large, but gigantic, and they were gigantic both in radar and laser-ranging images.

They *couldn't* have, she thought at once. The war simply hadn't gone on long enough for the Naxids to have built a squadron of giant *Praxis*-class battleships like those destroyed at First Magaria. Even under the accelerated building schedules produced in wartime, it would have taken ages to put one of those giants together.

She counted. There were nine overlarge blips. There had only been eight battleships in the entire Fleet, and they had all been destroyed.

The big ships had to be something else.

They had to be warships simply because they were here. There had been plenty of time for all nonwarships to clear the system. But the overlarge blips couldn't have been built as warships, they had to have been *turned into* warships.

They were converted transports, big ones like the vast ships Sula had seen in orbit around Magaria.

"They're converted merchant ships," she said, and immediately felt the relief that sighed through Command.

Merchants couldn't be much of a threat, she thought. In the days after First Magaria, when Zanshaa was expecting a conquering Naxid fleet every minute, a number of small private vessels had been requisitioned by or sold to the Fleet, given a few missile launchers apiece, and sent to patrol the Zanshaa system as "picket ships." Fortunately, the ridiculous craft had been withdrawn from service before the Naxids had the chance to wipe them from existence.

But these Naxid ships, Sula thought, weren't yachts and little transports and small merchantmen. These were the largest vessels in existence, bigger even than the old *Praxis*-class battleships, even if they weren't built for war. All that was needed to turn them to warships would be missile batteries, the addition of turrets for point-defense weapons, an electronics upgrade, and extra radiation shielding for the crew compartments and certain other parts of the ship. The craft wouldn't be very maneuverable, and damage control would probably be worthless, but there would be lots of redundancy. As missile platforms, they would be serviceable enough.

The conversion could probably have been done in a couple months. If the order went out after the Naxids lost Zanshaa, the conversions would start appearing about now, too late for Second Magaria. It was a desperate move, but a reasonably practical one.

Sula began calculating how many missile batteries could be crammed into a space capable of holding ten thousand citizens, like the transports she'd seen at Zanshaa.

The total was frightening.

She asked for a line to Chandra Prasad.

"Yes, my lady?" Chandra said. The camera showed her

properly suited, with her helmet in place. Sula, whose helmet was not in place, suddenly felt exposed.

"Those big blips," Sula said. "They're large converted transports."

Distance caused a few seconds' delay between Sula's words and the response.

"Yes, my lady," Chandra said. "We've worked that out."

There was the tiniest bit of condescension in her voice. *Yes, we know that, don't bother us.*

"Have you worked out how many missile tubes a large transport can carry? Something like six hundred."

A few seconds later Sula saw Chandra's face fall.

"I doubt they carry that many," Sula said. "For one thing, transport from the magazines would be incredibly complicated. But we shouldn't dismiss those ships just because they started out as merchants."

Her tone echoed Chandra's condescension. It was the least she could do.

"I'll tell the squadcom," Chandra said.

Ten seconds later Michi had joined the conversation.

"Six *hundred*?" she demanded. "How do you figure that?"

Sula explained. The huge hemispheric hull of a transport had a vast surface area. Each missile launcher took only so much of that surface area. Add it all up, there could be lots of launchers.

Missiles were cheap. Launchers were cheap. The offensive element was the cheapest part of a warship—the most expensive components were the engines, and merchant transports came with those already fitted.

The limitation on the total number of launchers wasn't a factor of the surface area, but of the amount of plumbing necessary to feed the missile batteries their reloads. Missile batteries needed to be near the magazines, and both the magazines and the batteries needed heavy radiation shielding, and the heavy shielding needed structural support. Sula guessed that most of the big ships were completely

614 • Walter Jon Williams

empty except where missile batteries had been jury-rigged to the exterior, all on special support struts.

"Thank you for this," Michi said. There was a little X between her brows, just beneath the bangs. "I'll give this some thought."

"No matter how big the ship," Sula said, "it still takes only one missile to destroy it."

Michi gave a weary smile. "I'll bear that in mind, Captain."

Michi had two days to think about the converted transports, because at the current rate of closing it would take that long for Chenforce to catch the enemy. The Naxids could always maintain distance, but they would still have to fight before they got to Naxas.

Sula knew the battle was going to happen wherever the Naxids wanted it to. If Michi had adopted her suggestion and pressed the pursuit without decelerating, she would have caught the enemy-before the reinforcement could have caught up with the Magaria survivors. She would have destroyed the Magaria contingent and then swept on to Naxas before the converted transports could have interfered.

She didn't mourn Michi's decision. At least Michi had reasons for what she did, not useless prejudices like Tork.

There was no reply to Michi's demand for surrender. Sula considered this yet more evidence that Dakzad was dead. She hoped his replacement was equally old and useless.

The two days to the Battle of Naxas was filled with activity. Officers and sensor techs scrutinized displays, trying to figure which return signal meant a genuine warship and which did not. The Magaria survivors were known quantities, but the reinforcements weren't. The nine overlarge signals were real ships, and it was decided that at least two of the others were genuine, though whether real warships or converted civilian craft, it was impossible to say. They seemed to be the size of frigates.

The analysis was all performed under heavy deceleration. Increased gravities strained bodies and slowed minds.

Sula stuck one med patch after another on her neck, twitched through dreams of disconnected horror, and fueled herself with coffee and sweets.

Michi gave Chenforce another three-hour break before the engagement, a few blessed hours under low gravity for the crew to have a hot meal and a few hours to relax the knots that heavy gravities had put in their muscles.

Sula called a drill instead. She was worried that Squadron 17 might have lost its edge in the long, dull prelude to the battle.

After the drill, she was glad she'd spoiled her crews' quiet moment, because her ships performed raggedly. She issued a series of brisk corrections, then had the crouchbacks' meal served at their stations.

She ate coffee ice cream on her couch, caffeine and sugar combined in a single efficient delivery system, and watched the Naxids come closer.

She was ready for whatever was to come. The converted transports might have large missile batteries, but they could be killed just like any other ship.

She was still the point of the spear. She was going to trust her luck, and trust Ghost Tactics.

This would be the last battle of the war, and she would be in at the kill.

Martinez watched the Naxids coming closer and didn't like what he was seeing.

Nine enormous missile batteries, screened by twenty-nine warships, or perhaps thirty-one. Worse, Chenforce was following them, in pursuit. When the shooting started and burning plasma began blooming between the two fleets, Chenforce would fly *toward* the radio-opaque screen, and the Naxids away from it. As the battle intensified, Chenforce would grow more blind just as more enemy missiles were launched.

He had seen this situation once before, as a tactical officer at Protipanu. The situations had been reversed then, and he deliberately used the missile splashes to dazzle and confuse the enemy, and to hide whole volleys of missiles.

The Naxids had not survived that battle. He'd killed ten ships in less than two hours.

He sent a message to Michi pointing out the similarities in the current situation. In response, he was yoked into an encrypted datalink with Michi and Chandra.

"Any solutions to the problem, Captain?" Michi asked.

"There are no choke points the way there were at Protipanu. The enemy had to line up to slingshot around Okiray, and we were able to swamp them with missiles as they came at us. That's not going to happen here—there's nothing between us and Naxas."

A curl of auburn hair had escaped Chandra's sensor cap and was dangling in her eyes. She grinned.

"You're suggesting that we go in on a broader front."

"Why not? We have the time and the distance. Tork made the mistake of feeding his squadrons in one at a time and lost more than half his force. Instead we send our three squadrons against the enemy all at the same moment. We can link our sensor data together, so that maybe we can see around those plasma clouds, and we can throw out pinnaces to extend our range. Each squadron can use the Martinez Method so as to maneuver on its own while still providing maximum protection for its own elements."

"The *what* method?" Michi asked.

Martinez blinked. "The Martinez Method." When Michi failed to react, he added, "I had to call it *something*."

Michi frowned at him. "You didn't think to name it after your highly supportive force commander?" she asked.

Dismay filled him. Michi and Chandra began to cackle. With effort, Martinez summoned his dignity.

"Would you *like* the tactics named after you, Squadron Commander? You're already going to get credit for the victory and for winning the war."

Michi affected to give the matter her consideration. "I suppose in view of my impending glory I can afford to throw out a few tidbits to my juniors." She gave a gracious wave of her gloved hand.

"The Martinez Method it is."

Engines fell silent. Ships made minor adjustments in their trajectories. Engines flared again.

Each squadron's deceleration was slightly different. Sula's deceleration was the heaviest, Martinez's the lightest, Michi's somewhere in the middle. Their courses began to diverge.

Communications and sensor techs fed the sensor data of all Chenforce into one vast, webbed system. The technology had existed for ages, but it was complex—the computers had to compensate for the amount of time it took the signal to arrive from each ship down to the merest fragment of a second, which meant that Chenforce's ships were continually bouncing ranging lasers off each other, and the data from these worked into the sensor feed calculations.

Chenforce didn't starburst yet, but Chandra Prasad assigned each squadron a starburst pattern based on Sula's formula. Each used a separate formula so the Naxids would have a harder time figuring out that the maneuvers weren't completely random; but each squadron knew the others' patterns, so the ships could continue to share sensor data.

"Engine flares!" Maitland's baritone voice rang in the close confines of Command. "Engine flares at Wormhole Three!"

Sula looked at the display and saw a whole constellation of stars flying into the system, plasma tails blazing. Probably the vast majority were decoys, but there were at least three real ships, giants like the converted transports.

Whatever they were, they were too late. Even though they were accelerating at crew-killing velocities, they'd still flash past Naxas a day after the battle.

If Chenforce won, they'd have the newcomers for dessert. If the Naxids won, the newcomers would be redundant.

Michi Chen, with her furious pursuit, had succeeded after all in wrecking the Naxids' schedule.

Chenforce raced on, Michi's heavy squadron now in the center flanked by the two light squadrons. The Naxids responded by deploying squadrons of their own. The nine giant auxiliaries were clumped on the far side of the warships, with the smaller ships as their screen.

The warships fired, a volley of over three hundred missiles. Sula checked the chronometer: 2314.

"Message from Flag, my lady," said Ikuhara. "Return fire at will."

"Right," Sula said. "Let's make sure this is the *last* battle, shall we?"

THIRTY-FIVE

Countermissiles lashed out. Antimatter fury raged in the space between the ships. More missiles were on the way.

Martinez looked at the display, the two light squadrons attached to Michi's heavies like a pair of wings, the Naxids in a formation that countered that of the loyalists. Everyone was in the same plane, just as they'd been at Magaria.

He messaged to Chandra. "Do we really want to limit ourselves to just two dimensions?"

There was no answer till the next salvos of missiles found each other, blossoming to create a screen, and then a series of orders came from Chandra. The two light squadrons were ordered to rotate about a common axis, with Michi's squadron joining them equidistant from the others. The squadrons were also ordered to starburst.

Martinez's acceleration cage creaked as it swung to the new heading. He could only imagine the alarm in the minds of the Naxids as they saw Chenforce swinging into its new configuration, the three squadrons rolling around one another as the individual ships darted and flashed in alignments that had never been prescribed by any tactical manual, the ships like chaff flying before a crazed typhoon aiming at their destruction. He wondered how the Naxids could possibly react.

Let's hope it's with panic, he thought.

"Message from the flag," Falana reported from the signals station. "All ships to volley in succession at fifteen-second intervals."

That would put a lot of missiles into the pattern over a period of time, create a lot of plasma splashes, and help mask Michi's movements. The maneuvers might look all the more ominous if the Naxids only glimpsed them between roiling plasma spheres.

"Fire Pinnace One," Martinez said. The little craft raced away, heading away from the mass of explosions between the opposing fleets. A set of sensors to peek around the corner of the antimatter curtain and see what was happening on the other side.

The Naxids took their time to respond to Michi's maneuver, and did so simply by matching it, one Naxid squadron planting itself in the path of each Chenforce element. The enemy were still in close formations, ideal close-packed targets for swarms of loyalist missiles.

Martinez felt a course change tug at his inner ear, and along with it a rising sense of optimism. The opposing forces hadn't yet truly engaged, but already Chenforce was in a much better position for this stage of the battle than Tork had been in Magaria.

"Missile flares, my lord!" Warrant Officer Second Class Gunderson, at the sensor station, spoke in a deliberate sonorous calm. "There seem to be . . . well, hundreds."

The nine giant ships had finally fired, and the number of missiles blossoming into existence on the tactical display was truly phenomenal. Hundreds, many hundreds. Thousands, perhaps.

Martinez's nerves began to cry a warning.

This wasn't going to be easy as he'd thought.

"Fire Pinnace Two," he said.

He had a feeling he was going to need more than one extra set of eyes.

Light Squadron 17 flew amid a riot of missile tracks as the weapons officers of each ship tried furiously to match the incoming missile barrage with countermissiles.

The first barrage from the converted transports had totaled around eighteen hundred missiles, which exceeded the average squadron salvo by a factor of something like fifteen. There were so many missiles that they were coming in from all angles, some flying direct, some swooping far out to drive in from the loyalists' flanks.

That first massive barrage had been followed by a second. Then a third.

Counterfire was complicated by the fact that Chenforce was now flying through the cooling remains of plasma bursts, which was beginning to fuzz sensor readings.

Squadron 17 had fired a pair of pinnaces well away from the squadron to provide a clearer view of events, but the two fragile little boats were beyond the range at which the squadron could protect them. If a group of the enemy missiles decided to target them, there was little Sula could do to prevent it.

"Message to Flag," Sula said. "Query: press the enemy? End message."

There was no point in staying in this shooting gallery any longer than necessary. The sooner Chenforce could buzzsaw its way through the Magaria survivors and destroy those huge missile platforms, the better.

"Message from Flag," Ikuhara said a few moments later. "Engage more closely. End message."

Sula gave the necessary orders, then copied to all other ships so the sensor net could be maintained. Ships swung on their axes. Gravities began to drag at Sula's heart.

"All ships," she ordered, "fire full batteries in succession at fifteen-second intervals. Target nearest enemy."

The sensor operators were working furiously with their counterparts in Auxiliary Command, and with the weapons station, to spot flights of incoming enemy missiles and take them under fire. Ahead was a vast irregular plasma wall, radio-opaque, toward which Chenforce was advancing and from which the Naxids were flying.

In the virtual display, she raced toward the plasma wall, gauging its shape and the areas where it was likely to fade and cool or brighten with new bursts of fire. She shifted the center of the squadron's movement toward areas where there were likely to be gaps, where she could see farther.

She sent her own offensive missiles plunging through the wall at denser points, to blind enemy sensors to their presence.

She wished she had a tactical officer to absorb some of the work. Commanding the squadron and *Confidence* both was a job worthy of two people.

Enemy missile bursts came closer. Point-defense lasers flickered out, seeking the missiles that wove and dodged to avoid their beams.

The converted transports unloaded another vast barrage. Sula began to taste desperation on the air.

She saw the enemy movement at the same time as Maitland's baritone rang out.

"Starburst, my lady! The enemy's starburst!"

The enemy force that had opposed Squadron 17 was flying apart, each ship trying to put as much distance between itself and the others as possible. Sula narrowed her eyes— uselessly, since her view was projected not on her retinas, but on her optical centers—and carefully studied their movement.

They were not moving within the free-seeming calculations of Ghost Tactics. The enemy were just dashing away from one another.

Relief sang in her bones. The enemy had seen Squadron 17 cut through Naxid formations at Second Magaria, but they either hadn't realized that its movements weren't random or hadn't had a chance to do a proper analysis. They'd concluded that battles were best fought from starburst formations.

Each enemy ship was now moving and fighting on its own. Squadron 17 was still a coherent entity that flew and fought as one.

She was going to pick off the enemy one by one.

Sula chose one of the enemy ships, reached into the virtual space with one gloved hand and stabbed it with a finger. It shifted from blue to white.

"Message to Squadron," she said. "Copy to all ships. Center formation on target vessel, beginning at"—she checked the chronometer—"twenty-four forty-nine."

Half a minute later *Confidence* swung to a new heading, its engines still blazing. Sula's acceleration couch swung on a short arc, then returned slowly to its deadpoint.

The hunt was on.

Martinez watched the radiation counter as the point-defense lasers of Squadron 31 flashed a dozen attacking missiles into a brilliant random pattern of overlapping spheres, like a spatter trail flung by a careless brush.

Thus far, he thought, the squadron had been lucky. Despite the vast quantity of missiles thrown at them, the enemy had been kept at bay. The Martinez Method was keeping the ships of the squadron within supporting distance of each other, and the overlapping fields of defensive fire were walling off the enemy attack.

So far, anyway.

The missile batteries were firing as fast as they could be reloaded. The sensor and weapons techs who shared Auxiliary Command with him, crew who normally sat out combat unless their cohorts in Command were taken out of action, were fully occupied tracking enemy attacks and plotting responses. Forty percent of *Courage*'s missiles had already been fired, mostly as countermissiles. If this expenditure continued, there could be dire consequences. Martinez found it ludicrous that he might find himself in a superior tactical position, about to administer the coup de grace to the last Naxid formation, and find himself with empty magazines.

Another flight of missiles soared in. Point-defense weapons flashed in answer. Another part of the starscape burned with plasma light. A few missiles, dodging and corkscrewing, survived, but were retargeted and destroyed within seconds.

Courage, already burning for the enemy under heavy acceleration, gave a swerve to dodge any theoretical Naxid beam weapons. The movement felt like a fist in Martinez's side.

The converted transports huffed out another vast barrage, like overripe weeds hurling a cloud of pollen onto the breeze.

Surely, he thought, they couldn't keep this up. Surely they'd run out of missiles before long.

Surely.

Anger flashed through him.

"Message to Squadron," he told Falana. "Each ship to fire one battery at converted transports. *Vigilant* to order a pinnace to accompany."

It was time the weaponers aboard those Naxid transports had something to do other than plot offensive action. And the pinnace would be in a position to direct further barrages.

Courage gave another swerve. Martinez's teeth clacked together.

"First blood to us, my lord." Gunderson's mellow baritone was filled with satisfaction.

Martinez looked at the display and saw a sphere of plasma where an enemy ship had once been. Sula's Squadron 17 had made their first kill.

The enemy's defenses were beginning to break down. All three warship squadrons had starburst, and their fields of defensive fire weren't nearly as efficient as those of Chenforce.

Martinez plotted a missile strike and ordered it launched. The missiles would dodge through a series of plasma bursts to strike the enemy from an unexpected direction. He didn't want Sula's squadron to get all the glory.

He looked at the tracks of his missiles looping around

the enemy warships to target the converted transports. A colossal number of enemy missiles were coming in the other direction. He clenched his teeth.

Courage ceased its acceleration, and Martinez's ligaments shrieked with relief as he floated in his webbing. His acceleration cage made a shimmering noise as the frigate reoriented, and then the engines flamed on again and he was punched into his couch.

Another of the random-seeming maneuvers dictated by Sula's chaos mathematics. The constant dodging and shifting probably looked deeply sinister to the Naxids, the application of some principle they hadn't been able to decipher.

The enemy were dodging as best they could, but without the relentless purposefulness dictated by Sula's formula. The only Naxids who hadn't starburst yet were the converted transports, which were still moving forward in their inexorable way.

Martinez began to wonder if they *could* dodge. The transports were so huge that they couldn't dart about like a frigate, they carried far too much inertia.

Which meant—theoretically—the transports were vulnerable to beam weapons.

The most formidable beam weapons in Chenforce were the antiproton cannons in Michi's heavy squadron. He couldn't command them, and they were already heavily committed in knocking down enemy missiles.

"Message to Flag," he told Falana. "Transports are not maneuverable. Suggest hitting them with antiproton weapons. End message."

The second kill went to Michi's heavy squadron, an enemy ship erupting in a furious burst of angry antimatter. Martinez clenched his teeth and plotted another complex missile attack.

Parts of his display fuzzed out as the squadron flew through an expanding cloud of cooling plasma. He couldn't tell where all the enemy missiles were. His heart boomed inside the confined space of his helmet, and his gloved hands dug into the padded armrests of the couch.

He launched his own missiles into the murk. He launched another barrage against the transports. He launched countermissiles against an enemy barrage that he could barely detect in all the fuzz. He launched countermissiles against a barrage he couldn't see but somehow knew was there.

The enveloping plasma cooled and thinned, and his tactical display glowed with the glorious sight of his own missile striking home.

He watched as three enemy ships were engulfed in silent flame. His heart shrieked with triumphant joy and he raised a clenched fist against the gravities that were pinning him to the couch.

"Three for us!" he shouted. *"Three for us!"*

Hardly immortal words, but at least they had the virtue of sincerity.

He'd just incinerated a neat thirty percent of the enemy squadron facing him, and that would make killing the rest a lot easier.

And he'd scored higher than Sula and Michi, who had only picked off one apiece.

Martinez plotted another series of strikes and sent them on their way.

Things were improving.

*T*wo. Squadron 17's missiles had found a second Naxid warship, now a bright, hot expanding sphere of plasma as its supplies of antimatter fuel and munitions went up.

Lovely, Sula thought. Another star.

She sought through the radio murk for another target. Orders flashed to missile batteries. Missiles leapt off the rails.

It wasn't enough to shoot missiles at an enemy, she thought. You had to shoot at the enemy's neighbors as well, so missile defenses couldn't combine to aid your real target. You had to keep every defense laser busy—*more* than busy. Overwhelmed.

Her attack raced away.

She was busy trying to coordinate the defenses against another massive strike by the converted transports when an enormous plasma bloom flared on her virtual display.

"What's *that*?" she said aloud, and refocused her attention.

One of the giant transports had just blown up. Massive amounts of antimatter had detonated, and the hot expanding plasma sphere was engulfing other ships.

Sula wondered how it had happened. There was no indication that any loyalist missile had even gotten close.

There were no secondary explosions, so it appeared that none of the other transports were destroyed. But flying through a furious bombardment of gamma rays, energetic neutrons, and blazing plasma couldn't have done the other squadron elements any good.

The huge converted ships stopped firing. They began to lumber through a series of evasive maneuvers.

Something had them frightened. Sula sent a pack of missiles after them to keep up the scare.

More missiles splashed white fire against the night. An enemy warship flared and died, leaving two other ships isolated.

She picked them as her next targets and began to plot her attack.

Michi must have followed his suggestion, Martinez thought. One of her antiproton beams must have destroyed one of the converted transports. None of the missiles had gotten close, but a lucky hit with the antiprotons must have hit an antimatter store.

Or an even luckier shot had hit a missile just as it was being launched, and set it and every other missile off within a fraction of a second.

He fired a salvo of missiles at the big Naxid ships, just to see if he could keep their luck consistent.

He picked one of the enemy warships in the opposing

squadron and ordered it to become the center of Squadron 31's attention. The entire squadron began moving toward the target, firing missiles as it went, and moving within the larger vector to the purposeful bob and weave of the Martinez Method.

Martinez was nudging the enemy. The Naxids had starburst and their response was uncoordinated, and he wanted to drive them farther apart and make them even less coordinated. But he couldn't simply fly into the middle of the Naxids, because then they could throw missiles at him from all sides. He could put his head only so far into the noose. What he had to do was threaten in one direction and then another, wedge the Naxids apart without committing himself in any one direction.

It was a delicate and subtle task. If only the ammunition supply held out.

He scanned the display. Elsewhere in the battle, the last huge barrage of the converted transports was being dealt with by coordinated antimissile defenses. Michi and her opposite number were involved in a furious duel, and it looked as if Michi was gaining the upper hand.

Sula's squadron, he saw, was threading its way through plasma bursts, striving always to fly through the oldest, coolest bursts in order to keep from completely blinding itself. Sula was in the process of isolating a pair of enemy ships and destroying them.

He looked at the enemy and saw what was probably an unintended pattern in the squadron that faced Sula. If she moved now, if she moved *immediately* with her entire squadron, she could detach a second pair of enemy while still keeping the first pair isolated.

Martinez considered sending Sula a message to that effect. He could imagine her scorning the message on its arrival. He could imagine the contemptuous response that would burn across the intervening space between their ships.

But she had to do it *now*. It would make a difference.

He was stumbling through his message, which he

planned to illustrate with a frozen three-dimensional image of the battle with some hand-drawn arrows added, when he saw that Sula was beginning the movement on her own. She'd seen the opening.

"Cancel that message, Lieutenant Falana," Martinez said. Sula was doing just fine on her own.

As usual.

His own wedging was working. He isolated one enemy ship and hammered it till it vanished in a flash of plasma fire. He began moving to drive another wedge between a pair of enemy and the rest of the Naxid squadron.

At that point the squadron of converted transports fired again. The two Naxids that had been engulfed in the plasma storm from the destroyed ship failed to fire, but the remaining barrage was formidable enough, and it occupied much of his attention for the next several minutes.

When he next had the opportunity to view the battle, he saw that Sula and her entire squadron had vanished into a colossal fireball.

She had miscalculated. She had killed two of the enemy and then shifted the squadron's center of mass toward a part of the oncoming plasma wall that she expected to cool and thin by the time she arrived, giving them all better sight lines of the enemy. But a salvo of Naxid missiles came racing out of a hotter part of the plasma wall and was hit by counterfire right in her path. She was flying toward a blazing hot, opaque, expanding sphere, and before long, Sula knew that she and the rest of the squadron would be blind.

Sensors from her own squadron showed nothing but a flaming hot wall in her path, but *Confidence* was still receiving sensor feeds from the other squadrons and the pinnaces. The feeds showed no threat, but any perspective on the engagement had its blind spots, and in any case the situation could change quickly.

Sula felt a growing obsession about the blind spots. She fired a volley of missiles into the hot spot anyway, in hope they would fly through the hash and find and locate any enemy missiles that might be about to plunge into the cloud from the other side.

Right. Fat chance.

For a moment she considered a starburst—a *real* starburst, each ship clawing for maximum distance from the others. That would reduce the chance of them all being hammered while cloaked in the plasma sphere, but on emerging they would have surrendered any advantages that Ghost Tactics gave them.

No, she thought. Just try to get to the other side *fast*.

She ordered all ships to blast through the plasma sphere at acceleration of ten gravities. The acceleration began as soon as they entered the plasma. *Confidence* groaned as the weight came on. An invisible hand began to close on her throat. She watched the radiation readings rise, and the hull temperature with them.

Darkness encroached on her vision. She felt the pillow press over her face. Perhaps she cried out.

An instant later the darkness seemed to fade. She was floating in her harness. A persistent, irritating tone sounded in her headphones. She tasted iron on her tongue.

"I have command of the ship," said a voice. Belatedly she recognized it as that of First Lieutenant Haz.

Someone touched her arm, her throat. She flailed at him.

"Are you all right, my lady?" There was an edge of panic in Ikuhara's voice.

Sula pushed him away. She heard the twanging sound as he rebounded off the bars of her acceleration cage.

"Display!" she called. "Cancel virtual!"

The limitless space of the virtual display was replaced by the soft lights and close confines of Command. Ikuhara, clumsy in his vac suit, floated over her couch. His face was a mirror of concern mingled with a touch of fear.

Something dark floated in the air between them, something round and shiny like little marbles.

"What the hell's going on?" Sula demanded.

"Acceleration canceled," Ikuhara said. "Health risk to an officer."

At quarters the state of the crew was constantly monitored by detectors in their sensor caps. Any threat to the health of the crew—any cerebral hemorrhage, blood pressure spike, or heart malfunction—was monitored, and action taken in accordance with a preset program. If enlisted crew stroked out during a battle or even an exercise, it was usually the pulpy's hard luck; but a threat to an officer could shut down the engines.

"Who was it?" Sula said. She'd have him off her ship the second they could shuttle the invalid away to a nice safe desk job, preferably on the most distant planet available.

Ikuhara's expression suggested that he was suffering some gastroenteric malady. "You, my lady," he said. "Your blood pressure was extremely high and—"

"Right," Sula said. "Get back on your couch, I'm fine now."

"You have a nosebleed, my lady."

She put a hand to her nose and felt the wet. A blob of blood detached itself from her nose and joined the others in the air, a formation of perfect spheres. She could taste the blood running—floating—down the back of her throat.

"I'll deal with it," she said. She looked at the displays before her. "Haz!" she cried.

"Yes, my lady."

"Light the engines! What is this *insanity* about cutting the engines completely during a battle, for all's sake?"

She groped for a tissue in the necessity bag webbed to the couch.

"It was programmed, my lady."

"Engine startup in fifteen, my lady," said Engineer First Class Markios.

"Accelerate at three gravities." Sula jammed a tissue to her nose.

"I am in command, my lady," Haz said in her ear. "Your blood pressure is still—"

"It isn't, and you're not," Sula said. "Three gravities, Engines."

"Yes, my lady," Markios said smoothly.

She enlarged her biomonitor display and saw that her blood pressure was returning rapidly to something like normal. Her heart rattled in her chest with fear, but at least it wasn't in the process of giving her a stroke.

This had happened to her once before, at First Magaria. There might, she thought with a burning resentment, be something wrong with her heart or its wiring that would make it impossible for her to stand high gees.

Make it impossible to do her job.

The engines caught and snarled. The droplets of blood in the air fell like hail, and spattered the breast of her vac suit.

Gravities swung Sula's couch through a series of decreasing arcs. Her blood pressure elevated slightly with the gravities, but within acceptable limits.

Other lights flashed on her display. She enlarged them and saw a big radiation spike, then another.

Somewhere in the radio darkness of the plasma bubble, missiles were finding targets.

Martinez held his breath. Only six of the nine ships belonging to Light Squadron 17 had flown out of the great furnace of plasma and sundered matter that had concealed them for several nerve-wringing minutes. A glance at the shifting sphere dictated by the Martinez Method showed gaps in the formation. Sula seemed to have lost a third of her command.

He wondered if Sula had been lost along with them.

And then a seventh ship flew out of the great dissipating bubble. The others regrouped, adjusting their formation to their new number, arranging around the late arrival like a flock of angry geese around an injured comrade.

Martinez sent out orders. He had isolated a pair of enemy and had them ready for the kill, but now he ordered Squadron 31 to shift in the other direction, toward Sula's squadron and the enemy they were engaging. He wasn't going to let the Naxids take advantage of the disorder in her squadron.

The Naxids seemed startled by this unexpected movement, and scattered before his advance. The two ships he'd cut off were too isolated to take advantage of their sudden reprieve.

Squadron 17, once it had resumed its formation, made a similar movement, toward him. It had likewise cut off a pair of enemy, and likewise ignored them.

Martinez and Sula now found themselves with scattered enemy between their two fires. The two loyalist squadrons moved, dodged, fired. It was as if, without communicating with one another, they were moving in accordance with some higher version of Sula's formula, one that encompassed the whole battle.

Martinez felt a stream of astonishment and delight. It was as if he and Sula were reading one another's minds.

The ships darted like swallows.

Sula *had* to be alive, he thought. No one else had the kind of genius that so thoroughly complimented his own.

The combat was like a ballet.

It was like telepathy.

It was like great sex.

Naxid ships flamed and died. The few that remained were scattered, and the loyalists could pick them off whenever they wanted.

Only the converted transports and the squadron facing Michi was still putting up resistance. Michi was fighting the Naxid heavy cruisers, better armed and better able to defend themselves, and though she'd destroyed four of them, she'd lost two of her own.

"Message to Captain Tantu," Martinez said. "Take Division One and go after the converted transports. End message."

Division 1 was four ships, including the two light cruisers. Division 2 was five frigates, including *Courage,* and he was going to take it to Michi's relief.

After expressing brief thanks for having at least half of his old command back, Tantu ordered his ships into a heavy acceleration for the transports, regrouping into a separate Martinez Method formation as he went.

Martinez swung his own five ships away from Sula's squadron, rolling down on the Naxid heavies. Joy danced in his heart as he saw Sula detach four of her own ships and roll away from him with the remaining three, coming to Michi's aid.

The Naxid heavies didn't last long, attacked from three directions and by superior numbers. After that, ignoring the few Naxid warships that still danced around the perimeter of the fight, all of Chenforce went after the converted transports with everything they had.

The big ships didn't last long either, particularly once they'd starburst. They were configured for offense, and their defensive abilities left a lot to be desired. In addition, Michi's antiproton cannon kept blowing big chunks off them.

After that, the remaining Naxid warships were hunted down, one after another, and dispatched.

An anthem of triumph began to thunder in Martinez's veins.

Chenforce had lost four ships to the enemy's forty. His Squadron 31 had lost none.

In the course of the war, in the battles in which he'd either commanded a squadron or had an influence on the tactics, he had lost only one ship, at Protipanu.

He was as proud of that as of the victories themselves.

He didn't count Second Magaria, where his advice had been ignored.

Tork could have that one, if he wanted it.

Before the last sphere of plasma had cooled and dispersed, Michi called for a simultaneous conference between herself and Chandra, Martinez, and Sula.

Michi and Chandra looked weary but exultant in their

virtual images, sagging in their vac suits but glowing with victory.

Sula appeared spattered with blood.

Martinez looked at her in shock. He remembered her appearance in bloody body armor after the Battle of the High City, and wondered if she'd decided to specialize in dramatic entrances.

"Are you all right, Lady Sula?" Michi asked.

"Yes. I had a nosebleed under high gee."

Sula's tone was curt and dismissive. Michi changed the subject.

"I need a report from all ships on the number of remaining missiles. I need to know if we can fight those three enemy ships that just entered the system."

"I happen to have the figures," Sula said. "My ships' magazines average nine percent of full capacity."

"My ships range between three and six percent," Michi said. Her gaze flickered to Martinez. "And Squadron Thirty-one?"

"Ah," Martinez said, "I'll check. But I don't suppose our numbers are much better."

Michi looked grim. "If those three big ships are like the others, they'll be able to fire off six hundred missiles in each salvo."

That, Martinez thought, was going to make fighting them very difficult indeed.

Stupid to die, fighting a trio of improvised warships, just because you're at the end of your logistical tether and you don't have anything to shoot at them.

"My lady," he said, "may I suggest that you make your surrender demand extremely convincing?"

Determination crossed Michi's face. "Yes," she said. "I'll make it clear that if we're fired on, Naxas burns. We've got enough missiles for *that*." She looked at someone off-camera—presumably Chandra, because Chandra also looked off-camera.

"I'll want a list of the twenty-five largest cities on Naxas," Michi said.

"Yes, my lady."

"Better make it fifty. And I'd like demographic data as well, so we can be sure to pay special attention to smoking any Naxid neighborhoods."

Chandra hid a smile. "Yes, my lady."

Michi's demand for unconditional surrender went out in the clear, both to Naxas and to the oncoming ships. It would be nearly three hours before Naxas could reply. Chenforce took aboard its surviving pinnaces, recovered the few missiles that hadn't yet found something to blow up, and began repairing the minor damage taken by some of the ships in the fight.

Martinez took a shower to wash off the scent of his suit seals and invited Captain Dalkeith to a celebratory dinner. That seemed fair, since after all he was dining in her cabin.

"I wish I had your cook," Dalkeith said in her breathless child's voice. She looked at the black specks in her fluffy scrambled eggs, which Perry had laid on a bed of fragrant preserved seaweed. "Are those truffles?"

Martinez didn't know.

He was back in Auxiliary Command at the earliest possible moment that Naxas could reply. No answer came, not even an acknowledgment.

Minutes ticked by. The air in Auxiliary Command began to seem hot and close. The bodies of the crew, liberated from the confines of vac suits, combined to give the room a sour, combusted scent, all save Khanh, who wore far too much lime-scented cologne.

Martinez heard chatter in the background as Chandra gave the weapons officers targeting information for the fifty largest cities of Naxas. He thought about how to fight those three big ships with their limitless supply of ammunition.

"Squadcom wants another conference, my lord." Falana's fingers jabbed at the touch pads on his display.

"I'll go virtual."

The same three faces appeared in the display. Michi and Chandra looked scrubbed and refreshed, but Martinez didn't spare them more than a glance. Instead he stared at Sula. She was breathtaking—beautiful and polished and perfect. She wore understated Fleet undress, and the dark sensor cap and its chin strap framed her face and made it seem to glow. Suddenly he could scent a phantom memory of her perfume.

"I've given them an hour," Michi said. Her angry voice snapped Martinez out of his trance. "I think that's enough. We'll launch our missiles for Naxas. Time the impacts for a hundred twenty minutes from now, so they can see it coming at them and have time to think about it."

"That will give them extra time to evacuate their cities," Chandra pointed out.

"The living will envy the dead," Sula said. Her voice was hard.

Martinez looked at her again, and wondered where that cold anger had come from. He knew her anger well enough, but he remembered it as hot. He remembered her as insecure, as clumsy in formal situations, as passionate in bed.

Clearly she had learned a few new social strategies.

"My lord!" Falana cried. "Message from Naxas!"

The others must have been alerted at the same time, because they were all gazing off-camera.

"Let's see it," Martinez said.

His virtual space was invaded by the image of a young Naxid. He wore the brown tunic of the civil servant, and he stood alone and faced the camera with frozen dignity.

"To Squadron Commander Chen," he said, "greetings. I am Lord Ami Yramox, Secretary to the Assistant Minister of Right and Dominion, Lady Rundak."

Secretary to an assistant minister, Martinez thought. Yramox lived pretty far down the chain of command to reply to an ultimatum as crucial as Michi's.

"All my superiors have committed suicide," Yramox

said. "Before their deaths they instructed me to surrender to you all forces under the command of the Naxas government. We await your orders."

The Naxid spoke on, but he was drowned by the cheers now ringing from the walls of Auxiliary Command. Even Gunderson, who throughout the battle had spoken with a deliberate, sonorous calm, was bellowing with undisguised joy.

Michi and Chandra were glancing left and right, off-camera, smiling, apparently enjoying a similar frenzied demonstration in the Flag Officer Station.

Sula remained cool, gazing at the camera with her jade eyes. Apparently there was no spontaneous shouting permitted in her control room.

A few hours later, when orders from Naxas reached the new arrivals, the three big Naxid ships began firing their missile batteries, hundreds and then thousands of missiles racing into the void. When they reached a safe distance, they exploded, a long series of bright expanding detonations, like fireworks celebrating the end of a long, bloody war.

THIRTY-SIX

There were a few hours for rejoicing, just enough time for the cooks to produce a feast and for the crew to drink to their own survival and that of their mates. The recreation tubes were very much in demand. Martinez dined with the officers of *Courage* while Alikhan packed his belongings, then he formally surrendered command of Squadron 31, and with it, his acting rank of squadron commander.

He sent a farewell message to his captains, praising their record of enemy killed without a single casualty, then said good-bye to Dalkeith and the other lieutenants. He arrived aboard *Illustrious* to the usual formalities. The corridors echoed to the same sort of celebrations he'd just left. The party was just getting started when alarms began to blare, and everyone strapped in for more hours of heavy gee. In order to stay in the Naxas system and avoid shooting off into space, Chenforce had to lose delta vee, and that meant more days of bone-hammering deceleration.

This was clearly unfair. The crews resented the fact that they'd just won the war but had to endure the heavy gees anyway.

Martinez resented it too. He had just enough time to visit his cabin—he found the Holy Family undisturbed, still snug with their cat and their fire—and then he had to don his vac suit.

Around them, as the gravities pressed the crew deeper into their couches, the peace began to take shape. The Fleet and the Convocation had worked out a plan ahead of time.

Non-Naxid officials who—the last anyone heard—had been on Naxas were ordered by Michi to take command of the government, provided they hadn't accepted jobs in the rebel administration. A disturbingly large percentage of them had and were disqualified. The remainder were not always the pick of the crop, but would have to serve till new administrators were sent out from Zanshaa.

The Naxids seemed to accept the situation quietly, which was certainly lucky for those who so unexpectedly found themselves in charge. The presence of three squadrons armed with dozens of missiles seemed a good recipe for social order, and those most likely to lead a resistance had just committed suicide.

The three Naxid converted warships, traveling too fast to decelerate completely, were ordered to proceed through one of Naxas's wormholes, dock at another system, and surrender themselves there. Michi didn't want them in the Naxas system, where they might tempt some unreconstructed Naxid into a misadventure.

A consequence of the sudden victory was that all the wormhole stations were suddenly open. For the first time in a year and a half, nearly all parts of the empire were in communication with one another, the communication lines broken only here and there where a wormhole station had been blasted out of existence.

Michi sent a brief report to Tork through the wormhole relay, the text wrapped in the Fleet's most elaborate code in case the Naxids were inclined to eavesdrop. It mentioned the bare facts of the battle—victory, a loss of four warships for thirty-eight enemy, a friendly government soon to be in place—but carefully avoided any details, such as the dire lack of ammunition.

A more candid report went to Tork via the more secure method of a relativistic missile, with another missile going to the Fleet Control Board. These reports featured a complete record of the fighting as well as a statement concerning the perilous state of the ammunition supply.

Because there were two reports, Michi received two replies. The first, which arrived fifty-odd hours after she flashed off the original brief report, featured equally brief congratulations. The message was in text, signed by a staff officer.

The second message, which flashed into the system on the back of a relativistic missile, was a video from Tork himself. Michi called off the squadron's acceleration, then summoned Martinez to her office to view it.

Ligaments creaking in the reduced gravity, Martinez came to her office and braced. Michi sagged wearily in her chair, a cup of coffee before her. The half-nude bronze statues towered over her. The strain of days of high gee lined her face, and there was something else as well, sadness and a kind of defeat.

"This concerns you," Michi said, "and in a burst of cowardice I decided that you'd better get the news from Tork and not from me."

"You've seen it?"

"Yes. Sit down."

Michi's servant Vandervalk was already pouring coffee. Martinez thanked her, sat, and took the cup. The coffee's sharp scent bit the back of his throat.

A pall enshrouded his mind. This wasn't going to be good.

Michi ordered the video wall to show Tork's message. The Supreme Commander appeared at once. He looked more healthy than Martinez had recently seen him—his skin was a healthier shade of gray, and no strips of dead flesh hung from his face. He was out of his body cast and dressed in a viridian dress uniform covered with more silver braid than Martinez had ever seen. Around Tork's narrow throat was a ribbon on which hung a simple gold disk.

"They gave him the *Orb*?" Martinez blurted.

Tork gazed from the wall without expression. "To Squadron Commander Chen, greetings," he said in bell-like tones. "Your full report has been received, along with your request for additional missiles. I can spare no missiles here, but will order as many as I can from elsewhere in the empire and inform your command when you may expect their arrival."

Can spare no missiles, Martinez thought. Who was Tork planning on shooting his damned missiles *at*?

"As you can see," Tork continued, "the Convocation has awarded me the Golden Orb for the recapture of Zanshaa and the victory at Magaria, and they have also honored me by making permanent my rank as Supreme Commander."

Which explained where all the braid came from. Martinez suppressed an urge to spit on the floor, and sipped his coffee instead.

"As one of my first acts," Tork said, "I will establish a Committee of Inquiry to analyze the tactical lessons of the war and to prepare a series of recommendations for the Fleet. This committee will be chaired by Fleet Commander Pezzini and will be headquartered at the Commandery in Zanshaa."

That figured, Martinez thought. Pezzini was a retired fleetcom, a Control Board member who had never seen a missile fired in anger.

Tork continued. His voice was a melodious chime.

"I therefore order Captain Sula, Captain Martinez, and Squadron Commander Chen to report at once to Zanshaa and place themselves at the disposal of the committee. *Illustrious* and *Confidence* will go into dock at Zanshaa for routine refit. Lady Michi's command will remain at Naxas under Captain Carmody, who is promoted Acting Squadron Leader. You will find the text of these orders in an attached file."

Martinez stared at Tork's image in shock. *He's taking my ship away?*

Ships that went into refit were turned over to dock superintendents and lost their officers and crew.

The harmonies of Tork's voice were implacable. "Because it would be premature to release any information regarding the battles, or the tactics employed, prior to the report of the committee, I must classify all this information as Highly Sequestered. Any publication or discussion of these matters will be deemed a violation of the Imperial Sequestration Edict and subject to prosecution.

"You will acknowledge receipt of these orders and proceed at once to Zanshaa."

There was a highlight to Tork's chiming voice that Martinez suspected was Daimong triumph.

It was all going to be hidden away, Martinez thought. The conclusions of the committee were foreordained. Innovations were a wrong path, and the orthodox tactics with which Tork had captured Magaria were going to be enshrined. Michi's victories would be explained away or forgotten.

He could imagine already what the committee would say about Naxas. It wasn't a real battle, it was fought against patched-together converted traders and warships heavily damaged at Magaria. Of *course* it was one-sided. Under the circumstances, Michi Chen was criminally negligent for losing as many as four ships.

He turned to Michi. "What do we do?" he asked.

Michi's look was matter-of-fact. "We obey orders."

"And then?"

Michi considered the question for a half a second or so, then said, "We wait for Tork to die."

"You could talk to Lord Chen. He's on the Fleet Control Board."

She nodded. "I'll talk to Maurice, of course. But in order for him to reverse an order by the Supreme Commander, he'd need a majority of votes on the board, and I don't think he'll get them. Anything he attempts on our behalf will just look like special pleading on behalf of his relatives." She pushed a plate toward him. "Almond cookie?"

Furious anger raged in Martinez. He put down his coffee cup before he crushed it in his hand.

"We can demand a court-martial," he said.

"On what grounds?" Michi drummed her fingertips on

the desk. "We're not being sent to jail or ordered to cut our throats. We're not being punished or reprimanded. That would cause a public outcry, and Tork doesn't want that. All that's happening is that we're being sent to Zanshaa in order to testify before an elite commission."

"I'm losing my ship," Martinez pointed out.

"A routine refit."

Martinez waved an arm. "There's nothing routine about it! There are dozens of ships damaged in battle that should go into dock before *Illustrious*! And we're ordered to dock in Zanshaa—the Zanshaa ring is a *wreck*. We *blew it up*! It will be *years* before the ship gets out of dock."

Michi looked down at the black, mirrored surface of her desk. "But there will be other ships. Many, many more. The Fleet's building program won't end with the war— Maurice told me that in a few years the Fleet will be nearly twice its size at the start of the war."

Martinez rubbed his chin and felt the bristles that had grown while he was webbed to his acceleration couch. "There will be plenty of ships," he said. "Fine. But will Tork give us command of any of them?"

Irony touched the corners of Michi's lips. "At least we'll have seniority over those he favors."

Martinez looked up at the bronze woman who was gazing down at him with eerie composure. He wanted to rise from his chair and punch the perfect, serene face.

"Have you told Captain Sula?" he asked.

"No. Though she may have intercepted the message and decoded it herself. Why?"

"Because," Martinez said, "once she hears Tork's orders, I wouldn't want to put her in the same solar system with Tork and a missile."

Sula's reaction to Tork's orders was far from violent. She had known that Tork would retaliate for her defiance at Second Magaria, and she was surprised only at Tork's moderation. He hadn't ordered her throat cut; he hadn't issued so much as a reprimand. She decided this was a measure of how weak Tork felt his own position to be.

If there was one thing she understood, it was the calculations of survival. Tork had killed forty or so enemy ships while losing forty ships of his own. Chenforce had killed nearly forty and lost only four.

Were the facts made available, Tork's ability would be called into question. In order to justify his Golden Orb and his new permanent rank, the inconvenient data had to be suppressed.

The only surprise was the ingenuity of Tork's response. He was a more subtle manipulator of the machinery of the Fleet than she'd thought.

After viewing his message, Sula took advantage of the break in deceleration to shower. As the water hammered her sore, gravity-torn muscles, and as the tiny metal-walled shower cabinet filled with the sandalwood scent of the translucent soap, she considered her future.

She had captain's rank, and captain was higher than she had ever expected to rise. She had her medals. She had a modest fortune.

She didn't have an army any longer. And very soon she would not have a ship.

She possessed fame, but didn't particularly want it. Increased fame could lead to increased scrutiny, and someone with her past couldn't afford that. Perhaps a few years in an obscure posting would be the safest alternative.

On the whole, she had little to complain about.

She had defied Lord Tork not out of a desire for glory, but out of pride. Her accomplishments were genuine. Her pride had not been compromised. Her pride was still alive. Tork could do nothing to take it away.

She had done well enough out of the war.

Then she paused in her scrubbing, thought of Martinez, and smiled. He was not the sort of person who would take Tork's orders quietly.

He must be going crazy.

* * *

"**Y**ou may not say that we won. You may not say that we destroyed the enemy at a ratio of ten to one. You may not say that we deployed superior tactics, or that any superior tactics even exist. These facts are to be forgotten until Pezzini's report is released—*if* it's ever released. And you must tell your crew that they may not speak of these things either. We don't want any of them to get in trouble."

Martinez looked at his officers and saw their surprise at his vehemence. He forced a smile.

"I want to assure you that the Supreme Commander is very serious about this. The Investigative Service will look into anyone found to be careless with this information." He gave them all a solemn look. "Careers may be at stake. I don't want to jeopardize any of your advancement through my failure to emphasize the absolute nature of Lord Tork's orders."

He picked up his fork. "Now that I've got these unpleasant preliminaries out of the way, let's enjoy our meal. I believe that Perry has done something brilliant with this tenderloin."

The others ate thoughtfully as they sat beneath the murals of roistering ancients. Martinez had given them plenty to think about.

And to talk about. He knew there was no better advertisement for a subject than forbidding it to be mentioned. Lord Tork's orders—at least as interpreted by him—would naturally offend the pride of every member of Chenforce. When *Illustrious* and *Courage* discharged their crews, and officers and enlisted made their way to new postings, they would take their offended pride with them.

It was ridiculous to command them not to talk about their accomplishments. They would talk in wardrooms over dinner, in drawing rooms over cocktails, and drunkenly in bars. They would boast of their time with Chenforce, of their service under Michi Chen and Martinez, of their own prowess.

They would not let the memory of Chenforce die.

Martinez had also made a point of giving his lecture while the servants were still putting plates on the tables, thus ensuring that the enlisted would also carry their full measure of indignation throughout the Fleet.

There were certain things that Tork could not do. He could not put a number of Peers of the empire under surveillance to make sure they weren't speaking of their wartime experience, nor punish them when they did. He couldn't follow the hundreds of enlisted as they moved through the expanded Fleet, or prosecute them en masse, or even discharge them. They too would carry the legend of Chenforce wherever they went.

Sometimes, Martinez reflected, the best way to sabotage a superior was to follow his orders in the most perfectly literal way.

Martinez's dinner with his officers was the first of several social events after the long, brutal deceleration finally ended, with Chenforce diving through the rings of a gas giant gorgeous with velvet-soft clouds of purple and green, then shaping a new course at a far more moderate deceleration. *Illustrious* and *Confidence* wouldn't have to part from the rest of Chenforce for three more days, and during that time there was constant visitation back and forth. Michi played host to a reception for the captains during which, through heroic effort, Martinez and Sula managed not to exchange a single word. Sula invited Michi to a dinner in her honor, and since Martinez hadn't been invited to accompany, he in turn invited his former captains from Squadron 31. He gave them much the same speech he had given his lieutenants, and with much the same effect.

The final day, Michi gave a farewell dinner for the captains of Cruiser Squadron 9, in which she thanked them for their loyalty, their courage, and their friendship, and raised a glass to their next meeting. Martinez, who sat at the far end of the table quivering with the barely suppressed impulse to deliver another tirade on the subject of Tork's order, thought he saw a tear glimmering in her eye.

Illustrious and *Confidence* set a new course and began their acceleration toward Naxas Wormhole 1 en route to Magaria and Zanshaa. Martinez braced for the inevitable, which came two days later when Michi invited him and Sula to supper.

Michi and Martinez met Sula at the airlock, where a guard of honor rendered the proper formalities as Sula stepped onto *Illustrious*. She wore full dress, the dark green of the tunic a subdued reflection of the emerald green of her eyes. The sight took Martinez's breath away.

Sula faced the squadcom and braced; Michi shook her hand and welcomed her aboard. A tall, bushy-haired orderly hovered behind her right shoulder, a young man Martinez would have been inclined to dismiss if it weren't for the ribbon of the Medal of Valor on his breast. He was taken off to be a guest of the petty officers' mess, and Martinez and Sula followed Michi up a companionway to her quarters.

"Interesting decor," Sula said, eyeing one of the trompe l'oeil archways in the corridor.

"All installed by Captain Fletcher," Martinez said. "The artist is still aboard."

He figured she wouldn't rip his head off if he stuck to the facts.

"That was a Vigo vase in that still life," Sula remarked.

Michi glanced over her shoulder. "Are you interested in porcelain, Lady Sula?"

Which led to a discourse that took them to the dining room and into the first cocktail. Sula had a mixture of fruit juices, and the others Kyowan and Spacey. Martinez, standing with tingling tongue and feigned nonchalance by the drinks cart, felt Sula's clinical glance burn like ice on his skin.

Michi turned to Sula. "Lady Sula, I was wondering if I could review the moment in the battle when you moved your squadron to engage the enemy heavies. I have some questions about how you knew which of the enemy to choose as your particular target."

Sula explained. Illustration would make the explanation more comprehensible, so the party moved to Michi's office, where they could use the holographic display built into her desk. The tension drawn between Martinez and Sula began to ebb as they reexperienced the fantastic degree of coordination they had felt in the battle, the balance of movement and fire, subtlety and force. Sula's pale skin glowed. Her eyes danced. She looked at him and smiled. Martinez returned the gaze and found that his laughter matched hers.

The party moved back to the dining room and continued the battle while plates, bottles, and napkins were deployed on the table like ships of war. Michi and Martinez described the Battle of Protipanu, and Martinez talked about Hone-bar. Diagrams were drawn in gravy. Sula recounted her adventures on the ground in Zanshaa.

"Weren't you afraid of dealing with the cliquemen?" Michi asked.

Sula seemed to calculate her answer for a half second or so. "Not really. I'd known people like them on Spannan, where I grew up, and—" There was another moment of calculation. "Well," she said, "it's like with everyone else. You have to calculate your common interests."

Michi seemed dubious. "Weren't you afraid that they'd betray you and . . . well, just take everything?"

Sula calculated again, then grinned. "Unlike good Peers like Lord Tork?"

Martinez burst into laughter. Michi's laughter was more strained.

Still, Martinez thought, Sula wasn't being completely candid about something. He wondered what it was.

The scent of coffee floated through the room. The conversation went on well past the tail end of dinner, well into the second pot of coffee. During the long course of the conversation, and with Sula's agreement, Martinez told her honor guard to stand down—she could leave the ship informally, with no inconvenience. When she thanked Michi, rose, and collected her hat and gloves from Vandervalk, Martinez offered to accompany her to the airlock.

"If you'll page Macnamara to meet me there."

Martinez did so. He walked with Sula into the corridor. It was late and nearly deserted; most crew were asleep. Their heels rapped on Fletcher's polychrome tiles.

Suddenly Martinez was afraid to speak. He was possessed of the certainty that if he opened his mouth, he'd spoil everything, all the intimacy that he and Sula had just rediscovered, and then the two would have no choice but to be enemies forever.

Sula was less shy. She gazed straightforward as she spoke, her eyes not meeting his. "I've decided to forgive you," she said.

"Forgive me?" Martinez couldn't help himself. "It was you who dumped me, remember?"

Her voice was flat. "You should have had more persistence."

She came to the companion and dropped quickly down the stair to the deck below. Martinez followed, his heart throbbing.

"You were very insistent," he said.

"I was upset."

"But why?"

That seemed the point. He had asked her to marry him, and she had refused him—with anger—and marched off into the Zanshaa night.

Sula stopped, turned, looked at him. He could see the muscles strained in her throat.

"I'm not good at relationships," she said. "I was afraid, and you wouldn't let me *be* afraid. By the time I got over the fright, you were engaged to Terza Chen."

"My brother arranged that without telling me." He hesitated, then spoke. "I called you all night."

She stared at him for a blank second, then reeled as if he'd struck her.

"I was upset," she said. "I was—" She shook her golden head. "Never mind what I was doing. I told the comm to refuse all calls."

They stared at each other for a long moment. Martinez felt as if an iron hand had seized his vitals and twisted them. It was like losing her all over again.

"I . . . forgive you," he said.

He took a step toward her, but she had already turned and was walking away, heading for the next companion. Martinez followed.

At the bottom of the stair her orderly waited, properly braced. The airlock door was only a few paces away. The words that were on the verge of spilling from Martinez's tongue dried up.

Sula turned and held out her hand. "Thank you, Captain," she said. "I'll see you again."

He took her hand. It was small and elegant and warm in his ungainly paw. Her musky perfume caressed his senses, and his nerves leaped with the impulse to kiss her.

"Sleep well, my lady," he said.

And dream of me . . .

That night Sula dreamed of nothing but the dead. She woke after a few hours with a scream bottled in her throat, and knew that she didn't dare rest again.

She used her captain's key to open *Confidence*'s databanks and edited out all references to the blood pressure spike that had shut down the engines during the Naxas battle. Instead she blamed the engine trip on a power spike in a transformer, a spike caused by radiation from a near miss. The transformer was scheduled to be replaced anyway.

There were anomalies in the cover story, and there would be her footprints in the record, but it would take a fair amount of detective work to find them, and she suspected that no one would ever be that interested.

The whole point of the elite commission, after all, was to bury everything that had happened on *Confidence*. She doubted anyone would look at the official records.

She resolutely refused to think of Martinez as she worked, and did her best to ignore a prickling of her neck hairs that told her he was standing right behind her, looking over her shoulder as she committed a lengthy string of electronic felonies.

I've done worse, Sula told the specter.

Martinez, she thought, strolled through life profiting from the death and misfortune of others.

She, on the other hand, was the *bringer* of death and misfortune. Make the two of them a couple, and the implications were chilling.

If we are ever together, she thought with a shiver, *one or both of us will die.*

She sent the revised database to bed. It was over an hour to breakfast, and she was still afraid to sleep. She sat up reading *The Greening of Africa,* another of her Earth histories.

She still felt Martinez standing behind her, silent and reproachful as the dead.

Martinez spoke to each of his staff in turn to find out if they were willing to stay with him after *Illustrious* went into refit. He was allowed to take servants with him from one posting to the next, but he wanted to make certain they were willing.

Alikhan accepted, as Martinez had hoped he would. He knew that Narbonne, Fletcher's formet valet, didn't like being Alikhan's junior, and he wasn't surprised when Narbonne asked for a discharge.

Montemar Jukes was more problematical. "I don't think I'm going to need an artist after this," Martinez said. "I won't have a ship to decorate."

Jukes shrugged. "I can save those plans for another day, my lord. But on Zanshaa you'll have a palace, won't you,

Lord Captain? You and your lady? And won't that palace need decorating? Perhaps with a full-length portrait of Lady Terza to match the one of yourself."

"Ah . . . perhaps," Martinez said. He didn't want to admit to himself that a future without Terza was a possibility that lurked somewhere in the back of his mind.

Jukes remained on his payroll, and began contemplating themes for the decoration of a large house.

The surprise was the cook, Perry.

"I'd like to request a discharge, my lord," he said.

Martinez looked in surprise at the young man standing opposite his desk.

"Is there something wrong?" he asked.

"No, my lord. It's just that . . . well, I'd like to strike out on my own."

Martinez regarded him narrowly. "There *is* something wrong, isn't there?"

Perry hesitated. "Well, my lord," he admitted, "sometimes I wonder if you actually like my cooking."

Martinez was astonished. "What do you mean?" he said. "I eat it, don't I?"

"Yes, Lord Captain. But—" Perry strove for words. "You don't pay attention to the food. You're always working while you're eating, or sending messages on the comm, or dealing with reports."

"I'm a busy man," Martinez said. "I'm a captain, for all's sake."

Determination settled across Perry's expression. "My lord," he said, "do you even remember what you ate for your noon meal?"

Martinez searched briefly through his memory. "It was the thing with the cheese," he said, "wasn't it?"

Perry gave a little sigh. "Yes, my lord," he said. "The thing with the cheese."

Martinez looked at him. "I'll give you the discharge if you want," he said, "but—"

"Yes, please," said Perry. "Thank you, my lord."

Feeling slighted, Martinez wrote Perry an excellent reference, in part so he could feel superior to the whole situation.

That evening, at his meal, he looked at his plate with a degree of suspicion.

What was so special about it? he asked himself.

Sula gave a dinner to thank Michi for her own dinner party, and Martinez, Chandra, and Fulvia Kazakov were invited. Martinez would have been the sole male at the affair if it hadn't been for Haz, Sula's premiere.

Sula's dining room on *Confidence* was metal-walled and painted a pale, sad shade of green. An overhead duct was a hazard to anyone tall. She had tried to make light of it by painting *DUCK!* on the duct in red letters. She served Hairy Rogers for cocktails, followed by wine and brandy. Martinez suspected that, as a nondrinker, her knowledge about how much alcohol people could actually consume without falling over was shaky. She was well on her way to getting everyone plastered.

Martinez sobered at the table, where he sat opposite Sula. Each cell in his body seemed to yearn toward her with every beat of his heart. He hardly dared look at her. Instead he did his best to follow the conversation, which was bright and amusing and concerned as little as possible with the war, Fleet business, or politics. The captains might be losing their ships, and all the officers might have a permanent black mark against their names for being a part of Chenforce, but the long, violent contest was over and they had all survived. Healthy animal spirits were rising, and on a pair of tubes soaring between the stars, there were only so many outlets.

Perhaps alcohol was safest, after all.

As the voyage progressed, he saw Sula frequently. There were only two ships, and the officers were social beings. Some kind of party occurred every day, though it wasn't always the captains who were involved.

Still, it was half a month before Martinez dared to invite Captain Sula to dine with him alone.

He met her at the airlock—she had a different orderly this time, a straw-haired woman, but still with a Medal of Valor. Martinez escorted Sula to his dining room, where he offered her a choice of soft drinks. She had a glass of mineral water, and Martinez, who out of courtesy to his guest had decided to avoid alcohol, had another. Sula looked at the Jukes portrait of Martinez, looking brave and dashing at the head of the room, and smiled.

"Very realistic," she said.

"Do you think so?" He was dismayed. "I'd hoped for better than that."

Sula laughed and turned her attention to the murals of banqueting Terrans, the bundles of grapes and goblets of wine and the graceful people wearing sheets.

"Very classical," she said.

"It only looks old. Let me show you another piece."

He took her into his sleeping cabin and ordered the lights on, to reveal *The Holy Family with a Cat*. Sula seemed amused at first, and then a little frown touched her lips, her eyes narrowed, and she stepped closer to the ancient work. She studied it in silence for several long minutes.

"It's telling a story," she said. "But I don't know what the story is."

"I don't either, but I like it."

"How old is this?"

"It's from before the conquest. From North Europe, wherever that is."

She gave him a sidelong glance. "Martinez, you are really appallingly ignorant of the history of your own species."

He shrugged. "Before the conquest it was all murder and barbarism, wasn't it?"

She turned once more to the painting. "Judge for yourself," she said.

He looked at the cozy little family around their fire, and a warm affection for the painting rose in him. "The picture belongs to Fletcher's estate now," he said. "I wonder if they'd let me make an offer."

Sula looked at him. "Can you afford it?"

"On my allowance? Only if they don't know what it's worth."

She glanced briefly at the other pictures, the blue flute player and the landscape. "Any other treasures?"

He took her into his office. She looked without interest at the armored figures and the murals of scribes and heralds. Then her eyes were drawn downward to the desk, to the pictures of Terza and young Gareth that floated in its surface.

Martinez held his breath. The moment crucial, he thought.

The light in her eyes shifted subtly, like a wispy cloud passing across the sun. Her lips quirked in a wry smile.

"This is the Chen heir?" she said.

"Yes."

"A healthy child?"

"So I hear."

"He looks like his father."

Her eyes followed the images as they floated over the desk's surface.

"How *is* your marriage, anyway?" Her tone was delicate and light, shaded with irony. They were both pretending that she didn't care about the answer.

"It seemed to go well enough for the first seven days," Martinez said. "Since then I've been away from home."

"Seven days?" She smiled. "Fertile you."

"Fertile me," he repeated pointlessly.

He fought the impulse to take her in his arms.

Not on Michi Chen's flagship, he thought.

There was the sound of footsteps in the dining room, Alikhan bringing in the first plates of snacks.

Sula brushed past him as she walked to the dining room door.

Moment passed, he thought. Moment survived.

He followed her. Alikhan stood by the corner of the table, immaculate in dress uniform, white apron, and white gloves.

"Master Weaponer Alikhan!" Sula smiled. "How are you?"

Alikhan beamed from behind his curled mustachios. "Very well, my lady. You're looking well."

"You're very kind." She allowed Alikhan to draw out a chair for her. "What are we eating tonight?"

"I believe we're starting with a toasted rice paper packet stuffed with a filling of whipped krek-tuber, smoked crystallized sausage, and spinach."

"Sounds lovely."

Sheltered beneath Alikhan's benign presence, Martinez and Sula managed a civil, pleasant meal. The conversation remained on safe, mostly professional topics, though over dessert he finally managed to deliver an outburst on the subject of Tork. He'd had a lot of practice by now, and his diatribe was exceptionally eloquent.

Sula shrugged. "The war returned certain people to power," she said, "and they were the people who had no use for us to begin with. What did you expect? Gratitude?"

"I hadn't expected to be treated so badly."

"We both have our captain's rank, and our seniority. Even under the best of circumstances we wouldn't be promoted to squadcom for years, so we've done better than we could otherwise have expected." She sipped her coffee. "They'll need us again, for the next war."

Martinez looked at her in surprise. "You think there'll be another war?"

"How can there not be?" She flung out a hand. "The Shaa put us all in the hands of a six-hundred-member committee. How effective do you think such a group could be in running something as big and complicated as the empire?"

"Not very," Martinez said. "But they're going to have the Fleet, aren't they?"

"Maybe. But *I* think that the only thing a six-hundred-member committee can agree on is that they should all have more and more of what they've got already. In the past the Shaa kept a lid on the avarice of the lords convocate, but the Shaa are dead. I think we'll have war within a generation." She placed her coffee cup carefully in its saucer and examined it in the light. "Gemmelware," she said. "Very nice."

"Fletcher had good taste," Martinez said, "or so I'm told."

"Fletcher had good advisers." She put the saucer and its cup on the table and looked at him. "I hope you're getting good advice, Martinez."

"About porcelain? I depend entirely on your expertise."

She gazed at him for a moment, then sighed. "A lot of it hangs on what you like," she said. "You're going to have to choose."

Sula stood in her miserable metal office, looked at the pair of guns mounted on the wall behind her desk and counted the dead in her life. Caro Sula, PJ Ngeni, Casimir.

Anthony, her almost-stepfather. Richard Li, her late captain, and the entire crew of the *Dauntless*.

Lamey, her lover on Spannan, who was almost certainly dead.

Thousands of Naxids, who almost didn't count because she knew none of them personally.

Each death was a roll of the dice. Against the odds, each time she had come up a winner. For others, luck had not been so generous.

Now Martinez was coming again into her orbit, and she wondered if he realized how much danger he was in. He was the luckiest man she knew—the luckiest in the universe, she had once told him. She wondered if his luck could possibly overcome the ill luck that she seemed to carry for others.

Certain calculations could be made. Fertile Martinez

had done his duty, and sired a boy on the Chen heir. Perhaps that meant that his family were done with Martinez, at least for the present.

She wondered how Clan Martinez would take the news if Martinez were to divorce the wife he'd known for all of seven days. Clan Martinez had most of what they wanted, access to the highest levels of the High City, and a Chen heir with Martinez genes. Sula also wondered if Lord Chen would object if his parvenu son-in-law were to decamp and leave him free to marry his daughter to someone with a more suitable pedigree.

Michi Chen also figured in Sula's calculations, but she had been sent into obscurity by the Supreme Commander and had lost both her ability to reward and punish. She had become irrelevant to the situation.

Even if Clan Martinez proved an obstacle, there were other ways. Sula now knew people who specialized in such ways.

She pictured herself the perfect, doting stepmother, dandling the young Gareth on her knee, letting his tiny fingers play with her medals. Replacing the mother he barely knew, the one who had died so tragically . . .

Sula basked in that picture for a long, sunny moment, then rejected it. Bloodletting was not a suitable way to begin a new relationship. One wanted to begin with hope, not slaughter.

And besides, she never wanted to put herself in the debt of someone like Sergius Bakshi. Only the worst could come of that.

If things were to proceed, they would have to move in a more conventional fashion, with drama and rage, anger and passion, sorrow and betrayal.

With her at the center of the storm, rolling the dice and letting them fall where they would.

The two ships raced on, accelerating at a steady one gravity. Decks and walls were painted or polished. Meals were cooked and consumed. Parts were maintained and replaced on a regular schedule. Drills were held occasionally, just so the crews didn't forget how to do their jobs. For the most part life was easy.

Communication with the outside went only so far and no farther. The wormhole relay station destroyed by the Orthodox Fleet, at Bachun between Magaria and Zanshaa, had not been replaced, and neither had other stations destroyed elsewhere in the empire by Chenforce and Light Squadron 14. Communication was perfect within the part of the empire formerly held by the Naxids, and that sphere was ruled absolutely by Lord Tork, from his new headquarters at Magaria. To reach any area outside that zone a courier missile was required, and the two ships generated no news of sufficient importance to justify sending one.

The halfway point was reached, and the ships spun neatly about and began the deceleration that would take them to Zanshaa. Shortly afterward they entered the Magaria system and rendered passing honors to the Supreme Commander on the Magaria ring. A staff officer sent a routine acknowledgment, and that seemed to be that.

Until, a day later, an order was flashed from Tork's headquarters.

The message consisted of new orders for Sula. After testifying before the elite commission on Zanshaa, she was to take Fleet transport to Terra, where she would begin a term as captain of Terra's ring.

It was intended as *punishment,* Sula realized with delight. Exile for two or more years to an obscure, backwater planet, off the trade routes, which coincidentally happened to be the home of her species.

Terra. Earth. Where she could see with her own eyes the venerable cities of Byzantium, Xi'an, SaSuu. Where she could caress ancient marbles with her own hands and touch the most venerable porcelains in the empire. Where she could bathe in the oceans that had given birth to all the planet's myriad forms of life.

Where she could walk among the carved monuments of Terra's history, with the dust of kings clinging to the bottoms of her shoes.

And this was a *punishment*.

Sula could only laugh.

If Tork only knew, she thought. If he only knew.

Martinez floated through his days in a haze of calculation. Or perhaps fantasy. In the ritualized artificial worlds that were *Illustrious* and *Confidence,* it was getting hard to tell the difference.

Sula was present, and tangible, and beautiful, and he desired her. He saw her every two or three days, but they were never completely alone. If he should kiss her, or even touch her arm for too long a time, someone on the ship— Michi, Chandra, a servant—would see, and within hours everyone on board both ships would know. When they were in company, he tried to avoid looking at her, so that he would never be betrayed by a spellbound gaze.

He distrusted the sense of unreality that surrounded his current existence, and he wasn't used to doubting himself or his senses, so his doubt made him frantic. The journey from Naxas to Zanshaa was a transition from war to peace, from fame to obscurity, from duty to irresponsibility. The temptation was to forget that there would be a landing at the end, and that the landing would be more or less hard.

In his mind, he bargained with Lord Chen. "You may have your daughter," he said, "for use as a pawn in whatever unspeakable political games you next wish to play. In exchange you and your sister will continue to support my career in the Fleet—that's only fair, I think you'll agree.

"And one other thing," he added, "I must have the child."

This fantasy, or calculation, or whatever it was, seemed perfectly reasonable, until he found himself at his desk and looked down at the floating images of Terza and his son, and then it seemed madness.

Sula had walked out on him twice. Giving her a third chance seemed the height of lunacy.

Then he would see her at dinner or a reception, and the fever would kindle again in his blood.

Illustrious flashed through Magaria Wormhole 1 and left Tork's isolated sphere. All the accumulated news, mail, and video communications from the outside arrived, and met the fantasy head-on.

There were dozens of messages from Terza, ranging from electronic facsimiles of brief handwritten notes to videos of herself with Young Gareth. When Terza spoke to the camera, the infant turned his head to look for the person who was so occupying his mother's attention, and was visibly puzzled to find no one there. Martinez was completely charmed.

I must have the child.

The one non-negotiable clause in his bargain with existence.

Terza's later messages showed her relief at the news from Magaria, and then from Naxas. "At least we know you're all right, wherever you are, even if we won't be seeing you right away."

In the very latest message she was aboard a ship. "I'm traveling with my father," she said. "The Control Board is moving from . . . well, one secret place to another, and I'm going along as his hostess."

Terza was going to some new place, he thought sourly, that Michi would know about but he wouldn't. Sometimes it was hard not to think of the entire Chen clan as a vast conspiracy designed to keep him in the dark.

The next day, Michi invited him for cocktails. The elaborate dinners that had for a month occupied the attentions of the officers and their cooks had faded, to be replaced by teas or cocktail parties or gaming functions. People were putting on too much weight, for one thing, and for another, the delicacies that had been brought aboard at Chijimo, and restocked at Zanshaa, were running low.

He found Michi in her office, not in the long dining room. A snack of flat bread, pickles, and canned fish eggs gave off a whiff of stale olive oil. Vandervalk mixed the drinks in the corner and poured them into chilled glasses. Michi gazed at hers, sipped, and gazed again.

She looked tired, and careful application of cosmetic hadn't entirely disguised the fine new lines around her eyes and mouth. She looked at her drink as if seeing past it to the end of her active career, and Martinez suspected the view wasn't to her liking.

"I've heard from Maurice," she said after a moment. "He was as annoyed as we were that the Convocation made Lord Tork's rank permanent. More so, perhaps—he'll have to deal with Tork at Control Board meetings, while we won't have to see him at all."

Martinez very much doubted that anyone was more annoyed with Tork than he was, but he managed to make sympathetic noises anyway.

"Maurice let me know some of what's been going on behind the scenes," Michi said. "Did you know that the government was in touch with the Naxids almost the entire length of the war?"

"Was it like Tork and Dakzad before Second Magaria?" Martinez asked. "Arguing the finer points of the Praxis with each other?"

Michi smiled. "Probably. I imagine they mostly exchanged surrender demands. The Naxids even took ours seriously, after they lost Zanshaa."

He looked at her, the astringent taste of the cocktail on his tongue. "Really?"

"They tried to negotiate an end to the war. But we insisted on unconditional surrender, and they saw no reason to accept that while they still had a fleet in being.

"After Second Magaria the negotiations got a lot more

serious. But apparently they decided to gamble on winning at Naxas, and that we'd accept more of their conditions if Chenforce sailed off into the unknown and then vanished without a trace. But it left them without a leg to stand on when we actually won."

"They had no choice but to commit suicide," Martinez said.

"Yes."

"I can't say I'm sorry."

She gave a little shrug that said she wasn't sorry either.

"I've got a video from Terza," she said. "She seems to be thriving. And Gareth is perfectly adorable, obviously a bright child."

"Obviously a genius," Martinez corrected.

Michi smiled. "Yes." The smile faded. "It's hard being away from them at this age, isn't it? I know."

"Have you heard from yours?"

"Yes. James has matriculated, finally."

"Send him my congratulations."

"I will. He'll be at the Cheng Ho Academy next term."

That was the Fleet academy reserved for the highest caste of Terran Peers. Michi and Sula had attended it. Martinez had settled for the somewhat less prestigious Nelson Academy.

Michi's face darkened. "I'm not sure it's wise to send him into the Fleet. I don't know what I'll be able to do for him, with Tork hovering over our careers."

"I'll do what I can, of course."

"Of course." He was family; that sort of thing was expected. She turned to him. "What about Lady Sula?"

His heart gave a lurch. "Sorry?"

"Do you think she'd be willing to take James on as a cadet?"

There was no reason to think that Sula would be enjoying a command in a few years any more than he would, but he answered that he was reasonably sure Sula would oblige.

"Though you may not want James's career to be entirely in the hands of those on Tork's shit list," Martinez said. "I'm sure we'd help, but you might want to find James a service patron who's not in the line of fire."

"I'll do that, thanks." Michi took another sip of her drink.

Martinez began to fret about his son. Young Gareth would go into the Fleet, of course, there was no doubt about that, and being a Chen, he would attend the Cheng Ho Academy. The junior officers who had thrived under Martinez would then be in a position to aid his son. A brilliant career was therefore assured.

Unless some malevolent force intervened. Of course Tork would be dead by then, but Tork would no doubt pick a successor.

Martinez sipped his drink, letting the burning alcohol fire trickle down his throat, and wondered if for the sake of his son he should hope that Sula was right, that there would soon be another war.

"That rifle? That's an improvised weapon, used in the fighting in Zanshaa City. And the other one"—Sula turned to him—"that's PJ's gun. He was carrying it when he died."

Martinez looked at her for a long moment, then at the long rifle with its silver and ivory inlay. "He got what he wanted then," he said. "He was trying to find a way to join the fighting."

"He was in love with your sister till the end."

She didn't have to explain which sister PJ loved. Not Walpurga, the one he'd married, but Sempronia, who had jilted him.

Martinez had been invited to dine by *Confidence*'s wardroom. The frigate's lieutenants hadn't heard his war stories yet, and he expected to enjoy himself relating them.

He had arrived early to pay his respects to Sula.

And to talk to her.

And to see her.

And to feel his blood blaze at the sight.

"Would you like some tea?" she asked. "I can have Rizal boil water."

"No thanks." The fewer interruptions by servants, he thought, the better.

"Sit down then."

He sat in a straight-backed metal-framed chair acquired on the cheap by some government purchaser. Sula's bare, small, functional quarters were far removed from his own luxurious, art-filled suite.

"Are guns your only ornament?" he asked. "I'd send you some pictures, but I don't think Fletcher's estate would approve."

"You've got an artist, don't you?" Sula said. "Maybe I could commission something from him."

"Perhaps a full-length portrait," Martinez said.

Sula grinned. "I couldn't put up with looking at myself hours on end, especially in a tiny place like this. I don't know how you stand it."

Martinez felt an implied criticism in this statement.

"I admire the artistry of it. The sfumato, for example." It was one of the technical words he'd learned from Jukes while he sat for the painting. "The balance of light and shade, the arrangement of objects on the table that helps to bring the image into the third dimension—"

There was a knock on the door, and Martinez turned to see Haz, *Confidence*'s premiere.

"Beg pardon," Haz told Sula, "but the wardroom is happy to offer Captain Martinez its hospitality."

"I'll see you another time, Captain," Sula said, rising smoothly.

As Martinez took her hand to say farewell, his mind finally received the message that his senses had been trying to send him for some time.

Sula's scent had changed. Instead of the musky scent she had worn since she'd joined the Orthodox Fleet, she was now wearing Sandama Twilight, the perfume that he had tasted on her flesh as, over a year ago now, they lay in the vast, hideous canopied bed in her rented apartment.

He looked down at her in shock, his hand still wrapped around hers. She gazed back, her face deliberately incurious.

He dropped her hand, turned to follow Haz to the wardroom, and felt a flow of sheer emotion as it rolled like a slow, implacable tide through his blood.

She's mine, he thought.

Sula had decided to roll the dice again, three nights earlier when she'd returned from a cocktail party Michi had given for the officers of her sadly reduced squadron. She'd stepped into her little office, her skin still tingling with the awareness of Martinez that she'd felt during the last few hours, and paused to look at the wall behind her desk, the wall with the two rifles.

There was the keepsake of PJ, she and the keepsake of Sidney.

It was only then that she realized that she had no keepsake of Casimir, nothing but memories of frantic nights filled with the sting of adrenaline, the tang of sweat, and the sound of weapons fire. She had put Casimir in his tomb, and sacrificed the *ju yao* pot to his memory. She had intended to join him, to seek her oblivion in a brilliant, clarifying, annihilating blast at Magaria, but pride had intervened.

Very well, she would let pride dictate her course. She would roll the dice on life, not death. She would roll the dice on love, not exile.

She would let Casimir stay buried, and hope that the fantastic Martinez luck would overcome the curse she carried with her.

In her mind, she bargained with Lord Chen. "I can arrange for the return of your daughter," she said. "Captain Martinez and I were in love before the marriage was arranged. I can arrange for that love to blossom again. The marriage will end, and you will not be blamed by Clan Martinez.

"In return I require your patronage of myself, and your continued patronage of Captain Martinez. And of course Martinez and I will raise the child, who I don't imagine you'd care to have around anyway."

And who I need as a hostage to guarantee your coopera-tion.

She looked at the matter from Lord Chen's point of view, and saw nothing to object to.

She knew better than to strike any fantasy bargains with Lady Terza Chen. The Chen heir had been born under cir-cumstances that valued her womb over any other part. She was a bearer of precious Chen genetics, to be mixed with other valuable genetics as her family dictated. That Chen genes had been debased by Martinez plasma was, as far as Clan Chen was concerned, a misfortune of history.

Terza had been born a mere carrier of genes, but mar-riage had turned her into something more formidable. Her social standing was higher than that of her husband, which made her valuable to the wealthy, ambitious clan into which she had married, and who would be inclined to defer to her. In fact—as Sula was inclined to read the situation—it was Lord Chen who was the pawn now, a pawn both of Martinez interests and of his newly empowered daughter, the mother of the new clan heir.

It was unlikely that Terza would wish to return to her earlier role as a mere breeder-in-waiting. Any such change would have to be decided elsewhere. Her husband and her father would have to be in agreement on these basics.

With these thoughts in mind, Sula shaped her new pro-gram. Her policy of pride demanded that she not cheapen herself in any way. She did not pursue Martinez.

Instead, she drew him a map. She gave up the Sengra perfume that Casimir had given her and returned to her earlier scent, Sandama Twilight. This, she noticed, seemed to produce an effect—Martinez looked as if she'd hit him between the eyes with a hammer.

Detail was added to the map. When *Confidence* was still two wormhole jumps from Zanshaa, she arranged to rent a spacious apartment in the Petty Mount, in the shadow of the High City. To give herself privacy she made Macnamara and Spence the present of a twenty-nine-day vacation at a resort on Lake Tranimo, two hours from Zanshaa City by supersonic train. "You're sick of the sight of me after all this time," she told them over their protests. "And though I love you both, I will be happy not to have to look at you for a while."

Her cook, Rizal, was given a discharge and permission to return home, though she kept him on retainer in case she needed to produce a meal.

She made certain that Martinez knew of all these arrangements, knew that she would be alone in a comfortable apartment away from the close confines and spying eyes of the High City. She wouldn't even have any servants around.

She drew the map, but it was up to Martinez to follow it. Pride demanded that, at least.

She received few messages once communication with Zanshaa was restored. The news programs from the capital consisted in large part of executions. She didn't watch them—she'd seen quite enough of that—but took note of the names.

With the peace, the information possessed by the enemy prisoners was no longer of any value, and batches of them were being flung from the High City every day. All the members of the government, both Naxids and others, officers of the security services, and the members of the ration authority whose lives Sula had spared so the planet would not starve. Now they were all condemned, their lives forfeit, their fortunes confiscated, their clans decimated.

Good, Sula thought.

The tiny revenant of Chenforce flew into Zanshaa's system, braked, fell into orbit around Zanshaa. Between the ships and the blue and white planet curved a vast section of the broken accelerator ring, a section so huge that it was impossible to tell from close up that it was a mere fragment of what had once been the greatest monument of interstellar civilization. The ring's smooth flank was studded with antennae, receiver dishes, and vast solar arrays.

In time, fragments of the broken ring would be nudged down to a lower orbit, reconnected to the elevator tethers, then stitched back together. Several large asteroids would be sacrificed to provide enough mass to replace the segments that had been vaporized in the antimatter explosions that had separated the ring sections.

For the moment, though, the ring was still a wreck. Tugs nudged the two warships to bays in the Fleet docks, where they would remain for months, perhaps years, awaiting their overhaul. The ring wasn't spinning, so there was no gravity, and the crew floated weightless as soon as they released their webbing.

There was no accommodation for officers or crew on the ring. Not only was there no gravity, but the vast empty tube had not yet been pumped full of air. A series of atmosphere shuttles approached the warships and hovered a short distance away while lifelines were rigged. The crew formed in their divisions, donned vac suits, and moved in small groups into the main cargo airlock, where they crawled hand over hand along the lifelines till they reached their shuttles. Their baggage came after them on lines.

Sula waited in the airlock atrium to wish them all goodbye. She stood before the doors, wearing her vac suit but without her helmet, and shook the hand of each of the crew as they passed.

It was harder than she'd expected. Building the secret army and seizing the High City had been her greatest accomplishment, but it had never been her ambition, and she had never trained for such a task. The covert war and the battle for the High City had been a frantic improvisation, and though she was proud of her decisions, it had been too much like a plunge into unknown territory for her to feel comfortable with the memory.

Her training and hopes, however, had always been aimed at the command of a warship, and *Confidence* was her first. The frigate was small and unlovely, and her quarters a metal-walled box, but she had grown to love this deadly waspish instrument of her will. She had won many victories in its close confines, and not all of them were against Naxids.

The officers and their servants were the last off the ship, and had a shuttle of their own. Sula nerved herself to put on the hated helmet, and managed to contain her terror long enough to slap the faceplate closed and step into the airlock. Seeing the huge blue loom of the planet to one side and the great dazzle of stars on the other calmed her, gave her a sense of scale and helped her forget the confines of the shoe box she wore on her head.

After the transfer, they had to wait on their acceleration couches for the officers from *Illustrious,* who took a longer time because they had more crew to transfer. Sula hated every second she was confined in the helmet, and was grateful for more than one reason as she recognized Martinez floating aboard. Even in a vac suit, those long arms and shortish legs were unmistakable.

Everyone webbed in, and the chemical engines ignited. The shuttle trailed fire across half the world before making a series of braking S-turns before Zanshaa City, after which it dropped to a landing at Wi-hun. Sula gazed out the ports and watched the sky turn from black to viridian green.

She was happy to wrench off her helmet as the shuttle taxied to its hard stand. When the big doors opened, they let in a blast of summer heat and the most wonderful air she had ever tasted. It smelled mostly of the volatile chemicals of the shuttle exhaust, but behind the reek she could savor greenery and summer flowers. The air aboard *Confidence* had been filtered and scrubbed, but still, over time there was a buildup of sweat and dead skin and hair, spilled food and lubricating oil and metal polish, and it produced a deadening musty odor.

In contrast, fresh air was wonderful. It was glorious. It was better than the finest wine.

Sula followed Michi and Martinez out of the shuttle. The docking tubes at the terminal building were incompatible with the doorways of Fleet vehicles, so the officers descended on a metal stairway that had been run out on the back of a small truck. She felt sweat pop on her forehead from the reflected heat of the pavement. Macnamara and Spence helped her out of her vac suit and stowed it in its container.

Final salutes were made, final good-byes spoken. She said her farewells to Haz, Giove, Ikuhara, Macnamara, and Spence. Some of the lieutenants piled into rented transport that had driven out to meet them, and the rest followed the enlisted on a walk across green grass to the train station.

For herself and Martinez, Michi had rented a pair of vast slate-colored Victory limousines, the same model that Casimir had painted eleven shades of apricot. Michi had offered Sula a ride as well, and she had accepted.

Alikhan, Jukes, and Michi's servants piled the luggage into the second vehicle. Sula, who had brought only the minimum number of uniforms and a pair of rifles, had neglected to acquire statues, figurines, and works of art, and possessed no porcelain blazoned with the Sula crest, no hand-cut crystal, no bed linen, no foam pillows cut to the shape of her head and neck. She simply asked Alikhan to put her vac suit into the baggage compartment of the first car along with her trunk and her rifle cases, and went to join Michi and Martinez in the passenger compartment.

A polite young Lai-own stepped into her path. He held a crisp creamy envelope in one hand, an envelope sealed with a ribbon and a blotch of wax, and a datapad in the other.

"Beg pardon, Lady Sula," he said. "If you will sign that you have received this?"

She signed the title "Sula" and ducked into the car. The inside of the limousine featured cut crystal vases filled with fresh flowers. The seats were maroon leather and very soft. Michi was dragging a bottle of champagne out of a bucket of ice, and Martinez helped her open it.

Sula opened the envelope, read the contents, and began to laugh.

"What is it?" Michi asked.

"Blitsharts!" Sula cried. "It's another deposition!"

Michi stared at her blankly. Martinez grinned.

"It's how we first met," he said.

Sula and Martinez explained to Michi how they had encountered one another on a mission to rescue the famed yachtsman Captain Blitsharts and his equally famous dog Orange. It was the first time they had worked together, the first time they had experienced the near unity of thought and action that sometimes seemed to make them a part of some higher being.

"Except that once I got to him, Blitsharts turned out to be a corpse!" Sula said.

A Fleet Court of Inquiry had ruled the Blitsharts death accidental, but the insurance company was appealing in civilian court, claiming evidence of suicide, and now a new round of depositions was scheduled.

Michi smiled indulgently as Martinez and Sula relived the past. When the torrent of memory had ceased, Michi undid the top button of her tunic, licked spilled liquid from her fingers, and raised her glass.

"I'd like to make a toast," she said.

"Wait a minute," said Sula. She found a glass of sparkling water in the little refrigerator, opened it and poured it into a champagne glass.

"To a campaign well fought," Michi said.

Sula rang her glass against the others. "And to our next," she said.

Michi raised her eyebrows at this, but drank in silence.

The limousine left the second vehicle still loading and

pulled away. Sula saw that saplings had been planted to replace the trees on the verge of the airfield, those the Naxids had cut to give their guards a proper field of fire.

The Terran driver took the Axtattle Parkway into the city. She had never seen the Axtattle from this point of view, and she looked for the building where she and Action Team 491 had laid their first disastrous ambush against the Naxids. She found the place easily enough. The facade of the building was still pocked by the thousands of bullets the Naxids had fired in response.

"What are you looking for?" Martinez asked.

She told them, described the disastrous ambush and their frantic escape. Other sights visible from the elevated highway triggered additional memories, and she described the Bogo Boys' ambush of the Naxid flying squads, her visit to the illegal hospital set up for the victims of the Remba bombing, the way she'd visited a Judge of Interrogation in her Green Park home and threatened her into releasing an imprisoned comrade.

She looked at Martinez as she finished this anecdote, and saw a deep, appreciative awareness kindle in his eyes.

It seems she'd impressed him.

Well, she thought. *That* was good.

"Will you be seeing old members of your army while you're on planet?" Michi asked.

"Yes," she said, "absolutely. Though I'm starting with a courtesy call on the lord governor tomorrow, to assure him I'm not here to overthrow him. After that I'm just going to be living quietly for a few days, get over the trip and the time change."

Another few details added to the map, to let Martinez know that she had no activities planned for the next few days and might be available for a rendezvous.

She'd already sent messages to Julien and Patel, and they were planning a raucous Bogo Boys reunion in four days' time. She'd visit Sidney when she could, and invite Fer Tuga, the Axtattle sniper, to pay her a visit. She'd also send greetings to Sergius Bakshi, though she wouldn't see him unless invited.

She wondered what Martinez would think of the more raffish element among her friends. She wondered what they would think of Martinez.

She was looking forward to finding out.

The Axtattle Parkway broke into several avenues as it approached the High City, and the driver chose a route that swept around the north flank of the cliff face and up the switchback road. The ruins of the Naxid bunkers at the base of the acropolis had been cleared, and the unsightly gun turrets at the Gates of the Exalted had been removed.

"Where shall we take you, Lady Sula?" Michi asked.

"Oh. I'm not staying on the High City. I've got a place on the Petty Mount."

Michi looked at her in surprise.

"I'll take the car back down, if I may," Sula said. "But I still have to deliver the data foils, and while I was here I thought I'd look around the High City, see what they've done with it."

"Certainly. Take the car if you like."

Parts of the High City still looked as if a battle had been fought there, and the empty cave where the New Destiny had stood had not yet been filled. But all of the parks and many of the palaces were bright with summer flowers, and dozens of new businesses had opened, none of them aimed entirely at the Naxid trade.

The limousine drew up to the Commandery, and Daimong guards snapped to the salute as they stepped out. The officers paid their ritual visit to the Fleet Records Office, where they deposited the data foils that contained their logs and the official records of their commands, and then returned to the car.

A few minutes later the Victory pulled up before the Chen Palace, where Martinez would be staying as Michi's guest, a temporary—Sula hoped—prisoner of his in-laws. The doors rolled in silence into the roof. Martinez stepped onto the sidewalk, and bent to take Michi's hand and help her out of the vehicle. Sula stepped out the other side, into the street.

"My lord!"

Sula looked up at the sound of the new voice, and saw a handsome, assured man of middle years walking forward from the Chen Palace front door. He wore the wine-red tunic of the lords convocate and was leading a party forward to meet the newcomers at the curb. Most of the party were servants, to carry the luggage.

But Sula paid no attention either to Lord Chen and the servants. She looked instead at the tall beautiful black-haired woman who walked by her father's side, her path a graceful glide despite the infant she carried in her arms.

Sudden bitterness stung her throat. Apparently the Chens had planned a little romantic surprise, not letting their son-in-law know that his wife and child had come to Zanshaa to meet him.

Of course the Fleet Control Board would return to Zanshaa as soon as it was safe—ahead of the Convocation, who had farther to travel. *Of course* the members would bring their families. *Of course* the new mother would want to show her husband their new child. It was foolish of her not to have anticipated it.

A domestic ambush. And from the secret little smile that Sula saw on Michi Chen's face, it was clear the squadcom had been a part of the plot.

Sula's eyes flashed to Martinez, who stood in complete astonishment, his big hands by his sides.

Terza Chen neared, her eyes glittering with profound, triumphant pleasure. Sula had never seen emotion so close to the surface of her face.

Sula could see Martinez only in profile, and she watched the rapid play of feeling that crossed his face, the shock and surprise, the dawning comprehension followed by the frantic sense that he had been trapped.

And then his eyes turned to the child, and they softened

in growing wonder. His face began to glow with awe and adoration. He reached out a hand. Terza stepped close and kissed him on the cheek, but his eyes were still on the child.

Sula knew she had lost. She had created a map that Martinez would never follow.

She had rolled the dice, and lost.

She lowered herself back into the car and pressed the stud to roll the doors down. She touched the pad that would open a comm channel to the driver.

"Drive on," she said.

**POCKET
BOOKS**

This book and other **Pocket Books** titles are available from your
local bookshop or can be ordered direct
from the publisher.

Please send cheque or postal order for the value of the book,
free postage and packing within the UK, to
SIMON & SCHUSTER CASH SALES
PO Box 29, Douglas Isle of Man, IM99 1BQ
Tel: 01624 677237, Fax: 01624 670923
Email: bookshop@enterprise.net
www.bookpost.co.uk

Please allow 14 days for delivery. Prices and availability
subject to change without notice